BLACK SEA
(Kara Deniz)

Trebizond

ARMENIA

Yerevan

mt. Ararat

Erzerum

Lake Van

Van

Bitlis

Urfa

Euphrates River

Tigris River

YRIA

Palmyra

Der ez Zor

Tikrit

Baghdad

scus

IRAQ

SRAEL

ders

iddle East and Armenia

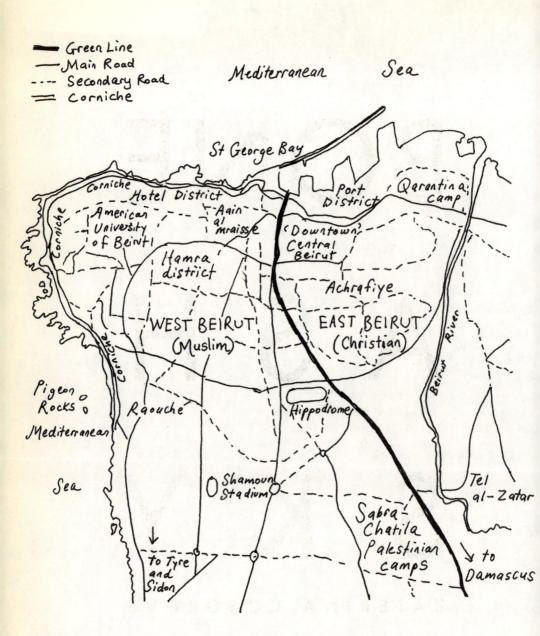

Beirut During the Civil War

BONE
ASH
SKY

KATERINA COSGROVE

hardie grant books
MELBOURNE · LONDON

Published in 2013 by Hardie Grant Books

Hardie Grant Books (Australia)
Ground Floor, Building 1
658 Church Street
Richmond, Victoria 3121
www.hardiegrant.com.au

Hardie Grant Books (UK)
Dudley House, North Suite
34–35 Southampton Street
London WC2E 7HF
www.hardiegrant.co.uk

Cataloguing-in-publication data available from
the National Library of Australia.
Bone Ash Sky
ISBN 978 1 74270 585 9

Cover and text design by Nada Backovic
Cover images courtesy Corbis (Damascus 1925, Aleppo 2012)
Author photograph by Sophie Haythornthwaite
Typesetting by Kirby Jones
Typeset in Adobe Garamond 11.5/15pt
Printed and bound in Australia by Griffin Press

This story is for the survivors and those who haven't lived to tell the tale.

Also for my sister, Annette Livas, 1965–2010.

�֎   The historic circumstances in this novel are real. Many of the characters are not. This is a work of fiction, and liberties have been taken with some dates, events and places.

The author does not seek to blame, defame or offend any race, creed or culture for their beliefs or their past and present actions.

There are no villains in this story – and no heroes either.

K.V.C., Sydney, 2013

Everything is in process of creation and destruction.
There is no here or hereafter;
everything is a single moment.

Bedreddin, 15th-century Islamic mystic

Book One

BONE

LARNACA, CYPRUS – BEIRUT, LEBANON, 1995

My back and legs and head hurt as if I've been travelling non-stop for days, and Dilek laughs every time I complain.

'Toughen up, white girl.'

'Who are you to talk?' I shoot back. 'This is the first time you've been home in fifteen years.'

She laughs again, slaps me on the shoulder, making me wince. We're at the port, waiting for the ferry. It's uncomfortable with both of us sitting on my backpack; my arse bones ache, and she keeps shoving me every time I wriggle.

This week in Cyprus has been full of bus journeys, dawn starts, nights spent on the kilim couches of Dilek's countless relations. She and I are tight, or used to be at school; my being Armenian and she Turkish–Cypriot seemed to bring us closer together. Even now, we understand each other's contradictions. We don't need to probe. She puts her thin brown arm tight around my waist.

'Anoush. Do you really have to go?'

I look at her; we're sitting so close I can see the way her mascara clumps on the ends of her lashes, the black down on her upper lip, just like mine.

'Yes, I really have to go. But I'm scared.'

'Is it safe? I mean, you're not going to get there and find a bunch of crazies sitting around a table with guns?'

'Oh, come on. The tribunal's run by the UN and the Lebanese government.'

'Yeah, that's what I said. A bunch of crazies.'

I don't give her a laugh. She cocks her head, holds me away from her with both hands on my upper arms, the way a mother would.

'See you back home soon, yeah? Don't stay in Lebanon too long on your own.'

I smile, brush off her concerns.

'Thank your relatives again for me. *Tessekur ederim.* Is that how you say it?'

It strikes me as wrong even as I open my mouth. That I speak so readily the language of the people who killed my ancestors. Yet Dilek's aunts, uncles and cousins have been warm, overly hospitable. My own uncles are dead, my aunts lost to Turks or Kurds or Bedouin, cousins unborn. My father, mother, grandparents, all gone. Dilek didn't tell her family that I'm Armenian. I'm not myself anymore. On the plane from Boston my life freeze-framed, then sped up. Beneath me, countries and cities blurred into countless dawns, floating, incomprehensible, until there was only white.

✿   I close my eyes, let my head rest against the window. Condensation drips down like tears. This Cypriot boat, the *Solphryne*, plying the same Larnaca–Beirut route for how many decades with its grimy seats and diesel aroma, a tired saloon with an espresso machine only used for the hot water it dispenses. Greek coffee and rusks, thin oblongs of dry bread wrapped in shiny blue paper. I've been on board five hours. My *Lonely Planet* said three and a half. An hour spent docked in Larnaca, among the shouting and swearing of Greek sailors, not understanding what the problem was. When the ferry finally started moving, its slow shudders made me think of a sick animal.

I'm afraid to go out on deck, where I can discern the red glow of cigarettes against the blackness that comes just before dawn. Too many men: Cypriot, Turkish, Lebanese, Greek. No tourists, except me. Though I don't really think of myself as a tourist. The smell of salted pistachios and sunflower seeds, crunching and breathing, snores. An old woman near the door mumbles to herself, never letting up. The man next to me rolls his eyes. Too many bodies. Passive, drowsing over muted TV screens, inhaling the same air.

Is this how it felt during the massacres? No modern tragedy, no large sacrifices. Only an ignoble irritation for the smells and sounds of other people, nothing so strong as disgust. Out the window, scattered stars look like a child's drawing: lopsided, full of possibility. Then why do I feel such dread? I make a line with my finger on the cold glass. It was at the port in Cyprus, with Dilek. That's when my dread began. Or was it in Boston, before I came? If I'm honest, it's always been with me, since I was born.

Approaching the place of my birth by boat makes me feel as if I'm going somewhere else entirely. Maybe I am. I've come the roundabout way from Cyprus, but that's how I tend to do things. I approach a problem from an angle, tricking myself into thinking I'm not really tackling it at all. The trick now is to convince myself that my father wasn't all that bad. There were massacres in the Palestinian camps in Lebanon's civil war. Three thousand civilians dead. Growing up, my family taught me not to believe it. Now I'm not so sure. Selim, my father, who was second-in-command in a Christian militia, is implicated in the killings. The tribunal aims to try the three key perpetrators – Ariel Sharon, Elie Hobeika, and my father – in absentia and nail them for good. I hope they don't nail him, and I'd rather not be there to watch – but it's like a car crash: I have to slow down, stick my neck out and see the blood for myself. Selim Pakradounian is long dead, but I'm here – wisely or not – to try to absolve him of blame, and myself of guilt. Fat chance.

I'm going back to Beirut because of a phone call.

✳ I had no intention of leaving the safety of Boston, the staid, comfortable routines of my exiled, unexciting life: new clothes, old music, pastry shops, roasting coffee. Which eggs or bread to buy, which milk: low-fat, full-fat, organic, walk-on-the-wild-side raw?

It was past midnight, everyone else in my share house asleep. I was lying on the couch, too lazy to turn off the TV and go upstairs. The phone rang, shrill in the dim room. An Old World, accented voice. Then I clicked: my godfather – a man I last spoke to when I was sixteen. No preamble. No *hello, it's been so long, how are you.*

I waited. Sarkis was always this way: a man of few words, and gestures that meant everything.

'I know something about your father,' he said. 'The war criminal.'

I flinched at that, but didn't reply.

'Anoush, listen to me. There is a tribunal in Beirut. It is happening now. I will give you money to go there.'

'Why? What's it got to do with him?'

'It is for the victims – of the massacres at Sabra-Shatila.'

My stomach dropped. 'He didn't do it.'

'You know he did.'

'So? What's it to you? Why do you care all of a sudden?'

'You dare ask me why! You?'

He was shouting, ranting, off his head. He always did that to me when I was a kid, and now he was doing it again. Fuck him. Fucking old man. I'd made up my mind to hang up when all at once he stopped. Wheezed, gathered himself together.

'Listen to me, child. I am sick. Come and see me. Tomorrow. We can meet somewhere public, if it makes you feel better.'

'Why should I? Why should I believe you?'

He was whispering, his breath so soft I had to press the phone hard into my ear.

'Anoush, I know how he died.'

❀ I arrive in Beirut as massed clouds reveal another day. Amber, violet, parchment. Ashes, bone-dry hills, a panoramic sky. The ferry skims across the Mediterranean, skirts a curl of foam on pebbled beaches; red ribbons bleed into the harbour and paint the pockmarked seaside apartments pink.

In a flash I retrieve a dozen images: parties high in the suburbs above the city, plates of chickpea and lemon, whole chickens roasted on beds of coals, pickled eggplants small as my thumb. Alcohol like you wouldn't believe. The city spangled and fantastic and deeply unknowable below us, faraway noise of cars and Israeli bombs mere background music to the chatter at the table. And looking down from the ferry at that chaotic mishmash I called home, I now remember thinking – if only for a pulsating moment – that the world was opening up for me alone, that passion and love and freedom could be mine one day. I watch the waves, their hypnotic rise and fall. Maybe I'm idealising the past. Surely it couldn't have been that good?

Thud of the ferry's red hull, and the cabin erupts in shouts and cheers, people happy to be home. When Lilit, my maternal grandmother, arrived back from any journey she would ululate in ripe waves of sound that carried me aloft, lifting me up to the joy of weddings and homecomings, the sight of a beloved's face. But I have no beloved here, nobody who recognises me anymore in this city.

The man next to me is silent, head thrown back and eyes open. He seems to be studying the ceiling. I want to share the hilarity with someone but he's impassive. Since the beginning of the trip I've sat next to him, an engineer on his way home to Byblos. In the midst of his crisp pleasantries he turned away to the view of the sea and I took in his profile, bit by bit: sharp nose, heavy brows, an overbite that made his mouth seem poised on a silent conversation. He looks a little like my father: that wiriness with an incipient softness beneath, those creamy-lidded, thick-lashed eyes, tanned skin fading to pink. But this is wishful thinking, with only photographs to go on. Cardboard poses, black and white camera smiles. He left me as soon as I was born, and it hurts too much to think about.

Now I want to say to this man, 'Let's turn back, forget about all of this: family, history, guilt. Let's hold each other and remember nothing.' But he's aloof and I smile tightly in the direction of the window, watching his hands on his thighs, waiting for him to reach across and open up another conversation. I'm tired but my eyes are open, head pumped full of adrenaline.

The port of Beirut gleams wetly now in a strengthening sun, corrugated-iron shacks refracting and mirroring its rays. Walking onto the ramp, I feel the early morning on my skin nostalgic as a caress.

I was born here. I lived here until I was sixteen. Part of me feels an incandescent joy. Yet as I enter the arrivals building my quick sense of familiarity fades, and I'm uncertain where to go next. It's understated, foreign in its hum of piped Arab pop and aircon. Nothing as I remember. Not the milling Beirutis in their new wealth, the ads selling designer bags, shoes, bras, faster cars, seaside villas, strip clubs. People with eyeless Gucci stares and flaunted bodies. As if the war never happened. As if I don't belong.

I'm held up, requested to take a seat and wait while my papers are processed. Officials go through my backpack with childish deliberation;

they're only teenagers after all. So many books – why did I bring them? – are rifled through with disdain, toiletries examined, camera opened, underpants held aloft so others can smirk and exchange the expected glances. Laptop opened, booted up. My grandmother's old Koran passed over. Stiff sepia photographs, an embroidered veil. One of the officials touches the fabric for a moment, letting the fine weave wash through his fingers. He looks up, quizzical. His eyes are a startling mountain blue. Not the blue of Lake Van but the colour of cedars in the snow, winter wildflowers from villages in the north.

'Where you from?'

'America.'

'No, where you from?'

'Here.'

He laughs with real warmth, and points to a chair. 'Welcome in Lebanon!'

Another official eases himself next to me, too close, and asks the questions I expect to hear. He looks my age, with his designer sunglasses and expensive haircut. Astringent face, afraid to crack. Gun fastened at his belt like a fashion accessory. He switches from English to French to Arabic randomly. 'Why have you come back after so many years?' 'How long will you stay?' 'Where will you live?' 'Why did you go to Cyprus first?' 'Do you have friends here, relations?' 'What do they do?' 'What do you plan to do here?' 'Do you have a return ticket?'

I answer without enthusiasm, matching his indifference. Deflect, give him the stock phrases he wishes to hear.

I'm apprehensive of my legal status, uncertain of the reception I'll receive in Lebanon, even with dual citizenship, two passports, a tourist visa if all doesn't go to plan. My entry card scrawled with *journalist*, a word that never fails to give me a self-satisfied thrill. But it also makes me far more interesting to government officials. I pass over a letter, crisply folded. It's from the editor of the World section of *The Boston Globe*. The official looks at it intently; I'm not sure he can read English. The editor has agreed to consider any feature pieces I write from Beirut, after I wrote a few articles for him in the previous year, mostly about 'the Armenian question' as he coyly terms it, and my family's close connection to the events.

The official opens my Lebanese passport lazily, flicking through the pages with the air of someone who's seen it all before. At my photograph he pauses, looks up and scans my face. I assume the blank, stunned gaze of my forefathers, going to their deaths. My face small, square-jawed, in the falsetto of the fluoro lights.

Name: *Anoush Pakradounian.* Hair: *Black.* Eyes: *Dark blue.* Height: *5 feet 4 inches.* Age: *29 years.* Place of birth: *Beirut.*

Before I turn away from his gaze, I will myself to look – carefully, without sentimentality – at myself through his eyes. My tattoo of Mount Ararat – I know, I know, what a cliché – is too confronting here; I cover it with my sleeve. Lips in a thin, disappointing line, slanted Armenian eyes that hide something. Everything. It's my grandmother's face he's looking at: her hair shorn ragged by a Turkish bayonet, cheeks burnt by rage and fear and heat, eyes narrowed by desert sun.

He looks through my health documents. All the right shots. But there are no vaccinations against this sickness, this compulsion *to find out.* Grandmothers, fathers, histories, wars. All these wars. I'm an American citizen, but now I'm home I feel as if I'm not deserving of this privilege.

The official gets up, taking my passports with him, and his dismissal scares me more than his words. How will I survive in this country, where cruelty is so casual? Too many years in polite, pampered Boston, writing articles about student housing or where to get a cheap meal, seeing reports on TV that failed to register, that managed only to be broken down into secondhand stories, subcategories of rage and pain.

I retrieve my laptop and begin to write. Maybe I can start on an article about 'the new Beirut', a flashy Beirut intent on forgetting the past. Yet this is no letter from home. It's a letter to the past, certainly, but it leaps out into the future: bold, precarious, with a strangled cry. Soon enough I'm tired of my stilted phrasing, my half-baked ideas. Leaning my head on the chair I try to rest, so the security guards, the arrivals and departures, the disinfectant odour, become a hum and burning behind my eyes.

I traverse west Beirut on foot. Noon, the sun so high in the sky it's become unrecognisable, a black circle spinning nowhere. I stop in the shade of palm trees, on stony squares so small they seem like afterthoughts, someone's idea of civic duty.

Beneath the paving stones of this city, behind building-bricks and those blinding white pieces of gravel, breathes an older, more frightening Beirut – a city hiding war and bloodshed, a little girl lost in memories I dare not speak. The civil war is over, and all those wars, but I still have trouble convincing myself. Only a matter of time before Beirut is blazing again. I know this in my bones, in the pulse of my hybrid blood: Armenian, Lebanese, Turkish. There's another, secret war, lodged deep inside. The battle between hating my father and loving him. Hating him for being a ruthless killer, for leaving me before I had a chance to know him. Grasping at this chance to absolve him, restore the fierce torchbearer to me again.

I pass a boutique on Rue Hamra and peer into its display. Thigh-slashed gowns with artificial blooms on the shoulder: bird-like, predatory. Sequins, stiletto heels. The sort of dresses I longed for as a teenager, watching other girls at dances, weddings, while my grandmothers would force me to wear little-girl gowns, puffed sleeves and a bow tied at the back. Today I wear a shirt with bone buttons – more than a decade old, reminding me of who I once used to be in this city. Camel-bone, like the carved Syrian earrings dotted with gold leaf that I wear in my ears. Another of my grandmother's treasures. Spoils of war. The shirt's been washed so many times it's become diaphanous. So comforting to wear something so frayed, full of holes: like my memory of those times.

When the saleswoman emerges from her dark interior, suspicious but expectant, I turn away to follow a crooked road downhill to the sea, elated by its promise of welcome.

I heave my backpack to the ground when it becomes too cumbersome. I haven't found my hotel yet, still on a sleep-deprived high from my night on the boat and my first glimpse of the city. I'm pushed and jostled by passers-by, standing my ground to squint up at a street sign that isn't shown on my map.

This Levantine sun, harshly hot, exposes every mote and speck of dust, corruption, hypocrisy. I promise myself to buy some sunglasses at the next street stall. A sad artiste caresses his broken oud. The street signs just as I remember, squares of hammered blue tin bordered in white, nailed onto buildings, fences, corners. There's something aesthetically satisfying about them: I imagine upbeat tourists collecting them as retro artwork to put on their living-room walls.

The musician is oblivious to me standing here, staring at the street sign in Arabic and French above him. The old man sings in a whine. *My violet city luxuriates in the light of dusk.* His instrument is only just being held together with peeling layers of tape. Behind him, crumbling colonial apartments: butter and rose and Nile green polluted to grey. Mock-Corinthian columns hold up rickety balconies that double as summer bedrooms, bristling with electrical wiring and outdoor plumbing, the ugliness of modernity obscuring beauty beneath.

And yet there's still a sense of grace to my city, in its narrow painted shutters, olive trees and jasmine sprouting from rooftop gardens. The ease with which high-rises marred by shrapnel stand like sentinels, the fretwork of balconies designed for women to see without being seen. I imagine how it would feel to touch those rusting grilles, stroke them as if they'll suddenly unfurl, revealing my father's face. Through the gate an Ottoman townhouse, its formal garden taken over by knee-high grass and weeds. Only a matter of time before it too vanishes by bombs or plain neglect. The musician keens. *My darling, my love, your sufferings and joys will be many.* The sea behind him white with heat and debris from the smoke-filled, hazy air.

I walk to the Corniche, to drink raisin juice on the promenade. It's something I did every Sunday. My grandmother Lilit would bring me here, still well enough to walk, both dressed in our church-going finery. She with her walking-stick, its staccato dance on the potholed path; me, conscious of my white eyelet dress and the oversized bow perched like a butterfly in my hair. I would wish my mother was with us too, my lovely mother who had looked so much like Lilit. I took after my father's side of the family, they used to say: the spitting image of Selim. Yet more and more, when I look at my face in the mirror now, it's only Lilit I see. Not in my features, but in the expression. Beggars and refugees and young men lifting their proud heads to look at me, steeped rows of apartment blocks above the sea lit silver and gold and all the shades of cream in morning sunlight. Behind them, bare mountains whisper their dark secrets. I would take off my shoes and walk in the pearl-pale wash of foam on the beach, while Lilit sat on the sea wall, watching. A *kaïk* vendor walked by with his long wooden pole wreathed in the warm, hollow bread. When I gave him a coin I could feel his palm smooth and dry with sesame seeds. The Orthodox liturgy insinuating its reedy refrain into my thoughts: *Profound mystery*, the congregation sang. The priest in an undertone, *I will wash my hands in innocence and go around your altar, O Lord.* We would leave my other grandmother, Siran, taking coffee with the priest and the rest of the old ladies. Crying over her lost son, Selim. Siran thought Lilit was blasphemous for keeping a copy of the Koran by her bedside as well as the Bible. I'd heard them arguing over Lilit's muffled past – her Turkish husband, her veils, that silver jewellery from Syria – as if the innocent green-covered volume was its entire manifestation.

Lilit was different, even then. She had a streak of danger I admired, something dark in her past that made her joyful and reckless. She could swim – in a huge, black, knitted bathing suit – unlike any of the other old ladies I knew. She joked. She sometimes even swore.

Now I poke with my straw at the pistachios floating on the surface of the ruby liquid, wonder what I'm really doing here. Already lonely, condemned to this fruitless exercise. Too earnest for companionship, for the quick darting smiles of these dark-cheeked waiters with their knowing bows.

Lilit arrived here in the clamour that comes with the end of war. Did she walk on this pebbled beach as a young woman, face exposed for only a moment to the sun, sit laughing at a cafe table? More likely she stood on her flimsy balcony in east Beirut, veiled in a Turkish yashmak, knuckles white against the rail. Her position in the city so precarious, her view of her future so small. Fighter ships in the distance would have seemed as small and inconsequential as children's toys. I can see them now, still lounging in the port. Are they American, or Israeli? Paper cut-outs against a sharp sky. The morning so still it makes no reference to war. Black-fronded palms crackle in the haze from car exhausts, the burning of garbage in the poorer parts of the city. A lone fruit vendor, walking crazily as if dazed by the heat, leads a cart laden with pomegranates down the road among the cars. They look like Christmas decorations, round baubles of painted wood. Everyone swerves to accommodate him. Traffic noise diminishes and all I can hear is the slap of feet on broken pavement, the tinkle of Lilit's cheap silver rings against my glass.

Down on the grimy beach, a blonde in a bikini stands poised against the horizon, her waist-length hair being brushed by a short, attentive man. I watch young women like myself choose a table, sit down. Their expressions muted by sunglasses in the latest fashions, extraordinary curtains of hair. Middle-aged men argue on mobile phones, shovel in pastries as they speak. My father would have been their age if he survived the war. One of those soft-paunched men with good humour and dirty jokes and a love of home-cooked food. Who would know just by looking at Selim Pakradounian that he was a militiaman? Someone who kills. Kills indiscriminately. If he were still alive, he'd sit with me in these cafes, listen to my hopes and doubts. We would eat more pastry than was good for us.

I watch other people, mothers and daughters, lovers and friends. The trickle of rosewater syrup. Crushed cardamom at the bottom of a cup. The tap of false nails on marble tabletops, clink of glass against raised glass. Do I have the courage to stop people, thrust my tape-recorder in their faces: *What did you do in the war? And you? You?* I know I can't do it, not yet. I need to travel further back, until there's nowhere left to go.

LAKE VAN, TURKISH ARMENIA, 1905-1915

white wall. It was the first thing she saw when her mother took her outside, opening her eyes wide into the sun's dazzle. A white wall. She looked at it and remembered everything she'd learnt to forget. Memory before memory had a name. A white wall. Its flickering light familiar yet distant, the same blankness she'd gazed at for forty weeks, the walls of her mother's womb.

irst a wall, whitewashed each spring. On its surface, shadows of a window grille in diamond shapes: close-patterned bands of light and dark as the sun moved. She lay and looked at it for a long time.

Her mother called her lamb, quince-bud, rose-petal. The infant responded to the sounds but did not understand the meanings. She cooed and held out her fists.

In time the child learnt to recognise numbers and letters, great black rounded vowels. She didn't know how to string them together but Mamma did; she would start to speak and a bracelet of sound would form itself into links of here and there, yes and no, right and wrong. Truth and lies. Muslims and Christians. Them and us. Turks and Armenians.

'There's a war on its way,' she heard Papa say. 'A world war.'

He said it in the same way he spoke of the weather, approaching rain. Her small head was tucked into the curve of Mamma's neck and shoulder and she burrowed in, rubbing the soft creases of skin with her lips and cheeks.

'Ssh,' Mamma said. 'The child.'

Mamma's breath smelled of apricots. Dragonflies swooped around her hair, her pale cheeks, her mouth with its constant uplift of surprise. The airy sound their wings made had nothing to do with war, fear,

ONE

14

what they were hearing. She fanned them away, stamped her bare feet a little in the long grass. When she moved closer to Papa, wet blades lay flattened and crumpled where she stood.

'Maybe it's already in the city,' he continued. 'Wars start there and seep into the countryside like blight.'

But Mamma turned away, spoke so low only her little girl could hear. 'There's always hope, do you know what that means?'

Hope. She made her daughter say it. *Hope means everything will be all right someday.* The little girl nodded and bit her lip, afraid to say anything wrong. Mamma sighed and swung her up into the trees, so high she was covered in leaves, while polished fruit all around threatened to fall. 'Pomegranates,' Mamma whispered. 'The fruit of our forbears. Remember that.' As she looked down through Mamma's arms, yellow and purple irises made a Persian rug beneath her, their two lower petals little sucking mouths.

She played by the lake while Mamma caught fish to sell. Pearl mullet migrated against the current at this time of year, leaping out of the water straight into Mamma's hands. She waded in with an apron bunched high around her hips, and algae trailed behind to catch between her legs, sinister green curls.

'You wait there, my lamb. Don't follow me.'

She nodded with her finger far in her mouth. She remembered a time, so much time ago it seemed, when she tried to follow her mother into the shallows, fell and cut her lip on the jagged rocks that hid beneath. Her blood fanned out into the water like wet hair, like the moving, sipping weeds on Mamma's thighs.

Mamma was gone a long time, so she pulled oval stones from the suck of mud and washed them until their colours sang dove-grey and pomegranate red. She didn't know those words yet but remembered the drowsy feel of pink and green and purple behind her eyes, when her mother hummed an old Armenian song as she bent over her at night. *My darling, my love, your sufferings and joys will be many.*

She learnt Lake Van was dangerous, more lethal than a split lip. Mamma told her the surface might look like a pale drawn-out sheet of sky, so calm and still it reflected the mountains above, but the depths were dead, so salty nothing could live there. *Be careful. You could sink to the bottom and we would never know.* The little girl poked her toe in the water, drew it away again. There was always fear around her in whispered commands: *Don't do that*, or *Watch out*. She moved imperceptibly so she wouldn't brush against Mamma's anger. *Mamma is very sad when you're naughty.* Or, *Wait till I smack you.* She was on guard against accidents: of gesture, thought, word. Perhaps that was why it took so long for her to speak. She learnt her name first: *Lilit*. Lilit Pakradounian. It was another litany against fear. Mamma made her repeat it many times, scolding if she stammered.

She was ashamed, bowing her head, afraid of letting Mamma see the sting of water in her eyes. Flat stone eyes, blue-black as the scum of silt marking her mother's feet in wavering lines. Van blue, Mamma called them. *You have eyes like the lake before sunrise.* Lilit didn't know if this was the truth; she'd never seen her own face. She turned the pebbles over, sleek round objects, comforting to hold. They warmed her hands, these little reflections of her, mirror shards polished by the lake at low tide. She looked into them, opened her eyes wide. Tried on different faces: sad, sorry, fearful, glad. She was bored. They stood all day together beside the pot of fish, throwing their arms out wide whenever a horse and rider or a cart clattered by, raising vapours of dust.

Sometimes they had eggs to sell. Mullet roe Mamma smoked then piled in tiny pyramids, amber orbs come alive again, gleaming in the slow sun.

'*Tsoug*,' they shouted at retreating travellers, making the sign of a fish with their hands, two fingers apart like a gaping mouth and forked tail.

One of Lilit's hands was clenched tight, holding on to the last pebble.

✳   At night they smelled the burning of fragrant grass. It went on for weeks but nobody in Van paid much heed, other than to bolt the shutters of their houses more carefully than usual at sundown. Only the ancient widow who begged outside church would point to the mountains, charred now, divested of foliage, and say: 'They stank like that the last time our people were killed.' Lilit looked up as she passed into the nave, lit a candle to hush her heart's pounding. Her little brother Minas poked at her with a cruel finger, before rushing to join the priest behind the altar to begin the liturgy. She didn't respond. The old, nameless fear paralysed any movement, the same fear that haunted her since she was a small child, the fear of never knowing enough.

The men milling in the porch narrowed their eyes to survey the barren peaks ringing their town. Rocks no different than before, sky-edged and veiled by inevitable mists, shy as a virgin bride – not that there were many of those now. What with Kurds carrying girls away as fourth wives after they'd already been spoilt. The tribesmen had begun acting like lords lately, requisitioning houses when they passed through these valleys for their wintering. Of course they had been here for centuries too, as the Turks had. It was an uneasy relationship: nomad Muslims, farming Christians, Ottoman overlords. Much as the Armenians wished to believe they were autonomous, they had always been subject to the Turks.

The Kurds had begun moving into Armenian houses with their pack animals, exhausting provisions then turning their attention to the women of the household. No Armenian man would protest when they carried off his daughter. She was soiled now, indistinguishable from the wild-bearded men who claimed her. Lilit hoped this wouldn't happen to her. She was old enough, now, for these violations. She peered sideways at the men, at their sunburnt cheeks, wondering how brutal they really were under those colourful silks and tassels, their wide-throated laughter. Surely they couldn't be so bad, with smiles like that. They even came to her church on holy days, Muslims venerating the same Orthodox saints.

'Look at the Kurds,' the Armenians told the widow. 'They respect us, we respect them. We even go to a mosque on their feast days to show our solidarity. Look at our mountains, our fields, our orchards. Nothing has changed. Look at our houses, our churches, our schools. They are still standing. Nothing has changed here for thousands of years. When have Armenians been killed by Muslims? Never. Not in our recollection or in our grandfathers' or great-grandfathers'. Nothing is amiss. Everything is the same.'

⌘ Minas knew the men were wrong. Or lying, to keep their women quiet. They hadn't read all the books he had. Most of them were afraid of the Kurds, bowing and smiling on the street, yet calling them the Turks' butchers under their breath. They did all the dirty work. The Turks paid them to crucify Armenians a long time ago, for being Christian. The old men swapped these ancient stories between breaths, wheezing in the high air as they cut wood for winter.

'We Armenians got our own back,' they joked.

Minas piped up – they didn't realise he'd been listening. Lilit sat aside under the trees, watching her wilful sheep, and thankfully out of earshot.

'How?'

'Ah, Minas,' one man sighed. 'You always want to know everything.'

Minas's teacher began to speak, now his tongue had been loosened by the recollections of the older men. 'Remember the Kurds in the 1870s?' He was shivering and sweating as he brought down his axe to the soft white wood. 'Remember what they did to us?'

The other men ignored him. Minas watched, his heart pulsing with a new understanding.

'Remember the Turks moving in and pushing us out? Remember the atrocities twenty years ago? Two hundred thousand killed.' He pointed at an old man. 'You? You must have lived through it. And you. You.'

The men muttered, looked down at the blades in their hands, wouldn't catch his eye.

'We're under occupation, I tell you. They're calling it a holy war.'

The men continued to evade him, shaking their heads and spitting on the ground.

'What about the massacre of 1908? Don't tell me you've forgotten that as well?'

One of the older men cleared his throat, spoke without looking up at the teacher.

'Enough, *effendim*. Enough now. We have constitutional rights again, after the end of that scoundrel Abdul Hamid may-he-burn-in-the-fires-of-hell.'

Another man chuckled.

'You know his mother was an Armenian dancing girl? Neglected him in the harem. Maybe that's why the bastard hated us so much.'

The older man frowned, deciding to ignore such levity.

The teacher cut in. 'She was Circassian. A blonde slave from the Trebizond markets.'

The man pressed on. He continued to address the teacher, laying a grimy hand on his shoulder. 'The Young Turk party are fine men, they are … they are … I don't have the words for it.'

'You mean liberals, intellectuals, reformists? In the lies they've been feeding us in newspapers and on posters?'

'They can't be liars. They're civilised. We can carry arms now, own property, even emigrate. What's there to worry about anymore?'

The teacher flung his axe down, threw up his hands. 'I'm going. I'm getting out of here before they start killing us again, even if none of you are.'

When a breathless youth came running into Van with stories of hanging and looting in Constantinople, only a thousand miles to the west, all the men turned away.

At any rate, by day they didn't smell the burning.

�֍ They still went to church each Sunday. They tied scraps of fabric to holy trees on the way and prayed guiltily to other, older gods, nature gods, fire gods: *Hope nothing like that happens to us.* Rag ribbons faded in sun and rain. The men fed their frightened beasts, or what was left of them. All pack animals had been seized by the Turkish army in the last few days, but the Armenians accepted this. After all, this was a time of war.

A night like any other, and Lilit's hair a shiny black hole in the light of the dying fire. Her father's seamed hands at rest on the blanket; her brother's profile, sharp, waxen, childlike; her mother's bridal earrings heavy on the pillow – all gilded by the last burning coals. She woke. Sobs wracked her whole body but she didn't make a sound. Tears welled deep inside, a formal, adult sadness that seemed to tear her stomach and lungs apart. She stayed very still, as if to move an inch would cause her to sever completely, to forget the dream she had the very moment before she opened her eyes: fires in the mountains, mossy boughs of oak and birch burnt black, charred in the shapes of men's bodies. She lay frozen in her bed, panting, while her brother, father and mother circled her and slept.

In the morning, she heard her mother wake before she saw her. It was just before dawn, the room they slept in still dark and fusty with lambs' breath and herbs, too cold for late spring. She opened one eye, worried she'd be called to help gather kindling and stoke the fire. A sliver of morning light picked out the pinkness of objects: rose-cheeked icon above the window, earthenware plates and bowls from last night's dinner, the brass coffee kettle on its side.

She watched Mamma sit up in her mound of blankets and don a heavy scarf, kiss Minas on the forehead, before she closed the door. He murmured sleepily and turned over. Even on a Sunday before church Mamma had to work. She cleaned the homes of rich Turks, most of them officers on leave with their families, or the feared gendarmes who patrolled the streets, neither police nor army, with no rules anyone could see. At night she hurried home with tales of cruelty, how the lady of the house had called Armenians bloodsucking parasites, an infection in the neighbourhood that should be eradicated now. But Papa urged her not to be so easily offended. Thus they could pay the infidel taxes imposed on them and still afford to send Minas to the missionary school, where he was taught the glory of the Ottomans and what his American teacher termed 'their passive brutality called justice'. But that was all in the past. The Young Turks were different. Secular, modern, pro-Western. And they believed this. They had to.

Now Mamma was away most of the time, Lilit learnt to cook, clean, string rows of walnuts in front of the house to preserve them in the sun. She watched how neighbouring women painted them with plum syrup each day until they were purple and fragrant, a faint wine-rich whiff of death. When she'd left them there a few more months they were packed in jars to lie unopened until autumn.

They all planned in this small way for the future, averting their eyes from the whispers and sighs across their mountains and lakes. They tried not to dwell on stories of their brethren in Constantinople: dangling from gibbets in city squares, stripped of clothes and jewellery. Mansions, townhouses, chapels burned. Tokatlians, the city's most famous Armenian restaurant, destroyed one night by a Turkish mob. Poets and merchants arrested and deported to the wild interior. City folk were different anyway; who knew what subversive behaviour they indulged in? Bringing retribution upon themselves. Artists and intellectuals, proud men with proud ideas. *Self-defence in the face of violence. Self-determination. Self-rule.* Self. Self. Count on city dwellers to be selfish. Writers of fantasies and lies. Setting up printing presses, talking of freedom and sovereignty from empire. That composer Komitas always big-noted himself; well of course they'd send him to a labour camp just to shut him up. They laughed at the paltry joke that did the rounds of town, shook their heads, went on with their patient work, the daily caress of the familiar.

Nothing much had changed in Van. The Pakradounians lived on the outskirts, to the east of the walled citadel. It was cleaner, Mamma said. *And safer too*, Minas mouthed, but didn't dare speak aloud. They lived in Aykesdan, the Garden City of fields and farms, where there was a great deal of space to run and hide. It had once been the granary and pleasure quarter of the old town, now reduced to a hamlet of huts and orchards clinging to the slopes. Nothing had changed there since the war began, except for the shape and colour of their worries. Minas still fed their pet lamb – the runt of the flock – with warm milk each evening, taking comfort in the small round head resting against his knee. Mamma continued to bake holy bread every Saturday night to be carried under Papa's none-too-clean jacket, and Lilit still put the sacrificial hen to roast slowly on the coals before they left for church. She twisted her hair in curl papers the night before, at her mother's insistence, and had angry, vengeful dreams from sleeping on her stomach with her face buried deep in the pillow.

Mamma was always pale from the early morning's work, her lips shut tight on her secrets. Papa strode well ahead, calling formal greetings to all his friends. Lilit halted every few paces to pull up her summer stockings, surreptitiously, under cover of her voluminous skirts. The stockings were old and thin, much darned, too loose for her now. She'd grown since last summer, cast off baby fat, and her legs were longer, trim-ankled, shapely. Minas trailed behind his parents, stepping on his sister's heels deliberately each time she stopped: a small diversion from the boredom of the long walk from home.

She uttered whispered yelps of protest each time but never looked behind or raised a hand to her brother. Yervan sauntered behind them with his parents, whistling his secret signal so she'd know he was there. She could feel his gaze burning into the flesh of her buttocks, hidden by her lawn tunic and layers of undergarments. She wore a linked belt her papa had made, embossed with inscriptions promising a good future and many children. She knew that if she married Yervan the belt would widen then diminish as she became pregnant, gave birth, whittled down to her girlish shape again. It would be her fortune: the only record of her life, years written in silver and underlined in gold.

In church she contrived to stand opposite Yervan, able to see across the thicket of heads to where he lounged against a wall among all the other men and boys, avoiding her eyes. A frescoed Christ rose behind him, robed in cloth of gold, pomegranate buds twined in his unruly hair. Woven designs of flowers and fruit, constellations of earth. Black skin from so many burning candles. His three fingers were raised in benediction, touching the top of Yervan's perfect head. She breathed a prayer: *Please let nothing happen to him.* In the next heartbeat, half-ashamed of herself for such frivolous appeals: *Forgive me, Jesus. But I meant it.*

She mingled with the other women at the end of the service, eating her morsel of blessed bread, careful not to scatter crumbs, when all she wanted to do was fling away those trappings, bread and all, stride across the courtyard to Yervan and kiss his half-open lips. The sun shone on snowy scarves and upraised faces, where whispered gossip bred darker each year. He loitered past her, head down, hands in his pockets. She turned to listen to what another girl was saying about dried meal being good for the pigs, and he was gone.

When they arrived home, the chicken was cooked through and dripping fat. Mamma placed dough on the *tonir* over a bed of coals as they washed and prepared to eat. The dough was elastic, so transparent her hands could be seen through it. Minas took out his schoolbooks, not before telling Mamma she should sprinkle a little water on the bread as it baked to prevent it from drying out. She replied that a young man shouldn't be so concerned over the doings of women, slapping the dough onto the hot surface, where it blistered. Yet Lilit knew she was pleased Minas knew about cooking and keeping house. She only yelled at him to keep Papa satisfied his only son wasn't turning into a girl.

Papa napped now near the smell of baking, his cheek cupped in one hand. Mamma went outside to pull up spring onions to have with their meat, and Minas sighed as he began to read from the light at the window. Lilit stood in the middle of the room watching them all; she could sense the mood of her family, of the town, concentric ripples of doubt under sedate Sunday streets. She was alone; she among them had nothing to distract her. A shiver of fear passed through her, but she was used to that by now. She unbuttoned her cuffs, rolled up her sleeves in prudent folds and sat at the piano.

In front of her stood another window and a low white wall marking the boundary of their property. Mamma had never planted a vine or flowers over it; she said the shadows of fruit trees were beautiful enough. Lilit cracked her knuckles and looked at it now. Moving light seemed to draw letters on the rough surface, letters more powerful than those she wore at her waist. *You will see him*, it said. The shadows weren't of leaves and branches, but of the diamond-shaped bars on windows that kept her inside. *He will love you above all others*. She began to play. Her fingers were long and brown and thin against the black and white keys. Two silver rings clicked against each other, point and counterpoint. The piano was badly tuned, some keys emitted no sound, some only creaked when she laid her fingers on them. But to her it was a wonder, singling her out to Yervan from the rest of the girls. She could play – granted, not very well – but she could play.

She knew Yervan's family would walk past on their way home, and she wanted him to hear her voice and stop, enchanted by its lilting beauty. *My darling, my love, your sufferings and joys will be many.* Mamma stopped to click her tongue.

'It's Sunday, Lilit. Aren't you ashamed of yourself, singing like a Turk?'

BEIRUT, 1995

There's a hum and burning behind my eyes. The hotel curtains let in too much light; I wake at dawn every morning and can't get back to sleep. I've been here three days now yet it feels more like years — or as if I never left. The same smells, sounds, undertone of anxiety. The bathroom tap drips in a slow, melancholy devotion. Yellowed sheets, threadbare with the washing of generations.

I chose the Mayflower because it was where journalists mostly stayed during the civil war. Now, its faded gentility makes me alternately nostalgic and irritated. The lobby sombre and outdated, stiff fake flowers bleached white by the sun. My room airless, windows nailed shut, balcony doors rusted by sea air. But the staff are welcoming, and there are always a few journalists at the bar downstairs every night. There's an uneasy excitement about the place, even with its shabbiness, the hotel incinerator under my room, the bathroom door that won't close all the way.

But I'm still only halfway here, still rising in the cold light of another sunrise, breathing the stale air of a Boston apartment that belongs to me now my godfather is dead. It's been willed to me, and I feel glad and surprised and slightly queasy. It's all happened so quickly: his phone call, his death, my journey back. He told me what he knew about the manner of my father's death, and who killed him, then the struggle was over. He was sick; he knew he was going to die. That's the only reason he decided to tell me the truth. I realised soon enough that it wasn't possible for me to listen to all the details. We'd arranged to meet in a restaurant, and I had to leave my seat and go to the bathroom to hide.

Yesterday was my second day in Beirut, and I went to the tribunal. It's already been underway for a few days, but once I got there I didn't feel as if I'd missed anything. Like a soap opera with the same interminable plot.

It was held in a provincial court building a long bus ride away from here – in an outer suburb of Beirut that may as well be another town. When I got there I took a seat in the back, not telling anyone who I was. My stomach was churning, I couldn't even have a sip of water. Couldn't swallow, couldn't ingest the reality of what my father did to these people. I had the illogical fear, as I sat there, that someone would recognise me, that one of his victims would turn around and point the finger, scream in my face. I saw Lebanese–Palestinians mostly, relatives of the victims, and a handful of Israelis. Even a girl, about twelve, sitting with what looked like her grandmother. There were no bearded militiamen of my father's generation there, no generals. Just a few tired-looking Belgian lawyers and two bored UN judges: one Dutch, one Swedish.

On the way there, I'd had visions of standing up, telling them I was Selim Pakradounian's daughter, confessing my part in their history. Atoning for my father. Asking their forgiveness. But what good would it do? I was worried I'd become emotional, that my memories of the massacre and my father's role in it weren't accurate enough to base anything on. So I skulked in the back and listened to Ariel Sharon's name, Elie Hobeika's name and my father's name repeated over and over by lawyers, judges, victims. Elie Hobeika seemed to get the brunt of the accusations – after all, he was the supreme commander of the Phalangist militia during the civil war. My father was only second-in-command, merely following orders. But isn't that what Eichmann said? I felt uncomfortable, itchy. That first day hasn't illuminated anything for me, except how unnerved I have the capacity to become.

Now there's a whiff of burnt skin and rot, the smell of sinks on rainy nights when drains are full. My pillow is hot at my neck. My shorts have bunched into a thick, irritating wad. I take them off and throw them. I count the things I know, the few, slight things I'm certain of.

One. I know there was a civil war. I was here for most of it, born in the midst of its paradoxes; as a child, understood no other life.

Two. I know it lasted seventeen years.

Three. The death count rose to two hundred and fifty thousand. And counting, though the war's officially over.

What I don't yet know is my father's part in it. His intentions. How he felt when he came home after a killing spree. His justifications. Did he lie in lumpy beds like this one and eat himself alive with guilt? I worry my past like the lucent amber beads Arab men play with in midnight cafes. The beads my father would have slid through his fingers, settling his scores. Same bed, same city. Not the same sector of the city, though his Muslim lover had a seafront apartment in west Beirut. He lived far away from Israeli bombs on the other side of the Green Line.

I know that much from my grandmothers, from the man I called godfather. He made it his business to know everything about everyone. Nothing about Sarkis – not his money, his clothes, his laughter or sadness – was innocuous. Tonight I want to go back to Boston, forget about this crazy quest for truth. Old friends wait for me there, and gentle young men who push and prod for more: passion, commitment, a house in the suburbs, three children, undying love. Are all these even compatible? They never introduce me to their parents. I'm not Jewish, or a WASP. I don't come from the elite of Boston's families. Since graduating, I've worked two days a week tutoring first-years in the craft of researching a topic, writing an article, hooking a reader. Most nights I work in the cafe making coffee for those same students, deflecting the attentions of pubescent boys. I sometimes get an article published, mostly in alternative papers and magazines: streetwalkers in downtown Boston, ten-year-olds on drugs, where to get the best meal in Chinatown. The sympathetic editor from *The Boston Globe* has only been a recent supporter; for once I was writing about something that related to me directly, and it was the only article I was paid decent money for.

Yet with all my hard work I'm still not the sort of girl the middle-class matrons of Boston want for their sons. I'm too socially awkward – though sometimes it drops away from me and I feel the fluidity of childhood: unselfconscious, untramelled, free. I speak with an undefined accent – though I can't hear it. The prim, glossy mothers, the large, haw-haw fathers, would be horrified.

Should I go back? Dilek is back there by now, working in legal aid. Then there are my former housemates – good-natured, herbal New Agers – to whom I no longer have anything to say. What else could I go back to? Other friends, already with jobs on major newspapers, in banks, law firms: the corporate cop-outs? Pressure, the trite imperatives, get a good job, compete, succeed. Who am I kidding? I can't go back.

On my last day in America I pained for Sarkis; too late, I know. Pewter drizzle of a Boston morning, fastening my army surplus jacket at my throat with fingers numb in anticipation. His bedroom abandoned, ghostly in its lack of furniture, grey marks on the wall where his Arshile Gorky reproductions hung. I'd stored them in the basement downstairs, scared of sleeping with the self-portrait of a teenage Gorky, his dead mother's memory veining his crazed eyes. Her closed-off, cowled face. The peony in his buttonhole, its answering pinkness in her bosom.

I feel a pang of regret now for my small, careful American life, the safe routines of walk and work and study; what was I thinking, leaving it all? Father dead – now godfather. Lilit died long ago, my mother when I was only an hour old. Nobody to stay in Boston for. Nothing there but my own petty flaws, my raw wounds. In Beirut the only link to the past is my other grandmother, Siran, and her grip on reality wanes by the day.

The kitchen was dark and airless; Sarkis's tea canisters and herbal remedies littered the peeling benches. A cockroach darted for safety into the shadows, living room windows sealed tight against the cold. I took a mug from the cupboard, gulped down water from the tap – ice on my fingertips, the back of my throat – left it unrinsed in the sink. My new tenant would wash it, dry it, put it away. I turned to face the apartment after I opened the front door, knowing how sentimental I was. On the coffee table, lilies in a vase I remembered from my childhood, their alien petals gone brown.

Before I hailed a cab I walked down the street, lugging my backpack and laptop, feeling rain on my hair. A hurried farewell to the extravagantly pierced girl behind the counter; the boy who was the best barista; my one-time employer, his arms elbow-deep in grey suds. Dilek and I worked there together; forgot orders, burnt milk, served those same derelicts with leftovers at the end of a shift, collapsed on the kitchen floor at midnight in hysterics at how tired we were. Dilek asked me to come with her to Cyprus right there, behind that counter. And I said yes, without telling her my real reasons.

I smiled, waved with my free hand. Fellow students just come back from a party, heads down and hung-over, coffee warming their palms. None for me, I was late already. And I knew they weren't sorry to see me go. I've always been the outsider in this university, the entire country. Or so it was easy to think, now I was leaving. I needed it to sound that way or else I wouldn't go.

At least I've established a routine of sorts in Beirut, a comforting pattern that bears no resemblance to my childhood in this city. I wake just after dawn, sprint up the stairs to the hotel gym and run barefoot on the treadmill, gazing far away beyond the mirrored image of my body into the past, where everyone is alive, where everything will be given meaning, where lake meets sky. When I get back to my room I wash the sweat out of my hair to the tinkle of those thick silver rings Lilit gave me before I left Beirut. Tap, tap, as they bang against each other with every movement of my hands, my fingers that look just like Lilit's, even down to the square, ridged, fragile nails – the metallic sound insistent, as if awakening memory. Responsibility. I sing in the shower, old Turkish wails, American jazz, so I won't have to heed its call. There was always so much jewellery to ask about, as if the tarnished filigrees and arabesques of silver rings and gold earrings, bridal necklaces and bracelets, held all the answers to Lilit's Armenian past. Bracelets. Whatever happened to my mother's bracelet, and the earrings Siran gave her on her wedding day? Nobody ever told me when I asked.

It's been a week and I've only been to see my grandmother Siran once. I thought I missed her when I was in Boston, but I have to admit I missed – still miss – Lilit more. I miss the silences of our Beirut house, the late-afternoon sun that lay thick on the surface of the marble-floored sala and lit pale icons and picture frames into shadow-jewels of silver and blue. Lilit's singing, which seemed part of the silence itself, Siran's low agreement as she listened to the radio. Siran always talked to herself, always forgot the names of things. It became a family joke.

I went to see her the day before I went to the enquiry, exhausted by lack of sleep since Boston – since Sarkis's death, really – and the cheap Greek coffee I ingested in such a quantity on the boat. When I woke at five, I couldn't settle. On the bus I closed my eyes, trying to rest, then noticed my hands locked into fists on my lap. The sky was a bruise in the first bars of light silvering the sea.

When I got off I was directed to the nursing home by a sullen shoeshine boy. I walked through carefully tended lawns and fragrant hedges to the Armenian Apostolic Sisters' Home for the Aged. Inside, the building reeked of disinfectant and an obscure stink of decay. Down grey corridors, I was tempted to hold my nose. The head nun clucked in sympathy. 'We try to mask it as well as we can, but it takes over every time.'

I was ashamed to be so transparent in front of a stranger. The nun opened Siran's door a crack and I saw an untidy shape under a cotton blanket, one foot poking out, small as a child's. The nun slipped away, her soft soles almost soundless on the linoleum floor. Siran's cheek rested on one hand. Her mouth half-open, as if she was on the brink of saying something that would change the course of my life. If only. On her flabby earlobes, my mother's earrings. They were the only point of light in the room. So that's what happened to them. She took her wedding gift back when my mother died. Can I blame her?

I knelt down beside her, afraid to touch. In sleep she was incredibly young, yet all the weight of the twelve years since I said goodbye was in her face.

'Grandma,' I whispered. 'It's Anoush. Are you listening?'

She didn't move. I reached out, laid my hand on her arm. Nothing. For a moment, panic filled me, and I thought she must be dead. But as I looked closer I could see the rise and fall of her narrow chest, her nostrils flare with every inhalation. I let my hand rest lightly on her arm, and as I bent my head to hers, wishing I was anywhere else but in this airless room, smelling her old woman's odour and the sour breath inches from my mouth, I was conscious of my ignorance of it all: Lilit's and Minas's fate, my mother's silent pain, the implications of my father's death.

Siran's slight, hiccupping breathing started to strip away the layers of denial I'd nursed in all my time in Boston, and in my first days here in Beirut. Suddenly the sweat was springing out of my pores, my mouth dry and my palms wet. I felt myself crumple at her feet and the sobs erupted out of my stomach, so violent I couldn't breathe. I didn't care about the nuns hearing, or scaring Siran if she woke. I was beyond caring about anything. For about five whole minutes I cried with the same intensity; then it subsided. I sat there drenched, panting. And still she slept.

I didn't stay. The nun said some days she didn't wake at all. That this day was one of them, and it would be better to come back tomorrow. I haven't been to see her since then. Haven't been to see my old house, visit friends, track down my father's fellow fighters, my neighbours. I'm wary of being pulled under, of becoming that little girl – longing, helpless, afraid – forced to flee Beirut with so many unanswered questions. Why did Selim leave me when I was born? Did he ever love me, or my mother? Was he the kind of man I can now try to love, or only despise?

The Beirut of my childhood seems as real as today's, yet more frightening. The Kurdish butcher I remember is still there, his lamb carcasses dangling like hanged men from hooks in the open air. The fish- and fruit-sellers with their improbable pyramids, buckets of rotting fruit and blood-spattered scales. So unlike the supermarket hush of Boston, housewives with lipsticked smiles, tennis bracelets, little white visors for the sun. The sun in Beirut is never so polite; it burns and shrieks at midday, fizzling out detail until all that's left to grasp are the bare bones of the city. Blackened sea, bougainvillea petals veined as a fair woman's wrists, frankincense and sweat in Maronite mountain chapels, pack donkeys with philosophers' eyes. The old men who live their lives in the cafes, their worry beads that sing lullabies. Those early mornings, getting ready for school after another sleepless night. Wetting my fingertips with water to place on tired eyes, coaxing a mere trickle from the shower in yet another water shortage. Olive oil soap that stained my hands green. Now I shower twice a day.

I lean over the dusty railing on the hotel balcony, letting the sea breeze dry my wet skin. I want some time to ease into the rhythm of the city, to take on its erratic pulse-beat as my own again: crazy cars, gesticulating hands, screech of vendors and beggars from the Sudan and Gaza, the Congo and the West Bank. Men, women, hordes of children lining the pathways, hands outstretched, little girls singing old love songs, their hip-swaying and come-hither eyes incongruous in childish faces. The rankness of trodden vegetables, open sewers and cigarette smoke, cripples and gypsies and tourist touts all jostling each other to get to the other side of the street, to the money, to Paradise. I ache for them, see my family in its own scramble for security.

Then a sudden fragrance and the falsetto voice I remember so well: the sweet-seller with his pyramids of acid pink and sour apple, his simple songs, dodging trolley buses and fruit barrows, mangoes and melons scenting the balcony with the promise of somewhere else. Somewhere less complicated. The manifold perfumes of my childhood, intensified by the sense that I have a limited time to enjoy them before the pull of the past takes me under again: to my ailing grandmother, a house that may be broken or bulldozed like so many others, a place somewhere in the Beka'a Valley where I now know my father was killed.

By mid-morning I'm in the Cafe de Paris. The main thoroughfare of Rue Hamra is close to the hotel and the breakfast offered by its oldest cafe marginally better. I can't stomach the hotel's day-old croissants tasting of the diesel truck they came in, the same flaccid figs refrigerated and brought out again day after day; I finally gave up after a few mornings of sitting and eating nothing. Here in the sidewalk cafe, old men sit at the same tables they seem to have occupied for decades. Above them, broken red neon lights mimic the follies of the Left Bank. The men cross and uncross their legs in a fury of backgammon, gulp down shots of arak with their muddy coffee. Argue. I sip sweetened tea, use my laptop.

'Move on,' I can hear my more esoteric friends say. 'Free yourself of these burdens. Meditate. Burn some candles. Get a tattoo in Armenian then make peace with it.' I always suppress the urge to laugh when they talk that way. But I got the tattoo, more fool me. And now I can't even summon an ironic smile.

I envisage the landscape of Lilit's stories. Was its dawn light or evening hush the same as here? I was never told much about the details before my family left Van, but Lilit waxed lyrical about Garden City, that white stone house with its painted shutters, the tender wheat fields and blossoming trees of their ancestral orchards. Lilit had never been back. Most of the town was burnt by the Turks after the deportations. Who knows if the old house is still standing or taken over by some Muslim family, oblivious to its bloodied past? I'm here in Beirut now, where Lilit's journey ended. Must I go further back, to the very beginning?

Today I hope my stomach – still upset by the boat trip – will allow me to eat bread served warm from the bakery next door, and a slab of mulberry preserve so thick I can cut it with a knife. The cafe owner proposes his house specialty without fail each morning, and each morning I smile and refuse. People come from all over the city for this dish of fried duck eggs and liver. Beirutis in their designer tracksuits with artificially whitened teeth. Their large appetites and gym-toned bodies fascinate me. I watch, listen to their swift talk. Their dialogue flits from Arabic to French to Americanisms, banter, ephemera: mispronounced symbols of attainment. They discuss television shows, nightclubs, manicurists. Complain about living at home with their parents, the price of waterfront property. One woman at the next table leans over and touches me on the arm.

'American, are you? We see you here two times.'

'How did you guess?'

'Your clothes. Hair. The way you so polite to staff. Is not necessary, you know.'

I stay silent, smiling hard. Take a sip of tea.

'I was born here. I wonder if that makes me a Beiruti, like you?'

'Of course. Once a Beiruti, always a Beiruti, eh?'

The woman laughs and turns to her boyfriend, and I laugh with her, despising myself. Yet I'm strangely drawn to that bright artificiality, liking to imagine myself safe in the same position: never having left Beirut, taking the smog, the noise, the heat and chaos for granted. The unpredictability of life in this city. The unhealed traumas of war. In a strange way these drawbacks flash the allure of toughness. I'd like to be so big and brash. I'd like to have such a large, uncomplicated smile, such white teeth. Large appetites. To go to the gym each morning and talk and laugh and make love with abandon.

Sometimes it's those we despise the most that we long to become. I'm deeply, shamefully envious of their shininess, their frivolity, their long muscular legs. I watch with a longing to join in that's almost sexual. They drink Diet Coke for breakfast. The man burps softly behind his hand and the woman cuffs him. Her long red fingernails reach up to her lover's hair, ruffle it, lose themselves in its strands. They hum together, surprisingly well. Listen to the latest hip-hop and watch MTV from rooftop satellites. Take holidays in Ibiza and Mykonos, in loud nightclubs and bars that stay open until dawn. They light unfiltered French cigarettes and exhale smoke into my face.

BEIRUT, 1981

As the city weakened, Sanaya grew stronger. She woke early each morning and stood on the balcony, leaning out onto the Corniche. Even in its devastation, as she greeted fruit stalls, hawkers, beat-up taxis skimming back and forth between luxury hotels, she couldn't stop a smile of possession from creasing the corners of her mouth. Beirut belonged to her. The country had already been at war for seven years and here she stood, on the knife-edge of another Israeli invasion. Yet she wasn't sure the Israelis were coming now, if at all.

She wasn't sure of anything in this war of rumours. But it might be the end, on a morning such as this. It was all too beautiful to last. The sea cupped the peninsula in a lover's embrace and waterfront apartments jutted out white and shimmering as if rising straight from the waves. Even the frilled edges of their shrapnel marks seemed to wink at her in the morning sun. She lit a French cigarette and called over her balcony to the apartment below.

'Hadiya! Come up here before you go to school.'

She had a surprise for the little girl: an old photograph she'd found of herself at the same age. Mirror images of each other, except for the enveloping chador Hadiya was forced to wear. Sanaya butted out her cigarette and went inside. The photograph was propped up on the kitchen windowsill, curling at the edges in the morning damp. She broke up half a bar of wartime chocolate into shards, stirring powdered milk into the saucepan. As she stood at the stove, she thought about what she would have done if Selim Pakradounian hadn't been so free these past few years with his gifts of food and clothes and cash. Starve probably, like everyone else in west Beirut. He was generous with his money, if not his time. She suspected he had other lovers. She'd heard rumours of an abandoned daughter, living in the Armenian quarter. But she'd learnt to wait and, if she cared to be honest, grown so accustomed to feigning indifference she began to feel it grow cold and hard in her flesh. A secret cyst plumped full of dissatisfaction and regret. She wasn't sure what he meant to her, or she to him, but it was enough for now to sit out the war together.

She prodded at the frothing milk with a spoon, watching swirls of grey powder turn brown. Not exactly the colour of real chocolate, but a close-enough approximation. Her former self stared out into the future with the same blank gaze Hadiya affected with strangers, as if hiding some delicious irony of childhood. The little girl had the same straight honey strands in plaits, the same self-conscious upright figure. The cheap chocolate refused to melt but Sanaya poured the lumps into a mug anyway, wishing there was more.

Hadiya ran in with her satchel on and her hair flying behind her.

'Where's your scarf?'

'Downstairs. It's too hot to wear today.'

'What will your mummy say?'

'She doesn't care. And you know Daddy's still in the south.'

Sanaya couldn't suppress an intake of breath. She never supposed the fighting would last so long and come so close, with the threat coming ever closer.

'Here.' She gestured to the steaming chocolate. 'Have this.'

Hadiya took the mug in both hands without wanting to betray her hunger, and sipped at the foam. Sanaya knew she wanted to slurp it all down in one ferocious gulp.

'Drink it quick, you're late for school.'

'Mummy's rushing to work, can you fix my hair?'

She sat the little girl on a kitchen stool facing out into the courtyard, so she'd have something to look at besides the sea, obscured now by a greyish viscous scum, all the detritus of industry and war. The fountain, tiled in Persian blue, splashed in seeming contentment under a solitary fig tree. This year the tree had borne no fruit. Around its perimeter, glazed pots of basil and rosemary had long since been plundered, even the square sweet-grass lawn plucked bald by enterprising cooks. Hadiya settled her buttocks into the seat with a wriggle, letting Sanaya brush out her hair, comfortable in their silent intimacy.

After a decent interval of brushing she began to speak in a dreamy, singsong voice. 'Our canary's so cute, isn't he? Hope the old man downstairs doesn't cover him up when there's an air raid.'

'There won't be an air raid, Hadiya. What makes you say that?'

Hadiya twirled her tongue around the last of the chocolate.

'You'll see. Back home, my pet birdie would sing especially loud during the bombs. He loved it.'

Sanaya brushed and looped the rough, lustrous hair that grew more magnificent the more malnourished the child became, as if in some perverse compensation. Hadiya's family were Shia Muslim Palestinians from the south of Lebanon, forced out of their camps by the Israeli invasion three years ago, exiled from their ancestral orchards for generations. They arrived in Beirut with two pans and a single blanket.

Sanaya suspected the Maronite Christian who owned the apartment below would murder her when he came back from Paris – if he ever came back – seeing the way she had aided the squatters. He'd been away since the beginning of the war – seven years – and it didn't look like he'd be back any time soon. Although she was Muslim, he'd trusted her to watch out for his property. He and her parents lived in such close proximity for decades, guarding each other's interests in fear of their own. He took her to church once when she was seven, the same age Hadiya was now, and she remembered the pale wafer he showed her, poking out his tongue. She'd wanted to try it, wondering if it tasted like a vanilla milkshake, those frothy concoctions she begged for on Friday afternoons after school, the paper straw too big for her mouth. Her parents had been more Western than he. No matter. She shook her head and rolled up her sleeves, not entirely convinced how she fitted into these categories, arbitrary labels that changed overnight.

She helped the Palestinians dynamite a three-inch-thick steel door the old man had installed against just such calamities, ripping up brocade curtains for sheets, pulling apart faux Regency couches for makeshift beds. There was something seductive in destruction. She even gave them a set of crockery once destined for her own dowry, rose-patterned ware her mother had ordered all the way from England. It didn't hurt as much as she expected; she'd given up on marriage. Especially with Selim.

Hope-chest pillowcases, her mother's honeymoon bedspread. All left to her in the convoluted will.

She didn't regret what she did. She saw the fate of others from the south camping in theatre foyers, alleys behind shops, in the few parks of the city, being robbed of the meagre possessions they had, the women raped, even knifed to death, by Christian extremists.

She and Hadiya's mother had become friends of a sort, especially now they were both living alone. Rouba's husband was fighting with a Shia militia against the Israelis, defending the port town of Tyre. No word from him for months now. She brought Sanaya damaged fruit from the stall she worked at; they washed their clothes downstairs together in the courtyard, hanging out sheets to dry in the sun, gossiping and worrying over their health, their hair, their sanity.

Sanaya looked after Hadiya when she came home from school. She'd grown to love the little girl, as though her existence somehow held the key to Sanaya's own continued survival. If Hadiya was all right, then everything would be. The city breathed along with her. So she fussed, scolded Hadiya when she sulked, made her walk to school with her back straight and toes pointed outward, heeding nothing, ignoring fear.

She kissed the nape of Hadiya's neck when she was done and the smell of milk and warmth brought on a renewed rush of tenderness.

'Now run and put your shoes on. Here's the photo. Hurry, we don't want to get into trouble from the teacher.'

Hadiya collided with a young man at the open door.

'Uncle Issa!'

Sanaya took in the spectacle of the man, not yet a man, almost still a boy: incongruous in his torn battle fatigues, tarnished cartridges slung about his hips, the lankness of his shoulder-length hair. He carried a Kalashnikov and couldn't have been more than twenty. As he sidled into the room, he scooped Hadiya in his arms and kissed the top of her head.

'I heard your voice all the way outside, Hadi. You're way too loud for a little girl. Where's your ma?'

Hadiya didn't answer but instead looked up at him with something like fear. Sanaya felt something in her retract. Although he spoke coherently enough to his niece, even tenderly, his whole stance revealed a terrible weariness and indifference, resignation bordering on insanity. He eased Hadiya to the floor and dropped to his knees before her.

'She shouldn't be out of the house. Setting a bad example again. And where's your scarf gone?'

At this, he put his head in his hands and rocked on his heels.

'I should never have gone and left you, now your father's—'

Knowledge passed through Sanaya like sickness. She had the presence of mind to put out a hand before he could finish the sentence.

'Go now, Hadiya. Samara's mummy is waiting downstairs; I heard her honk the horn. I'll look after your uncle.' She hugged Hadiya goodbye and led the uncle to the divan.

Hadiya hesitated for a second, spun on her heels and was gone. Sanaya hurried into the kitchen, trying not to let the young man see her consternation at his appearance. She looked out the window, to make sure Hadiya got safely into the waiting car.

'I'll get you a drink. Something strong?'

'Water,' he whispered.

From her vantage point at the kitchen counter she studied him without allowing him to see her. His eyes were hooded, surprising her, when he glanced up briefly, with their blueness. His hair so matted she could hardly make out its colour, but lightish and web-like where it waved at his neck. Small hands, girlish fingers, a hint of golden down on his exposed forearm. He was still a child. When she gave him the glass of water he drank so quickly some spilled on his front. She wanted to dab at the stain with a napkin, but there seemed no point amid the general disorder.

She didn't ask him how Hadiya's father died. Her instinct was to get him to take a shower, but she knew how this could be misconstrued. Instead she sat beside him on the divan until he fell asleep. She removed his boots and covered him with a cotton sheet. His body a dead weight at her touch.

As usual bombs fell and she could hear them far away across town. One explosion was fairly close that day and rattled the empty vase on the mantel. She put it in a cupboard. She'd latticed all her windows, the shower screen, mirrors and glass doors with masking tape. Only the picture frames, etchings of a faded pre-war Lebanon and solemn, pinched portraits of her forbears, were free of the patterns of potential annihilation.

She felt safe though; the bombs never came as close as here. It would be very unlikely if her block were to suffer a direct hit. Although she lived in west Beirut, it was the southern suburbs, the Palestinian camps of Sabra-Shatila, Bourj al Barajneh, that bore the brunt. Her city was divided by a no-man's land of crushed steel and toppled buildings, a Green Line not many had the courage to cross. The swarming camps of the Palestinians were teeming with filth and fear now, the Armenian quarter and Christian east, where Selim lived, still remaining untouched. But for how much longer?

She went out onto the balcony, trying to see. Nothing, only the sea before her: serene, limpid, a great swallowing eye. Sea draining colour from city and sky, sucking light from the pavement, the people, the pale, unhealthy fronds of the few palms still left standing on the Corniche. Hadiya, somewhere among those mismatched and rubbled streets, sitting up straight at her desk as Sanaya had taught her, mouthing her multiplication tables. A normal little girl at school, a normal day. Here, by the water, it was as if the war didn't exist.

Issa still didn't wake. Sanaya wandered around her apartment, straightening an ornament here, jerking a doily flat, rearranging the silk flowers just so. How pointless it all seemed. There wasn't much to do; she cleaned incessantly. She went into her bedroom, kicked off her slippers. For how many years, how many days and days had she looked at these same yellowish walls, these glossy brocaded curtains, the green upholstered chair her mother chose when she first married? It stood at a deliberately casual angle to the corner, the way her mother would place it when she was alive. Nothing in this room had changed. It was a monument, a mausoleum. Sanaya was born in this bed, napped under its covers. As a child, she would hide in the space between the bed and the wall, playing with her dolls, serenely content in a world of her own making. She never entered the room when she was a teenager.

Now she lay on top of the bedspread, staring at the ceiling. The plaster rose was cracked and flaking; a large grey moth nearby stayed very still, miming death.

Hadiya's father was dead.

She thought about breaking the news to Rouba, decided it was better for her to hear it from Issa. Was this cowardice or logic? Stupid men, always fighting. She wondered if Issa saw him die. She tried to nap. Restless. The vein in her right temple itching. She got up to make Arabic coffee, sipped it slowly while standing at the stove, watching the sleeping man. In repose, his face was gracious as a child's. She turned the cup over on its saucer to tell her own fortune, knowing this ploy could never work. Fate knew just who was cheating.

✳   Sanaya woke early the next morning and sat up in bed. She was so still she could hardly feel herself breathe: statue, column, pillar of salt. A pale dawn spread itself out over the sea, smooth as a fresh sheet. The few last stars shimmered on the horizon and wind from the ocean set the palm trees on the Corniche alight with the first of the sun's rays. She sat, holding her dressing-gown closed over her breasts with one hand and Selim's erect penis with the other. She studied his sleeping face, moved his foreskin up and down indifferently, then, suddenly changing her mind, crept out of bed.

She sat on her balcony overlooking the sea, alert to any noises from the bedroom, and lit a cigarette from a large box – Cuban this time. Another gift from Selim, her ritual before breakfast. She exhaled with a voluptuous slowness, happy if only for a moment to sit, to revel in her aloneness, in her seeming safety. Her apartment was intact, unlike the other blocks she passed on her walks, doll's houses with facades torn off, women bathing, cooking, hanging washing in full view, assailed by the honking of cars and trucks. It allowed her to feel contained, with its creamy ornate ceilings, flaking pink-papered walls, the concrete balcony that was beginning to crumble in the sea mist that sprayed over it every evening in fine silver beads. A pearl necklace just like her mother's, kept in a flat blue satin box. Tiny bubbles, like the faint sheen of sweat on Selim's upper lip when he grew passionate, when he made his pronouncements on politics and women, women and religion, when they made love.

She made some tea, drank it gazing at the horizon, now milky white, indistinct, heat haze emanating from the city like sleeping breath.

The tulip-shaped tumbler sparkled with refracted light. Hadiya always insisted on drinking her chocolate milk from one, entailing many refills. Yesterday morning she had pointed to the chandelier in the dining room and said she was drinking from the very same glasses that held those tiny electric candles. Little glasses filled with light. Little Hadiya, loved more with each passing day, loved more desperately because she was in so much danger. Her uncle Issa, out in the streets, fighting with Hezbollah against the PLO, against the Christian Phalange, against his own Shia comrades in Amal, and the Sunni Mourabitoun militia. Hand to hand for an alley or gutter, a few square inches of rubble to make the futility worth it for a while.

Sanaya shaded her eyes, peered closer, stood up. Planes. Planes arcing into the city, making for the Corniche, whirr and buzz of machinery flattening sound. Planes. Another bombing. She stood still at the rail, not daring to move. All around her, daisy-yellow pieces of paper dropping from the sky, so fast and thick she bowed her head and shut her eyes until the fluttering ceased and the silence was replaced by familiar sounds: horns honking, screech of tires, sough of sea, neighbours below exclaiming, leaflets in their clammy hands. She picked one up from the balcony floor: '10 June 1982. We shall capture the city in a short period. We have committed a large part of our air, naval and ground forces for the area of Beirut—'

She looked up. A series of quick taps at the door. Rouba came running in with more leaflets and the morning paper, already smudged by the sweat pouring from under her arms.

'Sanaya, did you see what those Israelis—'

She didn't finish. Sanaya ran to the bedroom and closed the door on Selim, carefully, so as not to wake him. She turned to Rouba.

'My little cousin is sleeping here. Her mother had to work overnight in the factory and couldn't look after her.'

Rouba nodded slowly, keeping up the pretence.

Sanaya crumpled all the leaflets and threw them in the kitchen bin, grabbed the newspaper and spread it out in front of her, reading the blurred headlines. She thought she might be reading the same line over and over but couldn't be sure. Her breath caught in her throat, a lump she pushed down with the heel of her hand. Her eyes filled. Was it fear?

It couldn't be. Anger? Nostalgia for the city that she knew now – knew in the quiet unshakeable way of the dreaded truth – would be destroyed again and again? *Operation Peace for Galilee.* Rouba grabbed one of the balls of paper and smoothed it out behind her back. Sanaya looked up.

'Tea, Rouba? Would you like some tea?'

'I need to go downstairs in a minute. Hadiya might wake and will be scared if I'm not there. Give me half the paper; you can have the rest.'

When Rouba divided the paper, Sanaya turned to the back pages and read the atrocities of the day: kidnappings, bombings, torture, interrogations. *Two hundred dead in a single Israeli air strike.* Another day in Beirut. Except for one piece of news confirming those floating missives: the Israeli land army was sweeping north to Beirut and would reach the outskirts of the city in four days. She stood, shaking. Her voice when she spoke was unrecognisable.

'Send her upstairs when she wakes. I have some fresh eggs.'

✳ She lived in the heart of the PLO enclave in west Beirut. Her waterfront promenade and the boulevards that radiated from it still retained the beauty of an Orient past so idealised and yet so corrupted in these halfway countries, neither East nor West: delicately amoral, carelessly imprecise, in an advanced state of decay. The scraggly palm trees were indicative of it, the heat that embraced then lacerated, the grit between her teeth from watery coffee sold by vendors at the seaside, overblown fruit hawked by peasants from the south.

In these last few days before the Israeli invasion she discovered – reluctantly, shyly, almost ashamed – how much she was bound to this city. In refusing to leave, in clinging to her flimsy life, she found something interior, precious and reserved, close to love, for the city that mirrored her every breath, her every moan and fear. At night she lay back on her kilim cushions and smoked shisha tobacco scented with apples, gazing out into the middle distance past crowds on the seafront, as if by doing this she might somehow avert their shared fate.

When she was younger, she thought she would travel as soon as she could, explore the whole of Europe – live on the fringes, flout moral codes, a fleeting sparkling citizen of the world. She would promise herself in those nights spent lying awake in bed, hearing the clock tick, hearing her parents argue: *When I turn thirty I'll be somewhere completely different, Cyprus maybe, Greece, or taking in the shimmer-heat of the south of Italy.* She envisaged days of lassitude and iced drinks, nights of tanned skin and cool passion. She had no ambitions; studying was always a chore. She wasn't good at anything in particular, and hadn't really minded. She liked dancing, music, was capable of putting people at ease. She didn't judge. That was her one shining achievement. Now she wished she had something: a hobby, a passion to occupy her days, to make life sing. She should have gone away when she had the chance.

She despised her parents and their small-minded existence, that bitter, hard-earned, middle-class wealth, a dirt-floor factory and its underpaid workers. Manufacturing cheap nylon pantyhose; sheer nude, opaque white, dirty black, she refused to ever wear a pair. She loathed the obligatory end-of-year appearance, the grudging line-up to shake her hand, such a good girl, such a compliant daughter, the pretty child of the boss. Handing out presents, meagre parcels of tangerines and roasted nuts. Her parents would bend down, whisper in her ears, twin conspirators. *You know all this is for you.* She knew it wasn't. If she were dead, her parents would still be doing it. Now they were dead in her place, and she felt as if she had killed them.

She had dreaded the petty rounds of protocol, decorum: endless afternoon visits to fourth cousins and distant friends of friends. Muslim boys chosen for her to marry one day, all on display like so many fake clown-heads at the circus. Aim for the mouth, pop in a ball, win the prize. They sat in a row on stiff high-backed chairs, gobbling down food, betraying their indifference to her with their lack of manners. She watched them, sipped, never smiled. Tea and syrup cake disappearing down their gullets, scent of rosewater, glasses of pure arak poured from a little green bottle for the ladies. She hated it all: Beirut the implacable hostess, Beirut the hypocrite matron, Beirut the painted whore. Now, at the age of thirty, she realised just how much she belonged to Beirut, and the city to her.

It could be because she was now all these things. The slapdash hostess, the failed matron, the virgin whore. Beirut and she had an understanding, or at least something in common. She finally appreciated – if not accepted – her role in a society that alternately condemned and praised her for the very same attributes on different days. And she was no longer ashamed. No, she was defiant. It was easy to be when there was no longer anything to lose.

By day she walked, if it was safe enough to venture out. She walked through her tiny neighbourhood of Ras Beirut, waving in complicit denial to the odd herb- or egg-sellers squatting on the kerb with their kitchen-garden wares, oblivious to the threat of bombs. She passed the young Syrian – a *Yezidi*, a devil-worshipper, her neighbours whispered – who sat in exactly the same position every day, on a corner in the shade. He was a beggar, dressed in rags like all the other beggars and gypsies she passed, but he begged for words, not money. All around him in plastic bags were words cut from newspapers and books, bus tickets or food packets, or written on tiny squares of wrapping paper. *War. Devastation. Kalamata olives. Sadness. Lux soap. One way to Jbeil. Futility.* She knew he'd gone mad, shell-shocked by the death of his wife and four children during an air raid two months ago. They had only moved to Beirut this year from their village in Syria. He was at work when it happened; a day labourer, a simple man. Now he sat in his unmoving position, serene eyes staring up to the sky, murmuring his broken mantra as people walked by. 'A word to give me, sir? A word to spare, young lady?'

She always stopped and gave him one, bending down to his level, where the smell of his unwashed hair and clothes overpowered her, dismayed by his black bare feet. Each time she forced herself to linger, smile and make small talk after he wrote down her word in his incongruously perfect handwriting. Sometimes she slipped him some money and ran away before he had time to protest.

She power-walked past the American University campus and cheap student cafes, now bricked-up completely by their frightened owners. She rounded the strafed Gefinor building, once the modern pride of Beirut, to the tree-fringed road twisting through the old, crumbling quarter of Ain Mreisseh, where the last of the city's Ottoman villas were being picked off one by one like toy targets. Their red-tiled roofs made them easy to spot, their cheerful character easy to justify bombing. What right had they to look so complacent in a dying city?

There was a certain tree on this route. Miraculously it had escaped the shelling and stood bent in the ruined courtyard of one of those villas.

BONE

43

Old and twisted, its trunk thickening to low-lying roots, a woman's legs and pubis with no torso. On the opposite side, as if merged into it, were the thicker legs and squat penis of a man. Twin lovers with no heads, no eyes, no hearts. She couldn't abandon this tree. Whenever she became tempted to escape – take her money, leave the apartment to looters, seek refuge with Selim in east Beirut or Cyprus – she thought of the tree, so brave, so foolhardy, so achingly beautiful in the face of decay. Then she knew she had to stay. The tree had become her Beirut.

Her city had become an amphitheatre of terror. Here in west Beirut, once home to the liberal intelligentsia and artists, where Christians and Muslims lived side by side, people now asked each other's background and religion before committing to anything, before buying a bunch of grapes, accepting a simple offer of help. Everyone had become adept at euphemism. She'd be surprised if anyone could ever speak to one another in plain, honest terms again. They'd lost the knack. Now there were code words for everything. Seven years of civil war were called *the events*. Shrapnel had become *confetti*. Wounds were *scratches*. Death, *our grinning friend*.

The sounds of bombs and guns and the whirring of Israeli planes echoed from the apartments terraced on the mountainside all the way down to the sea. Commercial streets became empty spaces between onslaughts. When there was a ceasefire called, for minutes or hours – never longer – men scurried out for anything they could find in the shops along Rue Hamra and the women stayed at home, trying to ignore this war they thought had ended long ago.

Sanaya didn't stay home. She cloaked herself in her blue abaya and a pair of sequinned sandals she'd filched from one of the overflowing bins lining the Corniche. Spoils of war, discarded last week by fleeing Christians bound for the east of the city. She imagined the woman's panic: *Leave this? Take that?* Making two piles: hairdryer, *reject*; hand-mirror, *must have*; sequinned sandals, *not sure* – this third pile for objects requiring the clarification of attachment. Her husband sweeping up the piles on his way to the car, dumping them in the nearest gutter, ignoring her protestations.

Sanaya walked blind and fast in her discarded sandals and she walked this way to keep hold of her sanity. She didn't allow herself to see, to really see this devastation wreaked by her own neighbours on each other. No matter she walked past bombed apartment blocks exactly like hers, through shopping arcades collapsed and folded like paper flowers, as gunmen followed her through neighbourhoods pockmarked by shrapnel, demanding her identity card; no matter she stopped and showed it to them repeatedly, either smiling or keeping calm, a split-second decision between life and death. She stood with them on streets guarded by other uneasy sentinels: a few palms, bare and spindly, their fronds blown off by car-bomb blasts.

※   She woke late in viscous heat to militiamen on loudspeakers. She was thankful Selim wasn't there; he'd gone back to east Beirut last night. She sat up, looked out the window. Syrians – she could tell from the tattiness of their uniforms.

'The Israeli leaflets are poisoned,' they boomed. 'Come down to the bonfires immediately.'

She put on a pair of rubber gloves, rummaging in the kitchen bin for the leaflets she had crumpled and thrown in there yesterday. She didn't believe the Syrians – or at least only half-believed them. But it wouldn't do not to be seen downstairs at the bonfire. She jumped at a sudden pounding on the door and opened it to a Syrian soldier who thrust out a plastic bag. He didn't speak. Her hands were shaking in their irregular pink gloves; it wouldn't do to let him see her shake. He would think she had something to hide.

He looked around the room as he stood at the door, weapon easy by his side. She turned to follow the trajectory of his gaze, suddenly seeing the room as he must see it: faded opulence, bourgeois pretension, chandeliers and fake-marble columns and iridescent urns so much evidence of her betrayal to the cause. *He's a socialist. Comes from some dirt-poor village in the desert. I could be killed for this in west Beirut.*

She pulled off her gloves, beckoned him inside. Now he turned his attention to her and again she saw herself as he must see her: an aging woman in a rose-coloured robe, breasts loose and sagging, a once-beautiful face raddled by sleep and humidity. A decadent imperialist. A whore.

'Coffee? Glass of tea?'

He slapped his lips together once, twice. The sound was faintly nauseating to her.

'Some water.'

She brought it to him where he stood, watched as he drank. Something in the way he held the glass reminded her of Hadiya's uncle. Issa too had drained the liquid in a gulp, pouring the water into his mouth from above in the peasant fashion, without allowing the glass to touch his lips.

'*Sa'laam aleikum,*' the soldier said when he was finished.

'*Sa'laam,*' she breathed.

When he'd gone she stood on the balcony, leaning over the railing. Rouba was in the courtyard, hanging out her washing.

'What was his problem, Sanaya?'

'Syrian. Wanting leaflets to burn. Do you have any?'

Rouba smirked.

'I have one, but I'm keeping it. Don't like the Syrians. Never liked them. Coming here telling us all what to do.'

Sanaya watched her shake out a pillowslip with a sharp, decisive flick. Rouba, too, was defiant in almost imperceptible ways. Gnarled and misshapen, another foolhardy tree.

BEIRUT, 1995

I left the city at sixteen during the height of civil war, and I can recall that dreary afternoon as if it were yesterday. One of the wettest winters on record, the Armenian quarter flooded by relentless rains. Trees twisted and buckled under the onslaught of shells, rotting trunks exposed bruise-yellow and blue in the downpour. Some took on fantastic shapes: stripped limbs, coupling bodies in a death embrace. But I was too young to understand this, or any of what was going on: a city turning on itself.

The airport had long since been bombed and reduced to rubble by the Israelis. I was booked on a UN diplomatic flight to the States, beneficiary of the machinations of an Armenian businessman of my grandfather's generation, genocide survivor made good. Yes, you've guessed. Sarkis.

He'd grown rich on something to do with oil, a new company with offices all over the Middle East and the Caucasus. Was it black market oil, terrorist links and shady arms deals? I liked to think so. It reinforced my perception of him as sinister, untrustworthy. My godfather in America, he called himself now. Lilit said Sarkis had been in the death camp with my grandfather, that they helped each other escape. I didn't believe it. Why wouldn't Minas have said so? Why was Sarkis never invited to our home when he was alive? There was something more to the story, something unnameable.

Ever since Minas's death, Sarkis visited us at Christmas and Easter with packaged food from London, duty-free whisky for Siran, a girlish gift for me. It was always wrapped perfectly, and something told me a shop-girl had twirled the ribbons, not him. He didn't look like he could fold anything straight.

'Say hello to your godfather,' Lilit whispered.

'But he's not my godfather,' I began to say.

'Look him in the eye when you speak; there's a good girl.' I saw the reprimand fire her eyes. Siran had already opted out, a crooked shadow in the corner. Sarkis always left early, pleading business commitments, but not before pressing damp American dollars into my reluctant palm.

'We have money,' Lilit told me, as she did every day. 'Enough to get you overseas and into a good school.'

I cried, anticipating my inevitable departure. Lilit remained unmoved. 'Study. Go to university. We're modern now. No men to look after us.'

I sobbed, burrowed my head into her lumpy breasts. 'But how am I going to leave you?'

She patted me on the back, hiked up my greasy pullover, kneaded my ribs, massaging my spine with weakened hands. I relaxed against the softness of her stomach; I was safe now, at least. I always loved her most. More than my mother, or my father.

There are so many moments, milestones, tragedies, small joys – all gone, unrecorded. This moment is lost, too, but in my mind's eye it's so clear, so familiar. I can see the dark, low-ceilinged room of my childhood, multicoloured rugs on the floor around the hearth. And the lake Lilit always remembered, even in the midst of the desert or the ravaged city: the Armenian lake where she was born. She talked to me about it so many times: that lake with its colours of bone and ash and sky. And I still haven't seen it.

When the time came to leave Beirut, I'd grown into what Sarkis called a young lady. I flinched from such undisguised admiration in his face, his outspread hands. Chucking me under the chin, brushing against the tendrils of hair at my temples. His fingers smelled faintly of fish, and so did the money he continued to give me. He limped as he walked, his body looked as if it had been broken long ago then awkwardly put back together again. There were bright scars, still fresh-looking, on his nape and neck. My arrogant teenage self kept asking, how could a man so ugly think I could even look at him? We posed for formal photographs on festival days; his pathetic hand – I can see him as merely pathetic now, and small, and frightened and sad – bunching up the slippery taffeta folds at my waist. I began to hunch forward when I walked, looking down at my feet and hiding my new breasts. Lilit chided me in the same way as when I was small. 'Don't be like that. Show him how grateful you are!'

There was so much to be grateful for. I was issued with identity papers and a Lebanese passport, assured by Sarkis I'd be granted refugee status once I arrived in America. At a later date, I'd be allowed to apply for citizenship. I didn't know at the time how Lilit had organised it. Maybe she bribed him. Or begged. Maybe he owed Minas a favour. Maybe they were children together in that mythical place called Van.

I couldn't suppress a shudder when he touched my elbow, leaned over to peck my cheek. I glanced at him sideways as he led me to the taxi. He looked young, for all that he was in his seventies. His curly hair fell boyishly into his eyes and was still black, so glossy he must have dyed it. His beard pointy and well-trimmed, emphasising the line of his jaw. Yet there was a smell about him, and I realised it wasn't fish, or dirty money. It was the desperation of a man who couldn't reconcile himself to his past.

We were driven from the Armenian quarter to the airport through checkpoints that distinguished themselves from each other with posters of dead heroes, Christian or Muslim, and dirty-coloured flags. Each time we neared the telltale ramps, the driver slowed down and passed his identity papers through the front window. He too had draped a makeshift flag over his dashboard, the customary soiled white towel signifying neutrality. Surrender. Or simple fear. I shrank in my seat. Sarkis appeared calm. The gunman, either bearded or freshly shaven, Islamic or Christian, wrapped in a keffiyeh or sporting mirrored sunglasses, solemn or smiling, would study my face for a moment, an eternity, then with a flick of his hand allow the taxi to move on.

We passed bombed shells of municipal buildings, entire flattened streets. A grim cityscape of wet soil and smashed glass, as if the city was returning to a primeval state, vegetation creeping thickly over to cover its nakedness. A final surrender to nature would be preferable to what I saw, all the sordid military-industrial waste: black smoke, chemical haze, slow-burning bonfires of clothes and cars. Without the plane trees once lining the kerbs, the boulevards were foreign and frightening, a mouth with no teeth. When I wound down the window, the stench of the streets made me itch all over. Weeds with tiny yellow flowers were the only luxuriance and they grew everywhere, from potholes and between mouldy bricks. Little children armed with paring knives flitted from corner to corner, gathering the hairy stalks in their hands.

The American University campus was the only green space of any size left untouched in west Beirut. The driver slowed down for us to see it. One last time. The place I always expected would be my destiny. No picnics now, no cheap drinks at sundown, demonstrations over what seemed laughably trivial now – student fees, longer opening hours for the library. Sarkis let me slip out of the car to peer at the manicured lawns, ancient yews and swinging palms. All around me, Mercedes and BMWs with their tinted windows, militia warlords safe inside, their opulence standing out among the destruction.

At the bombed-out airport, militiamen everywhere. They lolled about, eating bars of black-market chocolate, smoking Gitanes, rocking weapons in the crooks of their arms as if nursing babies. Cries of *baksheesh* drowned out the sound of scattered gunfire in the distance. I sat at the back of the plane next to Sarkis, trying not to cry, buried my face in the flight safety manual. *Brace for landing. Do not panic. Breathe.* Neither of my grandmothers had felt safe enough to come and see me off.

When the plane took flight I caught a flash of the city in a carmine sunset, before cloud cover obscured it from view. From such a height, I could see exactly how destroyed west Beirut was. There were few public buildings left standing: no roads, no telegraph poles, no traffic lights, no colour. Only blue of sea and grey of destruction, the refugee camps a splotch of huddled black. As the plane dipped down once before ascending, I saw east Beirut intact and gleaming white: new high-rises, pools, beaches, resorts fanning out on the coastline toward Jounieh. As the plane ascended, my city, my country, my childhood home became abstract, theory, mere lines on a map. I didn't feel resentful that I'd been sent away; after all, my grandmothers loved me – it was only a matter of time before Beirut would become more dangerous. For now, the Armenian quarter was still intact, Lilit and Siran safe. And my father? I was uneasy, in my stomach if not my head.

I sit now in the Cafe de Paris, head in hands. Behind the counter, raised voices and the slap of a pan on the stove. I'm so tired. It must be jetlag, the traffic, this yellowish strengthening smog. My bed in the hotel room beckons, dark curtains drawn, the noise of the streets neutered. The notes I've typed, these surmises about my grandparents' past, seem childish now, useless.

I unfold a map of Van, inexpertly drawn by Minas as a gift for Lilit before he died. It's soft and limp from being carried in my back pocket. I peer at the ghostly markers he's left behind, the imprint of wet ink on paper. There, the little Pakradounian house nestled in a spring-flushed orchard. Here, the Garden City church, its quince-shaped domes coloured a brilliant red. The ancient citadel, long since reduced to rubble at the end of the Great War, looms over the whole town. Houses becoming larger and more elaborate the closer they are to the centre of Van. The main square, some way in the distance, flanked by tiny shops where Minas has written *baker, bookshop, tailor,* then the town hall and its tree-shaded courtyard, scene of killing.

I've managed to take a few bites of my warm bread. I shut my laptop. The Lebanese woman and her companion wave goodbye, put their sunglasses on in one fluid movement and exit into the teeming street. A uniformed beggar with a withered stump sits at the front door whining, and they step over him. He's old and blind, probably a veteran of the civil war. Nails dirt-rimmed, patched trousers settling in sad folds at the backs of his knees. He babbles, stops mid-sentence to wipe his sightless eyes in an impatient, furious gesture. He's speaking in French. What's he saying? He still hates the Arabs. Demon Muslims, sons of goats; their bombs made him blind. Slashing light, he fell to the ground, all was black. There is no solution. Raze this city and start all over again.

I stay long enough to see the waiter shoo him away, remembering the thin white ribbons attached to landmines, the buzzing of the mosques all day, everyday, those pink and green and ash-yellow edifices of rotting rubble, all the erotica of a fallen city. My father.

I run to catch up with the blind man as he lurches across the street, leaving my glass of tea untouched, knowing as I run that I'm being stupid and sentimental. He slows down when he hears me, puts out a restraining hand. I let him touch my head, stroke my arms, up and down, exploring my closeness. A shudder of revulsion courses through me. If my father lived, would he be like this? The old man parrots his name, age and rank as if saluting a superior, then holds out his palm. I drop some liras into his hand, watch him finger the medals on his chest with tenderness, as if caressing a child's face.

BEIRUT, 1982

Selim walked home to his apartment in east Beirut after a night on the town. He needed the exercise, dismissed his driver so he could clear his head, become part of the early morning sounds and dawn light of the Christian quarter for the brief time before he'd have to become Selim Pakradounian again. Selim Pakradounian, second-in-command to Elie Hobeika; Selim Pakradounian, efficient killer; Selim Pakradounian, with so many men looking to him for guidance.

Now he could slink through alleyways, a lean cat sniffing the sea's trail. He stopped short at the thinness of a child's cry behind closed windows. A little girl? His? He liked to imagine peering in at his own daughter, ringlets damp with sweat, face rose-flushed against the pillow. She would smile in her sleep and know her daddy was watching. He hadn't meant to leave her for good when she was born; he was too young then, too angry. And now he was afraid to go back. What if Father wouldn't forgive him? What if Anoush rejected him? What if she cried and hid behind both her grandmothers' skirts? And what good could he do her anyway? A father just as absent even if he was right there by her side.

He could be of no use to her. Only the money he sent twice a year vindicated him. He wondered if she saw any of it, for study or clothes or music, or if his father squirreled it away for when she was married. Or worse still, spent it on the shop and the house. No matter. Sending it made him feel a little better, and that was all he could do. Perhaps it even softened his daughter's feelings for him, poisoned as they were by his aunt Lilit.

He saw himself reflected in the glass, only his moustache visible in a ghost-pale face. The heaviness of gardenias here on a low balustrade, and night jasmine thick as grapevines on Christian churches, Crusader castles, fountains, minarets across the Green Line. The wail of the muezzin from west Beirut, sharp as a needle in the clear morning air. A last star, hanging between two cypresses. He listened. A thrush, trembling on a low branch before launching into the same warble he'd heard every morning of his childhood in this city.

He turned his key in the lock, stumbled upstairs. He knew he'd suffer for his drinking binge, only time now for a quick shower and instant coffee before he had to report to Phalange HQ. He hated instant coffee, wasn't even sure there was a jar in the house. By Jesus he needed it, though. He pondered last night as he ripped off his clothes, remembered each detail with a lingering sensation of voluptuousness and a faint stirring of disgust. Those fleshy white women: journalists, aid workers, wives of businessmen, black-lace bras under corporate suits. How he loved to uncover them, in more ways than one. He left a pool of clothes on the bedroom floor.

While he stood under hot water – hot as he could bear it – he brushed his teeth with short, sawing motions, lost in thought. *Should be easier now the Israelis are coming to help out. About time too. For all their generosity, they haven't exactly been right by our side.* His gold cross became caught in his hairs as he soaped his chest. The chain twisted yet again. He bent his head under the water's stream, tried to disentangle those infuriating links. Gave up. Sanaya would do it tonight at her place. She was good at that sort of thing. He tried not to think of what she'd say if she learnt of these other women, chose instead to remember her creased neck smelling of talc and roses, the coil of caramel hair she freed from its pins to press like a river against his chest. Her superb jack-knifing spine when she spread herself out under him. She knew about his other women, even if it was left unsaid; she was worldly, not a child.

Invariably, as soon as he dwelled on Sanaya, he remembered his dead wife, while simultaneously trying to push the memory back, in the same way you struggle to fight off the onset of a cold. It was their wedding day that always came to him as clear – even clearer – as the first time they had sex. The sex had been rushed, icy, awkward. Painful for her. A death-knell for him. It was better not to remember.

Neither of them had smiled as they stood outside his father's house and waited for the priest to arrive. Such an honour, to be the first in the quarter married according to the old rites. 'And not a moment too soon,' the neighbouring women exclaimed, crossing their ample breasts. 'We arrived here fifty years ago.'

It had been hard, they conceded – chattering among themselves while Selim burned with boredom – what with the French occupation, famine in the twenties and two wars. They openly marvelled at the composure of the bride and groom. Selim and Anahit stood side by side, almost touching at arm and hip. First cousins, joined by blood. Behind them, fluted columns were festooned with tinsel and flowers, even the crazy outside plumbing draped with wreaths. 'Too much expense,' the muttering went. 'Who's Minas trying to impress?' Bougainvillea had been cut back to form a perfect bower, where Selim and his bride now stood. A shrewish wind rose high above roofs and aerials, away into the city. It flung petals onto Selim's shoulders, little flags of protest he brushed onto the ground. He didn't want to marry this girl – this cousin he'd known since he was born, seen bathe and eat and toilet, fought with and ignored. He looked at her belly under her wedding belt, still flat. He looked at the small, pinched mouth. He knew she'd been vomiting all morning, bending over the bathroom sink, quietly so nobody would know. Her cheeks were grey and white, ash and salt.

She didn't look at him. Guilty, maybe. She knew she'd trapped him now – with her mother's whispers, her pregnancy, her helplessness. She watched intently as the priest prepared to slit the throats of two white doves. The old man muttered, so the women had to lean forward to hear him. *Give the good news to the bride of light; thy groom is risen, go forth before him bedecked with adornments; sing a new song to him that is risen, to the fruit of life to them that are asleep.* He threw his beard over his shoulder in a way they thought far too irreverent, rolling up his wide black sleeves. The birds flapped in his hands, unblemished and perfect. *Selim and Anahit. Sacrificial doves.* Minas leaned over and whispered in his son's ear, clear and authoritative.

'Be good to her, my son. Don't shame me again.'

Selim had thought his father at least would take his part against the others. But no. There was something secret between Minas and his sister, something shiny and complicit. He'd seen his father's face darken when Anahit told him Selim had made her pregnant, but it was more in disapproval of his own son than in judgement of his sister and her daughter. Everyone blamed Selim. They said he was reckless, always had been, even as a child, that he should have known better. Everyone blamed him, except for his mother. He watched Siran now as she stood a little apart from Minas and Lilit, her face arranged into a studied neutrality. For the first time since he was born, he saw that her ears were naked.

Lining the street in a trailing circle were familiar faces, grinning under a trifling drizzle. Someone unfurled an oiled umbrella over the bride. She touched her rain-damp hair, smoothing it at the temples, checked to see the earrings Siran had given her still dangled cold and significant at her neck. Thickly gold as the hairs on her legs, turquoise as the veins at her wrists, the thin white skin over her breasts traced with blue. Her mother sighed.

Selim glanced at Lilit for a moment and a shadow of doubt passed over both their foreheads. *You forced me into this. Now you owe me everything, you owe me my life.* He knew what she was thinking in turn: *Will I be punished for wedding cousin to cousin? Will my daughter be cursed? The Arabs do it all the time.*

Minas coughed slightly and frowned as well, but Selim knew it was only because he was excited. Excited enough to say stupid things. He peered through the veil at the face of Anahit beside him, a face he'd known since his eyes could focus. Such filmy skin and translucent eyelids, such innocence, such trust in him. She wore the heavy bracelet his father had given her the day she arrived in Beirut. Selim looked down at his mirror-shine shoes, flinching from her gaze.

Now he shook his head to chase the memories away. This same bracelet circled his left wrist, caught and refracted the morning light as he rubbed at his neck with a flannel, scrubbed the back of his knees. It was a strange design, of bold interlinked silver squares and Armenian crosses, too masculine for a woman. One of the squares was slightly larger, and on it was engraved the surname *Pakradounian*, twisting along his inner wrist like a snake. It made a lozenge of light on the shower tiles. For a moment more, he was distracted from the demands of his day to stare at the pattern: *Look at the way I influence the world.* Then he turned his attention to his responsibilities. He mentally ticked off the least important items on his list: return telephone calls to the Red Cross, the Red Crescent, the UN, foreign-media news agencies; no time to attend to them now.

Enquiries about lists of Muslim deaths, casualties, victims of the Phalange. Unimportant. Anything they claimed could be censored before printing by the Phalangist office, anyway. The priority today was to boost morale. Although the other militias didn't know it, the Phalange had suffered a beating in the last few months. He allowed himself a chuckle. *The Israelis will soon help us reverse that. And they won't stay a minute longer than they have to. Just long enough to ensure a Maronite peace. Liberators.*

The hot water ran out within minutes. He jumped about underneath the dying stream, trying to wash the shampoo out of his hair and the soap out of his armpits without freezing to death. His penis had shrivelled to a dried date: insignificant. It was the only part of his body he forced himself to rinse thoroughly before he turned off the water. After all, it was the most important thing.

❋ *They're here,* Sanaya said to herself. *They're really here now.*

Scattered machine-gun fire reverberated through the corridors. It felt as though the gunmen would burst through the door in a moment, accuse her of everything and condemn her in an instant. There was a knock. She jumped. The door opened a crack and a black-veiled head poked through. Rouba's cheeks were rounder now, yet unhealthy, as if swollen by her grief. Behind her, Hadiya's flower-like face peeped into the room, eyes huge with fear.

'Hadiya's scared,' Rouba said. 'She kept asking for you. And I persuaded Issa to come up too. Do you mind if we—'

Issa squeezed through before them, hanging his head. Sanaya came with short hurrying steps, one hand outstretched to Hadiya as she fixed her gaze on him.

'Sorry, Issa—I—I'm surprised to see you here.'

She scooped Hadiya up into her arms, at the same time surveying Issa's face, attempting unsuccessfully to hide her stare. He was wounded, and blood seeped through an inexpertly tied bandage on his shoulder.

Rouba pushed forward. 'He won't let me look after him. Sanaya. Maybe you have some influence. He insists on bandaging himself.'

Issa squirmed under the combined gaze of both women, embarrassed.

'I haven't been out there at all today. My commander said I needed some time off after—after this happened to me. Of course I wanted to keep going—'

'Of course,' Sanaya echoed. Something in his voice wasn't right, as if he was hiding something. Lying. Yet why should he? She turned to the kitchen, put Hadiya down on a stool with a glass of peach nectar – Italian, a gift of Selim's. She rattled spoons and saucers. Who cared if Issa lied like everyone else? She lied all the time, most of all to herself. *I am strong. I am happy. I won't die like everyone else.* Any truth was a scarce enough commodity nowadays.

'I'm glad you're all here,' she said. 'I'll make some tea.'

The light bulb in the kitchen guttered and fizzled out, a faint rumble from afar and it shone steady again. Issa stood and cleared his throat.

'There's no water, Sanaya. Only what we've saved in the fountain. It's grey.'

'Damn, I forgot.'

'I'll go get some.'

'No you won't!' Rouba said. 'You're already wounded. I forbid you.'

'Who are you – a woman – to forbid me?'

'Be careful,' Sanaya said. 'We'll think you're serious.'

'I am,' he replied, and turned to go.

❋ On his way out of the building he patted the outline of his pistol through his shirt. He weaved through clumps of household garbage and stranded cars, others appearing stationary but actually caught in the eternal traffic jam of west Beirut. Some people were trying to get home before more bombardments, others trying to flee the city, even a few out merely for a drive because the incessant waiting at home to be hit was driving them crazy. Each driver's hand fixed permanently to the horn. Those leaving Beirut were jammed in, ten to a car, roof racks strapped with the accumulation of lifetimes: heirloom blankets, gas stoves, overstuffed mattresses, even a black goat that bleated in fury as it was forced to endure the dust, the heat, the smoke and ashes of a disintegrating city. The deserters were the most insistent honkers of all.

He hummed to loud radio music mingling with the honking, in rhythm with the gunfire, syncopating the faraway bombs. The petrol station on the corner was overflowing with people jostling each other to buy enough fuel to get them to the countryside. Taxi drivers loitered nearby, knowing those desperate enough or unprepared enough would pay any price to get out.

As Issa crossed to the seafront, he wrinkled his nose at the stink of raw sewerage thrown up by the tide and admonished himself for showing such weakness. A warrior of the Prophet must be as stone. No human emotion must touch him, only purified fire from the fear of Allah. He thought of his mother with painful affection; that in itself was weakness. He thought of that woman Sanaya, of her immodesty and imperious voice; weakness again.

Weakness. He knew too much about it, didn't want to go back down south. Not ever. He slapped his right hand to his heart. Through the dense haze of car exhausts he spied his regional commander's gleaming Renault. Could it be his? He dived behind a parked car and hid, trembling. He was shirking his duty, staying with the women tonight. He'd be sent back to the south as punishment if he was caught, and this he wouldn't – couldn't – bear. There was something there, something dark, that he dared not admit to himself.

He was letting down his friends, his fellow freedom fighters. He knew at this very moment they were running on foot into Israeli gunfire. The Jews were advancing into the city, by ground and air. His friends were launching homemade grenades at Israeli tanks, unafraid, spines tingling, shrieking the oath of Allah at their foes. *Allahu Akbar*. God is great. He too should be there. They were tearing pieces from their shirts and wrapping them about their foreheads like Khomeini's martyrs. His friends were within twenty feet of death. And here he was, hiding behind a car, twitching in fear.

When the Renault moved on, after what seemed like hours, he made for Rue Hamra. There was sure to be at least one shop open to buy some bottles of water. Those renegade shopkeepers would never pass up a chance to make a profit, even at the risk of being bombed. He ran down the street now, afraid the bombing might begin again. His head jerking to the right and left. Signs on the awnings showed more French, less Arabic, these days. Some were even replaced by Hebrew graffiti, no doubt scrawled by the Phalange.

Tattered posters of the Syrian president smiled at him. Assad everywhere: on the shuttered shopfronts, flapping in the wind from the sea, on the windscreens of cars alongside shiny pictures of Bashir Gemayel, the Phalangist poster boy, in his aviator sunglasses and a deeper shade of tan. Other posters, more garish: Yasir Arafat parting his fleshy lips in a leer and gazing toward the green-girdled fantasy of a free Palestine. *Butchers all,* Issa thought. *And that Arafat worse than all of them, pretending to do right by his people and all the while only looking after himself. Hypocrite.* Syrian or Lebanese or Palestinian, all they wanted was earthly power without the will of Allah.

He tore down the newer poster of Gemayel and tried to rip it in half. It was laminated, impossible to tear, so he threw it to the ground, stamping on it with his scuffed boots.

'Hey, son! What are you doing?'

An old man leaned out of his newspaper booth, upsetting straight rows of cigarettes and chocolate bars and Tic Tac dispensers.

'That's our future Christian president! What business have you to do this?'

'There's no God but Allah.'

'Are you crazy?'

Issa looked up and down the street. In a dawning joy he realised he and the old man were the only people on the rubbish-strewn, windswept street. Not even the foolhardy shoeshine boys had dared to venture out today. He scanned the booth, the old man, the pornographic magazines, the rows upon rows of bottles. Soft drink. Water.

'Give me five of your biggest bottles of water.'

He took out his gun; it peeked almost shyly from the gap in his shirt buttons. The old man saw it and started to cry.

'Don't kill me. Please don't kill me. I'm just trying to make a living.'

'Give me the water.' A weird, unknown exhilaration took hold of him. It was unlike the adrenaline and raw animal pleasure he took in operating the tank down south, in attacking Israeli soldiers, in hand-to-hand combat against a creature equally armed and dangerous with killing lust. This man was pleading and sobbing. His mouth opened and closed, pink as a child's in search of nourishment. Issa raised his pistol to the old man's smooth oval head and watched as bottles were arranged on the counter by shaking hands. He put the pistol back, hugged the water to his chest and strolled away.

✳ Sanaya doled out her daily ration of face cream each night before bed, frightened of the day there would be no more, yet at the same time ashamed of herself: others were already drinking salt water and eating garbage from the road. She knew Selim could get her some, even from Paris, but didn't want to ask. Why not? She asked him for almost everything else. Yet it was at these times she felt a jab of guilt. If he weren't so free with his largesse, would she want him at all?

She wiped off her make-up, spat into a cotton-ball and dabbed at her eyes. 'Spit's good for the skin,' Rouba said. 'Enzymes.' Tonight she was restless; she grimaced into her reflection and decided she looked older than ever, tired. Her eyes, once so bright and clear, were drooping, the irises a muddy colour. Wrinkles fanned out from the lids. She frowned, smiled, pouted at the mirror – and felt ashamed. She wanted to be frivolous like those Christian girls in east Beirut, wanted to see European films at the cinema, eat ice-cream at the seaside, travel north to a seafood restaurant in Byblos, white awnings pulled tight against a rising wind. She wanted to go with a man, any man, to that tiny two-seat cafe near the Pigeon Rocks, wear floaty dresses, string bikinis, have sex. She couldn't do any of these things in west Beirut. Except the last.

So she waited for Selim to knock on her door once a week, sometimes twice, if she was lucky. He could cross from one side of the Green Line to the other, unlike her. His militia protected him at checkpoints, with M16 rifles and Sherman tanks. She readied the apartment for his arrival: killed the spiders which determinedly spun their webs across her cornices, dusted the gilt-framed lithographs of Lebanese mountains and rivers she might be destined to never see again, mourned the loss of an old Beirut she half remembered, the one part of her childhood memory she allowed herself to dwell on fondly.

The rest was all falsity, the crumbling facades of the city's buildings, her frustrated dreams. Yet at times the destruction of Beirut pained rather than strengthened her resolve; at times she heard the tinkling of her mother's voice like a taunt. *Don't think you can fool me. The fall of Beirut will mirror your own decay.* She remembered her self-consciousness as a teenager, her creeping boredom, the frilled little girl's dress she was forced to wear that scratched at her new breasts and throat. Mother was always at home to welcome visitors on Sunday afternoons, with murmured gossip under rattling teacups, the low laughter of well-dressed women, a lone piano playing the latest sheet music from France.

She could feel it as she woke and made tea and sat on the balcony in her mother's dressing-gown, that pink silk grown threadbare under the arms: she'd become another forgotten member of the Sunni bourgeoisie, this new class of existential emigrants, homeless souls, internal exiles. Much as she despised them for their wealth and stupidity, their middle-class values, she'd become them. Become her mother of thirty years ago, a refugee of memory and the mind. She had something in common with Selim, at least. He always went on about being the son of an Armenian.

They had met at a party in east Beirut a year ago, when it was still possible for civilians to cross the Green Line and back again in a night. One of the many glittering receptions given by a leading hostess of the city. Tables so full of meze plates and serving platters and tureens the polished surfaces were no longer visible. More drink available than any of the well-stocked bars on the Corniche, and a record player pumping out a distorted version of the *Sgt. Pepper* album. It was one of those conspicuously wealthy parties, in appalling taste; the mood was jaded, edgy, slightly dangerous, and she found herself sitting alone near a potted palm, glad of the viewing screen it offered.

Her friend Amani had invited her. 'Come along,' she had said earlier that evening. 'My husband's away lecturing and I have nobody to go with.' Sanaya agreed, thinking the two of them would have a few quiet drinks, laugh at the antics of the other guests, then leave.

She needed a diversion; she'd been alone too long, spent too much time in her apartment, had even pleaded illness when her cousins insisted on their monthly drinks at her place. She wasn't sure why she felt so apathetic lately. Well, she was sure, but didn't care to admit it to herself. Somehow the bright girlhood dreams she once cherished had faded. There was no large future out there for her. There was no adventure, romance, success. This was it. Life was mundane and dangerous, and the realisation of this made her curl up into herself.

So that night she forced herself to swallow her social queasiness and dress for the party. She thought Amani would introduce her to a few friends, share some idle gossip. But Amani was out to have a good time – too good a time. As soon as they arrived, she disappeared into a side door with a tall man, a bottle of champagne and a wink at Sanaya.

Sanaya tried to smile when people walked past, raised their drinks to her. Others danced on the balcony, threw their empty glasses down, trying to skim them across the surface of the sea. They pointed and exclaimed at colours in the sky. Bursts of light from bombs and shells falling in other parts of the city were merely a backdrop to the view. Stars extinguished. Another explosion. Familiar war. The incessant crack of machine-gun fire, only a faintly off-the-beat bass line to the music inside.

Sanaya hummed along to 'Lucy in the Sky with Diamonds'. It was a strange choice. Out of date, ironic even, nostalgic for better days when there was no war, when Beirut was that much-lauded but true cliché: Paris of the East. Sanaya closed her eyes. She wanted to dance alone, oblivious to the ugliness around her, float among clouds with diamonds in place of pupils, a third eye shining bright. She let herself sway a little, opened her eyes. A man walking by raised his glass to her, self-deprecating, with a twist to the mouth. He was heavily tanned, like a construction worker, the whites of his eyes too bright. A woman behind him struck poses on the coffee table, in her own self-imposed trance, pushing aside the tiny, heaped plates onto the carpet with her stiletto heels. The man stopped in front of Sanaya, his body blocking out the other people. He was wearing a tuxedo, and although his dress shirt was half out of his trousers she thought him pretentious.

'Having fun?'

She raised her eyes up to him and smirked, sitting more upright on her chair, cross-legged, almost prim except for her bare, hose-free legs.

'Not really.'

His attention wandered for a moment; a blonde leaned backward over the balcony, screaming, her bell-shaped sleeves flying in the breeze. Sanaya looked, too, and grimaced.

'I haven't had enough to drink, maybe that's why.'

He topped up her glass with whisky from a bottle he carried under his arm. She didn't think it strange at the time. She was only conscious of him looking at her. His too-white eyes were now closed, the violet lids veined with thread-like capillaries. When he opened them, he didn't blink. From his vantage point, she felt he could see right down into her cleavage. She stood up, too close in the humid, smoke-filled air, uncomfortably close. Excitingly close. He didn't move, their torsos and faces almost touching.

'What?' she asked. 'Is there something wrong?'

He shook his head. Together in rhythm, they turned and downed their glasses of whisky. He shook out a packet of cigarettes.

'Smoke?'

'Sometimes.'

She let him lean forward and light the cigarette for her, smelled something from his hair, spice and sourness; a lock of it touched her face. She shivered, felt the pressing-down sensation of desire in her belly, runnels of energy, almost like anxiety, or ambiguous signals of distress. She inhaled, felt the smoke enter her brain in tendrils like another form of lust.

That had been a year ago, to the day. An anniversary of sorts. Tonight, Selim would be dropped off at her apartment by his fellow militiamen, after an evening session at the gym. It was always a different Mercedes, armour-plated, that she could see from her upstairs window: always a different number plate, but always with the same gleam, the same plushness, the same understated malice. He was still sweaty and red-faced when he arrived, clutching a half-full bottle of Johnny Walker and jumbo packets of Marlboros, tokens of the generosity and goodwill of Israel and America. No matter how many times he brought these gifts, she tried to make him take them back. But she still wanted them, regretted her scruples once again when he took them away.

The money he brought her she always accepted. He pressed folded notes into her hand in rainbow currencies – dollars, deutschmarks, pounds – citing her cracked ceiling, her mother's massive, mahogany furniture, the leak from next door's bathroom seeping into her hall. He never brought her Lebanese liras, worthless for anything but buying bread and newspapers. She conferred with him and nodded at his suggestions, but when he was gone she put the money away under the bed, separate from her own emergency stash. She had no heart for repairs and purchases. She knew Selim didn't even notice each time he visited that the apartment hadn't changed at all. She wasn't sure what to do with the money, but continued to stretch her hand out for more. There was tangible security in so many bills, even if they were worthless.

He eased her into his arms as she stood by the door and, further still, into a blanket of cologne. Under the green upland scent, something rancid as bacteria. She extricated herself from him and lit another cigarette, took some Valium from the packet he proffered.

'Sit down and stop pawing me. I need a glass of water with this.'

'I can paw you better in bed.'

She let him lead her by the elbow to her bedroom, swallowed her pills dry.

Selim, as second-in-command to the Christian Phalange leader, specialised in assassinations of key Muslims: rival militiamen, political subversives, intellectuals. The regiments within the Phalange sported religious titles evocative of the Crusades: Selim's was called The Knights of the Virgin. Whenever he – rarely – went into battle against the PLO or any of the other factions, he wore an enormous rose-red crucifix embroidered onto his breastplate.

'So they know where to hit me,' he told her. 'Right over the heart.'

He saw himself as a Crusader of old, defending Christendom against the bloody hand of Islam. His brand of idealism came with an essential pragmatism, his religion merely a sentimental exercise reserved for Sunday mornings and the lulling ritual of litany, requiring less a conviction of faith than a simple appreciation of the pleasures of incense and flowers. Certainty and absolution, strictly earthly concerns. The fact that Sanaya was born a Muslim didn't seem to pose a problem in this rough reasoning of his. It was as though he saw women operating outside religion: featureless, fashioned by man not God, neutral bounty, unwieldy spoils of war.

She didn't want to marry a Muslim. This was partly why she continued to see Selim. Even with his early paunch, his bloodshot eyes, his drinking, he was a good catch. His legs and arms were strong; in summer, with his tan, he looked like a man of the land. She loved this about him, the thrum of sinew and muscle beneath his flesh. She loved his thick eyelashes. She loved his glossy hair. Or so she liked to tell herself. He had power in this upside-down world of war. And some of his tarnished lustre brushed onto her, however briefly, if only when she lay in bed with him before dusk, saffron circle of the late sun clawing its way through her blinds. His palms were soft on her belly, her cheeks, through her hair, his thighs hairless and vulnerable between hers. It was the Armenian in him, he said. Pliable, but steely beneath.

Why should she marry a Muslim when she owned her apartment outright, bequeathed by her parents, in the family for generations? A Muslim husband would only take it for himself, depriving her of freedom. Why would she settle for a Muslim when she had an independent income? Old money hidden in tight rolls, withdrawn from the bank at the beginning of the war, still just enough, even with such inflation, for some luxuries. Gold and silver jewellery, her mother's rings and necklaces and brooches to sell on the black market if things got really bad.

But at the same time she knew there was no future for her with Selim. Their casual union was illegal, since civil marriages didn't exist in Lebanon. Even if they agreed to take the final step, they'd have to make their way to Cyprus to bind it. So she kept Selim a secret, from her neighbours, girlfriends, the cousins who came for cocktails once a month – such casual Muslims – and tried to arrange matches with her among their fundamentalist friends.

Her eldest cousin, Shahid, almost suspected. He drew her aside regularly to whisper in her ear, elbow resting on the kitchen counter near the knives as he watched her slice shreds of orange, mix drinks. His admission of violence all the more sinister for being so intimate.

'If you play with Christians, Sanaya, you know what you'll get.'

She shook her head, knife poised above the fruit's soft pale heart, mesmerised by her cousin's slow breathing. His face was calm when she lifted her eyes to him, his expression self-possessed. He trailed a pinkie finger – offensive, the long burnished nail – in a line from her eye to her jaw.

'You'll get your face cut, Sanaya. You know that's what they'll do.'

Despite the threats, she didn't stop seeing Selim. She was more afraid of the alternative: arranged marriage, unsought babies, the unwelcome clinches she'd be forced to submit to each night. No marriage to a Muslim, no sharing her man with another woman. Or three. No divorce whenever he felt like taking someone younger into his bed, throwing Sanaya out of the house and even taking away her children. Not that the Koran authorised any of this behaviour. She read the Koran every night before bed, even when Selim was there, even when he laughed at her. She read the Bible as well, but mainly for the Old Testament stories. It was the Koran she believed: the unassailable word of truth. She read it and cursed those mullahs and clerics, unscrupulous fools sanctifying man-made rules in their own interest.

BEIRUT, 1995

Someone is coming to meet me this evening – a contact I met through the tribunal. When I went back for my second session he got up to testify, in his role as project manager for the UN's post-conflict portfolio. His team spends a lot of time in the Palestinian camps in Beirut and the south of the country.

He'd been a UNDP finance manager during the civil war, so had seen the Phalangist militias assembling outside the camp before the massacre, asked them what they were doing, and in getting no real reply had called his superiors. Strangely, throughout his testimony he accused both Phalangists and Israelis, but I could also detect his faint distaste for the Palestinians. As if he thought everyone was as bad as each other, and that he was above them all. He mentioned my father's name three times as well and each time I heard those familiar syllables coming from his stranger's mouth, in that transatlantic, cultivated accent, I burned from my stomach to my cheeks, red with blood.

When he finished, he sat – I can only assume deliberately – right down beside me. His name is Kajetan D'Andrea, an Italian of indeterminate age. He could have known my father personally. I don't know yet. I haven't told him my surname, or whose daughter I am, just that I'm an American journalist interested in writing an article about the massacre for *The Boston Globe*. I've arranged to meet him this evening in the lobby. I was faintly alarmed, but not really surprised, at how keen he was to follow up.

The phone rings. Reception calling. 'A gentleman called Mr D'Andrea down here to see you, madam.'

'Already? Sorry, yes, I'll be down in five minutes.'

I put the phone down, suddenly sweating so much my singlet sticks to my body. D'Andrea said we could meet at ten-thirty, and at first I was put out by how late people stay up in Lebanon. But now the night has slipped away from me, and I'm not even dressed. Cockroaches scuttle into corners as I turn on the bathroom light, strip off, splash myself with water. There's no window, only an air vent with the cover torn off. The open shower drain emits a melancholy odour. I want something tough to wear, a man's shirt with unbreakable thread. A belt to tighten around my waist, so I won't have to breathe out and feel any ambivalence. Instead I slap on some deodorant, hide my tattoo with a blouse, fluff out my hair.

As I press the button for the lift and hear the eighties' muzak piped from downstairs there's my father, always my father's mystery, his hard knuckle knocking and demanding entry into my life. Selim, the evil martyr, whose face I sometimes can't remember, then conjure up in disparate shapes to comfort myself. Only some aging photographs, a scrawled note, to anchor him to his brief life. And all these years later I feel an illogical guilt: at leaving Beirut, joining with Lilit against Siran to erase his memory, not being there to save him. Yet he left me first, the day I was born. I feel no anger at this – at least consciously. He was so young. My mother trapped him by falling pregnant. He hadn't loved her, so Siran said. But did he love me? He couldn't have, surely, if he left me so soon then made no attempt to see me again. Even so, the smell of certain festival foods, batter, sugar, meat; the haze of quiet, sun-filled, dirty streets; the reiteration of a minor key in a woman's voice, all remind me of him: a man I never knew.

In the lobby, D'Andrea waits. He rises from his seat as I enter, puts out a slender hand.

'I'm sorry I came so early – I don't know this side of the city so well. Do you prefer English, Arabic, French?'

'English, if you don't mind.'

'Tea, coffee? Something stronger, yes?'

He pours, I accept whatever it is.

'So, how can I help you?'

'I wanted to ask …' I feel embarrassed, wonder if he can see it. He inclines his head, inviting me to speak.

'I wanted to ask whether I could get in contact with any aid workers at the Sabra-Shatila camps, and maybe some of the Palestinians who live there. I'm thinking of writing an article for *The Globe*. "Fifteen years later, the survivor's story" – something along those lines. What do you think?'

'A worthy story indeed. Very worthy.' He pauses. 'I can get you limited access to the camps, if you like. You can interview some of the women and teenagers. The older men are not so keen to talk to reporters, as you understand.'

I murmur my thanks. He looks around the lobby, back at me. His eyes lock with mine. Now I allow myself to really see his face: sharp nose, silvered goatee, short legs in expensive suit trousers with immaculate cuffs.

'Why don't we go somewhere … a little more comfortable? Have dinner, a few drinks. Have you eaten? We can talk further about the contacts you need.'

I hesitate, feel slightly pushed, but say yes. He hasn't given me any contacts yet.

We go to an exclusive restaurant on the Corniche, in a high-rise far above the city. Reflexively, as we sit down to dinner, I finger the recorder in my bag.

We talk half the night, on deep couches, under dim lamps.

✳ Back in my room, it's just past six in the morning. I'm not ready yet to fully remember what he did, what I almost let him do.

I blame myself most of all: for being too open, too empty, too trusting. For giving the impression that I liked him more than I did. I remember I was shaking on my walk back to the hotel, but I'm not anymore.

I can say that, after a few drinks, I finally told him my surname and whose daughter I am. He seemed aroused by that, suddenly leaned forward over the low table, his eyes alight. We went for a walk to the beach across the road, at four in the morning. All I can recall with any composure now are his final words to me, before I broke free, running away from the black pre-dawn sea. He said he knew who ordered the killing of my father, and could arrange to have the surviving family 'taken care of'. The subtext to this was, provided I do what he wants.

I listen to my voice on the tape, rising slightly, becoming panicked, and on top of mine his protesting drunken slur. My feet, soft at first, and harder as I make it to the boulevard. *Click.* Silence.

Now I have his voice on tape, saying something so incriminating as to be laughable. Why did he think he could trust me with his indiscretions? I'm almost sure he didn't know my recorder was in my bag, but did he really think I won't pass on what he said? Maybe he thinks I'm such small fry he has nothing to fear from me. I'm not sure whether to erase the tape now or call the editor in Boston right away. So I do nothing.

I'm exhausted, sweaty, soiled. Sitting on the bed, I call the UNDP number scrawled by him. I wonder if it's too early; but no, a woman with a Texan accent explains there are certain families whose homes are open to journalists. She tells me to wait on the line, and five minutes later she confirms that an older woman who survived the 1982 massacre is available next week. She says the woman seemed surprised when told my surname, that she may have even recognised it. Could this be a sensitive situation? Has anyone in my family ever been an aid worker, doctor, an English teacher in the camps perhaps? A sharp, cold column, like sudden sickness, passes through me.

'Please make sure you don't ask any difficult questions,' the woman says. 'Nothing political. We don't want to offend anybody. I'll be sending you the forms to fill and sign today. Please send them back ASAP. And obviously, as the paperwork will explain, we need to see any articles you write before anyone else.'

I write down the Palestinian woman's details. Her name is Bilqis Ali. I note bus routes from Rue Hamra. The woman wishes me a nice day and hangs up.

I'm shaking after this conversation. Everything is political, I want to say. Don't talk to me about difficult questions. A flash of D'Andrea's hands comes to me: the way he gripped my wrists with one hand and pushed down on my shoulder with the other. For a second, I'm inflamed by hatred for him. Then I start blaming myself again. And I'm anxious about the Palestinian woman who seemed to recognise my surname. Could she have known my father? He would never have been friendly with Muslims, let alone Palestinians. Maybe his Muslim lover knew these people, maybe he helped them through her in the past. At this point I'll do anything, put myself through thousands of tortuous equations, to prove that my father was not all bad.

I'm paralysed on the hotel bed. I stare at the table at my side, the fragile amulets I've grouped there to keep me safe. Unread novels, cheap hotel pens. Lilit's photograph, buckling in the humid air. I lie on my back among countless pillows that are too hard or too high or too thin and look at the ceiling: discoloured, a water stain the shape of a stunted tree blossoming out from the wall. Holding my elbows tightly, trying to stop from flying apart. I would like to believe I can find the truth here. That there's only one truth, and that my father's actions will be finally vindicated by the tribulations suffered by his race. I need to believe that the massacres, the deportations, the destruction of a culture and its people were not for nothing. That my father did only what he thought was good. If this is a made-up story I'm telling myself, then I can at least control the characters, their motives, the ending. This will be a happy ending, and I should be part of it. I can will this life of mine to flash into brilliance, unfurl a terrible beauty – exactly how I imagine my Armenian ancestors, struggling to retain their dignity, the child destined to be my grandfather trudging alone into the night. Selim dogging his father's footsteps, civil war raging around him, killing, being killed. I know all the details. Did I make them up? If I think too hard about my family I'll leave, never to return. All the while I know the end to this particular story can't be happy no matter how hard I try.

LAKE VAN, TURKISH ARMENIA, 1915

Minas bent over his history books, steeling himself to forget it was spring, to ignore the soft, painful scents of plum trees and dry grass, the niggling reminder of other boys on the bank of the lake, slippery in the setting sun. He could hear their shouts carrying through the evening quiet to his window, where he sat hunched over the narrow ledge with his schoolbooks spread before him, Papa's blunt nib seeping in the margins. He knew he could be punished for this by his teacher, but also knew it wouldn't be severe, as he was displaying *initiative* and *individualism*, both prized above anything else by his American teacher at the mission school.

To date, the glorious Ottoman Empire spans the Caucasus to Eastern Anatolia and as far as the Balkans, he wrote. *Unfortunately, the Great War has put a stop to any further imperialist ambitions. The Allies are doing enough of that.* He put the pen down, chin on hand. The other boys' shouts grew raucous. He picked up his pen again, inked out *glorious.*

Lilit came through the door, waving goodbye with her kerchief to someone who had only just run past below the hedge; she was still laughing, flushed with heat and vanity and the small, sweet deceits of her afternoon. Minas straightened up, peering through the cracked and flawed pane.

'Who was that, chasing you to the front door of our house?'

'Nobody. Anyway, Mr Nosey, you're too young to question me about what I do.'

'Wait till Mamma gets home and you'll have something to worry about. Mincing around here in your red shoes.'

She poked out her tongue, admiring the bright wooden clogs she wore, pointing her toe rudely toward him. He refrained from his desire to hit her, retreating into lofty disdain. He hadn't much respect for her nowadays; she was out all the time, neglecting her chores, hiding in overgrown thickets and caves with her boyfriend. He even saw her at it once, moaning and licking at this boy's face, eyes closed against the world. He came upon them by accident, glad they hadn't spied him and relieved to escape without a thrashing. They were high on the slope of the mountain, under the shelter of cliff-side carvings his teacher told him dated from the Bronze Age. Etched designs of knowledge trees and streams of wisdom. Spiral suns and moons shaped like curving prows, for navigating sweeter dreams. Van cats with eyes of blue and amber; every beast of field and steppe. Such beasts, his sister and that boy. It disgusted him, Lilit's open need, the slight whimpers she made as she turned her head from side to side.

Now she tore a thick crescent from the bread on the table and devoured it, keeping half an eye on him.

'Hey, I just baked that! It's all we have for tonight.'

She ignored him, proceeding to swallow her last morsel and tear another piece from the ashy, still-warm disc.

'Mmm. Needs some oil and honey, I think—'

He couldn't let her get away with this. He bounded in front of her and grabbed her high up near the armpit. The bread fell to the ground and she fell with it, gasping, still laughing, tickling him hard until he fell on top of the bread too and bellowed at her to stop with breathless, wound-up cries.

They scrambled to their feet in a sudden shadow cast from the open door. It was Mamma.

'What is going on here? I leave you two alone for an hour and what do I see?'

Minas picked up the bread from the ground and put it on the table again, giving the edges little pats here and there to squash it back into place.

✳ Lilit lay with Yervan in his father's stables. Sounds all around were muted: the low cackle of a broody hen, rustling of straw – 'It could be rats,' she whispered, but he shook his head – the high, limpid call of the shepherd to his few remaining lambs. She was almost content here,

Yervan's arm strong around her waist, her head carved into the curve of his shoulder. Yet at the same time not completely content; she didn't like his attention to be somewhere other than on her.

She'd traversed fields of green-capped wheat to come to his house, afraid of being seen by a relative or neighbour on the main road and questioned. She was especially wary of Yervan's father seeing her on his property, making haste as she climbed the fence to run toward the stables. The old man had been heard to say he would kill the boy himself before he saw him married to a Pakradounian, with no dowry to speak of and a mother who read American books when she should have been bearing sons.

Her skirt was soaked through to her drawers by the dew that lay thick on the crops even at noon; spring had arrived late this year and the earth still retained the damp and danger of winter. Her eyes were dazzled by the intensity of wild poppies and anemones thrusting out of the grass. She picked a few of the reddest for Yervan, and took off her sodden skirt when she arrived, as well as her stockings. There they lay now, faintly human still from the imprint of her legs, crumpled from being peeled off in such haste. She wondered if they were dry enough to wear again, although she luxuriated in this half-nudity, Yervan's rough wool sleeve against the smoothness of her belly.

She sat up and checked on her stockings, feeling the dampness of fabric between thumb and forefinger. The anemones were limp now, already shedding their petals. Yervan moved his body a little to the left, finding a more comfortable position. She took the flowers and began pulling the heads off poppies, scattering them over his face and torso. Yervan didn't stir. He lay on his back, eyes wide open, looking beyond the vaulted roof to something else. His mastiff slept beside him, snoring gently in its dreams, and Yervan kept one hand on the dog's coarse flank.

She lay down again, throwing petals at his hair. If she moved her head a little to the right she could see his profile: too close, even painful, the edges of brow and nose and chin sharp against the fading light. He didn't respond to her, merely kept gazing far away, his face still and unmoving at her side with its fall of crimson.

All afternoon he'd been that way, refusing to caress her when she undressed, not talking much, sighing too often. She had lain like that for hours now, shivering, exposed, and he hadn't said anything at all. No compliments. Not even pleasantries. Selfish. Wrapped in his big man's thoughts, while she curled up beside him, freezing. And hungry. There wasn't much food left at home anymore, what with Kurds coming on midnight raids and the Turks taking the spoils. Shopkeepers in Van had barricaded their doors and windows to no avail. The peasants in Garden City could do nothing when they woke in the morning to find all their fruit and vegetables gone. Yet Yervan's parents were rumoured to have stockpiles. People even whispered they were collaborators.

'I must go,' Lilit said. 'Mamma will be home soon.'

He continued to look upward, not heeding her movements as she rose and pulled on her skirt, an old velvet jacket far too tight, so she looked awkward when she walked and tried to swing her arms. It was not like him to ignore anything she did. She bundled one of her breasts further into her blouse and leaned over him.

'Yervan? I said I'm going.'

He passed a hand over his eyes, scowled at nothing in particular.

'I'm sorry, Lilit, I just feel so lazy – and what's the point of anything?'

She laughed, but not too loudly in case someone should hear.

'Has your papa been waking you too early for the chores?'

'No—no. He lets me sleep late when I'm not at school. But—I'm not well, I think.'

She bent down further, felt a wave of concern flood her face.

'Do you have pain?'

She pressed her palm to his forehead, pulled up his shirt to expose his belly.

'No, no pain. I think I'm—frightened. In my stomach and my head. Did you know the Armenians in the army have had their weapons confiscated? Papa told me they'll just be killed now.'

'Why would they do that, Yervan? The Muslims need us, always have. We're smarter than them.'

She scoffed at his fears and left, after kissing him on the mouth and demanding they meet tomorrow at the same time. The skin of her forearms prickled with impatience. As she turned to go, Yervan yelled after her, heedless of any farmhands hearing him.

B
O
N
E

75

'Lilit! I'm worried you and I are doing the wrong thing and we'll be punished for it too.'

The dog followed her to the boundary of his master's property, as if seeing her safely away, but she ignored him as she had ignored Yervan. Surely he was being silly, too sensitive. As if God were an irascible old prude, with nothing better to do than punish people who loved each other! Yet when she walked, scuffing her clogs on the gravel like any child, she wondered if Yervan was right. If God wouldn't punish them, the Turks would.

Now she'd seen him, she was somewhat bolder and scorned the wet way home through the fields. It was quicker to pass the central square but she didn't look in the shop windows as she always did. She was already late. Mamma might be home already, and Minas was sure to tell. Also, there were more soldiers than usual crowding the middle of the square, loitering near the bakery, squatting on their haunches with cigarettes as if their time was their own. Of course they were all Turks. A pair got up when they saw her and pretended to be on duty, tearing down some flaking insurgents' posters from the walls. *Better ten days' liberty than to die the slaves we've been.* She tried to avoid them by walking fast and keeping her head down. She couldn't help noticing the others tearing at freshly baked loaves, fluffy and white and unlike any bread she had seen in a long while, cramming it into their mouths. Others held *simit*, the ring-shaped sesame rolls she remembered Papa bringing home on winter evenings when she was a child. Before this war raging through all of Europe, before the Turks had taken over the town. It was all she could do not to beg them to give her one.

She didn't like the way the soldiers looked at her. *Is it wrong to let Yervan touch me? Can they see it?* Their stares confirmed her suspicions. They lingered too long on the flex of her breasts and arms, on her black-bright hair under a brighter scarf. She reddened, looked down at her feet. She knew Turks were afraid of blue eyes, thought they could cast evil spells. Who knew what they would do to her if they took it into their heads she was a witch? An Armenian witch. They kept staring. One soldier's fists were clenched at his sides. Lilit turned away. She began to stride over the cobblestones – hard to do in clogs. One Turk stood and leapt in front, barring her way.

'Hey, little one,' he said, stretching his arms out wide.

She dodged him, but now there were others all around, laughing at her and shouting in Turkish.

'Pretty whore! Pretty unbeliever!'

She crossed her arms over her chest, tried to find a way out of the crush of men's bodies, their sweat, their breath.

'Come on, *gaivour*, how about a look at this?'

The soldier in front made as if to unbutton his trousers. She ducked away from him, evaded grasping hands, running through the mass of stamping boots and kit and laughing faces. As she ran she could feel them pelting her with their pieces of bread.

✳   Bread at home became blacker and coarser and Lilit's hands hurt from kneading. She complained of it every day and Minas could see tiny cracks of blood in her knuckles when he looked hard enough. He would have baked for her but the jobs Mamma assigned him now were all out of the house. He grew tired of spotting the grains left behind on the threshing floor after the army requisitioned the town's harvest, hauling his meagre collection onto the table before stomping out to sit in the yard, head on knees, eyes smarting.

'Don't whine,' Lilit called to him, wiping the last of the grey dough from her fingers. 'At least you're not here when they burst in searching for arms.'

She took to hiding in the back storeroom whenever there was rumour of a search, a woollen scarf snug around her face. Minas felt sorry and brought her mugs of well water and even some of his simpler books; there was nothing else he could do. She had only finished three years of school before Mamma and Papa kept her home, so her reading of Turkish and even Armenian script was not very advanced. Minas sat with her some evenings and tried to teach her the harder words, but she became petulant and flung the book to the floor. He knew she hadn't seen Yervan for weeks. He tried to care, but couldn't.

There was more talk of killings at night, rape by the light of a lamp. Fortunately, nothing like that had happened to anyone in the Garden City neighbourhood, or to any of their relatives in the walled town. Only the poorer folk who lived near the army barracks. The streetwalkers who prowled the banks of the lake at night. The widows. The beggar women. But one could never be sure, Mamma said. So Lilit was banished to the storeroom for more and more hours each day, and Minas was ordered not to play outside with his friends from school. Most of them had joined the resistance, anyway.

Soon no one ventured out of the house unless there was no other alternative. Although Minas was considered small for his age, Mamma was afraid he would be abducted by the Turks for conscription in road gangs or labour camps, or even worse. School closed and his teacher fled to relatives far away in Dilijan, high up in the wooded mountains of the northern Caucasus. A combined force of Turks and Kurds besieged the centre of town and the Armenian insurgents hidden in basements were defeated in days. One hundred villages around Van were torched, they heard, but Mamma told Minas and Lilit not to worry, they would still be safe. Papa promised by laying his hand on his heart and poking his tongue out as he did when they were small, making them laugh despite themselves. Rings of fire danced above the trees and dyed the night sky red.

The men of Garden City still went to work each morning; they had no choice. The Turks had already conscripted Armenians to fight against the Russians in the Caucasus, against the British in Syria and Palestine. Minas had stood with Papa and watched them march by the house a year ago on their way to the front, in dun-coloured uniforms, proud rifles over their shoulders. One of the conscripts, a Syrian Arab, looked as young as Minas, though he must have been fourteen at least. He was being used as a *hamal*, a human beast of burden loaded down with supplies. He stumbled a little in his cast-off boots and a Turkish officer pushed him down into the mud with a foot between his shoulder blades. The boy spluttered and choked but the officer held him down until he lay limp and unresisting. Minas wasn't so frightened by the boy's pain as by Papa's reaction; he staggered to the table and placed his head in his hands as if he had already seen too much.

'If they're doing this to their Muslim brothers, imagine what they'll do to us.'

Minas was glad his father couldn't go to war. The Turks had taken four hundred of Van's men already; now they asked for four thousand.

Those who stayed home, like Papa, had a trade to offer. They were not paid in liras anymore, only in bread. Sometimes the flat loaf was slightly warm when Papa brought it home. More often than not it was stale, dry and tasteless. Whatever it was Papa would bring it out from under his jacket, place it on the table like an offering torn from his own body. He broke apart morsels that became ever smaller as the weeks went by, until they were insubstantial, almost transparent. Equal portions for everyone, and one extra ration for Papa, because he had to force his poor body to get up each morning and trudge to work. They ate in silence without chewing, swallowing the wafer pieces whole. Bread had become a symbol, a communion, a commodity more precious than truth.

Soon came a time when Papa did not arrive home with any bread at the end of the day. Before the war he'd been a jeweller, and a successful one at that, designing heavy collars studded with mother-of-pearl, repoussé earrings, wedding bands, showing Minas how to mould and twist white-hot threads of silver and gold. Now he was fortunate to find any work of that kind at all. In his spare time, he made ammunition for the freedom fighters from spent cartridges and shells. More and more he couldn't come home until the next morning, staying late if he was lucky to mend a travelling clock at a Turkish officer's townhouse or tinkering with the mechanism of a lady's watch.

'Stupid Mussulmen,' Mamma scoffed. 'They do everything topsy-turvy. Sleep at noon and work at midnight.'

Minas gasped as though his mother had uttered a blasphemy.

'Keep quiet! Who knows if they're listening?'

He knew from his studies that Muslims considered noon, not midnight, to be the most evil hour of the day, the time when the devil on his flaming horse could gallop away with the whole world on its back. At noon, he was foiled each time by the call of the muezzin, proclaiming Allah is great and banishing the devil with fear of God's name. He had studied Islam at school; he knew the names of the holy caliphs better than those of his Orthodox saints. He knew the histories of the Prophet's battles, knew of his flight to Medina. Mamma told him the story of the Christian Virgin on her journey from Egypt, burdened with a sacred pregnancy and her fluttering human fear. Something in him wanted to draw parallels, excited by common threads and like mistakes.

Now he stopped studying at night, as there were no candles or kerosene for the lamp. Mamma had used all the olive oil in her cooking long ago. The only light came from the fire, burnt down to staring red embers in the *tonir*. On the rare times it flamed up into brightness, for an instant he could make out the carvings on their ceiling cornices: picture histories of hermits and stocky angels, Byzantine dragons with tight mouths and curled tails. He was no longer afraid of them, as he'd been when he was a little boy; there were other, darker pictures to be afraid of now. He put aside his schoolbooks, running his finger down the length of each spine as he arranged them one by one on the windowsill.

Four Turkish regiments advanced on Van with artillery when the Armenians refused to deliver more men for their labour battalions. By now, even Lilit believed that conscription was another word for murder. Van was transformed into a garrison town, with soldiers throwing people out of their houses and moving in. The irregulars were the most feared; soldiers of fortune who claimed no responsibility to government or country, able to commit any atrocity without reprisal. Bombs fell on orphanages and churches. Even Minas's Protestant missionary school, its American and Red Cross flags a half-hearted bid for protection, burnt to the ground. Refugees from outlying villages came swarming into Aykesdan, bringing epidemic diseases with them. They babbled in dialect, eager to speak their pain – *only three out of three hundred villagers of Rashva have escaped; all but one of the monks on the fabled island have perished* – but the Van women, Mamma and Lilit too, soothed them with childish songs and dressed their wounds, silencing such words with tea and clucking sounds, unable to hear what lay in store for themselves.

Minas knew there was no point in learning history any longer from his schoolbooks. Now he dug trenches with the other boys around Aykesdan, watched the fighters use mud walls and orchard terraces as fortified outposts. They only had enough provisions, ammunition and weaponry to last until the Russians came to liberate them. The northern advance was their only hope. Minas walked about mouthing it, Mamma murmured it as she wept, Lilit sang it with hope settling like a saw-toothed stone in her chest. They had to hold Van against the Turks until then. Papa was withdrawn, merely stumbling home at dusk or dawn to sit at the window and make ammunition from the scrap tin Minas gathered.

There were hardly any young men left after the last conscriptions and defeats. Or any weapons either. All they had were hunting guns, antiquated matchlock rifles and Mausers unearthed from cellars, rusty from misuse. Minas sensed the trap closing in. The god of oracles and dreams had brushed Minas with folded wings, Mamma used to say. Even at birth, this scribe and recording angel had whispered close in his ear. The one whose role among many was to register when someone was going to die.

✼   Soon there were no more grains to glean from cropped fields and barn floors. Planting had been stopped, with such terror stalking the land. Now what little threshing to do was over, and the workers had gone home after their Turkish overlords had taken everything, even rusting tools. 'Could be used as weapons,' they muttered to the Kurds, encouraging them to see Armenians as a cow to milk, nothing more.

Minas saw fresh new posters pasted on walls and fences. Words daubed in haste and a drawing of a fat cow with an Armenian face. 'Turkey for the Turks.' The artist had made sure to make the nose large and crooked, the expression of lips and eyes furtive. Minas tore down the first poster he saw, weeks ago now, as red paint ran to the ground in puddles. There were flyers on every Turk's doorstep: 'The Armenians are enemies of our religion, our history, our honour. You must buy nothing from an Armenian or from anyone who looks Armenian.' He ripped up every one he saw. When he told his father what he had done he'd been scolded. 'Leave your energy for important things,' Papa said. Minas went to bed that night seething. Even his own father was weak.

Now there were no more cows in Van, or sheep or goats for that matter. They had gone to find the mules and horses that vanished months ago. The only animals flourishing now among the filth of abandoned homes and bivouacking soldiers were cats, beloved pets turned strays, Van breeds with eyes of startling colours and no fear of water. Rumour was that people were catching them like fish as they swam in the lake, roasting them with salt and grass. Minas had visions of skinned carcasses, thin as rats without their fur. Rumour also had the new governor of Van, Djevet Bey, throwing his victims into burlap sacks with the starving animals, until they were bitten and clawed to death.

Mamma refused to believe it, telling Minas and Lilit it was impossible for someone to be so evil – even a Turk.

Yet Minas knew it was the truth. 'The Armenians must be exterminated,' Djevet Bey had said in a recent proclamation. 'If any Muslim protects a Christian, first, his house shall be burnt, then the Christian killed before his eyes, then his family and himself.' He had visions of being lacerated, a skinned carcass himself, screams muffled by folds of fabric. His pet lamb was now skin and bone as well; Papa glanced at it more than once with a knowing look in his eyes but Minas threw himself onto the animal, pleading with Papa not to kill it. The lamb bleated, as if aware of the daily danger of being alive. Minas knew it was only a matter of days before he too would welcome the meat.

Lilit stopped baking at home other than on the rare times she was traded dried corn by Kurdish nomads trawling through town knocking on doors, willing to barter. Women with grinning faces and stumps of teeth; Minas couldn't help but discern a sneering complicity in their false smiles. *See what you Armenians have been reduced to.* A handful of husks in exchange for a piece of Lilit's dowry. Stiff linen meant for bridal sheets and pillowcases, embroidered squares of peach-coloured silk. A hank of wool she'd been planning to make into a vest for her shadowy, future husband. Yervan? No weddings now. Wiser to trade cloth for at least one night with a full belly. Bread was better than dreams.

She would grind corn into coarse meal then stir the mess into something like porridge, firing the solidified slab and putting it back on the *tonir* to be baked again. Now it was so hard Minas could throw it on the wall without it breaking apart. His gums cracked and bled from the repeated effort of chewing. His tongue grew great white blisters from the lack of fresh food, and Mamma was never home to comfort him. Nor was Lilit any longer, grown bold and reckless. 'If we're going to die anyway,' she told him, 'then what's the point?' She spent the daylight hours huddled in haystacks with her boyfriend, meticulous in making sure she was home before Mamma, face passive and bemused, hands busy working with nothing.

Mamma came home from the town bakery one evening after standing in a queue all day. She had her wedding earrings to trade. They were delicate – Papa had made them from soft gold and teardrop-shaped turquoise. She thought she would be able to get enough bread for the week at least, but she came home with the square package still wrapped in her apron. Her clothes reeked of sweat and fear and Minas shrank from her when she made to touch him, as if his mere innocence would keep her safe.

'I couldn't stay a moment longer. People started fighting over the last loaves and I was afraid I'd get hurt.'

'Where's Papa?' asked Lilit. 'You said he'd come home with you.'

'I couldn't find him. I waited. Maybe he has to work all night again for the Turks. I waited some more but the people at the bakery scared me.'

Minas couldn't stop himself.

'What will we eat tonight, then?'

Mamma furrowed her brow, a family trait.

'I tell you, I couldn't wait! A Kurdish woman tapped me on the shoulder and said, *The soldiers are selling Armenian orphans to the Turks as slaves.* She was laughing at us.'

She couldn't disguise the horror in her voice and Minas turned away from his own panic, standing up and banging his hand on the table as he'd seen his father do.

'I'll go find food. Maybe Papa. Don't wait up for me.'

✤ He walked down the silent cobbled streets of his childhood. Mamma had run out after him into the street, forbidding him to go. He hadn't looked back. Never before had he been out so late at night: he, usually in bed by eight under the yellow spool of the lamp, with a plate of preserved walnuts, with his beloved books. *Another time,* he thought, *another life. Another me.* This last realisation made him painfully happy: he walked faster, straightened his shoulders and set his tender jaw.

Neighbours' houses were strange and unfamiliar, leering at him with lighted faces, slanted Turkish eyes. He trudged his way between them, traversing fields and orchards separating the city from Aykesdan, finally stopping at the town square. The mediaeval walls of the old city grinned, conspiratorial. He regarded the empty displays of the bakery, the butcher, the seller of sweets and wine. His face reflected in curved glass, wavering, as if underwater. None of their windows were lit, not even upstairs in the sleeping quarters. A voice in his head wheedled, then spoke with authority. *A food vendor never starves.* He thought of ways to break into the baker's – never liked him anyway – to steal some flour, at least. The voice egged him on. *There must be sacks and sacks of it; he'll never miss it.* His stomach ached with a hollow pain, like death.

He walked to the back of the row, in a narrow alley where refuse was thrown, where stray dogs and cats marked out their territory. They hissed and spat at him, one dog barked, half-hearted, then resumed snuffling in the filth. He filled his pockets with whatever he could find. It was hard to see in the dark. He picked up a moist cake, mouldy on one side; it could be scraped off and toasted in the fire. A worm-eaten peach the animals hadn't yet found. He forced himself not to taste the food, even when his stomach began growling and saliva gathered thick and slow under his tongue. He'd wait till he took it home, present his gifts with a flourish to his mother and sister.

There was a noise of boots, the sharp *tap tap* of clubs and rifles echoing on the paving stones of the square. He fell to his knees in the rotting squelch, heard men shouting in Turkish. He crawled closer. The moon shed a weird, spectral light onto the square, houses and shops around it black, muffled, their protests mute and ineffectual. He flopped down on his belly, using his elbows to propel him closer still, hidden by the shadow of the building. The officer who could be heard shrieking sidestepped the prisoners, who now held each other's hands like little boys. He banged his club down on the ground each time he finished a sentence. When he turned to give orders, Minas glimpsed the side of his face, an open mouth with the glitter of gold eye-teeth in the moon's gleam.

The officer directed his men to prepare the prisoners. Minas's blood battered in his veins, thrashing through his arms, into his heavy, useless legs. *Prepare for what?* He watched the Armenians being bound to each other with thick rope. Made to hang their heads, some forced to kneel with a blow from a rifle butt or the jab of a pistol in the ribs.

He scanned the length of the company with his eyes. The butcher was there, still wearing his soiled apron. It was hiked around his waist like a skirt. Minas's godfather, too, his spectacles smashed but still managing to balance on his face. His nose emitted a dark-brown liquid, but he didn't wipe it away. The priest, lips moving in silent prayer. Lilit's boyfriend was there, with a torn shirt and bloodied chest. A wet circle spread slowly at his groin. He whimpered at intervals, amplified in the acoustics made by the flat square and the amphitheatre of buildings.

Next to Yervan, a grey-haired man. One eye open wide, the other pulpy and closed, swollen from a blow. *Oh, no, please God, not my Papa.* He knelt with the rest of the men, his blue cap pushed low over his ears. He was stiller than the other fidgeting prisoners; he seemed to be asleep, kneeling upright, or even praying with the priest. Minas struck at his own thighs, blocks of wood. *Get up! Get up, you coward!* But he continued to lie flat on his belly, eyes and ears strained to every movement. He tried to catch Papa's gaze. He watched the patient face, dwelling on it from afar, wanting to memorise every detail of its expression. He watched the men being lined up against the wall of a building, kneeling with their backs to the gendarmes and to Minas. He could no longer see Papa's tired, trusting face. A shot rang out, echoing long on the cobblestones. One man fell, dragging those on either side down with him to the ground. Another shot. The butcher was thrown forward, his head hitting the wall. Then another. Yervan slid to the ground, neatly, as he had done everything in his life. The shots grew louder and Minas put his hands over his ears. Papa fell onto Yervan's stomach. *How could that be?* He heard another shot. *Not my Papa.* Another shot, and another, a cacophony causing the stray dogs to throw back their massive heads and howl. He heard himself sobbing, too: a strange bubbling sound he was remotely aware of, as if coming from someone else. He didn't hide his face, didn't stop watching as the men were finished off in a volley of fire, slumped against each other, crushing the still-living to death with the already killed. He held his palms to his cheeks. He'd soiled himself.

The dogs grew quiet. Minas stopped crying; or at least, couldn't hear the sucking in and out of his breath anymore. He couldn't see Papa, his body was too entwined with other men's limbs and the gendarmes and soldiers, standing over the bodies, poking at them with their swords, checking if they were dead. The officer drew his pistol and stared at it. For a moment Minas thought he would use it on himself. Instead he lowered it once more as he strolled around the bodies, firing a last round into each man's head.

✳ When he collected himself enough to run home, it was dawn. Pale light fingered the roofs of houses and tops of trees, suffusing the hills with shattered hope. As he left the town and made his way to the outskirts he came upon a withered, ancient woman sitting by the side of the road. He didn't want to stop in case she needed help, didn't want to look at her in case she was sympathetic to his own pain and he burst into tears again. Yet he forced himself to slow down when she raised her arm at him. Her legs were bare and swollen, as if she'd been walking for days, and she sat with them stretched out before her in the dirt. A vein on her left foot beat like a pulse. She wasn't wearing a scarf and was completely bald, the dome of her head sunburnt and peeling. She was muttering something to herself and he bent closer, against his better judgement, to hear what she was saying.

'Oh my sweet Virgin, help me, the Turks are coming to cut my throat.'

Her eyes were glazed, darting about and alighting on nothing.

'My people have left me behind and fled into the mountains.'

She focused on his face for an instant and put her arm out to him again. The way she held it outstretched, so straight and still and unflinching, made him angry and frustrated and sad all at once.

'My boy, do you know where they've gone? My boy?'

'No.'

He surprised himself by kicking out at her and watching as the dust rained over her inert, lifeless legs.

'No. Don't bother me, old woman. I don't know anything.'

He began running away from her.

'No,' he repeated. 'No! No! No.'

He was still muttering the same denial to himself when he ran down onto the gravel road that passed his house. 'No,' he said, and kicked at the loose stones in front of him. 'No,' he repeated, louder now, as he slowed down and bent double, holding his side. 'No,' he murmured, panting and sweating, and it seemed the word came from somewhere outside of him.

Home appeared the same as before, squat and silent and screened by willows. He passed close to the whitewashed wall marking their southern boundary. It was a living pattern of sunshine and shadows; he remembered Lilit pointing it out to him when he was not yet at school, content to lie with her in the long grass for hours watching. Now he stopped and stared. It couldn't be the same now Papa was gone; it should be struck down, subdued, in mourning. This happy movement was travesty. It was like any other day, a morning of no import, the sky a high blue bowl upended above him. Green summer light played on the white wall. A swallow darted back and forth, making infinitesimal alterations to its daubed nest. Feathers, twigs, mud with flecks that sparkled like the lake in the distance.

He lunged forward, hammered at the wall with his fists. This went on for a perhaps a minute, or an hour, until his knuckles were torn and bleeding. He stepped back, surveying them as if they belonged to someone else. There was no pain. The shadows continued to flicker. He put his hands down and turned his attention to the house again. The yellow shutters were closed, smoke curled in a lazy plume from the chimney. Home was ignorant of Papa's death; smug and complacent, it couldn't help him now. He kicked at the wall one more time, smacking at grapevines overhead as he climbed the worn steps to the front door.

His mother and sister were still up when he burst into the room, whey-faced and drawn, waiting. Mamma ran to him, shook him hard. She didn't seem to notice his bloodied hands, the filth that stuck to his clothes. He glanced at Lilit for an instant; her eyes saw everything.

'My son, where were you all this time?'

He lied, looking up at her wrinkled forehead.

'As soon as I heard the news, I ran straight back to tell you, Ma.'

He told her a column of men had been taken by gendarmes and marched to the top of the hill overlooking the lake. His father was among them. He heard rumours they were being deported to a labour camp, far away into the interior of Turkey.

He watched his mother from the open door as she turned and distributed whatever she could find in the cupboards. Her movements were slow and easy, yet her face suddenly contorted in a spasm of helplessness. If it were not for the distortion of her features, he would not have thought she registered at all.

'Did you hear me, Ma? He's gone. He might never be back.'

She didn't answer. She was calmer than he expected, tipping the last of their dry cornbread into his open palm and a gulp of cognac to

Lilit: customary food of death and burial, though she knew nothing of what had really happened. *Ancient sacrifice,* came the voice in his ear and he slapped his forehead to drive the sound away.

Lilit grabbed his arm.

'Do you know if Yervan's among them?'

'What do I care about your boyfriend,' he bellowed. 'It's Papa I'm worried about.'

He hit her in the face, feeling all the rage and pain and disgust for the Turks who had killed his father find its outlet in the force of the blow. She stood there, unmoving, her eyes staring into his. When he drew back his hand, she untied her apron slowly. With shaking fingers and a swift glance at her mother over her shoulder, she was clattering out the door and down the path. Mamma stood in the middle of the room, holding her face in her hands. When she raised it to Minas, it was washed clean of any emotion.

'Run after her, my boy. It's dangerous out there.'

✳ Lilit made for Yervan's property. She plunged through fields of flowers, registering now at the edge of her awareness what those colours really meant, in all their shades of blood, from scarlet to deep blue, the arterial purple of emperors. Death, not love; pain in all its guises. Once they were tiny red banners of joy. Her cheek pulsed, she stripped the flowers and pressed their petals to her face.

When she got to the farm, she ran to the stable and pushed the thick doors open with both hands. Nothing. Even the hens were gone. She went to the house, her heart beating high in her throat. Maybe Yervan's parents were merely sitting in the kitchen, drinking tea, and would frown upon a young woman bursting in on them like that. Maybe Yervan was there, too, and would not be pleased to see her like this.

She stopped in the courtyard when she saw a crumpled shape lying on the ground. There were large stones scattered about, spattered blood nearby, and the object lay like a heap of old clothes, face down. The clothes were dirty, as if they had been dragged to where they lay. She didn't want to stop and examine the body; she already knew it was Yervan's father from the fine gold-seamed waistcoat he wore. Nobody else could afford a waistcoat like that. Not in time of war. A beat, an instant of quiet. She could hear her blood pounding in her ears. Could she hear him trying to say something? She peered closer against her will, breathing hard. His skull had been smashed open. She felt her voice fizzing out of her in a high, crazed laugh, tried to quell the sound by clutching at her throat. 'Oh my God, my God,' she could hear herself screeching. 'Yervan's father's been stoned by the Turks.' Her voice was long and loud in the silence. 'Oh my God, my God,' she whispered, and the hysterical laughter burst out again until she vomited the bread her mother had given her into the dust at the dead man's feet.

She sat on the dirt next to him for a long time. She made the sign of the cross, once, twice, three times, and her wrists were shaking so much she had to repeat the ritual a fourth, a fifth time before she did it properly. She gathered her strength and got up, drawing her scarf over her shoulders, mouth and nose, so only her eyes were visible. Her legs gave way, but she persisted. She was still laughing: a strange, low sound that seemed to come now from her stomach, not her throat. She tapped on the glass-paned door of the kitchen, trying to peer in. This habitual gesture of courtesy did not strike her as out of place at the time. A blurred figure sat at the table, head on arms, keening. Was it one of the servants? She could hear the thin, inhuman cry from the other side of the door. She turned the knob and entered, silent now. Her hysteria was crushed by the otherworldly sound coming from Yervan's mother.

The kitchen was in chaos. Bins of flour and grain had been overturned onto the floor, splashes of dark wine stained the walls. A half-dead farm dog – not Yervan's – lay under the table, whimpering in a child's voice. Yervan's mother stared up at her, uncomprehending, then put her head on her arms once more. Again the high, wailing cries began to fill the room. Her unbound hair was matted with men's urine, her bodice torn and filthy. Lilit tried not to follow the implications of her ripped skirt, the blood down her legs. She put her hand out as if to touch her, then drew it back again and ran out the door, leaving it swinging.

She ran to the town hall, making a high wail under the folds of her scarf. Maybe somebody there could tell her what had happened. When she saw a group of Turkish soldiers march past, she flattened herself against the walls of houses lining the road, trying to blend into the bricks like a moth. Furled wings, brown-grey. She convinced herself they couldn't see her this way, that she was safe. When they passed on, she made for the centre of town again, hiking up her stockings as she ran.

She hadn't been out of the house for months now. In her absence, the centre of Van had become unrecognisable. She felt strongly as she ran to the square that she was inhabiting a nightmare: her sleeping self wandering through the streets and laneways of her childhood home, yet a home that had now become strange to her, skewed, laid out wrong. The stately facades with their scrollwork and pediments were still there, the same trees and buildings and street signs, but the spirit of Van was gone. Shops hollowed out, with looted or destroyed stock and charred timber. Turkish graffiti. Old men – grandfathers she'd grown used to seeing with their chessboards at the cafes, under the shade of the square arguing – now lay silent under those same trees, their faces so haggard she could see the egg-cup shapes of their skulls. The children – she couldn't look at the children. Their faces were too crazed, or too accepting. All around her, a shuffling mass of the half-dead, begging and clinging to her skirt and sleeve. She batted at them in frantic misery, trying not to take in any more detail of the ravaged faces, making small sounds of protest between her closed mouth and nostrils, trying not to breathe in their stink.

She fled across the square, pounding on the doors of the town hall with both fists. From inside, a rise and fall of sound. It took her a while to register the sound as human screaming. Her legs turned to water and she crumpled against the steps, panting, overcome by blind fear.

'Try to breathe.'

It was a man's face, a man's hot breath against her cheek. She stood up, swayed against the door.

'Please, *effendim* – are you a soldier?'

A slight nod, the hint of a formal bow.

'*Effendim*, can you tell me, what's happening in there?'

'It's best for you to go home.'

'But my father—'

'Go home. Now.'

He came closer, put his arm out to her. He smelled of wet wool and dry sweat, a comforting, masculine presence.

'If you would only check if my neighbour—'

'Now. I'll take you.'

Minas arrived at the town hall to see a uniformed Turk leading his sister by the arm down the steps.

'Lilit!'

She gave no appearance of hearing him. The man saw him, turned around.

'Are you related to this woman?'

'She's my sister.'

'Well, take her home right now and don't let her out of the house again. How old are you?'

'Thirteen.'

The gendarme looked him up and down. Suddenly Minas was ashamed of his homespun trousers, Papa's old jacket held together with pins used for babies' diapers.

'You'll pass for eleven. Make sure that's what you say.'

Minas took hold of his sister as soon as the man had let her go. He watched him take the town hall steps three at a time and push the wide doors open with a crack of his cane. He seemed familiar. His carriage: that affected yet proud bearing. He turned around for a last moment and Minas saw his face. Gold flash of teeth as he smiled one last time at Lilit.

Minas had a vision of the Turk poking a limp body with his bayonet, turning it over to make sure it was really dead. He grabbed his sister's arm and propelled her down the street.

✳ The Vali of Van, Djevet Bey, leaned back in his chair with an expansive yawn. All was going according to plan. Any males of the town above twelve had been apprehended and shot three abreast by the lake. Only last night, Turkish collaborators convicted of sheltering Armenians had been hanged in front of their houses, then the houses themselves burnt down. The ringleaders of the recent insurrection had already been beheaded in the town square, and the remaining women and children were terrified and starving, ripe for deportation. He would promise them new homes in the desert, on the banks of the Euphrates. Two-storey houses, more gold than they had ever managed to hoard and Arab servants.

Djevet was approaching middle age, yet still ambitious – he wasn't afraid to admit that. Ideal for promotion, but in a strictly limited sense. He knew he was a safe bet. He'd already been assured a post in Constantinople if he made up the numbers from the province of Van and its neighbouring *vilayets*. His mother – his ancient, cantankerous mother – would be so pleased. Or so he hoped. *Allah the merciful, make her be pleased for once. Just this once.*

She never thought he could do it, do anything; he was a disappointment from birth. Gangly, unformed, with a big nose to boot, for her he only seemed to intensify an already burning dislike of his father. Poor Father, who shuffled from bedroom to table, table to bedroom in down-at-heel slippers, for his whole life. Even if the slippers were new, worn for the first time, he managed to make them look battered. It was the shuffling that did it, drove Mother mad. Head down, shaking hands growing worse and worse until he couldn't even fasten his own trousers. Djevet would wake early and help him dress before school, so poor dear father wouldn't be too ashamed in front of Mother's vulpine stare.

'You look just like him,' she would sniff.

As an adolescent, he grew weedy and retiring, like those indoor succulents Mother kept in her bedroom: insidious, with flat pale leaves that tended to droop with the addition of too much water. She would water them herself and then yell at him from her bed to do it once more, with a little blue-painted pitcher she had bought in Ephesus.

He married at fifteen, a rapacious girl his mother had chosen. Layla soon banded against him as well. They never had children. This could have been one of the reasons she, too, turned against him so soon. It was clear from the start: he was hopeless. He couldn't even give her a baby. Yet it was her elder brother, Enver Pasha, the Minister of War, who gave him this appointment in February, with the promise of a more salubrious position to come. He knew he was indebted to his wife, come what may. They were tied together by more than just the lack of babies. Policy. Propaganda. New laws. And still his mother considered him a failure on all counts, with no hope of retribution. Now at last he had his chance.

In the meantime he was biding his time here as a petty governor in the provinces, officiating over Armenian deaths and imprisonments, pleas and back-room bargains and the repossession of their assets by the few Turks and Kurds of the town who somehow found favour in his eyes. His spies told him he'd been dubbed 'the horse-shoe master of Bashkale' throughout the country for his exploits in the previous province. Horse-shoe master, he chuckled with satisfaction. He liked having this much power; it gave him an ice-dark thrill of accomplishment, made him wonder why he'd waited so long.

He leaned forward to cut a pomegranate in half from the platter at his elbow, fingering his pearl-handled knife with pride. A present from one of his beneficiaries. The platter had been an artful arrangement of Persian melons, Smyrna figs, tiny tomatoes and olives. His secretary was good for something. Now the figs lay mashed and blackened, olive pips scattered, pulp of tomatoes sucked so only the skins remained.

As he ate his pomegranate, Djevet was heedless of the seeds spilling onto his desk. His secretary, Mehmet, called for a plate but Djevet waved him away. He enjoyed the pretence of poverty, the frisson of being a peasant for a while. Just like those Armenians. He liked their folk dances, the girls' wide, smiling faces when he forced them to pretend they liked him. He enjoyed the aqua vitae of the region, drinking it secretly before bed so as not to offend his subordinates who were still devout Muslims, fundamentalist illiterates. He made sure the old men still continued to produce it, and among all the other privations there was always plenty.

He picked up one of the pomegranate kernels between his thumb and forefinger and put it in his mouth, savouring the tang of sweet-sourness on his tongue. As he dictated his daily correspondence, he continued eating them one by one.

'First a letter to my mother,' he told Mehmet. 'She'll be worried about me. Write it on the good paper with my crest. And make sure you date it first.'

The secretary scribbled 'April 1915', cocked his head and asked Djevet Bey which day it was.

'We pay you to know these things, Mehmet! Look, just don't worry about it. All right. Ready? *Dearest Mother, I have no work and much fun. The news from here is very heartening. We have killed 2100 Armenian males already, all of them food for dogs.*'

'I'm sorry, *Bey effendim*,' Mehmet said. 'My pen needs refilling.'

Djevet waited, tapping the desk with his ring finger, admiring the square-cut emerald.

'*Mother, I am safe and eating well. Our cook makes a superlative pilaf. Ask Layla to send my summer underclothes and tell her I kiss her eyes. May Allah bless her and you and Father.* That's all. Now turn to a new page,' he instructed Mehmet. '*Pay the butchers one gold lira per person.*'

The boy hesitated, as if unsure of what the Bey wanted him to write, so Djevet got up from behind his desk and advanced toward him. Mehmet cowered, expecting a slap. Djevet seized the pen from him and scrawled on the paper, using Mehmet's bent-over back as support.

'*Pay the halal butchers of the town one lira for each Armenian male they slaughter before Tuesday. I will not leave a single one standing.*'

He touched his knee with a short chopping motion.

'Mehmet, make sure you tell them we will not leave even one so high.'

He stabbed into Mehmet's clean gabardine suit with a final flourish of his signature, threw the pen down and looked out the window. Outside his office in the town hall, some of the gendarmes were amusing themselves. They were cutting down branches from the plane trees lining the town square. *Are they making an outdoor shelter? That would certainly be nice*, he wondered. They stripped boughs of their leaves with the points of bayonets. *A shady pavilion for hot afternoons. Tea and music.*

They were letting out the female prisoners locked in the basement: raucous women with loud voices who had come to the hall in the last few days demanding to know what had become of their men. He remembered being harsher than usual with his orders – they reminded him so of his wife. Nasty and ill-tempered, blaming everyone but themselves.

The gendarmes beckoned the women out of their prison. He saw them squint and cover their eyes, unused to such bright light. *Do they want the women to help build it?*

Some – the very old, lame, diseased – had already been shot at night in the courtyard; the others were being kept alive to make up the numbers of deportees. He knew it wouldn't do to have too many deaths in his *vilayet*. It could do his reputation more harm than good. He needed to appear efficient to his superiors, oh, yes, but Turkey itself also needed to appear not entirely ruthless to the world. The state needed to keep up the great pretence of the Armenian solution: women and children will all be spared. We're merely relocating them to somewhere better, for their own good, far away from the theatre of war.

'We Turks are civilised after all,' he liked to say to the gendarmes. He didn't quite agree with the ideology of the moment: reminiscent of the golden age of Turkic and Mongol warriors, fierce-bearded Genghis Khan and Tamerlane. 'We are the master race,' Talaat Pasha, the Minister of the Interior, had proclaimed in Constantinople. 'It is our duty to subjugate inferior peoples.' This glorification of ethnic Turkism irked Djevet, when he stopped to think. All that talk of blood and race, mystical. He much preferred the Ottomans, yet knew the boys screwed up their faces at him when he continued to refer to them as such. It was a term in danger of becoming obsolete.

At the same time, he knew the boys needed some diversion. It was hot and boring work guarding prisoners, feeding them, dealing with their constant cries and their smell. He watched the gendarmes throw off their embroidered jackets and roll up their sleeves. They began by stripping the prisoners down. Some women helped by doing it themselves, all the more fun to watch. It was slower, for one thing. More satisfying.

When the women were all lined up in the courtyard in the sunlight, some shivering, although it was so warm, the gendarmes stood aside and whispered among themselves. He could see their faces clearly: the boys were enjoying the situation. Some of the naked women were old and wrinkled in strange places and he turned his head away, not liking to look at those. They cried the loudest, short little quacks of fear.

The boys began whipping the women with branches. The more they wailed, the harder the boys struck them. He could hear the women praying and screaming, 'Lord, have mercy, Jesus help us, Oh dear God, why have you abandoned us?' The boys kept on whipping them, telling them to dance, to sing Turkish songs. 'Sing, *gaivour*, sing it loud. Dance, Armenian slut!' He could see they were in a frenzy of sex – pain and sex. He saw it was good for morale, a little healthy exertion before the long march they would have to take in the next few days. They forced the little children to stand in a circle around their mothers and sisters, and Djevet heard the high, reedy sound of their singing voices over the cries and groans. Soon the youngest children stopped, sobbing uncontrollably now, and one by one they all began to cry.

The boys let them be. They had run out of branches, having whipped the women so hard the boughs were breaking into bits. More trees were stripped, feverishly, with the leaves still clinging onto them. The prisoners were now nearly all on the ground, shielding their faces and those soft women's parts with their hands. Some were motionless, supine in the dust. *Perhaps the boys are going too far.* He opened the window and leaned out, enjoying the sensation of his ribs sharp against the wooden sill. *Perhaps not far enough.*

'Soon there'll be no trees left the way you're going!'

The young men stopped and looked up at him with open mouths. He shut the window to flick a pregnant fly from his shoulder. *Slap* – he killed it and kicked it under the rug for the cleaner to find.

'Idiots,' he muttered. 'I'll show them how it's done.'

In the following days, the remaining Armenian prisoners were shod like horses with nails driven into their soles. They were forced to dance to ballads set up on a gramophone in the prison courtyard. *My darling, my love, your sufferings and joys will be many.* Djevet Bey stood aside and clapped in time with the music, his ring flashing dark in the sunlight.

BEIRUT, 1982

Selim was driven back to east Beirut at dawn through a hail of hard rice and rosewater. Lebanese Christians welcoming the Israeli troops, heralding the end of seven years of war. Or so they thought. As he walked from his car to the Phalange HQ, women blew kisses to him as well, festooning the dour building with ropes of ribbon and hothouse flowers. He wasn't as flattered as he would have liked to be. He didn't think it was that easy. One young woman with crooked lipstick came close to him, simpering and mispronouncing *shalom*. He shouted at her.

'I'm not Israeli, all right? I'm Lebanese, like you.'

He felt a little guilty for not saying he was Armenian, after everything his people had suffered. Some of them had died rather than renounce who they were. But his guilt didn't last long. He walked home after a couple of hours spent shuffling paper and making telephone calls. People embraced in the streets. They made love in destroyed parks. They danced with Israeli soldiers, dragging the heavy-booted youths into whirls of movement and laughter.

At home he opened the fridge and drank four glasses of French champagne for breakfast.

'Here's to Lebanon,' he toasted himself.

When he was sufficiently drunk, he decided to ring Sanaya. After two unsuccessful attempts to connect to west Beirut he heard her exhale on the line before she said, '*Sa'laam*.'

'Be ready, *chérie*. My driver will come and get you. We're going on a picnic.'

In the hills above the east of the city, the Israeli-troop compound was filled with the sounds of improvised music from hastily assembled instruments. Sunni families watched in awe of the officers' antics, wanting to see for themselves what liberation looked like. Selim hoped this would be peace only for the deserving. These Muslims had no place here. He strode through the mess of children playing on blankets and mothers in deckchairs, to the knot of leaping, yelping, off-duty soldiers. They noted his cedar insignia and offered him a glass of something bubbly and pink, not worthy of being called champagne. He took a sip then emptied the contents behind his back.

Sanaya stayed in the car – she didn't like to be seen in public with Selim. So much for the fabled picnic. She could smell cheese and bread and cured meat on the back seat. His driver must have bought them quickly, without thought. Maybe they could drive somewhere secluded, up into the mountains; maybe Selim would lie down on the grass, his head in her lap.

She laid her head back and closed her eyes. She let herself imagine a future with Selim: the wedding in Cyprus, the simple cream dress. A spray of roses, lone drinks after the ceremony. A life together, away from the danger and filth. But what would they have left to talk about? Her mouth hung open; she dozed. The sun made red patterns behind her eyelids. She heard a tap on the window, sat stiffly upright, wound it down. An Israeli airforce officer leaned in.

'I've been watching you, Mademoiselle. You look sad.'

His Arabic was classical, affected, yet he was almost boyish, with frank eyes full of confidence. He seemed too young to be so high up in the ranks. Sanaya was taken aback.

'Not really. Just tired. Too many late nights.'

'Your name?'

'Why do you want to know?'

'I'm just making conversation.'

'Okay, it's Sanaya.'

'Mine's Alon.'

She shook his outstretched hand. As she sat, uncertain, neither pulling her arm away nor offering any warmth, Selim sauntered over to them and put out his hand. The Israeli released Sanaya and clasped Selim with feeling.

'Hey, I've seen you around. You've done some good work. Pakradounian, isn't it?'

'Selim Pakradounian.'

'Pleasure. Alon Herzberg.'

He smiled, and Sanaya could see his blind hope for the country, his beatitude. It dazzled her for a moment.

'Should all be over soon,' he said.

Selim leaned over and lit his cigarette for him. Sanaya was surprised at herself for despising the gesture, so deferent, so mercenary, a subject king bowing down before an emperor.

'You think so?' Selim asked.

'I know so. The PLO will be running out of here in days with their tails between their legs.'

Sanaya wondered how the Israeli soldiers could be so young, so touchingly naive, so arrogant. Their ignorance coupled with civility was unnerving. She watched Selim take a long puff of his cigarette, considering.

'What about all the rest of the troublemakers? Hezbollah, Amal, all the Shias. Push them back into Iran, I say.'

'They'll pipe down. Once they realise we're not leaving until Bashir Gemayel's firmly in power.'

'And then?'

Both men looked surprised. Neither of them expected Sanaya to volunteer an opinion. They turned around and stared at her, not answering. She repeated her question.

'Well? What then?'

Selim grew red in the face, threw down the butt of his cigarette.

'What do you mean, what then? What more do you want?'

'What's going to stop us all killing each other again as soon as the Israelis leave?'

Alon put his hand up between them.

'If you allow me, I think we will put enough structures in place to stop that happening.'

'Like what? Mossad agents? Shin Bet? More secret police? Suspension of civil liberties?'

Selim tried to light another cigarette, burnt his fingers, swore.

'Enough, Sanaya,' he said. 'What are you trying to get at?'

Sanaya shook her head, tears starting in her eyes. Alon looked from one to the other, with puzzlement and sympathy in his face. Sanaya waved him and Selim away with a flick of her hand. She stumbled out of the car, slamming the door. Before she walked two paces, she viciously ground the butt of Selim's cigarette into the ground under her heel.

The Israeli bombardments continued, increasing in duration and force. Sanaya was surprised Issa spent so much time at home, finding food and water, sitting on the divan smoking shisha, spouting rhetoric about a holy war. Then why wasn't he out there fighting it?

'Come on,' he said. 'In the corridor. It's safer there.'

'But—'

She took one last look through the intact glass from her window. Crimson fire from Israeli planes burnt the seafront in successive washes, bleeding out, fading, only to return again.

'It's safer there,' Issa repeated. 'I know. When the bombing gets really bad, there's no choice.'

As Sanaya followed Issa into thicker darkness, she heard her chandeliers breaking one by one with the force of each blast. Lamps of Persian coloured glass and gold filigree, shaped like Hadiya's tulip tumblers. Smash. Shards against her face. She ducked. A fragment in her hair. Issa plucked it out.

'It's okay. You'll live.'

She let herself smile at him, knowing he could hardly see her face in the dark. Downstairs in the courtyard, she could hear the canary trilling with desperation, an all-is-lost-so-there's-nothing-to-lose bravado. She felt the same herself tonight. Nothing to lose now. So why not enjoy? As if sensing her thoughts, Issa grasped her arm above the elbow. She pulled it away with involuntary petulance, suddenly realising just how much she resented the familiarity he'd assumed in the past few weeks. For a fundamentalist Muslim, his gesture was tantamount to ownership. In that instant he felt her rebuke and there was a moment of awkward silence until he covered it over by shouting in her ear.

'He's just like me, that little bird.'

They sat huddled together in the gloom: the old concierge and his wife, the Druze family from downstairs, refugees who had come to camp in the garden when their apartment block was reduced to rubble. They had three daughters, mouths open, dribble at the corners, deeply asleep. A baby boy sucking frantically at his mother's breast. The stone stairs were cold. Rouba lay on one of the shallow steps, bedroom pillows piled about her, Hadiya curled so close she seemed an extension of her mother's body. The explosions coming ever closer reverberated in Sanaya's heart, drowning out its trip-trip beat. She held Hadiya's hand where it lay, illuminated, each time there was a flash of white. The sound thudded in her lungs and throat and in her very marrow. Each time a bomb exploded, she felt that this time she should be used to it, that next time she wouldn't shudder in its impact. She cried out, an involuntary sound. Issa smiled, as if excited by her fear. Another explosion, closer this time. The ringing in her ears drowned out every other sound for minutes, so many long minutes she was afraid she'd be deaf forever.

The Druze man had a radio that worked.

'President Reagan has appealed to Menachem Begin earlier today to call an immediate ceasefire,' the BBC newsreader announced.

Sanaya cringed at another loud blast, cutting through the transmission. Israeli warships fired rockets into the Corniche. Shells fell in Hamra. This was Begin's reply.

After four hours of continuous bombing, the concierge produced a bottle of Scotch.

'I don't drink,' Issa said. 'It's against the will of Allah.'

Sanaya drank her own glass down, looking at him over the rim.

❋   When the bombardment ended they walked out into the heat of a morning tinged with the smell of burnt hair, ash, cordite.

'That was the longest we've had,' Issa said.

'We're helpless,' Sanaya murmured.

'What did you say?'

'There's no use fighting, Issa. They're too powerful for us.'

'Take those words back. It's a sin.'

'I don't see you out there with your fellow fighters.'

'Part of my duty is to protect my dead brother's wife and daughter. And you, if you want it.'

She strode ahead of him as if she hadn't heard, opening the tall iron gates with some difficulty and walking out into the street.

'Hey, you can't go out there! It's not safe.'

'There's nothing you can do, Issa. You might as well not be here.'

He ran out after her, grasping and pulling on her hand. This time she surrendered to him but let her hand lie limp in his. He was babbling like a child in the effort to convince her of his importance.

'I find food for you, I bring clean water, I fix the generator when it breaks down. I kill the rats in your kitchen, the cockroaches that come into your bed—'

She still let him hold her hand but remained firm against him, pushing forward all the while. They walked down the street – he let her lead him. The destruction of their neighbourhood was far greater than she had imagined. This celebrated district of seaside hotels and restaurants had become, overnight, a graveyard of twisted steel, slabs of concrete scattered like the ruins of Roman columns. She felt a hard bullet form in her throat; she wouldn't cry. Wouldn't give the Israelis that satisfaction. She looked around for familiar landmarks: the corner shop where she sometimes bought chewing gum and toilet paper, gone. The flower seller who swore at her whenever she brushed against any of his arrangements, pulverised. Nothing left. No, she would not cry. The debris of people's lives everywhere on the ground: a charred exercise book with no covers, broken pieces of crockery – some still with bits of food clinging to them – a nylon negligee draped over the bonnet of a car. Dust coated their faces and eyes and they both walked blind, holding each other close and then closer, coughing at intervals to expel the black particles from their throats.

'We should go back,' Issa said.

'No. One more block.'

She wanted to see the Khalidi hospital, to see for herself if it had been bombed. He clutched her hand tighter, anticipating the worst. It had been three days since Israeli troops had cut off water, food and electricity in west Beirut. As they passed open doorways, the sounds of children crying and women wailing for the dead were interspersed with more familiar, comforting sounds: slosh of reservoir water poured from jug into glass, the tinny French of the Phalangist *Voice of Lebanon* radio station, sizzle of potatoes dropped into a pan, the papery thin rustle of *L'Orient Le Jour* being opened to read news of last night's blasts.

They neared the hospital, Sanaya stony, white-faced. Gunmen from rival Muslim militias shouted at them to leave, 'Fucking leave, leave now', firing their automatics in the air for emphasis. They too were coated in grey dust, comic-book ghosts. As Issa and Sanaya turned the corner, a high red smell caught them unawares. Flies settled on their lips and eyes and the smell intensified until it became too sweet, suspending speech or coherent judgement.

The dead were lined up in messy rows with heads against feet all the way to the entrance of the hospital. A woman nearby lay on her back with one leg crumpled beneath her, tan stockings pulled halfway down her calves by the force of the explosion. An old man next to her had the top half of his face scooped out, his mouth intact and twisted into an incredulous smile. The hospital facade was gone, all that remained was the basement, where open-air surgeries were being performed. No electricity; Sanaya could discern the hum of generators beneath the screams of old people and young women. Relatives of the wounded, even of the dead, shrieking at doctors to save their loved ones, grasping at them, pushing them away from someone else and to their own people. Scuffles broke out. Guns fired. Babies and children in hysterics, their open mouths black with horror. A thin little boy with a halo of chestnut hair was having his leg amputated. Two blood-spattered nurses hovered above him like anxious angels.

'Let's go,' Issa said. 'I can't.'

Sanaya stood staring at the tableau. The doctors and nurses were so tired they looked as if they were about to cry. This couldn't be happening to her city, her neighbourhood. She could hear the doctors talking among themselves as they made their rounds of the wounded, their voices growing louder and more irritable. The hospital had no clean water, no painkillers, no anaesthetic. The syringes they were using were recycled. There was no gauze for bandages, only ripped-up clothes and underwear donated by the relatives of the wounded. Thick cloth stuck to open sores. The wounded lay on the ground, sweating and moaning in the sun. The hospital was running out of body bags for the dead.

Half the people who had lived here were Christian, more than half hated the PLO, aping the West for generations in their politics and lifestyle. They took holidays in New York and Paris, sent their children to German schools, their daughters to Switzerland. They consumed and went on consuming just like good Americans. They had done nothing to deserve this, except perhaps by being too shallow, or trusting. Sanaya made to go. Issa tugged at her arm. She stopped and he bent over and vomited. She held his forehead, murmuring to him as if he were a child. He pushed her hand away.

SYRIAN DESERT, 1915

Minas could stop himself from despair for moments at a time by imagining it all as one big game: last person standing wins the prize. As he saw the surging crowd thin, as the gasps and sighs and screams subsided, he knew he would survive the journey – if only because he lulled himself into apathy. The voice in his head conspired to keep it so. *It doesn't matter,* it said to him. *Nothing matters. It will all be over soon.*

He didn't dare look at Van behind him, houses burning, their mutinous crackle heard well into the fields, the fabled lake awash with fire. Mamma groaned and fell onto the dirt, knocking her forehead against stone, hand to chest in immovable despair. He couldn't help thinking it was all an act. If she really cared to survive, she'd be still and quiet, circumspect as he was.

He clapped his hand over his mouth so he wouldn't yell at her. Lie low, head down. The only way to get out of this alive. He imagined his schoolbooks burning in neat piles where he'd left them, in order of size, propped against the window. The voice in his head whispered, cajoled. *Isn't it ironic? The first novel ever published in Turkish was written by an Armenian.* He was holding a book to his chest when the Turks came, now he couldn't even think what it was. The officer in charge had arrived waving a *firman* from the Vali of Van and the Minister of the Interior in his hand. He dismounted from his horse, handed the paper to Mamma, who looked at it blankly. As Minas stretched out his arm to take the official document, one of the gendarmes knocked the book out of his hand.

He watched the book skid across the floor, pages unfurled and spine broken, then thud against the *tonir.* It made a sound like bone cracking. He stood with his back against the wall, unable to move, breathing hard. He thought he'd vomit – *please, God, no* – and, as if watching a stranger fall, he felt his body bend in half and crumple, both palms down on the floor. When he eventually looked up, the officer stood above him, face screwed into fastidious disgust. Flecks of bile on his polished boots and on Minas's knees.

Mamma came forward, knelt on the floor beside Minas. He felt her arms around him, but didn't dare look at her. She peered up at the officer, recognition lighting faint hope in her eyes.

'*Bey effendim*, I know you. You do remember me, don't you? I clean your home each Sunday. I know your wife, your children. Please, *effendim*, you're a family man, you understand. Your little boy always asks me to—'

But he cut her off with a slap to the face so hard Minas felt his heart jump in his chest. He was ashamed, so ashamed. Ashamed to see Mamma so helpless, and so hated. He watched her press her lips together, holding the tears in, resting her head on her knees, waiting for the pain, the disbelief to pass. After that he didn't remember much. He must have received a blow to the head as well, because his temples throbbed even now. He came to, still sitting on the floor, propped up against the linen chest. Mamma's right cheek was scarlet, head held high. She and Lilit were bustling about as the gendarmes shouted and cursed at them to leave the house, quick. They picked up one object at a time – a patterned plate, a daguerreotype, a discarded stocking – then laid it down and took another, until they were forced to drop everything they held in their hands. Mamma had placed a pale rose from the garden in the middle of the table two nights ago, when Papa was still alive and everything had been different. The flower fell to the ground now from its smashed vase, petals in disarray, blown. All blown away.

The gendarmes went through the house in a frenzy, finding money Papa had hidden behind the plaster walls, an old fob watch, some jewellery he'd been repairing, Lilit's silver-inscribed belt. They ripped icons from the walls and swept cups and glasses from the shelves to the ground. Minas watched Lilit stop at the door to slide her feet into her clogs as one of the gendarmes took them on the point of his bayonet and flung them outside.

He looked back at his home among the laughter of Turkish men, the tears of Armenian women. He was picked up and forced to walk, a gendarme on each side.

'Steady there, *janoum*,' one of them yelled. 'Get back into line.'

Janoum – he knew that word. It meant jewel in Turkish, used for darling, precious one, a term of endearment for sweethearts, beloved children. His mother sometimes used it when he was younger, with a mocking, half-reproving air. His legs refused to obey him – was it fear or sadness, was it the blow the Turk had given him? – he lolled between them like a man stuffed full of straw. His feet rolled outward and the gendarmes gave up in disgust and dropped him to the ground. He was drowned in the crowd of deportees, losing Mamma and Lilit, helped up by some neighbours and carried along. He craned his head over them to keep home in sight until he was forced to turn the corner. The windows – unshuttered now, open to wind and the sighing summer rains – flashed at him for the last time in the morning light: *You will never be back.* He fought to hold down the tears, wiping his eyes with his dirty sleeve.

Mamma kneeled like a Muslim, face to the sand, hands cupped around her ears. Now they were gone from Van, Minas tried not to look at her. He was ashamed of her: a deep, deathly shame he'd never known before. If she could alter in an instant, what would become of him? He sprang to her side, bent down and shook her by the shoulders.

'Straighten up, Ma! I can't breathe when you carry on like this.'

She flung herself away from him, wild-eyed, her weeping uninterrupted by his outburst. He could see her eyes questioning, trying to put it together in some digestible pattern, failing in the end. He glanced at his sister, telegraphed her a frantic message with his eyes. *What do we do now?*

'Ma! Why are you doing this to us?'

She looked up as if she didn't recognise him, unresponsive to his once-familiar voice. He felt her pain in his skull, at the back of his eyes. 'Stop it,' he mouthed. 'Stop doing this to me.' His mother continued to wail, hitting out when Lilit knelt to help her up. He bent down, gripped her chin in his hand.

'Enough,' he said. 'I can't stand it anymore.'

He let go of her face and watched her flop onto the dirt, walked away, lost himself in the horde of patient women and wailing babies, didn't look back. He was struck now by the silence of the gathering; except for the babies, nobody made a sound. They were being led like sheep to the slaughter. Wasn't someone going to scream, raise their fists, make a run for it? People shuffled around him, heads down, helping grandparents and children walk faster. A blind man walked alone, his arms held out in front of him, face untroubled and serene. The gendarmes must have knocked his stick out of his hand. Everyone was resigned. Everyone was quiet except his mother. He could hear his own spit being swallowed, the sucking sound it made in his mouth. They had all become one terrified, cringing organism, alert to any hint of danger, moving blindly toward some obscure goal. Only his mother could bring them all down. He could still hear her, louder and more unpredictable than the children's droning whine.

Please, God, make her stop, he prayed. *Make her stop, just make her be quiet.* They were all so vulnerable here. They were one slow-moving, brainless beast. His mother's cries were a buzzing of hornets in his ears, not allowing him to think. The time she bathed his ear with warm wax and water when he was stung in the field; the time she rocked him to sleep when Turkish girls snubbed him on the street, holding their noses at an imagined stink, for his being an infidel. She rocked him and rubbed his back even though he was already twelve and a big boy too.

He remembered his father's slumped body in red flashes of heat, shutters opening and closing in his mind, no connective thread to the story. Papa. Body soft. Falling. Poked in the rib by a Turkish heel. Sharp spurs. Cut. Gaping flesh. Papa. His mouth. Wide open. *I know what it's like. She doesn't.* He still hadn't told his mother or sister what he'd really seen last night. He hung back for a moment or two, eluded the guards, made his way slowly to the outer edge of the column to his mother. *Thank God she's stopped.* He could breathe again. She walked, unsteady, her face now composed in the mask she had always worn. Her cut forehead trickled a tear of blood into her eyebrow. Lilit put her hand out to wipe it but Mamma stopped her.

'It's nothing, not now. Here.'

She spoke without moving her mouth or looking at Lilit, passed her a handful of coins under cover of her clothes.

'Hide these.'

Then she unclasped her wedding earrings in a swift movement and made to press them into Lilit's unwilling hand.

'If I go—before you. Save yourself.'

Lilit gasped.

'No, Mamma, I couldn't!'

She pushed them weakly away. Minas lunged out at her and grabbed the earrings.

'What about me? Am I not to be saved?'

He ran further into the crowd, disappearing from his mother and sister as he clutched the earrings closer. He tried not to look back at them, desperate lambs bleating against the inevitable. The pet lamb he'd been allowed to keep now left behind, those trusting eyes consigned to ashes. Lilit's round eyes, growing wider by the second, as if only now had she begun to see. The glint of gold in her hand, a muffled movement and the money vanished somewhere among her skirts.

He strode further away. Where to hide the earrings? He thought of his tiny navel, his anus – so tight, impossible. *I could never do it.* The voice in his head whispered. *Pierce your nipples under your shirt.* He fingered the diminutive buds, pinched them between thumb and forefinger. He would have to do it tonight, under cover of darkness. *Heaven help me if they find the earrings before then.* He licked his lips, realised how hungry he was. His last meal had been at dawn, the coarse bread his mother had rationed after he saw his father die. *Don't—think of Papa.* He busied himself with food fantasies. *I'm strolling through stalls giving off the fumes of roast lamb, fried onions and herbs.*

He scuffed his shoes on thorny undergrowth and rock, calf muscles seething with the strain of walking uphill, of walking so quickly. The gendarmes cracked their whips at anyone not walking fast enough. He forced himself to pick up pace, dragging Mamma and Lilit behind him. They came to a rise overlooking fields and valleys, where they could look down in all directions, even on Van itself, marred by those bright, random patches of fire. Smoke stung their throats and eyes even here, even up so high.

'Look,' he said, pointing. 'Our neighbourhood's not burning.'

His mother and sister stared at him, open-mouthed, but he didn't care anymore what they thought. *I don't care about anything. Other than making the Turks angry.* From his new vantage point, he could gaze down as if drinking deep, upon Lake Van lying like an eye, gazing upward but seeing nothing. He could look upon the plain of sand stretching all the way to the horizon, marking what he assumed was the jagged boundary of northern Syria. They were being marched south-west, past Gevas, Mardin, Qamshile – places he'd only ever heard nomads speak of – then down into the blinding heart of Arabia. Ahead of him, the column of deportees trickled forward like a river toward the desert, sparkling in the afternoon sun, soon to be sucked up like water into sand.

He looked behind him. More people following, more than he could ever count. Gendarmes and soldiers rode on horses alongside, their bayonets pointed and shiny in the heat haze, lances of blinding light. Behind him, the mountains and grassy hills of Armenia beckoned. Before him, the desert lay still and sinister as a mirror at night.

✳ He didn't feel the days pass so acutely any longer. He was too obsessed by survival. He walked in his sleep, watched his shoes fall off blistered feet as if they belonged to somebody else. He trudged alongside his mother and sister through a moonscape of white stone and parched animal bones, tufts of saltbush he learnt to fight over for its sparse liquid. *Bowls of cherries and cheese white as a sheep's coat, scrolls of bread and peach brandy.* Sometimes he held the plant high above his head and wouldn't let Lilit or his mother share. Soon they stopped asking and let him walk ahead.

He made games of counting how many bloody footprints he could make each day. Lilit's cracked lips and burning face made him turn away. He didn't want to feel sorry for her. Yet at the same time he was amazed at her gritted calm. Only her hands betrayed her suffering; they twisted and pulled at each other as if she were trying to wrench them off, substitute one pain for another. Mamma's cut forehead turned septic in the heat and he told Lilit not to bother when she tried to clean it with her own saliva. He twisted the earrings in his nipples, regularly opening the wounds he had made. He thought the fresh flow of blood would stop them from infecting, so he continued to twist slowly each day, wincing at the pain. Some mornings he woke before dawn with the gendarmes, started off with them and walked alone at the head of the convoy, close to the horses.

Most times the Turks offered him a cigarette, which he took with a studied nonchalance and coughed over between cupped hands.

Sometimes Afet, who seemed to be the leader, allowed him to walk ahead of the entire convoy, and on these rare times he felt as if he were exploring new territory he had only dreamed of before. He was a solitary figure in an empty landscape. He was now a man, the new man. Nobody before him in history had ever experienced this. It made him proud, yet ashamed at the same time.

Sometimes, if Afet was in a thoughtful mood, he would talk to Minas, slowing his horse to a walk. He would explain how this was a duty for him, just a job like any other, that he had no choice but to fulfil it to the best of his ability. The future of modern Turkey was at stake here, even in this benighted desert. Minas could understand that, what with the world war and unrest in the cities and villages and those starving Muslim children Afet described so elegantly. It was only when Afet painted the Armenians and Jews and Greeks as greedy obstacles to this shining future that Minas had to blink hard and smile up at the officer to stop the tears from forming in his sandpaper eyes.

He wouldn't let himself cry as the others did. That would blur the clarity of his vision, muddy his purpose. Observe. Remember. Record. Do not forget. He was now scribe and recording angel made flesh. He had flashes of the past and then his future as he walked: himself as an old man, sitting on a chair soothing a baby. A little girl who mewled constantly, screwing up her face in anger. A daughter, a granddaughter? In this half-dreaming state he knew the little girl had been abandoned by her mother, just as he had. He tickled her under the chin. *Little one, you're not very pretty, are you?* And she made fists of her tiny red hands and punched at him as if in reproach, gulping in bubbles of air.

He blinked away the image, trying to keep his eyes open in the glare. There were no signs of life in the desert that he could see, except a solitary hawk high over the mirages of towers and plumed minarets, a stone seeming to take the shape of a djinn or an animal, a mythical beast out of a Crusader bestiary. Fine grains of sand through his fingers, falling, collecting in mounds, obscuring, so easy to hide any traces of killing in, as the blood simply welled up and disappeared.

So much blood. He let himself close his eyes for a moment and could almost believe they were walking through a sea of it, instead of sand. He was conscious of his own blood seeping at times from his pierced nipples, especially when a gendarme leaned over to speak to him; but among so much blood and dirt and so many people, he knew nobody would notice. He tried to calculate how many had died already, knowing he'd be asked at some point, when it was all over, when the Turks were called to account. He counted on his fingers, scratched figures of the marching dead on pearl-smooth pebbles. After two hundred, he gave up.

✳   The fifteenth evening – or was it the sixteenth? Lilit had lost count – they were ordered to stop by a desert well. One acacia stood guard, its spindle branches their only shade. The gendarmes and Chettis – Muslim criminals, mercenaries Lilit feared the most – flopped beneath it. They brought water up in a rotting bucket, drank their fill and replenished their leather flasks. Lilit wanted to drink; she was going crazy from thirst. If only she could have a drop, one drop. If only she could lick the outside of the flask, glinting wetly in the sun. She could suck at it. She saw drops of water glisten on one of the gendarme's fingers, his mouth. But she didn't move.

In time the Turks washed their faces, feet and hands, shook out their prayer rugs and faced Mecca. As the sun set over the sandhills, they pared their nails with the daggers kept at their belts. They ate from provisions of hard rusks and dried meat, while the deportees watched their every movement with increasing intensity as the hours grew: greasy index finger to mouth, white tongue visible for only an instant to lick, gristle tossed into sand behind them, where prisoners would not dare to venture.

It had been days since any of them had been given rations. Lilit assumed the Turks wanted as many of them to die of starvation and heat and thirst as possible, to save bullets and perhaps their sense of guilt. It was only at night, if the Turks seemed in the mood, that they taunted and killed with impunity. As she tried to sleep, she could hear the cries of women being raped. The grunts, the sound of heavy flesh hitting flesh. The mechanical precision. She shut her eyes tightly and tried to sleep, tried not to think of what she would do, how she would still manage to be Lilit – her very self – if she too was raped. She pressed Mamma's hands to her stomach, pulled Minas's arms around her waist. Welded like this with her family, she listened. She'd passed the point where she cared anymore about other people's suffering. She was not shocked. Only the crying of the children continued to pain her, but only hazily, only in theory. She was so hungry, so tired she could hardly muster the energy to feel anymore.

Minas had managed to find a few snakes and spiny-tailed lizards, trapped some rodents, eaten them fur and all. He hadn't shared with her or Mamma. They had been following the course of the Euphrates for the last week, so at least there was enough water to drink, when they were allowed to. The river was sluggish and narrow in these parts, silted by the grey pall of desert sands. At intervals it was filled with corpses, and Lilit could feel her lips grow slick with the fat that came off the dead, the white jelly of decomposition. She forced herself to drink and helped her mother kneel on lacerated knees to also cup her hands in the water. She overheard the Turks saying the river widened further on, became fast-flowing and red with the flame of the setting sun. But she wasn't interested in words anymore, even when she drank enough to vomit. Her hunger remained.

Now she watched her brother salivating as he followed the swallowing mouths. She saw how his body echoed the gestures of the guards: spasmodic, exaggerated, parodying the motions of eating and involuntarily partaking in their meal. When they ingested a morsel of meat his throat worked too, as if forcing it down. When they burped their satisfaction or hiccupped, he jerked back and forth as though it had been him. She knew his hunger was growing out of control, puberty taking over, dictating his need for nourishment. She saw him try to eat sand many times already, she even saw him contemplate his own excrement yesterday when he finished squatting. One of the Chettis crouched near him, combing through with his bayonet to see if there were any coins in it. Minas was oblivious. His knee bones strained through the skin, his shoulders broadened, that once-gentle voice was thickening by the day. He needed food and was half-crazed from the lack of it.

He seemed to be blaming all the prisoners, all Armenians, anyone who dared to fall down or cry or speak out of turn. At times she thought he was becoming one of them: a Turk. Or perhaps pretending so well he could even fool his own sister. He seemed to have developed an anxious tic, constantly patting his chest through his shirt, looking down at it, as if afraid it would suddenly disintegrate into his flesh. She noticed little flecks of blood, sometimes fresh, sometimes dried, on his torso. He would mutter to himself, as if answering silent questions.

She shivered. All she wanted to do was lie down, close her eyes for a long time. It was agony to imagine getting up again, talking, even thinking complete thoughts. The sun exhaled on the rim of sand and disappeared. The women held their children up to the darkening sky in both hands, an insane parody of a baptism ceremony. Lilit's heart squeezed in her chest: *Could I and Yervan have had—?* The babies wriggled and cried in whimpers, limp legs and arms jerking in the air, scalps glistening under the new moon with sweat. Some seemed half-dead already, their heads lolling back. The women continued to wait, arms upraised and aching. They were pleading for food: not for themselves, but for their children. Lilit saw Afet nod only once to the gendarmes and they began to move, slow as cats, then suddenly faster, upon the babies. The women screamed, fought, kicked. One woman took a blow to the head and got up again, blood pouring from her temples, to attack the gendarmes. But they were too weak, even with the crazed strength that came from defending their babies. Soon enough, the children were all taken away, some already dead, others wailing and struggling, crying for their mothers.

Hours later, when the women finally subsided, the gendarmes laid the tiny corpses out on the sand. All the children were dead, even those they last saw alive. The women were quiet. They caressed their children and other people's children, blessing them with Armenian psalms, fingers soft on foreheads, lips, on wide-open eyes.

Lilit shut her own eyes and refused to look. Part of her had wanted to leap up and stop the Turks, to die with those babies. But she held her mother and Minas close and he did not push her away this time. He shook with guilt, with shame. She looked at him, felt the ancient, nameless bond they shared. He knew what she was feeling, she in turn knew his suffering. Her fears, her selfishness, her private cruelties had taken shape and form, threatening to grow a face that was too much like her brother's.

✳   The action of walking became the only constant. One leg in front of the other, dry feet wading through sand. All Minas could see in every direction was sand. The undulations and waves and Arabic inscriptions in the sand. A holy Koran. An unholy verse of thirst and pain, hunger and sleeplessness. White sky and burning sand, melting and bleeding into one another in the heat.

The ache in his muscles subsided, only to be replaced by the unbearable lust of hunger and the equally unbearable agony of thirst. Even so, the act of walking soothed, gave shape to existence. He knew it was the only thing to count on, and he needed something. The rest of the days and nights were immense and frightening: capricious, a fine broken thread between living and dying or going mad.

Killings became more common, but he never knew if or when they would happen, or for what reason. He tried to avoid any confrontations with the Turks, tried not to speak to anybody unless he had to. He kept his head down and was the first to volunteer for anything the Turks wanted done. He listened to the voice in his head and it assured him this was the only way to survive.

Mamma had stopped looking at him, as if he weren't worthy any more of her love. He grimaced and capered in front of her and she merely turned her face aside. He fed her a bit of cured meat one of the Turks had given him but she spat it to the ground. Lilit bit her lip in sympathy yet shook her head to indicate how sick their mother was, how deserving of his forgiveness. He didn't acknowledge Lilit's gesture, merely picked up the moistened morsel and ate it himself. Nobody brought food to him, nobody asked him if he was all right, if they could somehow ease his fatigue or thirst. He watched Lilit trickle some of her own saliva into Mamma's mouth, he saw Mamma smile weakly and try to kiss Lilit's hand. *And what of me?* Confronted by this secret feminine tenderness, he steeled his heart. Stupid women. They could die in their sentimentality. Only he would survive.

One morning, when they veered away from the river, he watched soldiers laugh while they stabbed and played among the bodies of women perished in the cold of the desert night. He stood close to Afet, ready for anything the Turk needed done. He'd learnt to look when ordered to, yet taught himself to see nothing with his glazed, swollen eyes. He stood and watched with an impassive face, eyes squinting tight against the glare on the horizon. No visible sign of distress, except perhaps the sun tears streaking his cheeks. He beckoned Lilit to him, held her arm tight by his side and forced her to look as well.

Their mother lay naked on the sand in full view of the prisoners and Turks. By her left side were all her clothes. She was curled into a ball, her round back like a glistening pebble on the sand.

'We have no time for insubordination,' Afet said. 'Let this be a lesson to all of you.'

One of the gendarmes kicked out at Mamma as if to emphasise Afet's words, yet no sound came from her. Minas was only aware of the sensation of Lilit's cool hand on his back, the current that passed through her shaking body into his. She tried to put her hand over his eyes, to spare him the sight, but he pushed her away.

'This woman does not understand,' Afet said. 'She questions our motives. And yet, if you do what you are told, there will be no punishment. We young Turks are not unjust.'

Mamma's face upturned now, twisting and turning to avoid more blows, her palms open to the sky.

Afet leaned over her.

'So, I will ask you again, madam. Where is the hidden gold?'

Not a sound from Mamma. Minas could feel Lilit shaking harder, opening her own mouth to speak. He pinched her, and continued pinching until she closed her mouth and bowed her head.

'Once again, madam, where is the gold?'

Minas moved away from Lilit, still further into the crowd. Hiding among strangers, peering over shoulders and behind heads to catch a glimpse of the woman on the ground, watching indifferently, denying his connection, just another bored onlooker wishing it to be over soon, to stop. *My Ma?* Her body sinking, sinking, covered over by drifts of sand.

He saw Lilit look around, searching for him, wondering where he went. His mother convulsed for an instant, subsided again. *It's all her fault. Afet said so. She didn't believe they're taking us somewhere better.* This wasn't his mother, not the mother he knew. She was filthy, blackened, a beggar. Her hands and face were dirty, like a child's. Her feet a mass of bleeding sores. A hand was clamped over her head, Afet's cloaked body over hers.

'This is the last time I will ask you. Where is the gold you have hidden?'

Minas concentrated on her hands, her wrists, those strong fingers that had once scratched and rubbed him, massaged his tummy when he was ill. *No. That wasn't her. Not this stranger lying on the sand.*

There was a sound from the huddled shape. Afet put his ear to her mouth, nodding intently. He looked toward Lilit, then scanned the crowd for Minas, still nodding. Minas nodded too. He studied his mother's fingers again, the way they clutched and clawed at grains of nothing. *Not my Ma.* Long fingers, delicately turned. He was looking so hard he jumped at a sound that seemed to come from behind his ear. The jolt of a rifle and her body jerked upward. Suddenly he felt the tiny hairs at the back of his neck tingle. He hummed, a buzzing in his ears, a wordless song of no sound, *My darling, my love, your sufferings and joys will be many,* the shouts and cries diminished, the voice in his head loud, louder, *It's not really happening. It's not happening at all.*

His legs moved before he knew why, running, running toward her to the front of the crowd. Then beside him he felt a rush of air like the felling of a sapling. Lilit was spread-eagled on the ground. A fat Chetti bent over her.

'No!'

He heard himself say it, but the terrible motion of two bodies didn't stop. He mustn't have said it at all. The jerking, the painful burrowing, the thrust and pull would not end. Lilit fought, clutched at sand and hair. The Chetti swore.

'Daughter of pigs. Whore. Christian whore. Wriggling. Moaning. Shut your mouth.'

His hands were now inside her. Minas looked at his own hands, held them up before his eyes. His eyes were open, were they? Better to close them. He heard faint scuffles at his feet; the song reached a crescendo amid the ringing of imaginary bells. He opened his eyes once more. All he could see were burning spaces and blind white sky and the voice in his head took over, urging him on as he ran away, while the song swelled and burst.

He turned back heavily. How much time had passed? Lilit was still and mute on the ground, bared breasts flat against her ribs. Her cache of gold discovered hidden in her vagina. The Chetti threw chinking coins up and down into the sand. Her short pale legs blossoming bruises. He watched them change from white to black to yellow. *What funny colours. Never seen those sorts of colours before.* He concentrated on the spreading shades and wanted to cover them up; they were too vivid for churchgoing, deepening to purple and green. *Where are those summer stockings of yours then, Lilit?*

He thought of Lilit pulling up her stockings on the way to church, the sad little folds that invariably gathered around her ankles. He laughed and the other prisoners around him clicked their tongues. *He's mad, poor thing. Lost it.* Lilit gazed up at him, reproachful. He didn't care. He hauled her to her feet and arranged the ragged skirt around her thighs, patting fabric into place like broken bread on a table.

�֍   They were nearing settlements now, sickly villages carved out of sand and powdered rock. 'Shaddadie,' the old women whispered around Minas. Shaddadie. The name of the largest town seemed to hold some morbid significance. There were empty caves on its outskirts and the prisoners were made to sleep in one of them, they weren't sure for how long, while the gendarmes and soldiers rested.

'Not far to go now,' Afet yelled at them from the mouth of the deepest cave. His voice grew distorted before it reached Minas, changing into the howl of a jackal. 'A train will be along soon to take us all to Der ez Zor. You'll be well looked after there.'

More and more prisoners were herded into the cave, until there was no space to sit or stand or even breathe. Some began protesting at the entrance, and he heard shots, a muffled collective sigh, then silence. He was pushed to the back, where curved inner walls dripped condensation. He turned his head and licked at beads of moisture, fire-cold on his tongue. Old women crushed against him, all sharp bones and rotting teeth, and he grazed his chin on rock before he fell.

He was lifted, almost carried aloft by the pressure of other bodies. He craned his neck above them to try to catch a glimpse of Lilit. Sometimes he thought he saw her dark head, but it was always another girl, or a bald man, a trick of light and shade. When he finally settled against the wall, knees to chest, arms clasped tight around them, it occurred to him the cave stank of burning. A stink that penetrated into his nostrils, his ears, into his eyes. A suggestion of burnt clothes and hair and something else, something he'd never smelled before. Soft stones broke under his weight when he adjusted his position, ash stained his feet and the side of his face when he lay down to sleep. It was dark, save for the lantern strung up at the entrance of the cave, and when he lay down it too was extinguished by the shapes made by others' bodies.

He closed his eyes, although it made no difference to the uniform shades of black, curled up in his corner. Beneath him, the ground of the cave shifted and exhaled, disintegrating further into darkness.

� 'Minas.'

He opened his eyes slowly, not sure if the girlish voice was part of a dream. He couldn't see anything, but felt the firm grasp of a hand on his arm. His first instinct was to shake it off and place both hands on the earrings in his nipples.

'Minas, it's me.'

'Lilit?'

'I'm scared.'

He sat upright, took her two hands in his. They were cold, so cold, in the chill of the cave. It occurred to him there, in the safety of half-sleep, that neither of them had mentioned Mamma since she was killed. Or what had happened to Lilit. It was too much to bear. Too much. And now this? But her voice in his ear intruded into his thoughts.

'They've pushed us in here to kill us, Minas.'

He let go of her hands.

'Nonsense,' he muttered. 'You heard Afet. The trains are coming in a few days.'

'Minas, listen to me.'

Lilit's voice was low, and thrilling with a new, deathly intensity.

'I've been talking to the women. This is Shadaddie. This is where three thousand of us were burnt alive only months ago.'

Minas snorted.

'Why would they want to do that? They need us, our labour, skills, education, to help them build a new state.' He heard a shuffle to the right of his foot and felt her smear something dry and chalky onto his palm.

'Feel it. Burnt bones. Ash. Charred bodies. We're going to die, Minas.'

✳ Lilit woke tangled in Minas's limbs. For a moment, before she opened her eyes, she thought it was Yervan, a sleepy afternoon, his penis hard against her leg. But it was only her brother's hipbone, and she pushed him away and stepped over the sleeping prisoners toward the mouth of the cave, brushing ash from her arms and licking her fingers to wet her face. She wanted to stand in the cool air, away from the sour smell of sleep and unwashed bodies and excrement. Away from the memory of what had happened to her yesterday. And Mamma. The shapeless sense that all was not right with the world. The sun was not yet up and the desert retained the chill of night; she walked on tiptoe to the entrance and felt each grain of sand damp and clammy under her feet.

Only one Chetti guarded the cave, with a rifle across his knees. She was glad it wasn't the man who—but she wouldn't let herself think of that. He was smoking a long ivory pipe, but as he turned to look at her he placed it with careful delicacy to the ground and lowered the gun to her belly. She stood still, meeting him with a level gaze, until he placed it over his lap again and beckoned to her. She hesitated, afraid to come too close, but something in his calm, almost indifferent manner quietened her fears. So she stepped toward him and he offered her a puff. She shook her head, and seeing the hunger in her eyes he rummaged in his trouser pocket and held forward a hunk of dry meat.

She grabbed it, sitting at his feet and tearing at the goat's flesh with teeth that hurt, guilty at not waking Minas to share it with him, ashamed of accepting food from a Turk at all. As she swallowed the last mouthful she looked up at the burly man. He made no effort to smile or even acknowledge her, merely gazed ahead into the distance as Yervan had often done, but she felt safe curled up on the sand near his dusty boots; she knew the train would come now and they wouldn't be burnt, and for a moment she even felt they would be all right.

✳ When Lilit allowed herself to witness what happened to the last living baby she pushed away all sentiment. She told herself it wasn't her fault. She'd heard the baby cry in the cave at Shaddadie, seen it survive the suffocation and heat and cold with all of them. There was no bonfire, no mass deaths, other than the daily shootings and knifings that came as a matter of course. The Turks did it only last month, the old women told her, pushed Armenians into those caves and torched them with brush fires. They heard Afet talking, telling his soldiers that perhaps it wasn't wise to do it again; there would be too much evidence.

Many of the prisoners from Van and its *vilayets* were still alive. Only a few had been left on the damp floor of the cave, expired overnight with the scattered bodies of their compatriots, strangers, sisters, lovers in death and dark. She saw the baby taken onto the train with everybody else, hidden by his mother's long hair and rags, still sucking at her flabby breast. It was hard to hold on to Minas in the crush of bodies, gendarmes pushing people up onto the carriages with their rifles, women screaming, children falling underfoot. Many refused to get on, having never seen a train before, so the gendarmes dispatched them quickly – more room for the others, they said.

Minas held on to Lilit's arm so tight she thought it would be wrenched off. She felt herself lifted headfirst into the train, Minas bundled behind her. Only when all the prisoners had been packed into the sweltering carriages and the doors were bolted did the baby begin to cry.

It might have been the sudden dark and quiet that frightened him. Lilit breathed a sigh of thanks for the tiny chink of light up high in a corner. At the same time she felt she couldn't breathe. A man pressed on her, his beard grazing her bare arm. A girl had soiled her underclothes. In the heated closeness the odour was overpowering, making it difficult to think.

The train moved forward with a shudder. There was an unfocused brutality in its movement, in the sickening, shrill sound of wheels grinding on tracks. She opened her eyes wider in the dim, searching for Minas. Hadn't she been holding his hand? People started to scream; at least, those who were still well enough to expend the energy did. She screamed with them. The mechanical movement so final. It was more terrifying than anything else, this fiery beast that held them in its belly. She saw Minas in the periphery of her vision, his mouth open and eyes blazing, perhaps he was going to die, too. The shock of that thought made her stop. She curled up on the floor, dragging him down with her and cradling his head on her lap. The noise of the train and the shouting was deafening, the baby's cries even louder.

Soon people began complaining, threatening to denounce his mother to the guards if she didn't shut him up. They now wanted silence; they wanted to talk in whispers; they wanted to sleep. Lilit trembled at the fear that Minas might betray the woman, expecting a reward of food. She bit her bottom lip and, as if reading her thoughts, he looked at her and wagged his head, dog-like, from side to side.

Somebody flung the woman a jacket to suffocate the baby with. She let it stay on the floor. She continued to give her baby the breast, forcing her huge nipple into his angry mouth, stuffing him with it, trying to drown out his wails. The baby nuzzled at her for a moment then flung his head back again in disgust. The woman began to sing a lullaby, high wailing that filled the room. *My darling, my love, your sufferings and joys will be many.* Lilit wanted to scream again. *My mamma sang that to me. Where is she now?* Ossified in sand, bones picked clean by desert rats and birds. Her mamma. That cushioned lap, those strong hands, breasts she buried her face in against the cruelty of the day.

She knew the woman's milk had dried up, knew the baby would soon die. But there was nothing she could do. She thought of latching the baby onto her own small breasts, praying milk would come in sympathy, but, somehow, she was too tired. Too sleepy. Too indifferent. Too afraid of what the Turks might do again if they saw her.

Earlier in the day, before the train came, the woman had crawled over sleeping and sick prisoners to the cave mouth. The sun hadn't yet reached the rim of hills, and Lilit sat at the entrance to the cave, shivering. The woman patted her on the arm and asked her to help look after the baby.

'I saw you watching us. You care.'

Lilit turned away, frowned. The young mother became insistent.

'My milk's running out. Don't know what to do. He keeps screaming.'

Lilit looked down and pretended not to hear. The baby was asleep in his mother's arms, his mouth and nose crusted with scabs. She distracted herself with disjointed memories, scenes from girlhood fantasies. *I wore a narrow band of lace across my forehead and my too-tight bodice. Yervan took me for a walk.* Her shadow wavering then tight on the sand. She continued to look down, as if studying her own serrated outline, until the woman sighed and went away.

The train now stopped at the outskirts of another town and the gendarmes' horses were let out first. 'Malaria,' she could hear Arabs shouting on the platform. 'Malaria here. You must leave now.' Minas hoisted her onto his shoulders and she peered out of the tiny opening near the roof of the carriage, where timber slats had been pulled away for air – by former prisoners? Who were they? Where were they now? Little boys stood so close she could touch them, in long robes with gold-woven kerchiefs wrapped around their heads. Red dust flew about, settling in mouths and ears and the corners of their eyes. They held up white banners scrawled in green. *Malaria.*

The Turks didn't care. She watched them lead their horses to the well and let them drink. Amid the stamping hoofs and coarse shouts, she felt the young mother push her aside to lean out as well. She balanced on the shoulders of a thickset man whose face twisted with the effort. The baby, bound to her body with a wide length of cloth from her skirt, seemed asleep again or dead, his mouth pinched tight. Lilit jumped down, wondering what the woman would do next. She nudged Minas. The woman seemed to wait for a few minutes, perhaps until after the animals had their fill, then Lilit saw her beckon one of the gendarmes closer with a pitiful smile.

'I need some water, *Bey effendim*. Please. A few drops.'

'No water for deportees,' she could hear him announce. His voice bored into her head. 'No water until we reach our destination.'

Soon Afet let out the prisoners for a moment, if only to give them enough time to throw out any dead or dying from their carriages. Lilit saw the mother make for a well with the bundle of concealed baby under her arm. She was shaking now, her head jerking from side to side like a hen's, the movement of her legs spasmodic. The gendarmes glanced at her for an instant as if surprised by her temerity, then turned to their drinking flasks and food.

'No water for you either,' they said, 'so don't bother hanging around.'

But Lilit could see she was no longer waiting for their pity in a few sprinkles from soiled hands. In an instant of despair, she dropped her baby like a wishing stone into the well. He would bring her good fortune. He cried too much. She was too tired to carry him anymore. There was no milk left to give him. She wanted him to drown, have a swifter, easier death.

She could see the woman screaming now, slapping at her own face and hair and clothes, trying to fling herself down the well too and being held back by Chettis and gendarmes. It had become a loud, riotous game, the men competing to see who could hold her down long enough without being bitten or kicked. She had tapped into some superhuman strength, shrieking, scratching, teeth bared, with no fear of their whips or clubs.

Lilit tried not to look. Madness was catching. The woman seemed unaware of the blows, the bruises. Lilit studied the stones at her knee as she lay on the ground resting, flicked a lump of dirt from Minas's elbow. She picked up a smooth pebble, held it before her eyes like a talisman. Pebbles from Lake Van, oyster-grey and pink, she'd played with so long ago. The image receded, she was too tired to hold it. She wanted a pillow, soft, something she could sink into. All her energy and faculties trained upon this one pinpointed desire. A pillow. Only that. Somewhere to rest her head. She tried not to feel anything as the woman collapsed suddenly in the dust, worn out by her fighting, as the men shouldered her and took her away behind their horses. She heard nothing, but knew what they were doing.

She tried to make herself inconspicuous. *Poppies cut from the riverbank were made into bouquets bigger than I could hold. Yervan gave me one.* The woman was only heard at intervals now, a choked cry here and there. She lay, bloodied, a broken doll slumped on a gendarme's horse, finally inaudible as the prisoners were herded back onto the train, still further into the desert and to Der ez Zor.

BEIRUT, 1995

I wake at sunset, sweating in dreams of D'Andrea's hands and my father's imagined voice. I must have slept all day in my dirty clothes and my mouth is dry. The dust of the Beirut day is rising, making my nose tingle.

As I rise from the bed my movements are slow and wooden, and in my mind's eye I travel long and hard across desert wastes, across white sand so fine it looks like sugar, train tracks rusted and overgrown with the sharp, spindly stalks of thistle.

I pull off my clothes, stand and gaze at a ghostly face above my nakedness. Something in my own expression – dazed, passive, almost surprised – reminds me of my grandmother. Lilit looked like that in the days before I left. As if she regretted letting me go. Or was it more than that? There was so much left unsaid, so many memories untouched, left to moulder in chests like the poppy-embroidered veil – such fine woven silk – I once glimpsed under layers of goat's hair blankets. Now I have it, swaddling Lilit's Koran. I hadn't asked Lilit about it then, knowing any more questions would only hurt us both. Was it given to her by the teenage sweetheart or the Turkish husband? Did she wear it because she wanted to, or because she was forced? I see her aging face in an unknown future, marked by war and work and the loss of everything familiar. Her shortened girlhood, its petty joys and loves.

I know all too well the details of the deportations, forced marches through the desert, the cattle trains that came out of nowhere like noisy harbingers of Hitler's Final Solution. *Who, after all, remembers the Armenians today?* And who remembers my father? There's nobody left alive who knew him.

I laughed and joked in the dimly lit restaurant last night with D'Andrea, drank four glasses of arak, meandered to the beach across the road together. It was past midnight, past two, past three, the time when identities merge and fall apart, when alliances are forged and broken. As the evening wore on, after I'd told him whose daughter I am, he'd become brasher, larger, less complicated. I began to like him more; his former affectations seemed funny rather than condescending. So I let him hold my hand as we clambered over the rocks in the dark, almost falling over and laughing at ourselves. His palm was alert and cool in the dark, and I felt safe. I was open to any experience, felt maybe that was why I'd come here. I let him stop me with a hand on my upper arm, then slowly kiss me, his tongue a swollen muscle in my mouth. But when we got to the sea my mood became more sombre.

The strip of beach when we got there was a grave: dark and narrow. Nobody else around. I sat close to him on the pebbles. It was nice not to care, not to strive. I wanted to lie there and fall asleep, his heavy arm over my hip. I lay down, then got up again almost straight away, thinking better of it. I think he noticed, and I could feel the affront in him. His voice changed. He started talking about the man who ordered the killing of my father, without mentioning any names. Said he actually knew who it was, but needed to know that I could be trusted with the information.

'Trusted with information about my own father's death?' I blurted out. 'You don't need to tell me, anyway. I already know it was Islamic Jihad.'

'Yes, but who?' he shot back. 'I know the name of the man who effectively pulled the trigger, who arranged the whole thing.'

He told me he knew the family from his work in the camps, knew who the dead man had been, and who his child was, a little girl. I closed my eyes, put my head on my knees. I didn't want to hear it, not from him. Suddenly, I was scared. If I found out the name of this man, of his family, I would have to do something. I would have to befriend them, or make enemies of them. Either way, I would lose.

I think he felt my shutting-off, because then he licked his index finger – I could hear the wetness of his mouth in the dark – and placed it on my nape, leaning forward into my hair. I jumped.

'I can have them taken care of,' he whispered, his breath tickling my scalp.

I sat up, my hand still on the recorder in my bag, almost brought it out to show him how stupid he'd been. But he didn't give me time. He lunged forward, his leg hard over mine. I heard the catch in his breath, almost a sob, the bitter excitement, but I turned away, tried to get up. He held me down, swiftly unzipped his trousers. I saw his white, baggy underpants, the limp penis. Now I was panicking. The black night that was so still a moment before seemed full of our loud, rasping breaths. We fought without speaking. He pushed me back onto the pebbles, grinding against me with all the weight of his middle-aged body. My tight lips, his soft paunch against my belly. The pebbles felt sharper now, dangerous. He took out his penis, nudged it against my mouth. I bucked. All I could think of was my father, floating somewhere above us, outraged, and I broke free, sprinting across the sand, toward the lights of the promenade.

Now I lie back on the bed with my eyes wide open. I can't get up, can't even shower. I can't believe this has happened to me. Me, at my age. I think of how his unremarkable face looked, fuzzy around the edges from moonlight and arak, precise as a housewife when he unzipped his trousers. His eyes were open, searching my face for some intimation of what I felt. What did I really feel? Fear? Curiosity? Desire? Disappointment. I close my eyes and try to sleep again as the day's light fades, my pillow pressed like a stone to my belly.

DER EZ ZOR, 1915

There was malice and revelry in the faces of the Turks, their lewd jokes and swearing, the aroma of raki from their mouths colouring the air. *Not such good Muslims after all,* Lilit thought. She saw a man at the back of the mob puff out his weak chest and look about, smiling at the drunken gendarmes who grinned back, frowning at the white naked women who kept their heads lowered to the dust. Lilit kept her head up; she knew by now it was the way to survive. Many women were already mad, maimed beyond recognition, fingernails and toenails gone, disjointed puppets with burnt skin peeling in patches from their faces.

The man moved forward through the marketplace, brushing women with his shoulders as he walked. It was almost as if he had to touch each woman as he passed to steady himself. Most were naked, but some wore rags that were once underclothes: bloomers and corsets and petticoats now grey and disintegrating. Lilit still wore the skirt she'd been wearing in Van, though it hung in limp ribbons now. But she was thankful she had it. Her whole body was black with filth and she hid her breasts with her arms, conscious even in her terror to be ashamed.

She watched his face; he looked as though he would vomit. A woman close by gazed at him in sublime indifference, her proud lion's head created by the lack of a nose. Only a gaping hole remained, the bridge completely cut away. A gendarme saw him staring, too, and boomed in his ear.

'See this? I taught her a lesson. She kept screaming about her baby, her baby, her arsehole baby. Not a peep out of her now.'

Lilit tried to block out his voice. She squinted at the sinking horizon and the stippled sand dunes with the odd sensation of coming to a place where she knew she would stay. Dead or alive, she wasn't going anywhere. One woman lay on the ground, legs open in a triangle, palms upturned to the sky. The way she'd lowered herself down was careful and pathetic, like an old woman preparing for bed. Seeing this, an obtuse, dangerous anger took hold of Lilit. The light breeze irritating the hairs on the back of her neck seemed complicit, intimate as a lover's or an assassin's breath. Beneath it, the smell of sweat, of meat and blood. And something else mocking her – not rage exactly, but an emptiness, or a profound regret. The gendarmes made her line up in a row with the others, and she suddenly goose-pimpled as the rising wind hit her bare skin. A familiar panic lashed through her as one and two and three, thirty, more, were bound together, now beyond speech or thought or the shame she'd felt so acutely the moment before.

Yet she still stood straight, head held up. Her braid had been hacked off some days before, and she could feel the rough cut at her nape, the bite of the bayonet on tender skin. Her brother, one of the few boys left alive, closed his eyes and murmured to himself. She turned her head to look at him, maybe for the last time: he was growing, already had a faint smudge on his upper lip, reddish strands of hair. He spun around, oblivious, humming. *My darling, my love, your sufferings and joys will be many.* She pulled him to her to quieten him and felt his bones grind against hers.

But they weren't being killed, not this time. Only sold as slaves.

So many had already been killed in countless ways. Thrown into desert rivers, roped together by the waist so only one bullet would drag them down. Lines of dead women, the whiteness of their thighs. Caves nearby filled with the living, then torched by Turkish boys carrying bundles of wood. Charred stumps, blackened rock, matchstick bones. Mass graves of grandfathers, sons, children without names. Mothers and girls raped, strangled, pushed under clumps of sand.

The man that had been standing at the back now came forward and touched Lilit's arm. She lifted her chin, stared at him. His face was pale, as if he spent a great deal of time indoors, and he wore fine European clothes. She assumed he was checking for typhus or dysentery before he paid, pulling her lips away from her teeth. 'Gently, gently,' he murmured, studying the whites of her eyes. Pushing a finger into her distended stomach. He came so close she could smell his breath. He stank of desert wells, death and decomposition. The sand and sky and a lone thorn tree seemed to recede behind him into the distance, then come to rest between him and her, suspended in silence amid the chaos.

Lilit leaned forward, then spat in his face. For a moment he stood there, her spit dripping off his forehead onto his lashes. Then he sprang back, wiping it off with the edge of his jacket.

'Crazy girl,' he whispered. 'Who do you think you are?'

Three Turkish soldiers came running, bayonets ready. The man put both hands out wide, held them back.

'It's all right, all right. Nothing happened. She accidentally stepped on my foot.'

Twenty piastres they asked for her, claiming she was still a virgin. Those visibly raped and mutilated went only for five. Tarnished coins, tarnished women, passing from hand to filthy hand. He led her away. When they were out of sight of the gendarmes he placed his soiled jacket over her shoulders.

She looked back at the marketplace once, to see her brother for the last time, but by then it felt as if she'd already left him forever.

✳ Suleiman wasn't aroused in the least by the girl he'd bought; the sight of breasts, small or large or pointy or spaced wide apart, round or sagging, the details of thighs and hips and groins, the emaciation or dimpled fat, the hair under armpits and on legs was too confronting, pathetic. They had all become one strange mass of limbs and no faces. Animals. He had to cut out the expressions and the eyes; it was too much. Most of all, beneath the awe and revulsion he felt was a deep, profound sadness. He would never plumb the depths of this sadness. Women, these women – all women – were unknowable.

And he was distracted. He wasn't happy to be here, afternoon sun and flies, touch of heatstroke coming on, more accounts to do at home and the cook sulking yet again. Something about plates of food being virtually untouched at the feast last night. Did they not appreciate all her efforts? Only Suleiman could appease her. But the summons had come that morning from Zeki Bey, the governor of Der ez Zor, and couldn't be ignored by any Ottoman subject. Anybody disregarding the command could be called a traitor. Even the Syrian Arabs had come.

Only males were duty-bound, of course. It wouldn't do to let their women see such horrors.

He'd chosen a woman to buy not because he wanted one, but because not to do so would invite recrimination. The soldiers were so drunk all they wanted was more money to buy raki and wine. He wondered what his dead brother's wife would say when she saw him bring another woman into the household. At least Armenians were people of the book. Even if he did end up sleeping with her the Koran allowed it, though he didn't think it likely he would want to. She was not unattractive, though. She had a small round mouth so she would be tight, that was one good thing. Her thighs seemed thick and strong – she would be bold in bed. He decided to like her.

She stood straight beside him, head held up and with no expression. She was black-haired, which was normal for an Armenian. He preferred blondes: Georgians, Circassians, Northern Greeks. Her braid had been hacked off. At least she wouldn't have head lice if her hair was so short. She still wore a skirt, unlike most of the other women, although it was so ragged it hung about her calves in strips.

Her irises were a flat, serene blue that made him draw breath. They seemed to have no depth, only colour. She looked almost healthy, even robust compared to the terrible condition of the others, and incredibly young. She did have lice, though; he could see them crawling over her hair and under her arms. In her secret hair, too, no doubt. He suppressed the urge to part her legs and look. Her eyes stared at him with no plea, no recognition of him as a human being. He flinched inwardly at this. He didn't like to think she had the moral high ground.

He had given the gendarmes all the liras he had in his pocketbook, not caring how much he paid. After all, what was a human being worth? He had only let himself ask the question for a moment, as he watched the money being counted. He wondered again, with the panic of a man with no recourse, what Fatima would do to him when he walked through the door with another woman.

✳ Lilit accepted the offer of the jacket. *Jacket,* she said to herself. *That's the word.* She looked at the Turkish man without blinking. *Waistcoat,* she murmured in Armenian. *Baggy trousers. Belt of watered silk.* Her hand went out to finger the shiny crescent buckle, the gleaming pistol at his waist, but she stopped herself just in time.

They walked quickly as the sun balanced red on the horizon. In the dusk, full-skirted women and their many children sat on the verges, enjoying the creeping rumour of a new season. Light arced from the sea behind the citadel. Another walled city. *Where have I seen one like this before?* Palms were outlined against the sky like the pencil drawings she had seen Minas do. *Minas. Now where is he again?*

She turned her attention to the wet, shiny street. Tiled courtyards in the centre of houses were sprinkled with water to settle the dust of day. She remembered home now in a pale flash of images, the Turks of Van building watercourses and aqueducts, bathhouses adjacent to their mosques. Now she and the man passed shallow pools in gardens, glimpsed through elaborate stonework walls, and fountains in public squares. She stopped and concentrated on the sight as something valid and true, palpable reality to cling to. Her smooth forehead marred by the effort of thought. The Turkish man thought to bring her a tin cup of water and for this she was grateful, draining it and holding her hand out for more. She drank and drank, water pooling at the corners of her mouth, dripping down her chin. Women came with buckets to sluice their courtyards and children skidded on the wet road, avoiding her. He led her away by the arm.

'Please,' she said in Turkish when they had passed the curious stares.

'Yes?'

'What is this place called?'

'Der ez Zor.'

'I'm sorry I spat at you.'

He stopped, looked at her. Really looked at her, in the eyes.

'Why did you?'

'I don't know.'

He put his arm around her waist when she stumbled, she noticed he didn't flinch at her filthiness and it endeared him to her.

'*Bey effendim*, would you prefer if I walked some paces behind you? I must smell so bad you'll be embarrassed—'

'No. They'll think you're an escaped slave if I'm not nearby. Who knows what they would do to you. Anyway, I don't mind your stink.'

She nodded, keeping her gaze to the ground.

'What happened to your eyebrows?'

'The soldiers shaved them off. Wanted some fun one night.'

'Did they hurt you?'

'They moved on to a girl from Moush who cried and screamed. Cut off her breasts. She was more interesting than me.'

He concentrated on her eyes again as she spoke, and nodded carefully as if he didn't believe her.

✳ He brought her to a mere wall, a facade of peeling paint amid garbage from the street and the crush of people. In the centre, a tiny door. She hesitated, in an instant felt the dawning suspicion of loss and a bubble of panic. *Minas.* She remembered where he was now. Her fingertips tingled with the effort of being again in the world. For a moment, the grapple of sensation, the struggle of remembering, then the Turkish man pulled her to him in the crowd. Lips tight against her ear. Teeth the white of almonds when he smiled.

'You're home.'

When the door opened, as if by invisible hands, all was splendour and beauty and peace. No further thought of Minas, of her mother. Papa and his magic clocks the stuff of heroic legend, Lake Van a far-off fairytale. She stood in the centre of a courtyard among tiled fountains in diamond patterns of black and white. Drops of water silvered on the flagstones. A ginger cat lay in a puddle of sunshine on the largest fountain's rim, uncoiled itself and stretched. Lilit knelt down and cupped water in both hands, wetting her chest and arms. She turned and smiled at the man. Sun sparkled on her face. Then he hit her.

He had been so deferential as they walked, so solicitous of her comfort. As soon as he saw the other woman look down from the hidden quarters upstairs, raising her glittering veil and her eyebrow, he hit Lilit squarely on the cheekbone. She assumed he did it so the other woman would look upon her more kindly and would spare her future blows. Was she wife, servant or concubine? She looked like a mixture of all three.

Lilit looked at herself in the only mirror that night after he slept. He had taken her to his bedroom and, as she watched him draw the soft curtains around the bed, moving around her gently in the half-light, she had surprised herself by feeling both hopeful of being treated well and afraid of what would come next. But he hadn't touched her; said he could wait until the time was more propitious, it now being the waxing of the moon. She was glad of that. He merely brushed her forehead with his little finger and turned over to sleep.

The other woman was nowhere to be seen. Before he blew out the lamp, Lilit ventured to ask him. '*Effendim*, the other woman, with the veil? Is she your wife?'

His voice was muffled by pillows. 'My dead brother's wife. Now mine. She is my first wife. You may be next, if I like you.'

She couldn't settle when he fell asleep; the mirror flickered whitish at her in the dark. She hadn't looked at herself since she left home, and gasped when she saw her face. Thin lines where her eyebrows once were, a growing raft of black stubble. She wept at her reflection; there were too many shadows and recesses in this new, sepulchral face. No stars outside, no street lights. Only the moon swelling silent through the window. She examined her neck grown scraggy, breasts so slack, jumped up to catch a glimpse of her painful stomach. Her breath frosted as she leaned her cheek against the mirror. She wiped the gleaming surface with her little finger, a stroke for memory, just like that.

❋ In the morning, she lay on the divan in a soiled nightdress one of the servants had given her. The Turk asked her to call him Suleiman, not *Effendi*, not *Bey*, neither Sir nor Master. She nodded and closed her eyes, embarrassed by her ugliness. She was clean now, except for the dress.

After he hit her last night in the courtyard she'd been led away by one of the other women, older, fatter – another concubine or slave, she wasn't sure – and made to sit in a steam-filled room with a bucket of scalding water and an ancient scrubbing-brush. In a corner, razors and soap and pumice stones lay in a pile. She knew these were for getting rid of all her hair. She shuddered when the woman pointed to them, then at her armpits and groin and legs. She set to work, sobbing with the pain, hoping nobody could hear. The woman looked in on her at intervals and replenished the water level in the bucket, pouring the dregs over her as though she felt it was all taking too long.

The woman came in again finally after a greater length of time and spread Lilit out on her stomach, pressing her down hard on the slippery floor. She took Lilit's chin in her hand and showed her a small green vial she held; Lilit read the label as best she could, making out the Arabic phrase: *Oil of Lebanon.* The woman let go of her chin then and straddled her, massaging her back with the cedar-scented oil, working her way up from the buttocks to the tiny bones of the neck. The weight of her elbows was unbearable, but Lilit bit her lip and did not cry. The woman then turned her over onto her back, still looming above, fat face painted with red lips and gold lids and a moustache too close, sweat dripping into Lilit's eye.

She sat on Lilit's stomach and grasped both breasts in her hands, laughing and kneading them, saying something in Arabic Lilit did not understand. She pointed to her own flabby mounds under her housedress and shook her head. Lilit opened her mouth to cry out; the woman's fingers were tight, pinching her nipples, she tried to put her arms up to stop her, but the woman leapt up and was gone. She was left to rinse herself of oil and wait, naked, dripping sweat in the steam, for someone to come and dress her.

Now she suspected the nightdress belonged to Suleiman's second wife, the one she saw as she arrived; a cast-off she'd not even bothered to wash.

Suleiman sat cross-legged on the rug, smoking a water pipe. Its fragrance reminded her somehow of the peach orchards at home. She poked out her bare foot, studied the way it emerged from the threadbare cotton folds.

'Now, listen carefully,' he said. 'From this day on, your name will be Lale. Do you remember that? Yes? Good. Lale means tulip in our language – but I suppose you already know that. Yes? And you're not to speak anymore – ah, ah – Armenian. Just Turkish, all right?'

She looked at him, squeezing her eyes together so she wouldn't cry. His eyes were lowered, fiddling with the coals in his water pipe.

'So, Lale, my girl, tell me in your own words. How did you come to be here?'

Lilit felt this were somehow a test, an evaluation of her intentions.

'We were forced out of our homes in Van.'

'Why? What did you do wrong?'

'There was no reason. Except, I suppose, that we're Armenian.'

'Come, come – there must have been a reason. Was your father involved in political activities? I hear Van was a hotbed of subversion.'

She could hear her own voice grow softer, more indistinct, as if part of her half believed him.

'I don't know what you're talking about.'

'Well, then, what happened to you on the way here?'

'I was beaten and robbed of my money.'

She remembered something else had happened to her, wanted to tell him, wanted him to understand, yet wasn't sure how to say it. He didn't give her time.

'Your family?'

'All dead, I think. All dead.'

'What about that boy I saw standing beside you at the square? He looked just like you.'

Her eyes glazed over. She tried to recall his face, the little boy who was taller than her now and stronger, too, but the only thing she could remember were two spots of blood on a ragged shirt. She spoke so quietly Suleiman had to lean closer to hear her.

'I don't know what's happened to him.'

'What about the rest of your family? Mother, cousins, aunts? Couldn't they make the journey?'

'They were killed. The gendarmes tied them together, one behind the other, and shot right through them.'

The woman with the glittering veil walked through the corridor. Suleiman didn't raise his head, didn't indicate he was aware of her presence. He looked at Lilit properly for the first time that morning.

'You're making it up. Turkish soldiers would never do that. Unprovoked. To civilians? Impossible.'

Something in Lilit – a residue of her former self, an abstract sense of injustice – made her get up and put her face close to his.

'They were murdered!'

He hit her. She refused to back down, screaming, standing up again after he knocked her to the ground. He hit her again. When he was finished, she crawled across the floor to the side of the divan, leaning her back against it. Her face was numb, her ribs hurt with a pain that seemed to wait, crouching, for her to lower her guard. She felt her elbow carefully with her other hand. *I hate you,* she said to herself, not trusting her voice to speak it aloud. *I despise you, you imbecile Muslim.*

He sat again on the rug, took a long puff of his water pipe and looked at her, almost curious, or amused, through the fitful smoke.

'Well, Lale?' he asked. 'Where do we go from here?'

She didn't answer. The veiled woman shuffled toward them with a bundle of linen, poked her head in the door, hurried off again down the hall. Suleiman jerked his chin in her direction.

'Fatima. My dead brother's wife. She already hates you.'

She didn't know what to make of this offhand admission, their obvious intimacy.

�֍ Minas watched Lilit being led away with no emotion. It was his heart, not his face that seemed blank and cold. On his face he exhibited every natural expression of grief that could be expected of him. His eyes watered, his lips twisted, his cheeks slow-burned. But it was only his heart that remained still and lifeless, its beat ever slowing to a threatened halt.

He watched Lilit's cropped head bobbing through the surge of people as she followed the Turk. The man seemed gentle, a little bemused by the spectacle perhaps. A follower. A man who submitted to authority, who bowed down before those who knew better. A man capable of any cruelty if someone else told him to do it. Minas hoped he was not a cruel man. Cruel or not, he still hated him. The way he prodded and poked at Lilit as if she were a cow. The silly grin on his face when he asked her if she was all right. *Of course she's not all right,* Minas wanted to yell. *Can't you see for yourself?* But he hadn't. He stood beside Lilit like an idiot, helpless to change the outcome of the moment, helpless to alter the course of their lives.

When Lilit couldn't be seen any longer, he sat down in the dust to await what the rest of the evening would bring. He crossed his legs beneath him and pulled his shirt tighter across his nipples. He ignored the rigidity in his stomach, signalling either hunger or anxiety, he couldn't tell which anymore. All around him, women were being led away by Turkish men of the town, some by the hand, others resisting, with the aid of knotted rope or even a chain. A group of Kurds had just arrived on unhealthy horses; they dismounted and made a great show of inspecting the rest of the women, only to leave without buying.

He watched them ride away with something like envy. It wasn't really envy, it was more a wistful question or a wish: Wouldn't it be wonderful to choose a place and then go? Just like that. To be autonomous, to have choices. He looked around at the other Armenian prisoners. *We have no courage. We're letting them lead us around like animals.* But there was nothing he could do about it, except beg one of the Turks to let him die.

Again, the sick realisation that he was helpless, among others just as helpless as he, caused his throat to swell and his empty belly to revolt. He bent over and retched. A woman nearby wiped his brow with the back of her hand. He thanked her with a smile. It hurt to speak, he had no more words. He looked around him, looking for someone with strength, someone to lead them, a saviour. There was none. All that remained in the town square were the old, the very young, a few boys like himself and the disfigured or mad women, picking at their scabs. He curled up on the ground, at the feet of the woman who had helped him, and slept.

When he woke, all was grey. He could see the silhouettes of gendarmes standing about before the blaze of a dying fire, drinking. Dawn was beginning to break, and he was overwhelmed by thirst. He stood up, thinking to find Afet, perhaps some water. He approached the gendarmes, knelt in front of them with his hands outspread. Afet was nowhere to be seen. The Turks regarded him silently for a moment, then one of them giggled like a girl.

'Give him a glass, boys. Where he's going he won't last long.'

Minas sat on the ground sipping at the rough moonshine he'd been given. For a moment, he was content just to drink and sit, and not think about anything else. He looked at the sleeping and huddled forms of his fellow prisoners, vulnerable now in the rising light. One boy sat apart from the rest, with his curly head bowed so low to the ground Minas thought he might be dead or in a coma. He shuffled over and jabbed him in the ribs.

'You all right?'

The boy didn't look up. He gurgled deep down in his throat then a blob of mucus fell on the dirt, narrowly missing Minas's feet.

'Leave me alone,' he growled.

Minas swore at him in a whisper then looked up, alarmed. The gendarmes were yelling now at the prisoners to start moving. There was another long walk ahead of them, to a camp on the outskirts of Der ez Zor.

They passed mulberry trees shading the length of cotton fields. Dusty leaves on the ground. In the distance, peasant women in white kerchiefs worked in the early morning coolness. Did they not realise what was happening? He wanted to cry out to them, make them understand. He watched their steady movements, their worn, quiet faces creased by the sun. He knew that, even if he ran toward them, even if he made it without being shot, even if he spoke to them in Turkish, knelt and put his arms around their knees, they would not help him. They would not even believe his story. He was nothing to them. He was annihilated.

He continued to trudge along with the other prisoners through the strengthening heat. After many hours, passing the town and into the desert, he looked up and saw a shape he couldn't place. It rose before him like a spike in the eye. The tent compound came closer and closer as they walked, and then reared in front of him, cruel, glinting in a shimmering heat, hidden by a heavy set of gates. He stopped short, looking up at their curved and rusting bars.

From inside, he could hear a shuffling and wailing, a sinister, whispered sound like the gnashing of teeth, the howling of wolves, the sound of unnamed fears at night. He felt his stomach contract, leaned over and tried to vomit again. Nothing came, but one of the gendarmes slapped him on the neck and laughed.

'Time enough for that later. Wait till you get inside.'

The gates were opened by armed guards, and the prisoners herded into the compound. Within an instant, a naked man seized Minas's arm. He pleaded with him in Armenian for hope, escape, any news of outside. Minas saw burst pustules around his eyes, fat flies buzzing. He lurched backward in disgust, shook him off before he could finish what he was saying. The man fell to the ground and opened his mouth to curse, but no sound came out. A guard had lunged forward and stabbed a bayonet into his spine.

Minas hurried on with the rest of the prisoners, not looking back at the fallen body. *I must keep going. Won't let anyone stop me.* The guards increased the collective speed to a trot, barking out orders.

'Haircuts over here! Latrines there! Line up in rows for assignment to sleeping blocks!'

He tried to avoid the barber's long shears. He kept very still but the man still managed to nick his ear, graze his forehead, as it was all done in such fear and reckless haste. He could feel the barber's hands trembling as he cut down to the scalp; he was a prisoner too. The men lining the paths between the tents and outhouses were prisoners: gaunt, shiny-faced with sores, but they had learnt to talk in the half-chewed jargon of the guards. They held whips and clubs fashioned of desert thorn. They beat him as he ran from one tent to another, as if punishing him for arriving even a moment later to the camp, for suffering one iota less than they already had.

He saw the bathing room, swiftly put his mother's earrings into his mouth. He would not speak now, he would keep going, outwit them all. He tasted sour gold and blood on his tongue. The man assigned to help him wash was also a prisoner. He muttered without opening his own mouth as he doused Minas's head with cold water and kerosene for lice and rubbed all over his body and wet clothes with a cake of coarse brown soap.

He strained to hear the man's ceaseless patter: 'Don't get sick, they'll kill you, don't catch malaria, they'll surely kill you, don't let them see you vomit, they'll kill you right away, don't help anyone else, they'll kill you, don't look at anyone, don't raise your eyes, don't stop, don't sleep, don't lose your soul, they'll kill you.'

Minas set his jaw and suffered the man's ministrations, careful not to allow him to brush his hands over the wounds left by his mother's earrings.

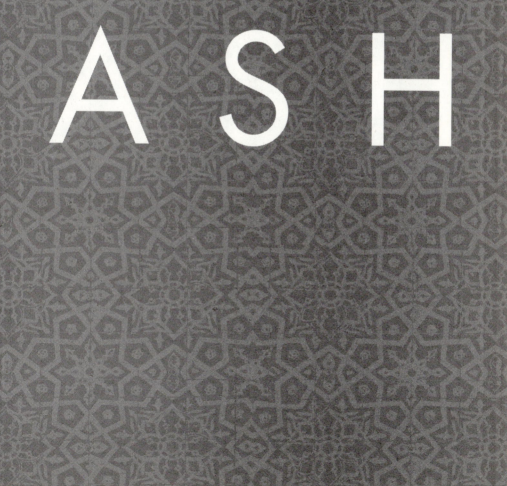

Book Two

ASH

BEIRUT, 1995

I wake with the phone ringing by my head, glance at the clock radio on the bedside table. It's past seven, and I need to be at the tribunal by nine. I slept badly after waking at sunset and trying to get back to sleep; spent the night stewing over my own stupidity.

'A Mr D'Andrea to speak to you, madam. Shall I put him through?'

'No—okay, yes.'

'Ms Pakradounian? I'm sorry to disturb you so early. I hope I haven't woken you?'

I'm disgusted by the formality in his voice. As if nothing happened last night on the beach.

'No, I'm awake. Do you have anything in particular to say to me?'

'Well, I wanted to apologise for—for, er, having too much to drink. And for my indiscretion.'

'Which one?'

I'm not giving an inch. He sighs.

'I *am* sorry, whatever you think. I was pushy and I frightened you, and I—said some inappropriate things.'

'Yes.'

Now he's exasperated.

'Yes, what? Don't even think you can blackmail me; nobody around here would believe you.'

'That's not my intention. But I do think people would believe me. And I don't accept your apology – for either of your blunders.'

I slam the phone down. My shoulders relax. He mustn't know about the tape. And I still don't know what to do with it. Incriminate him, or save him? Forget about it, or stay angry? I wish Lilit was here – she'd tell me what to do. We would lie like this before I left Beirut, her heavy flank against my hip, head turned so her cinnamon breath stirred the fine hairs on my arms.

I wasn't there when she was killed, but I know exactly how she would have slumped on her pillow when she was shot. Hardly any movement at all. Imperceptible. Smash of glass, car horns, howls, guns receding – silence. A sniper, a random death. Blood on her face, coming in a syncopated rhythm from mouth, nostrils, eyes; they would have darted about, flickered, then rested on one last point before her heart stopped beating. Was it the ceiling she saw last, with its cracks and damp patches, the open door, the lugubrious sunset outside her window?

She was always so sad. I'd tried to comfort her, to make up to her all the hurts that couldn't be articulated or explained. But it wasn't Beirut that made her so sad. I knew that, even as a child. It wasn't the brief, intense twilights or the sounds of hawkers from across the street. She watched them from her bed, day and night, calling out their wares to passers-by. She told me they hadn't changed since she first came here. Sometimes she'd trick herself into thinking the hawkers were singing. Singing to her. But it wasn't their voices that made her sad, or their undertone of painful resignation. It wasn't the caged monkeys they paraded from the north of Africa or their little sisters, teenage whores in the bars over the beach. It wasn't any of these things. It was other things, more intangible. Stray dogs like harbingers of death, smell of fish over open fires, the incinerating of garbage. Burning corpses.

Some were refugees, she told me, from camps on the other side of the city. Palestinians. Victims of infighting, revenge killings by PLO militiamen, swift deaths of traitors and Israeli spies. Also, victims of the Phalange. 'Selim. That stupid, stupid boy.' I blanched when she spoke like that about my father. They didn't like to discuss him too much, except when Siran tossed off a few too many Armenian brandies on Christmas Day and started wailing for her long-lost son, her patriot, her poor misunderstood boy. I sat aside with my unwrapped gifts and listened, made myself invisible under the heavy scented tree, arranging and rearranging the placement of the nativity figurines. Mary in the background. Joseph to her left. The baby Jesus in my right-hand pocket, where he'd always be safe. The dead mother. The lost father. The missing bracelet. Even then I was trying to make sense of my own misplaced trinity: *If I find just one of the three, will all the others fall into place?*

Now I turn my head on the pillow. Lilit's gone. In the photo by my bedside, she's posed against a fountain in a bone-yellow courtyard, tiles at her feet in black and white. A desert oasis, with a river close by that saw many bodies, many deaths. When I was younger, I didn't really listen to the explanation. I was more interested in the similarities I could detect in the young woman's face. Thin lips like mine, closed against a secret. A fringed veil thrown back over her forehead as if irritated by its weight, feet bare and ringed with beads. Under the gauzy fabric, rough-cut hair, fine as mine when I was a baby. I still chart my own features in hers: fingers just like mine, the sharp elbows visible beneath the sheerness of her sleeves, a dress in the dull green of Islam. Wrists dyed indigo, like a Bedouin. Her lapis eyes under the veil, the same colour and shape as mine, and my mother's, and my father's. Is that a slight swell under her clothes? A child's body heavy with a woman's burdens. A body that, in the wake of its mortality, is becoming increasingly hard to fathom, impossible to categorise. Hands and lips and eyes that have witnessed death, tranquil limbs invaded by brutality.

A
S
H

145

When she died, a box arrived for me in Boston from the Lebanese nuns who had looked after her. It was full of the debris of a life: photographs, letters, even a baby's caul. My mother's? At the bottom, a French–Lebanese dictionary. I was careful with the rice-paper thinness of its pages, sneezed as I opened it. So much dust. On the flyleaf, blue ink fading to grey: *Property of Minas Pakradounian, Bourj-Hammoud Refugee Camp, Beirut, 1922.*

My grandfather made sure none of the family forgot his heroics, reliving his youth at the table, in front of guests, how he made a grand escape from the death camp with Turkish guards in pursuit, and he, a mere boy of thirteen. He only stayed in Damascus a week, spurred on by his need to travel, to make his fortune on the trading coast. An imam he met in the Umayyad mosque carried him on his mule cart over the Anti-Lebanon mountains and down into the Beka'a Valley, then Minas hitched onward to Beirut. Fig trees and prickly pears growing on the verges gave him sustenance – sometimes a shepherd would share his midday cheese and bread. He drank fresh water from the Litani River, and his feet were grazed down to bone on the grit of the road. Even then, when I was only small, I knew his arrival in Beirut was inspired less by courage than by an all-encompassing fear.

I leafed through the dictionary that day, noting Minas's underlining of certain words and phrases. Then a note between the pages, dated 1966, the year of my birth, and folded many times. When I smoothed it out on my knee I couldn't place the inept handwriting.

> *Dear Papa,*
> *I know you'll be disappointed in me. Then again, you*
> *always were.*
> *I'm leaving. Maybe I'm leaving to prove to you that I can*
> *do exactly what you did. Maybe I'm afraid of being a coward.*

Here the ink faded and ran out until I had to hold the paper up to discern the rest of the words, etchings in angry relief against the light.

> *Maybe it's more cowardly to leave than to stay behind. Anyway,*
> *I'm gone.*
> *Selim.*

My father had held that paper in his hands, touched the pen that made those bright marks – now faded – on its surface. I have the note now, also hidden in Lilit's Koran. How my father would have hated that.

I also have D'Andrea's tape. It weighs on me now like the burden of my father's death, the annihilation of my people. I remember the slight wobble in his voice just now on the phone, his split-second vulnerability.

I get up, sit cross-legged on the bed, lay all my relics out on the covers like an incendiary game of Patience. Lilit's photograph, the veil, the Koran. The black and white photo of my parent's wedding. My father's note. The tape with D'Andrea's damning words. An inventory of objects that hold me back. I close my eyes, for a beat of silence. There's no way I want to be as vengeful as my father. I take the tape into both my hands, leaving a gap in the line of items. Push it into my recorder and press *erase*.

A
S
H

146

DER EZ ZOR, 1915

Lilit knew Suleiman wasn't sure how to approach her. She saw him lower his eyes when she chanced to meet him in the downstairs corridor, shuffle out of her way when she carried the brazier to his bedroom at sunset. After that first night, when she shared his bed as a sister or a child, he sent her to the latticed quarters upstairs and did not call her back again. So far he hadn't touched her. At first she thought he was disgusted by her Armenian blood – she was an infidel according to him, after all – or by her bedraggled state when he found her. Perhaps he only bought her as a cheap servant. Or maybe he was ashamed, his desire blocked before the reality of her great suffering. Yes, that was it. He felt pity for her because she wasn't normal any longer.

Often she thought of the initial walk home. He had said he didn't mind her stink when she asked him. At first, though, he had no compunction in calling her a slave. This had been the pattern of the past weeks since that day: he would say something compassionate then follow it with brutal logic that left her cold. As with that first beating, coming directly after his kindness with the jacket, the way he pulled her to him in the street. *Welcome home.* And yet – his avoidance of her, his awkwardness in her presence, the passionate beatings then contrition, told another story entirely. She didn't know what to think any longer.

She knew she'd regained some of her youthful attractiveness now. She had become plumper on a diet of spiced breads and pastries, sometimes worried she was even getting fat. She stood in front of the only mirror in the house and pinched her waist, made fists of flesh from her inner thighs. The older servants soothed her concerns, saying Muslim men liked their women to be squishy and soft as *loukoum*. Rose-pink and powdered with sugar. They commented on her black lashes and coral ears, her wide, spreading hips. The master would be well pleased with her. They didn't comment on her eyes; she knew they were afraid of the colour, and she tried to cover her face with her veil when she remembered. Only Fatima sat aside and remained silent.

Her hair was no longer cropped to the skull, although it was still far too short for a woman. Thankfully she had a large array of veils. She was given clothes and jewellery, even a pair of antique earrings the servants told her had been especially chosen by the master. She put them on before the mirror, screwing in the thick studs. Gold earrings. She remembered Mamma's. Minas had taken them. *Where is he now?* She closed her eyes. When she opened them again, she knew to concentrate only on her new earrings. She moved her head, watched the filigree glitter. From each stud dangled a scimitar, sharp and dangerous, tiny blades brushing at her neck. Her own curved knife-edge of desire.

She thought about Suleiman as she carried the brazier through the corridor to his bedroom, with the ginger cat shadowing her like a thought. For some reason the task had fallen to her to perfume his chambers each night with ambergris, living coals of fragrance. It was difficult at times seeing another woman from the household or even a tenant from Suleiman's fields lolling on the divan. She knew the women were peasants from the baggy floral pantaloons they wore. Catching a glimpse of brown shoulder, an arched foot. Suleiman in an unbuttoned nightshirt. His lax belly, the chosen woman waiting for him to disrobe. If it was Fatima in the bed she didn't even lower her eyes but invited Lilit's gaze, challenging.

She convinced herself Suleiman didn't desire her, that she would never share his bed. The realisation made her feel more discarded and worthless than she cared to admit. She was left spinning, lost without an anchor. She sat in the courtyard with the cat in her lap on most days, filled in her idle hours with the light household tasks assigned to her, polishing copper trays used for serving sweets, pruning the female date palm that stood over the central fountain, dusting the precious mirror. She looked at herself long and hard as she wiped the rag back and forth, and a sad stranger stared back at her. She was no longer the Lilit she thought she was. Yet who exactly she had metamorphosed into was another cause for anxiety. She was still growing, or being stunted inside; still in that amorphous, ugly state of flux between knowing and unknowing, past and present, exile and refuge. This was worse than being forced to leave home, worse than losing everybody, worse than being violated in the desert. She couldn't exactly tell herself why it was worse, but it was.

It wasn't until tonight, when Suleiman smiled up at her and said thank you as she placed the brazier on the floor beside his bed, when he clasped her bangled wrist and held her there, half-crouching, half-standing over him, that she realised what his problem had really been all these weeks. *He's falling in love with me.* It was impossible, comic and ludicrous, yet there it was. She was surprised to feel that she welcomed it.

She hovered above him in this position, light from the lamps all around illuminating the heat spreading from her chest to her face. She forced herself to look into his eyes and saw how they rested on her mouth, now moving over her cheeks, her spiky hair under the gauze veil. Not once did they travel to her breasts or her bare, goose-fleshed arms. *My God, he is in love with me. He's not sure what to do next.* She sat on the bed beside him and with her free arm drew the veil away from her head. They both watched it puddle at her feet. It seemed to take forever.

She lay down beside him, stretching out the full length of her body on the bed. In her head the shame and hurt and violence of the other man receded, paled into insignificance beside the tender breathing of Suleiman beside her, a musical breath whose rise and fall and expectation she could feel pass from his body to hers. She turned toward him and loosened the grip of his hand from her wrist, guiding his arms around her.

'Yervan,' she whispered in his ear, and knew he thought she was murmuring some endearment to him in Armenian.

If I do this now Yervan will be alive. I will make it so. Yet she knew even as she made the bargain that she was only lying to herself. This wasn't a sacrifice by any stretch. She wanted to do it.

'Suleiman,' she said, louder.

She felt him hesitate for an instant when he realised she was not a virgin. But his desire beat hot and deep now and was not to be slowed, and he took her with some of the painful love and hatred she felt for him already, the kindness and cruelty they shared. She breathed into her belly and held him inside her and his rising shudders jolted awake her memory again. *Turk. Another Turk inside me. Papa. Mamma dead. Oh,*

Minas. But it was only for a moment. Suleiman arched above her and spoke into her mouth in a caress.

'What is it?'

She closed her eyes and drew him deeper into her.

'Nothing,' she said in Turkish.

※ Suleiman gave her the Bible to read as well as the Koran. He taught her more careful Turkish than she'd ever known, and even classical Arabic, showed her how to wind the spangled veil over her face and breasts and leave her hands free to work, to cook, to pleasure him. To read the two holy books aloud, in those long evenings spent in the sky-filled courtyard amid the scent of water.

Sometimes they smelled burning and heard reports of Armenian deaths. Suleiman showed her newspaper articles discussing Talaat and Enver Pasha's latest statement in parliament. *La question Arménienne n'existe plus.* The final solution – *hall ve fasl* – had been successful. She wasn't sure what that meant. Did it mean the Turks would stop deporting the few Armenians that survived and repatriate them? *The Armenian question is no more.* What did that concede exactly? Acknowledgement of guilt? Or had they already killed enough Armenians to consider the task finished?

'Many are still being thrown into the Euphrates,' the old women muttered to each other in the market.

She turned her face away and the women spoke louder, knowing from gossip where she was from and to whom she belonged. Suleiman was always there to frown at them for her, to grip her hand with a careful, comforting pain. She had asked him many times to help her find Minas. After all, the work camp was not so far away. Surely Suleiman had some influence. But he looked afraid when she pressed him, telling her the authorities would punish him for prying, that her brother was sure to be dead already. It was not a work camp, he said. It was a camp of death.

Lilit stopped asking. She soon learnt to ignore any rumours and cultivate a sublime indifference to the public sphere. She concentrated instead on Suleiman and the moods of her growing body. Could there be a baby? Testing her belly for tenderness, learning to pad silently on bare feet through empty corridors with tea on the brazier, to wash the morning hush with songs of light. *My darling, my love, your sufferings and joys will be many.* With her new languages came new voids, clean surfaces one couldn't penetrate, rooms of meaning opened to the sun, bleached of significance then closed again.

✳ Minas rummaged in his tattered pants. A girl studied him with a smirk pulling at the corners of her mouth, the skin around it pitted with tiny sores from the dry heat of the day and the wind and cold of those desert nights.

He looked up, noticed her bug-eyed stare.

'What?'

'Nothing. Any food in there?'

He scratched at his testicles again, pinched and then held out something in his thumb and forefinger for her to inspect.

'Got it. Just catching lice.'

She smiled, disappointed.

'Eat it. Better than dead dogs and locusts.'

He made a face.

'I have my limits.'

'How long will they keep us here?'

'Forever.'

'What do you mean?'

A guard banged his rifle butt on the ground beside them.

'Enough talking, little rats!'

Minas spoke, hardly moving his lips.

'This is the end.'

✳ Later that day while he roamed the camp looking for food, the girl managed to slip beside him. He barely registered her presence, intent on scouring the fence line for new grass, which he held to his mouth and sucked until his lips and teeth were stained green. In the distance, he was aware of Bedouin tribesmen huddled around their camels, watching the camp with what he could discern as a mixture of fascination and fear. He turned to her and pointed.

'See those men? I wonder if they could help us.'

The girl wouldn't look.

'Them? What do they care about us? They're Muslims.'

She nodded toward the centre of the camp. He was surprised afresh at the sores around her lips, her lank chestnut plaits.

'A few women killed themselves just before,' she said. 'People are fighting over the bodies.'

What for?

'Fresh food.'

He flashed his teeth at her; made a fast, exaggerated, chewing motion.

'Should we join them?'

She laughed: a soft, strangled sound.

'I have my limits too. So far.'

They spent a while combing the ground for more vegetation.

'I love you.'

He looked around, startled.

'What?'

'I love you and want you close to me before I die.'

She looked straight ahead, licked her cracked lips with a violet tongue.

'Please.'

He took her little finger in his hand and nodded.

※   Fatima caught Lilit undressing for bed one evening by the light of an oil lamp. Lilit blushed and backed into a dark corner, hastily tying her robe together over her swell of stomach. Fatima followed her, until she was wedged into a corner of the room with the other woman pressing against her.

'Stop looking at me with those big round eyes. I'm in his bed tonight. So don't even bother putting on any of your stinking ointments.'

She nodded, her eyes grown wider in alarm. Fatima came closer until her breath was rancid against Lilit's mouth.

'Don't think I'll ever forget, even if he does. You're still an Armenian to me.'

Fatima left the room then, flinging off her veil so it trailed behind her as she flounced through the door. When she was gone and Lilit could no longer hear her rustle down the corridor, she untied her robe, watched it fall open across her stomach and slither down to the floor. She let herself follow its trajectory, sliding down the wall and squatting on her thighs in the corner. She rocked back and forth, some small comfort. She sighed; a broken, wavering sound. *Why does such a mundane exchange make me shake so much?* She splayed her hands open over her nude stomach and tried to quiet her fears with the faint human warmth from her child.

The next day, Fatima appeared distant from Suleiman at the morning meal. She and Lilit customarily stood behind him, one on either side, and waited until he finished before they could take a bite. Usually Fatima snatched morsels from Suleiman's plate as she leaned over his shoulder, making them both laugh. Yet today when she sat cross-legged opposite Lilit on the rug, she ate little of her bread and even less yoghurt, her eyes downcast. Lilit also noticed her hands trembling, but Fatima walked about the house all day with a strained smirk on her face.

Suleiman took Lilit into his bed the next night and the night after that. He praised her pearl-skinned buttocks and the roundness of her wrists and ankles, circled by henna. She floated about the house in a jangle of gifts: silver jewellery, linen scarves fringed with turquoise beads, shiny packages of cherry-scented mastic. Fatima's smirk began to smudge into a frown. At the end of the week she was so downcast Lilit forced herself to speak. She approached Fatima in the courtyard, where she stood by the main fountain looking into a swirling pool of water.

'Fatima.'

She looked around, saw Lilit and frowned.

'What do you want, slave? Go away.'

'I wanted to ask you why—why it has to be so difficult between us. If only—'

'If only you weren't here!'

Fatima sat on the rim of the fountain and burst into tears. She put her head in her hands and convulsed, shoulders shaking with the force of her crying. Lilit knelt down next to her. This woman had finally become human. Not lovable, but human. She wanted to place a hand on Fatima's shoulder, stroke her, comfort her. But she too couldn't forgive the pain of the past few months.

'Fatima, it's not my choice to be here.'

When Fatima lifted her head from her hands Lilit recoiled at the spectacle of her face. She was a fearsome sight, tears and mucus and kohl combined to tragic effect.

'I can't have a baby. I'll never have one. My first husband, Suleiman's brother – he threatened to divorce me, before he died. Now you're here, Suleiman will stop keeping me as well.'

Lilit looked around the silent courtyard, fearful of Suleiman hearing her. She heard herself hiss at Fatima under her breath and hated herself for lying even as she said it.

'Does he love you anyway? I don't see it. Does he love me? Of course not. I don't think he loves anyone at all.'

Fatima gulped, dabbing at the corners of her eyes with her veil. Lilit made herself come closer and put a light hand on Fatima's knee.

'See how he treats you already! Like a common concubine, not a wife. We should both be united against him, Fatima. It's our only hope.'

Fatima leaned over, fixing Lilit with her stone-idol eyes.

'Give the baby to me, Lilit. Then I'll help you escape. You can go back to Armenia.'

Lilit lowered her eyes and nodded. She was no longer sure where she belongs.

✳ Minas grew to know the camp and even respect its workings: the vomit-coloured sand, its erratic pulse of killing and torture and the few blessed hours at night of respite from terror. What gnawed at him was more than fatigue and the familiar grip of hunger; it was the constant mental strain of keeping alive.

Each morning at dawn the camp commander blared his refrain from a loudspeaker: 'Armenians! The lice crawling on you are less vermin than you are.' The prisoners picked at their sores, peeled the scabs off their wounds, exposing still more moisture for lice to feed on. Nearly all the inmates were naked, their clothes stolen by the guards or disintegrated into rags from the forced march through the desert. Minas had lost his trousers to another inmate weeks ago, trading them for an extra mouthful of gruel. Food was more important than warmth; that he knew. Yet he held on to his threadbare shirt, which still managed to hide the earrings glinting in his nipples.

With bared yellow teeth, the trained dogs were three-headed monsters guarding the gates of Hell. They watched the prisoners as if eyeing butcher's cuts of meat. Minas supposed he looked like that now: red raw, shapeless, moving slowly if at all. He couldn't see himself. He stared at the other prisoners and tried to imagine his own face in that man's hollow cheeks, this woman's sunken eye sockets. The formless fear he read in each person's eyes, the downward scrape of mouth. A few of his teeth had been knocked out by a drunken guard, and he had taken to sucking at the inside of his cheeks like an old man. Some days he rubbed his hand over his jawline and the manly rasp of stubble always surprised him. He'd lost all perspective. He saw a boy his age attacked by the pack of dogs, and guards standing by and laughing. That night he thought about the boy with the curly hair he'd sworn at in the marketplace, so long ago it seemed. Maybe he was already dead.

Some of the inmates were more frightening to him than the dead. They seemed to have withdrawn from the present altogether, men and women drifting from sleeping block to morning assembly and back again in a trance. Sometimes he was tempted to steal their food rations; they seemed so passive – he was sure it would work. Yet he put it off, alternately fascinated and repelled. They didn't speak, didn't answer when spoken to. They didn't make eye contact with anyone, indeed seemed not to breathe at all. The guards found it easier to kill them this way, no doubt. He wasn't so upset at those times; it didn't seem to matter if they were alive or dead. He almost welcomed the moment of disbelief, the swift dispatch. As if a favour had been done for them.

He'd been assigned a job these last few days. He was healthier than most of the other prisoners, one of the few young boys in the camp, and almost agile except for the blisters on his feet from the march. He had to help bury the dead bodies after they had been shot or knifed to death. Also those tortured in the interrogation centre – the only permanent building in the whole compound – with its barred high windows and twenty-four-hour lamps, burning, burning, a thread of fire glimpsed under the locked door. There wasn't so much to learn from such broken and diseased prisoners, he assumed. But he knew the Turks continued interrogating each arriving convoy for clues to hidden cash, heirlooms, the undying myth of Armenian gold. Some of the corpses he carried were twisted in death-agony, others serene and pink, placid mouths smiling at the sky. Yet they were all heavy, even the children. Heavy with the weight of mortality.

He felt a mixture of shame and disgust for the corpses. Confusing, his divided sentiments. He dragged the bodies from killing floor to mass grave, wrists threatening to snap each time and nails bleeding. The guards whipped him on the back and sometimes around the face and never ceased to abuse him. He grew to admire them for it – they articulated for him the punishment he couldn't inflict on himself: daily atonement for his guilt at still being alive.

Many of the older Turks were well disposed toward him, taking him aside to offer a bite from a hard-boiled egg, a cup of raki to fortify him. They asked him if he was tired, made him sit cross-legged at their feet. Some even commented on how beautiful a boy he was, so fair-skinned for an Armenian. They admired his glossy hair, the fineness of his eyebrows. He tried to smile through closed lips, ashamed of his toothlessness even among all this madness. One guard wiped the sweat from Minas's temples with a clean handkerchief then sniffed at it, and he finally knew. He began to realise they expected sex in return for such small kindnesses, and he learnt to avoid them. Yet he knew, even as he did so, that it was only a matter of time before he would do the unthinkable.

He buried dark-haired infants who looked somehow like his sister, surreptitiously stroking the ringlets on their damp, flushed cheeks. He covered over warm-bellied women who reminded him of his mother, obscured their eyes, suffocated them in sand. He carried teenage girls in his arms, tried not to look at their gaping vaginas and limp, blood-soaked plaits. He saw a younger boy killed for being too slow, with the spade he had held only a moment ago for digging graves. He saw the curly-haired boy again, but only on days when there was a particularly big burial. Mostly, from what he could see, the boy was adept at gaining favour from the guards, flirting with them and avoiding heavy work.

In the late evenings, after sunset, he returned to the inner camp and lay side by side with the pimpled girl. She always managed to seek him out. He was cruel at first, unfeeling and cold and reeking of shit and sweat and other, more sinister fluids he couldn't wipe off with sand or fingertips of water from the bucket in the corner. The girl revived him, made him forget where he was for a few seconds, even a minute or two, in those rare times he mustered the energy to enter her. He knew he was being selfish, using her body for his own brief respite. But she surrendered to him, and in the dark he felt her thighs and belly go soft and her breath exhale out, out, out, until she was still and quiet and finally at peace beneath him.

At night he felt the memory of hope weigh down on him like a great white stone in his belly. It would force him to act. The voice in his head increased in volume, singing, startlingly erotic in its lightness, uncaring of his discomfort, spurring him on. He breathed into the girl's ear.

'I've decided to try and escape. Soon. Maybe even this week.'

Two bodies in the dark, hers against his, his pressed against some sleeping stranger, never sure if the person next to him was alive or dead by morning except for the mushroom coolness that gradually infected his own skin. The girl was alive, though, warm and pulsating against his cheek and thigh in the darkness, her hair sweat-damp against his neck.

'How? Where to?'

'Don't know yet. But you must come with me.'

The desert temperature dropped at nightfall like the sudden closing of a door. Competing winds rose and flapped the sides of the tent in and out, like a giant animal breathing death. He could hear hyenas circling the camp, eager for the carrion it promised. The girl sniffed, as if the stink had only now penetrated her consciousness.

'I can't. They'd catch me and kill me. But first they would force me to betray you.'

'You'll die anyway.'

She leaned over and he felt the tiny pimples in contact with his mouth. His first instinct was always to recoil, but he opened his lips and allowed her to kiss him, her fingers on his back thousands of crawling lice, her breasts hot and slippery against his chest, her determination silent and painful to the touch.

'Please,' she said. 'Just let me die here.'

She slid on top of him, the weight of her body light, far lighter than the corpses he carried each day. He pulled her hair away from him so that her back arched and her face widened in the half-dark, hair slapping through his hand, mouth open in a soundless scream. Her bittersweet fullness of face, mouth agape in revelation – the presentiment of death firing her eyes.

✳ Lilit readied herself over the coming weeks to escape. Fatima helped her stockpile dried figs and walnuts and find a waterskin, even made her a new set of clothes. A pair of loose trousers and a diaphanous shift, fitting attire for a slave readying to flee.

She thought of her nightly readings with Suleiman: Hagar and her wild-haired son, cast out into the desert. Moses and his tiny barque of reeds. She had no idea where she would go once she was out the front door of Suleiman's courtyard. Fatima had given her a knife and a tattered map of the region she could hardly read. She also had a muslin pouch of coins Fatima had filched from the household allowance she was given each week.

She had vague plans of following the course of the Euphrates through northern Syria and back into Armenia. Of looking for Papa. She knew Minas was most probably dead by now, judging from the talk at the marketplace. Maybe she should go to Constantinople, lose herself in a big city. Become Turkish. Become anything at all. This last thought gave her a twinge of excitement and a downward lurch of remorse.

Days and nights passed. It was always the same: the daily morning trip to the market, which she and Fatima took turns at making with the servant girls. The baking of sweets, which they also took turns at doing week by week. Suleiman hired a cook for the meals and the baking of bread each day, but a proficiency in pastry-making was one of the hallmarks of a good Muslim woman. So she taught herself how to roll filo pastry and finely crush pistachios and dates, how to heat dark Marmaris honey until it poured liquid and gold. Almond puddings with saffron. And Suleiman's favourite, *kaymak* of Afyon Karahisar, rich buffalo cream, boiled until solid enough to slice. Suleiman sampled each pastry equally from these trays, day by day, making sure he didn't eat of the same woman twice in a row.

Much in the same way, Suleiman took turns at sleeping with them. She'd never have believed when she first arrived that she would crave his touch. And yet, there it was. Sometimes, late at night with the lamps dimmed by the servants, she could even close her eyes and imagine he was Yervan. Something in the mildness of his caresses alerted her to the similarity. Yet as the weeks and months progressed she no longer needed to imagine Yervan there beside her. Suleiman was enough. He had a way of inclining his head to the side when she straddled him, as if the pleasure was too much to bear head on. His body was opposite to Yervan's, dark and slight, hair matted high at his throat.

She never believed she would be jealous of the nights he spent with Fatima, either. The servant girls and peasant women he cajoled with gifts, the occasional whore from the markets – she didn't bother herself with those. She knew these dalliances were expected of him, even by the reluctant women themselves. But when she knew Fatima was sharing his bed she lay awake for hours in the women's quarters and burned with frustration and desire. She undressed and picked at her faults, finding more ways to make herself beautiful for him. She cursed Suleiman on those nights, telling herself it would be best if she left soon, so this torture would end, once and for all.

There were some weeks Suleiman turned away from them all and slept alone on the flat roof of the house. He couldn't breathe sometimes, he would explain to her. He needed the night wind and the stars. She'd read enough of the Koran by now to know he wasn't being a good Muslim. His duty was to satisfy all his wives. And he only had two, not like the other men of the town who had four women to care for, as well as an ever-changing array of concubines. Then again, neither Fatima nor she was really his wife. She was bought and paid for, a mere slave, and Fatima was something else. A penance, perhaps, a hastily promised favour for a dying brother?

Yet she couldn't shy away from the truth. It was Fatima who had a traditional wedding to Suleiman as soon as her husband died; she stood in the centre of the courtyard, swathed in sequinned veils, while the imam asked the customary questions of the assembled crowd. Suleiman stood aside and bowed at the end of each response, his heirloom dagger sheathed at the waist. Fatima had been carried to the bridal chamber on the shoulders of virgin youths, beneath the divan a broody hen for fertility. Suleiman was accosted as he made his way to her, scattering coins at the feet of well-wishers to bribe his way in. Fatima was the official wife. Lilit had no status.

When it was Lilit's turn to go to the market Suleiman always went with her, the servant girls lagging behind with their bundles. Maybe he was afraid she might run away. Find other Armenian slave-girls to conspire with. Or talk to people, learn more about what was happening outside the fortifications of the old city. No fear of that. She didn't want to excite his suspicions. Not now. She'd linger sometimes over certain stalls, fingering triangles of fabric or perfumed feathers from Africa, bottles of camphor and seed pearls piled in careless heaps. She would buy powdered orchid root for churning ice-cream, coastal sage for tea, the aromatic seeds of black cherry. Then she would invariably feel a tug on the ring slipped over her index finger. The ring attached to Suleiman's hand on a long thin chain. In this way he kept her close to him.

Even with his suspicions, his shadowing, the brass ring on her finger, in bed Suleiman seemed not to suspect that she would soon leave him. Now she did only what was expected of her, not allowing herself to enjoy his precise attentions as she had in the past. She almost didn't want to go at all. Life here was soothing, a faint lulling into apathy. Suleiman was slow and gentle in his night caresses, like drinking cool water. He sucked her through his mouth and nostrils, revelling in the smoothness and youthfulness of her body. She kept trying not to enjoy it too much, stopped herself from falling into his touch.

Some nights she wanted to tell him of the plan, confess everything. There were three more months to go before the baby was due. Maybe if she told Suleiman and blamed Fatima for the plot, he would banish her from his house altogether, leaving Lilit and him in peace? She knew she couldn't tell. So she merely sighed, and opened her mouth and legs to Suleiman, stiff and wooden, paralysed by the fear of giving up her baby.

BEIRUT, 1995

It's still so early the day hasn't had a chance to heat up. I've made it to the courthouse just in time, and now I sit, watching the caretakers out the window sweep the narrow paths and wet grass with short twig brooms. It must be hell on their backs. It's the last day of the tribunal, and nothing's happening yet, though everyone is seated and waiting.

Thank goodness D'Andrea isn't here; I don't think I could have faced him after our telephone call less than an hour ago. Yet I already feel less animosity toward him now I've erased the tape. Maybe I've forgiven him. I don't know. I settle back in my seat, look around. There's a different mood in the court today: expectant, watchful, almost an exhilaration running beneath the formality of cheap dark suits and carefully impassive faces.

Since coming to Beirut it's as if my life in Boston has receded, reduced to its essentials. Leaden skies. Raindrops on camellias, sagging petals crammed against the window of Sarkis's apartment – I still can't call it mine – the cold hands of a stranger on my bare back at night. I miss no one in particular, though I long for some human contact. Long to fill up my emptiness with somebody, anybody. Not D'Andrea. Not with second-hand memories of this place. Not my non-existent scenarios of who my father really was. Last night before I fell asleep I roiled in that terrible, familiar well of loneliness, and a jazz melody was playing on the clock radio by the bed – but it wasn't jazz any longer; it had changed into that eerie Armenian lullaby and there was a man there that wasn't really there, a man like my father with dark straight brows and a smile that could make me melt.

In a chilling moment, I'm struck by the sense that I'm merely existing here in Lebanon, only going through the motions to finish off something that began eighty years ago. And then what? I remember

Minas talking – an animated skull swathed in sheets to the chin – from the heights of an iron-barred bed. Was he already in hospital then or was it the bedroom on the top floor of the Beirut house? He was sick, dying. I must have been too young to understand the import of his statement because I continued playing with my dolls, moving them back and forth over the mounds and hillocks of his blanket, chattering under my breath. Yet what I did understand was the anger and shame in his voice as he began to whisper, 'Come, child, come closer, over here.'

I climbed onto the bed, conscious of his old man's smell and the dandruff flaking his narrow shoulders. He told me about a terrible place he was sent to when he was only a little boy. That's what had made him such a horrible grandpa, and I must forgive him. I nodded, pulling at my lower lip. He told me about gritty sand and heat haze as far as the eye could see, tents that bent and cracked like dry skin in red winds that came from the south, wailing that rose and fell like a descant day and night, until he couldn't discern whether it was women crying or his dead mother calling him, but it was a sound he couldn't – even now – escape. At that moment, I hated the people who had done this to him.

Once in Boston, I didn't have the time to wonder whether I hated – no, distrusted – Turks. But it was the first time I'd met any: petite girls with black hair like mine, skin as dark, eyes, gestures, songs, food, jokes – like mine. But I never became friends with them. *I've grown up with the sounds of bombs in my sleep,* I whispered as I traversed silent, empty classrooms. *I've dreamed through explosions. You wouldn't understand. I'm immune to loss. Warring factions live inside me, tribes at odds with one another, armed to the teeth.* I felt so sorry for myself it's almost laughable now.

Do I still feel sorry for myself? My grandmother became the slave of a Turk. My grandfather was incarcerated in a death camp: seven months of hell in the desert. How did he survive? My father – what exactly happened to my father? Somehow, the horror of his death fails to touch me today. I'm okay. I'm still okay. Here I sit, fed, clean, rested. I can smell the faint rosemary residue of my shampoo when I move my head, the fine soap I brought all the way here from Boston on the tips of my fingers. My pressed, crisply washed clothes folded artfully as origami before I put them on. The maids at the hotel so quick, I barely have time to give them my dirty linen before it's been washed and dried on the rooftop terrace.

My daily routines in these few weeks have become immutable; exercise at dawn, morning glasses of tea at the Cafe de Paris; the beginnings of those articles for *The Globe* that grow bristly with more questions. My marathon walks coming close, then closer to our old house in the Armenian quarter, yet never quite reaching its sacred, sinister arcs; exhaustion and sleep in the late afternoon; gin-soaked midnight conversations with journalists who spend more time at the Mayflower than on the ground. Each night, I lose myself in the intimacy of panelled bars and other peoples' stories, in the harsh, glittery edges alcohol brings. Each day, I come closer to the core of my history, the blackness.

The two UN judges come in, sit down. It's all so sudden, I don't feel as if I have time to take it in. The verdict: charges dismissed against Ariel Sharon, although Israel is shown to bear 'indirect responsibility' for the massacres. The biggest villains are the Lebanese Phalange militia, with special mention made of Elie Hobeika and Selim Pakradounian. No reparations to the families of the victims. Just an official apology made by the Lebanese government and Israel under the auspices of the UN. It makes me so ashamed I want to hide my face. I sit paralysed in my seat and all around me groups of Palestinian families stand, cry, hug: children, women, holding flowers from their gardens, their faces awash with conflicting emotions. I see the old woman and the little girl again. They stand apart from the others, then the woman takes the girl's hand in a slow gesture of resignation as they shuffle out to the street.

I raise my sleeve to hide my face. I know my father was a war criminal. I've always known it. But all along, I'd hoped that someone else would come along – someone from the past, someone with authority, and tell me I was wrong. As I wipe my eyes, I capture the indefinable smell of my childhood on summer mornings, when Siran would begin the day's chores just after dawn. A day exactly like today: dew still on the ground and moisture dripping from the thick-veined petals of bougainvillaea. My father's absence a continued knife-thrust, a sharp pebble in my throat. Streets stretching out into the distance, already flared white in a hot wind. Washing powder from a huge round tin and early sunshine, smooth as milk. Lilit in the kitchen making breakfast, hobbling out to the garden on her cane to tend our flowers. The scent of lime-blossom tea that hung, faintly cloying, in her withered hands and hair. It's here I sit, on my hard slippery seat in the courthouse, and begin to accept where I've come from – a place where everybody was a victim, or a perpetrator. Or both at the same time. I came here, wanting to make sense of it, and found D'Andrea instead. He was so desperate that night, beside himself. I know he didn't want to scare me, or hurt me. Nevertheless, he did. But I'm glad now that I erased the tape, because I'll do anything – everything – not to be like any of them, not to be a victim again.

BEIRUT, 1982

Sanaya decided that she wouldn't replace the glass in her windows again. She'd already had it done three times and was sick of avoiding flying fragments in the dark. Today she'd stand on a chair and tape plastic sheets over the window frames, just like everybody else. Around her she sensed the other inhabitants of her building, her city, her country, continuing to surrender to the instinctive desire to bring some order and comfort into life amid the chaos and death. A desire she had only this moment abandoned as hopeless.

She recognised in herself a loosening, a strange calm. Slowly, she was letting go of the need to impress. She didn't fret anymore if her clothes were dirty or if there was no water in which to wash. She stopped wearing so much make-up, tied her hair up every morning because it was so lank. Her days and nights were as slow moving as a dream, and as unpredictable.

She saw women washing clothes carefully with a sliver of soap or none at all, hanging grey underclothes between fallen facades to dry, throwing a pinch of spice into a courtyard pot filled with boiling seawater in which there was nothing but greens gathered from city streets. They scrubbed at rubble that was once a bedroom wall. Busied themselves smoothing threadbare sheets over torn mattresses, looted from ruins next door. This was what gave her city its distinctive and bizarre paradox: the nature of humanity to busy itself with the inane while denying the inevitable.

She forced herself to go downstairs with a bucket and spade to remove broken bricks and garbage from the once-proud fountain. Rouba helped her sometimes, but the others in the building merely conspired in filling it up again. Their concierge – the fountain and garden and its birds had been his pride and joy – was killed by a hooded gunman while crossing the street. Which militia the murderer had belonged to, nobody knew. Anybody could find a gun nowadays and patrol their corner of the street without fear of censure. Except, of course, when a bigger militia decided to claim the same turf. The dabblers and dilettantes would run inside to their wives and brag about their neighbourhood exploits for years to come, on their balconies in the late evenings, in the courtyard downstairs while playing cards.

The care of the canary had been taken over by Hadiya. In reality it was Issa who went with her each morning, changed the water dish and scattered grain, put down fresh newspaper. Sometimes he would take Hadiya by the hand and scour the garden and surrounding streets for a bud, a blade of grass, a rotten lettuce leaf to offer. He professed a deep fondness for the little bird, and was as gentle with it as he always was with Hadiya. Sanaya felt herself grow soft when she watched him with the little girl, aching at his youthfulness, the springiness of his brown skin. She wanted him to hold her hand instead, to touch her lightly, look into her face with the same glittering focus he brought to bear on the bird, the cup of water, a tiny flower he'd found. 'Our prophet loved animals,' he told her. Instead of getting up to disturb a cat sleeping on the edge of his robe, Mohammed cut the garment. But Issa was not often home anymore, so the bird's welfare was left to Rouba. She had no idea where Issa had gone when Sanaya asked her, all she knew was that he wasn't in the south any longer.

'Why not?' Sanaya pressed. 'Isn't that where the worst fighting is?'

Rouba looked away. 'He's somewhere in Beirut,' she replied, and Sanaya imagined him getting hurt or dying and was surprised at the chill that crept over her.

The concierge used to hang the canary's cage from the boughs of the fig tree on sunny days, but this tree had now been stripped of everything: not only its fruit, but its leaves and even its branches too. It had become a stump the neighbourhood children sometimes proclaimed from in their complicated games of cruelty and justice. Hadiya was kept away from those games.

Today Sanaya came to terms with the fact that perhaps she didn't want the war to end. If it ended, this ultimate distraction from real life and its pressures – find a job, choose a husband, accumulate wealth, have children, succeed, compete – would no longer hold any sway. Nobody was competing now, except to kill each other. Most people were living in the moment, helping each other in small, delicate ways to survive.

The only thing she was afraid of in this war was death. Living with the war had become a necessary distraction, a challenge of daily habit. It came closer each day, placing a hand on her shoulder like a friend. Dying in the war was another matter entirely. If she were younger, she'd say her youth rendered her invulnerable. But she was just old enough to be sensitive to the onset of decay. Just old enough to coddle herself the same way she fabricated her fantasies of the city. The twinned destruction of herself and Beirut, yet their resolute obstinacy to remain – as a city, and as a citizen of Beirut – gave them both just enough strength to continue.

Yet it wouldn't do to rely solely on this connection between herself and the city. She had rituals to perform, repeating them daily to protect herself. She never shook the tablecloth outside at night, never cooked without throwing a pinch of salt over her left shoulder. She would never remove the amulet she'd worn since birth, the gold hand of Fatima, from around her neck. In her long evenings of reflection, she mused over where she had learnt these superstitions and concluded that she had no idea. Her mother was never interested in rituals, in folk remedies or myths. The first port of call in any family crisis had always been a straight whisky at six and sleeping pills at bedtime. Western doctors, specialists' fees and potent creams for her beautiful, aging face.

The view of the sea from Sanaya's balcony lulled her, on some primitive level, into feeling the human war below couldn't touch her. Violent sunsets, the rush and boom of waves between marbled rocks, the silvery sheen of dawn on the horizon gave her an illusion of constancy. Yet the war of machines, the mechanical war of bombs and explosions, terrified her. Some mornings she didn't get up at all and stayed in bed all day reading old fashion magazines, telling herself this wasn't a form of absolution, of giving up. When Issa came back, after weeks of silence, she was deaf to his protests during air raids. She wouldn't go and hide in the corridor anymore, so he came to her.

Rouba, Hadiya and Issa sat with her in the bathroom for hours during the fighting, playing backgammon, eating, talking. Sanaya took note of the way Issa always let her win, watched the way he ate daintily, like his bird. She liked the way he sat, arranging his long limbs loosely on the floor next to her. Resting his arm against hers as he played, he smelled of sweat and spices, and she found herself surprised that she didn't mind – whenever she smelled Selim after his workouts, she always wanted him to shower right away.

'The bathroom's safer anyway,' Rouba announced, trying to make the best of the situation. 'And I wouldn't want to die all mangled up with our neighbours. It's better this way.'

Whenever Issa found food in defiance of the blockade, he bought enough for all of them, as much as he could carry.

'Why do you spend so much time with those backward Shias?' Selim would ask. 'Don't accept anything from them. I can source everything from the Israelis: chocolate, bread, orange juice, toilet paper, extra soft.'

When the water supply was cut off intermittently by the Israelis, Sanaya's neighbourhood dug its own wells; when electric power was out for more than twelve hours a day, they installed temperamental generators; when the police disappeared, they affiliated themselves with neighbourhood militias for protection. This was another reason she was still with Selim, even under pain of death by Muslim militias if they found out she was sleeping with a Phalangist. He seemed more effective than they. He seemed more powerful than Issa.

Of course, he was more powerful than any of the militias. He had the backing of Israel and America. Sleeping with the devil, that's what she was doing. A demon with a crooked smile, a soft moustache that hid his frown. A demon who came to her apartment in the middle of the night or the early hours of the morning, so nobody would see him. Especially Issa, though Sanaya didn't let herself articulate the thought. How would she feel if both men were in the same room?

Selim was so serene at dawn when they lay on their backs, talking. He knew exactly what to do when she became frightened: of the war, the onset of middle age, her lack of a child of her own. He kissed her, opened her up. Calm and efficient.

✴ Selim staked out the Armenian quarter late at night in the Mercedes. His driver didn't question the location, the post-midnight hour, or Selim's continued drinking in the back seat. He merely drove back and forth, from street to street and house to house, as directed by Selim's confused grumbling. Selim knew he was drunk, knew he was sad and confused, but on nights like this there was nothing else for it except to wallow.

'Show me Urfa Street again, Pierre.'

The car was wheeled around to a stop under the leafless plane trees at the top of the street. He didn't remember them that way. Maybe the war had traumatised their growth. Jazz played from the tape deck – Frank Sinatra live with Count Basie, his favourite – and he tapped out the syncopated beat on the window as he peered at the streetscape, lighted lamps ghostly in the humid air, filthy kerbs just as he remembered them, that rampant bougainvillea still festooning the facade of every timbered house.

'Pierre. You're new to us, aren't you?'

'Yes, monsieur.'

'You carry the name of our venerable founder, eh? Pierre Gemayel, what do you think? Is he genius or god?'

'Yes, monsieur.'

'Well, which is he, then?'

He took a quick swig of his whisky, not waiting for an answer. The man's silence unnerved him.

'Like the French, Pierre my friend, we Maronites have a civilising duty to this country. A mission. Without us, where would the nation be? Banging heads in mosques and shimmying up palms for dates, no doubt. None of this jazz from America, for one thing. Do you like it?'

'Yes, monsieur.' A scarcely perceptible sigh from the older man. Selim heard it and was hurt, yet it only served to make him more loquacious.

'Our Phoenician forbears, Pierre, defenders of the only real democracy in the Arab world. Such hopes we have, for the future of our Lebanon.' He gestured with the whisky bottle. 'Park in front of the two-storey house over there, the one with the rotting balcony.'

He watched the lighted windows of his father's house. Behind thick glass he could discern moving figures, voices, sounds of laughter. His father's cough. Or was he only imagining it? He always contemplated going in, arriving in the midst of a family idyll with only a swift knock at the door to announce his presence. Then he stopped. Yet another part of him wanted to punish them, even his unknown daughter. *I won't go in. Won't give them the satisfaction. Let them wonder about me. Let them continue to worry, to wonder whether I love them, the twice-yearly envelopes a constant reproach.* He'd been trapped, he'd been so young – and now they wanted him to feel guilty as well? And what of this little daughter of his, growing into a woman without a father to look to for protection? Not so little anymore. She must be at least sixteen by now. Tarred with her mother's brush, no doubt, opinionated and wilful. Complicit in her grandmother's ambitions.

Did I ever love Anahit? He took another gulp from the bottle and was drunk enough now to be honest with himself. *I never did.* He only wanted her the way a boy wants the touch of any pliable flesh, the way he needed his own left hand at night under the bedcovers. Nothing more. She'd tricked him into having sex, then got herself pregnant to trap him. That was all there was to it, and he absolutely refused – even now – to feel any remorse. He remembered the night mostly because it had been so cold.

It was early spring but the nights were still chilly. He made sure to dress in warm, dark clothes before he left the house. At the side door he wound a woollen scarf around his neck twice; his only concession to colour. Mother had made it for him last winter in his football team's stripes, and he knew it would bring him luck. He glanced at his watch, a New Year's gift from Anahit, nearly midnight. He hadn't told anyone at home, exams tomorrow and he had no intention of going back to the American University. He was no naive student, no idealist. He was a man of action, wanted to save his country. Or be a hero, whichever came first. He ran down Urfa Street and onto the highway, made it onto the last bus.

At Camp Marash he nodded to black-coated, capped figures. They were all men – no women were allowed at the meeting. *Of course*, he thought, but the thought was only a result of the habit of discussing everything with Anahit, internalising her disdain of men and their ways. *Why can't I join a liberation organisation if I want?* He could hear the rising frustration in her girlish growl. *Bet I'd be more ruthless than any of them.* He didn't doubt it.

The Secret Army for the Liberation of Armenia was the largest anti-Turkish organisation he'd heard of, in response to Turkey's official policy of denial. Archaeologists and academics in Turkey were employed solely to exhume Armenian bones from the killing fields and claim the muddy skulls were Turkish. Turning perpetrators into victims. The Turkish government was manipulating international opinion, with the press lobbied not to use the term genocide. Even the Americans and British called it the 'alleged Armenian atrocity', the 'civil war', or 'intercommunal warfare'.

So far the organisation hadn't managed to assassinate any Turkish figures of note, though not from want of trying. There were a few bungled attempts at government ministers and a few arrests of activists who had been caught, but it was still growing in size. For Selim, it had been hard to find out anything about them at first. They were notorious for their secrecy, even among fellow Armenians. Minas was uncharacteristically silent on the matter, telling him not to meddle. But Selim asked the right questions around the Armenian quarter, in underground bars and at the marketplace, was given the right answers. And so he was here.

He stayed at the back of the auditorium, pulling off his jacket and scarf. The space was quickly being filled with Armenian men, all with that shuffling, sidelong way of walking that betrayed a certain amount of suspicion. Nobody glanced in his direction, nobody spoke. He noticed one slight, boyish figure stand toward the back in the same way he did, shifting from foot to foot, keeping his cap on even in the rising heat. His boots looked just like Selim's best Sunday pair.

The speeches began. Much talk of suffering, persecution, the danger of being Armenian in an Arab region. Revenge. Many speakers. Finally, a tense, black-browed young man stood and shook his fist at the assembly.

'Down with Turkey!'

The rest of the men followed suit, shaking their fists. Selim did so as well, noticing from the corner of his eye that the boy kept his arms clasped behind his back.

'Armenia is now one-seventh of her original size. The Turk has overrun our nation and culture while the rest of the world sits idly by!'

The auditorium blazed with shouts.

'Shame! Shame!'

'I propose we begin this holy war on all enemies of Armenia now! I propose—'

Selim felt his attention wandering, much as he was warmed by the sentiments expressed. The reason he was distracted was the boy near him. He sidled along the wall and was now slipping his sweaty hand into Selim's.

'Excuse me?'

He tried to pull his hand away but the other boy only gripped it tighter. He tried not to cause a scene. He struggled without moving, using his muscles to exert pressure. Was this a spy, a Muslim bomber, or an internal test for new members? He ceased to resist and became limp. The boy came closer so his cap tickled Selim's cheek.

'It's me, you idiot.'

He pulled away from the hand. He whispered back, furious, spitting in his haste to speak. 'What do you think you're doing following me here? You could get shot.'

Only a girlish giggle in his ear. He yanked Anahit by the arm to his side.

'We're going. Not a word out of you – not a word.'

Past the guards at the door, who frowned but said nothing, past the floodlit courtyard, through the high gates that spelled *Camp Marash* in Armenian script. Anahit was convulsing with laughter in his grip, and this made him madder still. He shook her, savage in his embarrassment.

'They'll never have me now! My name's been noted, thanks to you.'

Anahit pushed the cap off her face with her free hand and suddenly her face had changed.

'Oh, Selim. I didn't realise. I just—wanted to surprise you.'

He turned from her and strode away.

'Wait, Selim! I'm sorry—I'll go back and tell them it was all my fault.'

He wheeled around and arranged his features into a scowl.

'Then they'll really think I'm a coward, letting a stupid girl do that.'

She ran to stop him from walking away again, gripping him by the lapels of his jacket. She was crying now, great convulsing sobs that embarrassed him still further.

'I'm so, so sorry. Selim, please—'

He hesitated, wanting to punish her somehow, then in the next moment hugged her to him like the little boy he knew he still was, the movement of his arms and head fierce against her body.

'Doesn't matter. Let's go. I'd rather fight with a real army than slink around stabbing people in the back anyway.'

They walked arm in arm to the highway. The last bus had gone. It was that time of the early morning when the sky would exert a slight, pale pressure on the eyes. Cars whizzed past, their headlights glowing in the dark. Anahit tightened her grip on him. He stayed passive. She took his arm in a decisive gesture and wound it around her waist. He then turned around, his arms still around her, until they were face to face. She was panting, her mouth open inches from his.

'So,' he said. He could feel the warmth of her breath.

It was the first time he'd ever touched her like this. It had always been her taking the initiative: flirting, caressing, even slapping him when she was angry. Now he felt how slim she was, almost frail, but with a core of muscle under his borrowed shirt and trousers, his second-best belt buckled twice around her. He bent his head and kissed her lips; they were like fire. Her teeth knocked against his, their tongues met, and through the kiss he felt her widen into a smile. Slowly, he reached behind her head and tenderly piled her hair up again under the cap; it was growing even colder now.

They reached Urfa Street after an hour and both of them stopped to stand on the rise of the hill, looking down on their home. The honey-coloured stone it was built with gleamed and beckoned, but they both turned, without conferring, away from it. They caught another bus, sat together with their legs twined, the only passengers. It made them giggle. They got out at the Corniche, the sea still and inky under a pre-dawn sky. Made their way to Selim's campus, lay down together in the middle of the courtyard. Damp grass hard on their spines. It wasn't cold anymore, or at least they didn't feel it. He plucked his cap from her and threw it as far as he could. Her breasts warm, the nipples alive. He loomed over her, looking down into her face. Her eyes were open, but she didn't see him – stony, focused on a landmark way in the distance. Her bare head in his hands was ice, clammy, as if her hair had soaked up all the cold of night.

A
S
H

173

✳ His aunt Lilit had organised it all. She showed her daughter how to get pregnant, to shame him, trap him into a marriage he was too young to want and too noble to refuse. And now this: Anahit's death, an abandoned child, a broken family. Such unrelenting guilt. *How did we all come to this?* He moaned, became aware of the driver's puzzled enquiry, and excused himself.

'I'm sorry, Pierre. Back pains. Always come on at night.'

Pierre nodded, self-consciously professional.

'Perhaps we should be heading back to headquarters now, monsieur? You have a 6 am tomorrow. Or should I say today, sir; it's already two in the morning.'

He pressed a couple of notes into the driver's hand.

'Please, Pierre. Let's stay here a while longer.'

BEIRUT, 1995

At the Cafe de Paris, dust motes trace their eternal dance on the table, the customers, the silvery evening air, my ringed hands. I've finished my fourth glass of tea. Yet I continue to sit, watching.

It's my third week in Beirut and I've spent most of my time at the tribunal or writing, not living. Walking with my head down, unheeding the pale spring sunset, a lemon sky fading to green. Last time I called the editor of *The Globe* he asked me where my big story on the Sabra-Shatila survivors was. So far my New Beirut story and one on the sectarian nature of the camps have been well received.

Tonight I need to interview the Palestinian woman in the camp. She told the UNDP worker she'd be available at seven. Flipping through my appointment diary, I check the address. I dread bumping into D'Andrea there, but it's more from embarrassment now than hostility. It's late, though; he'd be finished work. The article has to be written, and the woman is ready to talk.

I set off from the cafe thinking about my early days in Boston. I'd felt uneasy, careful not to reveal the underside of my history. Much as I imagine Lilit would have been with her Turkish—what was he anyway, husband, lover, slave-owner? I imagine her circumspect, secretive, not allowing the real, contradictory Armenian girl to be revealed. Her voice in old age was frail, wavering. When she called me in Boston I would picture her sitting at the tiny hall stand by the side door: the shadow of the pomegranate tree on the wall behind trembling, moving, changing; the old-fashioned telephone, so black and heavy, in her tender hands.

As I told her about my uneventful days, I felt the threat of that same obscuring, that effacement, happening to me. The boys I met wanted me to be compliant and happy but only on the surface or in public: sitting down to dinner in a restaurant, dancing at a party, letting them brush a hand across my thigh in a crowd. They knew nothing of my true nature. And I can't blame them – I was too scared to reveal something I'd regret later.

Lost in thought, I miss my bus. At the Hamra taxi rank, I enter a cab absently and sit in the front seat without glancing at the driver, not taking in anything about him: age, attractiveness, ethnicity. I tell him my destination in English, a reflex. Next thing we're speeding down an unknown highway. I strain to read the signs that flash past, the huge billboards for Chivas Regal and Calvin Klein jeans, the tattered posters of suicide bombers and beaming mullahs. Ayatollah Khomeini's wax-doll face. The driver puts his white, hairless hand on my leg, and I slap it away. A hot panic grips me as soon as I realise I'm helpless, at the mercy of this stranger – the car's going at a hundred; there's no point even contemplating jumping out. There is an instant, when my vision dims and the light amid the blackness narrows to a pin, where I can see Lilit's fate in the desert among the Turks, in Syria with Suleiman, hollow with pain in her Beirut bedroom. The taxi stops. Then the man simply shrugs, and I see the dark stains of sweat on his shirt as he leans over me to open the passenger door.

I stand on the kerb, ashamed, as if the whole incident has been my fault. Heart beating crazily, ears stinging with heat. I even paid him for groping me before I banged the car door shut. Threw some notes into his lap, trying to normalise the situation. This did not happen to me. I'm not that sort of person. Forcing myself to remain calm, I bend down to my laptop bag and take out my map.

I have no idea which suburb I'm in; it's not a suburb I'd ever been to as a child, but the street is shiny and clean, the shops orderly, the people busy and well dressed.

'Excuse me?' I begin, hopeful.

No answer. Some passers-by make as if to stop, and I step forward, my features arranged into what I hope is a neutral expression. They offer a false smile and a miming gesture of the hands – *I speak no English* – and are gone.

I wonder why they won't help. Of course they speak English. Everyone does here. Do I look so strange? My scruffy jeans and tight T-shirt are too grunge, too cobbled-together, in this enclave. I can't see any young women or children, only purposeful men in Zegna suits and the occasional old woman, head down, scurrying about her errands in head-to-toe black. The old women don't even glance up when I speak. In affluent America people understand my sort of dress: ironic, political, self-reflexive. Not so here. They just think I want something from them. I want to try my Arabic but something in me is afraid, as if it might reveal too much. To whom?

I'm being jostled and pushed by a crowd of intense, moustached men. They're not wearing Zegna. They're what I imagine fundamentalist Muslims look like. Shias. Fanatics. Suicide bombers. I walk further into the crowd, trying to evade them. There still don't seem to be any young women or children in the neighbourhood, except for beggar boys who plead and wheedle with me for spare change. They don't seem affected by my clothes.

There are domes of mulberries at a stall and I'm suddenly parched. I point, smiling. The vendor ignores me as well, tending to the pressing needs of other customers. He pours the berries into an antiquated blender that churns melodiously as it's filled, and I'm mesmerised by his blackened fingers as he scoops up a handful and crushes them with shards of ice, at the transformed jewel-bright sludge spurting into a glass.

'Je voudrais un—'

'Here, allow me.'

A man in khaki stops and points a thick finger on my blowing map to hold it down. For a second I think he's a soldier, then realise he's wearing cast-off military clothes with a self-deprecating, slightly humorous air. Under his vest is a black T-shirt with the words *Free Palestine* in English. His clothes seem incongruous next to his spiky greying hair, the whiter stubble on his chin and cheeks. Creases radiate from his greenish-grey eyes. He tosses a coin to the vendor from one of his many pockets, hands me a glass of juice. Glancing at the liquid as I begin to drink, he hesitates for a moment then reaches out for it.

'Do you mind? I don't have change for another.'

I shake my head, non-committal. I don't want to share with a stranger but it would be rude now to protest. *Free Palestine.* He must be an old leftist hippie, accustomed to sharing fluids and filth. Now I see he has a dog with him: a huge, black-tufted mastiff that places its paws on the man's knees and begs in whimpers.

ASH

177

'Don't bother looking at those tourist maps,' the man says in English, his mouth full of ice and berries. 'You got it from a hotel, didn't you? Useless.'

He slaps at the dog. 'Down, Julius. You won't like it anyway.'

He addresses me again. 'The streets are known by different names, locally. Where do you want to go?'

I open my mouth to speak.

'No, no, no,' he cuts in. 'Not the number, the building. Nothing's known by numbers around here.'

'I know that,' I say under my breath.

'Hmmm?'

I look at him but don't reply. Can I can trust him? Will he follow me there, take my money and passport, rape me? His accent is a hybrid I can't place: part American, part cultured, part something else. He seems to be in his early fifties, the same generation as my father. The same age Selim would be if he were alive. He's swallowed now and smiles through his stubble, as if sensing my hesitation. Hands me the half-empty glass.

'Aren't you going to finish your juice?'

Something about him looks out of place in the splenetic crowd, something as awkward as the way I feel. I suck at the straw, conscious of the stain of his saliva on the tip, and speak through a mouthful.

'I'm going to the Sabra-Shatila camp. The driver stopped here because I thought it was somewhere nearby. Well, to tell you the truth, he was overcharging me *and* making moves and I just wanted to get out of his cab as quickly as I could.'

The man whistles.

'Why are you going there anyway? Are you crazy? You could still get shot, even nowadays.'

'I need to meet someone,' I reply, taken aback. 'I'm expected.'

'Friends of yours?' He pauses. 'Okay, you don't need to tell me who they are. I was only joking before, trying to scare you. It's where all the half-baked journalists go for their taste of the real Lebanon.'

'Oh, well, I'm a journalist.'

'Are you now?'

He looks at me keenly, as if wondering whether I'm telling the truth. I feel the need to justify myself to him for some insane reason, and all the while as I'm preparing to speak I inwardly squirm at how naive I'll seem. I hand back the unfinished glass.

'Here, the rest is for you. I've had enough.'

He accepts it, regards me with his head tilted to one side. I succumb to the need to explain.

'I'm Lebanese. I mean, Armenian. Just back from the States. On assignment for *The Boston Globe*—'

He interrupts, throws the empty glass back at the vendor.

'Still want to go there? Okay. We need to get you another taxi. How can you carry that laptop bag around? You'll be robbed. Sorry. Here, allow me.'

I hesitate, shrug and gesture to my bag. The man exclaims at its heaviness and hails a cab, whose owner complains about the dog but nevertheless allows us inside.

✳ Back in the hotel bathroom, I turn on the light and scrutinise my eyebrows. They're more untidy than usual. I think of the man I just met. The way he talked about his lack of family, his engineering degree, without telling me where he was from, the way he finished all the juice between pronouncements. I left him in the taxi, still slurping at the dregs. He leaned out of the window, said I looked agitated, it was getting late, that he'd wait until I was finished. I was annoyed, but glad. I could feel him watching me as I stepped onto the kerb and walked fast toward the camp gates. When I came back twenty minutes later he was dozing, head thrown back, the dog snoring at his feet. I tapped him gently on the arm.

'They're not there. The woman and child. Nobody could tell me why.'

'You probably got the time wrong.'

'Believe me, I didn't.'

'Okay, you didn't. Who knows, maybe they chickened out.'

'Or maybe they're sick, or just running late. I think I should go back, wait at least another fifteen minutes.'

'I'll come with you if you like.'

I hesitated. 'It's okay. I've left a note.'

'Well, shall we go somewhere else now?'

'I know a cafe,' I suggested. 'In Rue Hamra, the Cafe de—'

He cut me off again. 'Terrible place. Where all the tourists go.'

Instead he took me to a tiny bar called Che Guevara's and talked through two local Almaza beers. The dog curled up at his feet, snoring like a man. I only allowed myself one arak, in order to keep some control. He was a stranger, after all.

He told me he's a minesweeper, pressed his business card into my hand. His job is to clear Israeli mines from the south of Lebanon for a non-profit organisation. He said he wanted to take me out on the town that evening, show me the new Beirut.

I like him. I like him a lot. His T-shirt has something to do with it, the solidity of torso beneath, his sunburnt cheeks and short, short hair. I trust his penetrating expression somehow. I tell myself to stop, not to romanticise him already. I always do this. Sometimes I despise myself for being so open, so ready to love. He has curiously thin brows, like Errol Flynn or Clark Gable.

I take tweezers and yank unruly hairs, one by one, from my own brows, pat down my hair. Put on some lipstick, stand back to look. My tattoo shows in my sleeveless dress, but I get the feeling he will like it. He's promised to show me a nightclub, stupidly fashionable, prohibitively expensive, rumoured to have been a torture centre run by the Phalangists during the war. I had to suppress a shudder. Surely my father wasn't involved? It's one thing to know intellectually the things he did, another to see them, touch them, participate in Beirut's continual whitewashing of the past.

'Call me Chris,' he said in the cab on the way to the hotel, paying the driver in American dollars. 'Most people can't pronounce my real name anyway.'

'I'm sure I could. Try me.'

'I'll tell you later. Meet me in the lobby at nine.'

✵ I meet him downstairs and his eyes light up when he sees me.

'I love a woman in a white cotton dress,' he says, and I don't know what to reply.

He takes my hand and instinctively I pull away before submitting. Never sure of the right way to be.

'Let's walk,' he says. 'It's a cool evening, for a change.'

The streets are uneven and narrow, shaded by high-rise apartments. Squat villas built in other, saner eras press up against the kerb like fat women craning to get a better view of the spectacle of sleek cars and damaged people. Painted shutters open to fumes and dust, in all their fading shades of lemon and leaf-green and rose. I peer into a bedroom, at its bare light bulb, brown-papered walls. Pages cut out of fashion magazines are pasted to the peeling wallpaper.

'Hey, don't be so rude,' Chris whispers.

I'm beginning to tire already of his familiarity, his arrogance, his opinions on everything. It's as if I've known him for years, already been made to endure all his theories. At the same time this sense of ease gives me comfort among so much that's unfamiliar in this new, shiny Beirut.

We pass more apartment blocks with open courtyards and broken fountains, baby olive trees planted in blue-painted oil tins. Grey scum on walls, grease on the pavement. We walk, slipping at times, following open sewers that lead us down to the sea. On the Corniche promenade, women stride past in heels and tight jeans, gelled glitter in bouffant hair. I can't help contrasting their stalking feline grace with my own diffidence, retreating under their gaze. Surely I can't compete with these beauties. I watch Chris appraising them, one thin eyebrow raised – yet his hand's on my arm; he's in step with me, making me laugh. I watch the way my shadow and his – elongated, elegant, long-limbed – walk beside us, like idealised versions of ourselves. Now he's switched from being fatherly to funny, I can let myself relax. Now he's looking at me in that appreciative way, a tiny glint in his eye.

I can smell the hot spiciness of his aftershave, the skin of his face and neck gold-stubbled in the last of the light. Waves lap against the sea wall like a lullaby. Above the noise of cars and mopeds and hawkers – all hushed now for this brief moment in the stillness of sunset – Beirut's waterfront apartments shimmer in the evening mist, telegraphing messages I alone can hear. I pause, looking up at them, and Chris stops in front of me.

'You all right?'

I shiver, a chill breeze off the sea.

'I'm—just remembering. Reminded of who I used to be.'

Now I take his hand, naturally, as if we've been doing this for years. As we walk, women glance down at my sandals. A quick once-over of the face and legs, then without exception down to my feet. I lean closer and whisper.

'Why do they keep looking at me?'

'You're not wearing a boob tube. And, horror of horrors, you're wearing flat shoes.'

'I don't remember it being like this before.'

'Before? You were just a kid. Isn't that what you told me? Image is everything now. Did you know they're one of the highest users of cosmetic surgery in the world?'

'I wouldn't think they'd have the money.'

'Back-room jobs. My theory is they're trying to forget the war any way they can.'

'And the possibility of another war,' I blurt out.

He's not looking at me. We pass a fish restaurant, its blackboard announcing 'Fresh Crab Strait from Sea', and the tuxedoed tout with his plastic-covered menu takes my arm in a surreptitious scoop. Chris gently steers me away.

'Well, that's something no one wants to discuss.'

I whisper again as we pass two young women who slow down and openly stare.

'They don't care whether I know they're staring or not. What's there to look at?'

'They're trying to figure out if you're poor, in those clothes.'

'I am poor.'

'Not compared to them.'

'Oh, really! How about all the BMWs and Mercs everywhere? The beauty parlours and fake tans?'

'Families think nothing of going into debt for a luxury car. These same families live in hovels with no running water.'

'You don't have a car?'

'I wouldn't dare drive in Beirut. I'm not crazy.'

'So you weren't born here?'

'Tel Aviv. And I holidayed in Eilat, in the summers.'

'I didn't know you were—'

He interrupts and points.

'See that man over there? He sits on this corner all day and night. We call him the man who wants words.'

I follow his gaze. An old man sits on the curb with his sparrow legs folded beneath him, arranging and rearranging bits of paper. He seems oblivious to the clattering traffic, the feet of passers-by, the billowing dust and grit blown in from the mountains and out to the sea. In the half-light I can faintly discern that each piece of paper has only one Arabic word written on it, either torn from school notebooks, written on the back of bills, bus tickets, cardboard, or print carefully cut from newspapers.

'What's he doing?'

'He's Syrian. They're all mad. He begs for words instead of money.'

As we pass the old man he looks up and smiles at me.

'He's crazier than most,' Chris mutters. 'A Yezidi.'

'A what?'

'A strange religion in these parts. Heretical Muslims. Didn't your grandmothers ever tell you about them?'

The old man croaks at me in Arabic, putting out his hand in the begging position.

'Any words to give me, little lady?'

I shake my head and look to Chris for assistance.

'Look, he's showing you the words he already has.'

I bend down near him as he spreads out his collection on the asphalt, careful not to make my knees grubby. He smells painfully of unwashed scalp. His white moustache makes two curly worms on his upper lip. Chris translates as the old man lays each piece out, saying the word in Arabic and nodding at me each time he hears the word in English.

'*Exile*,' Chris says. '*Grapes. Loss. Rage. Fresh eggs.* That's two words; his standards are slipping. *Identity. Futility. Denial.*'

The old man's face lights up when I indicate my willingness to give him a word. Chris passes me one of his business cards and I turn it over.

'*Truth*,' I write in English with the beggar's pen, get up and leave, not sure why I don't wait to hear Chris translate. I'm afraid of him for a moment, as if he's exposed something about me I'm not willing to see.

He catches up to me, holds my arm. 'Hey, are you okay?'

'I'm fine. Really.'

He shakes his head, disbelieving.

When we arrive at the nightclub, bouncers wave him through, assessing my clothes and hair for a moment then nodding. We descend many steps, into humid darkness shot with green light. Even this early in the night, people fight for space in the large, low-ceilinged room, ambushing the bar, overflowing into the middle of the floor where nobody seems to dance. The music hums and shudders, thudding hard, and people shove against each other in small, ever-diminishing circles, shouting in each other's ears over the din, swaying, wiggling their hips, while at the same time holding drinks out toward each other, flimsy barriers to intimacy.

I look around again – it looks exactly the dimensions of a torture chamber – and I shudder. 'Hey,' I shout. 'Can we find somewhere quieter?'

'It's great. You'll love it. We'll find you a secluded spot. What are you drinking?'

'Same as last time.'

We make for the bar together, with Chris using his elbows to propel us through.

'So tell me your real name.'

'My name's Chaim. But nobody calls me that these days – except my mother.'

'So you are Jewish.'

'And? Is that a problem?'

'No. No, not at all. Why would it be?'

He doesn't answer, instead takes my hand to pull me through the crowd.

'Good. Now we can have fun. Let's dance before we get a drink.'

'Wait a minute – Chaim.'

He turns to me, his expression changed under the pulsing greenish light.

'I want to call you Chaim from now on. Your real name. If that's okay with you.'

He hesitates, then smiles. In that wide smile, I see the little boy he once was, and I warm to him further.

'Well … thank you,' he says, stepping closer to me. 'I'm not sure what else to say. *Toda lach.*'

'What's that?'

'Thank you, in Hebrew. *Toda lach.*'

I repeat it. '*Toda.* And you're welcome – Chaim.'

He chuckles, grabs my hand.

'Let's dance.'

'But there's nobody else dancing.'

'All the better, then.'

I tug at his arm. 'Really, I don't think I want to—'

He ignores me, making his way through the people, greeting and smiling. I think of the old Syrian beggar and my word for him: *Truth.*

'Wait,' I say. 'Let's sit down for a minute. Tell me more about the old man.'

We've reached the outer row of people storming the bar. Chaim raises his hand over the sea of heads, signals almost miraculously to the barman. He lifts up two fingers and the barman seems to know what he wants. He turns to me, looking straight into my eyes. His pupils are huge and black in the dim light.

'Tell me,' I say again.

'Yezidi. They believe the devil's been forgiven by God and reinstated as the principal angel. There's no more hell, not anymore.'

'There's hope for us all then.'

'Don't laugh. These guys have been persecuted for thousands of years as devil-worshippers. They call him the Peacock Angel and it's his job now to supervise the running of the world. Quite a job!'

'He's not doing it very well.'

'Could you do any better?'

❋ I can do better, I think – much better. I've come back to this place to see if I can make a difference. If anything could be said to *make a difference* in these days of cynical obsolescence. What a worn-out, bankrupted phrase.

I walk through neighbourhoods of wild children and pyramids of garbage. Nothing has changed in Beirut except multi-million-dollar airbrushes of buildings and downtown districts, the influx of more money for the Christians from the West. I can still see the poverty, the camps, the shantytowns of the displaced, Shia Lebanese and Palestinians, pushed out once again by the Israelis from the south. I feel anxiety in the air of the city: the icy breath of change running like a current beneath early summer's heat.

The Israelis are still squeezing the south like an orange, with Hezbollah fighting them for the pips. Could these small, brutal wars escalate and spread to the rest of the country? I'm lost in thought, slipping more than once on tyre-tracked streets. A young man brushes past, gazing at my bare arms and short hair with startled, inquisitive eyes. He stops, murmuring something salacious in Arabic, and I want to swing him around and smash his face against a wall. I want to scream. I want to see Chaim again tonight and abuse him for doing this to my people. Doing what to my people? Are they my people? I only lived here for sixteen years. And why should it be his fault anyway? Of the two of us, he's the one actually *making a difference.* But the desire to pinpoint somebody else to censure for my own confusion remains. Would the Arabs be like this anyway, even without these skirmishes on their southern and eastern borders, without Israel flexing its muscles each time they utter a sound above a whimper?

Before I left Beirut, Lilit once said: 'We're not Arabs, even though we live here. We're Armenian.' She sat up straighter in bed, monitoring my expression.

'Where is Armenia?' I asked.

Lilit took time over her answer. 'Armenia doesn't exist anymore.' Her voice lowering, as if admitting a crime. 'Your grandfather was Turkish, but, never mind, you're really Armenian.' And she smiled, as if not quite sure of it herself.

I stop at a corner. The sea at the end of the street is obscured by heat haze and car fumes, a white backdrop to chaos. My stomach hurts. It's too far to walk back to the hotel. I'm lost, anyway. The city of my childhood has rearranged itself into new and confusing configurations. The worn stones at my feet claim no prior memory. I step out to hail a cab, think better of it. Don't want to be duped again, targeted in yet another reinforcement of my difference. Don't want another driver thinking I'm an American tourist, a New World Lebanese back for a tour of the old country. Easy pickings.

I pass a phone box. Chaim. Somehow I feel he can answer my questions, absolve himself. But why should he have to absolve himself anyway? He's done nothing wrong. I know it's not his fault; it's not the Israelis, or the Americans, not even the Lebanese themselves. It's this that makes me feel rage: nobody to blame.

I walk straight past the phone, start toward the direction of the hotel in short, determined strides. My face clotted in self-reproach. Chaim has insinuated himself into my life already; I've let him. An Israeli? Of my father's generation. And what of my life back in Boston? The only friend I want to call is Dilek. And even to her, I don't know what to say.

I wipe sweat from my forehead with my shirtsleeve, motes of dust float before my eyes. Part of me is pleased I feel so uncomfortable, as if this is in some way a confirmation of my anger. I like Chaim already. More than like. He's funny, he's sincere, he already seems like a still point of calm in the midst of all this chaos. Do I like him because he's the only man paying attention to me here? Am I that superficial?

I pass the American University, on impulse go in. At the gate I'm relieved of my bag by a bored-looking woman in a brown uniform. I walk past palms and manicured gardens, knowing exactly where I'm going now. To the library.

Air-conditioned cold hits me like a door in the face. I walk the length of the room, trailing the broken spines of French and Arabic titles on the shelves with my finger, sit at one of the computer terminals. The woman behind the counter nods, then connects me.

I click onto a search engine, type without thinking. *Minesweeping in Lebanon*. One hundred and forty-five entries.

I pull Chaim's card out of my wallet. *Chaim Herzberg: Mechanical Technical Advisor*. A crude line-drawing of a skull and crossbones on a scarlet background.

I type in the name of the company: *Mines Advisory Group*. Chaim's surname. Let's see what he really does for a living. His name appears among a list of other employees, a description of work being done in the south of the country, the funding they're hoping to get next year. I click onto the next hit under Herzberg. An article from *The Jerusalem Post* dated August 1982:

ALON HERZBERG, ONE OF OUR MOST ESTEEMED FIGHTER PILOTS, RECOUNTS HIS DAYS AND NIGHTS IN BEIRUT

Mr Herzberg recently joined a protest organisation in Tel Aviv to put a stop to the Begin government's incursion into Lebanon. He claimed the 'invasion' is both brutal and inefficient, entailing many Israeli military deaths as well as the expected Lebanese collateral damage. Yet Herzberg continues to fly his nightly missions into Beirut. 'I made a pact with my country,' he said. 'I can protest from a moral stance, but at the same time I must continue to do my duty.'

I read no further. Could this be Chaim's brother, an uncle, a cousin? I click on the next entry. It's an obituary notice, dated September 1982:

ALON HERZBERG, BELOVED SON AND BROTHER, DIED TRAGICALLY IN THE COURSE OF DUTY. MAY THE LIGHT OF ZION CONTINUE TO BURN IN HIM AND IN HIS SORROWING FAMILY. Survived and mourned by his mother Tova and brother Chaim. Memorial in the Great Synagogue, Allenby Street, Tel Aviv, Thursday, 2 pm.

I swallow my apprehension and take a taxi back to the Mayflower Hotel. The trip passes without incident. I grab my room keys from the grinning boy at reception. *Merci. Shukran.* Never sure which language to use. Which voice.

Another icy air-conditioned room, noise of traffic muted by thick crimson curtains. I switch on my laptop, comforted by its whirring welcome. The screen lights up electric blue. I freeze, hands poised over the keyboard. Am I falling in love with the father I never knew, again, in Chaim? A failed, dirty, doomed love from the beginning.

Downstairs a busker wails. I type. Type anything: the weather outside, the scraping sound of a vacuum cleaner in the room next door, the way my shirt-collar feels hot and sticky on my neck. I stop. I have no opinions. Nothing to say. Nobody to blame.

I've heard Lebanese point the finger at their Ottoman heritage for the civil war and for their continued factionalism, a five-hundred-year occupation with its precedents of corruption and tradition of public neglect. I don't believe it. Others bewail the sense of impotence left by the imperialist experience. The collective stupor of the twenties, or the present-day supremacy of America. I get up from the cramped hotel desk, turn on the sputtering TV. A Benny Hill comedy dubbed into Arabic. I pull off my shirt, loosen my bra. Relief. There's sweat under my breasts, stinging.

Many Arabs maintain the West still conspires to keep them in second-class status. That they haven't moved on from the mediaeval glory of their past. Arab culture continues to honour religion over reason, conformity over diversity, rhetoric over truth. Who's to say the West isn't doing the same thing? I kick off my sandals, lie on the bed and watch the antics on the screen.

A
S
H

DER EZ ZOR, 1915

Lilit scrubbed Suleiman's baggy underclothes against the ridged board in the tub outside. She rinsed them, wrung them out until she felt she could extract no more moisture from the heavy coiled folds. She scolded the servant girl responsible for the washing this morning; last week certain festival clothes had been folded and put away with sweat stains still on them.

She wasn't sure herself if she was truly angry with the servant girl or merely conspiring to be outside in the courtyard today, closer to the front gate and to freedom. She'd taken to wearing every item of jewellery Suleiman had given her all at once, pushing ring upon silver ring onto her swollen fingers and fastening bracelets all the way up to her elbow. Leave-taking preparations, the decisive gesture finished before the brain had time to realise exactly what it meant. Just as she had pushed the girl away today, warning her she would be beaten if it happened again, and announced that for the first time she would soil her own hands with Suleiman's dirty clothes.

She was surprised at her own audacity, she who only months ago was a scared and cringing slave in the household. She who now had the power to order the servants, to avoid heavy work and play the lady. A nameless doubt gripped her. Her hands were shaking, her lower spine ached. She straightened up and arched backward with her hands on her hips, stretching. The baby was nearly due. She could feel it rasp and fret inside her, a sharpened stone growing too large for its cavern, questioning, demanding to be let out, demanding to be free.

She wiped the soapsuds from her arms. Today was the day. She was going without telling Suleiman, without telling Fatima. She was going to leave them all and escape with her unborn baby. She reckoned on this time of day being safe: Suleiman at the notary's office, discussing the ongoing lease of his cotton fields and palm groves; Fatima on her pallet with a headache, shutters closed and a wet cloth over her eyes; the cook ensconced in the kitchen muttering to herself as she chopped up a lamb killed only that morning, squatting on her haunches, throwing the pieces into a pot at her foot.

The noon hour had only just passed and the town seemed still and drowsy as a drugged bee. She rolled down her sleeves, fastening them at the wrists, collected her meagre provisions and the jingling cache of coins. One rolled out of the pouch and fell to the ground. She grimaced at the sound as she bent to pick it up, belting the pouch at her waist. The ginger cat miaowed as if aware of her defection, and she knelt down to bury her face one last time in its fur.

With swift deliberation, she draped her veil firmly over her face and traversed the courtyard in silent steps, peering into the kitchen on her way. The cook's back was to her and she was humming. She unbolted the courtyard doors. Her hands were trembling again – she knew she made more noise than was necessary. The pounding of her heart louder than the fountains' splash. She slipped through the tiny opening she made and closed the doors behind her.

When she was outside, she stopped for a moment with her back against the wall. Her blood was still surging in her temples, thick with dread. *It was so easy. So simple.* The street murmured painful foreboding in the shimmering heat. She shaded her eyes, gazed up and down its length and breadth. *But what do I do now?* Her plans had seemed so perfect, so watertight when she lay awake at night beside Suleiman, his knee wedged between her legs, her body weak and yielding and moulded into his.

She would go back to Van and find Papa. There would be *khans* on the journey for her to sleep in, where she might remain unmolested. She might be able to give birth on the way. This terrified her. But to wait here would mean she would lose all hope, all freedom, become Turkish and give birth to a child who would grow up Turkish, knowing nothing of its true culture. She had to leave, for her child's sake if not her own. She would be protected, she'd have to be. A peasant woman would help her birth. A Bedouin, used to labouring alone in the desert. She would arrive home safely. She would reclaim their old house and live in it with only her baby if she couldn't find Papa. If the house had been burnt down by the Turks, she'd get someone to build it again. Yervan? He might still be alive. After all, it was still their land. Suleiman had told her all Armenian assets had been classified by the government as abandoned goods. She didn't quite understand what that meant in her case. Surely they couldn't take away her ancestral fields. Surely she would be safe again at home.

Now the street stretched before her in a terrifying spiral of doubt. *Where do I go? What if the Turks find me? They'll know I'm Armenian.* She looped another thickness of fabric over her face and made herself walk to the end of the street. Her legs trembled and threatened to buckle beneath her. She knew she looked odd; she couldn't help making little whimpers of fear she knew were audible through the veil.

Yet there was nobody around. The buildings moved closer together in the heat haze, conferring over her escape. Black palms swayed above her, although there was no wind. She looked up, squinted into the sky, blue as the indigo dye she saw for sale in the markets. Too blue, too perfect, sinister, like the cold glass eye Suleiman had tucked into the folds of her nightdress when he found out she was pregnant. She hadn't wanted to look at it. It reminded her too much of her own Armenian eyes, the colour of Lake Van.

'Keep this,' he said. 'It will protect you and our baby. Trust me.'

She fumbled in her clothes as she walked higher up the incline of the silent street. Her fingers searched between her breasts, in her underclothes, digging into her navel. It was nowhere to be found. *I've left it behind!*

She halted, her face twisting beneath her veil. *I can't leave here if I've left it behind.* The panic of choice held her down, deep in the belly. *Suleiman. Our child. Help me.* She remembered the way his face had looked last night in the moon's pale shiver. 'No,' he had said when she bent down and touched her mouth to him. His penis was a little furled bud, vulnerable. 'No.' His cheeks crumpled, like a baby hurting. He helped her put her clothes back on with jerky movements, fumbling with the buttons, tying the sash askew, and sat with her on the bed, saying he was too tired. 'The others,' he said, 'they demand so much from me. You, Lale—I can only be myself with you.'

Standing at the crossroads, torn by her indecision and the desire to scurry back to the safety of the courtyard, she saw a caravan in the distance, visible over the high town walls.

I could go straight back there now and nobody would ever suspect.

She thought of Fatima: all those barren years of longing, her reckless desperation. She thought of her child in the future, a son or daughter that would look just like its father, blank-eyed when she tried to tell the story of its origins, the suffering of its race.

The caravan was coming closer now, skirting the edge of town. She could see men in bright checked scarves, the fluid grace of camels, litters and palanquins carrying piles of clothes, rugs, thick bolts of rainbow fabric. Also women, perched high on the smaller beasts, unveiled and tattooed on forehead and chin. She thought their eyes sought her out, could see who she really was under all her veils and gold. For an instant she thought she would raise her hand and alert them to her presence. They would take her now, look after her. But her hands remained where they were, clasped loose on her belly. The child kicked; a sublime nudge into the present. She turned away and began to retrace her steps to Suleiman's house.

✳ Now the voice in Minas's head redoubled in its efforts. It was shrill and then there were more of them calling, brittle and insistent, sweet singing refrains from the community of the dead. They would not let him rest so he lay awake at night scheming, planning his escape. He pushed away the girl with the flat of his hand when she wanted to touch him. Yet he was selfish. He held on to her greasy braid as he plotted, the same way he had with his sister when their mother left for work each dawn in Van. Her hair a living reminder he was not alone in the dark.

He thought of the other boy, now assigned to the best sleeping block in the camp and given work in the kitchens. Minas had seen him some mornings in the back courtyard, throwing last week's slops to prisoners lucky enough to be there at the right time. Old and young men fighting over garbage, cradling it in cupped hands, taking it back to their sleeping block or behind the latrines to savour, mouthful by mouthful, deflecting kicks and blows from the others. He watched the boy eat his breakfast ration of gruel with fastidious slowness, brushing the curls out of his eyes, then wipe the tin bowl with his little finger to lick it clean. He seemed more energetic than most, even robust, with less prominent ribs. Working among food would have something to do with that, scrounging scraps left over from the guards' meals, stealing an extra mouthful here and there.

Minas hadn't approached him again since the time he was rebuffed; they hardly acknowledged each other's presence at all. Survival was hard enough without pleasantries. Yet tonight as he curled up beside the girl and tugged at her hair, he knew the key to his escape lay with this boy. He seemed to have retained a faint trace of dignity among the filth, some vestige of an intact identity from his life before; the rigours of the camp had not yet rendered it meaningless. This awareness was present in all his gestures: the unhurried rhythm of his movements, his sense of hygiene, the youthful arrogance Minas could also – faintly – recognise in himself.

The boy was the only other inmate in good enough physical condition, and perhaps even optimistic enough, to consider attempting an escape. He had access to water and provisions they could take with them for the desert journey; he could even steal a knife or two for their protection. He was younger than Minas, perhaps even young enough to be easily manipulated should anything go wrong.

He rose from the ground, stealthy, and the girl beside him grasped his arm.

'Where are you going?'

'Piss,' he muttered.

She let him go, her hand lingering for a moment on his elbow. He stepped over sleeping bodies, eased the tent-flap open. He strained his eyes into the desert dark, terrible and final as a blanket draped over the eyes. No Turks close by. Far away, in the direction of the kitchens, he could hear male voices singing, smashing glass, a girl's thin, insistent cry. He made his way to the next sleeping block, his ears painful with the effort of listening out for a patrolling guard's footsteps, the slaver of the sleeping dogs, his own cough.

Now he slipped into the other tent. How to find the boy among so many people? He stepped over recumbent bodies again, more careful this time of out-flung arms or legs. In a moment of panic, he realised he didn't know the boy's name. He waited until he stood in the centre before he spoke, hearing his own voice come back to him in a tight, controlled whisper. 'Is the young boy here who works in the kitchen? The one with curly hair?'

Nothing. Then from the darkness came murmurs and whispers like the rising of a tide. 'Why, do you want to fuck him?' 'No boys here, only men!' And a reedy woman's voice, 'Shut up, all of you, I'm trying to sleep.' One of the figures sat upright, pointing an accusing finger. 'I'll call the guards! Get back to your own block, you'll have us all killed.'

He quashed the instinct to flee, gulped and tried again.

'I beg you, I need to find him.'

Somewhere in the far corner, he heard a fretful voice.

'I think you're looking for me.'

He stumbled over bodies in the dark, all the while being prodded at and kicked in the shins. He knelt down so close he could smell the boy's breath, feel the tickle of those damp curls on his forehead. Anxiety and the fear of being found out made him garble and cough and spit out his words.

'Come outside with me. I need to ask you something – in private.'

The moon glinted through the tent flaps. The boy hesitated, flung his hair back. It seemed an affectation.

'You're not—you don't want me, do you? Because you know it will cost. In food.'

Minas breathed out, exasperated already.

'Just come outside.'

He yanked the boy up by the arm and pulled him through the tent and outside where they both crouched on the ground, shivering in the night air. The boy was gasping with what seemed outraged pride and fright. Minas tried to look into his face.

'Listen to me. I don't know you well but feel you're in the same mind as I am. I need to speak to you about—escaping from here.'

The boy stood up.

'You've got to be joking.'

He seemed recovered now, his tone and stance familiar.

'We can do it together. I've been thinking about it for months.'

'Why me?'

A
S
H

195

Minas decided to lie.

'I trust you.'

He felt rather than saw the boy nod his quick assent.

'But how do I know I can trust you?'

'Listen to me now and make up your mind. I'm putting my life on the line just by telling you, aren't I? I have a plan and need you with me. Will you listen? Just sit down again. Tomorrow we hide in the kitchens after the evening meal – you must know a good place – and when the back gates are opened next morning for the provisions to arrive—'

'They only come on Wednesdays.'

'All right then, the day after tomorrow.'

'I'll be serving Tuesday night; it will be easy for me to hide. As for you …'

'I'll think of something, if you tell me where you'll be.'

The boy seemed to be lost in contemplation, silent in the dark. Minas looked around him, acutely conscious of the time passing.

'Anyway,' the boy finally said. 'What's in it for me?'

'We can help each other in the desert. And when we reach Van. You are a Vanetzi, aren't you?'

'Yes. So far I'm helping you, but I don't see how—'

'We'll stick together. If we get out of here alive, I'll look after you. I promise.'

He felt the boy's thin hand on his leg. The high voice throbbed in his ear.

'You promise?'

'Yes.' Minas was becoming exasperated again. 'I promise. So, the delivery comes the next morning, and as they're unloading we make a run for it.'

'In broad daylight? They'll shoot us before we can run ten metres.'

'There's no other way.'

✳ They were squashed hard against each other in the kitchen storeroom. It was little more than a cupboard, so crammed with jars and sacks there was barely room for the rats that scurried over their feet and faces, let alone two grown boys. It had been more difficult than Minas first thought, evading the guards at the evening meal and managing to hide. A new

Turk had been on duty, a younger man who seemed to feel the need to be vigilant, counting prisoners as they filed into the tent for their evening meal and then out again. But Minas had created a diversion by spilling his scalding broth on the bare feet of another inmate, and in the commotion had been able to slip to the side in the shadows and join the boy.

Now, as he sat twisted up against the boy's heaving chest, he remembered that he still didn't know his name. He couldn't ask him now; any sound or movement could give them away. The Kurdish cooks were still in the kitchen scouring the huge pots that held every meal, morning gruel or evening broth, each day. Some inmates were busy sweeping the dirt floors, wiping down the thick slab of stone that passed for chopping board and serving counter. He could hear their whimpers and groans as the cooks kicked them in the kidneys to urge them to work faster. He moved his knee back an inch, and felt the boy flex his muscles in gratitude for the extra space.

They tried not to breathe too loudly, although the air was becoming staler. He felt the stolen knife dig into his thigh, but there was no way he could move again to ease his discomfort. The boy seemed to be gasping, then in a terrible moment, ceased to make any sound at all. He pressed his lips to the boy's ear.

'All right?'

A slight twitch was the answer. He let himself drift into reverie then, and the pimpled girl's face swam at his side in reproach. This morning he told her he was going to try to escape tonight. He saw in her careful expression she was hurt. Although she insisted she was too weak to come, his obvious hesitancy to take her now was unforgivable. Yet she still nestled into him to say goodbye and he moved away from her stink with a squeamishness he had never been aware of before. He was leaving her now, his body shrinking from contact before his brain even severed the bond.

Fastidious, after everything he had touched and seen. The rats stirred at his feet. Not as fastidious as this boy at his side. He saw him avoid certain inmates as if afraid to be infected by them. He saw how the boy cultivated the guards in the hope of favours. He pinched him to make sure he hadn't suffocated, and felt a flicker of response. He must have dozed then, or slipped into unconsciousness, because the next he knew there were shouts and sweeping shadows cast by lanterns held aloft, and thick Turkish voices in an uproar. He heard the commander's fractured voice over the loudspeakers.

'Two men missing! Search the entire camp.'

He could hear the sirens now, and dogs snuffling at the storeroom door, and his bowels turned to water. He felt the boy stir beside him, and try to stretch out. He held him fast in his grip. He manoeuvred his arm painfully to the side and clamped his hand over the boy's mouth. The boy struggled and flailed, and Minas knew they would soon be discovered. Still he nursed some faint hope, if he could only hold the boy still long enough.

He felt the warm stench of vomit seep through his fingers. He tightened them on the boy's face, resisting the urge to let go. More liquid bubbling out of the boy's mouth – it seemed to never end. He felt his fingers relax their grip somewhat; the boy's face was slippery now, unmanageable. In an instant he wrenched out of Minas's grasp and yelled.

'He's in here, my lords! He took me hostage against my will.'

✳ While Minas was in solitary confinement he wondered why the Turks hadn't just killed him on the spot. He supposed they needed labour, and he and the boy were two of the very few inmates at this point healthy enough to work so hard. There hadn't been new convoys for many weeks now. He had also seen some of the older guards stepping forward and pleading for leniency on their behalf, the very same guards who had propositioned him by the mass graves.

Both boys had been bundled out of the storeroom, landing at the feet of the assembled company. Minas would have laughed if he hadn't been so terrified. The knife had skidded across the floor in a wide, shining arc, evidence of his guilt and the boy's betrayal. Although the Turks had only half-believed his babbled story, the boy had been whipped and left out in the sun for a day and a night as an example to other prisoners. Minas was spared the sight of his oozing, blackened body at assembly and taken to solitary for three weeks.

Thank God they hadn't stripped him before throwing him into prison. His mother's earrings still pressed into the flesh of his nipples, all but healed now, and growing over the piercing. A voice he learnt to rely upon soothed him in these confined quarters, his cage of steel wire. Sometimes it came to him in the guise of his mother at bedtime, her black hair redolent of bergamot and her temples damp from the bath, an open window at his head to let in the lake's summer breezes. *My darling, my love, your suffering and joys will be many.* At other times it mimicked the voice of Lilit, hissing and swaying and not allowing him to forget. *There is hope*, she said, *hope means everything will be all right someday*, and the familiar girlish voice echoed somewhere deep down in his gut.

He couldn't lie down or stretch out, only crouch with his head tucked into his chest and his knees buckled up to his ears. The sun beat down on him constantly during the day, and in the chill of the desert night rats, lizards and scorpions sought some warmth in the recesses of his body. He killed the smallest lizards with the flat of his hand, watched their pale bodies blacken and shrivel as he waited until he was brave enough, or starving enough, to partake of them.

He felt he was slowly dying, moment by moment. Yet the voice lulled him to sleep, sang him lullabies.

He busied himself with more escape plans. They became ever more elaborate and improbable, yet they helped him brave the buckets of camel dung thrown over him by jocular guards, the clump of dry gruel flung at him once every two days, the incessant evening chatter of the younger soldiers on duty. At three-hour intervals the guards kicked him awake so that he never enjoyed a full night's sleep. Five days into his confinement, after a surprise meal of mouldy bread, he thought of the Bedouin. Perhaps the extra nutrients jolted his brain into some semblance of logic.

Before the failed escape, he'd seen some of the younger Bedouin from nearby tribes loiter around the periphery of the camp in the mornings, looking for some work, a handful of liras in exchange for an hour's menial labour. The guards sometimes used them and their camels to transport prisoners out to the middle of the desert to be shot and buried on the spot. He would have to befriend a Bedouin when they let him out.

In the meantime, he tried to exercise, but there was no room to move. He wriggled his fingers and toes at strict intervals, kept himself from total boredom by tightening each individual muscle he could detect then relaxing it again. After the first week, this began to tire him. After the second, the most he could do was wake throughout the day and night from longer and longer periods of unconsciousness and open his mouth – *yes, I am still alive, because my jaw hurts* – then close it again. This in itself was an achievement. At the end of his third week, he was hardly aware of his body at all. He floated above the cage, borne along by the ear-splitting, painful accents of his mother's voice. *My darling, my love, your sufferings and joys will be many.*

✳ His first morning back at dawn assembly, he was so weak he could hardly keep from falling down. His arms and legs would not obey him: his impotent brain confusing signals. His torso was bent double. He tried to straighten up a little and gasped with the pain. The other inmates stood apart and watched, waiting for him to fall so they could jeer at him. He tried to walk, but found he couldn't. He leaned against another man, who elbowed him in the side and glared. He stumbled and managed to right himself, panting and clutching at his chest. He felt as if he'd run for days, lifted the weight of worlds, been stretched out on a rack. Every inch of his body, every muscle, rasped and burned and screamed for relief.

Before the commander's tirade began, he squatted in the dust and scrutinised his arms and legs, holding them out in front of him in the sunlight as if seeing them for the first time. Skeleton bones, shreds of yellow skin, reddish in places. Now he looked like everyone else, or even worse. A walking corpse. No longer himself. When was the last time he knew who he was anyway? The little boy who used to sit by the window in Van entranced by his schoolbooks. He searched for the pimpled girl and couldn't see her. Maybe she was dead, he thought without emotion. Maybe she was avoiding him, afraid to be tainted by his botched escape and subsequent ordeal.

He kept to the outer reaches of the crowd of prisoners, trying to see without moving his head if there were any Bedouin waiting on the outskirts, beyond the barbed-wire fences. There were. He knew that to walk across and speak to one of them openly would mean certain death. And he wasn't entirely sure he could walk that distance unaided.

He knew no Arabic. He would have to trust they spoke at least some Turkish, would have to trust they would listen and not betray him. And would they even want his gold earrings?

Assembly ended with the usual curses and oaths from the commander. Minas was selected, as always, to go with the youngest team far into the desert to carry and bury corpses. He didn't think he would be able to bear the dead weight, not now. They were given extra rations for this job – two ladles of gruel instead of one – and, even in his consternation, he was glad of that. During breakfast, the guards sat to one side and were never overly vigilant, slurping their tea from huge metal panniers, eating food the inmates of the camp could never dream of: fresh goat's meat, frothy milk, eggs. He knew the Bedouin supplied them with such luxuries in exchange for a few more coins. The milling crowd of prisoners worked in his favour; it was easy to wander, be unpredictable.

He waited in line for gruel, using his fingers to scoop it into his mouth. He saw the boy who had betrayed him squatting behind the main cauldron, being fed by another inmate. The older man seemed to be cajoling him, one hand clamped on the boy's scarred thigh. As Minas came near, the boy was in the act of opening his mouth wide to the spoon, like a baby bird. Minas caught his eye, made a growling sound in his throat then decided to ignore him. He was beneath contempt.

As he ate he walked in circles, feeling the strength come back to his legs and lower back, stretching, straightening, adjusting his spine. He walked, giving the impression of rumination, a man in the morning sunshine with nothing much to do. He caught the eye of a young Bedouin close by, a boy with a fine hawk's nose and copper skin. The boy edged closer, twining his fingers in the mesh of the fence. His eyes were sharp beneath his red and white headscarf. Minas walked up and down, up and down, skirting the boy, always coming closer into his vicinity. When he passed him for the last time Minas slowed down, speaking between gulps of his gruel in rapid, slurred Turkish.

'I have gold if you'll help me.'

The Bedouin didn't move, didn't register a flicker of interest.

'Do you understand?'

The Bedouin closed one eye, a lizard's reflex. When he spoke, his Turkish was accented, melodious.

'Show me the gold.'

Minas pulled up his shirt in a flash, then down again.

'I need you to help me get out of here.'

The Bedouin made to walk away, not before making a clicking sound with his teeth.

'Tonight, *insh'allah*, I shall come for you. Wait near the latrines.'

✳ He waited, shivering in the cold air. If he were caught outside his sleeping block so late at night he'd be killed on the spot. Mauled by those dogs. The Bedouin hadn't mentioned a time; he could be waiting here all night. He'd volunteered to be the one to empty the slops out in the shallow ditch that served as a latrine, to rinse out the bucket, to bring it back where it stood stinking all night by the door.

He'd been here many minutes now, maybe even five. Ten. Too long. He squatted in the ditch among the turds and felt his bare feet sink into the moistness of earth fed with excrement. He didn't hold his nose; after the corpses he managed to carry all day, this was easy. Still, he didn't like the sensation of it on his soles and worming around his toes. He fought the need to retch, but there was nothing in his stomach. *Maybe the Bedouin has been and gone. Maybe he's going to betray me too.*

Barking. The soft, crunching sound of bare feet on sand. He crouched still further into the ditch, until the spongy mass of it touched his nose. He covered his eyes with his hands. *If I'm mauled, I don't want to see it coming.* He heaved, tried not to cry. *After everything I've seen, why am I so scared?* A light hand on his arm.

'Quick, Nazarene.'

It was the Bedouin.

'I managed to come in on the pretext of bringing them some *mansaf*. Run now. They will not be eating it for long.'

He swathed Minas in a dark bolt of fabric, winding it around his face and neck.

'Good. Now you look more like us.'

He followed the Bedouin's swishing robe to the very perimeter of the camp, on the south side, which the Turks usually manned with only one or two men. He saw a guard holding a gun and panicked.

'I can't,' he panted. 'I'm scared.'

The Bedouin put his finger to his lips, miming sleep. Minas looked again. The guard – just a boy – was indeed sleeping upright, head sagging, the gun almost slipping off his shoulder.

The Bedouin smiled, a flash of teeth and grimace in one, and cupped his hands low to the ground. Minas looked up at the barbed-wire fence; it was too high, but he saw that the Bedouin had thrown a saddle over it to ease his passage.

'Come. Use my hands. Jump up high. My cousin is waiting on the other side.'

He jumped, scraped his torso against the barbed wire, wincing at the sound, and managed to climb over, lacerating his whole body. When he landed in the sand on the other side, he felt his right leg buckle and knew he'd sprained an ankle. The cousin helped him to his feet. Limping, quietly sobbing, he clambered behind him onto a spitting, groaning, exasperated camel.

✷   Minas remembered his sister: her half-smile, the way he laughed at her long plait and pulled it hard so she screamed. There was not much else to do, except think and remember. He thought of the girl he left behind at the camp. Her own greasy braid, cold as a snake between his fingers at night. He tried not to think of her again. He'd been hiding now in the litter under a pile of rugs for too long. His thigh muscles ached, his neck permanently twisted to one side, his throat tickled then shut down completely from lack of fluid. The Bedouin gave him water twice a day with his food but in this heat he craved liquid constantly. The dried strips of unidentifiable meat they gave him increased his thirst only the more.

On the first night, they pressed a cold, mealy compress of some desert herb on his ankle, bandaged the swelling and left it to heal. He reached inside the swaddling now and scraped some of the paste onto his fingers, tasted it and immediately spat it out. It did not quench his thirst and was decidedly bitter. He regretted the loss of saliva. He moved his ankle cautiously now, flexing it back and forward, feeling the warning twinge of pain all the way up his thigh.

At sunset he was let out for a few minutes with a handful of dates. He balanced on one leg, holding his penis, pissing in a trickle and gazing at the promise of a new world. The Bedouin had laughed at him the first time; they all knelt to urinate in an attitude of prayer. He continued to stand, heedless of their remarks, gazing out at a landscape with no horizon. The colours of the dunes and pillars of sand became softer, although at the same time more distinct: shimmer pinks and beaten gold and tinges of night blue. Clay dwellings in the distance were shaped like helmets fashioned of copper, ancient headdresses for long-dead Armenian men. His dates were fresh and plump, syrupy. The sensation on his tongue overwhelming. While he ate them, they alone constituted the sum of his existence. He kept the few date pips in his mouth until he had extracted every last molecule of sweetness from them, until they resembled pellets of bone, sparking a jolt of memory.

The young Bedouin hadn't accepted the earrings after all. He waved Minas's offer away with wide smiles and clicking sounds and said he was as glad as Minas to be going far away from those Turks, to be travelling to Damascus to buy kilim saddlebags and tea sets and iridescent veils for the long journey back to Baghdad. They had gold enough this season, he said. Their trade was good. They sold their wares for twice the price the further east they went. Better than any amount of gold was the coinage of heaven. And by saving him, hopefully the Bedouin had paid some of his dues.

Sometimes people would sit on top of the pile of rugs and woollen saddles and he almost suffocated in the odour of hot flesh and drying sweat. At those moments he felt the Bedouin were torturing him for their own pleasure instead of aiding his escape. He cursed them under his breath as vile Arabs, traitors, sadists as bad as any Turk. He waited until the next meal, the next morsel tossed from camel-blackened hands. He begged for more water, clutching at his throat, but the boy assigned to him didn't understand, or didn't want to.

When they left him in Damascus he had no idea what to do. They had provided him with a clean set of clothes in the Arab style; it took him several days before he grew used to feeling the loose fabric swirl across his calves, the uprush of air on his genitals as he walked, limping at first, then slowly gaining in strength. Even in all his fear and confusion, sometimes the airiness of his new clothes made him desire another's body. He wandered the streets in this way, patting the beard that had grown sparse and wispy as a grandfather's in patches over his cheeks. Reddish, he assumed, as his father's had once been. He had no mirror.

He tried to catch a glimpse of his reflection in shop windows or in mounds of scattered glass on the road but he never managed to see any detail or colour, only his smudge of a face, features clouding, insubstantial. He bared his teeth at himself like an animal. Over the last months in the desert and with the Bedouin he had become a man.

He scavenged in piles of refuse for discarded food and drank full to bursting from the elaborate fountains on every street corner. He didn't want to sell the earrings, not yet. He had sewn them into the hem of his garment before he left the Bedouin, with needle and strong thread they gave him. He wasn't sure where he wanted to go next, or what to do with the money if he sold them. At the same time he grew to like Damascus and was loath to leave. Its open squares and fountains were bathed in early morning light, where he washed fully clothed with the city beggars. Spikes of sun came through the high palms that shaded its thoroughfares. The water raining over his body made cataracts of silver that fanned out into the circling streets, wetting flower sellers, donkeys laden with watermelons and boiled sweets and bananas, or the derelicts that seemed more affluent to Minas than himself. The mosques and museums offered shaded courtyards where he could sleep and rest in the noonday heat, sometimes even eat a meal when pilgrims and mourners dispensed their largesse of crescent-shaped cakes and jellies to all the beggars.

He made a habit each day of walking through the dim archways of the gold souk, wondering how much his earrings would be worth. He pressed his nose to the polished-glass fronts of jewellery shops, street upon street. They were all the same. Tiny bands of gold for newborn babies, miniature fragments of the Koran on thin chains, garish belts of carnelian and chased silver. *Papa's were better than these.* He straightened up, caught a blur of his own reflection in the glass. *I can do better than these.* He wondered if he could stay in Damascus, settle into life as a shopkeeper and fashioner of gold. In the next breath he dismissed the thought. *I'm a refugee, for God's sake. I don't even have any shoes.*

He passed a stall on the corner near the Umayyad mosque and begged for food by placing both hands together and bowing his head.

The vendor gave him a dried husk of corn, assuming he was a Muslim pilgrim. At noon when the sun reached its zenith he entered the mosque compound and lay with believers in the shade of jasmine vines that ran riot over gates and crumbling stone walls. He slept with the scent of his mother all about him. He dreamed of her, a pale shade dead for little less than a year now. His sister gone with a Turk seven months ago. Probably dead as well.

He knew he must leave soon; Damascus was not far enough away from the Turks, the great maw of the death camps. The straight road to Der ez Zor like a character meaning death. Those long evenings in the sleeping blocks, with nothing to do with other prisoners except reminisce, mourn the death of their culture. The Ark foundered on the shores of Lake Van, or Mount Ararat? Some of the old stories did not stick. He was living the myths now, writing in his body a new narrative of suffering. Surviving the deluge, as they had. Their land of Hayastan, now gone forever. Only the women had kept the old words alive. The tenacity of wives and mothers and sisters: women scratching letters in the sand as they marched, teaching their children the Armenian alphabet so it would not be lost forever.

The Armenian alphabet, milky words flowing like hidden springs in the desert. Mamma had told him a story, when she sat in the slight breeze from their Aykesdan window at dusk. How the creator of their alphabet, Mesrop Mashtots, died and was to be buried on a mountain far away. The walk to the burial site was long and hard, much as Minas now knew the forced marches were. The mourners suffered with thirst. They were fatigued, could go no further. His body was laid on the grass, and from the place at his feet appeared a spring of cold, bubbling water, pure as truth.

No miracles in the desert this time. The women suffered great thirst, great hunger, watched their babies pushed deep into sand, not laid to rest on grass. They took the holy manuscripts of mediaeval Armenia with them, cut in half, buried them with rituals, psalms for the dead. Tears mixed with blood, with sand, words fragmenting into syllables, cries of uncoded meaning. The letters remained in the sand for an instant, only to vanish in the careless desert wind. The women died. The children perished without language to guide them.

Minas broke off a thin branch from the jasmine above him and knelt in the dirt. *Armenia is no more*, he wrote, in the squat, round script Mamma had taught him. Near his foot, he saw a wet blade of grass, a yellowing jasmine leaf, its striations as curved as the Armenian alphabet, the white squares of light between the mosque walls – and he had to stop. There was a litany of names, dates. A dirge. Lilit. Mamma and Papa. Yervan. The pimpled girl. So many more. And what of the shadowy ones, the unknown?

The voice in his head reached a higher pitch. It taunted him with his apathy. He rubbed out his previous sentence. *Minas Pakradounian is no more*, he wrote. He would have to go away from here, to the farthest edge of land bordering the sea. He would go to Beirut.

❄ Lilit stopped short when she saw Suleiman coming toward her. She thought of turning around and going the other way but it was too late – he'd already seen her. She drew her veil tighter around her face but knew he would recognise the cut of her clothes and her swaying walk, the advanced pregnancy singling her out from other women of the neighbourhood.

He came alongside and pressed his mouth to her veil.

'What are you doing away from the house without my permission?'

She felt flecks of his saliva on her cheek through the fabric. She didn't know how to begin, or even if it was wise to begin at all. He hauled her into the courtyard, gripping both her wrists in one of his hands.

'You're hurting me, Suleiman! Don't pull so hard.'

'Where have you been? What have you been doing?'

She unwound the veil from her face, let it fall to the floor in a heap. Suleiman came closer, thrusting his face into her line of vision.

'Tell me why you were out of the house. Bringing shame onto me and my household.'

From the corner of her eye she saw Fatima by the door, woken by Suleiman's shouting. She was wearing bathroom clogs, looked awkward without her jewelled slippers. Lilit remembered her own clogs, once bright as pomegranates, drifted for a moment, wondering where they ended up after the gendarme speared them with his bayonet and flung them into the garden. She had a vision of hundreds of shoes sprouting from tree branches, dangling fruit of painted wood. Looking into Suleiman's eyes, illuminated by the memory, there was a moment of tenderness, of possibility. *I don't have to be afraid of you.*

Fatima moved slower than usual, as if a small part of life was drained out of her body. She made her way through the courtyard, reached up to touch the trembling fronds of the date palm as she passed. The cook shadowed her, wiping streaks of sheep's blood on her apron, wearing the same neutral expression she always cultivated when in the presence of a man.

Lilit whispered, 'Not in front of them.'

Suleiman slapped her twice, once on each cheek.

'Yes, in front of them! I want them to listen and learn.'

She straightened, looked Suleiman in the eye. Her cheeks were pulsating; the sudden pain gave her power. *There's nothing to lose now.* She made her voice high and shrill and fast so she could be carried away by its insistence, unafraid of what would happen when it stopped.

'Fatima wanted me to give her our child then run away and leave you, and we've been planning it for months now and I couldn't bear to give my baby away to her so I decided to leave today but then I came back because I was afraid and now I'm scared she'll punish me and so will you, and I don't know what to do.'

She stopped, felt the fear she'd kept at bay filling her lungs. She prepared herself for a beating, a swift drowning in the shallow pool, or a public death with the imam nodding in assent. Suleiman wheeled around, beckoned Fatima to him with a crook of his finger. She took her time responding, her powdered face suddenly flushed red under her transparent veil.

'Kneel down,' Suleiman told her.

She knelt in front of him, ringed hands flat on her thighs, waiting. She didn't look at Lilit.

'Now bend your head and kiss Lale's feet.'

Fatima gasped, made as if to rise, but Suleiman held her down with one hand on her shoulder.

'Go on. Lift up her robe and kiss her feet.'

Lilit's knees turned to water. She saw Fatima look up at Suleiman imploringly, her eyes filling with tears under the veil. He remained impassive. She stood very still as Fatima crawled on her knees toward her, a bare shuffling on the wet tiles of the courtyard. It was an indecent, naked sound. *Oh God, she's going to kill me after this.*

Fatima lifted up the dusty fabric of Lilit's travelling cloak with one hand. Her breathing became heavier; it filled the courtyard. Lilit kept her eyes lowered, almost shut. *I should not have to see this. This should not be happening.* In a furtive movement, Fatima pressed her lips to Lilit's toes. Her mouth was warm and moist, too intimate. Lilit tried not to breathe as loudly in the ensuing silence.

Suleiman clapped his hands, once, then twice, as if summoning a slave. He knelt beside Fatima and placed his open hand on her head, forcing her to stay down. Lilit felt Fatima's jaw push hard against the delicate bones of her foot. Suleiman spoke precisely then, without emotion.

'Never, ever think you can abuse my love, Fatima.'

He stood up and turned to Lilit; she felt rather than saw the flash of his teeth.

'She will never hurt you again.'

Fatima stayed in the same position, lips pressed to Lilit's feet, a moment that seemed to last an eternity.

BEIRUT, 1982

There was a pall of silence over the whole city now. Even in Selim's suburb of Achrafiye, where brave cafe owners once served spiced-meat pastries and coffee to tired gunmen, the shops were shuttered, curtains drawn. With the PLO forced to leave Beirut the previous day under multinational supervision – dodging the hailing bullets of their own guns in pretence of a victory farewell – Sanaya felt her allegiances shift like an involuntary shiver down the spine.

They were shooting in the air for five days prior to their final leave-taking, with Arafat embarking on a Greek ferry for Tunis, now safely out of the way. She didn't go with all the other Muslims of west Beirut to see him off, afraid of being accidentally shot at in the clamorous streets, or of being too clear about her political loyalties. If she had any at all. By now she was too tired to be angry at herself for any lack of conviction.

For weeks, even months, she'd joined with the other inhabitants of west Beirut in tolerating, if not supporting, the presence of the PLO in their sector of the city. Of course she didn't want them there – it was common knowledge they were the cause of all the trouble. Yet she didn't want to hand them over to the Israelis either. It was all bound up in her refusal to abandon west Beirut. Leaving now would be conceding defeat. It had become a matter of pride in the streets to tape a poster of Abu Ammar – the people's Arafat – to the door of every building. For a brief moment, he was their undisputed hero.

Now she was in no-man's land once again. She tore down her poster of him, used it to duct tape over the smashed bathroom window, blank side looking out over the street. She thought resignedly that now she must endure his leer as she showered, his wide-armed gesture pointing not in the direction of an occupied Palestine, as before, but down the plughole. After two days she took out a thick felt pen and coloured in dark sunglasses over Arafat's greedy eyes.

Issa was no help. He taunted the retreating Palestinians as much as the Christian Maronites did. He rejoiced when the freedom fighters were nearly all gone, a wild look in his eye she had never noticed before.

'They're not true Muslims,' he said. 'Apostates.'

She questioned him, puzzled by such factionalism. Or revenge. Rouba had told her once that Issa had sought work with the PLO time and time again, but had no connections. He'd never been able to find a job, and before the war had believed he never would.

Now he leaned into her and whispered. 'I shouldn't be telling you this, Sanaya, but our future lies with Iran.'

Rouba told her he stayed up all night reading the Koran, then would leave at five for morning worship at the mosque. Not even the old, pious men made it to the dawn prayers. He muttered *suras* to himself as he shaved, as he ate the meagre breakfast Rouba forced upon him, as he stood for too long under the shower's trickle. He would only speak to Hadiya. She told her mother she'd grown sick of his favourite *sura* – and now she too knew it by heart, he'd chanted it aloud so many times. *Such is the paradise which the righteous have been promised, it is watered by running streams, eternal is its fruit, and eternal is its shade.*

Sanaya saw him in the corridors sometimes when she went for her walk, his cheeks more hollow than ever, dark rings punched beneath the eyes, his manner both wary of her and obsequious. *But the fire shall be the end of the unbelievers.*

'Issa!' she called to him, putting out her hand.

He was already gone.

The two women discussed him as they hung up the washing to dry one morning in the courtyard, hiding their concerns behind strung sheets and crumpled pillowcases. Hadiya sat in the shade cast by the wet washing, placed her five precious dolls before her in a perfect row. Their pink plastic faces were inscrutable, like little cats.

'Don't speak so loud,' Rouba said. 'He's right up there, watching us.'

Sanaya looked up over her line of pegs; Issa sat cross-legged on the window-seat of Rouba's living room, Koran open on his lap, eyes fixed, staring at her. She waved, smiled. He signalled back, a slow sweep of the

A
S
H

211

upper arm, but his expression remained unchanged. She turned away from him, shook out a shirt before hanging it up, murmured to Rouba.

'Is he going south again soon? To fight?'

'I have no idea.'

'Won't he tell you?'

'I don't think he knows himself. To tell you the truth, I think he's scared. Terrified. Something happened to him down there.'

Sanaya laughed; it came out as a high, hysterical snort.

'Well of course it did, Rouba! He killed people and saw his own friends being killed. Even his own—brother. I'm sorry. I didn't mean to …'

Rouba gave Sanaya a frigid stare, indicated Hadiya, who seemed unaware of their conversation, now making muddy tea for her dolls in pebble cups. They let the comment pass. Rouba hung up a pair of trousers, made Sanaya wait.

'No, I mean something more than that. I hear him in his sleep sometimes. He frightens Hadiya. Screams, calls out someone's name.'

'Whose?'

'I can never make it out. It's almost like he's pleading with someone to leave him alone.'

'Have you tried asking him?'

'I wouldn't dare to.'

Sanaya finished hanging up the clothes, her basket empty. She balanced it on one hip, made to leave.

'Well, then I will.'

'Don't even think about it! He'll know I told you.'

'I'm going up now to ask him. I need to know what's wrong with him.'

Rouba stopped Sanaya, grabbed her arm. Her voice had altered, a low growl akin to Issa's when he was threatened.

'I can't believe how selfish you are. Why do you always need to know everything? It doesn't look to me as if it's really about what's wrong with Issa at all. How about what's up with you?'

Sanaya could hardly find breath to speak.

'What do you mean, selfish? I—I care about him. He trusts me. It might do him some good to talk.'

'To you?' Rouba sneered. 'You wouldn't know the truth if it hit you in the eye.'

✳ She was shaken after Rouba's words. She went upstairs to her apartment, taking the steps two by two. She let herself in, flopped on the divan, looking around the living room. *Am I selfish?* She surveyed the splotched Turkish rug, an accident with wine, smoked salmon and Selim a few nights ago, the kitchen sink piled high with dishes. She looked through the open bedroom door at her slatternly, unmade bed. All those trivial, mindless tasks, unimportant to her, waiting for someone to transform them into imperatives.

She made herself some tea, spooning in less sugar than usual. Her precious store was dwindling in its little paper sack. After two glasses she recovered enough self-composure to dismiss Rouba's criticism. *Well, of course she'd think that. So different from me. She's only jealous.*

Growing up in a refugee camp south of Sidon, Rouba never knew a home other than that seen in postcards: out-of-date, grainy daguerreotypes, a mythic Palestine in scenes of the harbour and citrus orchards. Fabricated memories, second-hand grief. Old stories embroidered by a phalanx of women, generation upon generation. Of course she would resent Sanaya, who had never known displacement, except of the psyche, never known death, except in peace, never known hunger, except of the soul.

She should feel sorry for me. I might appear to have everything, but I have less than she does. She felt sorry enough for herself as it was. It had become sickening, a low, dull ache in regions undefined.

She remembered Rouba's ambivalent expression those nights during the air raids, when she would sit back and watch Sanaya and Issa joke, laugh, fight over winning at cards and backgammon. Sanaya put it down to the loss of her husband. There was something in the set of her jaw: not jealousy exactly, nor ill will, but a bitter wistfulness, as if Sanaya in her own lack of suffering was lighter, easier, more desirable to men. A blank page, an open book, a sheet drawn tight and pure against the past. She got up, went downstairs to the courtyard again, telling herself it was only to check if her washing was dry.

She looked up; Issa was still there, in his position at the window, except now he was chanting the Koran aloud and rocking back and forth. 'On that day they will all share in the scourge. Thus shall we deal with the evil-doers, for when they were told, *There is no deity but*

God, they replied with scorn: *Are we to renounce our gods for the sake of a mad poet?'*

She tried to tell herself this was normal behaviour for a devout man, and that even her father, a fair-weather Muslim, would do the same sometimes at the mosque on holy days. Nevertheless she was disturbed. Issa seemed to be in a trance. A bubble of ecstasy which no one else could penetrate. *If there was a wall in front of him, he'd bang his head against it. Fanatic.* She couldn't reconcile his apparent fundamentalism with his youth, his humour, his many kindnesses to her, his gentle hands.

Nor could she understand his hatred of America and Israel when she could also see his obvious devotion to Hollywood films, like any teenager: *Rambo* and *Terminator* and old black and white war movies, his collection of music tapes and videos. Those absolute pronouncements and professions of holiness, living as he tried to with the example of the Prophet, and then his absolute commitment to violence at any cost. A *shahid*, that was what he wanted to be. A holy martyr. He continued to rock, getting faster and louder, oblivious to her, staring up at him among the fluttering washing.

In all her fear, all her perturbation, something in him called to her.

❋ She watched Issa each day when he left the building at dawn. She told herself she wanted to do something for him, to help. By each afternoon, when she was finally honest with herself, she realised it was less about helping him than making him notice her. She'd become curious about him, now flattered by his small, almost unconscious attentions. She suppressed a thrill of something – she couldn't yet call it desire – when he leaned close to brush a mosquito from her arm as they sat outside on the balcony, when he asked her how much olive oil she liked drizzled on her beans when she brought them to the table.

There was more to it than that, she admitted. She heard how his voice dropped and wavered when he talked of the fighting, when she asked him who were his closest friends at the front. His insistence that his Iranian commander was a prophet, exactly like Mohammed himself, unnerved her in a way that contrasted with her indifference to Selim's professions of love for Bashir Gemayel. There was something in this desperate intensity that didn't ring true. And she wanted to be the one to unravel it. Show Rouba a thing or two. She wanted to buy Issa's trust so he would take her into his confidence.

Today he was later than usual. She stood in the shadow of the balcony and craned her body over the railing to see which direction he would take. He was wearing civilian clothes and could have been someone else entirely without his faded battledress. His jeans didn't sit well on him; she could see him attempt to pull them up around his waist as he walked. Couldn't Rouba find him a belt? She watched him cross the road toward the sea wall, look to the right and left as if afraid someone was following. He bought a plaited sesame bun from a hawker, walking brisk and sure toward the southern suburbs.

She flung off her bathrobe, dressed without giving any thought to what she should wear. Ripped clothes off their hangers, buttoned her blouse askew. Slid her feet into flat sandals. Before she left, she dropped to her knees and rummaged under the bed, shoving rolls of Selim's money into her pockets, stuffing them into her handbag. She slung it over her shoulder and sprinted down the stairs.

She was afraid she might have lost him already. She ran, swerving around cars and trucks, an abandoned tank, crossed the road, dodging the hawkers and beggars blocking her path. She couldn't see him. She ran faster than she ever thought she could, handbag banging against her hip. Patted her pockets at intervals to make sure the money was still there.

She saw his figure, far away, a speck against the sea.

'Issa!'

He didn't look around, if it was indeed him. She spied a taxi idling nearby, signalled to it and got in the back.

'Only down the road,' she said to the driver.

He shook his head at her without turning around. She peeled off a US ten-dollar note from one of her rolls, waved it at him in the rear-view mirror. He put his foot on the accelerator.

'Stop over there,' she said. 'Just behind that white car.'

She got out, almost falling into Issa's arms. He brought his right hand to his heart.

'What's wrong, Sanaya? Are Rouba and Hadiya—'

'No.' She was still breathing hard. 'I just needed to talk to you.'

He was perturbed, even slightly embarrassed, but motioned to the sea wall. They sat and she looked down at her feet, not sure where to start. Issa followed her gaze and looked down, too, apparently mesmerised by her toes with their chipped, pearly polish.

'Let's go somewhere and have a drink.'

Issa frowned.

'Not in a bar, please.'

She stood up, scanned the row of shops across the road.

'There's a place over there that looks all right.'

Once inside and seated on cushions, they ordered tea. She placed her hands flat on the low table. Mirroring her, Issa placed his palms down as well. They were nearly touching hers. The ends of his fingers were stained with henna, in memory of an obscure Shia martyr's blood. They were in the private family room of the restaurant, where gauze curtains partially hid them from the other patrons. In the corner against the wall, a group of heavily veiled women ate from ten different meze plates. The man with them stared hard at Issa, but said nothing. Sanaya whispered.

'I just want to help you, Issa.'

He straightened up, looked ahead at the polished counter through the curtains, the glass drinks shelves with nothing left on them to sell.

'You can't help me. I don't need your kind of help.'

'But your militia does.'

At this, she began taking the rolls of money from her pockets and thrusting them into his lap under the table. Issa recoiled, pushing them aside.

'I don't want your money! What are you doing, woman? Anyone could come in and rob you here.'

She sat back, shamefaced. The money lay strewn on the carpet. Methodically, Issa gathered it up. He fixed her with an unwavering, fanatic eye.

'How do I know how you made this money?'

She smiled.

'It's all above board, Issa. No drugs, no corruption.'

She knew she was lying and wondered if he did as well.

'You're not a—'

'A prostitute, Issa? Is that what you're trying to say?' She breathed out. 'Thank Allah, no.'

She thrust her handbag at him.

'There's more in there. I just want to help you.'

He drew the bag toward him and crammed the rest of the notes into it. For a moment she thought he would throw the whole lot at her. Then he slid the bag onto his lap. He looked about him at the room, avoiding the women, bowed his head at nothing in particular.

'Today, Sanaya, for the first time in your life, you have done something good.'

✖ Selim passed from woman to woman at the luncheon party. He was not aware of flirting, would be terribly embarrassed if the epithet were applied to him. Yet he did know he was working the room. It was his duty. His silk tie and tight collar made him itch in the hot August sun that came through the concertina doors. He dabbed at his face with a monogrammed handkerchief; women always found this quaint and endearing. As they did his imperfect French.

By sunset he'd ended up on the front terrace with a daughter from one of the north's most stately families, a teenager with ashy hair – he could see it had been dyed by one of the best – and an impossibly short dress. He became distracted counting the number of frills on such a small piece of fabric, all the way from plunging neckline to hem. She kept asking him to hold her glass while she pulled the skirt down over her speckled, dimply thighs. Surprisingly, she made him think of Sanaya with fondness and something like regret.

Women tended to do that for him: got jumbled up, faceless, all lips and breasts and eyes. Even the one he married, blurred now, unrecognisable. There were small, insignificant scenes that stayed with him, but they always featured her young and wild, when she'd been a rebellious teenager and crept into his bedroom each morning at first light. He filled the girl's drink, lit her cigarette, looked out with her over the glistening, pristine coastline of Jounieh, but his thoughts were elsewhere.

The girl was speaking about the new colourist she'd found in Milan. He tried to extricate himself from the conversation, asked if she would like him to fetch her another drink. He was trying not to appear too attentive to any woman, or any one man, tonight; his instincts were trained on Bashir. The party had been held in his honour, to celebrate his election and rise to power. Bashir Gemayel, new president of the Republic of Lebanon. Devout Christian, militia leader, elegant killer, Selim's idol. He would like to kill so well, to speak French so fluently, to charm women with a flick of his hair.

Through the terrace doors, Selim could see Bashir on a brocade armchair in the middle of the room, sipping champagne from a crystal glass. His florid, high-coloured face smoothed by a sun-lamp tan. He threw back his head and laughed at something a man beside him had said, and Selim could see the blackened fillings in his molars.

He made his excuses to the princess, not before making sure she had somebody else to talk to. He made his way through the doors and across the room to Bashir, sank to one knee before him and kissed his outstretched hand. Nearby, he could sense his commander Elie Hobeika staring at him – was it in approval or distrust? – with his deathly cheekbones and frowning eyes.

'Monsieur,' Selim breathed. 'An honour, as always.'

Bashir tossed his glass to a servant, helped Selim up with both hands.

'None of that! Well, Selim. Selim, my good soldier. Are you enjoying our little gathering?'

'Immensely, monsieur. A pleasure to be in your presence.'

Bashir waved away the compliment.

'How do you like the barman? We brought him all the way from Paris.'

Selim watched the little man pouring drinks with a sullen expression and mechanical flourishes of the wrist.

'I see the Israeli officers are all here.'

Bashir looked across at the bar, where the Israelis had gathered. Selim thought he could perceive a slight wrinkling of distaste in the perfect nose, the full, pink-tinged mouth.

'Yes, indeed they are all here, Selim.'

He followed Bashir's gaze to the officers, noticing the relaxed gestures of their arms, their wide-open stance as they lolled at the marble counter. They handed around drinks to the socialites who milled and fluttered about them like bedraggled birds of paradise. One of the officers elbowed Bashir's barman out of the way and now stood in his place, mixing cocktails with far too many different spirits, and cutting up indecent wedges of fruit.

At the end of the bar Selim recognised Alon Herzberg, the fighter pilot he'd met – it now seemed so long ago – on the hills above the city when the Israelis first arrived. He lounged by himself, picking at pistachios. The Israelis appeared so at home here, in Bashir's villa, almost as if it was they hosting the party and not he.

He saw Bashir's father, Pierre, sitting in a corner with an Israeli commander. Two old grey heads conferring close together, two boys plotting mischief. Combined cufflinks gleamed. They seemed so immersed in each other he thought twice before approaching, but the old man saw him and beckoned him to them.

'Ah, Selim! How good to see you here, my boy.'

He knelt in front of the old man, bowing his head for a moment. He made a curt salute and put out his hand to shake that of the Israeli, murmured his name and position.

'Pleasure.'

Pierre looked from one to the other with crinkled, beady eyes.

'What a happy day this is, gentlemen. The culmination of all our beleaguered dreams.'

'All our dreams,' the Israeli echoed, and smiled with satisfaction at Selim.

✳ At the news of Bashir Gemayel's 'election' as president, Sanaya told herself she should continue to side with the winners while still helping the losers. That way she could do so much more. At times she wondered why she bothered anyway. Wasn't everyone looking after their own interests, just trying to survive?

'Bashir is our father,' Selim said at night in bed. He sat up and smoked, absent-mindedly flicking ash on the sheets. 'He's closer to being the son of God than Christ himself was.'

She sighed, rubbing at the ash mark that only seemed to spread. She took off her dressing-gown, sat on the edge of the bed with her back to him.

'You're mad. He's a thug and a killer.'

She said the words automatically, knowing they made no impact, not sure herself whether she could any longer recognise the truth. As she lay beside Selim in her satin-sheeted bed she told herself yet again she wasn't really a traitor. She'd helped Issa's Shia militia with money from Selim and, by default, with money from their worst enemies the Phalange. She'd attained her fortunate position, neither Christian nor really Muslim, through less than scrupulous means, she accepted that, and this little outburst was just a continuation of her habit of taking no side. If any of it would drive out the Israelis, then so be it. Yet this was the first time she'd dared to question him outright since their meeting with the Israeli pilot.

'Operation Peace for Galilee,' she mocked. 'They've come here to bring *peace.*'

'Exactly. Terrorist targets are under attack. And I don't know why you're laughing like that.'

'Am I a terrorist?'

She couldn't stop herself from laughing, as if all the fear and bitterness of the past weeks could find only one outlet – the high, hysterical snort of a mechanism beyond her control.

'I keep telling you to come and live in east Beirut. And it's no laughing matter.'

'Oh no, Selim, it's no joke.'

'Isn't it?'

And he'd wrestled her back onto the bed.

'The shelling's smashed our water pipes,' she said.

'*Bon,*' he growled. 'Now you'll have to come live with me.'

'I'm getting a rash,' she whispered in his ear. 'You won't want to touch me.'

She submitted to his large caresses, let her body drown in this brief state of luxury, of such careless irresponsibility. *Four hundred civilians blasted to death in their waterfront apartments*, she murmured. Or did she only think it? Selim was intent on his own breathing. Her limbs were inert and heavy while her mind floated on the waves of his proximity: *slowly, please; no conscience, faster; no opinions; frenzied until he was finished; no guilt.* Only the strong yet gentle force of his two thick legs between hers, his face and torso blocking out the light, the sounds outside, her own tenuous arguments.

When he left, she fantasised about telling him it was all over. *Never come back, I don't want you anymore. Your politics sicken me.* Didn't she always tell people she was apolitical? It had been easier to say before the war. Now, in her deliberate flitting from side to side – Christian Maronite to Muslim, Phalangist to Shia freedom fighter – she'd split her allegiances, fractured her sense of self.

✳   Selim was driven back to east Beirut once again by a different militiaman. He said his name was Gilbert when Selim questioned him. The driver knew the routine, briefed at dawn by the others: Monsieur liked to take black coffee and brandy in the morning before reporting to HQ. Gilbert waited in the car, eyes trained on Selim's every movement, pistol at the ready in case there was trouble.

Selim watched the driver from the corner of his eye. It was good to be protected. Good to feel safe. He ordered another brandy with an understated gesture. A man used to getting his own way. The waitress smiled at him when she placed the glass on the marble top. He pressed a crisp note into her hand, smiled back. He liked to feel attractive, it made him strong. He watched the girl's tight black skirt and swell of buttocks as she bent over an empty table to wipe it clean. Sex with Sanaya always did that to him: a heightened consciousness of eroticism in the most innocuous of places. The girl turned around to smile again, she had dark, short hair and a milkiness to the skin not often found in hot climates.

He liked her. He called her over to him again. He liked her very much. She was about the same age as the daughter he never knew. Sixteen. Maybe seventeen. Maybe she even looked like his daughter, the way she was now. Anoush, they had decided to call her. Well, he had nothing to do with it – it had been Anahit's choice the moment the baby was born. That in itself alienated him from his daughter – she wasn't really his; she was some interloper Anahit had manufactured all on her own. She had wailed without stopping for an hour after her birth, writhing and slippery, refusing to nurse at Anahit's breasts, as if she had some intimation of her mother's impending death. Selim had tried to hold her but she flailed and wriggled so much her swaddling came off

and the nurse took her away. He called for the nurse to bring her back –
he wanted to hold his baby again, skin to skin, but the woman ignored
him, and his aunts ushered him out of the room. He could hear the baby
crying as he left, wondered if she smelled him, missed him, sensed who
he was.

When he had left that next day, he didn't say goodbye to anyone.
Not his mother, nor his father, especially not his aunt Lilit, that scheming
bitch. It was all too much for him. He'd been trapped.

What is it about me? Selim had thought, as he stood behind Anahit
and watched her puff out her cheeks and strain, the tendons in her neck
double their size. *Why do I have to suffer?* He placed his hands under
her arms and held her spine upright against the bedhead, but her whole
body seemed swollen and inert, as if she were drowned. She pushed and
pushed but the baby wouldn't come out. Her breathing was violent,
unbearable to listen to. She slapped at the nurse's hands when the young
woman tried to massage her belly. She wanted nobody to touch her
anymore.

She moved about the room like a caged animal, changing position,
crouching, rocking her pelvis back and forth, crawling on all fours. She
swore in Armenian and Arabic. She grazed her cheek on the rough wool
of the rug. When she vomited and clutched at a chair leg, beating at
the floor, Lilit guided her back onto the bed. Selim helped her lie down
again, then went and sat on a chair in the corner. Anahit's eyes followed
him, but she didn't speak. The accusation was foremost in her face, plain
for all to see. *Accusation of what? That I made her pregnant? That I'm here
at all?*

She'd been trying for twelve hours now, it seemed more like days.
She didn't want to go to hospital. Selim thought about ringing an
ambulance, hauling her into it even if she screamed and kicked, but he
was too tired. Maybe it was time now. Maybe she was ready to birth, and
he would be interrupting the process. He was beginning to feel tired and
sweaty, couldn't remember the last time he washed, or had something to
eat. *Why are they all looking at me like that? It's not my fault she can't do it
properly.*

The oldest nurse didn't want him present at the birth. She said
it brought bad luck and punishment for the masculine and feminine

principles to be confused at such an amorphous time. Demons would surely come up to earth and take over. Now it seemed as if she was telling the truth. Even his aunt and mother drew him aside and shook their heads, saying, 'It's not right, Selim. You should be waiting outside.' He was tempted, but now he was here; to leave Anahit at this juncture seemed too close to cowardice. If he upset the order of the universe by being at the birth, it was already too late. He helped tie hot towels around her lower back and belly. He brought buckets of steaming water from downstairs and arranged them around the bed. What they were for, he wasn't quite sure. Perhaps, he told himself as he sat back in the corner, he was expiating in this way for some future sin. Abandonment and escape. It had to be done. He couldn't survive in this household. But this was not the time.

On the bed, Anahit kept her mouth shut tight against the pain. Now she would not scream. The nurses begged with her to help a little by letting out a breath at least, or by grunting and moaning as other women did, but she kept silent. Her bright rabbit's eyes stayed fixed on Selim as if he were the only answer.

An hour later, she was dead. He tied the shoelaces on his boots with shaking hands, bending over with one eye on the door in case someone walked in. His bedroom. For a few months, his and Anahit's. There were still traces of her there: the damp imprint of her head on the pillow next to his, her nightgown flung over the chair when Lilit had undressed her and wrapped her body in a stiff, crackling sheet.

He could hear the keening of the old women his father had engaged, murmured conversations beneath, rattling plates and forks being passed back and forth. The new baby tugging then pausing to scream at the wet nurse's breast. They christened her Anoush while Anahit was still alive: the choice of name her mother's last wish. There was a hasty baptism at her bedside by the priest who married them, in case the baby died, too, so at least she could follow her mother to heaven.

Selim buttoned his coat high at the collar and wound his scarf doubly thick around his neck. It had become a ritual for him, comforting as a child's blanket clutched tight to the chin. The lambswool soft and yielding, like a mother. He scrawled a hasty note, wincing at how trite it was to leave such a banal record of his existence, to apologise in advance for causing grief. The pen bled onto the page then ran out, scratching at the paper. He shook it for a moment, then decided he'd written enough. He left the note on the end of the bed, weighted with the edge of the coverlet.

He took one last look at his bedroom as he stood at the open door. Anahit's red shoes lay discarded: the right one under the bed, the left one heel up near the window. He knelt down and put the two shoes together at the foot of the bed, as if she'd just stepped out of them. This made him feel as if he wasn't abandoning her at all.

He planned on slipping out the side door under the pomegranate tree. He hadn't packed much: one change of clothes, his identity papers, a thick envelope of money given to them both at the wedding. Yet he took the silver bracelet Anahit had worn since she was a child, stripped it from her wrist before the women undressed and sponged her. He knew Lilit would miss it at some point and take note. Take note of what, his selfishness, avarice, cruelty? Who cared anyway? The bracelet was some reminder of his cousin at least, a cheap, glinting token of her girlish need. He wore it now on his own wrist, far too tight so it bit into his flesh, but he told himself he deserved the constant reminder, the sensation of pain. *Let me bleed too.* Or at least it allowed him to pretend he had suffered as she had.

He took a moment to look in the hall mirror, smoothed the fine down on his upper lip with a lick of saliva. His hands were shaking again and he ignored them, instead looking more intently at his reflected face. His mouth so close to the mirror he could see a small circle of fog, his breath frozen on the glass. It was a necessary distraction, so that he wouldn't have to think too deeply about Anahit's death, his new baby daughter, what he was about to do. Look in the mirror, concentrate on the easy problems of the material, of pores and pimples and hair. His features did not please him – had never pleased him. He didn't look Lebanese enough, or tough enough. And militiamen needed proper moustaches. After all, didn't Father once sport one, soft and bushy, in those grainy shots from his fighting days? Selim was on his way to becoming a hero too. He'd already been given his first rifle by the Phalangists in secret, and offered military training in the Catholic monasteries of the north. If he showed talent there, he would be sent to Galilee with the Jews for specialised training in the techniques guerrilla commandos used. He would have to convert from Armenian Orthodox to Maronite, but that was a small sacrifice. Already he'd been to confession, knelt in a box with the faceless priest, but couldn't think of any sins. The old man had been kind, taking him down into the crypt afterward to show him all the armaments the church had agreed to store for the Phalange. He was struck by how much like a simple, work-worn peasant the frail Father looked.

'This is a sacred war we're fighting,' he whispered, his breath rank on Selim's cheek.

He suppressed a brief stab of regret as he closed the gate behind him. He expected to feel something more for his newborn child, or for Anahit's death, but it was his father he suddenly pained for. *I only married her to please you, Father. Honour. To keep that stupid shop in the family too. Because we all know who really owns it, don't we?* And yet it wasn't good enough. Nothing was ever good enough. *Don't shame me again, my son.* Father had slapped him on the back and settled the marriage crown more firmly on his head. Selim winced at the gesture: uncareful, off-hand. It was then he thought: *Fine. If you really think I can't measure up then I'll leave.*

As soon as Anahit took her last breath, the family's accusation was worse. He could feel the disapproval in their eyes. *If it weren't for you she would still be alive. You made her pregnant too early. Then you had the audacity to be present at the birth.* Little did they know. Or maybe they did. He knew Lilit had something to do with it. Anahit seemed so sure that night at the university that she had her period, she was used to this, knew what she was doing. He even saw her blood, smeared it on rough concrete with his fingers. She said she didn't want anything from him, that it was just fun, harmless fun. After all, wasn't this the sixties? Americans in the movies she watched were doing it all the time.

He paused on the pavement outside the house. Inside, he could see figures moving slow and trance-like before the windows, could hear the low, painful pitch of women crying. He made a gesture as if to brush something aside, and stepped out onto the road to flag a taxi.

The waitress stood before him now, almost awkward, balancing a laden tray on her hip. It was crammed with half-full coffee cups and crumbs.

'Monsieur, did you want anything else?'

'Put your tray down; it must be heavy.'

'I'm sorry, monsieur, I can't. My father is watching.'

He raised his eyebrow at the little man behind the counter, who nodded. He touched the side of her face with one finger, got up and sauntered toward the car.

�   More leaflets. Pink and tan, less shocking than the first, now the worst prophecies had been fulfilled. They piled in a snowdrift on the balcony, carpeting the streets thick and silent with the non-sound of shoes impacting on soft paper.

Men of Beirut
If you value the lives of your women and children
take them and leave the west of the city now

They're not addressed to me, Sanaya said, and tore them up.

✷   Issa came back for sporadic visits now he was officially stationed in Beirut, fighting Israelis and Phalange with combined Shia militias on the borders. It was early September now; the sea swelled in anger and appeared even more blue, but the days and nights were hot as summer past. Only at dawn when Sanaya woke and then couldn't get back to sleep, when she sat on the balcony nursing her tea and a cigarette, did she draw her mother's dressing-gown tighter around her against the breeze. Then she felt the possibility of autumn, the hope for peace in the promise of cool air.

Rouba still stayed away, barely acknowledging her in the courtyard or corridor. Nothing sincere had passed between them for weeks, nothing more than a swift nod and a puzzled stare. It hurt. She couldn't stop herself from turning away, hiding the sudden sting of tears at such overt indifference. Rouba still sent Hadiya upstairs to her, though – or did the child beg her mother to visit each morning? At any rate, she was thankful she still saw Hadiya once a day, was allowed to give her chocolate milk and brush her hair. Yet Rouba's disapproval remained heavy. It was more than the conversation they had at the washing line.

Rouba couldn't pretend she condoned Sanaya's relationship with Selim, now she guessed its true nature. She assumed Issa too knew of Selim's clandestine visits, from Rouba, yet hoped he would keep her secret and not betray her to his superiors. There was no use thinking about what they would do to her, no use being frightened. She had to trust Issa, Rouba too. At the same time Sanaya felt that Rouba was not exactly pleased about Sanaya's recent friendship with Issa. She avoided speaking about him when Sanaya asked.

Sanaya allowed Issa to visit again, even welcomed him, more so now Bashir Gemayel had been assassinated – by the Israelis? Palestinians? Syrians? By his own? – after less than a month in power. It looked as though the Muslim majority might govern Lebanon after all. Issa spent most nights downstairs with Rouba, and Sanaya stifled a pinprick of jealousy when she thought of what they did there together, all alone in the dark.

She tried to draw Issa out when he was home, sat him beside her on the divan and asked about fighting in the south, the militias he aligned himself with in Beirut. She polished her nails when he was around, brushed her hair, darned underwear, treating him in the familiar fashion she would a female confidante, or a household pet she spoke to from time to time. Issa sat with his legs drawn up under his knees, bit his nails in a reverse mirroring of her movements.

'Is it hard for you, Issa? To get up every morning and know that today you might die?'

'It's the same for you. You could be bombed today, or any other day.'

'It's different, and you know it. I have no control, but you do.'

'How?'

'You choose to go out there and fight. You can decide how many you kill or don't kill.'

He smiled at her, a tight, patronising smile.

'You lie to yourself if you think I have control. My life is in Allah's hands, just as much as yours.'

She flounced up from the divan, gathered tea glasses from the low table at his side.

'I'm tired. Time for you to go now.'

'Why? What's wrong?'

'I'm sick of being sneered at, Issa.'

'Who's sneering?'

'You are. Condescending to me.'

'I'm merely telling you the truth.'

'Your truth! Allah protect me from your lies then.'

She strode to where he still lolled on the divan, put her face inches from his.

'What really happened to you down south, Issa? Why do you keep having nightmares?'

Issa half rose, then flopped down on the divan again when he saw she wouldn't move.

'Who told you that? It's a lie.'

'Bullshit.'

'Don't swear in front of me.'

'Who are you to tell me I can't?'

'Nobody, Sanaya. I'm nobody, if that's the way you want it.'

With that, he pushed past her and slammed the door behind him.

✳ Issa sat downstairs on the spare-room bed, nursing his Koran. He looked up at the ceiling, Sanaya's bedroom right up there above him. If he jumped up, he could touch her ankle, wind his fingers around it, drag her down to him here.

He opened the holy book randomly, chanted aloud. 'But the true servants of God shall be well provided for, feasting on fruit, and honoured in the gardens of delight. Reclining face to face on soft couches.' He stopped reading and thought of Sanaya's questions. So many questions, what did she want? And how did she know about his nightmares? The way he called out his commander's name every night and woke, sweaty and shivering, afraid Rouba and the child had heard. Chief, his men called him. His hands were strangely soft for a soldier's, clammy and spongy, knuckles constantly ridged with unhealed scratches. His grip was tight, though, on shoulders, wrists, around other soldier's necks. Issa saw him strangle a young boy, only to teach him a lesson, just long enough to knock him unconscious, not long enough for him to die.

Then there were those nights. When the moon was new and frail, so enveloped by scudding cloud that the consistency of dark would muffle sound, self, coherent thought. That nameless fear again. On those nights, Chief's grip was tight on Issa's hair, his waist, over his mouth, choking him so he wouldn't scream.

Now he looked out the spare-room window. Through the mess of buildings and balconies and aerials he could catch a glimpse of sky, blood orange fading to rose. Nightfall, and with it the advent of Selim, that bastard.

He ran up the single flight of stairs, tapped on Sanaya's door. She opened it after what seemed like too long, stood peering out at him through a sliver of light.

'Open up,' he pleaded. 'I was wrong.'

'Now is not a good time,' she whispered.

Behind her he could sense candles being lit, shuffling in the room, jazz playing.

'But I want to tell you something. I need to tell you.'

'Not now.'

'It's about what happened to me—down south. I need to tell someone.'

She looked panicked, harassed. He could see a thick vein pulsing at her neck. Pulsing, pulsing, telling him to go away.

'I can't. Some other time.'

'Is he here?'

She nodded, resigned. He put his hand out, brushed the side of her neck where the jugular throbbed, and left.

✳ Sanaya mused over Issa as she wandered around her apartment with nothing to do. After their talk that revealed nothing at the half-opened door, something had altered between them. There was a subtle respect revealed, an unspoken tenderness. As if Issa were the little brother she never had.

Part of her knew this was wishful thinking, idealism, her own special brand of naivety. There was an undercurrent of danger to his laughter, a hot iciness to his gaze, an edge to his monopoly of her time.

He lounged on the divan now on most afternoons, sharing whatever treats he scrounged at the borders with her, and read parts of the Koran aloud, bullying her to adopt the veil. He never mentioned Rouba, seemed unaware of any coolness between the women, and for this Sanaya was thankful. It was Hadiya she still missed most of all. The morning visits were never long enough, and she took pleasure in every opportunity to ask him about her. He ignored her, continued intoning classical Arabic in the singsong voice he affected when respectful.

'Enjoin believing women to turn their eyes away from temptation and to preserve their chastity; not to display their adornments (except such as are normally revealed) to draw their veils over their bosoms and not to display their finery except to—'

'My adornments are normally revealed, Issa. And it's time for you to go. I'm sure Rouba has something fresh for you to eat from the stall. All I have are pickled turnips from last year.'

'Are you waiting for someone else?'

'Why should I be?'

'You seem in a real hurry to get me out the door.'

He got up and walked to the window.

'What's this I see? A big German car in front of our block. A man in a flashy suit getting out. Looks Christian to me.'

'Don't forget Christians once lived here too, Issa. Don't forget you're living illegally in a Christian's home.'

'Illegally! There's no law anymore but that of Allah. And you're flouting it by sleeping with that man. I should tell my comrades to come and stone you both.'

'So why don't you?'

As soon as she said that she regretted it. He came closer and put his mouth against her neck, with contained violence.

'Because I want you alive more than I want you dead.'

A languid knock on the door. His lips still pressed to her throat. She hesitated, paralysed by indecision.

'Open it,' Issa said. 'I'd like to meet him.'

'Please—don't say anything.'

She rubbed her neck in a swift motion, opened the door, took the bottle Selim held forward with a pleading glance at Issa.

'Selim, this is my neighbour Issa, from downstairs.'

Selim put out his hand but Issa stayed where he was. He was examining Selim's tanned face, his large hair, the heavy silver bracelet that peeked out from his shirtsleeve. *Pimp. Pretty boy.*

'We've never forgiven you,' Issa said suddenly.

'Excuse me?'

'You Maronites.'

'I'm Armenian by blood. A refugee, just like you.'

'You are nothing like me.'

Issa swept through the door, almost knocking Selim off his feet.

✳ Issa found himself out on the Corniche without knowing how he came to be there. Sanaya. Her round upper arms, her soft thighs. He could see it; he saw it all. Not only did she scorn the veil, she walked around her house in sleeveless blouses, nightgowns, flimsy dresses. In all her glorious sexuality. She was beautiful. Beautiful in any light, at any time of day. He would not let himself think about it. He fixated on her imperfections, willing himself to stand back and see her as she really was, to rid himself of her honeyed influence: her less-than-perfect breasts, the slight hint of a double chin in profile.

He wandered around the seafront boulevard, gruff to the soft-drink vendors who made to approach him then stopped, cowed by his menace. He was ill-shaven, trying to grow a beard, heavy-lidded, stern-mouthed. They backed away, muttering, but not too loud. They were afraid of him. He liked that.

He sat on the low sea wall and allowed his back to be soaked by flurry after flurry of sea spray. He looked up at Sanaya's balcony, half-hoping to see the lovers in a static Hollywood embrace that could fuel his loathing of them and his own self-pity ever the more. A bleeding sun disappeared behind the mountains and thick hot night settled on the city with the consistency of grease. He watched Sanaya light candles, small stars against the balcony doors, saw her silhouette merge into shadow then stab itself into the glow as she glided about the room. Closer, then further away, her blurring outline pressed into relief.

He closed his eyes and listened to the waves for a while. When he looked up at the apartment again, Selim seemed to have gone, although he didn't remember seeing the car come to pick him up. Should he go to Sanaya? Would she welcome him the way she melted for Selim?

He glared at the narrow rectangles of light denoting living room, kitchen, bedroom. The apartment was aflame and she was alone. Her flickering figure moved back and forth from room to room, a body cloaked in dressing-gown silk, a wobbling inconsistency in the smoke from so many candles. She'd become unrecognisable to him. Not Sanaya. Not a woman he knew. Not even human, not fleshy, composed only of light.

She came outside and leaned over the balcony, puffing at a cigarette. He could see the ember glow through the outside gloom, see the towels she'd draped on the rusted railing, little white flags of surrender. He'd told her not to do that, even when others in the neighbourhood tied white sheets to aerials and rooftops in a vain attempt to deflect more Israeli bombs from civilian buildings. There couldn't be any surrender now. She was a traitor to her multiple causes, an idealist bent on satisfying illusion.

He saw her speak on the telephone, dragging the cord all the way out onto the edge of the railing until it could go no further. Who was she speaking to? Not Selim, surely. For a moment he thought he heard her laugh, high above the traffic. She saw him, yes? Her eyes were trained in an instant to the point where he sat, head upturned. He stood up, waved with one swoop of the arm. She went inside. She pulled the blinds down in the bedroom and the lights were extinguished, star by star, until all he could see were shrapnel wounds on the facade of her building, tiny mouths open in horror.

He spent the night at Hezbollah HQ, sleeping on the cool concrete of the floor under a desk. In the morning, while worrying over a cup of instant coffee, he decided to see his mother in the camp.

✳ Issa's mother was not expecting a visit, without even a crust of bread to welcome him with. She lay in bed by the paraffin stove as late as nine, for now autumn was approaching the mornings grew colder. Or seemed colder here perhaps, in this one-room concrete hut. She surveyed the damp walls with sleepy eyes: dust, spider webs, runnels of moisture from countless leaks in the roof. Maybe it was warmer outside. But there was nowhere to go, anyway. No shops or markets other than the same UNRWA tent selling carcasses of sheep or goat dangling on hooks and garlanded with flies, the same shopkeeper – 'Half a pound of stewing mutton again this week, Umm Issa?' – no public squares, no parks, no gardens. Nothing other than the same jagged main road, unpaved, rutted, looped with the same anti-Israeli graffiti, alongside anti-Hamas, anti-PLO, anti-Hezbollah slogans.

Her eyes closed again to block out her surroundings. She lay in bed and dreamed, roaming the travelling markets of her youth. It was a favourite pastime of hers when alone – which was often, except for the few aid workers or journalists brave enough to drop in and see how she was doing. It was always the same fantasy. In reality, she wouldn't have been allowed to leave the house without her mother or aunts or the servants to escort her, yet in her memory she was always free.

The markets had only come to her home in Jaffa on the days of great festivals, along with the fire-eaters and puppet shows and gypsies, but she remembered them as if it were yesterday. As if they alone defined her childhood before the Catastrophe, *Al' Nakhba*: the flight from everything she once knew. Her younger self moved under laden orange trees, balancing a basket low on the hip. She flicked her plait over her shoulder, straightened her best abaya to show more forehead. Swayed as she walked. She passed dried fruit in pyramids of improbable colours, was offered a handful of currants by the vendor. A crooked smile. She smiled back at him, lowering her eyes as she knew she should. Chunks of roasted sesame glowed with honey alongside aged cheeses, thick blue skins like the veins on a woman's thighs. She bought two of the knobbly rounds and placed them in her basket. She tasted spoonfuls from vats of yoghurt in various stages of setting, swirled by a broad wooden paddle. A blanket spread on the dirt with country bread and nothing else, for those too lazy to make their own. Only the very old women bought these. This younger self didn't know, didn't know she would one day be one of those women without a home.

Today she remembered a man she had actually met at the markets. She was out of her mother's grasp for a moment, old enough to wear the veil yet still young enough to resent it. An American Jew, tourist to the Holy Land, bored with guides and grinning touts. He stopped her under a stunted tree, asked her name. She wasn't married then, hadn't yet given birth to sons to mark her with their existence.

'Bilqis,' she said, blushing. 'Bilqis Al-Mansour.'

She was pleased he knew she was named for the queen of Sheba. He smiled and recited a phrase from his Bible in sonorous and strangely stirring tones. She was too young then, didn't understand his loss, a Jew with nowhere else to call home. Now she repeated the line to herself from half-closed lips. *A land of wheat and barley and vines and fig trees and pomegranates, a land of olive oil and honey.*

She stopped in the shade of an olive tree; *rumani*, she called them, legacy of the Roman invaders – the first invaders. She hesitated at a hand-lettered sign she was only just competent enough to decipher: *Baqlawa by the kilo*. She bought a whole tray, saw it wrapped in layers of paper, a hot cinnamon parcel at the top of her basket.

She didn't linger by the sheep marked red for slaughter. Lamb hearts quivered in glass cases, flapping fish in clear liquid. Bones like those of a mythical beast, gnawed by stray dogs. A swift kick from the vendor, followed by curses. She rattled her house keys as she walked, making tinkling sounds the men glanced up to. A younger man, dishevelled stranger from another town, cursed her with a verse from the Koran as she walked past: 'And let them not stamp their feet when walking so as to reveal their hidden trinkets.' She smiled, above any bitterness today, and walked on.

The wedding loaves at the entrance were coiled in wreaths of birds and flowers, highly polished. These weren't to be bought, only admired – and coveted by all the young girls except her. She was marrying Taleb tomorrow. There would be wedding loaves – better than these – made by the virgins of her family, blessed by her little sister Amal, by nieces and cousins and spinster aunts. There would be trays of henna for hands and feet and hair, clay pots of kohl and all her mother-in-law's jewellery, starred with candles and scattered with sweet basil. She would wear a silk abaya strewn with rose petals fashioned of pearls. She stood looking at the currants and lowered her mouth to her hand, nibbling at them, careful not to drop even one.

Now she fingered her house keys as she dreamed. They were heavy and made of iron; they made a satisfying clink when she moved them through her fingers. She opened her eyes but continued to block out the room she was in: draughty corners, blackened ceiling and dirt floor. She studied the keys as she'd done countless times before, fixing the Arabic inscription, the filigrees and curlicues in her mind. *Jaffa*, their house was called. Like the oranges they grew in their orchards above the sea, the orange she segmented with reverence and ate each morning of her brief girlhood in that house, its quick spurt their life's blood. She hid the keys in a rusty tin that once held pale China tea, the very same container she carried her wedding jewellery in on the flight from Palestine.

How fierce she was then, how she refused to back down. When the soldiers came she waved her keys at them and flaunted her swollen belly, shouting, 'I'm coming back. With my newborn baby. In two weeks we'll all be back, you bastards.' Her mother and sister chided her for using bad language. Mother died soon after, when they reached the camps in Beirut. The tents were erected on a swamp, which in the heavy rains became an open sewer, a torrent of disease, carrying her mother and others along in its wake.

She kept going. With her first baby, a little girl dead soon after from the same disease, and still unmarried, she threw stones at soldiers, becoming a shadow, a silent link in elaborate signalling systems warning of the approach of Merkava tanks. Hiding men during midnight searches, pretending each sleeping figure was husband or father or son. In time one of them did become a husband, and she gave birth to another child. Mahmoud, killed far in the south of the country fighting the Jews. Then Issa. The third, longed-for child, his mute blue-eyed gaze at her breast. Those dainty pink feet, skipping through the puddles and potholes of the camp.

She braved the constant identity checks. Her sister Amal lay with her on the makeshift bed, silent and pregnant, a grieving sixteen-year-old widow within a year. She was promised to the younger brother of Bilqis's husband, a firebrand boy dead in an Israeli attack. Then she was given to the eldest of the Ali sons, according to Islamic tradition, yet she feared him. She hated living with his other wives, Lebanese Shias who looked down on the family and mocked her Palestinian accent. She came to live with Bilqis, discarded by her husband for being sullen, not swift enough in the household tasks. And what of the child in her belly, Bilqis demanded, when she saw her sister was too sad to resist.

But there were more pressing problems in the camp than the future of Amal's unborn child. Israelis and Phalange shouted obscenities at both women in Arabic, wanting them to falter, flush, betray any small indiscretion. Amal merely sat and stared at them blankly. Bilqis shouted back. They confiscated the bread she just baked, splattered her walls with the bean stew she cooked, trampled her precious stores of flour into the floor with their boots. She merely bent down when they were gone, gathered the flour up and proceeded to bake on the coals once again. She forced little Issa to eat that night, picking grit out of the bread morsel by morsel before he would swallow it.

When Issa and she were in bed with Amal, the same soldiers came in again and beat her without passion. They spared Amal, perhaps because of her youth, or her straining belly. All Bilqis could think of while they were hitting her was Issa's safety. She could sense him standing in front of his aunt in his pyjamas, eyes wide with terror, both hands clenched into fists as Amal held him back. Neither husband was there to help: always political meetings and committees to attend, dealing with the mediocrities of camp life, rationing, sewerage, factions, allegiances, armaments.

The Israelis left her on the floor of the hut, bleeding. It took all her courage to get up again that night and make light of it so Issa would not be so scared, to make jokes with Amal about Mumma's split lip and cut forehead in order not to frighten him any further. And yet – she knows it now, feels the guilt and pain of it – the hatred she felt for those soldiers transmitted itself through her body to the boy.

Her husband died too. She sat up in bed now and looked around, as if unaware how she came to be in this place. Photographs? None – lost or stolen by soldiers or Shin Bet, probably burnt. Husbands died. That's what they did. There was no solace there. Husbands, sons, soldiers; they all blurred together, those blank-faced, boyish men with the fury of killing and all the intensity of children playing games. Children with gleaming toys of destruction and visions of glory, ephemeral dreams of exalted pain.

She was startled from her reverie by a tap at the door. Who could it be? Her blue-eyed boy, after so many weeks? No, only the UNRWA counsellor on her weekly rounds.

She called from the other side of the door. 'Still asleep, Mrs Ali? That's not like you.'

She pushed the door open without being asked. Bilqis cursed these prefabricated huts for not having any locks, and struggled to sit up straighter in bed.

'Never mind. I'll just plonk myself down right here, shall I?'

'Speak Arabic,' Bilqis said. 'Please.'

The smile did not leave the young woman's face.

'Of course. You speak English so well sometimes I forget you disapprove. And how is your son – Isfan, wasn't that his name?'

'Issa. His father died the night before our wedding.'

'Yes, I know, Mrs Ali. You've told me before. No, wait a minute, it was your first child's father who died then, not Issa's. Your little girl, the one who died. Don't you remember?'

Bilqis ignored the contradiction. Who cared about chronology?

'He was shot by his own people.'

'Yes. All that infighting, PLO, Amal, Fatah, Hamas, Hezbollah, I can hardly keep up.'

'Thank Allah I was pregnant, although I didn't know it. *Alhamdulillah*. Thank Allah a little good came out of such sin.'

The young woman's smile tightened as the door was flung open.

'Mumma!'

Issa burrowed into Bilqis's body in a raw intimacy that made the UNRWA worker look away. It was incongruous, a tall, grown man acting like a child. He noticed her staring. 'What are you doing?'

'I—I was talking to your—'

'Enough. We don't want you here.'

Bilqis saw how his face changed when he spoke to the foreigner. In his dismissal of the young woman was a childish desperation, an anxiety that she would not obey him, and his identity would thus shatter at the challenge. But she went, not before putting a hand on Bilqis's shoulder.

'If there's anything you need, Mrs Ali, you just make sure you tell us, okay?'

Bilqis nodded and even smiled at the young woman's humiliation, half wanting to reassure her, half to join in taunting at her discomfort.

BEIRUT, 1995

I miss Sarkis sometimes, now he's dead. After all, he was the only one who filled in the gaps in my stories. By the end of his last week, he had almost made me feel whole.

I know now from the hints he dropped, from questions I liked to think were subtle on my part, that he was the boy who betrayed my grandfather in the death camp at Der ez Zor. And that calling me out of the blue that night in Boston was a crooked part of his atonement. When he called I didn't know he would be dead a week later. He knew, of course. He wouldn't have contacted me any other way. The cancer had already gone into his liver and lungs and bones, was reaching his brain. But I didn't know that until after, at the funeral.

We met at a restaurant over a long weekend. He'd chosen a neutral place, perhaps so I wouldn't cry, shout, make a scene. But his unshed tears were enough to silence me. Outside the plate-glass windows, night rain turned the sky to black and silver. Diamond points in my hair, his old eyes. I sat opposite, playing with my cutlery. He sipped wine between sentences, didn't touch any of the food on his plate. His hands were trembling, and a thin curl of spit stayed just on the side of his mouth the whole time we were there. I wanted to wipe it off. Every now and then he would open a pillbox and swallow two or three large white pills with his wine. Now I know it was morphine. On noticing my expression, he merely raised his eyebrows, or what was left of them.

He told me what he knew of my father's death. He didn't know the real name of the man who had ordered him killed, but he knew the man worked for Islamic Jihad, and that he was a suicide bomber, and a rival of Selim's. He also knew the name of the Lebanese town in which my father was buried.

He told me all this without glancing up once. Each sentence was a short, pithy fable engineered to impart some important message. The moral evaded me – I was just hungry for the details of my father's life, any small clues as to who he really was. I asked Sarkis how he knew all this, and he finally looked up at me, his mouth twitching.

'I've spent the last ten years finding out.'

'But who told you? Do you trust them?'

'I found some old men, like me. They used to work for Islamic Jihad in the eighties. One of them was Algerian, he lives here in Boston now. I trust his account the most. Do you want to meet him?'

I shook my head. 'I trust you.'

Sarkis lowered his head again. 'And I trust him, because he was there. He was the one who pulled the trigger.'

'What? Who is he? What's his name? How can he still be roaming the streets, a killer?'

'He was nothing. A foot soldier, following instructions. He isn't to blame. The man who told him what to do is the one you should hate.'

'And who was he?'

'I don't know. Only the Iranians in Islamic Jihad knew his real name.'

This final version added something new to the flesh and fat and bone of my father's character, but at the same time made me sick to my stomach. I had to go to the bathroom and hide my grief. By the end the bottle was finished but our plates were untouched. I had to help Sarkis home. Through slippery streets in the dark, he seemed half-alive, insubstantial, an old man finally empty of guilt.

He'd aged so much since I saw him last. No more the courtly flirtation with its hint of menace, sly intimations of something more. I didn't confront him that night with how uncomfortable he had made me feel as a sixteen-year-old – it seemed another life. Even as a teenager I'd managed to overcome my dislike of his attentions, allowing him in weak moments to manhandle me, only this much and no more – a flutter of the hand here, a sly tickle there – as he introduced me to Boston's Armenian community as his goddaughter. I would plaster a smile on my face. By then I'd learnt the necessary coquetries. Poor little orphan, the powdered ladies clucked, jangling as they moved in their old Armenian gold, their bright new American diamonds, and I would let my own forehead crumple in mimed pathos.

I would sit on his sofa when he released me, away from the other guests, and watch the cable news channel that beamed in live footage from the Middle East. I would think of my unknown father. Where was he? Looking for my own features in this or that militiaman's moustached face. The money had stopped suddenly, Lilit said in one of her letters. Could that mean he was dead? Or in trouble? Now I know that by then he'd already been killed.

Sarkis was so vulnerable that week before he died. His body – long broken by the torture – was folding in on itself. He spoke plainly about the death marches, the camp. He regained some energy in the lobby of his apartment when we got there, his stick wobbling wildly as he righted himself, re-enacting the pain, twisting his body, pulling at his own fingers until they turned red. *They did it like this. Like that. They hit me like this,* and I watched the white saliva foam again at the corners of his mouth as he worked himself into a frenzy, as he mimed the mechanical efficiency of the blows, hatred steady as a metronome. I begged him to stop, his breathing so laboured, chest and scalp slick with sweat. His bones were shell-light, his skull shiny and hairless, except for a few baby curls at the crown.

When I got him into his apartment he told me his housekeeper was asleep, her door shut. Now I know she was a night nurse. I helped him bath, averting my eyes from the welts and marks of his torturers as I soaped his back, held a towel out for him to slowly, precariously step into. His long shanks, his Armenian leanness. The harmless penis, curled like a snail.

He died at home in the apartment, not in hospital. The nurse called me, and I saw him when his body was still warm. It was the first time I'd seen a corpse so close – a corpse that wasn't mangled, or covered in blood. The thin, bluish hands clasped over his breastbone were getting colder, stiffening even as I watched. I bent over his body, my warm tears on his dead cheeks, and surprised myself by kissing him softly on the mouth. Now I make myself believe that his lips retained a final tremor. As if he was going to tell me the last piece of the puzzle, the one name that would change everything.

✳ Chaim comes every other evening with the dog, Julius, and waits in the lobby of the Mayflower hotel. He gazes wistfully at the glass doors of the Duke of Wellington bar on the ground floor, but resists temptation, knowing if he goes in there among the smoke and laughter he may miss Anoush.

He doesn't want to ask reception to call her room, doesn't like to appear complacent of her arrival or, alternately, stupidly desperate she won't come. He wants to arrive at her hotel room, watch her open the door slowly with a smile of recognition on her face. He wants to take her in his arms and kiss her, rough and hard, as if there's nobody in the world but the two of them. Yet it's shame that keeps him from doing it, shame and fear and disgust at himself. He's old enough to be her father. She's never indicated that she has any interest in him other than as a guide, a support, maybe a friend.

He's been anxious lately and, if he cares to pinpoint it, it's ever since he met her. Before her arrival he revelled in the voluptuous anonymity of his floating existence in Beirut: no past, no family, no friends other than the men he worked with, drinking companions and nothing more. No morality or the cringing need for guilt. Now with her probing about his Ashkenazi background – his father, mother and brother; his childhood in Tel Aviv and Eilat; his military service in southern Lebanon – he feels shallow and exposed. As if there's nothing for her to find beneath the tally of dates and names, nothing to redeem him. Or too much.

He hasn't allowed himself to dwell too much on his military career for years. Or on his dead brother Alon. Anoush's open curiosity doesn't allow him to turn away from the memory any longer, like a cavity in a tooth that must be probed. Those summer days and nights of longing and tears, patriotic songs. Shabbat dinners when he and his mother were alone except for the Muslim servants, breaking challah into four pieces, slurping stew, his elder brother's absence at the head of the table a silent accusation. By then, his father's early death was a wound long closed over. Television footage of fighter planes over Beirut, his brother, the tragic knight in tinfoil armour. Down, down in flames.

Will Anoush continue to respect him when she finds out where he really comes from? How even as a teenager he idealised a heroic brother and a pointless war? Is he here in Beirut to atone for all of them: his father's Zionist beliefs, his mother's passive racism, Alon's naive sense of entitlement?

He sits on one of the musty chairs in the lobby. But is it really such a pointless war? It's a war that can never be won, that will only breed more pain, but would he or his mother be alive without it? Driven straight into the sea, where the Arabs want them? Where else could they go? The only home his family has ever known is Israel. And Israel must protect itself – or it will be annihilated. They can't let that happen again. He's the grandson of a Holocaust survivor, his friends' parents, his neighbours, all survivors of a genocide so painful it can hardly be borne. And here he is, helping his friends' enemies, his parents' enemies, to destroy his own people. If his mother knew what he was really doing in Lebanon, she would turn her face to the wall and will herself to die. How can he make Anoush understand this?

Julius lies down just outside the swinging doors to the street, head resting on his paws. Chaim's already hot; he rolls up his sleeves, tries to distract himself by watching the young clerk, Jean-Michel, arrange faded postcards on a stand, fill his ledger. He's wearing a black bowtie and a dress shirt, ridiculous in this Edwardian squalor. This squalid city. What was it like for Alon, flying over the sea and checking, double-checking the coordinates, readying himself to bomb an already ravaged city? A city so similar to Eilat, the Red Sea resort town of their childhood summers. His brother was university educated, debated the ethics of such a war with his libertarian friends, talked equality and justice, words Chaim couldn't understand then, or refused to understand. His politics back then were more rigid, more simplistic than Alon's. In his mind, any means to rid Israel of its enemies were justified by the end. Alon even began attending the protest marches in the last months of his life, and Chaim mocked him. No Palestinian or Lebanese soldier would question the conflict or be so touchingly naive, so academic.

Alon would gather his university friends around him in the evenings, with wine on the table from their fathers' vineyards, the glow of Chinese lanterns strung on a trellis mingling with the red warmth in Chaim's belly. On the smudged horizon, silhouettes of oil tankers competed with a perfect sunset. His brother sat in the circle of rosy light and spoke of the need to avoid civilian casualties, of helping the people of Lebanon decide their own future. He spoke of Israel's 'purity of arms', that their army only ever attacked military targets, while the Palestinian fighters embedded themselves among hospitals and schools and homes. He never talked of the crushed bodies he saw, of the impossible rubble he helped create, rooms that once housed women, families, children twisted into terrible shapes.

One evening Chaim stood aside in the shadows watching his brother's lean, mobile face, so like their dead father's, waiting for him to beckon to him as he always did, still talking, still trying to convince his friends of the morality in this war. In the next breath he was crying and babbling about the immorality of what he was forced to do. This time, Chaim leaned against his brother's ribs, the long, hard arm still tight around him, the friends' faces closing down now, embarrassed, Alon's sobs distorting the fine words he'd uttered only a moment before. It was the first time Alon had touched him with tenderness since he was a baby.

He sits and waits, remembering the hard skin of his brother's arms, the smell of red wine and dry heat. He can still feel Alon's hands on his shoulders, their heft and weight, the fractured sound of his sobbing. He wishes Anoush was here with him, wishes he could explain everything. And then, she is there, and he doesn't know what to say. As usual, she comes down to the lobby at eight and they conspire in denying this is a planned meeting, a rendezvous, even an assignation. He sometimes takes her elbow when they cross a particularly busy street. She looks down at him in her high heels – she's bought some now, succumbing to the pressure of strangers' stares – and tells him each evening that she'll wear her old, flat sandals tomorrow. He can see her trying not to walk too tall and he laughs to himself.

'What are you looking at?'

'Nothing. Really. Okay, I was looking at you. Don't hunch like that.'

He suspects she's offended, but he didn't mean to offend. What he wants to say is how lovely she is, heels or no, how happy he feels to walk alongside her. But at times he can see her tiny ripples of irritation at his customary glibness, like a cat in a foreign room, pawing at the furniture and looking for a way out. He doesn't allow her to begin, what with his ready charm and laughter. And anyway, what will she rail at him for? For not being what she wants him to be? At least he's not his brother all over again, drifting between two worlds, unhappy with both.

They always choose one of two places every night, a basement eating house owned by exiled Turks or a waterfront restaurant in one of the few restored Ottoman villas in Beirut. Most often the eating house, as he can see Anoush is watching her spending and he doesn't always succeed in paying. Although he insists every night, sometimes she stops him and lays her credit card between them on the table.

Tonight they go to the eating house. She paws at her food, and not even the jovial Turkish owner can tempt her with more. Chaim can sense that something is brewing, that she's unhappy. He eats her leftovers, picks parsley out of his teeth. She drinks instead and he urges her on, though he's not sure why. He assumes that he wants to break down her defences, get deep inside. Stop that unblinking beam of hers from shining on his innermost thoughts. It's not so easy. She lets pearly arak slide down her throat, glass after glass, but never changes into something softer for him to lean against and forget himself.

He's never heard her mention anything much about her parents. Then again, he's never asked. He knows she's an only child but isn't familiar with the circumstances. She does speak of her Armenian grandmothers. It's always *Lilit said this* or *Siran did that*.

Tonight she shows him some photographs she carries with her: poised old ladies wearing headscarves, a laden pomegranate tree in a slip of garden. And one of her grandmother Lilit as a girl, with an expression he can only classify as terror. It was taken in a place called Der ez Zor, back in 1915 when the Armenians were getting massacred.

Looking at the photograph, he can see the resemblance between grandmother and granddaughter immediately. The effect this has on him doesn't diminish, looking at it more closely: their twinned faces confuse him as he takes in the solemn woman's rounded cheeks, restless eyes, rough-cut hair, the blossom mouth, as he looks across at Anoush, who seems anxious now, trying to snatch the photograph away. He hands it back to her without comment. Worlds apart, yet so similar: resigned household slave and defiant granddaughter, traipsing through the city armed with her search for something resembling truth.

Now one grandmother is dead and the other might as well be, here in Beirut in a nursing home. Such orthodox guilt. He can relate to it. He rings his mother – now eighty and still living at home with a new generation of Arab servants – every day. Anoush has told him she sends money now and then to Siran when she can spare it: small change for facial tissues, trinkets, bedsocks, sweets. She makes excuses to him about the old woman not recognising anyone from moment to moment, dribbling and babbling like a child, spraying food everywhere.

'Let's go together,' he offers.

Anoush shakes her head. She shows him another photograph, as if to change the subject. Her grandfather, Minas, and Siran on their wedding day.

'The only photo ever taken of them both,' she whispers fondly.

Their faces are broad and stunned, the grandfather looking somewhat doubtful beside the beaming young woman, black curls falling into her brow, across the polished silver coins strung on her forehead.

'Look at those earrings she wears. Gold and turquoise – his mother's. He hid them all the way through the forced march in the desert, then in the death camp and to Beirut, before giving them to her. Twenty-five years he kept them. True love.'

She says the last two words in an ironic tone but he can see she's touched by the fifty-year-old love story.

'They married late. How old was he?'

She laughs, looks up at him for an instant with a face full of coquetry.

'Doesn't matter, does it? You're not married yet. He was nearly forty. He'd been through a lot.'

'Like me,' he laughs.

Her face changes, and she doesn't join in. 'What have you been through? Looks like your life has been easy enough, to me.'

'I was only making a joke.'

'It's not funny. Why should you or any other Israeli have anything to complain about?'

'Whoah! What's all this about? Were we talking about Israel?'

'We are now. Surely you can't still think you're the victims. With your state-of-the-art weapons and your targeted killings. Who made Israel the great moral arbiter of the world?'

'Listen, Anoush. I didn't want to get into this, not now. But I'll tell you something, and maybe you'll be smart enough to hear me out. They want to wipe out Israel. Do you get it? They want us all dead. Israel doesn't want to wipe out anyone. We're trying to defend ourselves. We're yoked together with the Palestinians, brother to brother, and can't see any resolution. And yes, I'm here to make my own amends. I'm not the bad guy, nor is Israel.'

She won't look at him. As he pays for the meal and they leave the building his frustration is so great he wants to hit her. She's shut down. He stops, faces her, wills her to look into his eyes.

'You and I come from the same pain,' he says. 'The same struggle. Can't you see that?'

She doesn't reply, but halfway home she steps closer, links his fingers in hers. He can feel her body softening against him as they walk. They stop under the blue neon letters spelling Mayflower, and kiss goodnight. The kiss, as always, is not long; he doesn't linger. She keeps her mouth closed, chaste.

He turns aside and makes his way down the street, whistling for Julius to follow him, wishing she would stop him, drag him into her bed. He wants to get inside her head more than any clear desire for her body, cut through her anger and dreams and unravel all her questions: silent figures of grandmothers and absent fathers, the obscure grandfather that started all this pain. Sometimes Chaim would like to kill her father, or at least annihilate his memory. If he wasn't already dead. He makes Anoush so distant, half-alive, yet sublime too in her indifference to the present.

BEIRUT & DER EZ ZOR, 1915

Once in Beirut, Minas stumbled through narrow lanes and knocked on the doors of porticoed villas, looking for work. Servants opened the door, faces composed and smiling, then looked at him properly, and the smiles immediately faded from their faces. One maid shrieked. Minas ran away.

He began running everywhere, more and more afraid of himself. He ran away from lumbering trams, afraid the roaring beasts were searching for him in order to finish off what the Turks began. He became lost in star-shaped streets, passing the American University and not stopping, intimidated by its neoclassical facade. A new French school beckoned, but it too looked innocent and pristine, and he felt unworthy of its hushed pallor, with his torn feet and now-ragged Bedouin robe. After a few hours, he was too tired to run any more. He lay supine again as he had in Damascus, safe in the shade of white streets softened by flowering trees.

That evening he found his way to the seashore, thinking to learn from the beggars on the Corniche how to cajole and whine. He sat on a low wall near the promenade; painted fishing boats behind him jostled its smooth flank. He watched beggars prostrate themselves before gentlemen in frock coats and cravats out walking their daughters. Girls decked in finery he'd never imagined: lustrous scarves thick as tapestries around their hips, stiff taffeta skirts in sunset colours, square veils so tiny their kohled eyes and rouged cheeks could be seen. One girl looked at him for a moment and he smiled. She screwed up her face at him, satin cap tilted over her forehead, mocking him with its jaunty angle.

Most of the beggars were ignored, stepped over or kicked. A few, mostly children and young mothers, were given a coin or two. Some women were obviously prostitutes, leading men away behind the sea wall.

When the sun set behind the tall villas, Minas grew cold. It began to drizzle. He watched the beggars who were now squatting under the palms and counting their day's takings. They had set up a brazier and he inadvertently edged closer, rubbing his hands over the damp fire. A young woman with a blackened mouth saw him, spat on the ground and began to shout.

'We want none of your kind around here!'

He didn't remember how he came to be running and crying, fleeing through the streets away from the shore and rubbing at his eyes, trying to stem the flow of tears that only made him colder. After what seemed like many miles, he could no longer distinguish between his tears or the rain that had soaked through his clothes. *A man of no substance*, he thought, as he continued to limp and run, walk and stumble; *I am a man of water and sand.*

He stopped at a street corner high above the harbour, holding his side. He looked about him, at the curve of the Corniche promenade and the steep roofs of houses, far away in the distance the blink of ships' lights. All was dark below, except for the full moon casting a silver line of light from rooftop to rooftop. He began to cry again. He had no idea where he was.

The next morning he woke to the sound of many feet over his head and all around him. He opened his eyes and sat up to see he had fallen asleep on the steps leading to a tenement. Somebody cursed; he felt a kick aimed at his groin. He stood up then, favouring his bad ankle, leaned against the building. He stayed there, watching the tide of people swarm and increase in number, tea boys hurrying past with embossed brass pots on their backs, women balancing baskets and babies, lottery ticket hawkers thrusting their long festooned poles into the air, smacking at ribs if someone got in their way. Near him, a gang of children muddied their bare feet in potholes of water left from last night's rain. He swayed with weakness. He was hungrier than he'd been on the marches, or in the camp. He was hungrier now than he had ever been.

He drifted through the climbing streets, dodging children with stones and angry mothers sluicing pavements with soapy water. The incense wafting from their houses hurt him with the memory of his mother. In Van she would burn the silvery coals every Saturday night in preparation for the Sabbath. Anointing the icons with fragrance, leaving the Byzantine holder smoking at their front door in case evil entered. *Oh, Mamma.* Somehow it didn't feel right to ask her help any longer. As if he didn't deserve it now. His feet were wet and his ankle throbbing. She wasn't here to comfort him.

He sat on the ground and checked his wounds, only to see that his whole foot had swelled and become an angry red. He sat where he was, cross-legged, oblivious to the insults about him, the strange faces and threats to call the gendarmes if he didn't move on. He continued to sit, until the women and children left him alone and went inside. Their men came home from work at lunchtime and then again in the evening, not even glancing at him, hurrying inside to warmth and dinner, sleepy childish voices.

He rose then, trudged with care toward a main road, some open-air markets with rows of festive food under strings of coloured paper. There was a performance going on, with gypsies who beat hide drums and capered between the spectators, faces painted in crimson streaks and their children treading a tightrope strung between two plane trees. He was intimidated by the noises, and the mechanical gymnastics of the little girls unnerved him. He squinted beneath the bright lights and the scampering, hopeful children, being elbowed out of the way as if unworthy of their attention.

He knew if he didn't steal something to eat he would faint. Yet he was afraid to act, hopping on his painful ankle between the stalls, aware of the sidelong glances, concentrating on smelling, really smelling the aromas of cooking – juice of burnt meat, grilled gilt-head bream, orange-flower sherbets tingeing the aisles – hoping he might obtain some sustenance through his pores. Low tables and cushions were laid under the spreading plane trees, and the perfume of black tea and baking thickened the dusk.

At one stall he was accosted by an old Armenian with ears cocked for a sale. When the man took in the parlous state of his feet, he waved him down the road.

'Go to the Red Cross,' he said in Armenian. 'They've set up shelter and free food.'

Minas nodded, bewildered. The old man gestured to his wares, dried fruit and nuts and jars of sesame paste.

'Take something before you go. Please. You are my countryman.'

Minas lunged at the food. He grabbed a handful of almonds, stuffed them into his robe, then another handful, a packet of raisins, knocked a basket of figs to the ground in his haste. The old man opened his hands wide, told him to take more. Minas hobbled away, cramming all the food into his cheeks at once, swallowing it all down without tasting.

The Red Cross relief post was set up in the centre of the sprawling refugee camp of Bourj-Hammoud, built on stilts to rise above the constantly shifting, gurgling marshland. He didn't like that word. *Camp.* Something in him wanted to turn back, continue his aimless existence in Damascus. He thought of his father, his mother, his shadowy sister, either alive or dead. Yet he was alive. He owed it to them to make a life. Only in this humped building teetering on matchstick legs could he get some hot food, wash perhaps, even sleep in a proper bed. He remembered starched white sheets and lambs' wool blankets, and stepped forward with a new energy through the door.

There were signs in different languages everywhere. Armenian, Arabic, English, French. *Queue here to be processed. Identity cards to be collected between 12.00 and 16.00 hours.* Only here could he be processed and given an identity card. *Processed.* He made his face blank and pushed through the melee of bodies.

There were desks under the low ceiling, bare oil-wick lamps throwing dirty puddles of light on faces and hands. Many hands writing, recording names and birth dates and ages. Armenian records. Armenian lives. Evidence of their continued existence. He felt a slight upsurge of something akin to vindication, even joy. *They tried, but they didn't get all of us.* Precise voices could be heard whispering, in French and English and Arabic; he could understand a word here and there.

A French woman gestured to him, tight-lipped. He stood before her, nodded when she guessed from the way he pronounced his surname which *vilayet* he was from. His voice was rusty; he hadn't used it for so many weeks. It hurt to form the sounds. He coughed, tried it out once more.

'Are there many here from Van?' he croaked, incredulous.

'Not so many,' she replied carefully, wary of his response.

He watched her write his name in cursive script, fine and bold. *Minas Pakradounian.* She penned his age and blacked in the special box: *No dependants.*

'Any skills?' she asked.

He was just about to shake his head when he coughed again and cleared his throat.

'Jeweller. Gold- and silver-smithing.'

He watched her write the words, and somehow this made what he had just said more real. She nodded at him, flicked her wrist to the other side of the room. Stained screens of army canvas hid men shouting and laughing. Someone sobbed in strangled gulps like a baby. Thin, greasy blankets on all the beds, in various shades of ash.

Minas inched his way to the other side. All around him were tin hipbaths, some with nude men in them, soaping themselves and blowing bubbles, others empty, with the water still swirling from the movement of a body standing up and stepping onto the brown, dusty floor. Muddy footprints of bath water everywhere in the dirt.

These were Armenian men, his countrymen, but never before had he felt more alone. Not on the march, not in the camp, not with the Bedouin. These men were definitely Armenian; he could see that from their hard, rangy bodies and sloped, elongated heads. But they were laughing, making jokes, flopping their penises about at each other and guffawing. He choked. *How can you do this? Have you seen what I've seen? So many have died, are still dying.* One man with a smashed face and hairy back stood up in his bath, sloshing water on the floor and yelling. He waved his arms around as if conducting an orchestra, wriggled his hips like an odalisque and used his penis as an accessory to the dance, until a nurse hurried over to stop him.

He wanted to shake them, strike them, burn them all, upset their bath water over the floor and shout: 'Don't you know why we're here? Armenia is gone forever if we forget!' But he didn't. He hung his head, ashamed of his own sparse nudity, carrying his rolled-up clothes under one arm. He clutched his mother's earrings, they bit into his palm. An American nurse saw him and took his hand. She propelled him to the far side of the room.

'You all right?'

He nodded, although he didn't understand what she'd said. He spoke to her in Turkish.

'A mirror, please?'

She raised her eyebrows, shrugged her shoulders. She switched from English to French.

'*Je ne comprends pas.* I don't understand.'

'*Un miroir,*' he repeated, and touched the side of his face with one finger.

She grinned brightly and marched off to somebody else who was pissing in his bath, making a yellow fountain rise up from the murky water. When she came back, she held a jagged sliver of mirror in a clean cloth. He waited until she was gone to look at himself. He held the mirror out at arm's length, afraid of what he might see.

The way he held his jaw had changed, clenched and tight as if constantly chewing at the inside of his mouth. Maybe it had something to do with some of his teeth having been knocked out in the camp. His face seemed twisted in a perpetual state of suffering. He tried to smile at his reflection, found he couldn't arrange his features satisfactorily. He bared his remaining teeth again, as he had in Damascus; it made him feel stronger somehow. Then he became distracted by his hair. It was lank and brushed his shoulders, the new, patchy beard a fiery gold. He looked closer, yanked a white hair from his nostril. He brought the mirror down past his nipples, angry red and weeping fluid, past his genitals, pale and brushed with scurf, down to his rickety knees. *I'm an old man at fourteen.*

He put the mirror down and stepped into a bath. It looked a little cleaner than the others. Around him, scores of other men were doing the same thing. Testing the water for heat with the tips of their toes, knowing even as they did so it would be lukewarm at best, heated only by the memory of another's body. Armenians exchanging the fluids and the filth of each other's destiny. Stepping in, stepping out. Shaking the water from their skin in a rain of drops like dogs.

He stood in the bath. His feet were on fire. The cake of soap balancing on the rim of his tub was lumpy, yellowish. He picked it up, weighed it in his hand. Pork fat. Animal fat. Human. He sprang up from the water and lay very still on the dirt floor. Hiding. In the camp again.

Another nurse came past with rubber gloves, brisk. She wrenched him from the ground, ignominious, balls flopping, tears squeezed out of his shut eyes. She smiled fiercely, stroked his head when she sat him on the rim of the tub.

'There's a good boy,' she said in English.

He didn't understand. He winced as she smeared hard soap all over his chest, over the wounds in his nipples left by his mother's earrings.

⌘ Lilit squatted on the birthing rug and pushed, holding on to the midwife's arms. Hot, hairy arms, easy to grip on to so as not to fall. Fall, falling into pain. Blood spattered the flagstones, drops of blood on sand. She remembered murmured prayers at nightfall, Mamma crying, snatches of Armenian song. A bluish half-moon fell from the Der ez Zor sky. Her mouth was dry. She panted, holding it all in. Then one last push. There was not a cell in her body or brain that was not consumed by this agony. She was finding it hard to remember who she was. Another push. 'One last push,' they kept telling her, the liars. 'One last push.'

The baby flopped on the ground like a fish, squirming once then lying still. She put her hand out to touch the tiny body, then drew it back, afraid. Blue scrap of bone and tissue, throbbing cord tight around his neck. Pulsating, coiling, a snake come to strangle her baby. She was paralysed, staring at the little puffing face trying to breathe.

'Help him,' she yelled, and time seemed to warp, elongate, until she was no longer there in the room anymore. She fell back on the pillows and shut her eyes, shivering with cold. At her feet she could hear swearing, muttering, women's hands scratching and slapping at flesh – were they tugging inside her or dismembering the child? – but she was too tired to move or look or even open her eyes. She suspected the midwife for colluding with Fatima to bring her down. What if Suleiman cast her out when she failed to bear him a son? At times like this, when the anodyne routine of daily life ruptured and changed, when Suleiman threatened to become morose and distant again, she remembered she was Armenian. Whatever that meant.

The midwife knew she was Armenian, as did everyone in Der ez Zor. They had all been poisoned against her by Fatima, by her carping at the market about favouritism in the bedroom, the way Lilit cut a tray of *baqlawa* into far too few pieces, the way she held her spoon. Fatima, who stayed by the door all the while, watching under her veil as the baby was born. Fatima, with her muttered invocations and *suras* from the Koran, curses instead of blessings. Lilit opened her eyes then. It was Fatima, rummaging inside her, pulling out her womb and killing the baby too. She watched Fatima blow into his face, slap him, but he would not breathe. Lilit didn't pick him up, didn't hold him. She tried to stand, held down by the midwife.

'Don't touch him!' She pointed at Fatima. 'Don't touch my baby. You've already cursed us.'

Fatima stopped inches from Lilit's face.

'You dare blame me? It's your bad blood that's killed him. Christian blood.'

Lilit staggered off the rug, tearing at Fatima's upper arms, breaking her fingernails on the sparkling clothes. Sequins scattered, beads rolled across the floor. Fatima didn't resist, letting her tire. Lilit breathed out and sank to the floor.

'You poisoned me because you can't have one!'

Fatima wrenched herself away.

'You broke a promise and now Allah's punishing you for it.'

Lilit curled up, scrabbling for her baby. He was cold already, turning black. So many babies, all dead. *Why should I care if one more baby dies?* He wasn't even Armenian, as the others had been. Marred by Turkish blood. Maybe she was being punished for what the Chetti did to her on the march. Damaged her inside, made her worthless. A faulty womb. She stretched out her arm to touch the baby's head, his face twisted toward her in the gaze of Suleiman. In the next moment she drew away and screamed up to the ceiling, drumming her feet and fists on the stone floor. The hell of loss was too much to bear without noise to cover it.

It had been hard coming back from her aborted escape and accepting that Suleiman already had a wife in Fatima, even if he debased her daily; that she, Lilit, was a slave, a servant, an exalted concubine at best. And yet, as weeks and then months passed since Fatima's humbling, Lilit could see her own status in the household improving. Some mornings when she lay in bed with Suleiman, late and drowsy, his hand a gentle arc over her belly, it was Fatima who was summoned to bring them tea. She did so, grumbling and not before cursing them both under her breath. Lilit could hear her in the kitchen banging coffee pots and copper trays, smashing a glass under her slippered heel and leaving it for the cook to sweep up.

Suleiman often tried to explain the situation to Lilit, propping his cheek on his elbow and watching her for any signs of sadness. She lay very still and quiet, her face at rest as white as the pillow.

'I've grown to love you more,' he said. 'I know you can feel it. But she's family – and you, you'll always be different from us. Even if you decide to convert.'

'I know, *effendim*.'

'No, you don't know. It's hard for me to be mocked in the marketplace, to be sneered at for treating you so well, while your compatriots are killed in the—'

She put her hand over his mouth.

'Don't! I am not one of them now.'

Then she collected herself, smiled at him. The gesture was effacing, gratuitous, and she hated herself for it.

'Suleiman, I want to be your wife.'

She remembered these words, going round and round her head as she laboured to give birth and tried not to cry out. It was shameful for Muslim women to cry out, she was told by the midwife. Only Christian women sobbed like children in the midst of their pain. She could remember thinking: *Am I his now? Oh, yes.* And the strangest thing was, she wanted to be. His wife, his only. She had wanted to be his wife and wanted Fatima gone.

Now she screamed again.

'I hate you, Suleiman!'

There was no answer. Fatima turned toward the wall, as if embarrassed.

'I hate you all! I hate you, Suleiman!' she repeated, screaming the last word louder than the others. She tried to get up again, but was too weak now. She lay huddled among the pillows shivering hot and cold, feeling her tears beat onto her breasts.

Suleiman rushed into the room, grabbing Fatima on the way and planting himself above Lilit's body. The midwife hurried to cover her.

For what seemed like a long time, Suleiman stood looking at his dead son as if he couldn't believe this had happened to him. He turned to the midwife, still holding Fatima by the arm. His voice a breath.

'The child?'

'Strangled, *Bey effendim*, with his own cord.' She gestured to Lilit, helpless. 'A difficult birth. A fragile mother.'

Suleiman reached down to touch the top of his son's head. It was a moment, no more. He stroked the soft skull with the fingers of his right hand. The women stared at him, silent now. He caught his breath. Turned to Fatima.

'And you! Making trouble again?'

He dragged her down to Lilit's level and hissed through his teeth.

'Whores and bitches, daughters of dogs! Apologise to each other. I will not live in a household divided as this.'

The two women glared at him, forgetting each other for a moment.

'You choose,' Lilit growled.

He turned on her, incredulous.

'You? You—whom I rescued from the gutter? You ask me to choose?'

She looked from his face to her baby. Hers? Dead. Not hers anymore. She leaned forward and pushed the tiny corpse toward him.

'I don't want to look at him. He reminds me of you.'

BEIRUT, 1982

More Israeli air raids came to terrorise Beirut with their soprano whine. Bilqis sometimes thought her own laughter was a challenge to that sound: she laughed in the same unstable way, an out-of-breath gurgle and a screech. The raids targeted Palestinian camps in the southern suburbs with American-made cluster bombs. They exploded indiscriminately, showering anyone close by with perfect steel balls and jagged metal fragments.

Bilqis hobbled out of the camp's air-raid shelter screaming at the planes still hovering above, watching them retreat with the whirring motions of startled pigeons. 'Bastards! We're still alive!'

Children chorused around her.

'Still alive!'

They hugged each other: teenage widows, militia fighters, those stick-limbed, hysterical children, shaking in disbelief at their own good fortune. As the planes circled the camps once again then left, the refugees fell apart from each other to hug themselves, revelling in that moment of aliveness, still watching as the planes disappeared into the light sky.

�֍ Still more leaflets. Printed on crinkled paper of yellow and green, cellophane flowers. Most of which were dropped over the Corniche, only to fall into the churning water or to hang limply, dampening inch by inch on the knife-sharp rocks.

**You in west Beirut should remember today
that time is running out and
with every delay the risk to your dear ones increases. Hurry up.
Save the lives of your dear ones before it is too late.**

'It's already too late,' Sanaya said, as she threw it in the bin. 'I have no dear ones to save. Except Hadiya, and she's not even mine.'

She was scrubbing the shower recess with the last of the detergent and dirty water.

What about Selim? She hated him. She loved him. No, it wasn't that. She hated the public Selim, the one who killed. She loved the private Selim, the one who made her feel safe. She hadn't seen him for a long while; he was never home when she phoned. What about Issa? Crazy. So was the whole city. He fitted in well.

In the evening, gold streamers of light appeared around the edges of west Beirut. They were from jets firing flares over the rooftops, a carnival of the grotesque. Israelis sputtered on loudspeakers in bad Arabic. 'Leave the west of the city immediately,' they droned on and on into the night, disturbing Sanaya's sleep until she stood on the balcony and shouted back at them. 'You fucking leave the city! I'm staying here.'

It was her city now, more than ever. Now, in its decrepitude, its clamorous pain and filth, it begged her loyalty as in no other time. When she was younger, when Beirut was vibrant, flaunting wealth and power, she did not feel part of it the way she did now. When the restaurants were filled every night, casinos glittering, swimming pools floodlit and lagoon-blue, actors and directors swanning into waterfront clubs, the city did not need her.

She saw it now from her balcony and suffered. Most buildings were shells, open to sky and rain. Furniture and electronic goods had been carted away from abandoned houses, the only items left behind too sodden or soiled to be contemplated. Cooking pots and saucepans filled with the shit of retreating Israeli soldiers. Vandalised beds and clothes. Walls pitted with scars and graffiti, last-ditch pleas for justice. She couldn't leave, not now. Now, more than ever, the city relied on her for its very existence.

She sat through the next day and slept through the next, waking only for sips of cold tea. She slept through the beginning of the siege proper, through the electrical power circuits being switched off, water supplies cut totally, no more food allowed into the city from any channels, black market or otherwise. She sipped her tea and saved her dry bread for later, when things would surely get worse.

✳ Two weeks into the siege, she decided to risk going outside. She'd been kept alive by her store of canned food and shrivelled potatoes, scary tubers in the dark of the cupboard. Yet she had been kept from total malnourishment by gifts from Selim: army rations of brittle chocolate and shortbread, oranges and day-old pastries. He'd been coming around much more now, almost every day, checking if she was all right, gently solicitous of her comfort. Something in him had died, she thought. He seemed older and more wary of emotion.

Issa was nowhere to be found, and even Rouba had no idea where he was fighting, or for whom. Sanaya had broken the silence between them. One morning after she saw Hadiya go out into the courtyard to play, she made her glass of tea, put her stale croissant on a plate to have for breakfast. She sat on the balcony to read the paper, as she always did, regardless of the danger, then suddenly thought of Rouba directly downstairs, maybe with nothing to eat at all. She knocked on the door then, watched Rouba open it in her crumpled nightgown and silently handed her the plate.

Now she shared her treats with Rouba most days, pressing food into her hands, sweeping away her feeble protestations. *Take it. Eat it in front of me.* Both women had grown thinner, sallow and pinched and perpetually hungry. Hadiya's emaciation was heartbreaking, as if her hair had now sucked all the life out of her. She no longer went to school, waiting until the teacher could resume small classes in her own apartment.

Sanaya tried to wash before going out, an exercise in exasperation, as seawater was all they had now, trickling it over herself, leaving her hair and face greasy with a slick of diesel oil and salt, and hardly reaching the rest of her body.

She walked out into a nightmare. Crooked piles of burning garbage, streets stinking of shit and blood, children running to her with rivulets of snot from both nostrils, begging for coins, scabies reddening their hollow cheeks. The Israeli bombardment had been both discriminate and accurate. Finally those ritualistic words 'surgical precision' had become blazingly real to her. True, they were usually meant to denote the targeting of military buildings and few, if any, civilian casualties. Yet as she walked she saw the Israelis had targeted every civilian area possible:

schools, mosques, churches, hospitals, apartments, hotels, shops, parks, even the city's only synagogue.

She walked further, past the Hamra district, toward the Green Line into the dusk. She checked her watch – already nine. The light from the sky didn't diminish, rather became more distinct with every step. The other people appeared undisturbed by it, yet for her it was like being hunted, found and examined under glass.

She grabbed a young girl by the arm.

'I'm sorry, why is the city lit up like this?'

The girl looked at her askance, scanned the crowd for assistance. Somebody cut in, shoving her aside.

'It's the Israelis, up to another one of their tricks.'

'But why?' she asked. 'Why?'

The people around her shook their heads, tried not to stare, drifted away as she continued to ask why, exchanging glances among themselves, nodding at each other to convey the woman's strangeness.

By nightfall, the west of the city was robed in a halo of white neon from searchlights erected on the hills, a long-suffering saint under interrogation.

She sat on her balcony the next morning, sipping tea and smoking. More black-market Marlboros brought by Selim. Better than the Gitanes he would bring her last year.

She opened yesterday's newspaper: *17 September 1982.* Somehow the date surprised her; she hadn't been conscious of so much time passing. The city still retained its summer heat, in the pavements and between building bricks, as if drawing a blanket around itself in defence against some new atrocity.

It had been hard to sleep last night; she sweated in her airless bedroom and considered calling Selim, but in the end decided against it.

She jumped when she heard Rouba's voice behind her.

'You scared me. I didn't hear you come in.'

'You were humming to yourself.'

'Was I? I didn't realise.'

Rouba sat on the chair opposite.

'Sanaya, something's going on in the camps.'

'What do you mean?'

'Something horrible. My friends who live near there said they could hear dynamiting all night.'

'But the multinational forces are here, Rouba. Surely—'

'The marines have left us too early, and those bastard Israelis are doing whatever they want.'

✳ Selim and Elie were on a mission with their men. They rode in jeeps through the clean morning and ate rations from US army tins, a welcome change after tinned hoummus and stale baguettes. The Israelis had supplied them with these rations – as well as fizzy sodas and new guns.

They sat around, enjoying the brightness, basking in the sun. They ate, drank and argued. Some said the Palestinians had murdered Bashir Gemayel, as the Israelis had always maintained. They wanted revenge. They wanted to begin right away, but the others cautioned, waving their cigarettes. They countered with their own stories. Bashir was not dead at all, no – he'd been seen walking out of his wrecked car, covered in blood, into a waiting ambulance. He was biding his time, only to appear again when his country needed him.

In the meantime, they prepared for his arrival. They'd been sent to *flush out terrorists*. The euphemisms were inventive. *Neutralise the camps, cleanse the area, mop up insurgents, disinfect the region of aggressors*. To kill. They had been instructed to kill every living thing in the Sabra-Shatila camps: old men, women, girls, children, babies, stray dogs, pet birds in cages. They were all to be knifed or machine-gunned to death; no explosions until nightfall, the men were warned, when the dead could be bulldozed into mass graves with their shacks dynamited on top of them. A quick way to hide the evidence. Calm and efficient.

By afternoon, Selim was preparing to begin. Elie had long since retired to the Phalange HQ, after giving the men a rousing speech. Orders had come from the Israeli High Command to start at 5 pm.

Selim's boys were quiet now, some asleep, others staring into space. Most were high on hashish. Their movements could certainly be slower under the influence but were usually more deliberate. Their judgement was clouded, but that too could be useful. Today he felt as if he'd like a little himself. As second-in-command he operated as if he and the boys were one organism. His desires and needs were communicated to them almost by hypnosis, slow-moving unconscious, epiphany. His movements and expressions suggesting more than his spoken commands could elucidate. Today, the boys' instincts were trained on him with more intensity and fervour than he'd seen in a long time.

He stubbed out his cigarette in the dirt and led them to the first row of huts near the gates. Behind, more jeeps screeched to a halt and the rest of the Phalangist forces stumbled out into the dust, all in silence and something like veneration. The sky was empty of clouds, the colour of the Madonna's robes.

'Advance!' Selim shouted. 'In the name of the Virgin!'

He glanced down at his gun butt and the Virgin Mary sticker he'd placed there gazed at him with adoring plenitude. He made the sign of the cross, looked away.

The first Palestinian he saw was a pregnant woman, younger than twenty. She wore a sky-blue scarf and her feet were bare. When she saw the Phalangists rushing into her courtyard she began scurrying here and there like a beheaded hen, always covering the same ground, cowering before them in a cursed circle. He watched one of his boys stop in front of her then saw her crumple to the ground before him, as if accepting her fate. She looked like she would have done anything: kissed his feet, let him rape her, maim her, if he would just let her live long enough to give birth to her baby. The boy put his boot on her neck, then leaned over. Blood shot out of her mouth in small, unpredictable spurts. She made no sound, part of the afternoon's conspiracy of silence. *Maybe it doesn't hurt her as much. Maybe she's just too different from us.* Was it just like slitting open a pig? An Easter lamb, sweet and pliant? Maybe she wasn't human after all. Or maybe she was screaming deep inside.

Selim entered the hut and killed her husband with one shot.

'I'm doing you a favour,' he said. 'So you don't have to see what happened to your child.'

He didn't stop to check if the man was dead on impact. He could hear a gurgle escape from him, the rush of a deflating tyre. He felt no obvious hatred for the dead man, no acute ache of revenge. His hatred was chronic by now, like a back ailment he just had to live with. A justifiable impediment. A personality trait, like an irritating laugh or stammer.

Revenge was part of it, always had been. Still, the sense of injustice, the heat of anger, was not his motivating force. Nor the memory of his father's tirades, the red, dragging suffering of his persecuted race. Mostly it was a job he must do, he reminded himself, a task in which he brought his best training to bear.

Even so, he felt at times that killing was like the twinned sickness and satisfaction he felt while masturbating. Secretive, but a performance, no matter how intimate. Like the twisted lozenge of light his bracelet made on the bathroom tiles each morning, killing another human being was the way in which he made an impact upon the world. *I'm alive and I can take away your life. In this way I'm doubly living.*

Surely it was more than that. After all, the act wasn't always so pleasurable. At times he felt illogically diminished by this very exercise of his power. Then it *was* Papa and his tirades; it must be. Something in those whispered taunts, at night in bed when he was half-asleep already and couldn't be sure he heard right. The signalling cough down the corridor. His father standing by the door with a circle of light around his head. Selim sitting up in bed, still navigating his dreams. *What is it, Papa?* And Minas bending over with a hand heavy on his cheek. *Nothing, my son, nothing at all.* Then he would sit at the end of the bed and abuse Selim for not being a good enough son.

After that, long after all the swearing, the disappointment and anger, came the maudlin reminiscences and the crying. And Selim, in his love and shame for his father, would try to keep his eyes tightly closed and keep dreaming, allowing Minas's voice to weave into his own private images of suffering and war. He became his father: holding the girl from the death camp in a last grasping embrace, retasting her sweet insistence. *And I flinched away from her filth, did you hear me, son? Even though I was just as dirty as she was.*

Why now, why all this guilt? Selim could remember wanting to say it, yet not having the courage to ask. Papa survived because he had to. She succumbed. He comforted his father with these arguments – or did he? – and Minas repeated them after him so the girl wouldn't come to him in his nightmares. She wanted him to survive. Yet he left her behind, ran away from her. *Just as you, my son, are going to do to me.*

Selim lay in bed then and tried to stop the tears escaping from his eyes. It hurt his chest, his cheeks, to hold them back. His father told him to stay home, be good, marry an Armenian girl – but never his cousin. It was wrong. The Arabs did it. At this point Selim's fatigue got the better of him and he fell into open-mouthed sleep, his father curled up, too, lightly snoring at his feet. And their dreams fed off each other: Selim lying in a gutter somewhere in the warring south of the country, bleeding, calling for his Papa. Or running, running at night when Minas's own legs shuddered and strained with the effort of keeping up with him. And Selim saw two boys, hand in hand, wading through deserts riven with blood. Two boys; twin Minases and twin Selims, crying and laughing in a crisis of fear and freedom.

Selim knew now what he meant, the cruel subtext to all his father's ranting. *You've never suffered, my boy. You don't know what it is to be Armenian.* His father's voice descending to a hiss. *Food on the table, tucked into bed, coddled all your life. You have no idea what we went through to get you here.* So as the years went by, he fulfilled the prophecy and withdrew from his father more and more.

Minas, meanwhile, complained to anyone who would listen: Lilit, a worried Siran, bored neighbours, to customers who wandered into the jewellery shop expecting only a glass of tea and some small talk. He contrived to repeat the same thing every time, and Selim would hear it second-hand from Anahit: Selim was always such a good boy. Seventeen now, old enough to know better. And it was dangerous out in the streets, what with Palestinians and Muslim Lebanese running all over the place with their new guns. Another war, just like all the others. It wasn't really a full-scale war yet, but the Israelis were already rumbling over Arab borders. They even talked about nuclear power. Wipe out the whole region with one flick of a switch. Then those crazy Muslims from all over the region going on about pan-Arabism, socialism, decolonisation. Selim knew Minas only understood enough of those words to dislike them, so he didn't even try to explain to his father the very real threat Muslims posed to the whole of the Middle East.

Selim thought back to one night he remembered so clearly, perhaps because he'd been so ashamed. On this late summer's night Minas sat in his chair looking out over the same landscape, muttering the same platitudes as every other night. Telling Selim to look after his family. Wishing he would just stay home and do well at school.

'It's your own fault,' Lilit would interject from her bedroom, where she sat in the breeze that came from the open door. 'You're the one who's been stuffing his head with hatred for Muslims since he was in swaddling clothes. And my daughter too.' Selim and Anahit exchanged wry smiles.

Minas didn't want his son to fight. He always said Selim was too precious to be wasted on an idea. Of his own fighting days he said little, only that it was a necessary war, to establish French control in the region. Assisting their only protectors at the time. Now these same great powers had their own huge armies and allies from all over the world. 'Why should Selim be called upon? Let the French and English and Americans be killed for a change,' he replied to his sister. Lilit called these justifications, then threw back her head and laughed. When she did this Selim felt all of four years old, and secretly hated his aunt for being so prescient.

Selim knew that Minas approved of Anahit. He thought it was a good thing Anahit was so adamant, so fundamentalist, so very Armenian. Gone were the stories she was fed by her mother about her Turkish heritage. She spoke Armenian and Arabic and French fluently, did well at school but stopped to work in the jewellery shop. Her mother urged her to go on and try for the American University, but Anahit said she would rather work with Uncle Minas. She professed to hate Muslims as much as he and Selim did, screwing up her nose in disgust when she spoke of them. She hated the way they drank their muddy coffee, the way they spat in public at her feet, the way they treated their women. Selim had watched his father in the jewellery shop countless times. Whenever a rich Muslim came into the quarter expressly to visit their shop, having heard how fine Armenian craftsmanship could be, it was all Minas could do to prevent Anahit from refusing to serve him. 'I hate them as much as you do,' he whispered. 'But we need them in business, they need us. See?'

On the summer night Selim was now remembering, Anahit came between Minas and him, handing her uncle goat's milk and honey. She knew he needed it to soothe his stomach ulcers before bed. Selim watched her silhouette as she leaned over the old man. As she sat down next to him. He studied the way she clasped her hands around her knees, holding her slim, braceleted wrists, and rocked forward, looking into the patchwork of lighted windows and roofs as if she could somehow discern something in the sloping streets. As if sensing his thoughts, she turned to him and sighed.

'I hope you're safe out there at night.'

'He should be home every night reading his schoolbooks,' Minas grumbled at them both. 'It's his last year.'

She pouted. It was something Selim noticed her doing often these days.

'Uncle, you know you're proud Selim's such a patriot. And so am I.'

His father huffed but resumed sipping his milk. Selim sat still, willing himself to be cold as moonlight. She continued.

'I love my cousin a great deal, you know that, Uncle, don't you?'

Selim waited for the reverberation her sentence made to be over, his embarrassment acute. Rivers of shame and desire coursed up his throat and into his cheeks, and he was thankful the night was dark and the balcony lit only by a guttering lamp. She stood, leaned over Selim and kissed his forehead.

'But your son, my dear uncle, is single-minded. And high-minded. He never even looks at me.'

Minas drained the last of his milk and gave the glass back.

'Anahit, he's your first cousin. I've told you before, we're not Arabs.'

Now Selim began walking again, conscious that some of his men were looking at him strangely. Usually he was one of the first to instigate violence, to push the boys into higher and wilder states of frenzy. Usually the fantasy of his Crusader forbears, crashing and straining in their mediaeval armour, buoyed him. But today he felt strangely sickened. He forced himself to move from hut to hut, checking how quickly the camp was being cleared, watching the shooting and knifing from afar, taking care of rhythm and structure. He blocked out the cries and screams, the swearing. There was always swearing from both sides. He settled his mirrored sunglasses more firmly in front of his eyes. *Terrorists. Refugees. Same thing.* He never once thought of himself as refugee; he was a Lebanese citizen; he was born in Beirut. He was Lebanese, they weren't. *Dirty Muslims. Stink of sweat. What are they doing here anyway, living off our land?*

He stopped again in the middle of the street. Of course he thought of himself as a refugee. Every day, in fact. At school, in his father's jewellery shop, on the street, in the stiff volumes he was forced to read on the genocide. He spent his Sunday afternoons looking at the glossy photographs in those weighty, expensive books, a reluctant voyeur. *Sasoun, Bitlis, Kars.* Dead Armenians hanging on meat hooks. Well-groomed Turks in fezzes, looking on and smiling for the camera. Skulls on tables. Heads on sticks, freshly killed, with the same expression of bewildered affront he saw – and had inflicted – many times since. Dead babies piled in baskets like rotten fruit.

He was ashamed to be looking at the corpses along with those men, somehow complicit in their hermetic grins. At the same time he knew it was necessary, this collective memory – no, more than that, this collective guilt at not being there to suffer too. *Sivas, Trebizond, Diyarbekir.* Armenian heads displayed on shelves like trophies. His father's guilt at surviving to tell the tale. *Der ez Zor, Rakka, Ras ul-Ain.*

He remembered Minas quoting the Turkish gendarmes: 'No man can ever think of a woman's body except as a matter of horror, after Ras ul-Ain.' And the double shamelessness of those men, blithely photographing such horror. Armenian mothers and babies eating the flesh of a dead horse by the roadside. Stick figures with blank, unaccusing eyes. *Musa Dagh, Urfa, Erzerum.* He was conscious as he leafed through those books that his was a responsibility to look, to re-emphasise the ordeal, to bear witness to the memory.

Of course he was always a refugee. Mount Ararat on the wall in the parlour, the same cheap reproduction hanging in every Armenian house. Ani, ancient city of a thousand and one churches. Stories of Lake Van and the grandparents he'd never known. Displaced, wiped out, cursed to be forever far away from home. This loss was present in the drawn, haggard faces of the men here in Beirut, on streets named after destroyed villages, in the women's insistence on feeding their children until they grew as fat as those Easter lambs they gorged on each year. It was heightened each time he left the Armenian quarter and ventured out into the city. He skulked about the Corniche or downtown, hands in pockets. Wondered if this one or that was a Muslim, a fanatic, a bloodthirsty gunman. At first it was fear, yet as he grew into his teens it became swagger, bravado, hatred. *I'm the son of a genocide survivor. I have every right.* He picked fights at streetlights, in queues, at anyone who dared look sideways at him. Palestinian, Lebanese, Muslim Druze. He had no idea whom he was fighting. Now he stopped in the middle of the camp and thought perhaps he was fighting his father all along.

One night, not long after the episode with Anahit, he found his father alone in the kitchen. Minas enjoyed cooking late at night when everyone else was asleep, liked to listen to the radio and perfect ever more elaborate recipes as the clock ticked into another day. Dishes Selim's grandmother had cooked in the half-forgotten days before the genocide, when there was a sense of plenty and no fear. Milk-fed lamb with almonds and apricots. Trout baked in parchment. Selim loved those dishes. Special yeasted recipes for feast days, with fat raisins and far too many eggs. The secrecy of his father's act enhanced its pleasure.

That night, Minas looked up from his kneading, fingers glued together with bread dough, and saw Selim standing at the side door.

'And what time do you call this?'

He gestured with one hand to the clock on the wall and a blob of dough fell to the floor. Selim bent down, picked it up and placed it on the table.

'It's not so late, Father.'

He picked out one of the raisins and chewed it thoughtfully, trying to act unconcerned.

'You have university tomorrow! What am I going to do with you?'

'Nothing. I want to leave and join the army.'

'Which army? Not one of the militias?'

'I don't care, so long as they're not Muslim.'

Minas fought to get his hands free of the dough.

'Fighting! More fighting. No, I can't have that at your age.'

Selim straightened up and poked a finger at his father.

'You fought with a militia when you were younger than I am. You escaped one of those camps. You fought for years. And look at you now, reduced to this—' He broke off, gesturing at his father's handiwork helplessly.

'My son—'

Selim shook his head, not wanting to hear any more.

'Don't. You—I looked up to you. Now I'm ashamed of you.'

Now, all these years later, Selim could imagine what his father had felt, thought. Now, being a grown man, he could cringe with the poignancy of it, the loss. After he went upstairs, his father would have sat down, leaving his dough to dry out on the table. He would have clasped his old hands together on his lap and looked at them. Gnarled, criss-crossed with cuts here and there, pale dough caught under the fingernails. Hands that could fire a gun, kill, maim women, children.

Was there any use thinking about it? Selim didn't want to torture himself, but the image came unbidden. His father sitting there, weeping with the futility of all he had ever done. What was the point of joining, killing and being killed, if there would only be more wars?

Selim remembered hearing him call down the hall, not caring if he woke anyone.

'My son!'

And there he was, stumbling in the dark to Selim's bedroom, blind through his tears, those old man's hands of his groping for the door, the rattling knob. 'You have no idea what it was like,' he shouted. 'You would never have made it. You would have died out there – not like me.'

But he had said all this to Selim before: in those late-night rants when he collapsed on the bed, in lectures when Selim came home from school with ruined clothes, in admonitions when he played out on the street too often and didn't study, at formal dinners when Selim merely stared at his plate and ate nothing. A smack on the side of the head. Tearful protestations from his mother before the guests. His father's glare at the two women and the young girl whose anger sparked the air: Siran and Lilit and Anahit. Minas was unrepentant. 'At your age, Selim, I had nothing. Now go upstairs hungry and think about that.'

That night, with Minas in his room, Selim shifted awkwardly under the glare of the overhead bulb. He was already undressed, ready to jump into bed. Minas stopped and Selim could see, uncomfortable, how his father slowly surveyed his heavy, marbled chest, the tapering waist. Those muscular arms. All those nights spent at the gymnasium.

Now Selim thinks, *I was only seventeen.*

'What is it, Papa?'

He hadn't called Minas Papa since he was a little boy, when he would take him to the markets, teaching him how to haggle with Arabs – *they pretend they're poor but they're richer than we are* – showing him how to count out the exact amount of change for the Palestinian cab driver and no more – *they don't need tips, they get too much money from our government as well as working on the sly* – telling him how you could pick a Muslim girl just from the way she walked, even if she wasn't wearing a veil – *they walk like they're teasing you, do you know what that means, son?*

Selim repeated his question.

'What's wrong, Papa?'

Minas merely stood there, tears gluing his lashes together. He turned and left the room.

✳ Selim stalked now through disorderly lines of huts, looking for somewhere to hide. But he couldn't. His soldiers needed him.

He told them he was sick, something he ate. He started throwing up, his composure shattered, at the same time trying to direct them to other areas if he felt they were too immersed in one killing, too fixated on one woman or a crying child. The well-oiled machinery mustn't bog down, mustn't slow, no matter how he felt. When he saw a soldier being self-indulgent, he barked out a reprimand and watched the boy leave the job half-done, unsure of what to do next.

'Finish up!' he boomed. 'Get onto the next thing!'

He was panting. He estimated the time this would all take before they could stop and let the bulldozers in. A day? Two days? He kept an ever lower profile as he advanced further into the camp. He was becoming more and more afraid to be involved at all. At the same time frightened to become the deserter, the enemy they might turn on. On this day, any call to mercy – or even efficiency – could be construed as betraying the cause. So he stood aside, lit a cigarette to settle his stomach, and gave the impression of monitoring their progress without allowing himself to look.

He didn't feel as if he was missing anything. There was always a terrible sameness to the appearance of dead bodies, or half-dead bodies, the wounded, the unvarying expressions on an anguished face. It became tiresome after a while. An older woman stood her ground and screamed.

'Animals! Filthy swine!'

She was crying from rage, not fear.

'You're worse than the Israelis. I spit on your mothers' graves.'

He watched one of his men drag her away. He was feeling better now, detached again. Must have been the cigarette. He strode down the main road of the camp, into streets where the killing hadn't started yet. Phlegmatic now, seemingly unconcerned. He lit another cigarette, forced himself to inhale with measured calm. Yet there was something wrong with his breathing again. He usually cultivated a studied indifference in these situations; it was the only way to survive. Battles, bombings, assassinations, massacres. He slowed down and caught himself. *Did I say massacres? Is this a massacre?* No, it was a mission, an operation, that's what it was.

A young girl ran into his peripheral vision. She didn't look Muslim, wasn't wearing a scarf. He threw down the cigarette, pulled out his gun.

'Stop right there!'

Her arms flayed wide as she wheeled around to face him. She pulled out a wad of cash from the folds of her skirt, and he could see even this far away she was holding close to ten thousand lira.

'Please, please,' she cried.

For a moment, her incredible fragility stayed his hand. A moment, and her upright body rested weightless on the earth. She let the money fall. He shot her in the chest and she swayed into the dirt, her full skirt scattered like a blowsy tulip. It was the image of Sanaya. It was the pimpled girl from the death camp. He had one chance to honour his father's memory, and he'd blown it. He stumbled across to her and fell to his knees, cupping her lolling head in his hand. If it were only the girl from the death camp, he would have saved her. He wouldn't have left her there to die. He bent closer to her face. Her plait touched his cheek and he shuddered.

'Please,' he said. 'Are you awake?'

She exhaled. The sound broke his concentration. He shook himself, let her head fall back again to the ground. When he got up off his knees, his first thought was to light another cigarette. He tossed the empty packet down, stood above her and watched ash fall on her bright chest, the barest hint of cleavage.

'I had to do it,' he told her.

He finished his cigarette and pulled a notebook out of his pocket, walking away from the young girl to some shade and noting down the time, 5.25 pm. He calculated how long he would like it all to take and noted down that time as well. He prided himself on his precise nature, calm and efficient under any circumstances.

�֍ Candles guttered in all four corners of the room. Outside in the southern suburbs, distant flares of a mandarin hue shocked the camps into seeming daylight.

'Selim?'

'Hmm?'

He was busy unfastening Sanaya's blouse. Calm and efficient.

'I heard the news on the radio.'

'Which news?'

His gold crucifix glittered in the half-light.

'The massacres. At Sabra-Shatila.'

'And?'

He cupped one of her breasts, watching the way it stayed full and round in his palm, let it fall. Overhead, Israeli planes crisscrossed the night sky, raining shells down on the south coast.

'Were you part of it?'

'You know what I do.'

She turned away, threw her blouse over her shoulders.

'Sanaya! Don't blame me like this. We had our conversation, the night that Palestinian was here. Enough. It is what it is.'

'How can your grand ideals be corrupted so much you're killing mothers and babies? Your own neighbours?'

'Is your Palestinian friend any better?'

'I'm not saying that. All of you, you're all the same.'

'My dream is of a Christian Lebanon.'

'What about me?'

'I'll make an exception.'

'You make me sick.'

'Don't be so dramatic. It's not worth all this.'

'This—this what? This myth of an equal Christian and Muslim country everyone wants to believe because it's such a nice idea?'

'I'm not advocating equality, except when I talk to diplomats and journalists—'

'Let me finish. This dream you espouse reinforces everything you like to think yourselves to be: civilised, urbane, compassionate, reasonable. But you're none of those things.'

'I'm not pretending I am. I'll say it again: it's your Palestinian friend downstairs who pretends to be so concerned about the welfare of his fellow human beings when all he wants to do is kill everyone – Christian, Jew, Sunni, Syrian, anyone who's not Shia. We get more trouble from those Shias than any other Muslim faction combined.'

He leaned over close to her face and she could smell the stiff pomade, sourly sweet, that he put through his hair. Or was it something else she could smell? Had he washed since he came back from the camps? She could hardly hear what he was saying.

'Listen. My father was a survivor from one of the worst genocides the world has ever seen. And who did it to him? Muslims. It's my duty to fight them and avenge my family's honour.'

He pulled down his underpants.

'Come on, I don't have much time.'

✳ When the horn honked downstairs before dawn, he was dressed and ready in a minute. Sanaya noticed his hands looked old: splodgy, soft-knuckled. She looked away. He gave her a light kiss on the shoulder, pushed her down onto the bed.

'Sleep now. You look terrible.'

In the rear of the Mercedes, he settled back but somehow couldn't find the right position. He looked out the window at the deracinated palms, the first intimations of heat-shimmer on the sea. He looked down again at his hands folded in his lap. *I'm the son of a genocide survivor. I have every right.* He tapped on the glass dividing him from Gilbert.

'Stop for a coffee in Achrafiye. At my regular place.'

He looked at his old bracelet, fingered the large silver links with affection. He checked his watch. Still early, he could stop for a while before reporting to headquarters. Gilbert was driving fast, racing to the Green Line before shooting for another day began in full force.

Selim smoothed the tiny creases on his pants near his thighs precisely, with the tips of his square-cut nails. *We've suffered so much we're absolved of all guilt.* He looked down at his hands again, clenched and unclenched them in his lap. *My hands are clean. I didn't rape any of those girls pleading with me, didn't torture any men. Even that last girl, she didn't suffer for a second.* He bit a hangnail from his thumb, spat it onto the floor of the car.

He remembered the blood rush to his head, the euphoria of power. It came on especially strong after the doubt he had experienced earlier, hot on the heels of his creeping shame. He had run into the centre of the camp after the killing of the young girl, barking further orders, weaving between the hovels and alleys behind them and the winding stairways that led to flat roofs. It was just before sunset.

He stood high up on one of those roofs, legs wide apart, surveying the swarms of militiamen advancing like a black fire into the camp. He could see no opposing gunmen, no terrorists, only old men and women and hysterical children. No answering shots rang out. There was no resistance from the inmates of the camp. Subtly and insidiously, the shapeless doubt took hold of him again.

He'd swerved, scanning the lane below. Heard a rat scurry to his left. A woman looked up and saw him and started running away. Her fat behind waddling. He'd bounded down the steps, his rifle banging against his shoulder. She turned her head and he caught a glimpse of her face in profile, a flash of eye and cheek. He stopped at the foot of the stairs panting, aimed his rifle but didn't fire. She had seen him, looked him straight in the face. And he just stood there, wiping the sweat from his forehead with one hand, the violence of his breathing causing the gun to shake in his grip.

He stared vacantly out the car window now, the streets blurring into unrecognisable movement. *I just eliminated them. That's all I did. Except for that woman. I let her run away. Don't know why I did that. Maybe she wasn't worth chasing. She'll drop dead of her own accord, anyway, when she sees all those bodies.*

They were just Muslims: Palestinians, Lebanese, Syrians, Turks. All Turks, his father would say. Good for nothing other than killing. Selim went one step further. No race has a monopoly on cruelty. *If they hurt us, we will hurt them a hundred times worse.* His argument flowed sluggish in his veins and he closed his eyes, thinking of Sanaya, of his daughter.

✳ All day Bilqis and Amal could smell corpses from their hiding place. It was a high, stinging smell that cut into their noses and forced them to breathe through their mouths. It even cancelled out the discomfort of staying crouched together in so small a space behind the bed, in the mouldy concrete hollow they found.

Throughout the day the smell drove out any question of pity or compassion or even fear: in the morning, when they were too cautious to get up and forage; at midday, when they were too sick to contemplate eating; at sunset, when Bilqis forced herself to gnaw at a UNRWA biscuit.

Amal was in shock. She sat, her back against the wall, shaking. She couldn't eat. Bilqis tried to give her a cup of water mixed with sugar, but she couldn't swallow and the liquid dribbled over her chin. As the sun began to go down Bilqis wrapped her in blankets, told her to lie on the bed and sleep.

'I'm going outside. Don't worry about me. I'll bring you back a hot drink.'

All that was left in Bilqis now was a white-hot anger: against the Israelis, the Christians, the Syrians, the PLO, even against the corpses themselves. She wanted to push the smell away, forget it, if she could, distance herself. She hated the corpses, who forced her to smell them. She hated the corpses with the same level of passion she assumed the perpetrators did when they killed living, breathing, fleshy, human beings.

As she opened the door, she could see her porcelain and glass figurines crowding the windowsill, taunting her, mocking her luck at being alive. These gifts were from grateful journalists and UNRWA workers she spoke to honestly and without taking sides. There was the Swedish correspondent – a young woman with a grave face who came with a local translator Bilqis knew was an Israeli collaborator. There was the American journalist who tried to trick her into saying she hated Jews. And the aid worker from Italy who clasped her hands together and cried. No more gifts. It was time to take sides. They shone like avatars from some unwritten past, these smiling shepherdesses and solemn china cats and glass ovals, incarnations of divinity.

She walked out of her hut, unsteady, in a daze of humid evening heat. Flies settled on her nostrils, the edges of her mouth, in the corners of her eyes so she could hardly see where she was going. A massacre. An atrocity. A war crime. None of those epithets let even a glimmer of understanding in. No understanding, no analysis. Only the rotten, sweet air filling her nostrils and choking her breath deep in her throat. There were Mariam and Maha, young women with blank faces and torn undergarments in the yard next door. Were they raped in front of their husbands and sons? The rats had already arrived, scurrying over their bodies in the too-bright moonlight.

She walked further down the main road of the camp. Her knees had turned to water. Scattered school shoes, a tarnished spoon with a dent in it, old photographs charred black and frilled around the edges. She picked one up, marvelling at the composed faces and high, rigid collars. She carried the photograph with her as she reached the middle of the camp, where most of the Shia Lebanese lived. *Had lived.* Where her in-laws had lived.

She stopped, looking down. She stepped back, dropped the photograph. It was easy to miss the corpses in the half-light, grey as those desperate rats, they were too mixed up in the garbage and detritus of a retreating army: half-eaten rolls of bread, empty soda bottles, ration tins, ammunition stamped with 'made in USA' and torn clothing, fluttering, fluttering over the faces of the dead.

She peered closer. She sat down in the rubble for a moment to be nearer to them. Perhaps she could comfort them, stop their crying. Wasn't that a baby's wail she heard behind that building, carried on the wind? She found the old photograph again at her feet, studied the black and white faces with intent. Were they from Jaffa too? They looked like her own mother and father, could even be her grandparents posing for a wedding memento, the only photograph they could afford their whole lives.

She looked up and became distracted by the patterns made by bricks on a wall, some crooked, laid slapdash, some already crumbling, and she wished to set them straight. Who did such a bad job? She was sitting like this, staring, still rearranging the bricks into neater configurations in her head, sobbing softly, when another woman helped her to her feet, clucking, and ushered her away.

There was panic among the few survivors on this, the first night of the massacre. Rumours the Phalange were coming back to finish their work. With the arrival of the foreign journalists Bilqis relaxed somewhat.

They spoke to her in English and French, in incomprehensible German. 'There were also Israelis at the massacre,' she told them. 'I heard them speaking in Hebrew while I hid.'

She wailed now, flung her hands about, pointed to the corpses and pronounced the names she knew. The journalists wrote them down in fat notebooks with diligent flourishes of the pen. Named. This one small gesture of respect at least.

✸   She was silent most of the next day and following night, seated at the window in Rouba's kitchen. Not even her granddaughter Hadiya, with her child's wit and dolls and laughter, could rouse her from the blackness. Amal was in bed in another room, still shaking as she lay there. The canary filled in the silences with short, exhausted trills whenever somebody moved.

'Issa?'

'He's somewhere fighting, Mother. He told me he'd be back next week.'

She subsided into silence again. Rouba turned on the radio and after much fiddling with the dials tuned in to her favourite station, Radio Monte Carlo.

'At last count, more than three thousand Palestinian and Muslim Lebanese residents of the Sabra-Shatila refugee camps have been killed or have disappeared. We suspect those not yet accounted for have been taken to unknown destinations in Phalange army trucks.'

Rouba turned off the radio.

'I'm sorry, Mother.'

Bilqis twitched; she seemed not to have heard.

'Some noodles? Or maybe you should go to bed? I've made up a sofa in the room where Amal is. You haven't slept at all.'

Bilqis sighed and turned her face to the window. Rouba persisted, against her own better judgement.

'There have already been demonstrations against this even in Israel. And all over the world.'

A smile – could it be a smile? – played across Bilqis's lips.

'You know, Rouba, I'm remembering this thing. It will not leave my head.'

'Please try to forget, Mother. I'm sorry I turned on the radio. It's not good for you.'

'Listen. A British journalist once asked me, *Why are you in such a hurry to leave the camps? The children seem to really love it, such a perfect playground for them.*'

'Yes?' Rouba asked gently.

No answer. Bilqis was back there, beside the journalist, listening to his clipped BBC tones and answering the interpreter in monosyllables. She stood at the door of her hut, sun westering behind the hills, one hand shielding her squinting eyes. The photographer took many shots, told her to pose with her hand on her hip, leaning into the doorframe as if she were tired. Mahmoud and little Issa played in the dust at her feet with intermittent squeals of frustration at the sharp stones, those eddies of dust, at cockroaches that crawled over their legs if they stayed down there too long. Bilqis looked at the squalid dwellings all around her, their roofs of corrugated iron weighted down by bricks, their home-made walls of squashed petrol cans, herbs growing in rusting tins, clouds of flies, stink of animals and shit, the long line of women just like her queuing at the UNRWA truck for a small bag of rice, kerosene, or a few kilos of flour. She felt a shudder of desire for her childhood home: that small bare orchard overlooking the sea. Then she merely looked at the journalist. He understood her contempt for him, and left.

BEIRUT, 1995

Today I can't get Siran's voice out of my head. That reedy whine she punctuated with coughs, the melancholy inflection I wonder if my father inherited.

It saddens me that I've never heard his voice. Never seen him move, or laugh, or dance. When I think of him he's always static, caught in a noiseless dream. I would hear Siran nag Minas in that voice, and I hated it. I wanted them to be happy, wanted all of us to be, and had no idea how to do it.

Minas, killed in 1967 by his own rage. Before he died, he spent hours staring at the wall, only jolted out of his reverie by Siran with bowls of warm milk for his stomach. The tumours didn't kill him, so she said; his guilt and grief did.

'I'm dying,' he would scream. 'I'm dying for all of you.'

I take the bus to the nursing home early, forgoing my cafe breakfast, stomach a tight knot of misery, head teeming with memories, fragments of conversations, disjointed scenes. I've picked some jasmine on the way to the bus stop, thinking to give it to Siran. Crooked streets warp then bulge in the strengthening heat, fragile structures creak on wooden poles. The swamp where the Armenian refugee camp once stood continues to bubble beneath.

The nursing home looks smaller, more dingy than I remember. As I pass open doors, catch glimpses of bath-robed, shuffling figures, I remember with a new clarity all those years of secretly listening to Lilit's mumblings of massacres and deportations, the death of her family and friends.

When I turned to my other grandmother for confirmation or response, Siran merely looked away over the Beirut rooftops then back again at my face.

'What was it like for you, Grandma? How did it feel?'

Siran laughed, nodding at Lilit. 'Oh, darling. It was like a bad dream for us, exactly like a dream.' There wasn't any weight of blame in her version of events. It was like a moving picture she'd had the misfortune to watch.

Now she sits on an old pink-frilled bath chair with an expression of childish malice. Near her, a plastic bowl containing a sop of bread and milk, food for infants. A fly buzzes, settling on the rim. I start with an involuntary shiver at the sight of her awake, and one of the nuns puts a cautious hand on my arm.

'It's the drugs she needs for her diabetes, her sleep, to control her bowels. They give her that look.'

I advance toward her. What can I bring to this brittle wisp of skin and bone? Yellowish hair balding in patches, scrofula reddening her scalp and the back of her neck. Dangling from her ears again, my mother's earrings. Turquoise and gold, somehow obscene on her soft, drooping lobes. She's murmuring and rocking, repeating the phrase *where is my son, where is my son* in rhythmic flutters that don't stop or waver in intensity. I tuck the jasmine into my blouse. She wouldn't know what to do with it.

'She says the same thing over and over all day,' the nun whispers, solicitous.

I'm aware of smiling stupidly, conscious I have nothing to say, naught to offer.

'Grandma? I came to see you before but you were asleep.'

I kneel, kiss her upraised palm. Siran flings it away, querulous.

'Where's my son, little girl? I was in the shop on the corner buying some bread, stale bread for soup, and he skipped past in his uniform so long ago. He'd gone to be a soldier, he was holding a dead baby in his arms and it was screaming – but where is he now?'

Her new, loud voice and the nonsense she shouts shocks me.

'I don't know where he is, Grandma. I thought you might tell me.'

The nun makes a discreet gesture, mutters something about bringing some glasses of tea back, takes the bowl of uneaten food and closes the door behind her. I get up from the floor, sit opposite Siran in another chair. She seems to be half-asleep now, her anger subsided, slippered feet tapping in a soft rhythm on the linoleum floor. Flecks of green and cream, the bottles of pills arranged in a row on the dresser, the narrow, girlish bed with its corners tucked in. There are no ornaments from home, no photographs, no icons. A life wiped out. The cheap chipboard furniture, the threadbare woven blankets, stains on the floor of—blood, urine, faeces? I'm letting my grandmother die here? The blank pale-blue walls, the grimy windowsill, the trapped fly that bangs itself against the pane and then alights on Siran's lap, twitching. Siran might as well be dead.

I open the window, flick the fly away. Leaning out, I take deep breaths of fresh air cooled by arcing sprinklers on the lawn.

I sit down again. Decide to leave but don't stir. The nurse might come back with the tea. But there's nothing I can do here. Yet I feel a drag of responsibility for the wall-eyed, mumbling woman beside me.

Siran is talking in her sleep about the saucepan lid that was dented and needed to be fixed and the dress he bought her one Easter that fell to her hips. She was so thin nothing fitted her anymore. I assume she's referring to Minas. I listen and sit and wait, wondering when I'll have the courage to get up and go, hearing the rattle in her throat as she snores, watching a thin trail of spittle form on her chin.

Finding a tissue on a side table, I dab at it without any force, afraid to wake her. As I wipe nausea rises to the roof of my mouth. I try not to gag, making a small noise at the back of my throat. This seems to rouse her.

'What do you want here, little girl? The men have already come and killed our fathers and the rug from Persia needs cleaning with expensive soap. I told her I could do the washing better than her and she went ahead and did it, then I had to do it all over again.'

'I'm here to see you, Grandma. It's Anoush.'

The old woman is silent now, face averted to the window. I have the urge to chatter and gossip, fill such obscene quiet with meaningless words. I lean forward and put a gentle hand on her arm.

'Are you comfortable, Grandma? Can I get you anything – a glass of water, maybe? A biscuit? The nuns have been so nice and hospitable. You know, it's so lovely here in Beirut, I'd almost forgotten how perfect the city can be in summer. Grandma, I've met someone in the last few weeks – he's so kind, I think you'd approve. He's a little older than me but it doesn't seem to matter when we're together. After all, you always used to say—'

Siran nods then, suddenly knowing. She leans forward and spits out her words.

'You made my son run away, little girl. It was you who did it.'

I want to protest: *I was just a baby when he left us. A newborn.* Instead, I wait for her to continue.

'He would have stayed if it hadn't been for the scheming of that Lilit and her brother, God curse him. My own husband conspiring against me, little boy and girl, throats cut, thrown in the river. Tell me, did that lamb have to be so charred? My dead beloved silly boy. And your mother Anahit, my girl, all roses and cream, but tarred with a Turkish brush. Curse them all. Especially Minas. Gave me a hard life. All those soiled sheets, what to do? Soak them and boil them and put them in the sun to dry. Hanging like dead men. Get rid of that other woman's smells. A pimpled girl, dead now. He dreamed about her, spoke of her in his sleep. A husband needs loyalty to his wife, not his sister. And not to some nightmare girl from the desert. Even the Bible says it. *A man shall leave his father and mother and cleave unto his wife.* Not that Lilit was truly Christian anymore, what with all that time spent in an ungodly country. Dirty spoons, they fell on the ground. Lick them quickly.'

'What did Lilit and Minas do?'

She's stopped now, going over her words again, muttering, repeating her phrase from the Bible. She lapses again into the wail for her son and I come forward, without knowing what I'm going to do, and take her by the hands.

'Tell me what happened, Grandma.'

Siran shuts her red-rimmed eyes, obstinate. 'Where is my son, where is my son?' she whispers and shouts, fading and then growing in fervour. I shake her, gripping both shoulders. I shake her again, shake her some more.

'Tell me, Grandma! I have a right to know.'

She's blank-faced, lolling in my arms. She should be dead, she deserves to be dead, she's limp now, useless. I can't stop shaking her, she's complicit, her neck so easy to snap, my wrists burning with a rage that's almost sexual. Suddenly I see the livid eyes and the fear in her mouth and release her, going back to my chair, exhausted by my own violence.

'I'm sorry, Grandma. Forgive me.'

She hangs her head, unmoving. I kneel again at her feet, kiss the mottled hand. She looks up.

'Go now, child. Go, Anoush. What a silly name they chose.' Her voice so lucid now it seems to belong to somebody else.

'But—Grandma. I didn't mean to hurt you.'

She unclasps my mother's earrings in a swift, irritated movement, shoves them at me. Her pink lobes ravaged now, as if she's taken a knife to them. I look at the gold and turquoise lump in her hands, still warm from her pulse.

'But Grandma, Minas gave them to you so long ago—'

'Yes, child. So long ago. Then I gave them to your mother—before she died. Time for you to have them now. Go quickly. You're late for school.'

She hangs her head and waves me away.

I leave the nursing home with blurred vision, walking through the narrow intimacy of streets, not knowing where to go next. I stow the earrings away in my daypack, shuddering at the thought of ever wearing them. Siran, reduced to a dry husk, an insect's carapace, an absence of broken memories. And what did I do for her? Nothing. No compassion, no pity. Instead, I tried to force the truth out of her. A truth I already knew. Lilit conspired with Anahit to get her pregnant, so she could marry Selim. My birth was the result of two women, their whispered secrets and lies. Immaculate.

In a moment I have an intense desire to look for my childhood house. I keep walking, my feet hurt in their high sandals; I rub at my red eyes with my fists, ashamed to appear so weak to passers-by, who ignore me and continue on their way. Not sure where I am, the streets have changed, been made wider, more accessible, new apartment blocks everywhere now, casting their long shadows in the early morning sun.

I give up too soon on the house, search for my grandfather's jewellery shop. There it is, gilt letters underneath new Armenian script. *Minas Pakradounian – Jeweller Extraordinaire*. It's shut, opens at ten. I stay at the window, dazzled by row upon row of identical gold wedding bands.

No more silver and carnelian bracelets, inlaid mother-of-pearl rings. No traces of Armenia. Only the same gold jewellery found everywhere in the city.

I drift through the quarter's busy thoroughfares, stopping to read the street signs at every corner. Ani. Erzerum. Van. I can't find Urfa Street but don't want to ask. Some of the old neighbours may remember me and I'm in no mood to talk, to explain why I'm here. I can't help but think of the Armenian houses burnt down in Van, just like these: timbered, graceful, with wide carved balconies and sloping roofs. Mulberry trees, charred, with stunted, bitter fruit. Clogs the colour of fire, worn by a young girl going to church.

I sit on a bench in Municipality Square, watching the same meagre plane trees shed the same thin-pointed leaves I monitored each year when I was a little girl. Lilit would bring me here in the autumn when the leaves glistened. I must have been very small, before I started school, because Lilit could walk and didn't even need a stick. I held her hand and we played wild, screaming games with the drifts of leaves, which slowly blackened as the day wore on, catching them then kicking at the street sweeper's piles to make them dance in the air.

Once, sitting on this very bench, between Lilit and Minas, I heard them talk. I would have been about three. They were in one of their sad, quiet moods, and I'd wanted to get up and play but was clutching a huge sugared doughnut and Lilit wouldn't let me eat and run at the same time. So I sat, licking wet sugar from my fingers, and they talked on, half in Armenian and half Arabic, while I was alternately shocked and bored. They spoke of my dead mother, my father who was gone. Something they called a 'shotgun wedding'. And Lilit saying the jewellery shop belonged to me, without a doubt. They blamed Selim, Selim all the time. Until Minas stood up finally, the sky a lurid orange behind him.

'Whatever he is, whatever he's become – I want to find my son again before I die. I can't bear not knowing where he is each night.'

'Please, Minas. He knows where we are, he sends money – don't you think, if he cared for you, wouldn't he come?'

I watched Minas crumple into Lilit's arms. I could see he was trying to hold back his tears, but they came in retching gulps. Lilit looked over his shoulder at me and pressed her lips together as if she didn't know what to do. Something in the twitch of her mouth made me think she wasn't as upset as she should have been about her brother crying, that something in her was happy about it.

The wind picks up now and fallen leaves flurry around my feet. In the middle of the square is a children's playground, all rusting slides and swings that look too dangerous to play on. A broken fountain. No children. One yellow and red plastic slippery slide, banked up with the sodden leaves. A rocking horse balancing crazily on its bouncing coil, half-uprooted from the ground. There was none of this when I was growing up. I get up now, brush leaves off my shoulders and skirt, walk to the main road. I press some liras into a bus driver's hand, don't tell him any destination. Anywhere. Away from here.

I get off the bus at a corner that looks familiar. Walk as if I know where I'm going. Don't hesitate. I set off at a brisk pace, taking care to keep to the side of the road, away from shacks and ramshackle buildings, open doorways revealing sharp-bearded men and squalling babies, young women squatting over paraffin stoves, the smell of raw meat and unleavened bread. I squelch through mud and refuse, but keep to the verge. An unshaven man offers me a cigarette and a leer and I avert my eyes.

Soon I find myself in the vicinity of the Sabra-Shatila camps. A little boy of about twelve runs down the incline to the street when he sees me. He stops, awkward, one hand clutching a jagged stone.

'Mademoiselle?'

I look around; we're alone. *How did he know I'm a foreigner?* I think he may throw the stone at me. The zip on his trousers is undone or broken, I can't tell. He comes toward me and begins his patter in a servile voice I know he's used on others countless times before.

'Mademoiselle,' he says. 'Mademoiselle, can you spare a coin for a poor Palestinian?'

I fumble in my daypack, careful not to open it too wide.

'Wait a bit, not sure I have any coins.'

'Notes are good.'

He comes closer. I notice my hands are trembling. I know he can see this, wonder what he thinks of me, whether he despises me for my fear, my suspicion or merely my perceived Western wealth.

'American dollars are better.'

'I'm not American.'

'I can see that. You speak Arabic too well. But you're not one of us either.'

I fold some lira notes into his open palm and surprise myself with the vehemence of my words.

'Now leave me alone.'

'It's all right,' he whispers. 'I won't hurt you.'

I walk away, sense him watching my gait all the way down the potholed, empty street. I walk faster, forcing my legs to obey, afraid that at any moment they'll buckle and let me down. Now I'm shaking all over, with fear, disgust, another shame that's harder to define.

✳ I don't mean to come to Chaim's apartment. My feet lead me here; I'm upset over Siran and the Palestinian boy, and not thinking straight, and now I'm hot and exasperated from walking so far, sweat soaking my lower back, making stains on my blouse. I need to sit down for a minute and Chaim's apartment is on the way to my hotel. I only want a glass of water. I only want to wash my hands. I want to sit in his living room and look at him, simply look at him.

I press the bell and try to scrutinise my face in the glass doors leading to the building's foyer. I can't see a thing and lean closer, rearranging my irritation into something like serenity. Chaim's voice cuts through.

'Yes?'

'It's me, Chaim. It's A—'

'I know it's you. Come up.'

He buzzes me in. I sit for a while in the marble dampness of the atrium, on the imitation Regency chair for visitors. I can hear Julius in the courtyard playing with children from the ground-floor apartment, can't imagine what these Muslim mothers with their cultural disgust for dogs think of him; he has a tendency to drool and bark at the slightest provocation, yet he's gentle and calm even with their toddlers, who slap at him and pull his ears. I know Chaim is upstairs waiting for me, know also that I need this brief, silent time alone to sit, cool down, examine why I'm here.

I trudge up the shallow stairs, feeling his gaze burn the top of my head as he waits at the open door. With the light of the midday sun behind him, he's transfigured, an angel of mixed tidings.

When I reach the landing he's vanished into the apartment. I want to hold him, rest my tired head on his chest. Let him comfort me, as my father never did, never will. I tiptoe onto the bare boards, careful not to make any noise. I want to call out to him, run through his rooms, but to do this would break the fragile, spinning game he's initiated. Instead I let my laptop bag fall onto the sofa with a graceful thump, peer into the kitchen and bathroom, discarding my sandals as I go. My heart's flailing in my chest, a painful rhythm I attempt to control by breathing out slowly, then in.

When I reach the balcony I lean over the railing, hoping he'll steal behind me, push his face into my nape, end this stupid vanishing trick. I breathe, counting the length of my inhalations. Nothing. As I move inside again I'm struck by the quality of light over Beirut: the heavy silvering pall that heralds a storm. The sea is flat, a blank page waiting to be inscribed.

I open the bedroom door.

'Here,' Chaim says.

He's standing in front of the bank of windows, his body an indistinct shape against the glare. I can't see if he's smiling or solemn, or how I'm supposed to respond to the flat sobriety of his voice. He lets me wait, turning away to draw closed the dark floor-length curtains. His bedroom shrouded now, the brilliance of the sea neutered. Far away on the horizon the low growl of thunder.

'Kiss me, Chaim?'

He does so, hesitantly, afraid of my resolve. I shiver at the sensation of his moist lips on the dryness of mine, catch the specific, genetic smell of his mouth, his tongue, the recesses of his throat and stomach: too intimate. A phrase from the Armenian liturgy plays through my head. *This kiss is given for a bond of fullness. The enmity hath been removed. And love is spread over us all.*

Sacrilege. Blasphemy. Shouldn't I be with an Armenian man, erasing our combined past with this simple act? I turn my head away, walking to the tall, pointed windows. When I open the curtains an inch a line of light splits his body in half. Divided man. A brief fizz of lightning and his face and hands are white. Scent of gardenias from the balcony, semen-sour. I go back and kiss him again, blinding myself to the particularities, frenzied, biting, wanting to peel back the skin of age and gender and culture. He grabs my hands, holds them to his cheeks.

'Anoush. Can you tell me what you're doing?'

I kneel and bury my face in his thighs. He puts his big hands on my shoulders, murmurs under his breath.

'Please tell me what you need. Surely not this.'

I stand and put my fingers on his eyes, his mouth, closing them. He sighs, enfolds me.

'Okay. But think about what you're doing.'

He begins to undress me, button by button, as if he's never done this before. But I'm impatient again; stepping out of my skirt, pausing as it rests at my feet, a perfect circle. He sits on the bed and I can now see the top of his head, hair slightly thinning, the small, vulnerable circle of his skull. Is this how my father looked down upon those women? Is this who he was in private, how he played the sexual game? This is no game. I unpeel my bra, proud yet half-ashamed of my youthful breasts. His arm goes around me, pulling me close. As soon as I've slid out of my underpants I'm suddenly unsure. Angry. At him, at myself. He's not of my tribe, my flesh. His hands on my breasts are square, wrinkled, wiry hairs all the way down to his fingertips; surely I should have noticed before? My father had pale hands, smooth as a pianist's. Siran told me.

I turn my head sharply, push him away. 'Always get what you want, do you?'

He whispers, hurt. 'Isn't this what you wanted?'

'Why are you even here, Chaim?' I cover my breasts with my hands, flop to the floor. I'm aware of the smell of my sweaty armpits in the close, dark room. 'Why don't you go back to Israel?'

'Why do you keep taking it out on me?'

He's crumpling now, still in his trousers.

'What was it like doing your military service, bulldozing houses and bombing civilians?'

'What are you talking about? I didn't do any of those things. I tried to help. If you really want to know, suicide bombers tried to blow up our checkpoint twice. Once, they succeeded. I was nearly killed. That's when I decided to leave.'

I stand, looking for my blouse.

'You with your *Free Palestine* fucking T-shirts. What a hypocrite you are. Why didn't you stay behind and do something?'

'It was traumatic. It had nothing to do with me at that point, it was like, like a—it was just like a film in slow motion.'

'Don't be so naive. You're just like my grandmother in the nursing home. *Only a dream, my dear, only a dream.* Of course you're part of it. Part of the occupation. You bastards have been here for nearly twenty years, let alone in Palestine.'

'It's nothing to do with me.'

'Oh, really! What about your brother? Don't you worry, I've been doing my research.'

'And what did you find?'

'Your big brother was a fighter pilot during the war. He helped bomb Beirut.'

'My brother is not me, Anoush. And you know what – if it wasn't for people like my brother, and my father, there would be no Israel. There would be no me.' He spreads his arms out, savagely. 'There would be no Chaim for you to kick around.'

I catch a sob in my throat.

'Oh, Chaim. I never meant to—'

'Listen,' he says. 'Listen to me just for once, and get your victim crap out of the way. My people were almost annihilated, right? Just like yours. Genocide. We've all suffered, agree?'

I nod, ashamed.

'And,' he continues, 'my family have nowhere else to go. We're not occupiers, we're refugees. Do you understand that?'

'But your family didn't have a right to go and take over someone else's land. There were people living on it, before you.'

'According to many sources, the Jews were there first. Thousands of years ago. How can you say whether the Turks or Armenians were in your country first? If we go down that line, nobody would have the balls to settle anywhere. We all have a right to a home. A right to defend ourselves. And we all have a right to feel safe.'

'And you feel safe – here? I find that hard to believe.'

'I'm making a sacrifice to be here. And I didn't choose to be born there. I'm not going back.'

I stand up now, move closer to him, arms folded across my nudity. My anger deflated, voice grown weary. I have a headache that makes me close my eyes.

'Please come here,' I say, with my eyes still shut. 'Please come to me.'

He comes. I unfold my arms and let them fall to my sides.

'Kiss me and tell me I'm an idiot.'

He kisses the top of my head.

'Anoush,' he says. 'You're an idiot.'

Later that afternoon we lie together on the bed. He's opened the curtains again, and the floor-to-ceiling windows seem not made of glass but water. We sprawl side by side on our backs, touching only at the curve of the hip. Like this, we reflect sea, ceiling, sky. The sun hits our bodies now in planes of blue shadow and quivering light. My head on the pillow a mirror, indistinguishable from his.

✳ I walk back to the Mayflower, grateful to breathe in the cool dusk air. For almost a month now, I've felt inviolate, contained in my own private world of the past. After sex with Chaim I'm now permeable, my hard edges blurry, bleeding into the landscape and its people.

Do I resent this? What I feel is probably closer to panic. I linger at the sea wall, gazing down at murky waves splashing, receding, breaking again. A few beggars – young boys with downy upper lips – jostle me as if on purpose, pluck at my sleeve. I elbow them back, suddenly fierce.

Chaim was rough, insistent after his initial hesitancy. It was as though he were claiming me, touch by touch, with his hands. Or maybe punishing me for the mockery I'd indulged in only a moment before. I was aware of a sense of shock as well as arousal. I'm no prude. Yet he put half his thick, square hand right inside me, burrowing, as if seeking something I haven't yet revealed. His expression heated, questioning.

'Stop,' I said. 'You're hurting me.'

He kept going until I took his wrist in my grip and wrenched it away. I hadn't thought of him as that kind of man before, yet, there he was, driving into me with all the will and force he possessed. In my afternoon fantasies at the Mayflower he'd always been liquid, bodiless, resting between my legs, effortless as air. Yet in his bedroom he positioned me exactly the way he wanted, spread-eagled with my calves up around my ears. He growled at me to move sideways, arch my back, take him in deeper – *no, not that way; like this* – to grasp the sides of the mattress with my hands.

My inner thighs ache now. My vagina feels alien: wet, pulsating, bruised with my own ambivalence. I begin walking, taking an almost pleasurable pride in the dull grind of muscle. He wanted me to stay. I sprang from the bed as soon as the sun went down, splashed myself in the ensuite with cold water, one leg high on the sink. All over my belly and chest, his stray hairs were glued to me with our combined sweat. I wet my head, dousing my hair under the tap. In water, the crushed jasmine I wore in my blouse smelled of cigarette smoke, acid and sweet at the same time. He sat up, watching me through the open door.

'You all right?'

'Mmm.'

I answered without giving him anything to go on, came back into the bedroom, and with my face averted pulled on my clothes. The yellow stains under the arms of my blouse, the limpness of the fabric, made the whole room and what had transpired feel suddenly sordid and wrong.

'Where are you going?'

'Back to the hotel. It's getting late.'

'Why not stay here tonight?'

I stood, poised at the bedroom door with one arm out of my sleeve, looked at him and smiled. It was a smile that closed the door on him. I'm not sure even now why I didn't want to stay; I wanted to feel him near me again – I even wanted to have sex with him again – but my more urgent need was to be alone. It was something to do with a tardy modesty, a feeling of being profoundly alien to each other, even a lack of love. Beneath it all, a strange disappointment. What was I expecting? My father intact, as in my dreams?

I walk faster now, stepping out onto the middle of the road. Taxi drivers slow down and ingratiate themselves. I had a hard time persuading Chaim not to walk me back to the hotel. He kissed my

A
S
H

291

hands, my forehead, looked on the verge of tears. Yet I was adamant, possessed of an unformed desire to be rid of him straight away. As if I'd betrayed some vast contract with myself by letting him so soon into my life, my body. I walk and three selves come with me. Far too many for Chaim to tag along as well. Armenian, Turkish, American: split into a secular trinity. Which was he making love to? Which one did I surrender up to him, with my own naive ideals? I accused him of naivety when I'm surely worse. He showed me how much we share: family pain and historical guilt, that burden we both carry every single day. And now I feel ashamed. Which Anoush am I now, striding through the odorous dusk, gratified against all my better instincts by the warm flush of pain spreading from my inner thighs?

I stop at the last corner before the Mayflower, look behind me, banishing the ghostly figures that trail in my wake. Three women, or maybe more: Lilit, Siran and the Lebanese woman my father once loved. Or had he? Hadn't Lilit said he died for her? A secular Muslim, if there can be any such thing. A woman of simple desires, for children and home and security. Am I imagining this conversation? More likely a woman of bold passions, who remained unsatisfied by the bloodless couplings of a Christian militiaman.

And what of Anahit? My own mother, often overlooked. Did anyone love her? And were there any more women? Any dalliances, any dead girl-children? Victims, perpetrators. D'Andrea and his butting, thrusting, middle-aged man's desire. That moment on the phone when I felt a piercing sadness for him. When I pitied him enough to forgive. How to take up my own steps in this shuffling, complicated dance? I pat my hair down close to my scalp, settle the seams of my skirt in a straight line from waist to knee. This mundane gesture resolves something, if only to integrate these capricious and warring selves.

BEIRUT & DER EZ ZOR, 1925-1946

Beirut changed for Minas as he grew older. At times he wasn't aware of it, yet at other times, especially at night, he felt the silent, quick lurch in his belly. He couldn't call it anything else but excitement. Here he was, finally, in this city full of promise. It was 1925, and he had been here ten years already. In that time, Beirut had become a blessed icon of the Virgin mother carried through his every moment, waking or sleeping. She was like no other, this mother. She bled and soothed, beat and caressed, kissed and spat. She taught Minas to win and lose, to make a pyrrhic victory and never count the cost.

There were more wars, always wars in Lebanon. Now the Great War had finally ended, now the French controlled most of the Levant and the Ottomans had been scuttled away, war still seemed the only mode in which these big men could talk to each other. Yet he almost liked it that way: war made it clear to him whose side he was on. The French were strong leaders, rebuilding the ravaged city with wide boulevards and official buildings, raising a tricolour flag. They were clear who the enemy was: Muslims. Minas cultivated a grainy image of the enemy in his mind: foreign eyes and screaming mouth – a dimmed mirror in which he didn't once see himself.

Yes, he liked the idea of war. Killing the enemy was as good as any revenge. Small skirmishes in the mountains, frantic assaults on the higher slopes. Hand-to-hand combat in the slime of city streets.

He finished his breakfast, swallowing the last dregs of powdered milk. He liked the sweetish grittiness it left between his teeth. He wiped his tin mug out with his shirtsleeve and placed it on the shelf above his bunk bed, coughing with the sudden movement. He was older now, well past his teens, with a chest complaint that wouldn't go away. Was it from the damp of those long-ago caves, or the subhuman conditions in Der ez Zor? No matter. That was all in the past. So many years ago now. Ten years already, and it seemed a lifetime. He'd grown used to the cough, hardly noticed it anymore. He'd grown used to news of war. He fiddled with the dial – a radio he inherited from a dead fellow refugee – and put his ear to the fine mesh of the speaker.

He had also grown used to the Red Cross camp. *Another camp*, he thought. It seemed now as if he had known no other life, these barbed-wire fences, to keep enemies out now instead of inmates in, this icy sleeping block and that radio.

In all the years he'd spent in Lebanon, not once had he attempted to go back to Van, see if the old house was still standing, find Lilit. He justified it to himself when he nestled on the bunk for his afternoon nap, told himself he needed the rest, still weakened by his ordeal, still traumatised. He had no passport, anyway, only identity papers issued by the government, couldn't leave Lebanon because they'd never have him back, the house probably burnt down, Lilit no doubt dead in the desert, dishonoured and buried in an unmarked grave.

He hadn't received any money these ten years. Not once had a roll of cash in his pocket, to peel off for drinks and playing cards, women's trinkets to buy some respite from loneliness. He'd never worked for money, in fact, except for his childhood forays selling crickets to schoolmates in those faraway Van summers, trading stolen eggs. He'd worked hard, but it had all been for the Lebanese and American and French governments. The League of Nations, the Red Cross. He'd been given meagre rations and health care and clothes, shuffled with all the other men in the camp from bed to table to bath, one day indistinguishable from the next. He laughed and mocked himself in the long nights spent lying awake, listening to other men's whimpers and nightmares and snores. *If I thought I was an old man then, I must be dead by now.*

He scratched his head, wheezed in the cold spring air and settled his ear more firmly to the radio. In all the fighting, there was always one constant. Muslim against Christian. Whether it was heretic Druze against Maronite Catholic, Shia Muslim against Eastern Orthodox,

Sunni Muslim against the French liberators, it was always the age-old dichotomy. Them and us. He liked it that way.

He wanted to side with the Christians in their assault upon Islam. The Allies didn't make good on their promises of restitution for the Armenians during the Great War, so he wished to do it for them. He thought of their empty speeches as he got up each morning in the dawn light, walking with other refugees to the communal bathrooms to wash in cold water and then back to their huts to eat.

The other men all knew he was militant, prone to spouting the same daily rhetoric and pouring scorn on England and France. They listened to him, cautiously respectful, even though he was much younger than them. He held the floor every morning at breakfast, as they all sat on their carefully made beds eating, legs dangling in the damp air. He drew his bare feet up under his thighs and mocked, through mouthfuls of dry semolina.

'Ha! Those so-called Great Powers in 1915. *The Allied governments will hold all members of the Turkish government personally responsible.* Ha! Lloyd George again in the same year. *We guarantee the redemption of the Armenian valleys forever from the bloody misrule with which they have been stained.*'

They had done nothing. There was no international tribunal, no compensation, not even a symbolic gesture from the new Turkish government.

'I've had enough,' he would say to his fellow refugees in finale. 'Enough of them and their empty lies.'

One wag decided to challenge him.

'Well, what are you going to do about it?'

Minas wasn't exactly sure.

He switched on the radio again when the other men had gone outside. There was work to do in the camp: seedlings to plant, huts to build, hospitals to clean. The compound was already beginning to look a little like a prosperous suburb, an Armenian quarter that would continue to flourish. Armenian women from camps as far away as Aleppo and Iraq had begun to enter and stay, training as nurses and teachers, clicking past Minas on high-buckled boots, swaying in tight white uniforms. Some were marked by indigo tattoos on their wrists and ankles, signifying their incarceration and escape from a Turkish harem.

He'd seen them scrubbing at the designs with lemon juice and vinegar to lighten the load of shame. Others – the unmarked – were marrying his friends in quick civil ceremonies, as there were no Armenian priests yet in Lebanon. Orthodox clergy had been the first to be killed by the Turks. There was even talk of the Lebanese government giving this land to the Armenians sometime in the future, so that permanent dwellings could be built and taxes paid.

Minas was absolved from most physical duties, as the other men deferred to his intelligence, his superior reading and writing skills. He also helped most days in the kitchens, doing what he could with tinned and packaged goods from aid agencies. It was difficult to make do with what little they were sent, yet they still fared better than the locals. So many Arabs had starved in the last few years during the Allied blockade, while many Armenians had survived.

The men swore Minas's bread was the best they had ever tasted, even if it was made with third-rate flour. Though there were always some who spat it out, claiming it was not salty enough, or too dry; they still clung to the memory of their mother's baking as if it held the secret to their future. Many of them were farmers, peasants, survivors from mountain villages that hadn't been entirely razed by the Turks. Most of them couldn't even sign their own names. Minas was one of the few who could write to government agencies to search for missing relatives, to Turkish banks in order to try to recover stolen funds, to fill in forms and decipher statements.

Often when he was sitting, bent over, writing someone's letter or reading a land contract, part of him was transported back to the little boy at the windowsill in Van with his pile of books. He could feel the excitement coming from that little boy in sickening waves through his body. Then he would stop and look up beyond the window, beyond the sleeping block, beyond the fences, wondering yet again and with more honesty why he never tried to find his own sister, as he had attempted to do for so many other refugees. Something held him back, a dread of finding out the truth like a tremor of physical pain.

He didn't hear the voice in his head as often anymore; perhaps it wasn't needed. He had enough to survive here without voices. He had ample food, friendship, even novels sometimes. The aid workers were kind enough to lend him their own books in French and Arabic, even

English. He didn't like that language as much, perhaps because he wasn't as proficient in it. He wasn't exactly happy, but there was time enough in the future for that. For now it was something akin to revenge he sought. At times he was tempted to bring forth the voice with strong drink or prayer, beseech it for news of Lilit, or for advice concerning his life's path, but he pushed away the desire.

He still had his mother's earrings, hoarded in a pouch sewn into his pillow to wait for the day he could sell them and use the money. Sacred money, to put towards a deposit on some land, or open a jewellery shop that would cater for the demands of Armenian weddings and christenings. Traditional ornaments: lockets and crucifixes and Virgins on fine chains, beatific smiles on beaten gold. Tangible memories of home. A late legacy of Papa, so he would not have been killed in vain.

He hadn't held the pliant tongs, the hammer, for years now, since Papa had leaned over him in the tiny Van workshop guiding his hands, seducing still more heat from the forge. Minas would fan the guttering fire, murmuring to it in a childish whisper, wanting it to obey him in just the same way it did his father. Now he wondered if his cold fingers would remember what to do. Blazing metal. The hint of transformation on his clothes. Would a woman grow used to that, or would she be disgusted by his daily filth? He hoped to marry an Armenian, have many children to replace the countless ones that died. Of the girl in the death camp he never allowed himself to think.

The radio presenter's drone cut through his musings. He put his ear closer to the speaker and frowned. Muslim Druze in the Chouf Mountains had revolted against the French mandate. They didn't want Christians ruling them, accustomed as they were to the supremacy of their chieftains and the strength of a community based on intermarriage. They were barricading their villages, had already begun firing, a precarious balance of power threatening to shift. Minas straightened his collar and spat in his palm to smooth the hair off his forehead. *We'll be overrun by those barbarians if we don't stop them now.* He switched off the radio, strode outside into the morning air, coughing slightly into his sleeve. He didn't need a disembodied voice to tell him what to do anymore.

Maronite militiamen came into the Red Cross camp that afternoon, rounding up support against the Druze. French officers stood behind

A
S
H

297

them, nodding and making clear exactly whose money and weapons were involved. The militiamen appealed to the Armenian refugees as fellow Christians, repositories of Western civilisation, keepers of the faith.

'We don't see you as strangers any longer,' they yelled in French through their megaphones. 'We embrace you now as our own! Christian and Lebanese.'

They promised spanking new uniforms and immediate rank for those who volunteered.

Minas was one of the first.

He heard his commanders barking at their inferiors in badly accented French. He made a point of learning all the new, unfamiliar phrases, practising blasphemy at night in his tent as if mouthing a rosary of supplication.

'Kill them all,' he heard his superiors say. 'Women and children. Violate them.'

There was to be no mercy for a fellow Arab. And the French were there to protect the custodians of their colonial heritage, so they turned a blind eye to any atrocity committed in their name. 'After all,' he heard the militiamen say to each other in the long nights spent sleeping in mud and goat's turds on the mountains, 'we are not Arab. We are Phoenician. Our civilisation is different to theirs: our backs to the desert, our faces to the sea.'

The Christian Lebanese had always been in danger, a minority in an Islamic region like the Armenians before them. Catholic Maronites looking to Rome for the concerns of the spirit, and Paris for the flesh. A wealthy mountain-stronghold of monks and militiamen in the north of the country, under siege for hundreds of years. It was their turn now, to rule Lebanon as they were always meant to. And Minas would help them.

He slept within hearing distance of the others, but kept apart from the discussions. He was still only a refugee, even after his ten years in Lebanon. Who knew when they'd turn on him as well? He said his prayers and crossed himself three times in the mornings, alert, conspicuous, washing his hands with care before he ate so they should see him and take note.

He didn't let himself think of the Bedouin who helped him escape from Der ez Zor. That was a long time ago, and he had only been a boy. He simply loaded his rifle, aimed and fired. Fired at whoever he was told was the enemy. See her? Fire. Him? Fire. He went out on all the most distasteful excursions, the fuzzy, grey-area jobs nobody else had the stupidity or the spleen to do.

Today he was in a Druze village in the Chouf Mountains and it was colder than he'd ever known. He hit a chicken coop, the squawks of hens and shit-streaked feathers flying into his face. He flapped one arm about him wildly to disperse them. A woman ran away from him: *Another hen, only bigger*, he thought. He had to laugh, which brought on a coughing fit. *If I don't laugh, I'll only cry. And then what good will I be?*

She panicked, ran ever closer to him in a frantic effort to escape. Realising her mistake, at the last moment she turned away. Black scarf slapping at her neck. He aimed between her shoulderblades, felt the *thud-thud* of metal on his collarbone as he stumbled after her. She collapsed among the chickens as he leapt past, his boots avoiding her face, contorted in a last soundless curse.

He fired to the right and left, covering his advance. Behind him he could no longer hear or sense the rest of his unit. Something in him now was afraid. Should he hide until they found him again? He kept running. Quiet village, empty streets. A few corpses lounged in open doorways: all women, it seemed. The men were fighting higher up on the peaks. Fearless warriors, unafraid to die in battle, for tomorrow they would be reborn and suckling at yet another mother's breasts. Reincarnation, that fixed magic number of Druze souls already in existence. Heretics. If the same people would keep dying and being reborn, well, he'd just have to keep killing them again and again.

The women's faces were stretched beyond recognition. He avoided the black holes of their eyes. He looked around swiftly: nothing. The other militiamen liked to shoot them first and then bayonet them to make sure they were dead. Minas couldn't do that. He shot first and then ran.

He slid on discarded fruit, burst tomatoes. An overturned cart. The dead women watched him, unimpressed. *They're not the same as us.* He tried to look away from the accusation slashed across their faces, in their blown-up limbs. The women continued to stare sightlessly, neither

A
S
H

299

agreeing nor disagreeing. A solitary shot rang out, ricocheting against a building. He flung himself to the ground, propelling his body by the elbows out of range and vision. Snipers, hidden in those seemingly abandoned houses, guarded by their dead. It wasn't until he crawled behind the cart, heart pounding painfully through his breath, that he realised he'd been wounded. He rolled onto his side, wincing. There, the dark, wet stain seeping through his trousers. The stink of squashed cucumbers everywhere.

Oh, Jesus. He ripped apart one of his shirtsleeves, made an inadequate bandage for his calf. *Oh, Jesus.* A child walked out on the road in front of him, holding an old brown dress fast to her mouth. *Her dead mother's? Oh, my Jesus.* The spread of her saliva widened on the rough fabric. He stared at her through his rifle sight as she came toward his hiding place. *Is she two? Three?* She was crying, sucking at the dress like a teat. He knew if he let her she would scream and betray him to the snipers.

He peeked out from behind the cart, beckoned the little girl to him with a crook of his finger. He smiled in what he hoped was a fatherly fashion and nodded many times. He fumbled in his chest pocket, still with the fixed grin on his face, found a half-eaten mess of dried figs wrapped in paper. The little girl inched closer, cautious. Her mouth still working at the dress, frantic sucking. She put out her hand for the food. He gave it to her and watched as she tried to unwrap it without letting go her grip on the dress. He lowered the barrel of his gun. *Am I really doing this?* Her fair head swam then focused into vision. *Murderer.* He swung the gun at her head once, twice, then closed his eyes.

�֍   Time passed in long, slow doses. Minutes, seconds, heartbeats, a fly crawling on the bedhead. Lilit stretched her neck back and watched it progress, millimetre by millimetre, until it reached the highest point, where her evil eye dangled from a plaited ribbon. She studied the fine, iridescent wings and intent, magnified eyes, twins to her beaded talisman. Her sleepy cat, a fourth-generation successor to the ginger beauty she befriended when she first arrived, made to claw at the buzzing insect. Lilit restrained her. When the fly reached the pillow, she slapped it away herself. Minutes passed as she turned her head to watch it die. Many minutes, as she lay in her canopied bed and waited for the servant girl to bring sour yoghurt in a tall glass, as she counted the minutes before another day would begin.

Minutes then hours. Hours of careful washing and folding she couldn't trust the servants to do, putting festival clothes away for winter, taking pleasure in layers of smooth linen and seamed silk. Seasons turned. Wearing those robes again, fragrant folds on bare skin, greeting unveiled female guests for amber tea and ices in her inner quarters. Whitewashing summer garden walls, a team of local men with their paintbrushes and folk songs. She bent down with a tray of drinks for them, looked up: there, the shadows of fruit trees, window grilles, a spasm of memory. Somewhere far away, where another white wall danced in sunlight. No time for that now. There was always baking to do, weaving, slow bathing of tired limbs. Another baby, soapy with vernix, plaster-new.

Only a girl this time, yet Suleiman was pleased. He named her Ayse, after his dead mother. Both he and Lilit loved the baby with a trepidation born of tenderness, taking her into bed with them, watching her small fists clutching and releasing Lilit's nipple, her nightdress, her hair, conscious of a dearth of time to enjoy her. She was so waxen, so pink and white, so frail. She hardly ever cried, simply gazed up at the quilted canopy as if seeing the heavens.

She died at three months, limp with meningitis. Lilit tried not to let herself believe it was her punishment for sleeping with a Muslim and renouncing her faith. She made a bargain with God. *If I have another child, I promise to give it an Armenian name.* Suleiman was shaken by her grief and her terrible insistence, told her to name the next child anything she wanted. He assured her that he was pleased she herself was healthy, and still alive.

She took to her bed, afraid that any movement at all would make her lose the next baby, or the next. She dreamed of infants: their drained, ancient faces as they lay stillborn on cold tiles, Suleiman's dazzling tiles of blue and green. She had been here ten years now, ten years of high walls, and murmured voices, a grudging affection for Suleiman that often felt too much like effacement, nothing else. Weeks later, she walked out into the courtyard one evening, wearing only her nightdress, into a wall of desert heat. The call of the muezzin, melancholy in his devotions. She remembered Lake Van, smug and mute as Fatima's lips.

Children, and blood on its banks, the column marching to who knew where; the blotting out of lives, names, faces; their bones, white then yellow then black; the sharp hairs on the back of Suleiman's hands, his hands all over her, when he took his pleasure.

He was always pleased now, it seemed. Even with the Ottoman Empire waning, dwindling, dying; 1925 now and the treaties after the Great War left them in no-man's land, no longer Asia and not yet in Europe. The last sultan was deposed and exiled to some obscure Italian town Lilit had never heard of. Now the Syrians were pressuring them to leave the newly independent country, yet Suleiman elected to stay. With the few remaining Turks, colonial widows and doddering men, he approached the Arab headman of the town and bowed his head in humility.

Lilit questioned the wisdom of this, remembering what certain races did to those they considered outsiders. But Suleiman waved his hand at her in dismissal.

'Too late now to think of resettling in Turkey. I was born here, Lilit. My father came as a youth with the Imperial Army. If they can't accept me, then I'd rather die here than go anywhere else.'

It was all the fault of this new general, Mustafa Kemal: the splintering of Empire, the lack of social cohesion, his scraping servility to Western powers. It was only a matter of time before the French marched in to occupy the country. Or so Lilit thought. Yet Suleiman worshipped him.

'Ataturk,' he said, 'what a saviour. I feel as if I know him already.'

'But you've never met him, Suli,' she would reply.

'Ah.' He would lean over and fix her with a dogged eye. 'Kemal is a man who knows my own heart.'

She felt a faint intimation of chill, then suppressed it in the next instant: the closing of the door on a draughty room. She remembered the Turk on the death marches, the captor Minas trusted the most. Now this new captor was threatening her world. He was forcing women out of the home and into work, abolishing the veil, making her feel that without education or employment she wasn't worthy of being called Ottoman any longer. There were no longer any Ottomans anyway; now they were all Turks. The new political slogan was 'Happy is he who was born a Turk'. Kemal had even changed the language, switched the

Arabic script she laboured over for so many years to Roman characters, just as she was beginning to be fluent enough to write without Suleiman correcting her at every turn.

Turkey was proclaimed a republic. Suleiman rejoiced, with musicians brought from the town and feasting that lasted three nights. He even rose from the divan himself, tracing dance steps with Fatima on careful feet. Lilit sat aside on the rug and watched, diminished by a sadness she couldn't explain. Perhaps it was change, perhaps foreboding, even the first intimations of memories she had long learnt to repress. The drawn-out beat of the tabla.

Suleiman tossed away his grandfather's fez, a family heirloom, learnt French, even began stumbling through Schiller's German. He rejoiced at the capture of Smyrna from the invading Greeks, although Lilit cried, thinking of the burning villas, the sea caught up in waves of fire. Old women praying, then dying in the flames. *To whom are they praying?* she wondered. *One Allah. One God. Jesus the prophet, or was He the Son?* Suleiman saw her weeping and caressed her face.

'Ah, my little Armenian!'

The word no longer held its old sting; in truth, no longer held any meaning at all.

Fatima, also, had lost her sting of old. She still cursed, still grumbled, but she too was caught up in the thrills of modernisation. Although it was hard for her, she confessed to Lilit, to really see any changes in a backward little town like Der ez Zor. Lilit opened her mouth to say; *Why then, Fatima, don't you go home to Turkey?* But she held her tongue. Perhaps Fatima would leave under her own volition, and she and Suleiman would finally be alone.

Fatima did not go. Within two years the French had arrived. She stayed behind, became a favourite with the occupiers for her provocative belly dancing. She threw off the veil, was given a gramophone by one of her admiring officers, even went so far one day as to announce she was going to bob her hair and become a flapper like the Western women she admired in fashion magazines. She took to parading the markets of Der ez Zor in her new cloche hat and skinny, beaded dresses, scandalising the Syrians and answering their jeers with a defiance born of her protection by the French.

Suleiman waved his hand at her when she would come home, indignant and red-faced, after one of her altercations.

'Do whatever you like, my dear. I don't really mind.'

More and more it was only the two of them in the house: Suleiman with his newspapers, Lilit with her memories, faded now, like worn-out slippers. Their servants all gone except for the loyal cook; it had become too expensive to keep them. The economy was undergoing radical reforms, so Suleiman said, now the French controlled its currency. Lilit didn't understand. All she knew was that once he'd been rich and now he was struggling in this new Syria. His estates were being leased at lower and lower prices now the Empire had splintered, now the Pashas and Beys had fled. Labourers willing to work merely for food and shelter were becoming scarce.

Most young people were moving to the big cities now: Damascus, Cairo, Istanbul or the new Turkish capital, Ankara, to work and study. Suleiman was pleased at the news of women in universities, learning English and history and mathematics. Lilit was not so sure. Men didn't like their women to be so conspicuous, so capable. She was only unequivocal in her praise of the practical benefits: sparkling sewerage drains and electric lights in every room.

She begged Suleiman again to allow them to move to Turkey, where they could sample the benefits of democracy. All they had in Syria were the same old lamps that spat oil and fizzled, the same squat outdoor privy, buzzing with flies.

She and Suleiman had become intimates, almost without realising it. They shared the same battered brass spoon as they stirred their tea in the morning – Karadeniz tea they brewed so black it needed a cupful of sugar in each pot – they enquired after each other's health and sleep, the contents of their shared dreams. They'd long since built bridges to each other's childhoods. Lilit told him of the birds she grew up listening to each summer in Van, stilts and herons flying to the lake from colder climates; he regaled her with tales of the bald ibis, now extinct, that his father claimed to have seen when he first arrived in the desert. She remembered for him the fragrances of inky blue iris and pink orchid, the many-petalled poppies she made into wreaths for her brother and his friends. She never mentioned Yervan, had almost stopped thinking about him altogether.

Fatima retreated into her bedroom to listen to her gramophone when she was at home, which wasn't often any longer. She bought French furniture and papered the walls in Louis XIV patterns of embossed rose and gold. She took frequent trips to Pamukkale with the French soldiers for her health, the same women's problems that had always plagued her. She brought back photographs of them all bathing in calcium pools and wearing the absurd trunks she knitted, meandering arm in arm along the ancient paths.

Suleiman dispensed money and good advice, told her to settle in Turkey, closer to the healing waters. Lilit knew he wanted to be rid of her for some peace at last, but Fatima had her eye on his estate when he died. When Lilit thought of him dying, her abdomen tightened and her knees turned to water. She realised Fatima was well advised if not justified; she was after all the first, and the legal, wife.

✳ Minas sat alone on the steps of his sleeping block, smoking. An aid worker had given him an American cigarette that morning and he saved it all day until his afternoon break from the kitchens. He inhaled now and coughed, then exhaled with pleasure. The smoke was rich and dark, heavy in his lungs. Nothing like the cinders that passed for tobacco here, wrapped in little smirched squares of print.

He took out his week-old newspaper, opened it. It was an Armenian weekly someone had bought on the black market – a rarity. He was pleased. Nobody told the truth about the world like the Armenians. He turned the pages and scanned the headlines, not really reading, worrying about tomorrow, what he should make with the few tins and sacks of grain they still had left until the next shipment. He remembered Mamma's cooking in those early war years: famine food. She'd stir together a soup of cracked wheat and yoghurt, arch backward with her hands on her hips and sigh. That's what he would do tomorrow, remind the men of hardship, their mothers, the harsh comfort of the past. Bulghur soup.

He stopped short in his musings, holding the cigarette low at his side so that some ash fell to the ground. The headline on the third page read:

MONDAY 24 OCTOBER, 1946: DJEVET BEY, FORMER
VALI OF VAN, CAPTURED YESTERDAY BY ARMENIAN
REPUBLICAN FORCES AND SENTENCED TO DEATH. THE
BEY, FIFTY-FOUR AND IN BAD HEALTH, WAS FOUND
HIDING IN AN UNDERGROUND CAVE IN THE CITY OF—

He stopped reading and looked up at the sky, feeling tears, hot,
angry childish tears, start to his eyes. This was the man who condemned
Papa to death, drove them all out of their homes, deported them into the
desert. He had a vision of the old man now: unshaven, filthy, wild-eyed,
tortured maybe, at the mercy of his former victims. Yet he too had only
been obeying orders from higher up, a factotum himself, merely a petty
bureaucrat immersed in paperwork.

He had an image of himself leaning over and staring into that
flabby, bluish face. Eye to bloodshot eye, a picture so strong it caused
his throat to parch and the hand that held his dwindling cigarette to
tremble. *What would I do?* Drawing his lips together to spit into that
face. 'Help me,' the Turk would mouth, 'please help me.' And Minas
would turn away, without revenge, yet without forgiveness either.

He had entertained a brief notion of returning to Armenia, of
joining the Republican forces. But something small and lost inside him
caused his stomach to turn jelly-like whenever he contemplated going
home. Was it shame for Papa's death, Mamma's unmarked burial in the
sand, the broken memory of his sister? Anguish at his own helplessness.
And where would he go now anyway? To Yerevan? The new capital city
of the Armenian Communist state, a satellite of the Soviet Union. He
wouldn't dream of going there, to be sucked into yet another empire
bent on glory. Or Aykesdan, with its fertile fields and orchards? His
home in Van was officially in Turkey now, the house they once lived in
taken by Kurds, no doubt, filthy nomads who had no idea how to sleep
straight in a bed.

He glanced up and saw a young woman standing before him, leaning
sideways to read the same headline. She was a stranger, a newcomer to
the camp perhaps. He didn't recall seeing her at the communal table or
at the weekly meetings. He spoke before he could think.

'I saw him once.'

'Who?'

'The man they're going to kill.'

'A Turk? They're executing a lot of them these days.'

'Not the masterminds, of course, only the lackeys.'

'Do you think they should execute this one?'

He looked at her again, without seeing. All he could take in was a smear of mouth, her soiled apron that melded into the grit and dirt and grey sky around them.

'Without a doubt. Did you need to ask?' He flung the newspaper into the mud. 'You can have it. I'm finished.'

She picked it up with motherly concern and grinned.

'I never learnt to read.'

'But I saw you reading just then.'

'I can recognise some of the letters but can't make them into words.'

He held the stub of his cigarette toward her, inclined his head to get a closer look.

'Smoke?'

She shook her head. He drank her in now, his hungry gaze hidden by the screen of smoke and his hands. She was short, ample-hipped. Her hair curled around her ears and into her eyes. No etched designs of slavery on her face or hands, no marks of blue. Her shoes were scuffed and old, the stockings darned; she balanced on one heel, waiting for him to speak, like a little girl.

'I can teach you,' he said.

✳ The days passed swiftly now for Minas. He met the young woman in the dinner hall every evening after the meal was cleared, and they sat close together at the long table, heads almost touching. Her name was Siran; her parents and three sisters had died in the first of the Constantinople massacres. She was the youngest, hidden by her mother with a Muslim neighbour who then tried to betray her, but she escaped. She told him this with absolute purity and acceptance. She showed him the welt on her neck from a Turkish knife. Her broad, pale face made him marvel as she spoke.

She pronounced new words, as they read, with childish care, and he coached her with his silence and approval. Within weeks she'd let her shoe fall to the floor and rubbed her silken foot – he couldn't know if her movement was deliberate or merely habitual – to a quiet rhythm on his leg.

Some evenings they talked of the future, children, a house, without mentioning themselves by name in the equation. Impersonal chatter. They merely discussed possibilities, sounding each other out. He mentioned his mother's gold earrings and how much he could get for them on the black market. Siran spoke of the Lebanese and French governments' new scheme, good land going cheap in the camp. She said she had no dowry, her parents' possessions had all been taken by the Turks, and looked down at her stockinged feet in shame.

The next morning he found her at the other side of the women's communal latrines, washing her hair in a bucket. She was cross, he could tell, her customary curls dripping lank around her cheeks.

'You shouldn't be here, Minas. Can't you see—'

He held out the earrings in a twist of paper. 'Take these. Keep them until I ask for them back.'

She took the package, opened it to see. 'Do you mean—'

'What? That I want to marry you?'

She breathed in, squeezed some water from her hair in consternation. 'I'm sorry, Minas, I didn't mean to push you.'

'This is your dowry, Siran. And it will come back to me.'

She flung herself at him and he felt the wetness of her face and hair at his throat, in his mouth. He wanted to kiss her but something stopped him, perhaps the memory of another's look in her face. He drew away and unscrewed the earrings, putting them with slow formality in each of her ears.

'I have to go now, clear away breakfast. Wait for me tonight. And after today, hide those earrings until we have our own home together. Until we're safe.'

That night Siran laughed and clapped her hands when she managed to read a whole page of Charents's poetry in Armenian, and Minas leaned over and kissed her warm, springy hair. It was only then he thought of the girl at the death camp with clarity and drew away.

✳ Fatima had come back home to Suleiman, disgruntled. She'd been home for years now. She still complained of how the French had duped her in that brief golden period in the twenties. The French were stupid, the French were shallow, the French only liked young girls with no morals. They had let the Syrians gain independence. Not once, but twice. Once in the twenties and now, with the onset of yet another world war. If this is what one could call independence: lip service to the idea but fighting among themselves in the streets.

They would be here a long time yet, Suleiman told her. Free French fighting Vichy troops who were loyal to Germany. Many Vichy soldiers were fleeing the country, and Fatima was suddenly afraid. They shelled Damascus in one last blaze of resentment. She refused to believe they killed Syrian civilians in the blasts, snapped her mouth shut when Lilit waved the newspaper in front of her face. There were other soldiers on the streets now, in the *hammams*, in the marketplace: British and Australians with cold faces and red, capable hands. They were here to keep the French in tow. The local Arabs fawned over them, called them liberators.

Fatima let her hair grow back, resumed going to the mosque with Suleiman. The gramophone lay under an embroidered cloth in her bedroom until it was forgotten and used as a table for tea and halva when she had guests. Lilit stayed away from the centre of town and the sight of the foreign soldiers with a fear that paralysed her limbs and on some days made her brain cease to form coherent meanings. She spent more time in the courtyard among the date palms, taller now, dwarfing the high walls around her.

She continued to share Suleiman's bed. Even now, when she was past forty and her breasts soft and limp, her thighs wasted. He still wondered at the beauty of her body, drank her long in his gaze. She let him swallow her, inch by inch. She lay still and ecstatic in his arms, felt her tenderness for this man change and grow, pricking her into sensation. She cried out in pain and he soothed her, murmuring words of forgiveness that she mouthed along with him. Then she became pregnant once again. A child of her waning moon.

This time, the baby lived. The midwife was Syrian Christian, well schooled and kind. She lit a votive lamp in front of the icons by the bedroom door, garlanded the image of Saint Hripsime, Armenian virgin, with roses from the garden. Lilit was nourished by a herbal broth, acrid with leaves and twigs, to prevent bleeding. The midwife carried church incense through the house and left it burning, redolent of gardenias, by the bed. She chanted Aramaic low under her breath as she massaged Lilit with olive oil, her belly, her tight shoulders and thighs.

There were no curses, no suspicions. Fatima was impotent, flabby, preoccupied in tending to her ailments. The baby squalled when the time came, latched on to the breast within seconds. A morsel of date flesh was placed in her mouth so she would find only sweetness in life to come. Lilit named her Anahit, and Suleiman stood aside with one hand on her glistening head.

✳ More time passed. Suleiman grew fat and tired. He settled into his fifties with some of the resignation Lilit had seen in an old dog preparing to die. His breathing grew short and ragged, his heart gave him moments of pallor and panic that he dismissed with jokes and waves of the hand.

'My heart has always given me all kinds of trouble,' he said, and reached over to rub Lilit's cheek with a smile.

She held his hand there, alarmed at how cold it was against her skin, and went for the doctor. Suleiman swallowed the pills the doctor gave him each day with his tea, grew quieter and more careful in his movements. He played with their new daughter desultorily, as with everything he did. He just couldn't be bothered much any longer. The young Arabs of the town tolerated him, waved at him, half-respectful, half-disdainful, as they passed the house, where he reclined on the rooftop under a shirred canopy.

He had become a relic of ages past, like the fat belly dancers they trundled out at festivals, like the sense-memory songs of the wailing oud.

Lilit served Suleiman iced sherbets and sweetmeats with the same reverence she had always exhibited. It had been thirty years since she came into his life. He was pleased she was there, he said. Allah willed it.

BEIRUT, 1982

Hadiya was in a bad mood at breakfast. Her chocolate milk was too hot, the *labneh* on her bread too runny. Sanaya almost yelled at her to go back downstairs. Was this what it was like being a mother? This helplessness, this exasperation? There were so many shortages now, hunger in the streets, and this selfish child was taking food out of all their mouths by being so fussy. She set her jaw, peeled Hadiya some of the last precious fruit she'd been given by Selim. A tangerine, golden in the autumn sunshine. A floury green apple with mottled skin. She tried to brush Hadiya's knotted hair, while the little girl wriggled and squealed her protests.

'Off to school with you now,' Sanaya said, irritated again. 'Your uncle's walking you there today.'

She watched her go through the door, the swayback walk that reminded her of a pony, the wobble of her lovely, soft child's flesh – watched her tearily as if in the cut-glass light of some nostalgic afternoon.

When she was gone, Sanaya was at a loss. She picked at the half-chewed fruit on the plate, stood on her balcony watching the sea. Where was Issa now? Had he come straight back home after dropping Hadiya off at her teacher's apartment? She didn't want to admit it, but she missed him – even though he was living merely a floor beneath her, sleeping in his narrow childish bed, lost in thought as he washed under a trickle of water, sharing small morsels with Rouba and the child. It was almost a physical pain. She woke with an ache in her stomach for him, a dryness in her throat. Selim she never thought about when he was away from her, as if he ceased to exist the moment he walked out the door. They'd had so many arguments now about what he did in his public life, and yet every time she heard his quiet rap on the door, at midnight, or two or three in the morning, she always opened it. In private, in the dark, he was another man. If she made a pact with herself that she wouldn't talk about the war, all went well – for her and for him. But after Sabra-Shatila, she wasn't sure if she could swallow her distaste much longer, if she could bear to see him again.

At lunchtime, Issa and Hadiya didn't come home. Sanaya tried not to imagine what could have happened, what might be happening at that very moment. There had been so many more casualties in the last few months, car bombs and kidnappings, so many incursions from the air. Only last week she read of a non-denominational nursery school bombed by the Phalange. A mistake, they said. Friendly fire.

She stood by the telephone – who to call? – pressing her fingers hard to her eyelids. She dialled the number of Hadiya's teacher at her apartment. She couldn't get through. Of course. She tried again. The connection continued to drop out. Surely Issa and Hadiya must have eaten at a friend's house. That's right, little Samara. She tried the number of Umm Ibrahim's house, thankfully heard the woman's slow *sa'laam*. She sounded calm, no traces of panic in her voice. Must mean they were safe. Must mean they were there.

'I'm sorry,' the woman said. 'Issa and Hadiya aren't here. Samara didn't go to school today. I thought it wasn't safe enough.'

With hands that wouldn't stop shaking, she wrapped Hadiya's portion of rice and lentils in baking paper and placed the package in the coolest part of the kitchen. *Maybe if I do this carefully enough she'll walk through the door.* Part of her was comforted, lulled by domestic ritual, the mundane motions of hand and eye. *If I do this properly, she'll be all right.* Another, denying part of her thought: *She might like a snack when she comes home from school.*

She ran down the street to Rue Hamra. *Must find Rouba.* That was all she could think of now. Rouba's face swam before her, placid and untroubled, unaware of all this danger, on the kerbs, in gutters, crawling over flesh. Her wide eyes, made wider by the thin pencilled line of her eyebrows. Her slack red mouth when she laughed and ate. Her daughter's, pliant in the mornings when she licked warm milk from her lips. Sanaya dodged taxis and ice-cream barrows and limp calla lilies expiring in buckets of water.

She arrived breathless at the fruit stand where Rouba worked. Smoking and chatting with customers, Rouba was busy arranging grapes and figs and sliced watermelon into orderly rows, spraying them with a pump full of water to make them look fresher in the wilting sun.

'Hey, what's the matter?' Rouba flicked some cigarette ash from her jeans, rolled up the sleeves of her abaya and didn't wait for an answer. She helped a customer, cigarette hidden among the folds of her robe, smiled rosily as they left.

'Issa and Hadiya aren't home yet,' Sanaya said. 'Did they come see you at lunch?'

※ At sunset Issa came home. He said he'd spent the whole afternoon looking for Hadiya in the hospitals. Rouba seemed too distraught to be moved so the Druze neighbours from the ground floor were called in to make glasses of tea and try to put her to bed.

Sanaya and Issa were almost out the door when Rouba shouted at the neighbours to leave, throwing off her blankets and running into the hallway. She wrapped her arms tightly around her breasts, pacing, pacing up and down the hall, one hand beating the other arm harder and faster – an ancient gesture, tragic. It was hard to restrain her from rushing out into the street in her nightgown, to help her put on house slippers and throw a shawl over her head and shoulders, to stop her from ripping at her own clothes and skin in her haste to find Hadiya.

Sanaya tried to dress her, pulling limp arms through the sleeves of a cardigan, tying her hair back away from her face. This enforced proximity with another woman's body, with the animal aroma of her mouth and the slick of sweat on her forehead and chest, made something in her alternately attracted and repelled.

'Come on,' Issa barked. 'There may not be much time.'

Sanaya looked up at his face over Rouba's prone head; there was an inflection in his voice that betrayed him, something more than simple shock or grief. He looked back, challenging her to speak her doubt aloud. She lowered her eyes, keeping still as she knelt on the cold floor of the bedroom. Rouba writhed in her arms. Issa's gaze on the back of her neck, laser-like. *Oh, Hadiya.* A moan almost escaped her, before she suppressed it.

Rouba was crumpling onto the floor, scratching at broken tiles as if trying to bury her daughter. She tore at her cheeks, pulled out the band from her hair. Sanaya tried to hold her arms down, wrestling with her, until Rouba slapped herself twice on the face, leaving a stripe of white against the jagged scratches she'd made.

In a taxi on the way, she was quiet. Her pale hands lay folded in her lap; she could have been asleep or dead herself, if it wasn't for the hiccupping sobs she made at intervals. As they neared the hospital she began to convulse, her whole body moving in a discordant rhythm to the shudders of her sobs. 'God forbid,' she muttered. 'God forbid.' Sanaya took her arm, stroked it up and down. Hadiya. Flesh of her flesh. How could Rouba sit there now, merely leaning her head against the window? How could she not run out into these tired streets, scream at everyone here, blame them, take a gun and kill them too for the death of her husband and the pain of her daughter's life? Rouba just sat there, shaking. When they reached the hospital, a long, inhuman cry seemed to issue from her stomach.

She wrenched free of Sanaya and opened the car door, running into the hospital and down the ward. Hurrying after her down the crowded corridors, Sanaya tried to contain her panic. This couldn't be happening. This didn't happen to little girls. The war couldn't touch her. She dodged hysterical patients and anxious nurses. The odour of bodily fluids and antiseptic made her want to retch. At her feet, swirls of fresh blood where a wheelchair had skidded on the linoleum. The whole building breathed fear, in the echoes of countless conversations, the click of broken-down machinery, the stamp of harried, exhausted feet. There were narrow chipboard coffins lined up against the wall in a row. Near them, a little boy sat upright, trying not to doze, his head falling onto his chest each time before he jerked it up again. She could feel Issa behind her, his breathing heavy. She tried to keep well ahead of him. In the taxi she noticed that he stank of ingrained dirt and lack of sleep, and for a slow, sickening moment she couldn't ever imagine touching his body, lying next to him in a bed.

Hadiya lay on a mattress placed on the floor, with a sheet beneath her that didn't fit to the end. The blueness of the linen made her head look unnaturally large. Sanaya had a flash of a premature baby, tubes coming out of nostrils and mouth, stick-like arms. The peace of deep sleep. Hadiya didn't look peaceful. Her face was screwed up into an expression her mother would have called peevish if all had been well. The cotton blanket thrown on top of her was so threadbare Sanaya could see the shape of her hipbones under it, the almost imperceptible rise and fall of her breath, the fragile planes of her little girl's chest.

Her teacher's apartment block, supposedly housing a member of the PLO, was hit by an Israeli cluster bomb at one in the afternoon. Its five floors smashed like a child's hand through a mound of jelly. Hadiya was on the ground floor, saying her farewells in the foyer, waiting for Issa to come and pick her up. That's why she didn't die on impact or end up buried alive in the rubble. She had the presence of mind to run into the street when they all heard the familiar drone of aircraft. That's why she was still alive. The doctor explained there were tiny needles now swimming through her body, tearing at her organs even as they spoke. They were difficult to detect, even by X-ray – which the hospital couldn't get to function any longer – and thus difficult to remove.

Rouba lay down beside her daughter. She didn't try to speak to her, didn't kiss her cheek or hold her hand. She got under the blanket and pressed the whole length of her body against Hadiya's: inanimate, as if resigned to dying with her, intimate as warming her in bed on a cold night. She closed her own eyes, reached across and laid Hadiya's limp hand on her slack belly, umbilicus of their twinned lives.

'Mmmm,' she sang under her breath. 'Mama's here. You're okay. Everything will be okay. Mmm, Mama's here now, mmm,' a murmured buzzing that frightened Sanaya more than anything else had. 'Mmm. Mama's here. You're okay. Mama's here now.'

Rouba had given up. Sanaya could see that now. *No*, she wanted to yell at her. *If you do this, there's no hope for her. For any of us.* Then she was ashamed. She could see Hadiya's trembling lids, her small brown hands, dead birds, little thrushes at her side. Her hair – that coppery plait Sanaya had so carefully woven this morning – was still glorious, attracting light to it even as the child sank away, diminished into herself. Issa slumped to the floor, put his grey face close to hers. The doctor moved away to another patient, with a resigned shrug of her shoulders.

'We've made her comfortable,' she mouthed at Sanaya. 'I'm sorry. It's all we can do.'

Issa didn't say anything to his niece, just watched the rise and fall of her chest as she breathed, the shuddering of eyeballs behind those veined blue lids. Sanaya stood close to him now, one hand, without meaning to, resting on top of his head. He looked up at her and the whispered words seemed squeezed out of him by hatred, close to bursting.

'She's going to die and there's nothing we can do about it.'

All she could do was nod. Once, twice, too many times. Afraid that if she spoke, if she moved the rest of her body an inch closer or further away, she'd scream, lash out, go mad. They waited, silence closing in on them. It throbbed, pulsated. At the end of the corridor, a woman flailed and bucked as they took her dead son away from the ward, but her high-pitched, eternal scream was also part of the oppressive silence. There were distant shots, too far away to perceive as gunfire. At one point Issa turned his face up again to Sanaya and she had to avert her eyes from his, to the neutrality of the wall behind him.

'You watch. That fucking Arafat and his cronies, they'll let this happen again and again.'

His voice paled in the silence, as if afraid of itself. They waited, the two of them: he, bent double over Hadiya's body; she, watching herself standing frozen above him, until the narrow chest faltered and stopped. There was no emotion; nothing left to think. Rouba continued to lie pressed against the tiny body. Her voice resumed its thrumming. Issa pressed Hadiya's eyelids down with his fingers and they left Rouba alone with her daughter.

✳   Issa stood precariously on bare feet. His upper lip trembled and one eye twitched fast as he tried not to stare at Sanaya. He'd spent the last few weeks trying to forget her, fighting hard, banishing her memory. Avenging Hadiya's death. Sanaya wasn't good enough for him, wasn't worth the effort. Hadn't Mumma always said it was his duty to marry a Palestinian girl, virgin-pale and swathed in fabric? To give birth to more Palestinians for the cause. To replace Hadiya's life.

But now he was here, standing before Sanaya, trying to keep the shake out of his voice.

'I was wondering—'

'Where have you been all this time?'

'Fighting. Going to mosque. Sleeping at HQ.'

'I never thought I'd see you again. Rouba needs your help now she's alone. And your mother—'

'I know. I've already seen her. I was wondering …'

It was early; he could see his knock had forced her out of bed. Without articulating it to himself, he was glad he'd woken her. It put him at the advantage. She wouldn't want him to see her like this, hair clumped to one side and mascara streaks down her nose. She drew her dressing-gown a little tighter across her chest.

'I was wondering if you'd like to go out with me sometime.'

It came all in a rush and he flushed scarlet.

'We used to go out all the time, Issa, on our walks.'

He hated her condescending tone, its overriding familiarity.

'Take me seriously, Sanaya.'

'How old are you?'

'It doesn't matter!'

'Come on, how old are you? You know I'm past thirty.'

'Don't you see it doesn't matter? All I want to do is take you somewhere to eat and talk – when there's a ceasefire long enough. We could go to the Commodore Hotel.'

'What will your fundamentalist friends say to that?'

'I don't care. I just want to be somewhere, away from here – alone with you.'

She shook her head, smiling, and shut the door. He waited there, disbelieving. He could hear nothing on the other side. He watched her open the door again, saw her right hand reach for his and hold it for a moment, not showing her face, before she closed the door again.

✳ Issa read the Koran in Rouba's bathroom. He read it through without really attending to it at all. He knew the *suras* so well by now he could recite them while standing to attention, while pissing, while thinking about something else. He thought about sex. Those moon-thighed virgins with downcast eyes that Mohammed spoke of. Seventy-two supple houris to wait on him when he died. *They shall sit with bashful, dark-eyed virgins, as chaste as the sheltered eggs of ostriches.* White thighs, bruise marks, foreign tongues. American women, journalists and aid workers he still saw in bombed-out bars and restaurants on the seafront, sucking at cigarettes and swallowing beer.

Sanaya. She'd like to be one of those women: amoral, unfettered, living moment by dissolute moment, will o' the wisps, little balls of fluff. She was lost to him already, blurry, ambiguous, like the West. Lost to him even before he had the chance. He could see – could still see – her potential to be a good Muslim wife. 'Ah, the spirit is willing, but the flesh is weak.' That's what she said to him when he questioned her beliefs. 'Where's that from?' he asked, puzzled. She laughed, flung out her arm at him in self-deprecation. 'You're right, Issa. I'm not a real Muslim. It isn't even from the Koran.'

He lay awake in the spare room at Rouba's, thinking of Hadiya and her pointless death, feeling the pain and frustration of his helplessness eat at his sanity. He'd been the one who dropped her off at the teacher's apartment. He had been the one who let her go. He should have waited at the street corner that day, watched her at the teacher's window saying her lessons, however long it took, kept her safe with the mere presence of his body. He should never have left her. He tried not to think of it, lay back on the bed and his thoughts led him again to Sanaya. Was she upstairs, right now, with Selim? It hurt him, pained him in his bones. He groaned aloud then writhed in embarrassment in case Rouba woke and heard him. He couldn't believe Sanaya had let that man touch her. Let him touch her all the time. Have sex. Sex. He didn't really know what that meant. Except the little his commander had taught him.

Why was everyone in the West having sex? Why were the men so gentle, hairless, child-like? Why were men having sex with other men? *They will pass from hand to hand a cup inspiring no idle talk, no sinful urge; and there shall wait on them young boys of their own, as fair as virgin pearls.* He passed his hand over the muscles in his legs, pinching, aggressive to his own flesh. He was a real man, even though he let his commander touch him that one night – *what choice did I have?* – in the steamy dark of the underground garage they slept in down south, keeping his eyes wide open in the hope that, if he looked hard enough at the other sleeping militiamen, they wouldn't hear him whimper and plead no.

'Please, Chief,' he had said, his eyes straining into the dark. 'It hurts me.'

'Keep quiet,' his commander replied, easing closer to him on the straw pallet, clamping a hand on his shoulder, rubbing himself against the back of Issa's thigh. His rubbing started slow, then increased in intensity, rhythmic, broken, shriller, like his commander's splintered voice.

'Keep—still.'

His voice became higher, frenzied, fragmenting into little balls, like liquid mercury spilling on the ground. Issa had seen it happen, a thermometer fell and broke once. *Where was it? At headquarters? In Beirut?* He tried to remember, tried to force his mind to concentrate on something, anything, so that he wasn't really lying *there*, not in that fumbling, frenzied moment, with the other man's body pushing now soft, now hard, into his.

'Slowly, slowly,' Chief had said, as if telling himself.

He grew to hate his commander's Iranian accent, all their accents. *Bastards*, he let himself think. *Idiot Persians. Poofters. Fags.* He thought of all the words, all the evil, offensive, foreign words he could use to describe his superiors. Especially Chief. At the end, when he caught his breath, he could hear Chief shuffling over the floor away from him, rolling himself in his own blanket by the garage door.

That next morning Issa woke with a burning soreness, yet his mind was clear. *It didn't happen. Didn't happen to me. Someone else got it last night.* He was the first to salute Chief, the first to offer his services, polishing muddy boots, washing battledress in cold running streams, preparing meals. No trace of his night anger left. Chief was fine, Chief was brave, Chief knew best.

On the Holy Day of Mourning Chief tore the skin on his chest in remorse and blood splashed over his bare feet. He asked everyone for forgiveness of any sin he'd committed against them in the past year. Issa turned away, blushed, murmured, 'Nothing, Chief.' Chief was devout, a holy martyr. He knew how to run such a strong, disciplined organisation. *Iran is our future.*

He lay awake now in the spare-room bed. He tried not to think of Selim and Sanaya. He caressed his gun. It reposed by his side like a silent woman.

※ He picked up Sanaya in a borrowed Renault. International peacekeeping troops were everywhere now, back to keep half an eye on the Phalange and the Israelis. American soldiers sat on the side of the road, well-polished rifles balanced on their knees, and tried to engage passers-by in conversation. Everyone in west Beirut ignored them. Issa released the clutch and the car made a strangling noise. The soldiers clapped and he cursed loudly in English, not caring if they heard him.

On their way to the Commodore the car went at walking pace and nearly blew a tyre from all the shell-holes, ordnance casings and building debris from bombings. When they finally arrived, Sanaya laughed.

'We would've been better off walking, hmm, Issa?'

He glared at her, and then regretted it. He dampened her natural ebullience, weighed her down with his need for perfection. At the bar he swayed back and forth on his ripped plastic stool, looking down at the carpet, pitted with cigarette stubs and burn-holes. Through the plate-glass doors to the inner courtyard he saw Sanaya look at the hotel pool, a thick swamp of weeds and journalists' garbage: broken generators, abandoned satellite phones. Issa didn't care about his surroundings. He focused his eyes only on her, taking in every detail of her dress, her hair, her deliberately blank expression. His new, fashionably tight jeans sat incongruously on his fighter's body, and he felt embarrassed.

'I'll order,' she said.

He made to stop her with his arm.

'It's shameful for a woman to do what a man can do.'

She shrugged him off.

'No Muslims here, Issa. Nobody cares.'

He watched as French and Italian soldiers crowding the bar turned and looked at her with appreciation as she made her way to the front. She returned their stares, smiled, accepted their murmured compliments.

She watched him with a maternal eye as he took a sip of his drink. 'Like it? I chose something sweet for you.'

'It's exactly like rosewater syrup.'

'With an edge.'

'Like me.'

At the door of her apartment he attempted to kiss her. She let him, submitting, but kept her mouth slack. He bit her bottom lip, giving out an involuntary cry, the squawk of a bird. The smell of death and sex and sour mouth were too great – it hurt him. He drew his lips away but continued to hold her, wedged together, groin to groin and face to face, pressing tight as if without her he might fly.

✳ The women danced slowly in broken circles and Issa sat by the window brooding, gazing down at the foam-lashed sea. Celebration. He wanted to join in. A celebratory dance. But he knew better. He knew the war wasn't really over yet. Sure, Lebanese politicians were talking of holding a reconciliation conference in Switzerland. Sure. He knew nothing would come of it. What, to let Christians and Jews run the country? Never. The war wasn't finished – not if he or his militia had anything to do with it.

An old Armenian song played, recorded in Arabic. *My darling, my love, your sufferings and joys will be many.* Both Rouba and his mother had started wearing colours tonight; enough of mourning for Hadiya, enough of mourning the massacres.

A new year and the end of sorrow at last. He knew better. More sorrow, more pain. He smiled up at his mother, didn't want her to fret. She even wore a flowered scarf on her head. Her ancestral anklets jingled. She held her hands out to Sanaya and Rouba, they spun together and turned, the three Graces in bas-relief. He'd seen them once on a postcard at the beach, hadn't bought it when the hawker thrust it in his face and wheedled. Nude women. Pornographic. Swelling hips and moulded buttocks, arms pushed forward in exultation.

Sanaya glowed in and out of wheels of candlelight, slashes of red against white: crimson taffeta, creamy upper arm, red-ruched sleeve, white goose-pimpled breast. Her vermilion lips mouthed the song, her powdered cheeks put him in mind of Marie Antoinette. Cut off her head. Impale her. He looked away again. *You don't love me.* Such flamboyance was mere vanity, after everything they had been through.

'Here's to 1983,' Sanaya toasted.

The others joined in raising their glasses. He flicked his wrist toward Sanaya, pale amber punch sloshing in his glass.

'I hope there's no alcohol in here,' he said, and smiled morosely before she should become upset by his melancholy.

She danced toward him, hips wobbling, that circling stomach tight against his face.

'Come on, Issa. Just a little cognac. I waited for hours in a queue to pay far too many American dollars for it.'

He turned his head up to look at her, took a measured, quaking sip.

'Dance with me,' she said.

He shook his head, held the glass in front of him to block her. She pulled him up by both hands. The canary chirped in its shrouded cage, woken by the music. Sanaya dragged him to the middle of the room, cajoling, blowing air kisses. He resisted. His glass smashed to the floor and Rouba and Bilqis looked around, startled. In the silence of the record's end they heard a leisurely knock on the door. Only one person knocked like that. And if Sanaya didn't answer, he had his own key.

She sprang forward, opening the door.

'Selim!'

She stood awkwardly, blocking his entry, a schoolgirl reprimanded for playing with her friends.

'Ah—come in and watch the fireworks. You know Rouba, Issa ... and this is Madame Ali, Issa's mother. I don't think you two have met.'

�֍   They all crowded against the window – it was too cold to go out into the balcony. Selim's shoulder was pressed against the old woman's head, the Palestinian boy's mother; she was so short he felt he should reach out and pat her. *God, she looks familiar.* She glanced up and nodded, he saw her broad, square teeth. Then, in a slow instant, she looked at him again, and quickly looked away. He sipped his drink. She raised her empty glass. The sea abruptly lit up by balls of pink and green. Fireworks this time, not bombs. She looked over her shoulder at him again. His drink suddenly was not strong enough, and he felt a little sick. He swallowed the rest in one gulp and Sanaya noticed.

'Top up?'

He shook his head, choking on the last of the liquid. He looked again at the woman. She looked straight back. He thought of all the Palestinians he'd killed: in the camps, on the street. Their hands outstretched as they ran. The cries, the pleading. And the ones he'd let live. He smiled at the woman now, faintly, non-committally, seeing a glimmer of contempt in her returning nod. Behind him, he felt Issa's presence as a malevolent intelligence, a sixth sense wiser than the boy himself.

'I need to go,' he said.

He waited in the dark on the stairs for Sanaya to follow and ask what was wrong. He waited a few more minutes, then left.

✼ 'Why have you brought me here?'

Sanaya didn't answer. On the edge of the refugee camps, the Muslim cemetery seemed to stretch, brown and dusty, all the way to the mountains. But it was an optical illusion. In reality the cemetery was small and poor, enclosed by chicken wire to keep the dead inside.

Selim scanned the horizon without looking any closer, as if to deny where he was standing, shielding himself from any confronting detail: the forlorn tombstones, scarred graves with corpse buried flat on top of corpse, this evidence of mass burial in mounds of baked soil. On the outskirts of the cemetery, Israeli patrols could be heard faintly, distorted by wind. *We have come to cleanse your area of terrorists.*

'Are they going to kill us as well?' Sanaya shouted.

'Be quiet. You don't know what you're talking about.'

'Leave me alone.'

'Sanaya, tell me why we're here.'

'Are they going to kill me as well? They'll spare you. You're such a good friend to them.'

'What's wrong with you lately?'

'What about you? You've killed women, babies. Innocents. And you nearly killed Issa's mother on your little rampage. She recognised you.'

Selim stared at her, shocked. She waited, enjoying his discomfort. 'Are you going to kill me too, Selim? I'm Muslim.'

'No, you're not. Not really. You just think you are. You like playing the game.'

She stopped, considering his comment.

'I can't do it anymore, Selim.'

After so many nights of agonising, after so many days of playing and replaying the scene in her head, now she said it she felt flat. Cheated. As if she should somehow be feeling something, feeling more.

'Why?'

'I can't keep pretending it's not happening.'

'Is it the little girl? I had nothing to do with that.'

'But you could have. Isn't that right?'

'Is it him then?'

'He's nineteen, Selim, for Allah's sake.'

'I wouldn't put it past you.'

'I haven't seen him for months. Since that night you ruined our party.'

'I didn't—'

'It's not because of him. Just you. Okay? Now go. I can make my own way home.'

✳ Selim left the cemetery quickly. His driver didn't ask him why he was there, who he met, didn't question his short visit. He merely took him home, and Selim let himself in with a sigh of relief. The phone was ringing as he opened the door, had been ringing for a while; he bounded over to it, hoping it was Sanaya, knowing it must be Sanaya.

'Hello?'

'I think I'm going to kill you today.'

He could feel his heart rate quickening, breath caught thick in his throat. He sat on the floor holding the receiver to his chest. When he raised it again, his voice was still not steady.

'Hello? Who is this?'

'I'm coming over to do it right now.'

'You fucking bastard! It's you, isn't it, you little Arab?'

He could hear the other man thinking. *Why kill him outright? He won't suffer enough.* He seemed to sniff out the fear in Selim's voice, like a dog. A phrase from the book Sanaya would read aloud before bed flashed through his head; disjointed, nonsensical, out of context. *Those that suffered persecution for My sake and fought and were slain: I shall forgive them their sins and admit them to gardens watered by running streams.*

The other man made his voice into a growl and whispered.

'Or maybe I won't. Kill you today. Maybe I'll leave it for later. Something to look forward to.'

Selim put down the phone. He got up from the floor, tossed back a glass of whisky. Showered, shaved, sprayed on cologne. He dressed with consideration, as if for a new lover. Strode downstairs, ignoring the trembling in his knees, and hailed a taxi.

✳ Sanaya went to bed early, exhausted by her decision. Yet she wasn't sad, not at all. For the first time, she felt as if her past could be expiated, that there was a future waiting. She wriggled between the cold sheets, luxuriating in the slipperiness of satin on her cheeks and bare breasts, and was asleep in minutes.

Sometime in the blackest part of night she moved onto her back, flung one hand out to the side of the bed and felt a man's leg. New jeans, stiff to the touch, not washed enough. Was it a dream? She was wide awake now, fought the urge to scream.

'Selim?'

Darkness. Her senses of hearing and smell painfully alert. Unnatural quiet: not a car screech, nor a voice from the Corniche, even the sea below still and waiting under a black moon. Not even the sound of a breath. It couldn't be Selim. Could it? She'd taken away his key. She let her hand explore the leg, curve itself to the thin, muscular thigh. Then she relaxed, let out a huge sigh of relief. It was not Selim. Another man had arrived at the side of her bed in utter silence. Had she ever given *him* a key? He didn't give her time to consider. He was in the bed now, jeans off, his slight body grown monumental around her. She felt herself unbuttoning his shirt, fumbling, smelling the damp sweetness of his armpits, grazing the wiry curls of hair on his chest with her mouth, peeling thin cotton off his body as if somebody else was performing these actions, while her real self lay inert on the bed, transfixed with emotion. She turned on the bedside lamp, it hurt her eyes. His limbs and flesh and face a fire flickering from groin to cheeks, aflame in confusion and desire.

He muttered, 'There's less of you than I thought.'

'More bones now,' she whispered, and turned out the light.

Once he was on her, she could feel his frailty rather than her own. She counted the notches in his spine with two fingers, tread lightly on his fierce virginity. *Virgins as fair as corals and rubies. Which of your Lord's blessings would you deny?*

She murmured into his neck, 'Issa?'

'Yes?'

'I think I love you.'

He subsided into her, one hand guiding him, her mouth a bird on his shoulder.

BEIRUT, 1995

The Beirut waterfront where Chaim lives is neutral territory. Or at least that's what he calls it when he explains the current situation to me. None of the rival religious or political factions can lay claim to it, not now. The city is still divided spiritually into east and west, though these days you can easily take a taxi downtown or tread the fashionable, refurbished area once known as the Green Line. At the same time there are still boundaries – emotional perhaps, unacknowledged – furrowed deep into the heart of Beirut.

The Corniche is another city in itself. It's the haunt of the lost, the dislocated, the in-between, the untouchables – prostitutes, hawkers, beggars, tourists, the ultra-rich. Swiss-owned luxury hotels compete for space with hovels made of cardboard and hammered tin. Construction projects pollute the sea air with concrete dust and jackhammers, resorts and high rises, tax breaks begun with the express intention of never being finished. Beiruti high society – French-educated, expansive, cruel in its vulgarity – rubs shoulders with leprous touts; Syrian labourers lounge about eating gelato after a day's work; women accost tourists in perfect French, whores with university degrees giving everything they have of themselves. Palestinian children selling trinkets and concertina postcards – *six views of beautiful Lebanon* – hassle backpackers who shade their wide eyes from the sun, striding through the filth with open mouths and wads of greenbacks.

Chaim and I sit in plastic chairs on his tiled balcony, arms akimbo, faces upturned to the sun, absorbing the dust and heat into ourselves in order to become so dusty and so hot it can no longer annoy us and we're immune, ready to enjoy the last hour before sunset. His hand is on my knee, and I can't help but think it's a gesture of ownership. But I let it rest there, and the film of sweat between my skin and his is in some way a confirmation of my conflicting desires.

His balcony is sea-deep, generous. It has room for a wrought-iron table and these various plastic chairs, Julius's kennel, a summer daybed, broken and sagging in the middle, wet washing strung on a makeshift line. His pots of gardenias, the only flower he cultivates, waxen and shiny with blossoms all year round. He lives in one of the few French-era apartment blocks left in the city: neoclassical beauties complete with cornices and architraves in the guise of Roman temples, dizzying ceilings, windows of arched and ribbed glass in the Levantine style.

I've slowly succumbed to my need to be closer to Chaim, and to his single-minded desire for me. I want to be with him, near him, drink in his smell and speech and habits. But I feel guilty at wanting this so soon, and in such circumstances — a lover, or a father? Someone to rely on, someone to love. He thinks I don't care for him. He thinks my hesitation is indifference, when in fact it's my last-ditch attempt at retaining some final shred of my original purpose in coming to Beirut.

'Move in with me, it's cheaper,' he'd said. 'I'm hardly ever in Beirut anyway. Julius needs someone to look after him when I'm away. There's plenty of room. I'd love to have you here.' And, finally, one night as he raised himself on his elbow in bed and looked into my face: 'Please, Anoush. I know you don't care for me the way I do for you.' He held up his hand to silence my protest. 'Ssh, listen to me. I can help you out.'

'Chaim, I do care for you,' I whispered. 'More than I want to.'

'And I—' he said, coming closer, 'I think I'm falling in love with you.'

I felt a deep, discordant thrill at his words. At the same time, I couldn't help but think of Lilit, what she would think of us, he and I, a couple. I cast my mind back to the girl she once was, stoking a fitful fire; then a young mother in Der ez Zor, eating a bite of *loukoum* before bed; and in Beirut as an old woman mouthing her garbled Christian–Islamic prayers. Then I knew she would approve.

Over the past few weeks I've moved in, increment by increment. First it was my herbal shampoo, left behind in the shower recess. I saw him notice and try to hide his smile. Then my nightgown, a matted hairbrush on the dresser next to his. For me, these are testaments of love. For him, they mean only that I need refuge. Well, maybe that's what love is. A temporary refuge.

I've checked out of the Mayflower. I can send the money I save in hotel bills to Siran, for better conditions in the home, extra care from the nuns. My backpack with its entrails of clothes and shoes and paperbacks lies scattered on Chaim's bedroom floor.

We sit and drink tonic water; it seems to help settle my stomach. Chaim pours a finger of gin into his own glass and gets up to lean over the railing, squinting into the dazzle off the sea. I can hear the cracking sound of the ice in his glass as it bumps against the sides. The sound of a Beirut summer, on these very same balconies with my school friends. Drinking lemonade made with waxy-skinned garden lemons, spring water from the mountains, sugar syrup mixed with rosewater. I'm serenely happy in this brief sunset time to sit on the white plastic chair – buttocks sticking to it with sweat – to drink tonic water, remember and muse on those days when time ceased to matter and life was a little interval, the time it took for the crack of an ice cube against a glass. Chaim speaks softly into the silence, not turning his head to see if I'm listening.

'Those palm trees – ever seen them in old photographs? From before the war. The ones planted all the way along here?'

'Only in postcards, the black and white ones they sell down on the Corniche. What about them?'

'My brother used to bomb them every time he came through here.'

'And the Beirutis would keep planting them again each time, right?'

'Right. I don't think he ever knew they'd become so ...' He pauses, uncertain.

I speak for him, my voice low. 'I know, Chaim. So symbolic.'

He clears his throat, and I can see on his face that he's wondering whether to tell me something, or not.

'I've seen the same thing happen back home, in Tel Aviv. Whenever the terrorists bomb a cafe, or a service station, the trees are the first thing to come back: before the foundations, before the rebuilding. We're all the same. All the same, at heart.'

I know it's taken a lot for him to say this to me. So often when he speaks of Israel, or his family, we argue. Less these days, though. He's shown me patience, and a form of peace. I'm starting to learn. He half-turns away from me, looking out over the balcony.

'Your mother?' I venture. 'Is she safe?'

'Safe as she can be,' he replies, looking back at me. 'She stays in her apartment a lot. I worry about her, though. Anytime she goes shopping, or walks down the street, it could happen.' He shrugs. 'We've learned to live with it, over there. We try not to hate, all the time.'

I beckon him to me and we sit on the sticky plastic chairs again, holding hands over the divide.

BEIRUT, 1948

Lilit got off the bus in Beirut holding her daughter's hand. This was the Corniche, this narrow, crowded strip of cafes and stalls and beggars, refuge for the flotsam of the city. The few palms were stingy with their shade, a mere circle under each tree where people huddled close as if sheltering from rain instead of sunshine. Some laid out mats and slept. Others squatted, ate, washed children, shaved. Old women screeched at her and tried to palm off sugared pistachios, glinting pink and wet in the heat. A little boy flapped around her knees crazily, using a piece of cardboard and a mirror to distract her from his pick-pocketing. She smacked out at him in shock and he spat, running through the crowd. Another boy stood blankly by a set of scales, waiting for customers to weigh themselves and give him a small coin.

Lilit hurried past, wanting to get away from the crush of bodies. Men in turbans and long white robes frowned at her; reminiscent of Suleiman, they made her long for home. Throughout the journey from Der ez Zor to Damascus she did not allow herself to sleep, musing instead over the serene house she'd left behind, its fountains and clean-tiled courtyard, missing Suleiman, even Fatima. Mourning the graves of her two dead babies. Dead babies, soldiers, wars. She was one of the few passengers awake at midnight when the driver stopped in the desert for cigarettes and tea; she accepted his own refilled glass and held the steaming liquid to her lips, not drinking.

Endless sands stretched out black and windless in the cold night. Away in the distance a pale-blue flush heralded stars, but when she pointed it out to the driver he smiled with a dazzle of teeth and said that was just a trick the desert djinns played on you – to give you hope and make you lower your guard. 'No,' he continued, 'the moon is what we should be watching for. Our desert, Badiet-es-Sham, is treacherous, like a woman.'

Lilit blushed, thankful he couldn't see her face in the dark. He leaned toward her and his breath stirred the thread-like hairs at her neck. 'But the moon is like a mother,' he said, 'and she will guide us to the coast.'

Lilit scanned the sky, but the pall that enveloped them was immense, with no beginning and no end. She was glad to crawl back under her blanket in the bus, resting Anahit's hot cheek on her lap. The desert had made her aware, for the first time since the deportations, of her own insignificance.

She must have dozed for a while as they traversed the valley road from Damascus to Beirut, past the cedars and the Chouf Mountains, because her memories became more distinct then, with no logic of narrative as before, yet with an intensity of images flooding her eyes. Suleiman's faint shudders, his long, veined arms twisted in death. Fatima's thin mouth as she stood at the gates of the courtyard and watched Lilit leave the house.

She woke with the jolting of the bus and saw the sea. She'd never seen it before in her life, this great silver sheet of light. She grew up near Lake Van, of course, mirror-blue and ruffled by wind, became sick and afraid of the sand-silted Euphrates on those forced marches, sloping banks the colour of old blood. Then, slowly, she grew to love it over the years as she once loved the lake of her childhood. At times she even plunged with Suleiman into its summer coolness under cover of night; he, leaping and teasing, teaching her to swim.

Yet this sea was alarming and ecstatic all at once in its proximity. In the dawn starkness it snaked alongside the coast road, growing now closer, now further away. The fishing village of Damour glimmered bright with its flat whitewashed rooftops, a blinding extension of the sea itself. Festoons of fishing nets, purple and indigo, were strung between balconies and beaded with spray like diamonds – or tears. She longed to stop the bus, give up her search for Minas, live there in that peaceful place with her daughter. She even roused Anahit to show her its beauty. The little girl grizzled, hugging her doll still closer to her, opened her eyes for a moment then closed them again.

When the bus stopped on the Corniche in Beirut, she smoothed Anahit's sweaty curls off her forehead and straightened her own wool skirt over her stockings. It was the first time she'd worn European clothes in three decades.

'Dolly needs comb as well,' Anahit said. 'Her hair all messy.'

Lilit combed the black doll's frizzed locks down with her fingers. Its glassy eyes betrayed no sentiment. She bent down as she gathered their luggage and peered out of the bus window at the city outside, and as she did so a surge of excitement made the tears start to her eyes. Minas was out there somewhere. The Red Cross in Der ez Zor had confirmed the survival of another Pakradounian. It could only be him. He had been waiting for her all these years.

'Keep close to me and don't even think of running away,' she warned her daughter.

She was afraid she'd lose Anahit in this throng of people: street vendors calling their wares in mournful voices as if they despaired of any sales today, beggars screeching and pulling at her mourning garb, foreign men in the uniforms of many armies sitting on the sea wall, eating what she now knew was Western food – chemical-red sausages, minced patties of meat, oily fried potatoes – from the busy braziers that took over the footpath and made it difficult to move.

'Let's get away from here,' she said, and pulled Anahit down past lighted shops and restaurants to the edge of the water. It was slow-going, especially for Anahit: the decline steep and consisting only of pebbles and smashed shards of rock. Finally, they reached the shore. Here at least they could breathe. Anahit was silent, looking about her with wide, shocked eyes. She held her doll in the crook of her arm and checked now and then that the painted porcelain mouth wasn't crying. Lilit squatted on the smooth pebbles with her daughter and the doll on her lap and whispered in her ear.

'We're fine here for a minute, aren't we? We'll just catch our breath then go find your uncle.'

They sat, swaying against each other with tiredness, for a few minutes. Lilit picked up one of the pebbles and felt its cool heaviness in her hand.

'Anahit,' she said. 'Watch Mamma.'

She tossed it away and they both watched as it skimmed over the water, barely making a ripple on the surface.

'Mamma used to play with pebbles on the shore of a lake, far, far away,' she whispered.

Anahit didn't answer; she'd fallen asleep again. Lilit took in the fresh air, felt it cleanse her. It was calmer here, the sea spray covered their faces in a fine mist and the ragged fishermen further down the beach called out to each other fondly. The palms behind her rustled with invitation. It was easy to like Beirut, here.

A solitary figure came walking toward them, crunching his boots on the soft surface. Lilit narrowed her eyes in the sunlight and saw he was a soldier, wearing a uniform she couldn't place. She could see the gun in its holster, see the determination in his huge jaw. In a sudden grip of fear, she hauled Anahit into her arms and began running up the incline to the road. Her luggage lay abandoned on the shore, forgotten. The pebbles thwarted her, they slipped and rolled under her feet and it was all she could do to stop from falling down.

'Hey,' the soldier was calling in Arabic. 'It's okay. I'm not going to hurt you.'

She kept scrabbling up the incline. Anahit had woken fully now and was protesting with high, sharp cries. The doll fell to the ground and Anahit squirmed to release herself from her mother's grip, kicking out with legs and arms.

'Dolly gone,' she wailed. 'She fall down!'

'Here,' the soldier said, holding out the doll to her. He caught up with them in a few long strides and now stood before Lilit, his bloodshot eyes peering into her hot, sweat-streaked face. 'Are you okay, madam? Is there anything I can do to help?'

She shook her head. 'No,' she murmured.

He looked at Anahit, standing now at his feet and squinting up at him, clutching at her doll.

'Is your mamma telling the truth?'

Anahit looked up at him, tears still wet in her eyes. She was silent. Lilit felt a sob choke her, swallowed it down.

'Can you help us find my brother?'

✳ Minas gazed at the little girl as if to try to commit to memory all that bound him to her: the silent surge of blood and her single Levantine curve of nose and chin. She had arrived out of nowhere with her mother, as if they had materialised out of the ground. He hadn't had any time to bark at Siran for coffee and sweets from inside the house.

He merely stood by the door, dropping the tangled necklace he'd been repairing for some extra cash, its frail links broken. He blinked at the illicit curls and gash of mouth he imagined to be a legacy of the girl's Turkish father. A static scene flashed through his head. Another little girl, bright-haired too, lying among smashed vegetables ground into dirt. She had looked asleep, if it wasn't for her smashed skull, red of tomato, pale yellow, soft grey—*Enough. That was more than twenty years ago.*

This little girl was glaring up at him with all the ferocity a two-and-a-half-year-old could muster. She knew her mamma was upset and it could only be this strange man causing her to tremble so.

'How could you have let him touch you?'

Lilit stood open-faced before her brother's fury. One hand rested on her daughter's forehead, shielding her pale skin from the sun.

'He was my husband, Minas.'

'What did everyone die for? For you to be slave to a Turk?'

When Lilit thought of Suleiman her voice grew slight, like a little girl's. She waited for the wave of grief to pass, looked at her brother. He refused to acknowledge her, continued staring at Anahit as if she might suddenly spring up and bite him.

'He was an *odar*,' Minas finally said. 'Not like us. A heretic.'

'Really, brother, you're as bad as a Jew.'

He seemed not to hear her, choking on his words.

'Far better to have been killed than succumb to that.'

Then he realised someone else had said that to him, once, a long time ago. *Mamma.* And he had turned away, leaving her behind in his desperation to survive. Lilit leaned forward and pointed her finger at him.

'Don't you dare say it! You—you don't know what I went through. You have no idea.'

'Keep your voice down. Standing out here in full view of the neighbours, arguing like Arabs. Come inside.'

'No.'

'I would have escaped, Lilit, if it had been me.'

'You know nothing.'

He recoiled at the disdain in her voice, sat down, shaky, outside his house. A few bougainvillea blossoms fell about his face and he brushed them away with a show of impatience. He gestured to the other stool. Siran peered out from the gloom of the interior, frightened by her husband's shouting. Lilit continued to stand while the little girl sat down.

Minas tried not to look at his sister, at the dark spots of pigmentation under her eyes; she had aged. Where was the merry, laughing, fibbing girl of that vanished summer? Replaced by this dour woman in widow's weeds, eyes dimmed, too Islamic even without the scarf. At length, he spoke again. His voice came out in a croak.

'How did you find me?'

'The Red Cross in Der ez Zor. They told me there was a Pakradounian here.'

Lilit saw Minas gazing at her daughter with mingled fear, confusion and wonder. She had no idea what he saw. Anahit reached upward where she sat, fat hands opening and closing, grasping at air. She was trying to catch one of the papery blossoms that rained down on her from the sudden wind. The bougainvillea vines around her stirred and flickered, sun making splashes on her upraised, cameo-shaped face. Minas concentrated on the movement of shadow across her half-familiar features; he blinked once, her ancestry blurred, eyes and mouth watery, sliding in and out of focus like one of those new Leica cameras he'd seen downtown, a shutter on slow speed.

'She looks so much like our mother,' he breathed.

'You're imagining it.'

The little girl decided to smile, vaguely, in no particular direction. *She could be smiling at the sun,* Minas thought, the Beirut sun beating hot as a hand on their backs and the crowns of their heads.

'Her name's Anahit.'

Minas put out his hand.

'Say hello to your uncle.'

Minas stood aside and watched his sister decide – after much cajoling by Siran – to stay the night. Siran made up a bed on the floor before Lilit's eyes, said she wouldn't hear of her leaving, brought out iced water and spoon sweets, stroked Lilit's fine, grey-threaded hair.

Lilit protested, trying to help, saying a pregnant woman shouldn't be exerting herself so. Siran smiled and hugged her, saying she missed her own sisters, that it was so good to have another woman in the house. Minas watched his sister acquiesce to his wife's boundless innocence. She led Lilit around the tiny two-roomed house, showing her bits and pieces picked up at market sales, chipped jugs and bowls and tablecloths she now afforded heirloom status. He saw Lilit inwardly turn her nose at them, remembering her own fine Turkish things, no doubt, trying not to let her arrogance show.

What riches have you left behind, eh, Lilit? Blood money. He laughed out loud and Siran rebuked him for scaring the little girl. But Anahit was not scared. Something about him fascinated her so she allowed him to take her hand and introduce her as his niece to the curious neighbours that crowded the surrounding streets.

They walked through stone-arched alleys to Municipality Square and took tea with his elderly employer at the jewellery shop, exclaiming together at the turquoise studs and rows of gold rings Minas had fashioned. Anahit chose a beaten-silver bracelet for her very own at the shopkeeper's insistence. It was large, with heavy links and a design of Armenian crosses, and meant for a grown woman: they looped it twice to fit onto her baby wrist. Minas engraved the bracelet with the family name: *Pakradounian.* The name not of her father but her uncle.

He showed Anahit crooked rows of Armenian titles at open stalls, couldn't resist stopping to look at the new volumes, his boyhood thirst for books still unslaked. He shopped for fresh lamb at his usual butcher in the covered market. There wasn't much for sale anymore, what with the war still on, but his friend always managed to find some good meat that wasn't all fat or bone.

He didn't mention little Anahit was half-Turkish to anyone. He merely told the truth, he reasoned with himself. All they needed to know was that her father had recently died. On the way back to his house he stopped at every corner, hoisting her into his arms and pointing out the street signs.

'Look, Anahit. Kars Street. See, Adana Avenue. Every single stone here is named after a vanished Armenian town. Look down there. Rue Erzerum.'

Anahit didn't understand but liked being held up high, and gurgled her laughter. She was still laughing when he brought her home to Urfa Street. Lilit had been helping Siran, whose large belly hindered her movements. They piled warm flat bread on the table, which Minas broke and handed first to his sister and then to his wife.

'Not as good as my baking,' he said, and they all laughed, nervous with each other.

They sat in the evening gusts from the open door and he passed grilled lamb in to them on skewers from the bed of coals outside, proud of his skill with spices.

✳ Lilit and her daughter lay huddled near the door while the couple slept stretched out on mats near the central hearth, just as in Van. The timber shutters creaked and kept Lilit awake. Minas snored and then coughed as if ashamed of the old man's noise he made. Webs of silver from the full moon outside came through the slats and rippled over Anahit's smiling, sleeping face. Her new bracelet's glitter mingled with the lines of light until Lilit didn't know any longer which was Anahit and which was the night. She drew her daughter closer to her in the crook of her arm.

Minas continued to snore. How he had changed. That thin, drooping moustache he affected didn't make it any better, either. Not like Suleiman's: silky, short, just brushing his lips. He'd never snored, not once. Hard to believe he was dead, that there was nothing any longer for her in Der ez Zor.

She had left the house three days after his death, a week ago now. She closed the front gates behind her as she did that faraway day when she was pregnant with her first dead child. She left behind her bedroom furniture and the bolts of silk she planned only last month to have made into new Eid robes. She abandoned the loom she once chose with so much care and the fine, heavy trays for baking. So many sweetmeats for Suleiman. Gone were the heavy tunics laden with embroidery and gold thread, the sequinned slippers. Those thick unguents and perfumes that had littered the inlaid mother-of-pearl dresser by her bed.

She thought again of Fatima at the open gates, gloating. Fatima was back in favour with the French now, the remaining troops who had managed to rout the Vichy soldiers. Her household was guaranteed food and basic supplies while the other inhabitants of Der ez Zor could die of starvation for all she cared. Behind her huddled figure, Lilit saw billeted men sorting through furniture, making up makeshift beds in the courtyard. Suleiman's body still lay in the bed Lilit shared with him, in direct disobedience of Islamic law. Fatima wanted the French to help her with an elaborate funeral and ostentatious memorial. Lilit didn't wait for the burial. Suleiman was dead now and could do no more for her, nor she for him. She could discern a triumphant smile on Fatima's face as she stood with her spine pressed against the doors, ringed hands folded over her withered breasts.

She sighed so loudly the child stirred in her sleep. She had so wanted to be free of Suleiman in those early years, and yet at the same time felt a fierce tenderness for his slim body, his fits of laughter. She wanted freedom and now she had it, and it was bitter and unrelenting in her mouth. She had left the house where she had spent most of her life. Another house abandoned, like the one in Van.

The morning she left, her cat lay wrapped in a square of morning sun on the fountain's marble edge. The sound of coffee beans being ground by the cook woke the animal and it yowled, scratching at Lilit's leg, leaving bubbles of blood through her stocking.

'Is that the farewell I deserve, puss?' she'd asked, but didn't have time to lean over and caress the cat in a last goodbye. Fatima was going to be up and about soon and Lilit had known she wouldn't be able to leave then without Fatima becoming angry and causing a scene. The cat had continued to wail as Lilit and Anahit closed the gate behind them and stood outside in the street.

Now she raised herself up on one elbow to look at the pregnant moon. She couldn't sleep, couldn't rest her eyes in such light. Now another animal abandoned, as Minas's lamb had been left to the flames. She left Fatima behind too, left her crawling on the floor and counting out the wads of money she found under Suleiman's bed. But she hadn't found it all, Lilit saw to that. She kept a cache of her own, more money than Fatima ever dreamed. She tried in this way to make herself feel better about leaving, kneeling at the courtyard doors and taking Anahit's face in hers. *What a good husband I shall find you with this!* She hugged her daughter in silent vindication. Anahit merely frowned, looking up at the blank-faced sky. Other than that, she made no signs of grief or confusion. Lilit led her away by the hand, taking only what they wore and whatever trinkets they could carry between them, and made for Beirut.

❋　Before dawn the next morning, Lilit took over the heavy duties of the household, washing her brother's soiled work clothes, kneeling at the outdoor tub with Anahit curled up at her side, another sleeping cat. She bent her head and sniffed the metallic stink of tools rubbed constantly at Minas's side pockets. Sour smell of Papa. In the folds of his clothes, silver dust.

As the sun lifted itself from the horizon she went inside and began kneading with Siran's coarse ingredients – *I must teach her to haggle for the finest flour* – baking plaited loaves and pastries, delicacies she learnt to make in Syria. Siran had never seen the like. She protested, making weak, ineffectual movements with her hands, but Lilit gently pushed her aside and made her sit on the only kitchen chair and watch, with Anahit resting on her lap, in the small space left by her high, tight stomach.

'Here, try this. It's a special recipe for pregnant women. To ease the pain of labour.'

She stood before Siran with the ladle upraised. Siran peered into it, took in ground cinnamon, milky blandness, and cautioned a sip. Anahit nodded in her babyish way, encouraged her.

'Mm, I think I like it,' Siran mumbled between mouthfuls.

'Have some more. It's an old Ottoman dish.'

Siran took the ladle herself and began to slurp. Anahit looked on, impressed.

'It's really very good. I like it a lot.'

'You won't when I tell you what it is.'

Siran looked up, bewildered, her mouth full.

'It won't harm the baby, will it?'

'Of course not. Semolina, sheep's milk, rosewater … and chicken breast.'

Siran spluttered as Lilit and Anahit laughed.

Siran needed Lilit's help more and more as her pregnancy advanced. Minas was away all day and sometimes most of the night, making himself indispensable at the jewellery shop. Lilit taught Siran everything she had learnt in Syria and the younger woman tried her best to absorb it, at first clumsy and suspicious then enjoying the strange new tastes and meticulous Islamic routines of hygiene and superstition.

It was Lilit who assisted with the birth of the baby. The birth was easy and quick, the pain manageable. Within two hours the baby's head crowned and Lilit and the midwife were ready to catch it. The baby was placed straight on Siran's breasts and latched on in an instant. Selim's name came to Siran at that moment like a blessing, she told Lilit. It was not recognisably Armenian and Minas was quietly furious, but the women reasoned it would allow the boy to assimilate into Lebanese society.

Minas walked home from work for the half hour he was allowed to take the midday meal with his family each day. Today he walked faster than usual; the boss had proposed something to him he must consider right away. More and more as the months passed he found himself wanting to tell Lilit of his concerns, to confide in her, ask her advice. He watched himself regress into the little boy he had been in Van, jeering at his sister over the little things, yet trusting her to guide him when he stumbled under the weight of major decisions. He hoped Siran hadn't noticed.

He was getting thin, approaching middle-age. While his friends were growing paunches and double chins he was becoming emaciated; he regarded his forearms as he lay at rest in the mornings, knotty hands almost as brittle as the newspaper littering the bed. Something was eating away at his insides; he was sure of it. He confided in Lilit and she looked at him with those great cow eyes of hers and laughed.

'Guilty conscience, Minas,' she whispered.

He thought about her remark as he walked home. The new frailty of his body reminded him of fears kept hidden, a young boy starving, of his vulnerability and isolation. His limbs couldn't support him when he went downstairs to the outhouse: hollow legs, yet restless, when he lay back in bed, to be in some place far away. Twigs for arms, a thatch head harbouring only memories. He closed his swollen eyes and discovered a thousand images burnt into his retina. Soft slime of corpses, staring mouths, the high, wailing pitch of dying babies. Some days he screamed at Lilit and Siran to shut Selim up, smother him with a pillow, strangle him so his whining wouldn't lead into more nightmares. Minas's yelling brought on coughing fits that lasted all night, so nobody got any sleep.

The pimpled girl came to him often now, naked and bruised, with trailing hair. She came at dawn most of all, crying without sound. Her eyes were blind, she lay on top of him, her mouth open in a final ecstatic O. He tried to speak and his throat rasped with the effort. *Why isn't your hair bound?* She didn't answer but indicated with her fingers that she'd been strangled to death. He remembered her weak affections, her tiny laughter, those clammy hands on his chest. His cheek wet against hers as she slept and sobbed and he lay awake and plotted escape. *Why am I here, fed and rested and tended to by other women, while she lies dead and alone in Syria?*

He came to the gate now and peered into the courtyard before entering. He saw the pile of gardening tools lying abandoned in the corner, a tumble of red fruit near the side door. The two women had their backs to him, crooning and laughing over Selim. He saw their bent heads, Lilit's dark braid with its glints of gold in the sun, Siran's two plaits, black and wound into a crown, with curls escaping at the nape. He experienced a bright surge of pain at the sight of them, his family: *Whatever has happened, whatever will happen, I have this for now.* He watched their hands flash in the sunshine as they dandled his boy, one woman holding on to each arm, coaxing him to stand on his chubby bowlegs between them and take his first step unaided. He saw the gold of the chain he'd made glint on his boy's neck, the tiny crucifix hidden in creases of baby fat. Selim threw his head back to the sky and laughed: a full, adult belly laugh. Minas couldn't help laughing too. Anahit saw him then and clapped her hands in delight. She loved her uncle.

After a lunch of flatbread, soft white cheese and the jewels of pomegranates, he had to rush back to work. He put his hand out to his sister.

'Feel like a walk?'

She nodded and tied a scarf over her hair. Siran was busy putting Selim down for his nap. He flailed and fought and screamed, and she looked up as they passed and blew a kiss to her husband. He couldn't bring himself to blow one back; he felt too guilty at his desire to tell his sister of the news first and not his wife.

They hurried down Urfa Street to the jewellery shop. Anahit clung to her mother's and uncle's hands, skipping between them to keep pace. She looked up from one to the other as they spoke, keeping quiet, listening, although she couldn't understand much of what they said. Minas spoke in an undertone.

'Boss offered me the business today.'

'He did what?'

'Wants to retire, has no sons, thinks I'll follow in his footsteps and keep the family name.'

'Will you?'

'Course not.'

'Is he giving the shop to you?'

He laughed, increasing his pace.

'Lilit, I didn't think you were so naive.'

'How much does he want?'

'We haven't discussed terms yet, but I'm sure he'll look after me.'

'Well, how are you going to pay for it? Will you sell Mamma's earrings?'

He stopped mid-stride, breathless.

'We should keep those in the family. After all, we lost so much else.'

He coughed and a bright-red particle flew into his cupped palm. He showed it to his sister silently as if he were still a little boy, then flung it to the ground. She made as if she hadn't seen it.

'So how else to pay?'

'You told me that you—'

'Minas, that's my daughter's dowry.'

'Please, Lilit! I'll pay you back.'

'What if you can't?'

'I'll make it up to you somehow. You're already living in our house, eating our food—'

'I knew you'd waste no time casting it up to me! I'll have you know, brother, that I more than earn my keep.'

He loosed his hand from Anahit's, laid it on Lilit's shoulder.

'We want you here, Siran and I. I don't know what she would do without you. But can't you see, if I own this business, how much better it will be for all of us?'

He studied her face, she seemed more troubled than he had expected.

'Come on,' he said. 'I'm already late.'

He began walking around the corner, his sister and her daughter running behind. At the entrance to the shop, Lilit stopped him with a hand on his arm.

'Minas. I'll give it all to you. But promise me one thing.'

'Anything.'

'You'll look after my daughter as if she's yours. All your life.'

He kissed her on the cheek, lightly.

'You will give her the shop when you die, Minas.'

'But my son—'

'You will give her the shop. She needs a dowry. Your son can make his own way.'

He nodded, deep in thought. He knelt down in front of Anahit and took her face in both his hands, looking up at his sister.

'I promise.'

'And you'll give her the earrings when she marries. Whomever she marries – whether he be Muslim or Christian.'

He hesitated.

'Minas! Do you promise? Do you promise to look upon her as your own daughter?'

He entered the shop, called out again over his shoulder.

'I promise!'

'If you don't,' Lilit shouted back, 'I'll curse you worse than Mamma did.'

BEIRUT, 1995

I lie in Chaim's bed, stretch my legs and arms out wide to reach the cool parts of the sheets. Then I realise he isn't there. He's always working. Yes, so am I, but it's not all-consuming the way it is for him. I resent him for it – knowing how illogical my resentment is – yet my old sense of abandonment sours our brief time together. And he realises how fragile our state of coexistence is, how easily his behaviour can slide into shades of an absent father. But he doesn't know what to do. I know I'm being overly sensitive and unreasonable. How do other women cope with being the one at home, the one who waits, who cleans and cooks, making the private sphere bearable?

My grandmothers never had any expectations. At least, Siran didn't. Minas practically lived at the jewellery shop, especially after Selim was born. Lilit, on the other hand, seemed to expect much more from her men. Yet she didn't keep any of those men. In the meantime here I am, aping the tired dance of a generation ago. So how far have I come?

Chaim has again told me he loves me, and I was surprised at how right it felt for me to answer right away, 'I love you too.' As a young girl, I thought all this would be mawkish, awkward, when it inevitably happened to me. Yet now, in the thick of it, I swing from elation to confusion: daily, hourly. When he's here with me, there's no tomorrow, and my spirits soar. When he's away, I plummet, doubt him and myself.

Much as I battle against it, my daily routines have settled into long-established forms. I wake most mornings to find Chaim already gone. Even if he's not stationed in the south, he's usually at the company's Beirut headquarters by seven, filling in reports and checking files. He phones by half-past to wake me.

'Morning.' I cradle the receiver in the hollow between my ear and shoulder, eyes still closed.

'Hello there.'

Against my will, his voice lulls me into security.

'Come home early today. I miss you already.'

When the phone call is over, I luxuriate in the softness of the mattress, the slight tinge of sweat left on his pillow. I need to go to the camp again today for the interview, but my grandmothers' voices sing me still further to sleep, into a state of drowsy contentment where the outside world and its pressing duties somehow don't seem so important any longer. I sleep for an hour, two hours more. In my dreams, the insistence of my father's memory recedes, changes, billows into illusion.

When I finally get up, it's as if my dreams have given me an answer. I'm ready to find the place where my father died. Was murdered. By a suicide bomber, an old rival who wanted him killed. Or so Sarkis said. I'll go today, after I see the woman at the camp. And I won't blame any of them for what they did. Anyone can become a killer if they find themselves in a place where killing is necessary. Yet, as I rise from the bed, these justifications seem ramshackle, deliberately obtuse.

As I tidy the bedroom, wash and dress, I'm distracted by the physical manifestations of Chaim's existence: crinkled hair, butterscotch and grey, caught in the shower drain, rings of soap left in the bathroom sink after he's shaved. His boxer shorts discarded on a chair. Mounds of clean, curled-up socks, forgotten between the cushions on the couch. I wear one of his T-shirts as I make my way to the kitchen, drink out of the mug he's rinsed and left on the draining board. It's still wet on the rim.

I miss him. I love it when he tucks the bedclothes around me at night, a single sheet-fold soft on my nape, a blanket wedged beneath the angle of my spine. As I float further into sleep, the careful way he arranges the various weights for comfort suggests a memory – my grandmothers fussing about me as a toddler when they put me down for a nap. Part of me knows these traits of his will soon pall or even begin to irritate me. A day will come when I'll wrinkle my nose at the manifestations of his age, or simple maleness, shout at him over petty tasks like washing up and wiping bathroom mirrors of shower steam. I've never seen it first-hand with a father or mother but I've heard about it from Dilek and other girlfriends, watched it in enough films and books. Running beneath my pleasure at this new, elated state of being is the threat of its eventual demise. Some nights I feel it like a tight thread beneath my passion: disgust laps at me briefly when he rolls over after we've made love, a baby ecstatic and sated after the breast, when he burps unashamedly after a meal, looks slyly at other women. When I wash his dirty clothes.

Yet I stay in the apartment, revelling in his closeness. I move between wanting him here, and feeling ashamed to show so much need. I want to stay here, waiting for him, yet at the same time know my purpose in coming to Beirut is for something else, something larger. I look at maps, brush up on my written Arabic, read historical texts, tell myself I'm justly preparing for the journey to my father's truth.

I've finished my article on the new Beirut, and one about Shia and Sunni Palestinian clashes during the war. What next? I can wait until I've seen the Palestinian woman, ask about the massacres, do my human-interest story fifteen years on. Beneath the distraction of activity is a deep, nameless and guilty fear. I try to ignore it, drink in Chaim's presence with abandon, and in his absence worship the imperfect amulets he leaves behind. Discarded watchstrap grown too frayed to wear. Amber bottle of vitamins, a year out of date. Threadbare silk underpants from a kibbutz trip to China – so long ago – crumpled under his pillow. I go shopping with Julius at neighbourhood markets that set up each morning at the end of the street and then dismantle at dusk within twenty minutes, ephemeral treasures. Julius and I run together through fleeting summer rains. I buy rainbow-coloured shellfish, extravagant shapes so unlike the Atlantic clams of Boston, and two whole sardines to grill in vine leaves, a traditional Constantinople dish Siran would make in summer. I know I won't be able to eat any of it, with my stomach still unaccustomed to the bacteria of Beirut.

When I'm done cooking, I curl up on his broken sofa with a book on the civil war and stare out at the sea, slick with rain, without reading a single word. Do I trust him? He's Israeli. So what? I'm Armenian. Turkish. American. A citizen of Lebanon. So many warring identities, I'm surprised there's anything left. When I lie in bed beside him, his face pressed against mine, I feel as if we blur into each other. He's not other, he is me. When he leaves, the man walking away changes, becomes someone else again. What do I offer him? Am I so selfish that all I can think about is what he can give me? Then what hope is there? Why do we care for each other at all?

It's crazy to sit here worrying about it. He won't be home till late anyway. I turn off the simmering stew, cover the pot as securely as I can with a mismatched lid. I call a cab, having found the drivers are more reliable that way.

On the way to the camp I clasp and unclasp my hands in my lap, twisting my fingers together. When we get there, I make the driver promise he'll be back in an hour. He looks surprised to find himself there but lights another cigarette and nods, making a U-turn back into the city.

I unfurl my umbrella. The streets have become dirtier, children more ragged, the presence of women less prominent. The camp is behind a row of Chanel, Gucci and Versace posters, torn and papered over with the faces of bearded mullahs and boyish bombers, grimly gazing into Paradise. The jagged silhouette of the camp buildings rise behind the hoardings, limp clothes and even limper models displayed behind Koranic phrases in fresh green swags of paint. Advertisements from Paris and Milan, skeleton women rendered irrelevant, immoral, by the faces of the pious and the dead. A slapdash concrete wall topped with barbed wire. Heavy gates and guard posts, the stink of sewerage and hopelessness emanating from it with the black smoke of burning rubber.

I walk toward it purposefully, conscious of my high strides on the greasy footpath, my posture crumpling in the rain. I called the Texan UNDP worker last night and asked why the family hadn't been there last time. There was some excuse: illness, the little girl, hospital. The Palestinian woman finally agreed to another day. Is it only because I'm a Pakradounian? That the woman seemed to register my name? The suspicion sends waves of apprehension through me.

I wait for a gap in the flow of traffic, decide on the fatalistic approach I've seen others take, running and dodging, trusting drivers to slow down or swerve. A late-model Mercedes misses me by a few centimetres.

In a few minutes the rain has stopped and I'm sweating. The street stinks of car fumes, potatoes fried in cheap oil. My stomach begins to cramp, at first imperceptibly, like an ant labouring up a hill. I'm an ant. Labouring. The pincer motion increases. I double over, holding onto a corner wall for support. I'm going to die. I'm going to vomit and shit out everything inside me. The panic increases. I moan. People don't stop but I'm dimly aware of sidelong glances. A crazy man babbles to himself, eating red jam out of a jar with his fingers. I turn to the wall of an apartment building, doing everything in my power to stop from letting my bowels go. Please let there be a cab. A welter of people, fluttering by like the old Syrian man's words on paper. I squat down like a beggar, like the Syrian on the corner in the rain.

A man sitting on his apartment balcony above me calls down and waves.

'You okay?'

His wide gesture leaves no room for refusal; he's beckoning me to his home. Saviour. He'll let me use his toilet. I find the entrance, clutching my stomach, still doubled over in pain. The waves intensify, then suddenly subside. Blessed relief. I stand on his front step, face wiped clean with the agony I experienced only a second ago, my forehead wet.

The man opens the door, stands with me and closes the door behind him. My heart sinks.

'Are you pregnant?'

'Umm, no, no.'

'Good. Here, take one of these. It won't harm you.'

The man holds a smooth white pill in his hand. Seeing my expression, he thrusts it further, close to my mouth. In the other hand he holds a glass of water.

'This will fix your problem. I see this all the time for tourists in Beirut. Don't be afraid, I work at the American University Hospital.'

I take the pill into my mouth and keep it hidden between my gum and cheek. A voice screams in my skull: *This is the truth you must swallow.*

'Don't need water, thank you,' I mumble.

I hope the pill won't dissolve. Not opening my mouth, I nod my thanks and almost run in the other direction. I don't need to go to the toilet any longer. I feel drained of everything: fluid, energy, will. Once out of the man's line of vision I spit the pill out onto the ground and take a cab back to Chaim's apartment.

❊   As I spoon dog food into a bowl for Julius, I call the UNDP worker, give my apologies, almost retching when the meaty stench assaults me. When I explain my physical state, the woman's attitude alters in an instant. 'I get it all the time too,' she says. 'Damn this place. I can't eat a thing except dry potato chips. It's debilitating. No big deal. I'll try to smooth any ruffled feathers. Any time you feel fine.'

I don't feel so fine. I let Julius out into the downstairs courtyard and crawl into Chaim's rumpled bed to await his evening return from Nabatiye. He's been away for a week, still clearing the south of landmines planted by his own country's army.

At sunset I call him at work, impatient.

'I'm already in bed.'

'Good, can't wait.'

'I mean I'm sick. The usual thing. Are you coming home soon?'

'Yeah. Don't fall asleep until I come home, okay? It's been such a frustrating week. I keep removing these mines and the bastard Hezbollah just keep using the cleared space to launch more bombs into Israel. Seems pretty futile, doesn't it?'

'At least you're trying. I just ran away from my responsibility.'

'Tell me when I get back. My driver's waiting.'

❊   I smile at the woman, who smiles back. She says her name is Bilqis and I reply in Arabic that improves as I gain confidence. As I watch her prepare to make tea, I marvel at how long a simple domestic act can take without running water or electricity. The little girl ignores me, drawing complex patterns in the dirt outside the door. Watching them like this, they look so familiar it hurts. I lean forward.

'Bilqis? Was it you, with a little girl, that I saw at the tribunal recently? The war crimes tribunal?'

Bilqis places a battered saucepan on the primus stove, kneels down before it.

'Why? Were you there?'

'Yes. Just in my capacity as a journalist. I knew I recognised you from somewhere. I felt that it wasn't a very good outcome for families of the victims – no reparations.'

She looks at my recorder.

'Is it off? Good. Understand me. There will never be reparations for people like us. We are not human to them, so why should they treat us as such?'

She turns away and spoons tea-leaves into a copper pot and sugar into small glasses. I'm not sure whether she's annoyed with me. We sit in silence watching the water boil. Finally the tea is made and she reaches under the bed for a tin of high-protein, dust-flavoured biscuits, courtesy of UNRWA.

I turn on my tape recorder.

'You don't mind if we start the interview now?'

Bilqis nods many times, suddenly looking nervous and overly hospitable.

'How long have you lived here, if you don't mind me asking?'

'Since 1948. Except for a period in the early eighties.'

I look around the low-ceilinged, flimsy room. This woman has lived in the same hovel for close to fifty years.

'What happened in that period?'

'My sister and I lived with a relative for a time while the camps were rebuilt.'

'Rebuilt?'

'There was some destruction of buildings.'

I look at the opened UNRWA boxes under the bed, away from her face.

'The Phalange?'

'Yes. And the Israelis.'

I decide not to respond to the wider criticism.

'And how old are you now, if you don't mind?'

'Too old to remember. Nearly seventy.'

'Is this your granddaughter? She's very beautiful.'

Except for the hair, I want to add. The girl's ponytail is matted and sticky, unwashed for what looks like months. She pretends not to hear the spoken compliment but a grin appears at the corners of her mouth. She tries to appear mirthless when she catches me looking at her, intent on concentrating elsewhere and not looking into my eyes.

'She turns twelve in November. Both parents dead.'

'I'm so sorry.'

'Her mother was blown up by a car bomb. CIA involvement, they say.'

'Who says?'

I can tell she doesn't want to say any more. I turn off the tape recorder, she notices and relaxes visibly.

'Our newspapers suspected the Americans were involved. Then made it look like the Muslims did it.'

'I'm sorry. If it helps a little, I'm an orphan too. My mother died giving birth to me. My father was murdered when I was sent to America. Casualties of war, eh?'

Bilqis doesn't laugh and I press on, feeling a growing sense of desperation, the hypocrisy of playing this chatty, cheery role I don't believe in.

'Have you any ongoing help? Welfare services, counselling?'

'There's a young woman – a welfare worker – who comes once a week and talks to us. She's from the Red Crescent. We like Rowda, don't we, Inam?'

The girl sidles over to her grandmother and places a hand in her lap. It seems a strange gesture for a girl her age: deliberately childish, theatrical. She nods, dramatically shy. Bilqis ruffles her ponytail and continues.

'Rowda's Australian-born, with Lebanese parents. We feel she understands us.'

I lower my chin. Does this mean I don't?

'So, she's a counsellor? She helps you speak your pain?'

'She tries. It is hard for her to make a difference. Too many deaths.'

I swallow.

'Is there anything I can do?'

Bilqis seems not to have heard.

'Too many deaths in our family.'

She shakes her head, tears pooling in her eyes. The girl wags her head too, making fun of her grandmother's solemnity, winks and pokes her tongue out at me. Again, it's such a self-consciously childish gesture I laugh. Bilqis notices.

'Inam, if I catch you doing that again!'

The girl smirks and points at me. 'My uncle's in prison.'

'Inam, go play outside. That's no news to be telling everyone.'

Inam bangs the door behind her, bare feet slapping in the dust.

'She's very sharp.'

'Too sharp for her own good. True, she heard me say I wanted to ask you about her uncle, my sister Amal's only son. She had him late in life, when nobody thought she would have any more children. I ask all the journalists if they can help, and some of them write a piece here and there. Not many. Though you, being an orphan yourself, can understand that if Sayed doesn't get out of prison there is no family to look after Inam when I am gone. The poor boy has been wrongly accused. Could you help him?'

'How could I do that?'

Now I realise why the woman was so eager to meet me initially. She needs help and thinks I'm gullible enough to believe her.

'Let me tell you about Sayed and you will understand.'

I shift in my seat. Immediately Bilqis notices and looks me in the eye.

'You do not think I am telling the truth?'

I hesitate, falter before I speak. 'I don't know what to think.'

'Then I will tell you. My nephew was – is – a good boy. He was bored and disillusioned, as are all young men. Especially Palestinians. What do they have to lose? I ask you. He became involved with the wrong people and they pinned this lie to him. They were jealous he was able to go and study in New York for a year. Now they say he bombed a building there. I ask you, how could a mere boy do that? He is misguided, yes, but never a militant.'

I cut her off.

'What's his surname? Have I read about him in the papers?'

'What does it matter? Sayed Ali.'

The name seems familiar to me, I'm not sure why. I've read so much on the war by now that everything has blurred. 'Is that a common surname?' I ask.

Bilqis stops stirring her tea. 'Why do you ask?'

'I've seen it referred to in my reading. I can't remember in which context.'

'Many Palestinian and Shia families have this name. An old and renowned name. What is the matter?'

'Nothing—I … I need to get more information on your nephew before I can do anything. But I still don't know how I can help you.'

Bilqis puts her hand on my cheek.

'Just by writing his story. He's innocent.'

❧ Bilqis gazes after the journalist when she is gone. A good girl. Sincere. She even looks Arabic, except for those non-existent eyebrows. Her name is Pakradounian, and Bilqis suspected right away who her father was. She had a distinct feeling when the UN worker rang and asked if anyone would be available to meet an Armenian–American journalist named Pakradounian, new to the country after a long absence.

Now that the girl has confirmed her identity by speaking so openly about her past, Bilqis knows for certain. Her father was Sanaya's lover, the Phalange militiaman. The man Issa killed. The girl is on a quest; it's written all over her face. No matter. Her need for atonement will spur her into helping Sayed. Maybe she can get him out then poor Amal can see her son again, and Inam can have her uncle back. He was always good to her, treated her as his own child.

She can't rely on me for much longer, Bilqis thinks, bending to fetch a beaker of water for her cooking. The bucket is nearly empty and she has to go outside and down the street to the pump. On the way back, water spills onto her wrists and feet, the bucket growing heavier with each step. She stops, puts it down. *Look at me, trembling at the slightest exertion. I'm getting old now. Time to die. Seen too much. Forgiven so much.*

Once inside again, she measures two handfuls of rice into her only, blackened saucepan, trying not to drop any grains on the floor. It has become harder over the last few weeks to do anything without some slight mishap. She eases the pan over the stove. Rice again. Boiled rice with condensed milk and sugar, a stick of cinnamon, a splash of rosewater, cloves for flavour. *At least we have our spices.*

Inam likes that dish. Issa liked it too. It was one of the only meals he would eat with relish, without picking at it like a three-legged sparrow. That and eggs. Fresh, if they could get them. None of that powdered stuff. And then only if the Israelis didn't confiscate the hens over some imagined transgression, if the poor birds hadn't succumbed to the weather or the lack of grain, or hysteria caused by the bombs. *Thank Allah there are fresh eggs now. And no more bombs, not for the moment anyway.* Fresh eggs every morning, the hard-boiled yolk so perfect, a shiny crescent moon.

Issa, her blue-eyed boy. She can still see him at the breast, his mute gaze following every twitch of her muscles, every facial tic. That little topknot she kept unshorn at the crown of his head, easy handle for the angels if he should die, to swoop down and take him up to Paradise. Dead for all these years now, twelve already, and yet when something funny happens she'll still say to herself, *Must remember to tell Issa that.* Or if Inam makes a joke, or acts silly, as she often does, Bilqis will turn around and nearly say, 'My darling Issa, did you see your crazy daughter?'

What a pure boy he was. Pure and committed to Islam. Not that she condoned the violence. He killed too many people, too many women, children. 'Holy war, Mumma,' he would say. 'The Prophet tells us to fight against infidels if they threaten our religion. And they have.' She would shake her head, knowing it was useless to argue. 'Killing is killing, Issa, my boy,' was all she allowed herself to end with. 'No matter who is doing it or why.'

When Issa killed himself she covered her face with her veil and did not stir from bed for days. She felt abandoned by Allah. The only person who could rouse her was Sanaya, with her tender face and the promise of a grandchild. Sanaya, who she'd hated and distrusted at first, judging her liaison with the Armenian Phalangist. Rouba had told Bilqis all she knew.

She stirs the white glug in her saucepan. It thickens; she pours in a drop more milk, turns off the heat. She sits on the end of the bed to catch her breath and watches Inam come in the door, after having seen the young woman off to the edge of the camp.

'What took you so long, child?'

'She bought me an ice-cream at the shop. We sat outside.'

'Do you like her?'

Inam puffs her cheeks out in that way she affects, considering. 'I like her enough.'

She puts a finger into the bubbling saucepan with a sidelong glance at her grandmother, grimaces at her then licks it clean.

'I warned you – next time I see you do that, no supper! I'll eat it all myself.'

Inam steps up to her, placing her head on the ample lap.

'Play with my hair, Grandma, and tell me those old stories.'

Bilqis twirls a lock with her finger, her mind elsewhere, then pushes Inam off.

'You're wriggling like two fish in a bottle! Enough. No playing until we manage to brush that hair of yours. Come on, get me the comb.'

Inam flounces away, through the front door.

'You can't catch me,' Bilqis hears her shout, before she's turned the corner and gone. 'I'm a freedom fighter and I've got a gun!'

BEIRUT, 1983

Issa slept late every morning now. He told Sanaya the mosque could wait. His mother could wait. She was still living downstairs with Rouba, at times frightened by his liaison with Sanaya. He repeated all her dire warnings to Sanaya, and she wasn't sure whether he was doing it to make fun of his mother or to warn her himself. *She's dangerous, my boy. She could hurt you. She's too old for you; she's Sunni; she doesn't wear the veil.* His mother's moods changed hourly, he said. Last night she was hostile to Sanaya when they met in the courtyard; at other times, she seemed to welcome her as a sane influence on her son.

Sanaya lay awake by his side now, one hand resting on his chest, listening to him cry and shout in his dreams. She would have liked to think he had fewer nightmares now they were together, but she knew they had increased.

She wanted her love to enfold him, buffer him, keep him safe. The Israelis had finally left the west of the city, but had handed over its jurisdiction to Phalangist militiamen – not before giving them the honorific of Lebanese Army. It was not safe for Issa to be out on the streets alone, as the Christians were rounding up and imprisoning Palestinians and Lebanese activists and militiamen. There had been rumours of gross beatings, torture. Nobody came out of the prisons alive.

Yet Issa seemed unable to accept her concern most days, scorning it as an illusion, a temptation, an invention of the devil to plunge him further into the dark. He went out each morning for a week, returning late at night with a haggard expression in his eyes. Told her he'd been to the mosque again. She pleaded with him. He lowered his eyes and muttered. 'Orders. I have to.'

But he didn't leave her. If anything, he began to ensconce himself still further into the apartment, cooking up messes of condensed milk and eggs late at night which he slurped in bed, sleeping with Sanaya, reading to her, bathing together, making love. Those were the good times, the sane times, when he didn't give credence to his many fears.

Sometimes she'd wake in a panic, feeling her love for him more akin to that of a mother than an equal partner. Then she disturbed his sleep silently and held his penis, feeling it grow and pulse like a tropical flower in the dark, talking to it, stroking it into life. She convinced herself by her actions that her love for him was sexual, and adult, and whole.

He sobbed in his sleep. She patted him, soothed him, murmured in his ear.

'It's all right, Issa. I'm here. It's all right.'

She could tell he was still ashamed of his fears. On particularly bad mornings, when the nightmares had been relentless and violent, he took his Koran into the bathroom and sat on the toilet with it until lunchtime. She usually ignored him, hoping he would resolve it himself, continued with her small tasks, waited for Rouba to come so they could sit and talk in the kitchen in whispers.

Today she kicked the bathroom door and banged on it with her fists.

'Who are you in love with, Issa? Me or the fucking book?'

He rushed out through the door, almost knocking her over, brandishing the Koran over his head.

'What did you say?'

'You heard me.'

She was already walking down the corridor to the kitchen. He ran after her and pinned her against the wall.

'Blasphemer! How could I even think you would understand?'

'Understand what? That you're a fanatic? Ha! If only I'd listened to my reason.'

His grip tightened on her upper arms until he was pinching into her flesh.

'It's not too late,' he said.

His voice was squeaky, uncertain, the anger squeezed out of it.

'For what?'

'To throw me out. I'll go now if you want me to.'

She felt his grip relax on her arms. The Koran was wedged between her ribs and the wall, an unwieldy barrier to any comfort. She sighed, letting the anger wash out of her. Issa followed suit, breathing heavily into her neck, his head lolling on her shoulder. He seemed exhausted, tired out by his struggle over who he wanted to be.

✳ Selim walked down the rutted pathways of the Armenian quarter with firm strides. Streetlights were turning on one by one; it was nearly dusk. One last strip of sky on the horizon, alive in a wild-rose glow. He stopped to watch it fade. He was surprised the lights still worked at all in this part of the city. Each time he passed beneath one, it lit around his head as if he was controlling its flicker pulse with his own forward thrust of movement. His determination. In the lineaments of his body. To see his grown-up daughter. To see the baby he abandoned. Anoush.

He wanted to atone to his family, his daughter – for something; he wasn't sure what. Everything. He wanted to explain to them that he wasn't as bad as they thought. He peered into open doors and windows, stopped again in mid-step at the smell of meat cooking, children crowding around the stove demanding their dinner. Home-reared lamb in a rich cream sauce. Pearl onions and herbs. Shrill sounds of television, cartoons dubbed into Arabic. The smell of Armenian food made his eyes water, rather than his mouth, memory hurting too much for the quick response of simple pleasure. He walked past families in brightly lit rooms, safe from the outside, oblivious to his rheumy gaze.

Nobody else hurrying along the street gave him a second glance. He must look Armenian, then. He'd never been aware of it growing up. He was dressed in civilian clothes, a loose beige jacket and tie, linen trousers. All that sacrifice coming to nothing. Better to find Anoush now, explain. See her face. See if she bore any traces of his genes. Ask her forgiveness.

He carried a terracotta pot of pink cyclamens under his jacket in the hope that she would accept it – and him. He thought of bringing spirits or wine, but the gift would have seemed too worldly, too disrespectful of her youthful position. Flowers, more than anything else, signalled the humility of his intentions. He would give her back her mother's bracelet too. It belonged to her more than ever now.

When he reached the marketplace and its crooked row of awnings, he seemed to know where to go. He made for his father's jewellery shop, remembered exactly where it used to be. *Could Father still be in there?* It was late, he would have shut the shop and walked home to his dinner. He pressed his nose against the glass. The shop was dark; at first glance he saw only his own face, reflected against rows of silver bracelets just like the one he wore, and drops of turquoise startling his eyes.

He could squint and see the long wooden-and-glass counter he would sit on as a boy. He could dimly see the outline of the cash drawer, gleaming display cases ranged against the far wall. He remembered the little boy he'd been: too solemn, tow-haired, precise, counting out the money at the end of the day and handing it to his father, who wrote the amount down in a large, leather-bound ledger. He squashed his eye against the cold glass. The ledger wasn't sitting at the left end of the counter as it always did. Not like Father at all; he was such a stickler for order and tradition.

He looked around at the teeming street: *Now, where is my father's house from here?* He'd been driven here, certainly, but it had always been night and he had always been drunk. Now he was disoriented and afraid of what he might find.

An old man in a felt fedora brushed past as Selim looked up to the street signs at the crossroads, Armenian script blurring in the pale rain that had just begun to fall.

'Need some help, son?'

Selim cupped one hand over his forehead, trying to stop the rain from trickling into his eyes and mouth.

'Urfa Street. I'm looking for the Pakradounians.'

The old man slapped his own thigh and whooped. Selim stepped back, alarmed at his enthusiasm.

'I knew you were one of them! I said to myself, Bedros, old man, if that's not a Pakradounian, I'll milk my own goat! I saw you looking in the shop window and decided to follow you and find out. So, which one of them are you, now?'

'Selim. Minas's only son.'

'You? You're the wild one that ran away! And to think that I, old Bedros, have the pleasure of taking you back into the fold. Talk of prodigal sons! And to think you've gotten so fine too, so handsome, so—I don't know how to put it.'

'Lebanese?' Selim suggested.

'Well, I wouldn't have put it that way, but now that you've mentioned it—'

The old man cocked his head to one side in the rain and surveyed Selim critically. He seemed to have run out of things to say.

'How is my father?'

The old man pursed his lips, licked them sympathetically.

'You didn't know? He's passed on, my dear boy. Died many years ago. Fifteen or sixteen, it would be now, I think. He's well at peace now. I'm sorry.'

Selim caught his breath. 'I left—so long ago. It's just hitting me now—'

He slumped onto the street sign, wiping the rain from his cheeks. The old man took his arm.

'Come, come, I'll take you to your aunt Lilit.'

'Her?' Selim's voice was low, frightening. 'I don't want to look at her. Is my mother there?'

Bedros hesitated. 'Ah, my boy.' He patted Selim fondly. 'Your mamma is in the nursing home. You can go visit her tomorrow. She's forgotten who she is. Your aunt Lilit says—'

'I don't want to know what Lilit says.'

'Come, come then; rest at my house. I'm only next door. You'll catch your death if we stay out here jabbering. And whatever you think, Lilit will really be so pleased to see you; she's not so well either these days …'

He trailed off as they came to the beginning of Urfa Street. Selim stopped and could faintly discern his childhood home in the drizzle and approaching darkness. The bougainvillea was still there, luxuriant, flinging deep magenta blooms onto the upstairs balcony: flat, dark foliage dripping moisture onto the eaves. The window shutters and French doors were still unpainted, rotting further in the rain.

'Uncle. Uncle Bedros. I meant to ask you—I had a child with my cousin Anahit, a little girl. Is she—?'

Bedros squeezed Selim's arm.

'She's gone to America, my boy. As soon as she turned sixteen, they packed her off to some expensive foreign school. A little less than two years ago now. She never stopped asking about you, I heard—hey, where are you going?'

Bedros stood at the corner of Urfa Street, hands outstretched, watching Selim vanish into the rain.

✵ Selim sat at home on the carpet. A dark wet stain spread under his buttocks. His clothes and hair were sodden with rain but he couldn't seem to get up and change. He had an open bottle of whisky between his legs and another on its side, rolled near the door. The cyclamen lay discarded, limp and waterlogged, smelling of sorrow and sweetness.

His daughter had gone away and he hadn't even known. Could he not have sensed it? That she was no longer breathing the same sea air, hearing the same bombs and artillery in her sleep? To America, where she would forget her language, her culture, him. He should never have left her. Could he go and find her now? But he couldn't leave Beirut. And now it was too late, everything too late.

He pressed the receiver to his ear and listened to the shrill ringing as he gulped down another shot.

'Answer the phone, damn you.'

The telephone continued to ring. Sanaya was not at home.

'Damn you, damn you, damn you!'

He put down the receiver and smashed his glass against the coffee table. It made a teeth-aching, unbearable sound. He drank from the bottle. The painful sting of liquid warmed him inside and gave him clarity, cancelling out the cold and damp and confusion of his body. He tried the number again. This time, it was picked up after only one ring.

'Stop calling or I'll kill you.'

He recognised the voice.

'I need to speak to Sanaya.'

He could sense the muffled sound of a hand cupping the receiver, as if the other man was afraid to be heard.

'I said I will kill you. Don't make it happen sooner than it needs to.'

Issa's voice was frail, intimate. Selim shocked himself by sobbing.

'I don't care if you kill me. Just let me speak to Sanaya.'

There was silence at the other end of the line. Selim brought the receiver closer to his mouth, stood up as best he could and yelled into it. 'Sanaya! Listen to me! I've been wrong. Everything's wrong. I'm sorry, I don't know what to do.'

He put the receiver down on its cradle, whispered, 'I don't know what to do.'

BEIRUT, 1995

After finishing a new article by working solidly for five hours, I perch on my stool at Che Guevara's, imagining commuters hurrying back to work from their afternoon naps, shopkeepers pulling up cranky roller doors, unfurling awnings. Arranging displays of fruit or flowers or lining up cups of Arabic coffee. Like so many open wounds.

Stop it, I tell myself. *Don't be so negative.*

A day of writing and no human contact always does this to me, makes me cynical: all that work with the awful possibility of it slipping straight into the void, never to be seen. I've put aside the article about the Sabra-Shatila massacres; my editor needs a travel piece about Beirut for the weekend supplement, its history and architecture, a paean to the city full of post-war hope.

I steady myself to read the information I found yesterday and photocopied at the American University library. Somehow I feel these reports might contextualise the situation of the prisoner Sayed Ali, help me understand what I need to do.

I order olives and bread from the barman, at the same time knowing I won't be able to eat them. There are sliced cucumbers and chunks of white cheese on the countertop, free meze that have obviously been there all day. The smell is overpowering. I try to read through claims made by Human Rights Watch, the Israeli Human Rights Coalition, Amnesty International statistics on prisons in the Occupied Territories, as well as in occupied south Lebanon.

I called Sayed Ali this morning, ostensibly to ask him if there was anything I was allowed to bring when I come to conduct the interview. He's being held in the south of Lebanon at the Khiam Detention Center, prior to a mention hearing, when the judge will allocate a date and place for the court case. Sayed said he expected to be sent to the

Russian Compound in West Jerusalem after the relevant documents were exchanged, unless his defence lawyer could think of a good reason why he should stay in occupied territory to be tried.

Not that there is any virtue or respite in being held in occupied territory. I've now read all the reports: Lebanese and Palestinians detained without charge, teachers, clerics, teenagers, journalists just like me. The 'clean' beatings to the head and belly with rubber hoses, sandbags, open hands, jets of water, beatings that leave no visible marks. The videotaped rapes and threats of blackmail, so there's no chance the victims will ever tell their families, preoccupied with their unrelenting shame. Sleep deprivation for weeks as an interrogation technique, intimidation at gunpoint, humiliation at the hands of young, female Shin Bet agents, detainees hooded and made to stand wet and naked for hours in the air-conditioned cold of their cells. Swelling feet, dehydration, bursting kidneys. Again, there are no bruises, no blood. Nothing to point the finger at. Little food. Less water. I had an image of Sayed Ali being tortured in this way, but the calm masculinity of his voice on the phone belied it.

A
S
H

365

'Anything allowed in?' I asked.

'For people like me? With American friends? With media scrutiny? A lot. For the other unfortunates, not much at all.'

I was silent.

'Packaged food,' he continued. 'Magazines. Smokes. Marlboros, if you can get them.'

He seemed modern, educated, his Arabic accent barely recognisable when he spoke English. I asked him for details of his lawyer, legal aid provided by the Israeli government, wrote down the phone numbers of his university professors, the Pakistani man he worked for in America, selling sweets and chewing gum and cigarettes between lectures. He was born in the Sabra-Shatila camp but spent his final college year in New York on a scholarship arranged by Hezbollah. He'd been studying Industrial Design. I asked him what made him come back.

'The Americans wouldn't let me stay,' he replied.

There was nothing I could say to that. I didn't want to probe any further about his alleged crime and incarceration, at least not before I managed to contact his lawyer, ask more questions of Bilqis, of Amal, his teachers and friends. I made to end the conversation then, unwilling to implicate myself. And he had already mentioned that the guards were listening, and that the phone was more than likely tapped.

'Shin Bet and Mossad crawling all over this place,' he whispered. 'They train the jailers.'

Yet there was one thing Sayed said that kept me there and continues to stay with me now. I asked him if he was at all religious. He hesitated before he spoke and I grew impatient at the silence, as if he were falsely striving for dramatic effect. When he finally spoke he hardly answered my question.

'Well, Islam means surrender, you know? I never believed it as a kid in the camp. What, submit to our oppressors? I was fighting them back then with stones and taunts and rotting vegetables, since I was six years old. And I'm not surrendering now.'

Sayed seemed unafraid yet acceptant of his privations: a dangerous combination. I turn back to my notes, give up after reading three paragraphs. I'm not taking in a single word. I lean both elbows on the table, look around, can't see any of the commuters I take such pleasure in conjuring. The tiny bar has red plywood in place of windows, for no reason I can imagine. Instead I look around the room, as I have so many times before, at the smoke-obscured posters of Che and Fidel, Marx and Lenin, and the former Druze leader Kamal Jumblatt darkening the walls.

I stop here most evenings now, ever since Chaim first introduced me to the place weeks ago. I usually arrive at six and drink one or two shots of arak, feeling that the alcohol settles my stomach for my one meal of the day – my poor stomach that has protested at the very air I breathe in Beirut. It can only be that; I drink bottled water, boil everything I eat to death, take supplements like a good American. I wonder why my stomach can't remember I was in fact born here, lived here for sixteen years. Instead it reacts with the flutter of every tourist: the drawing-in of breath, the surrender to blackness, the rush to the toilet, then such fleeting relief.

'What have you been writing today, little Miss?'

The barman leans his mutton-red elbows on the glass surface, trying to peer over my shoulder. I note his low-slung gun with a shiver of apprehension, as I do every time I see it.

'I'm trying to find a Samaritan to interview. Do you know any?'

'Aren't they all in the Bible? Long dead now.'

Chaim pushes open the heavy doors and the barman retreats. He leans to kiss me on the cheek and orders a drink in that way he always does, with a crook of his finger and a nod.

'What's he saying about the Bible?'

'I want to find some Samaritans. There are about five hundred of them left.'

'They're Jews, aren't they? I might be able to find someone my mother knows.'

'They speak Arabic but pray in Hebrew. I don't know if they're Muslim or Jewish. Maybe some hybrid of the two.'

'Hybrid of the two? How can they believe in Mohammed being the Prophet and be Jewish as well? And why would that be interesting enough for an American paper to pick up?'

'Such a potent symbol of peace, Chaim! They claim to be both Palestinian and Israelite from way back.'

'Rubbish. Impossible.'

'What's wrong with you?'

'It's just an outlandish claim. They must be cracked. How can they be both? It goes against what this whole conflict is about. Either they're Jewish or Muslim. Either they got to Israel thousands of years ago as Jews or they didn't. Who cares which language they pray in?'

He downs his beer. 'Listen, Anoush. I'm an Israeli, and I live in Lebanon. I identify with Arabs, and the Palestinian cause. But no matter what I do, no matter how sensitive and helpful I am, nothing changes the fact that I'm Jewish and Israeli first.'

I decide not to argue; he could be right for once. Then I catch myself in my cynicism. For once? He's right most of the time, and I already begrudge it. Especially when he speaks of the conflict, of the need not to hate. He's right. And I'm resentful. Are we becoming an old married couple – after only a few weeks?

'Want another drink?'

I nod, finishing my arak. Chaim comes back with another two glasses and a bowl of pumpkin seeds.

'What about the story you had about that terrorist guy?'

'I don't know if I believe he's innocent.'
'Only one way to find out.'

✳ Sayed walks down the corridor to meet the journalist woman they call Anoush Pakradounian. She seemed okay on the phone but not the least bit compassionate of his plight. Yet she's been sent by the family. Aunt Bilqis vouched for her. 'She's sensitive to our cause; she could get you released.' She hadn't said any more. Wasn't her name familiar? But his aunt said she was trustworthy, was even born in Beirut. She's Christian – he knows that. Armenian, Orthodox, Western, no matter where she was born. She told him she spent her college years in America, just as he had for that one anxious year, along with his brief stint at a *madrassa* in Peshawar, learning the finer points of Islamic jurisprudence and how to assemble a dirty bomb from ordinary household substances. The Harvard of Al Qaeda, some would call it.

He sighs. Such a long time ago it seems now, so many fine ideals, so many dreams ago. He adjusts the regulation pants around his crotch. Sniffs his underarms. Wouldn't do to give the wrong impression. He needs her to believe him. Does he believe what he's saying himself? Maybe. He didn't do it. But he would have done it if he'd had half a chance. He sits on the ripped plastic chair provided for him and waits.

✳ I go through my notes on the bus taking me south to Sidon. The driver stops for a toilet break at a pastry shop and passengers troop back in a reek of rosewater, holding boxes of cakes. One veiled woman offers me a crumbly pistachio biscuit like the kind Lilit would make. I smile, refuse. My stomach is churning with dread.

Again, I read the legal report on Sayed Ali. I had a hard time finding any credible information on him: searching the Web, finding his college records – he was a middling student – talking to the infuriatingly impenetrable Israeli defence lawyer from legal aid, appealing directly to the Israeli prosecution, trawling through old newspapers on file. I talked to a committee that supports Lebanese prisoners in Israel. They were helpful, then roughly realistic: 'You can't help him.' I left their offices in a plummet of despair.

The report eventually arrived from legal aid, a photocopy so bad I can hardly make out the words. It doesn't reveal anything incriminating of Sayed. I try to read through to the end but it's hard to concentrate; the sun gives me a headache. I lean back, close my eyes. By far the most important information thus far has been volunteered by Bilqis and Amal, by cousins and uncles with explicitly divided motivations. Some, I soon realised, were out to blacken Sayed's name, perhaps to avoid any investigation of their own activities. The old grocer in the camp was too obviously effusive, the sort of man giving cash freely to Islamic charities whose funds went straight to the training camps and bombing operations. Others pronounced the facts so slowly and carefully, with such close attention to detail, that I was wary of disbelieving them.

Fatwas against Israel and the United States faxed by Osama bin Laden, a wealthy Saudi dissident, were found buried under Amal's shed in the camp. Amal and Bilqis both admitted this. Sayed allegedly transmitted the faxes throughout Lebanon to other operatives last year via email. Also found was a CD-ROM version of a key four-hundred-page text, *The Encyclopaedia of the Afghan Jihad*. The most damning evidence of all: Sayed knew the supposed operational leader of the bombing of the World Trade Center in 1993, Ramzi Yousef, personally. Thus he is implicated, along with some one hundred other Middle Eastern men, as a co-conspirator. This could mean any involvement ranging from financing to recruiting, to engineering to keeping records, or being an unpaid cook in a training centre in Syria or Pakistan.

I feel the familiar throb of a headache return. Am I getting in too far? I have no stomach for politics. It's the personal I seek. My father. Only him. Not these cold-blooded killers, men who can care for their loved ones with such tenderness yet blithely end the lives of other people's children with the flick of a switch. Yet he was a cold-blooded killer too, and he didn't even care for his loved ones: not his mother and father, his wife, not even me.

I go over my notes one more time. The estimated cost of the bomb that caused half a billion dollar's worth of damage to the World Trade Center was all of three thousand dollars. Why am I doing this at all? This is way beyond my scope. I've been drawn in to the combined plea of the old woman and the glorious, indifferent child. I don't know how to explain why I feel the need to help Sayed. Atonement? Maybe. Wiping out my father's sins with one grand gesture? I reason that it's for the child's sake, at least.

From the bus stop, I walk to the Israeli detention centre. *Prison.* I wonder why Sayed is being kept in occupied territory, why the Americans haven't extradited him to be tried on the very soil he supposedly helped destroy. Maybe it's easier to keep him here, where anything is permissible. Interrogation, intimidation, torture. 'Torture lite' I've heard it called, or 'enhanced interrogation': exhaustion exercises, choking in water, violent shaking, forced standing, noise bombardment. I almost begin to run. What if they do it to me? 'Stress and duress' techniques: coffin cells, tear gas pumped straight into the eyes, inmates shackled and forced to squat or crawl, the devastating cumulative effect of all those tiny humiliations.

I stumble through the centre of Sidon, past orchards of oranges and banana palms and unkempt verges of grass and wildflowers, stinging gravel roads. There aren't many locals about except for the shopkeepers, stirring themselves from their noonday lethargy when they see me, hoping for a sale. I try not to make eye contact with the Israeli soldiers and their Christian–Lebanese South Lebanon Army auxiliaries. They loiter in groups of two or three, baby-faced, impeccable in their stiff uniforms and polished-mirror guns.

I wave my press card at the guards manning the prison gate: young Israeli boys, good-humoured and in the mood for some talk. I smile tight, walk on down the drive, my sandals slapping against my feet as I hurry away from their stares. Run my hand over my cropped hair, my bare neck. Salt flecks on my fingers.

As soon as I sit across from Sayed at the pockmarked formica table, the headache I've nursed all the way from Beirut settles on my left eye. I'm surprised to see he's clean-shaven, full-mouthed. Young, maybe younger than me, with a sensual crease to his eyes and in the deep lines running from cheeks to chin – not the bearded fundamentalist I was expecting. I like the way he looks and distrust myself for it. Then I force myself to take in the grainy texture of his skin, the heaviness of his eyelids, the open pores on his chin. His square shoulders strain against his prison uniform, yet his shirtsleeves are floppy and too long for his arms, an oversized collar stained by what looks like the remains of a breakfast egg.

I put out my hand and decide to speak English. It might appease my headache, requiring less thought.

'Sayed? *Sa'laam*. Pleased to meet you finally. Is English okay?'

He nods, glancing in small bursts at my cleavage, arms, throat. Each time he drags his eyes away they seem drawn back by some irresistible force against his will. I follow his gaze and he blushes.

'Sorry. Haven't seen a decent woman for a long time.'

I swallow something. My pleasure at his words? I make my voice steely and impersonal.

'Well, let's get started, shall we?' I place my tape recorder in the middle of the table and turn it on. 'Do you mind?'

He shakes his head. I speak quietly but with force into the recorder. 'First interview with Sayed Ali. Khiam Detention Center, Sidon, 25 August 1995.'

Sayed coughs; it could be nerves.

'Can you tell me what you're in here for?'

'Supposedly instrumental in the bombing of the World Trade Center in ninety-three.'

'Right. And what do you say to this claim?'

'I didn't go near the building. I was working that day. Some jihadis say it was one of the CIA's dirty jobs.'

'Let's not get into the conspiracy theories – yet. If you didn't participate, why are you a suspect?'

'I'm Palestinian. I'm educated. I own a computer.'

'That can't be it, surely.'

'Okay – turn off the tape. This is off the record. I once pledged an oath of allegiance to bin Laden.'

I turn it off. Then I decide to play dumb, interested in what Sayed has to say about the shadowy figure.

'Who?'

'A jihadi in the Afghan war, a financier of pan-Islamic movements. I was young, stupid. He paid me a good wage for training at one of his camps, more than I could get anywhere else. I needed to help my mother, and I had no work. I looked up to him, though I never met him in person. He was my *emir*, my leader.'

I speak quietly. 'I've spoken to some of your relatives.'

'All liars. Except for the women.'

I stare at him, forcing myself not to look down. He resumes speaking in a gentler tone. 'Okay – one thing is true. When I was a teenager I was trained in guerrilla warfare here in Lebanon, by Ali Mohamed.'

'What for, if you didn't do it, or didn't have any intention of doing anything like it?'

'I was angry. Disaffected, isn't that what they call it? That's all. No way would I bomb a building. I won't risk my life for anyone or anything.'

'Then why all this evidence?'

'I'm a likely suspect, that's all.'

As he continues talking, he rolls up both sleeves to his elbows and calls out to the guard.

'Hey, it's getting hotter in here. Any chance of a fan?'

The guard shakes his head without any change of expression on his face. I watch Sayed's muscular arms waving about, admiring them in the back of my mind, catch the glint of a silver bracelet on his wrist. Heavy links, elaborately masculine. Multiple crosses. Armenian ones. As he continues to speak I'm not listening any longer. I can feel myself flushing to my temples. Sayed notices my colour.

'You hot too?'

He turns to the guard again.

'Look, man, the lady's about to faint. Can't you do something about it?'

The guard grimaces as if to indicate his helplessness, and Sayed resumes his story.

'My cousin was the suicide bomber who blew up the US embassy in eighty-three. Issa Ali. History matters around here. Just my name is enough to incriminate me. Didn't you do your homework?'

'I'm sorry, I—didn't realise.'

I reach across the table to Sayed's wrist.

'Do you mind if I get a closer look at your bracelet? It's a woman's, isn't it? Antique?'

'Could be. My aunt gave it to me when she knew I was going to prison. It used to be Issa's. There's something written on it in a language I can't understand. Could be Greek, or Russian.'

Sayed unclasps the bracelet and hands it over. I take it in both hands, feel its weight on my palms. I study the large silver links fashioned in the shape of Armenian crosses. Delicate, but strong. I read the Armenian engraving, murmuring now, hoping to appear normal to Sayed, losing my train of thought, the bracelet growing hot in my hands.

'From what your aunt and mother have said this is a simple case of …' I trail off as he begins speaking again. I'm reading and rereading the engraving on the bracelet as if the next time I sound out the vowels in my head it will change to something else. Please God, a miracle. As if the next time it will not read *Pakradounian* anymore. How did Bilqis get it? I remember Lilit saying Selim ran off with Anahit's bracelet as soon as she was born. I squeeze my eyes shut. Sayed is oblivious.

'It's okay. You're not expected to know everything. My cousin was a pretty committed guy. He kidnapped key members of the Christian militias, had them executed. Here's a story for you – Issa ordered one of those Phalange guys to be killed at the exact same moment as he drove his suicide truck through the embassy building. I can't remember the guy's name, but he was high up. Some personal vendetta.'

I turn on the tape recorder. Sayed looks startled. I make an effort to keep my voice steady.

'What was your cousin's name again?'

'Issa Ali.'

I have images of taking Sayed's head and breaking it open on the table. Calm and efficient. Then walking away. I want to say it in Armenian: *That man he had killed was my father.* I lean forward, staring at him. It's then I decide not to say anything, and hand the bracelet back.

�֍ After leaving Sayed I feel the headache squeeze tighter, a rubber band around my eyes. The bus journey back to Beirut passes in a blur. The last moments of my interview with him swirl, recede, then press forward and clamour for attention. He didn't want me to leave so soon. He sat behind that flimsy table, holding the bracelet in both hands, as if he wasn't sure what to do with it. I told him I'd come back, just needed some fresh air, but I knew he didn't believe me even as I said it.

I read the report again now in the bus, unable to progress past the typed name in the heading. Sayed Ali. His cousin Issa. The name of the man who ordered the death of my father. Issa. A name meaning Jesus in Arabic. A Christ-like figure who surrendered everything: love, a child, life itself, for a twisted ideal. Was there any redemption in his death? Or only the resurrection of hatred? I sigh again at the implausibility of the situation. How did I stumble into this? Was it a trap? Did Bilqis lure me into the camp – and for what? Surely Ali is a common enough name, as Bilqis told me, like Brown or Smith in the West. But had Bilqis known who I am, who my father was, all along? And why hadn't she told Sayed?

Once I arrive in Rue Hamra I call Chaim from a phone box, leaning over and dislodging a pebble from my shoe. Again, I can't shake the disconcerting feeling that I'm aping someone else's movements, mundane gestures refined for generations. I think of Lilit in Van, gasping with the reality of her new, cruel world. Think of Sayed Ali, his solemnity and quiet deference. Suddenly I'm afraid, with a deathly chill. Sayed and I are connected, by blood, history, ancestral guilt, and nothing can change that now.

Chaim picks up the phone at work.

'Anoush, are you okay?'

'Yes, I just—I just wanted to hear your voice.'

'You sound upset.'

'No, I'm okay. Come home early tonight, yes?'

I hang up on his voice, take a bus to Municipality Square. I want to be somewhere that feels like home, a place I feel safe. I berate myself – for coming back to Beirut, for caring about the past at all, for knowing too much and too little about the truth of my origins. My God, why did Lilit and Minas decide to stay in this place? Why didn't they go back to Armenia and begin a life free of all these lies? They never felt like Arabs, never fit in. I could be in Yerevan now among fellow Armenians, lulled by familiar songs and food. My father may not have left us then, my mother may not have died. Lilit most certainly would not have been killed by a sniper. I could be anywhere, could just go now, forget about all these deaths, these secrets.

The bus stops. I've reached the end of the line and the heat of the day is mellowing. There's a slight breeze, the sound of water. The plane trees on the square are decked out now in their summer finery, beneath them the fountain with only one spout working: a pert Cupid with big belly and trickling penis. There are many people, not like the last time I was here. People sitting on park benches, strolling, children playing and splashing in the water, little dogs with round eyes. A cherry seller. Strawberries in huge peaks. The late sun westering behind stone buildings, rendering them ripe gold and rose and orange.

I squeeze onto a bench, close my eyes. Next to me, I can hear a man and woman arguing in an undertone. She's telling him he doesn't understand, he's asking why she has to over-analyse everything. I open my eyes and he leads her away.

Now an old man is shuffling toward the bench cradling his walking stick, with a fedora pulled low over his forehead. He sits heavily beside me, breathing a sigh of relief and comfort. I close my eyes again, let the children's shouts and the sounds of fruit sellers and traffic in the distance wash over me.

A
S
H

375

I feel a hand on my arm. Jerk upward.

'Tell me, daughter, are you a Pakradounian or am I much mistaken?'

I turn to look into the face of the old man, close enough to see the lines etched so deep they're white against the tanned face, the insignificant eyes circled by pouches of skin.

'Yes, I am. Who are you?'

'It's Uncle Bedros. Don't you recognise me? You look exactly like your father. I knew you would come back, I knew it.'

I look into the milky eyes again, and press his old man's body to me, kissing him formally on both cheeks. He's twig-thin, with a bent back and huge-knuckled hands.

'It's been so long – I don't know what to say. You look so well, Uncle.'

'I'm ninety-two this year. And my wife – bless her soul – is convinced I'll not make it to my next birthday.'

'Oh, I'm sure you will, Uncle.'

He inches closer to me, takes my hand.

'So what are you doing back here, daughter? Surely you know the state your grandmother Siran is in?'

'I've seen her. Do you go?'

'My wife does. I—well, it upsets me too much to see her like that. I remember her when she was sharp, full of energy. You're not here to stay, are you?'

'No. Well, maybe. I'm here for work – but I suppose my real reason for coming back was to see whether I could find out more about my father. About how he died.'

'You know how he died. He was killed – by the Muslims.'

'Yes, but I know nothing about him. How it happened, how he felt, whether he was to blame—'

'Let me tell you something. He came here in eighty-three, not long after you left for America. I saw him with my own two eyes. He came looking for you.' He chuckles and wipes his face with an open palm. 'How strange that I should see him, out of the blue like that, after so long – and now you, my child! It's a miracle. Like something in a book.'

I turn my head away, ashamed of letting Bedros see the tears that are starting to my eyes.

'It can't be true. He came looking for me? I can't believe it.'

'Yes, daughter. He came looking for you before he was killed. He always cared for you. He loved you. But he was a man scared of his own shadow.'

✳ I don't know what to say to Chaim. If I reveal why I'm so moody lately I'll have to tell him the whole story. I'm not sure I can. The bald facts are so unpalatable. *My father was a Phalangist militiaman.* The movement had ties to the Nazi Party in the thirties. Neo-fascists. The Israelis conveniently forgot this during the civil war and helped the militia in their supposed struggle against Islam. My father thought he was better than the Arabs he lived with all his life. He unthinkingly swallowed the prejudice of his own father's trauma. It started when he was a young boy, this hatred of others. Maybe because he was other, in this foreign place, from birth. Is that why he left us?

I can't imagine what he was really like away from the guns and shells, the carnage he helped create. The wedding photograph doesn't help. In it he looks false, a mannequin grinning murder. He killed thousands of Muslims. Civilians. Children, babies. He thought the

Israeli occupation was the answer to Lebanon's problems. Other Muslim factions resented this, especially the Shias. Issa Ali was a Shia. My father died due to his own arrogance. And yet—and yet he'd done all that, then came looking for me in the Armenian quarter, to tell me, what? That he loved me? That he was sorry? Uncle Bedros said he'd come in the rain, a pot of pink flowers under his coat. That he asked about me and cried. I can't deny the pain this erases, the feeling of warmth and lightness it gives me.

Chaim asks me why I'm so quiet lately, so preoccupied.

'Too much work,' I say. 'I've finished four articles and now they want another by the end of the week.'

He shakes his head, miming disbelief. 'You can't fool me, but I'll let it go this time.' He chucks me under the chin and goes off to work for days and weeks. I can't tell him.

I go to see Bilqis in the camp but remain silent about what Sayed has revealed. I wait for Bilqis to talk first, look at her now with suspicion, even hostility. I accept tea, choke on more of the dry biscuits. I meet Inam at the school gate, even though she's old enough to walk home by herself. But Bilqis says she's afraid of Inam getting involved with the stone-throwers and militants, so Inam is accompanied to and from school. Now Bilqis is often too tired to walk. It seems that she becomes breathless now, even when walking only as far as the shop. Weeks pass. Still I don't tell her of the reason for my withdrawal, an interior reserve I know she's too wise not to notice. I leave as soon as I can, while Inam begs me to stay.

I call Sayed Ali and apologise for not coming back. He's cautiously respectful, and strangely sheepish. I tell him I'm working on the article about him. Assure him I believe in his innocence. I'm not sure if I'm lying. I'm still not sure why I'm so obsessed now with helping him, why I need to convince myself day by day, word by word, of his purity. The link with my father? Some way of finding out more about the way he lived his life? Or severing the bond in this small way between Sayed and his cousin? If Sayed Ali is innocent then maybe I can begin to forgive Issa Ali for the poison he inflicted, on my father and grandmothers and myself, the uncertainty that's eating away my life.

Sayed comments on my reticence, asks if there's anything wrong. I deny it, deny everything. When I hang up I'm conscious of feeling empty, wrong, as if I should have said more, gone further. I'm tempted to call again but instead stay by the phone, looking out at the view of the sea from Chaim's windows.

Chaim is still away. I'm left alone to my looping thoughts. I dream of Issa Ali, the faceless assassin. He comes to me at night and puts his curved knife to my throat. A scimitar, Ottoman, gleaming as a half-moon. His face changes to Sayed's, the pained expression twisting into a smirk. *Don't tell anyone what you know*, he says in Arabic. *I forbid you.* Then Issa comes back, floating, silent as the clouds around him. I hold my hands out in the dark, want above all to forgive. Only by forgiving him can I rid myself of his presence. *How can I know why you did it?*

I let myself mourn my father's absence. Did he love me? Did he love me after all? I remember peering at my parents' photograph on tiptoe when either one of the grandmothers wasn't looking. Holding it to my chest as if the manufactured warmth from my father's black and white gaze would permeate in this way through my skin. I caressed his poreless cheek, ran my finger across the inky length of his eyebrow. *Oh, Daddy.* He smirked back as if he knew he would go away someday soon. My mother remained a cipher, pale forehead wrinkled in doubt under a filmy veil.

I know Selim was second-in-command to the militia led by Elie Hobeika, responsible for the massacres of the camps. The war crimes tribunal confirmed that. I know, I know, I know. But it makes no difference. On one level, a deeper, darker level, I know nothing at all. I know the details of the atrocities, the rapes, the subsequent denials. The window-dressing enquiry run by the Israelis, the Kahan report. No condemnation of anyone at all, except perhaps the victims. When I found out in first-year college, it didn't stop me from continuing to love the ideal father, so young and handsome; it only made me hate myself. *How can I love someone so evil? How can I absolve him of guilt?* I shuffled through college corridors with my head down, fought not to vomit when confronted with a lunch plate of cold cuts. It reminded me too much of the dead bodies I mutilated in my nightmares.

Who is victim and who perpetrator? Now I hold two men in my arms, side by side in bed, stuck inside the body bags of Chaim's sweaty sheets. I hug them to me, twin spectators of my suffering. I cry out in sleep and hush myself like a mother comforting a child. *Hush, hush, it'll be all right. There's hope. We can all remember. Or choose to forget.* I torment myself with outdated notions of right and wrong. I don't know how to condemn my father for who he was, nor do I know how to forgive his murderer from taking him away, stealing him from me before I had a chance to confront him with my own flawed existence. And what of Issa Ali's family?

I field countless calls from the UNDP. 'The woman is asking after you. She wants to see you again. The girl misses you. Apparently she likes you, which doesn't happen often with anyone at all. Don't know what you did to charm them so.'

※ One morning the phone doesn't stop ringing even when I turn over in Chaim's bed and resolve to ignore it all day. It stops, begins again. I put the creased pillow over my ears. Finally, I crawl out of bed and pick up the receiver.

'Yes?'

'Ms Pakradounian? UNDP.'

I wait, sighing audibly.

'Ms Pakradounian, there's a parcel here addressed to you. Seems to be from a detainee at the Khiam Detention Center. Should we send it on?'

'No. I'll come and get it.'

※ In the tampered envelope, I find my mother's bracelet. There's one line, on paper torn from a child's exercise book, printed carefully in English.

> *I spoke to my aunt and know whose bracelet it is. None of it is*
> *your fault or mine. Sayed.*

※ I sit on the floor in Chaim's living room. Julius gnaws on a bone in the kitchen, now and then giving tiny grunts of satisfaction. My laptop beckons, but I have nothing to give today. My legs are folded beneath me, palms flat on the keyboard, an absent meditation. I look out at the sea. It's evening already, the light from the sky that blinded me all day has dimmed and all that remains is a pearl lustre at the edges of my eyes.

I make yet another beginning on the Sayed story, mull over the opening sentence for a moment. Pause, my hand hovering, then press the delete button. I'm making no progress, haven't been for days. There's a singular impossibility in writing even the first line, the first paragraph introducing the issue. Too many dimensions, and I know I'm not wise enough or experienced enough nor convinced enough to unravel them. The political. The personal. The blurred space of misunderstanding in between. A tangled heap of coloured threads.

Sayed's note has alternately comforted and unsettled me. As yet I haven't replied. Deep down part of me feels he's wrong. Of course it's our fault as well. The sins of the fathers. The responsibility to create good out of such evil. Has he tried? No. Have I? I wonder if my father ever really did love my mother. They were first cousins, after all. Tied by blood if not by desire. It was the other woman, that Muslim woman, who meant most to him. The contradictory woman of his other life, that flickering momentary life he conducted apart from his family. It's hard to swallow, hard not to resent him for such a blunt betrayal.

I get up, water Chaim's gardenias laboriously with a drinking glass I fill and refill many times. The petals are yellowing, tissue-paper dry. I snap the spent blooms from their stalks and drop them into the street far below. There's an evening breeze coming off the sea, a rarity. I stay at the balcony rail, let the wind clean away my frustration, the smell of exhaust and construction dust, the fine silt that settles on my eyelids from the ash that comes from garbage burning in the camps. In my silent, meditative state, this ash seems so potent. I don't want to wipe it off. I lick my finger, taste its bitterness. It's the bodies of my people, and Chaim's: in Der ez Zor, Sabra-Shatila, far-away Auschwitz. Death isn't personal. Violence moves through us, and is gone again.

I go inside, watch street lights turn on, one by one, over the whole curving promenade. Tiny starbursts of light. I play the recording of the interview again: play, pause, rewind. Play again. I've played the last three seconds of the tape so often I've memorised the timbre of Sayed's voice, the resigned, out-breath in the way he said his cousin's name. Issa Ali. His voice comes to me when I lie in bed, when I'm under the shower, when I move a morsel to my mouth. Issa Ali. A line of song. A refrain. My reply to Sayed cut off, a swinging pendulum in the darkness of no sound.

BEIRUT, 1983

Issa knelt during Friday prayers along with everyone else. It was satisfying, this abasement of the body, the tender skin of his forehead knocking against cold stone floor. The assembled men lamented the martyr Imam Ali, cradling their ears and wailing to the heavens, holding each other upright when the sadness and sense of injustice of his death was too much to be borne. Issa floated in a world all his own, buoyed by the collective suffering, grown majestic in its bodily expression all around him. *Allah is great.* He murmured along with the rising tide of voices, drew his faded-blue robe more tightly around him. It had grown chilly, just after sunset, here in the domed, cavernous mosque.

They sat cross-legged on their threadbare mats when prayers were over. The imam climbed like a great crab to his high seat. He was so slow Issa closed his eyes until the old man had finally shifted his weight and sat down. He commenced a long-winded, vague address to the congregation that caused most men around Issa to shuffle and yawn, examine the state of toenails and fingers, adjust caps and pull at their beards. Only Issa was attentive, gazing up at the imam's brownish, wrinkled face. Only he could decipher what the imam was really saying.

The imam was speaking in code. Each time he quoted *suras* from the holy book – *the fruits of Heaven, the sin of the unbelievers,* or *the date groves of the Prophet* – Issa received further confirmation of his new mission for Islamic Jihad. This was the way the Iranian leaders of Hezbollah communicated to their warriors in Lebanon. It was the only way that had been proven completely safe and foolproof.

He knew the selection of these phrases could mean nothing to the imam himself. He might or might not be judged committed enough, or clever enough, to be privy to the plan. The sermon had been written for him by his leaders in Iran and transmitted to every Shia mosque in west Beirut.

Issa listened carefully and decoded the key phrases. He now knew the date, the time, the three major steps of the operation assigned to him. He'd already prepared himself for the forty-eight hours he would spend entirely alone in a windowless room before his duty must be fulfilled. Solitary confinement, to ensure there was no turning back. He pictured himself sitting at a scratched desk, inscribed with the initials of so many others, writing brief letters to his loved ones. He sighed then, bowing his head to the ground. His duty had never been clearer than today.

✳   Sanaya walked brisk and free through numb blue streets. Yes, there were still checkpoints belonging to militia upon militia, but they let her pass without demanding papers. Some gunmen even smiled. She smiled back, unthinking. Everyone was as dulled as the weather, testing the new lightness of their city. The Israelis had agreed to withdraw their troops from the whole of Lebanon. Even the Christians were happy about this. An end to things, come with the cold of the previous winter still in the air. Now even a beginning, she let herself hope, in the first warmth of spring breaking frost on the pavement. She hummed to herself, still smiling. A smile was no longer an arbitrary decision between life and death.

She picked her way through the garbage on the Corniche, where newly planted palms bent in strong winds from the north. She was on her way home, hugging her eggshell belly close under her coat, thinking, *I won't tell Issa until I'm really sure*, as she stopped at a newsstand and bought the paper. She was going home to Issa, to kiss his nape as he leaned over the stove making tea, to watch him hand it to her, sweet and scalding, as she sat with her feet curled up under her on the divan. He would bring a basin of warm water and a handful of sea salt, he would kneel in front of her – head bent so low she would see the little-boy down on the back of his neck, the breakable bone at the base of his skull, further evidence of his amazing vulnerability – and he would grasp each foot in turn and knead it, snapping apart her stubborn toes. He would immerse her foot in water and bring it out into air again, a secular ablution he repeated five times.

She bought the paper, stood at the newsstand jiggling up and down against the cold, waiting for her change. She skimmed the headlines.

ISRAELI GOVERNMENT TO WITHDRAW FROM LEBANON
ON CONDITION SYRIANS WITHDRAW SIMULTANEOUSLY.

She turned to the next page, hands deadened by the wind.

SYRIAN TROOPS REFUSE TO LEAVE LEBANON.

She hurried up the stairs to the top floor, making tiny grumbling noises against the cold, unbuttoning her coat before she reached the landing, ready to fling it over the hooks near the door. The fur collar itched; she sweated. When she turned the key in the lock, calling out to Issa, he was not there. She could feel the chill of aloneness in the room. As if he had never been.

�֍ Issa parked the Renault in front of the gym, two other militiamen in the back. They could see Selim through the plate glass, his puffing and pounding of weights, his tight buttocks in absurdly small shorts. They sniggered among themselves, quietly.

Issa had been apart from Sanaya since early February. A little less than two months. He wanted to see how long it would take for Selim to come sniffing around the place. He wanted to see how long it would take for Sanaya to have the Armenian back and to forget that she once loved Issa. It was a test he needed to set her.

✖ Selim left the building, showered and dressed now, heading to his car. He began to cross the road, planning his afternoon appointments in his head. He was ashamed about this morning. He had tried to call Sanaya and she had refused to speak to him. She hung up, albeit gently. Their relationship hadn't resumed but he was willing to wait. In truth, he was a little afraid of what could transpire between them now. He'd seen her eating at the new Italian place on the seafront. She told him to go away. She was heavier around the hips and thighs, and this comforted him somehow; she was earthbound now, enmeshed in his protection again. *I'll keep asking her if she needs my help; I'll keep asking until she says yes.* He stopped at the kerb and noticed a car, adjusted his collar in the smoky glass of the side window, something black in fast motion on the periphery of his vision. His leg stretched out to step off into the slowing traffic when two hooded men grabbed him. Slits for eyes. Once in the car, he was hidden from view by a curtain pulled over the rear window, his torso bent crooked across their laps. Face in someone's groin, soap-smelling. The car started and he was flung back and forth as it skidded over gravel, righted itself, increased in speed.

A man chuckled. There was no mirth in the sound.

'Did you really think she'd go back to you?'

He tried to raise his head toward the voice. He was held down firmly, but without brutality, so his voice came out muffled and unassuming. 'What? Let me out of here!'

'I've been watching her. I suspect she's carrying my child.'

'Who the hell are you? I know your voice.'

Issa ripped away his hood with one hand and turned around for a fraction of a second.

'It can't be yours,' he said. 'I've done the calculations.'

Selim caught the blue glint of his eyes and thought, *I'm a dead man.*

✳ The kidnappings usually happened at noon. Sanaya knew; it had happened to her partying friend Amani. She was making lunch for her husband and herself, looking out the kitchen window and thinking it was such a beautiful spring day, perfect for meeting her new lover in the park. But her husband was working from home that afternoon, correcting essays and sniffling every minute with a head cold. She was trapped, frustrated; she thought she would go mad if she heard him blow his nose one more time.

'We had white wine from my uncle's vineyard,' she told Sanaya. 'I was getting it out of the fridge, pouring a glass for myself as I cooked. There was a knock on the door, very quiet, very gentle. We almost didn't hear it. My husband went to answer; I could hear him speaking in a low voice, normal tones, blowing his nose. I hurried out into the entry hall, arranging my hair. I even remember stopping at the mirror near the door, checking my lipstick hadn't smudged. I wanted to ask the kidnappers to lunch. I didn't know who they were, maybe colleagues from university or my husband's students.'

Then they each put a pistol to her husband's head.

Sanaya never thought it would happen to anybody close to her. She was Muslim; surely that gave her friends some protection. She lived in west Beirut. Then again, so did all the journalists and university professors who were kidnapped every day on their way home from work. Most of all, she didn't think it would ever happen to Selim. Not with his assortment of rifles and pistols, his armoured escorts, his swagger and his flash. Not with his powerful superiors, warlords of such talent they made money in everything from trading stolen antiquities to raw opium and hashish grown in the Beka'a Valley.

As Issa did not come home, so Selim vanished. Soon posters of Selim's smirking face appeared on street corners under direction of the Phalange. Sanaya waited a day, two days, a week. Maybe Issa was out fighting. Maybe he was on a secret mission to the south and had to leave without telling her. She looked for a note or a sign on every surface in the apartment, under every ashtray, in every book.

It could only be him. She listened to the radio for any reports, crowded into the ground-floor apartment of the Sunnis downstairs and watched their television at night. Nothing. She questioned Rouba, railed at Bilqis for bringing up such a son. Issa, the dainty kidnapper. All three women ransacked his old bedroom in Rouba's apartment. When he'd moved upstairs with Sanaya he hadn't bothered to bring anything with him except his clothes and his Koran.

They found crumpled tissues under the bed, a dirty white towel, Islamic Jihad instruction manuals and cassette tapes. Detailed steps on how to conduct kidnappings, assassinations, suicide bombings. She played them all in vain for any hint of Issa's voice. She took the towel upstairs with her, ringed by semen stains in concentric circles, like the timelines in the trunk of a tree.

Shattered hearts, lives. She felt she had betrayed Selim to Issa and his torturers. At the same time, illogically, she felt betrayed by Selim. But strangely not by Issa. She kept the towel nearby, made sure the rest was burnt. She hugged her belly at night, lay on her side praying to Allah, then turning to the other side, pleading with the prophet Jesus that both men would miraculously reappear. That she should not be the instrument of their suffering.

She went to the Phalange headquarters, taking care to remove the thin gold chain and hand of Fatima from around her neck. She didn't let herself think what these Christian militiamen would do to Issa if they found him with one of their men. Her first duty was to the man she told to leave her. Her second duty was to the father of her unborn child. In repeated formulae of skewed logic, she justified it to herself. *Because I don't really want Selim, I have to find him. It's all my fault this happened. If it wasn't for me, they would never have met.*

She set herself the task before she could find absolution. *I must do the right thing. Then Issa and I can be truly happy.* What was the right thing? *I have to go against what I really want in order to find it.* Selim's disappearance was punishment. Punishment for her denial of his love, for her betrayal. For her desire for Issa. She must sacrifice herself for pleasure, bleed for peace. She didn't deserve Issa without atoning, debasing herself, trying everything to get Selim back.

She pleaded with the Phalange gunmen to find their man, their illustrious member. *He had medals, you know. He commanded a whole unit.* She tried not to think of the massacres in the camps as she sat there across from these soldiers, handbag clutched to her slippery belly, watching the tired, paunchy, middle-aged men smoke, half-finish the cigarette, fling it down, absent-mindedly pick up the telephone, offer her a glass of tea. She accepted, forced down the sugary liquid. Sat and sweated.

She pleaded again and, after an hour of small talk and pleasantries, became pushy. But Selim was unimportant. The men behind their desks were forced to tell her the truth. Selim Pakradounian was not worth the trouble of upsetting Islamic Jihad. *We do not negotiate with terrorists,* was the mantra. The excuse. For anybody. He had outgrown his specific uses. All they could do was print more posters, more glossy leaflets – she could even hand them out if she wished.

'There must have been people there who saw,' she said. 'They must have seen where he was taken but they just ignored it.'

The men shook their heads at her as if in sympathy, then resumed shuffling paper at their desks.

At home she sat on the divan in a haze of disbelief. She forgot to put the hand of Fatima back around her neck. It lay coiled in her handbag. Of course, she didn't tell the other two women where she'd been. Rouba sat cross-legged on the carpet, silent for once. Bilqis made tea, crying so much her tears fell into the scalding liquid. Salt tea. Tea nobody touched.

'Where is my Issa?' she asked the walls, the windows, the sinister, gleaming sky. 'How can he be so cruel to us?'

Sanaya surrendered to a fit of sobs, intensified by her inability to decide who she was crying for.

✳ Selim couldn't stand the beatings any longer. As soon as he thought they were done for the day, another team of men came in and resumed. They strapped him to the table in the corner, stretched him out on his back and tied his ankles to a pole with rope. This was the worst time, when he was unsure what would happen next. Then they attacked the soles of his feet with whips, belts, clubs. One day they must have used a chain. He knew this from the way his feet swelled up when they had left, with a greater speed and intensity than he'd ever witnessed before.

He couldn't stand waiting for the next administering of *falaka*, the interminable uncertainty, the warped, elongated time frame of the beatings themselves. The only constant was Issa's winking, elfin face in front of him, coming up close, receding, until Selim was never quite sure he hadn't been imagining the whole thing. Some days he saw Anahit's bracelet on Issa's wrist and wanted to leap up and rip it off. Tear it from him, bite through it like an animal. Yet he had no strength. When Issa was in the room he couldn't even speak. His throat closed in fear and he writhed in the silence of his impotence. In a strange way, this appropriation of his past seemed more violating than anything else.

They were not trying to find out any information from him; of that he was sure. There was no attempt at questioning, at any form of interrogation. Only the daily brutality of the beatings, conducted in silence. He learnt to be thankful they only beat the soles of his feet. So far they hadn't touched the rest of his body.

When they left him he lay slumped in a corner for the rest of the day. Sometimes he heard the rustling of rats but never saw them. At night he fancied he could feel them pawing at his face, waiting for him to fall asleep so they could nibble through his eyes and nose. He jerked upward then, making his chains jangle, and the guard on duty rushed in and slapped him like a mother admonishing a wayward child. *Shush, go to sleep now*, in harsh Arabic.

Some mornings he could hear the angry bleating of goats and knew there would be fresh milk for him to drink at breakfast. It always came to him warm as blood, with globules of yellow fat floating on the surface. He slurped it down greedily, looked up at the standing guard ashamed of his baseness, at the crust of milk stiffening the sides of his mouth. Sometimes they forgot to chain him from the night before so he could try to crawl around his room, examining every single floorboard, every speck of dirt and every mote of dust for some clues as to where he was. He comforted himself with elaborate frameworks of justice. *If they haven't chained me up today, it must mean they're going to let me go.*

He never thought of escape or if there might be any prisoners kept in other parts of the farm. He never thought of Sanaya. Only rarely of his daughter, the faceless stranger who visited him at night through the darkness. The fact of imprisonment had become his whole world, the sum total of his waking and dreaming life.

Today his feet throbbed more than usual. He looked down at them: black, speckled, swollen to almost three times their size. His tendons had burst. He shuddered, unable to repress a hint of revulsion at this self of his, reduced to spectacle. He put his hands in front of his face, close enough to see dirt caked in the fine wrinkles on his palm, in the dry cracks between his fingers. His nails were nicotine-yellow and far too long. He couldn't see his face but could feel the growth on his cheeks and chin, soft, almost downy, matted with olive oil. They never washed him, but one young boy routinely oiled his new beard and head and face. There was a pimpled rash on his forehead from the lack of hygiene; he could feel its knobbly ridge under his fingertips. He'd been here weeks, even as long as a month. There was no way to calculate time, to know whether it was night or day.

He looked around. Sheets of hammered metal on what used to be windows, high up near the beamed ceiling. He could be in a disused barn. There was a faint trace of ammonia in the musty, dust-laden air, the rich, hot smell of living beasts. He heard a scuffle at the door. Somebody unbarred it and advanced toward him, bearing a bowl with the promise of something savoury emanating from its surface.

He tried not to look up this time. Yesterday a new guard had objected to his swollen gaze and threatened to kick him with those steel-capped boots. He concentrated instead on the floorboard directly in front of him. A cockroach was making its slow way to his foot. He didn't dare flick it aside, didn't dare move. He tried to send it telepathic commands. *Turn the other way! Leave me alone.* He felt the guard set the bowl down beside him, then kneel down to Selim's level himself.

'Eat. Good.'

His accent sounded Moroccan, even Algerian. Candid features, even with the scarf pulled over his forehead and around his chin. His Arabic careless and slurred. Selim took up the bowl and shovelled fava beans in with his fingers, burning the roof of his mouth. *If he's nice to me it must mean I'm going to be released.* He felt better then, ate with more appetite. The beans were earthy and soft, finely spiced. He closed his eyes, resting them. Then he put the bowl down as another thought took hold of him and paralysed his ability to move, eat, swallow. *If he's this nice to me it must mean he feels sorry for me. Because I'm not going to be released, never going to be released.*

The guard watched Selim intently, furrowing his brow.

'Good? You wan' something else?'

Selim croaked. It had been a while since he had to speak and his voice was almost gone from all the screaming during the beatings.

'Some water, please.'

The guard returned presently with a beaker of water. Selim drank it in small sips.

'You wan' anything else?'

He thought for a moment and shook his head. There was nothing he could think of, nothing he wanted anymore.

Book Three

SKY

BEIRUT, 1995

This time on my way back to the camp I carry calla lilies in a blue-glazed pot, bags of fruit. Hair-ties and a brush and thick chapter book for Inam, with stories of latter-day Scheherazades and wicked kings.

'I haven't finished the story yet for *The Globe*,' I tell Bilqis over tea. 'I should be done by the end of the week.'

'*Insh'allah*, it will help.'

Inam sits in a corner of the hut and reads her book. I remember those endless childhood days, when half an hour of reading felt like delicious forever. It could never end, as the next moment didn't really exist. Time was elongated, elastic. A game outside in the park with friends was an entire lifetime of achievement. When I was happy as a child, it was as if this sensation could never finish. When I was sad, my life became indecipherable and overwhelmed the promise of any future. When I was reminded of the loss of my father, this sadness became bound up in who I thought I was. Real joy eluded me, every day.

'Here, sweetheart. Let's see if I can remember any written Arabic.'

Inam comes and stands by me, leaning against the chair. I smile, gesture her closer.

'Sit on my lap. Unless you think you're too old for things like that.'

With a glance at her grandmother, Inam climbs into my lap, settles in comfortably. She's small for her age, and wiry, and I can easily bear her weight. Nervous as well as excited, she chews at her bottom lip.

'Let's see. Which story shall we start with?'

Inam giggles at my pronunciation, helping with harder words. As the story progresses she forgets herself entirely and presses her rose-petal cheek against my face. We could be sisters. I feel a sense of lightness, grace, as if she and I, here together, are all that matters.

There's a knock, forceful, insistent. Inam springs forward to open the door.

'Wait,' Bilqis says. 'It could be anyone.'

Inam stands aside, suddenly showing fear.

'Soldiers?'

Her grandmother doesn't answer, shouting through the closed door. 'Who is it?'

'Only me,' a girlish voice lisps. 'Rowda.'

A young woman pushes the door open, takes Bilqis's right hand and raises it first to her lips then to her forehead in a gesture of respect. Why didn't I think to do that? Inam immediately runs to her, jubilant, and I'm unexpectedly jealous. The young woman takes time over her greetings, as if purposely ignoring me. She takes Inam into her arms and swings her around. Inam's thick wedge of hair spills out of its binding and falls over her shoulders. Bilqis chuckles and makes ineffectual swipes at furniture getting in the way of their antics.

The play stops all at once when the young woman has had enough. Inam looks rebuffed, puffing out her reddened cheeks. The woman rests her hands on her narrow hips and surveys the ceiling.

'Phew! That's my workout for the day.'

She collapses onto Bilqis's bed, gives every impression of having only just spied me.

'Hi, I'm Rowda. You must be Anoush? Inam talks about you all the time.'

'She does? All good things, I hope.'

'Of course, but—'

Rowda seems to be withholding information she would dearly love to divulge. She fiddles with the buckle on her belt – black as her hair, with thick silver studs. I bark out a forced laugh, lightening the pause.

'Well,' Rowda begins. You're the one going with an Israeli, aren't you? Asking questions? People around here talk.'

'So? I don't understand.'

I look around the room. Bilqis seems very busy making tea, her back turned away from the conversation.

'Oh, nothing. I just don't think a Jew – or an American, for that matter – could have anything much of value to offer us here.'

I face her square on. 'Excuse me? The Jew I know is out there right now, disarming your country's landmines, saving your citizens from being blown up. I don't see you doing anything like that.'

I take a scalding gulp of my tea, and leave as soon as it's polite to do so. Inam hugs me briefly at the door, but soon joins Rowda on the floor, playing cards. Rowda stares after me for a moment, then resumes playing the game.

※ I cube lamb off the bone for a stir-fry and Julius whimpers, pawing at my feet. I throw him a morsel of fat.

'Patience, Julius! I'm keeping the bone for you.'

I swear under my breath at these Beirut butchers, selling whole legs of animal, no shrink-wrapped pre-cut packets. Struggle with the unwieldy shape. String of tendon, white muscle, resistant flesh. Cubes of red meat. Cut. Move finger. Chop. Move finger. Cube. Knife flash. Bone. Cut finger. I shake my hand out the window, trying not to drip blood onto the chopping board.

As I jiggle my finger in the air my thoughts turn to Rowda again: at the lisping, confident way she'd passed judgement on a stranger. Her long, crossed legs, the arched foot swinging back and forth. The dark lipstick she reapplied, turning her back on the three of us with studied ostentation. The mannish, forceful gestures that belied her statements about modesty, sensitivity to culture, fitting in with the local population. 'First step to making a difference,' she said. 'Not standing out.' Is she making a difference? And what about me?

I'm happy with my article on Sayed. It's finished, and *The Globe* has also allowed me to offer it to the local *Daily Star*. I wrap my finger in a napkin; blood soaks through in an instant. I throw it away, take another. Do I believe what I've written? Is Sayed really innocent? As innocent as Issa Ali was? What a lame joke. I actually say it aloud, hear my voice duplicate itself in the silent room.

I walk to the oval mirror over the fireplace, wishing Lilit were here to make some sense of it all. Siran was worse the last time I went to visit. The nurses implied it wouldn't be long now; she was deteriorating by the day. I despise myself for thinking that if she dies I can at last bring

S
K
Y

395

myself to wear the earrings, feel their burnished weight against my neck. Am I as selfish as my father was?

I continue to look in the mirror, keeping my expression neutral, trying not to put any feminine mask over my bland reflection. Boyish. In certain moods, definitely my father's face. He personally murdered dozens, even hundreds, of civilians. Yet I can forgive him for that. After all, he was my father; we share blood, history, too many personality traits. Lilit would tell me so when I was naughty as a child, weary and disapproving. *But which traits, Grandma?* Lilit wouldn't say. *You'll find out when you get older. You'll just know.*

I unwrap the napkin from my finger. Is it ruthlessness? The ability to inflict pain? I could easily get up and leave Chaim today; I know I have it in me. I could walk down the Corniche with my backpack, even wave at him in a friendly, off-hand gesture. He'd stand, gazing after me, on the balcony. His grief wouldn't hold me back. I could, if I had to. I'd leave him without regrets. As I've left my friends in Boston, those admiring boys, as my father once left my mother – and me. I could switch focus, try another life. Get Sayed out of prison, get to know him. Now wouldn't that be resolution of the best kind? Cousin of the killer, daughter of the killed, coupling under a Beirut night sky. At least I'm his equal, whereas with Chaim I often feel naive, diminished. Yet at the same time he gives me hope of change. That with him I can rise above myself, and my background.

Bright blood wells from my jagged cut, runnels of red in the creases of my fingerprint, the faint, fluting throb of my pulse. Dislodged flap of skin exposing white cells beneath. Cruelty in the same whirling DNA. My father was cruel; I've come to accept that. But he thought he was doing the right thing. Yet what of Issa Ali? Much as I wish to forgive him, this longed-for absolution eludes me, night after sleepless night.

And what of Chaim and Sayed? I can feel, even in all his cautious politeness, that Chaim distrusts the Palestinian. But there's nothing to be afraid of. Or is there? In the cold light of reality, I tell myself I feel nothing more for Sayed than the camaraderie of youth. Some admiration. Pity. A healthy dose of outrage at his plight. Why should Chaim feel threatened by that? But there's something more, something dark and shameful. I think about Sayed too much. I can't stop thinking about him.

As the light fades, Chaim comes home. I'm sitting at the table, sucking at my bleeding finger, quickly put it behind my back when I see him.

⌘ Chaim's gone south for another fortnight. Dinner together was hard last night; he asked again and again why I'm so preoccupied lately.

'Is it me? Have I done anything wrong?'

'No,' I said. 'It's not you. It's everything.'

He threw up his hands then in exasperation and went to bed.

I stayed behind at the kitchen table, studying the rhythmic way grilled lamb juices dripped onto pita bread and stained it the colour of old blood. Something in its slow deliberation reminded me of my father, although I never knew him to be deliberate in his actions or otherwise. But something in me suspects he was methodical at the very least. Armenians were famed for their attention to detail, their love of the precise. Jewellery, illuminated manuscripts, architecture, the thousands of upright stone grave steles called *khatchkars*, carved into minuscule patterns with a passion that could be maddening. Of course Selim was finicky. How else could he have risen up the ranks of the Phalange?

I went out onto the balcony after what seemed like an inordinate length of time, watched the Corniche slowing down after another hot day and night. Only a few tourists remained, probably young oil heirs from the Gulf, stumbling out of bars. Most lights had extinguished in shops and restaurants. The beggars had long since huddled under their cardboard shelters on the beach. I stood for a while, letting my arms hang limp and my neck relax. When I crawled into bed sometime in the early hours of the morning, Chaim was cold and unresponsive. At first.

Now I wake with him gone, yet with the memory of his arms around me all night, my back raw from his stubbled cheek pressed into the hollow between my shoulderblades. Meanwhile I dreamed of Sayed: his muscular, dark-flecked arms, his rough face on my skin. There's something slightly distasteful about my attraction to him. How can I condone his acceptance of hatred, his hardness, his connection with Issa Ali? Or is that an intrinsic part of the attraction? It feels such a betrayal to take pleasure in thoughts of his body, the promise of his flesh – a betrayal not so much of Chaim, I'm ashamed to admit, but of my father.

I get up with a growing aversion to myself and the day, jerk open the curtains. The new sun warms my skin and I dress after my shower in its slanted glow. Now I feel almost restored, part of the empty morning hush of these five rectangular rooms. Stripes of light echo the designs of the tiles at my feet: triangles and starbursts and diamonds in faded shades of ruby and sapphire and clotted cream. I've grown fond of Beirut again, and I love this apartment more than any place I've lived in, more than my childhood home. I belong here. In my saner, quieter moments, I can accept that I belong with Chaim too, that we can build a good life together. Then I think of Sayed, or of going back to Boston – and don't know what's good for me anymore. As for Sarkis's apartment – well, I haven't lived there long enough to know. I might want to sell it when I go back, find something with no traces of the past.

Chaim's home is a haven of calm amid the traffic noises below, motorists honking and swearing, hawkers whining, the sea booming on the Pigeon Rocks. I love the cubbyhole kitchen, the bedroom with its tiny Juliet balcony and narrow French doors, the huge balcony that comes off the living room. I love the worn Turkish kilims Chaim has thrown on the floor. I love his low futon with its vanilla-hued sheets, his large white wicker baskets for clothes and shoes and books, peeling posters on all the walls proclaiming their memories of old marches and protests: world hunger, minority rights, the end of war.

I feed Julius, who seems less hungry than usual, then take him for his daily walk through the noisy streets. Chaim is mad to keep a dog in Beirut. Julius strains, wanting to run. Surely a mastiff wasn't bred for this dust, this chaos, this blazing sun? I take him off the leash and let him run in and out of waves on the shore.

When we arrive home I pull an old leather rucksack out of Chaim's cupboard – legacy of his college days – and pile a jumble of supplies into it: wool sweater, water bottle, a packet of raisins, feel for my wallet in my jeans.

'No, Julius, I can't take you with me,' and I stoop to pat his massive head.

I'm apprehensive about leaving him behind, if only for the day, when Chaim has explicitly entrusted him to my care. I tell the women downstairs I need to go out; they nod in their practical fashion and promise to feed him if I don't come home before nightfall.

There's nobody to leave a note for. I'm going to the Beka'a Valley. There's no choice to make anymore. I'm going to see the place where my father died.

✳ When I arrive I find it difficult to suppress the rising gorge in my throat. Maybe it's merely hunger, or the swaying motion of the service taxi for the past hour. I shared it with a malodorous old man, whiffs of decay from empty gums, who used every opportunity of the vehicle's lurch to lay his hand on my knee. His veiled wife and daughters didn't seem to notice or care.

I squat on the side of the road, eat a handful of raisins. Their mustiness only makes me feel worse and I spit the half-chewed remnants into the dust. I take to wandering aimlessly up and down the dry, deserted streets. No idea where to look. All I know, from Sarkis, is that my father was taken to a disused barn in the Beka'a and killed. I'm certain the barn is – or was; it could be burned down now, for all I know – somewhere close to this transit town, a few miles out of Ba'albek. There's nobody to ask for directions. They all seem to have been swallowed up by the dust-filled, echoing street. The gap-toothed old man and his brood disappeared into a walled house long ago without a backward glance.

I have vague notions of finding the barn, examining it for some trace of my father's time there. A marking on the floor, some faint initials carved into the wooden beams. A message to me that would vindicate him. Sometime around noon I sit under the shade of an olive tree and drink my whole bottle of water, knowing I'll regret it. I make my way into a field and squat, hoping no one will see me. When I'm finished I walk across the field to where I can see a small hut made of timber, partly obscured by mulberry trees. Even if there's nobody home, at least walking through grass is preferable to walking in the dust. And the mulberries might be bearing fruit at this time of year – I'm getting really hungry now.

As I walk, a man emerges from the side of the hut. He's zipping his trousers. I come closer and see him go inside, come out again with a plate and a paring knife. I stop under the trees, peering at him through bright sunlight. He's tall, maybe fifty, with a creased forehead and leathery brown cheeks. A farm worker spending the hottest part of the day in the shade. His movements seem restricted; he lumbers back and forth on the threshold of the hut like a dog patrolling a patch of territory. His eyes are blank, unfocused, and he seems excited, as a child would be, to have me here. He must be mentally challenged, what I would have called in my childhood *slow*.

He comes toward me and stretches out his hand – I recoil, thinking he's going to strike me – but all he's offering is a tiny morsel of rolled-up pita bread. He advances. The black nails are close to my mouth now. I shake my head but there's no way I can refuse his food without offending him. I open my mouth and chew, realising that inside the bread is kibbeh, raw mince pounded with lemon juice and parsley and cracked wheat. I force myself to swallow it down, tears springing to my eyes with the effort, and sit down gratefully on the plastic stool the man has provided. I know I'll soon have to vomit, know it and at the same time try to convince myself otherwise. I look around for some distraction, up at the mulberries glinting like dark eyes among the leaves. The man follows my gaze and picks some. I watch his awkward, bear-like movements as if he's far away, in another frame, another time.

Was my father buried here, somewhere under these thick-leaved trees? Did Issa Ali dig Selim's grave before he drove the truck to his own death, or did one of his fellow fundamentalists? Did my father have to sweat in the hot sun himself, fear of death making his hands shake as they held the spade? I look around wildly. Should I knock on every door in the village, ask if they know of a man named Selim Pakradounian? Am I failing my father – just as he failed me – by even stopping here, giving up?

The slow man smiles at me, burbles something in a language of his own making. The berries fall into my lap; I stare at them stupidly. He motions for me to eat, taking one and snapping off the hard stalk. I raise one to my mouth and in that instant I'm running to the other side of the hut, bringing up meat and bread and raisins, and behind me I can sense the man's hot, wet hand on the nape of my neck and his soothing murmur, and I know in that moment there's nothing to be found here.

BEIRUT, 1983

It was 6.12 am on 18 April 1983.

Issa woke in a nasty mood. He'd worked himself up over the last few weeks to feel this way. Brittle, full of hate. Spitting venom. Even abusing the poor peasant boy who came each morning with a basin of water to wash his face and feet and hands, towel him, hand him glasses of tea. This morning he waved the boy away. He wanted nothing to eat or drink. He wanted to sit alone on the floor in the corner of the room and pray. Read the Koran. *Believers, why is it that, when you are told, 'March in the cause of God,' you linger slothfully in the land? Are you content with this life in preference to the life to come?* He wanted to meditate on the next twenty-four hours. Maybe he'd even let himself cry. Just this once.

He told himself his motives were purely political. He wanted the peacekeeping forces to know they were defeated; helpless in Beirut's maw. He'd been sucked in then expelled; why shouldn't they? He wanted the Americans, British, Italians and French to know their stupid little sortie in Lebanon was doomed. And what better way to do it than by bombing the US embassy? He too would die, but round-armed virgins awaited him. And he was sure his mother would be proud and grateful, if only for the best Iranian rice, flour, sugar and coffee Islamic Jihad would give her in compensation. And the cash he'd negotiated? He was sure she'd share it with Sanaya. Sanaya had told him she was pregnant and at first he'd been frightened, worried for them all. Then, as he watched her quieten over those days, and soften toward him, all he'd felt was tenderness and regret that he had to leave her and their unborn child. He knew his death would shock Sanaya into loving him completely, drive his memory straight into her heart so she would never be able to forget him.

But there was more to it than that – and he only allowed himself to admit so when he was in the barn with Selim, watching the beatings. He must sacrifice his earthly joy with Sanaya to gain eternal life. Only by being a martyr for Allah could he hope to be with her forever. Her face would be in that of the houris chosen to wait upon him. Her hands would caress him through their pearl-tipped fingers. He would taste her mouth through the fruits of immortality. Her arrival in Paradise by his side would be inevitable as long as he kept his given promise in this life.

His only twinge of doubt was in the impossibility of seeing his child born before he died. To see its tiny rosebud fingernails, its ten perfect toes. His own tinsel eyes staring out at him from another face. Some days he thought Allah compensated for his approaching death by giving him the gift of prophecy. He could see his earthly future in front of him as he slept, hold the gurgling baby and at the same time breathe in the fragrance of Paradise. His dreams were sharp, clear-cut as reality. They were spiritual dreams, sent down by Allah, not the mere inventions of a tired brain. He saw huge phoenixes with green plumage taking him up into the clouds, an inky sky that flaunted all the arabesques and flourishes of a Koranic inscription. The birds sang in classical Arabic, *Chosen one, you will see your child in Heaven.* Even with these manifold spiritual gifts, some days he feared the inevitability of his own annihilation. Yet he was committed to Islamic Jihad, had told them he would do it. And he knew now that violence was the only valid path to freedom. There was no other way.

He was chosen for the job long ago, although he hadn't known it until now. From the beginning of his appointment to the organisation, he was marked for suicide. He was given the easy jobs, the sure battles, in case he accidentally died in combat and ruined their plans. His decision to accept this project months ago reverberated higher and higher up through the organisation into Iran. To back out now would mean certain death. Death without glory. At least this way he would be a holy warrior for the cause and be lifted straight up to Paradise. He would also wipe out the stain of his weakness with the commander, the memory of his cowardice down south.

It was a hushed spring morning, the beginning of Easter Holy Week for the Christians. The fervid light of the Beka'a Valley had woken him too early. He walked outside to the well, pumped up some brackish water and splashed his face. Unbarred the barn door and kicked Selim into consciousness.

'What are you doing, pretty boy?'

He saw Selim swallow, force the thick sounds out of his mouth through dry lips. 'Praying. Praying you'll spare me today.'

'You'll need it,' Issa answered. 'Pray for all you're worth, which isn't much.'

Selim groaned and turned to face the wall. His chains clanged, giving off a vile smell. Issa muttered under his breath, 'No more French cologne for you, pretty boy.'

It was 9.30 am. Sanaya woke later than usual and banged her alarm clock down on the side table. Dead again. She sat on the side of the bed. Sleep pooled around her, dragging her down once more, caressing her heavy eyes, melting her limbs under warm flesh. Ever since her pregnancy had become established and the nausea had abated, all she wanted to do was sleep. Sleep and dream of Issa and the baby. Together in a sunlit field of flowers. Red poppies, irises, forget-me-nots. The cleansing aroma of thyme, its miniature purple buds. Blades of wet grass sticking to their bare legs. She contemplated lying down for a few minutes longer, until she remembered. The shock each time she woke and remembered Issa–Selim, Selim–Issa always paralysed her for a few minutes.

Today she stood up and decided to do something, anything. If she surrendered to despair, she might as well die now. She set her jaw, opened the blinds. It was a shimmering spring morning and she dressed lightly, packed some toiletries in a bag, wrote a note for Rouba which she would leave under her door. *Not sure when I'll be back.*

She was sure Issa had taken Selim to the Beka'a Valley. She read in the newspapers that this was where Islamic Jihad took all their victims eventually. She had only to make it across the Green Line without some trigger-happy sniper shooting her in the back, and grab a taxi. She had only to mention Issa's Arabic name to one of the Muslim drivers, or to mention Selim's Armenian surname to one of the Christians. Her dilemma was to decide which was the wisest choice.

She ran downstairs and placed the note under Rouba's door. Coming upstairs to get her bag, she felt a swell of nausea and rushed to the bathroom.

✖ It was 10.37 am when Sanaya gathered together her bag and keys and made for the door. As she opened it, the proximity of Rouba's face made her utter a small, confused yelp.

'Come on, Sanaya, I don't look *that* bad when I've got no make-up on.'

'You startled me. I thought you were at work.'

'I just got your note. Where are you going, may I ask?'

'To visit some friends for the day.'

'Which friends? Do I know them?'

'I need to get out of the city.'

'Do I know them?'

'No—no, they're old friends from school.'

Rouba walked to the divan and threw herself down on it.

'You're pregnant; you're not thinking straight. And I know you're lying.'

Sanaya crossed the room and sat alongside her, holding her travelling bag to her stomach.

'There's no point going anywhere, Sanaya. They're going to kill him anyway. For all we know, he could be dead already.'

'Selim?'

'No! What are you talking about? Issa. He won't be doing exactly what they tell him, I assure you.'

✖ At 1.03 pm she hurried to the taxi rank on the Corniche. Bombed apartment buildings rose against the flat, yellow sky. The streets had been smashed so many times by shells the tar had turned to dirt, brown dust coating her arms and face whenever a car drove past. She'd been fighting with Rouba for what seemed like hours. Rouba had insisted Sanaya eat something. She took her downstairs and packed her a lunch.

Now she rushed through the crowds – why did they all seem so frantic? – her handbag upending and spilling all its contents. She left the lunch on the ground. As she bent with difficulty to gather the rest, she was shaking. *My God, it may be too late to get through the border into east Beirut. I may be shot. Killed. And my baby.* She hesitated, pressed two fingers to her yielding belly. A taxi driver smoked a cigarette as he waited, saw her and opened the car door.

'*Merhaba.* I need to go to east Beirut.'

The driver shook his head.

'No way, madam. I haven't been over there since the beginning of the war. Eight years!'

'Please. I need to get to the Beka'a. It's important.'

He ignored her, pointing upward. Black smoke curled into the sky from all directions. Down near the embassy road, a red flame as tall as a building uncoiled itself from the earth. She left him and ran in its direction without knowing why.

✳ It was 1.03 pm. Issa had been given a Chevrolet pickup truck in unintended irony. American made, built to last. There was a militia car in front of him, in case he grew frightened at the last moment, blocking any escape. Another car behind, with more explosives in case his attempt failed. He waited around the corner for a while, composing himself, breathing in exhaust fumes, dust, the momentous air all around him, deep into his lungs. *My lungs, my heart, my lips, my body.* He opened his Koran and read aloud a few soothing *suras. Each soul is the hostage of its own deeds. Those on the right hand will in their gardens ask the sinners: 'What has brought you into Hell?'* He couldn't concentrate. He put the book down. *My body the weapon.* He passed his hand over his eyes. After a short time, he took a piece of paper out of his pocket. The instructions were typed in bold block letters.

BEFORE DRIVING INTO THE EMBASSY, PRAY:
    Oh, Allah. Open all doors to me.
    Oh, Allah, who answers all those who seek help.
    I ask you to light the way and lift the burden of this life
from me.

He pulled out from between the two other vehicles, manoeuvred the truck, smiling and with eyes closed, straight into the front doors of the embassy building.

⌘ Now it was 1.13 pm. She slipped in pale blood mixed with water and smashed glass. She fell onto a suited torso and was helped up by a faceless man in a surgical mask.

'Are you family?' he demanded.

'No. I mean, yes.'

'Just get out of here.'

So many parts of bodies the horror did not touch her. They weren't people; they were only leering heads and severed arms and legs tangled in a sick fantasy. The live ones were more frightening. They convulsed, they lashed out at each other, clutched at her ankles and pleaded with a stranger's name on their lips. She shook her head at them, trying to breathe normally, trying to wipe away the water that flowed down her cheeks. She wasn't aware what the liquid was that blurred her vision, and continued wiping it from her face, not conscious of crying, walking through the wreckage, swollen feet through her sandals shiny with blood.

⌘ When it was 1.17 pm, Selim was shot in the back of the head by the Algerian guard. He lay face down near the wall he'd been chained to for the last two months. He didn't make a sound, but his right hand spread itself out after he stopped breathing, as if attempting to contain the dark pool of his existence.

BEIRUT, 1995

I take a service taxi from the Beka'a Valley to the south that same afternoon. After leaving the strange man and the mulberry tree, I feel somehow lighter, floating without any goal. I haven't yet expiated my father's death, far from it, but I've somehow silenced the insistence of the unknown. I've done all I can, now. I've been there, where he died, and found him somewhere else instead. My father's right beside me, always has been. With his bloodied hands, his many contradictions, the pink flowers under his jacket. He's part of me now, and he's all mine. As I sit in the taxi my body is entirely relaxed for the first time since I came back to Beirut.

When I arrive at the compound where Sayed is held it's already evening, the floodlights on and Israeli soldiers' faces bathed in an eerie underwater glow. I had tried to phone first and arrange a time to see Sayed, but there was no answer. Now I beg to see him for five minutes at least. It's not a visiting day and the hour is late. The soldiers confer with each other, call their superiors, shake their heads. I sit on the steps of the sentry box.

'I'm not going until I see him. Please. I only need to say one thing.'

After two hours, and after the soldiers realise I'm not going to move, I'm allowed in to see Sayed.

'Three minutes,' the guard tells me. 'I'll be timing you.'

Sayed leans over and puts the back of his hand on my cheek. The coolness of his skin, its tiny black hairs against me, is unbearably intimate. I feel either I'll hit him or embrace him. Yet I stay still, waiting for him to remove his hand. It feels to me as if with this casual gesture he's marked me out as one of them. A Palestinian. I think of Chaim, and don't want to take sides, not anymore.

'You're wet,' he says.

'Sweaty. It's been a long wait.'

The guard nearest us steps forward.

'No touching between detainees and visitors.'

Sayed grimaces and leans back into his chair. 'Forgive me?'

'For what?'

'Being the one to tell you.'

'Like you said, Sayed, it's not our fault. Neither of us.'

There's a silence neither of us wishes to fill. Sayed puffs out his cheeks in the way I've seen Inam do.

'Which reminds me. Your article? You said on the phone you had it published.'

'Yes, in *The Globe*. And here in Lebanon. *The Star*.'

I unfold the cuttings and let him read them. He leans over the table, his head nearly touching mine, and the Israeli guard moves forward again.

'No touching.'

Sayed springs back.

'If only.'

He catches my eye and I smile, not sure whether to be pleased or sad.

✳ Chaim is back in Beirut again. To celebrate he suggests a daytrip to the ruins of the temple of Ba'al. We stop at Chtaura for lunch, eating with leisure under vine leaves, slow burble of irrigation channels at our feet. The waiter pours more wine. I put my hand over the glass.

'No more for me. I'm already tipsy.'

I'm dazed with heat and alcohol. I finish my curd cheese, scooping it up with bread, pick at the last of the purslane salad. Shafts of light pierce through the leaves onto the white tablecloth, the white plates, Chaim's greying hair turned blonder in the sun. I want to tell him what Rowda said, and about Sayed's note, but don't know how to go about it. In a strange way, I fear that either sentence once spoken will open a chasm between us that can't be forded again. So I'm quiet, letting him finish the bottle of wine, take my hand and lead me to the car. Our driver is happy too, singing ballads under his breath as he drives. Along the highway huge posters of sheiks and mullahs, holy martyrs, contemporary, smiling, raise their hands in benediction at the buses and cars and trucks filled with women and children and farm animals. The closer we come to Ba'albek the bigger and shinier the posters become, the more beatific the smiles.

Close to the town the mountains begin to shimmer with an otherworldly light. The Beka'a Valley when we enter is hot and sticky. As we pull up at the ruins, crippled men thrust forward with trinkets, T-shirts, keffiyehs, cheap postcards in long concertinas trailing behind them in the dust. Some have fake Hellenistic and Roman finds they try to palm off as original: tarnished coins, fragments of mosaic, tiny busts of Aphrodite. Chaim stops to examine a terracotta perfume vial, atmospherically grimy, and a votive candle-holder redolent with its newly applied history. They are mostly Hezbollah fighters, wounded family men, home from battle to eke out their existence in the vegetable patches and fruit orchards the same way their grandfathers and great-grandfathers did. When they're well enough they will go south again to fight the Israelis on the border. I fend them off with shakes of the head and outstretched arms, stride through and up the steps to the temple compound, leaving Chaim to question and cajole, and in the end buy nothing. The men are friendly; I can hear them. They want talk more than a sale, but I'm tired from the trip and enjoying the solitude of the cavernous, weed-choked space between the huge temples too much. All around are fallen Corinthian columns and pediments, graceful statuary: a rounded arm, a breast, a carved pomegranate tinged red, still so insanely red after millennia. I bend to the ground and rub some pigment onto my palm.

Chaim joins me and we walk together through the ruins. The merchants have long since dropped behind. Before us the main temple of Jupiter appears rosy and pale gold in the afternoon light, dwarfing the surrounding landscape of concrete two-storey houses and shops, crazy aerials and cypresses. Away to the right, sitting in the shade, an old man with a twisted staff watches over his few goats grazing among the ruins. He waves at us in a slow greeting as we come closer. We climb up and into the entablature, careful of falling pediments and broken columns scattered at our feet. Chaim helps me over a fallen frieze. His hand stays in mine, tight. A carved Medusa's head stares up at us.

'She's not much fun,' he says.

'Oh, but look at him.'

We bend down and look at another bas-relief that has fallen: a black-winged Eros with one leg thrust forward, his quiver full of red-tipped arrows like tiny nipples. Chaim's breath caresses my ear and I shiver.

'Any response in the US to your article about Sayed Ali?'

'Yeah, mostly negative. What did I expect? But I'm interviewing him again, for an opinion piece, trying to contextualise his predicament. I like him.'

'Like him? In what way?'

'Well, he didn't do it, I'm sure.'

'Hmm. How can you be so sure? And you haven't answered my question.' Chaim stops walking with me, turns around and blocks the narrow path. 'Tell me, Anoush, who the hell in this conflict hasn't been persecuted? If you talk to my mother or her friends they'll tell you the persecution began long before they arrived in Israel.'

'But he's being persecuted *now*.'

'And what of the kids in Israel who can't go to school without an armoured guard? Aren't they being persecuted? *Now.* What of the bits of blown-up people I've had to scrape off the pavement? The orphans and widows?'

'Okay, okay, I get your point. We're both on the same side here, Chaim.'

'Are we?' He fixes me with a cold stare. I've never seen him so angry.

'Yeah,' I say. 'And you and I both know there are no sides. We're all persecuted. All victims, all the time. And sometimes perpetrators too.'

'Well, I don't see how your Palestinian friend is being persecuted. If he's not guilty, he'll go free.'

'It doesn't make him any less heroic, Chaim.'

'I don't see any of these guys as heroes. Just as I don't see my Israeli friends in the army as heroes either. Come on. I'm sorry I shouted at you. Let's not talk about him now.'

He pulls me into the shade of a column and bends down to kiss me on the neck. My body recoils almost in reproof but I keep myself passive, shoulderblades pressed hard against dry stone. I'm afraid of this overt act of intimacy in so fundamentalist a place, cautious in case we cause offence. Chaim seems excited by the danger. I notice the old man with the staff watching from far away.

❋ The next day I see Sayed again. I don't turn on my recorder when we're talking, merely sit opposite and let him speak, not saying much until the guards say our time is up. He speaks freely and I wonder if he'll pay for it later, whether the Israelis will punish him for his indiscretion. Or whether he's suffered so much now he's become unafraid, immune to more pain.

He speaks in Arabic of what is called *Shabeh*, being told to crawl on all fours like a dog each time he asks to go to the toilet. Of *Qambaz*, the Frog, being forced to squat until his thighs scream and his back is about to break. Of being bound to a child's chair. Sunflower yellow. A kindergarten chair. Made to sit on it for days, then fainting, being revived. The constant headaches, the confusion. Of lying over a high stool backward, so that the small of his back is pressed onto the edge. Of being beaten with hoses on the face, the belly, the testicles, then shaken, shaken again; of relentless noise: shouts, demands, swearing, American pop music on loudspeakers. Music so sentimental, so romantic, it always makes him weep. Weeping along with the songs of love, those slow refrains of longing. He apologises to the guards for being so weak, so suggestible, then hates himself for it.

He speaks of hooding. Of it being the worst torture of all. The first time, he could hear another man through the hood – not one of his usual interrogators – whispering in Arabic, in a cultivated voice. Saying to the others: *Hit him around the eyes, not in the eyes. Hit him in the soft parts, not on bone. Bone bruises.*

I look at Sayed, my voice a croak.

'Show me. Surely there must be one mark?'

He rolls up his shirt. I see nothing. Is he lying? Am I being duped? Yet I want to write about him, about every aspect of his suffering. What chance of a piece about Israeli torture techniques? I can at least try. Sayed makes me promise to come again next week, to come back every week.

I arrive home that evening in a downpour. I can't stop thinking about him. The last time he was hooded, he said he could hear a child

– a little girl – screaming. Was it a recording? An inmate's daughter? Could it be Inam? He tried to put his hands over his ears but they were useless, limp as gloves. 'We'll make her scream louder,' the Israelis said. They ripped off his hood and winked at him.

✳ The gardenias on Chaim's balcony have upturned their waxen petals to the rain, dilated cells drinking in the fragrance of wet soil. I can smell them as soon as I walk in the door.

'I'm home.'

No answer. I fling off my sandals onto the mat, run to the bathroom, come out rubbing a towel through my hair. Walk to the living room, into the kitchen. Julius is curled up in the far corner, he cocks one ear up but doesn't deign to rise and greet me. I kneel and run my fingers through his coat.

'Hey you, not even a welcome wag of the tail?'

I drink a full glass of water, that chlorine-bland taste at the back of my tongue. He follows me down the hall to Chaim's bedroom. The door is closed. I tap lightly, ease it open. Chaim is lying face down on the bed in the dark with the curtains drawn.

'What's wrong? Are you sick?'

His voice is deadened by the pillow and the rain. 'You're not still seeing that terrorist, are you?'

'I've told you he didn't do it, Chaim. He's not a terrorist.'

He's huddled like a child, closed against me.

'Wait a minute, you were the one who encouraged me to interview him in the first place.'

'I didn't know then that you'd be so fucking enamoured.'

I sit as heavily as I can on the side of the bed to disturb him, but he doesn't move. I put my hand on his back.

'Oh, please. You're too old to be the jealous type.'

As I say the words, a flicker of guilt in my belly. He sits up then and stares at my face, taking in my smudged lipstick, damp hair standing up in spikes, my dress with the top two buttons undone.

'Look at you. All dolled up to see him.'

I get up and walk to the other side of the room, then abruptly turn to him again.

'What are you trying to do to me, Chaim? Do you really think I'm playing around?'

'No.'

'He's in prison, for God's sake. He's being tortured.'

'I don't believe he's telling the truth. I think he's lying to you. Taking you for a ride.'

'You've read my article. Seen the evidence of his innocence.'

'Which evidence? It's a triumph of wishful thinking. Total crap. Your editor must be as stupid as you are.'

I stalk out of the bedroom, pick up my bag in one hand and my sandals in the other, and stumble blindly out the door into the rain.

✳ I wait by the phone in a room at the Mayflower, knowing he'll call. I don't leave my room at all that night, going to bed early and trying, unsuccessfully, to sleep. Countless times I pick up the receiver, hold it to my ear, put it down again, banging it against the old-fashioned dial in the dark. I rise the next morning at dawn, shower for as long as I can, killing time. One ear cocked for the phone. I dress carefully in the same damp clothes as yesterday, anticipating the inevitable ring.

The phone shrills.

'Hello?'

'It's Sayed.'

'Oh.'

'You sound disappointed.'

'No, no—it's just—I was expecting another call. How did you know I was here?

I rang the number you gave me and some guy said you're probably staying at the Mayflower. Sounded like a foreigner to me. Who is he? You haven't told me about him.'

'Sayed, please, I really can't talk now.'

With those words, I know I've betrayed him for the first time.

'Sayed, sorry, I'm sorry. The other call can wait. Are you okay?'

'I'll be quick,' he whispers. 'They've just told me my tribunal comes up in four weeks. Can you find me a good lawyer? I can't use legal aid, I need an Arab–Israeli, someone who sympathises but can also represent me in Hebrew.'

'How will you pay?'

'I'm ashamed to ask, but I thought maybe—'

'Of course I can try and help you. But I won't be able to pay the full amount. I don't think I have that sort of cash, without selling something back home.'

'I know. I'll ask my mother, some of the elders in the camp. Or Hezbollah. Believe me, if I'm represented by one of the army lawyers I'm done for. They're moving me to Israel for the trial.'

'I'll come with you.'

'You don't have to do that—'

'I want to do it. I believe you're innocent.'

'I—you don't know how good that makes me feel. I—Anoush, I've been wanting to say something to you. But—I'm afraid to say it.'

I wait. A flush of excitement from belly to chest. Then I hear the click at the other end. One of the guards must have decided his time was up.

'Fuck. Fuck it.'

I throw the phone to the ground, where it lands with a strangled ring. Scramble to my knees, retrieve it.

'Hello?'

The line is dead.

✳ Chaim doesn't call. Sayed tries again the next morning, but is further constrained by who is listening.

I go to visit him every day, but am not allowed to see him. I worry, think my articles, my presence, my lack of discretion have jeopardised his chance of winning the case. I wait a week in the hotel, then another. I buy new toiletries and a few clothes, unable to bring myself to go back to Chaim's apartment and claim my own. I feel my anger against him solidify until it settles like a stone in my stomach, the same stone of my father's absence and my mother's and grandmothers' deaths. It irritates me by day until I can't swallow food or water, bears down on me at night. I won't call him, after what he said. And there's nothing I can say to bridge the distance between us. He knows I'm at the Mayflower, knows I'm here alone. How can he get rid of me so easily? I know why. He can sense that I'm not really there for him, not fully his. I know how hard it must be for him. But my position hardens too until, after two weeks, it seems as if there's no other option available to me but silence.

I go to see Bilqis and Inam, making light of my predicament. Talk about going back to America, finding permanent journalistic work, resuming a life; there's nothing left for me here. Suddenly it's all become too difficult. I even mention my mixed feelings for Sayed. I'm not sure what to say about my father and Issa Ali, refrain from telling Bilqis anything. How can I say it? Not yet. And it's not as if Bilqis doesn't already know, hasn't known for years. I suspect Bilqis knows everything and that nothing can surprise her anymore. Inam's there in the corner as well, always listening, and it's not something that can be discussed in front of her.

Surprisingly, Bilqis seems most perturbed by my feelings for Sayed. I thought she would be happy. She seems unconcerned about Sayed being hurt, instead asks me about Chaim.

'Is he good to you?'

'What do you mean?'

'Does he care for you, do things for you, think of you when you aren't there?'

'Yes. Yes, yes.'

'Does he drink? Does he beat you?'

'No.'

'Go with other women?'

'No, I don't think so.'

'Then what is it?'

I pause.

'He's Israeli, that's one thing. Sometimes I feel as if I'm such a hypocrite. Other times, I feel as if he and I are so close. Like one person. And then—there's Sayed.'

Bilqis nods then, closes her eyes.

'I understand. But you will not have a good life with Sayed. I know this. On the other hand, the Israeli is too old. Better to wait.'

I close my eyes as well, let them rest for a moment. Inam rustles paper and hums tunelessly in an undertone. When I eventually speak it's in a whisper as quiet as Inam's shuffle and murmur.

'Bilqis. Why do you care so much about me, anyway?'

'How could I not care for you? We are both tied together by the past. Both suffering for it.'

A small moan escapes me. Somehow I'm more embarrassed before Inam's silent regard than Bilqis's gaze.

'I don't think I love either of them. Or maybe I love them both.'

Bilqis tuts.

'Love? What's love? Who knows nowadays? In any case, you won't feel it till you've had children.'

She invites me to stay. I offer to pay board but she shakes her head, puts her large spotted hand over mine.

'You're family now. Part of us. It's the least I can do, after what my poor son did to your father.'

I lean forward, studying her. Everything seems small and pinpointed in this dark, dingy room, her face, this throbbing instance. She smiles – a sad, lopsided smile.

'Family,' she repeats. 'Too much blood between us, good and bad.'

'What? Did you know Sayed told me?'

'Of course Sayed told you. And of course he told me what has happened between the two of you. The very first day he met you he said, *Aunty, I think I'm falling in love with that Armenian girl.* Do you think he doesn't talk? That's what got him into prison in the first place.'

I lean back again in disbelief.

'And you still want me to stay here?'

Bilqis laughs.

'It's you that should be cautious, my girl, not us. My son – I think he hated your father, more than just a wartime battle. But I don't think he would have wanted that hate to poison the next generation. He wasn't a hateful man.'

'I'm sorry – I can't believe that. I can't forgive him. I wish I could. I really wish that. But I can't. And yet – I feel no animosity toward you. None.'

Bilqis pulls me into her arms. I lean onto her lap, smelling the strong, herbal scent of her clothes and skin and hair. In that moment my tears begin, huge all at once. I'm heaving, crying so hard I seem to be outside my body. I think of her, having the heart to be so open to me, not being vengeful, as her son and my father were. I think of D'Andrea and my forgiveness of him. I cry for a long while. After a time, Bilqis slowly draws away. I can see tiny points of light in her eyes, tears she won't let fall. Inam is standing, watching us.

'Come, come, enough of this,' Bilqis says. 'Let's drink a glass of arak together.'

Her grip is a little less firm than it was a few weeks ago. One side of her torso shakes, causing her to spill drinks and rattle plates when she serves. I move to help.

'Are you okay, Bilqis?'

'Feeling my age. I'm sixty-seven this year, you know.'

'Still young.'

'Yes.' Bilqis smiles at Inam. 'Still strong enough, Allah willing, to raise this one here a little longer.'

Inam stays in the corner, doing her homework and pulling faces. When I hold out my arms she runs to me in a wild rush of dirty hair and legs.

The three of us establish a routine over the coming days and weeks. In the beginning I am constantly on edge about bumping into D'Andrea, but after a week or so I realise that, if I do see him, I'll merely smile and greet him. I've forgiven what he said and did.

In the morning I encourage Bilqis to lie in bed late, behind a sheet she has strung up for privacy. She has periodic bouts of numbness in her neck and arms, making it difficult for her to get out of bed. I urge her to see the camp doctor, but she says it's nothing, just old age. I make breakfast and Inam and I eat sitting on wooden crates outside the front of the hut in our nightgowns, watching labourers pile onto trucks bound each morning for the south of the border, to work in road gangs for the Israelis. The men wave and blow kisses, dressed in filthy blue gear, caps pulled low over their eyebrows. Inam smirks her delight at such flattery but I can see she's old enough now to also be embarrassed. I feel myself wanting to protect her more and more: from strange men's gazes, hardship, suffering, from pain. She leaves her crusts behind for the sparrows, shooing her grandmother's hens away when they come too close, and licks fig jam from her thumb. I learn how tightly she likes her flatbread rolled, which sweet spreads to buy at the camp's only shop.

Inam drinks instant coffee every morning with evaporated milk and four teaspoons of sugar. I'm in no position to discipline her. She makes it herself as soon as she gets out of bed, and a mug for me and her grandmother as well. I don't have the heart to refuse but spill most of mine in the dirt when Inam isn't looking. The hens seem jerkier than usual on the days I do this.

Rowda comes once a week. I've grown accustomed to her presence but this doesn't stop me from resenting it more each time. I'm used to her faded-black jeans – tight but not too tight; that would be culturally insensitive – the cinched-in waist and shining buckle. Her rants about Israelis and white people and Western academics, the US conspiracy to keep the Arab world down. I agree with some of what she says but will never admit it, and my agreement doesn't go so far as to condemn anyone who isn't Arab, or black, or oppressed. And then there's Chaim – and what he's taught me about not hating, about questioning everything. So each time Rowda begins one of her rants I cut her off. If she speaks of Palestinian civilian deaths, I tell her of the latest bombing in Jerusalem or Tel Aviv. If she speaks of the rights of a dispossessed people, I counter with the image of those tattered remnants, survivors of the Holocaust, who found the only place that would have them. It does no good, of course, but it makes me feel that little bit closer to Chaim, allows me to miss him less if I speak in his voice. Even though I've tried so hard to banish him from my thoughts, as he's seemingly banished me in turn. It's been three weeks and still no sign of him.

Inam doesn't come home for lunch, as UNRWA provides stewed lamb, oranges and fresh milk for the refugee children at school. In the afternoon, I make her take off her school clothes to keep them clean. We wash her hair in a bucket every three days, trying to untangle knots as big as burrs. Inam moans about me hurting her, twists and wriggles; she's not used to doing what she's told. Bilqis reprimands her, yet more and more has become reduced to a painful whisper, slurring her words slightly, making quiet demands from the safety of her bed. Eventually we get to a point where Inam does it herself, and I don't have to help anymore.

Finally, when Inam has combed her hair, scraped it back with her favourite hair tie and dressed in the discoloured Bob Marley T-shirt and baggy shorts she wears every day after school, the three of us stroll out of the camp and toward the mountains towering above the city. Bilqis ties a shawl around her shoulders, girding herself for the first time she'll get out of bed all day. I hold hands with Bilqis, who walks with irritating slowness, and Inam demonstrates how she can twirl three times around her grandmother in the time Bilqis can only take one step. Sometimes we meet Amal at the crossroads and she ushers us into her hut, fussing about with tiny wooden stools and tea glasses. She's particularly careful of me, patting my hand and smoothing my hair, offering walnut biscuits she's bought fresh and warm from the sole pastry vendor who dares venture into the camp.

'So, Anoush,' she asks each time. 'When is my poor boy to be freed?'

'Patience. We need patience. Everything will be all right.'

And I think about my unsaid longing for Sayed, my hard lesson of patience for Chaim's return. But do I really want either of them? I have to admit that I'm not sure. Chaim feels right for me in so many ways. And I miss him, more than I've missed anyone before. More than I've longed for Lilit, or my mother and father. Sayed is something else: the possibility of a new future, the ability to wipe the slate clean.

When we reach the edge of the camp, we turn back to cook dinner and Inam tells us lurid stories about the other children at school, between demonstrations of acrobatics in her long-legged grace.

Without meaning to, hardly realising, I feel I'm recreating my life with my grandmothers here, in yet another ghetto. Armenian quarter: Palestinian refugee camp. The boundaries blur, wash into each other as I sleep and wake and cook and eat, walk arm in arm with Inam to go shopping, buying meagre provisions and taking a second-hand skirt or singlet donated by the compassionate West. I'm truly at home here, I realise. I continue to miss Chaim, and the beauty and repose of his apartment, but here I feel needed, and strong.

I do exactly as I did until the age of sixteen: feeding and tending Lilit's failing strength, turning over the old body, sponging it, massaging the clawed yellow feet, kissing the parchment forehead before nightfall. Reading aloud by the light of a lamp, curled in bed. The only difference now is that the reading and talking is in Arabic only, and the cadences of Armenian are merely a phrase I wake from after a dream.

✵ I decide to take Inam with me to see Sayed. It might be easier that way. Might make it harder for us to distrust one another – or like one another too much. Might make it easier just to be friendly, neutral. Now I've been able to pay for Sayed's lawyer with help from Amal, I feel more entwined with him, and I'm not sure I like the sensation.

I buy Inam a bag of striped sweets at the rest stop. We stroll across the highway to the sandy strip bordering the sea, the silver-nude sea that's followed us south all the way from Beirut, a winking conspirator on our journey. Inam balances a large white box on her knees, bird's nest pieces of *baqlawa* hand-chosen for her uncle.

When we arrive at the prison gate, there are two guards on duty that I've never seen before. With them, trained dogs with hyperactive movements. The men decide to hold us up, inventing excuses, telephoning superiors, being difficult. They're bored, hot in the sentry box, ready for some quiet fun. They're young, teenagers really. I feel sorry for them at first. Pretending to go and photocopy my press pass, the older one disappears. The other – younger, more handsome, brash – waves my passport and Inam's soiled identity papers in the air. She has no passport, only a *laissez-passer* given out by the Lebanese government. The guard hands the papers back as if they've infected him and bends down so he's level with Inam's face. 'What's a little troublemaker like you doing with an American citizen?'

Inam grips my hand tighter. She stares straight ahead as if she's gone blind. The other guard comes back with my press card, in time to catch his friend's last remark.

'And such a sexy American at that,' he says.

I hold out my hand for the card. He makes as if to hand it over then, just as I reach out to take it, hides it behind his back.

'Say please. No, not just please. A kiss. A kiss for a card.' He addresses Inam. 'That sounds fair, doesn't it, little Palestinian?'

Inam continues to stare straight ahead at the wall of the sentry box, painted in the muted colours of the Israeli flag, her feet planted firmly on the ground like a little soldier herself.

'Aren't you ashamed of yourselves?' My voice wobbles. 'Aren't you sick of teasing and harassing women and children?'

I lunge at my card, grab it from the guard's hands. I'm white-hot now, reckless. He steps forward, menacing.

'You better watch your mouth. We have the authority to stop you from coming here, ever again.'

I turn on my heel, dragging Inam toward the prison. I'm shivering all over from fear and rage. I can hear the dogs barking, can feel Inam's small hand shaking in mine. The other guard yells.

'Don't worry, Avram,' he shouts to his friend, louder over the dogs, so I can hear. 'She's just a *shiksa* whore, a fucking Arab-loving whore!'

Inside the prison, we sit down to wait. I'm still flustered and Inam takes my hand, caressing it in gentle circles as if she's the elder. A guard enters the waiting room and I half-rise, while Inam grasps my skirt in anticipation.

'Detainee Sayed Ali will not see you today, Miss.'

'I'm sorry? Why?'

'He said he does not wish to see anyone today – and you in particular.'

'Please. Can I speak to him for a moment? I've been coming for weeks and haven't been allowed even a glimpse of him.'

The guard shakes his head, impassive.

'Does he know his niece is here, at least?'

The guard nods, winking at Inam with a changed, boyish face.

'Well, can we leave him this box of cakes then?'

Inam hands over the box with great ceremony. As she does, she looks from my face to the guard's in appeal, as if we've made some mistake, as if either of us can make some swift remark or gesture to change her world. Nothing comes. Inam gives the *baqlawa* one last, longing glance. We stumble out of the prison into the bright, sunlit world.

'Anoush, did they really tell him I was here? Of course he'll see me if he knows.'

I turn around.

'Didn't you hear, you silly girl? I asked the guard! He must be sick. Or angry with me. I have no idea why. Don't be difficult now, let's just go.'

In the next instant I'm ashamed of speaking to Inam that way. But I can't help myself, and even as I inwardly cringe I take her hand in a rough grasp and stride to the perimeter of the prison. I try not to let stupid tears run down my cheeks. Was the guard lying under orders, because of my altercation with the others at the gate? Has Sayed rejected me? Has he given thought to the past and decided it's folly to campaign for his release? Is he just depressed? And what of his responsibility to Inam?

I run past the guards at the checkpoint, dragging Inam alongside. There's nothing I can do right. Chaim's gone. And now even Sayed has abandoned me. Was this how my father's lover felt? I finally feel a sharp prod of sympathy for her; pregnant, vulnerable and alone, both protectors dead.

BEIRUT, 1983

Sanaya came home and rushed into the bathroom, leaving the front door wide open. All she could think of was the blood. All she could think of was to wash the blood off her feet and legs. She clicked the latch into place on the bathroom door and wet a facecloth at the tap. Holding it, feeling its cold slowness seep into her hand, she sank to the floor. Now all she could think of was her baby floating in its flesh prison, contaminated by other people's fluids. The fear made her wooden, sleepy, limbs turned to lead. The trickle of water from the washer was warmer now, pooling at her wrist. She couldn't move, could hardly breathe, until she heard Rouba banging on the bathroom door and began swiping at her ankles with the cloth.

'So you didn't go?'

Sanaya hesitated before answering, couldn't remember what Rouba was referring to.

'No.'

'Open the door.'

'No.'

'What are you doing in there? I saw blood on the stairs—'

'No.'

'Let me in then.'

Rouba banged at the door again, rattling at the loose latch, finally kicking hard enough so it dislodged and fell open. Her eyes widened at Sanaya sitting on the floor with her legs splayed like a doll's in front of her. She fell to the tiles and took her shoulder.

'Talk to me. Tell me what to do.'

Sanaya continued dabbing at her legs with the bloodied face washer.

'Nothing. I'm not losing the baby.'

'Then why—were you anywhere near the explosion? I was downstairs listening to the news when I heard you running up the stairs.'

'Somebody blew up the US embassy.'

'I know. Islamic Jihad just claimed responsibility on TV. They could be lying. They're saying it was a suicide bomber.'

Rouba took the cloth and rinsed it at the tap, kneeling down and wiping Sanaya's feet and ankles, lost in thought.

'Do you think it—' she began.

Sanaya looked up at her, caught a sob in her throat. In that instant both of them remembered the tapes they found. Issa's tapes: all the detailed explanations of death.

'No. It couldn't be.'

Rouba rinsed out the cloth methodically and placed it to dry on the edge of the basin, before turning to face Sanaya.

'I'm going to make some calls. I know a few of those men, friends of Issa's from the mosque. If they'll speak to me. We have to find out.'

✳ Issa's body was not found – well, not all of it. When the Red Crescent workers had been and gone Bilqis and Sanaya went searching too. 'All genetic materials have been taken away,' the officials assured them. 'You will find nothing. We've even isolated hair, teeth, fingernails, shreds of skin. All classified. All in plastic bags, labelled *unidentified*.'

It was dusk now and puffs of smoke from disturbed rubble darkened the pink-tinged sky. Rouba stayed home. She couldn't face it again, she said, not after her husband, not after Hadiya.

Now that Sanaya was huddled on all fours, searching for something, anything, to connect her to Issa among the ruins, she couldn't stop thinking about his part in this carnage. Rumbling like a half-formed song in her brain was the old traditional term of endearment he would mumble as they made love. 'My eyes, my eyes,' he would say in a voice clotted with passion, and she would feel exquisite, in the moment, wholly new. 'My lion,' she would reply, and the pleasure she saw on his face blotted out the whole world – all that she didn't want to think about his past as a militiaman, his nightmares, his suffering, his daily unexplained absences from her. She was certain it was him now. The killer of so many innocents. Unless Islamic Jihad was lying, or using him as a decoy, there could be no other conclusion.

She thought of her shock when she found out. When Rouba had gone downstairs to telephone Sanaya had hurried after her. They found Bilqis sitting on the divan with a videotape in her hands. She held it straight out before her as if it were alive and could do her untold harm.

'It was on the mat in the hall when I went to take the garbage out,' she whispered.

Rouba snatched it out of her hands and turned it to the side so she could read the scrawled inscription.

'It says *Issa Ali, 1964–1983.*'

Now Sanaya couldn't stop thinking about Issa's appearance on the tape. He was flat, bloodless, like a man already dead. Gone was the fire of his convictions, the inflamed passion of hatred he'd nurtured since a child. As he spoke to the camera, eyes lowered to his boots, he cradled his gun in his arms as if it were an infant. Behind him, grainy scenes of training camps were spliced with his passive face: close-ups of men in bandannas and black scarves that only revealed their eyes, boys face down in the mud crawling to some unknown destination, leaping up and shooting targets shaped like bodies, chanting an unidentifiable phrase that drowned out Issa's modest, mumbled speech.

She now found herself engulfed by rage as she bent over the charred evidence of suits and desks and building materials outside the embassy – those damned Iranians were using Issa's death for recruitment propaganda. She had watched him farewell his mother on the tape, kissing the fingers of both hands in an unconvincing gesture, murmuring goodbye to his brother's wife, to his unborn child. She'd caught a glint of silver on his wrist, but dismissed it. He then punched his right fist into the air and his gun clattered awkwardly to the floor. There the tape ended; with the sound of metal on concrete. He made no mention of Sanaya. Was this to protect her? Even so, as she sifted through the rubble in the dim half-light, she was devastated by his omission.

She and Bilqis found a severed finger, a hexagonal lump of flesh: powdery, disintegrating into soot in their hands. Bilqis said she knew these were Issa's remains, even when at home Rouba told her they couldn't be, even when Sanaya's face betrayed her quiet disbelief. Bilqis had them laid out in a plain pasteboard box, covered them in stones, blue and grey pebbles, marbled from the sea and gathered at low tide.

S
K
Y

425

'Exactly the colour of his eyes,' she whispered to Sanaya.

Before the box was sealed Sanaya bent over the remains, touching the pebbles with her mouth. Their smooth surfaces were blank, inert. They betrayed no secrets, no mythic instructions for the rest of her life. At that moment, slow and eternal, death seemed preferable to life, to grief, to rage. She couldn't imagine being normal again. Like a numbing of the limbs in cold water, she began to understand in some small way why Issa had chosen to die. Part of her wished to join him, if it weren't for the unborn child. In the instant she pressed her lips to stone, the slow curdle of life became too much to bear and she was drawn to him with more intensity than when he was her lover.

She stood still, hunched over the makeshift coffin, breathing hard. *If I breathe, in, out, in, out, then it must mean I'm still alive.* In the end, she left Issa to his death. She took two pebbles away with her and carried one to the Corniche, stood in the wind and threw it into the churning water. The other she put aside, unsure why she needed to keep it.

BEIRUT, 1995

Bilqis hobbles inside where I'm helping Inam with her English-language homework. She's only up once a day now, either to accompany us on our afternoon stroll or to feed the manic hens. She scatters grain from her hands in haste as she closes the door behind her, and we look up from our books in alarm.

'There's a strange man outside. I'm worried.'

I rise from the table, wiping my inky hands on my thighs. Inam shadows me. I squint at the setting sun, cup my hand over my eyes. A thick-set silhouette visible at the end of the yard. One bent leg as he leans against a wall, carrying all the weight of his body.

'Chaim.' His name feels alien to my lips. I walk forward without realising what I'm doing, without meaning to show him how he still holds me in his thrall. The hens at my feet squawk and peck at dry earth, sometimes missing their targets and tapping at my bare toes, but I don't care.

'Go inside, Inam.'

She stays where she is, glued to my side.

I feel no time elapse between my loneliness and being engulfed in the warmth of his body. I allow myself to melt, ebullient with relief, elated by his open-handed touch.

'I'm so glad you found me.'

'Are you? Then why did you run away?'

Strange, this new mouth light on mine. I'm flexible in his grip, changing into somebody else. Inam stares up at us both and tugs at my arm.

'Anoush, Anoush! Come back inside with me.'

I wave her away, disentangling the furious hands. Inam plants her two feet between us, wriggling her body through.

'Go away! Leave her alone.'

'Inam, don't be silly. I told you to go inside.'

Inam punches me in the belly. Chaim gasps.

'Traitor!' Inam shouts. 'Traitor. I hate you.'

She runs inside and slams the door so hard the hut shakes on its flimsy foundations.

✳ We huddle together on Chaim's futon for days. Somehow the guilt of quitting the camp, leaving an enraged Inam and mildly acceptant Bilqis behind, of not working, not writing, not answering the telephone, not being responsible to anybody but each other, renders the time we lie there in artificial darkness ever more potent. We play games with intertwined arms and legs, make a tent of the bedclothes, giggle at each other's fiercely rumbling stomachs, ignore our hunger pangs for a day as we kiss and press against each other: new love now, tender and slow.

Finally Chaim gets up at sunset, only to bring back stale date biscuits and a jar of bergamot preserves – all he can find in his empty kitchen cupboards – brewing watery Arabic coffee to keep us awake. We eat the preserves with our fingers, licking Nile-green syrup from each other's wrists and chins. He burrows beneath the bedclothes, his rough, grey-flecked head between my legs.

'Don't,' I'm tempted to say, but I stay still, frozen, as his tongue finds me. This is the first time he's done it. Yet something makes me shudder, something in me wants to recoil. I push his head away. He sits up.

'What's wrong?'

I can see his age now in the harsh glare of the bedside lamp, the wiry white hairs around his groin and the soft rolls of fat, belly to hip.

'Aren't we together again? Why are you holding back?'

I feel guilty at betraying Sayed, wrong to leave Bilqis and Inam, but I can't say this. He's telling me what to do again, and I'm a little girl who can't help but comply.

'Lie down again,' I say. 'Come on. I'll rub you.'

He mumbles, his voice flattened by the sheet beneath his face.

'All that time without you, not knowing where you'd gone, made me realise—'

'You didn't even come to the Mayflower to find me.'

'How could I? I didn't know who you'd have in the hotel bed with you.'

'That's a low blow, Chaim. Sayed's in prison, for God's sake.'

'So it's the Palestinian you think about, is it?'

'Please, let's not start that again.'

'I'm sorry. Forget it. I'm just scared. Scared that I'll lose you.'

I continue rubbing, pressing my thumb into the hollows of his spine, leaning closer.

'You won't,' I whisper, next to his face. 'You won't.'

He turns over in the bed to kiss me, his cheeks wet against mine.

'It's hard for me, Anoush. Here I am, feeling that I'm betraying my family and my people by being here in the first place, and then feeling as if I'm betraying you if I'm truly myself. I'm just making it up as I go along.'

I stop, exhale.

'I still want to help him, Chaim. All of them.'

'I know. I'm sorry I was so suspicious. It's hard to trust, and just accept them as people. Too often who they are gets covered over by their own prejudices against me.'

I pause. 'I'm hoping Inam hasn't had time to fully identify with any race, or religion. Or have any prejudices. I hope she can learn to move between all these worlds. But she won't have anyone after Bilqis and Amal are gone. I don't know how I can help. I just feel that I need to go back there, be with them.'

He's sitting up now and pulls me by the neck toward his chest. I submit, laughing helplessly.

'Okay. Okay, I'll stay here for a while. Just a little while.'

My arms high up in the air. He imprisons my wrists in one hand, and takes me down with him.

✳ We're all here in court, dressed sombrely, hands clutched tight in laps, eyes averted from each other. The trip down to Israel was fraught with difficulty: Amal taken sick with apprehension and having to go back, silence and sullenness from Inam, a two-hour hold-up at the border. Israeli soldiers with designer sunglasses and condescending grins who treated Chaim as if he were some sort of traitor.

Now the waiting is unbearable. Inam asks to go to the bathroom ten times. I don't realise until the fifth time that this is because it's the first time she's seen a flushing toilet. She comes back after each trip dripping with pink liquid soap and wetting her only dress.

Weeks ago I'd asked to report on Sayed's trial for *The Globe*. My request was refused. The tribunal is under military jurisdiction, subject to security and anti-terror legislation, making it difficult for any civilian to attend. The best lawyer I could find for Sayed is an Arab–Israeli, educated in a Jewish university yet adamantly pro-Palestinian, a man with one precarious foot in both camps. His mother still lives in the Occupied Territories. Chaim couldn't help but cringe at the term, and I hated him for a brief moment.

I accompany Inam on her latest visit to the toilet. She spends an inordinate amount of time in the cubicle humming, and I have to shout above her garbled song.

'Are we friends again?'

Inam stops at the end of a verse, taking her time before answering. 'No.'

'Please, Inam. When you get older you'll understand.'

'I am older.'

'Big girls need a man sometimes.'

'I know *that*. But not one like him.'

She comes out of the cubicle, washes and dries her hands, using dozens of paper towels, turns and looks at me.

'How could you leave us for him? He's Israeli.'

'What does that mean, sweetheart? Does that mean he's a bad man? You know better than that.'

'No, I don't.'

I squat down and put my hands around her tiny waist. 'Yes, he's Israeli, and he's also a good person. Not all Israelis are bad. And not all Palestinians are good, true?'

She won't look at me.

We walk out of the restroom in silence. As we approach Bilqis and Chaim, Inam slips her fingers into my palm. She glares up at Chaim and wriggles her behind between us on the bench outside the courtroom.

Bilqis whispers, 'Are they going to put him away forever?'

'He has a good lawyer,' Chaim soothes.

'How do we know if it's a fair trial if they won't even let us in to see?'

'Shh,' I warn. 'He's coming now.'

Sayed's lawyer looks relaxed, almost too relaxed. He slouches about in front of his prosecuting colleague, adjusts his suit trousers, surveying the anxious families in the corridor with a self-consciously puzzled air. He smiles broadly at me as if we share some secret, and I smile back, encouraging. Chaim jiggles my arm over Inam's competing, resolute presence.

'What's his problem? Why's he acting as if he knows you so well?'

'What do you mean?'

'You know I don't want to be here. You know I'm here against my better judgement.'

'All right!' I whisper furiously in his ear. 'Go back home then.'

Chaim settles back in his chair, glancing at Inam. She's put her hand on my knee in a proprietary fashion.

'You know I'm only doing this for you,' he says.

'Don't trouble yourself, please.'

Inam smiles at nothing in particular. I turn away, blocking Chaim from my line of sight. Sayed is being led through a side door to the courtroom, less than ten metres away. His eyes are blindfolded.

✳ In the days following the verdict, Bilqis grows somehow frailer, more transparent. I move back into the camp to be with her, lacerated by Chaim's protests. I'm flat, worn out. Sayed has been sentenced to twenty-one years in the infamous Russian Compound in Jerusalem, with little hope of appeal.

I stroke Bilqis's arm where it rests on the faded, floral sheet.

'Don't worry. I'll visit him every week. I'll write more articles.'

Bilqis protests, 'How can you go there? They won't let you in.'

'I have two passports, Aunty. I can use one for here and one for there.'

Bilqis mutters into her nightie, 'That's not what I meant. It's your safety I worry about.'

'I can take Chaim with me.'

At the mention of Chaim's name, Bilqis sniffs and turns her face to the wall. She's become more critical of him since their meeting. She thinks he's too old for me, too jocular, too confident, too Israeli. And she's been more emotional lately, dwelling on the past – her dead son, Inam's mother – as though unaware of the tears streaming down her cheeks. I lean in further so my lips touch her cheek.

'We've already arranged for a counsellor to see him once a week. Medical care and visits from the Red Crescent.'

Bilqis continues to stare at the wall. I stand, brisk and falsely cheerful. I put my hand out to Inam, who's still clutching the now-bedraggled book I once gave her.

'Should we let Grandma take a nap, sweetheart? Let's go for a little walk.'

✼ I hurry home with Inam in the deepening dusk. People on the street jostle us as we run past; taxi drivers slow down, honking their horns, recognising me always as a foreigner. They keep up a meaningless patter of entreaty as they cruise alongside: 'Is very hot, mademoiselle, you need hat for your beautiful skin, you want I take you anywhere, is cheap, is cheap.' I grow tired of shaking my head at them.

We're both starving; it's past dinnertime. We stop at a sudden scent of spice and salt, a stall selling hot thyme bread. I buy four and we stuff them into our mouths as we run. I think of Bilqis opening a tin of something, trying to heat it on that tiny flame.

We come back to the hut to find her mumbling incoherently, evidently in a great deal of pain. Her right side is locked in a curve, almost completely paralysed. I run to find the camp doctor. He massages her arm and shoulder, gives her an injection, takes to pummelling her after fifteen minutes.

'Stop!' I scream. 'Can't you see you're hurting her?'

'She can't feel a thing, believe me.'

'What's wrong with her?'

'It may be the onset of multiple sclerosis or motor neurone disease. We need to run some blood tests and scans to see. Either way, she needs to get to a hospital tonight. If it's either of the two, she'll eventually lose control of her limbs, bowels and bladder. In extreme cases, her mouth and throat, and even the ability to speak.'

I cast a swift glance at Inam to see if she's listening. She sits cross-legged near the open door, leafing through the same dog-eared book. She gives no appearance of having heard but I know better. I come closer to the doctor's face.

'How long will it take for this to happen?'

'Weeks. Months. Maybe even years before it takes over and ends her life. There's no cure, no real treatment. She'll need a full-time carer. Unfortunately we don't have those facilities here in the camps. She'll have to be transferred to another hospital or a hospice as soon as we get these tests done.'

He calls an ambulance. Inam and I watch as it takes Bilqis away. She can hardly look at us.

Her last words are covered over by Inam's voice, but I think she says: *I'll be back tomorrow.* Inam is sobbing, screaming, hitting out at me.

When it's over, I try to get her to bed, lie down on top of the covers next to her. She holds my hand until she falls asleep, her fingers tracing my veins in an eternal circle.

I dream. Chaim's face. Sayed, smiling. I run, keep running through night-filled streets. Cats screech at me from alleys. I'm breathless and sobbing. Out of the gloom, the figure of a man. I stop, not sure who it is, tears drying on my cheeks. Before I can catch a glimpse of his face, he's turned away.

❋ I dread supervising the move to the hospice. The hut now empty, hollowed out. I'm shocked at how quickly one can remove any traces of a human presence, even after so many years. All that's left now are two single mattresses stripped down to their sheets, the dented saucepan for making tea. Concrete walls bare of any decoration. All of Bilqis's bibelots have been stored in cardboard boxes by the door, and her old house keys from Jaffa are nowhere to be found. Nobody except me knows she's hidden them under her nightdress, clutched tight against her belly so they don't jingle and give her away. They're too precious to be shown to strangers.

She's back from the hospital. The tests were conclusive: she has motor neurone disease, middle-stage. She lies on her bed, waiting for another ambulance that will take her to the hospice, and confronts the inevitability of her own decline. Inam stands outside in the yard, scowling. When I try to touch her she springs back and snarls.

'I'm too old to be in an orphanage. And even if I was, I don't want to go to any *French* one.'

She pronounces the word *French* with distaste. I kneel in front of her, try to convince not only her but also myself of the wisdom of this decision. Rowda's presence is only making it worse. She stands aside, arms folded across her breasts like a bodyguard.

'You don't have to go, Inam,' she says to the sky. 'Nobody can force you. You can go to the Hezbollah orphanage with all the other Palestinian kids.'

'Listen, Inam,' I whisper. 'It'll only be for a short while. I'll try and get you into a good Muslim school where you can board as well. Chaim will help me.'

I know I've made a mistake mentioning Chaim when I see Inam's face. She's flounced away, kicking at stones with her scuffed and broken sandals.

'I don't want anything from him,' she calls over her shoulder. 'I'd rather die.'

Rowda snorts, unfolds her arms.

'I'll go after her.'

'You won't.'

I'm standing face to face with her now.

'Look,' I say. 'I've spoken to Bilqis and she agrees. We discussed this months ago, before her illness got so bad. This is none of your business. We don't want Inam going to a place where there's no clean water or food and she could catch anything. Bilqis has signed the papers, okay? So you can just leave now.'

'What?' Rowda rages. 'What are you going to turn her into with your expensive, private-funded fucking orphanages? A Palestinian Uncle Tom?'

She sticks her head into the open door of the hut, leaning against the jamb.

'Did you hear that, Umm Issa? Your granddaughter's going to become a Jew.'

I rush up to her, smack her hand away from the door.

'You idiot! Are you trying to kill her? Come away.' I pull her into the yard. 'Can't you see that Chaim and I are trying to help you people? What more do you want?'

'We don't need you!' she snarls. 'You and your Jewboy trying to come in here and telling us what to do. We're perfectly capable of looking after ourselves.'

'Look around you,' I say. 'Look at this place. Are you serious? Of course you need help. Stop hating everyone and take a good, long look at yourself.'

Inam stares at me and Rowda. I can see she doesn't know who to turn to, what to believe.

✳ I can't sleep anymore. I lie awake on my back listening to Inam's murmurs, Chaim's increasing snores, Julius's whimpers and yelps as he dreams. I've brought Inam to Chaim's apartment until there's room for her at the orphanage. Now that she's here, sleeping on a mattress on the floor, I can't face sending her away. But where would we both live? Chaim's home is out of the question. I'd hate to be so much in debt to him. Over these past few weeks I've watched myself detach, as if to sabotage my own happiness. I've seen myself bicker, shout, be nasty. I've pushed him out and he's helpless.

Could I find an apartment to rent, settle for a while in Beirut? A few days ago I was offered a permanent position at *The Daily Star;* they like my work, said they could trial me as an Arts writer, also a few pieces in the Politics and World sections. I asked for a week to think about it. I could still write for *The Globe,* feature pieces that would build on those I write for the Beirut paper. Saying yes would mean I'm committed to a year in Beirut at least. But with a permanent job I'd be able to help Inam.

I'm still not entirely sure why I want to save her. I'm so tired. They're all so noisy. I fight the urge to kick out at them, even though they're not the ones keeping me awake.

I turn over, sigh, finally sit up. I look at Inam's serene, olive-skinned face, striped by moonlight coming through the gaps in the curtains. Could it be possible that I want to adopt her? Once I've entertained the thought, it builds. Soon the pressure is so great I want to wake Chaim and tell him. But I don't. I keep watching her. If I adopt her, if I help her now, everything could change. For the better, for all of us. It could be our only chance to set things right. But how can it be done? Aside from the practicalities of money, schooling, geography, is it wise? Am I ready to look after a child? And such a child! So aggressive, wilful, even uncontrollable at times. Is it in her genes? Can I trust myself not to blame her for what her father did? She may be violent when she grows up, unpredictable. Will I look at her and say, this girl is the daughter of the man who killed my father? I get up, walk to the windows, open the curtains an inch. Inam is quiet now, deeply asleep. She sleeps with both arms raised over her head like an infant. The moon rises over the sea, a lugubrious eye. It watches me watching it.

I entertain the brief fantasy of me and Sayed, out of prison and prosperous, bringing up Inam in the thick of her culture. A nice, easy ending. Surely I can't be serious. But part of me wants him as well as Inam. Yet how can I leave Chaim, after we've been through so much together in such a short time? But I can't see Inam being happy with a Jewish stepfather. I can raise Inam with Sayed, and we can, all three, comfortably stay in our boxes of 'us and them', Jew and Muslim, Israeli and Palestinian. Or I can raise her with Chaim and bridge the divide. I can teach her what Chaim has shown me. But how? Go back to Boston? Can I take Inam away from her language, culture, shared identity? And what of her grandmother?

I think of Bliqis lying in that rickety hospice bed, silent, uncomprehending, overwhelmed by the fluorescent lights and the constant clattering of feet, her demented, dying bedmates calling the nurses in querulous tones. Staving off the hour of death with the dubious comfort of strident young women. Women who at times can't even understand Arabic, sent by well-meaning aid agencies to further confuse the troubled journey into oblivion. From fretful sleep to the nightmare of being misunderstood. Annihilation itself.

Her right side was clawed and twisted. Her mouth constantly hung open, a trickle of saliva spreading over her chin. I leaned over with a tissue, wiped, kept wiping as the stream of dribble grew. I thought of Siran: another pang of grief and failure. I haven't seen her for more than two months now; it's easy to forget she's still alive. Here I am with Inam's grandmother and what about my own? I wiped Bilqis's mouth again, gave up after the tissue box was empty. The more agitated Bilqis became, the more she relinquished control of her failing body.

Inam stood at the end of the bed, not wanting to touch her unrecognisable grandmother, or to touch the blanket, the scratched bedposts, the peeling wall, nor the railings as she and I fled down the stairs. She held tight onto my arm and waist as if she too were falling into oblivion.

✳ 'I won't do it,' Rowda says. 'I just won't.'

The fan at her elbow whirs at a frantic pace. The desk in front of her is larger than life in its dustiness, its messiness and its mountains of billowing paper. On the far edge near the telephone I see a carefully rolled joint, with little wisps of grass escaping from the tight wad.

'Please,' I repeat. 'I've been to the lawyer, and I've nominated you as the home study counsellor. You have to come and make an evaluation of the apartment I've just rented before we can go ahead.'

'I see. The apartment you've rented is in the very same building as your Jewish boyfriend. And I know the procedure. You don't have to explain it to me.'

'Look, I've got all the paperwork.'

I empty my bag of photocopies: my and Inam's birth certificates, letters from a local doctor confirming my physical health, a psychological evaluation, confirmation of my freelance work with *The Globe* and my contract at *The Star*, bank statements, tax returns. Rowda waves it all away.

'Why are you showing me all this? I'm not the one you have to convince. Anyway, have you thought of asking Sayed's mother if she objects? She *might* want to have the option of looking after her own flesh and blood.'

'I've spoken to Amal and she agrees. She's too old now, she understands that. She has no money. Inam needs me and I can give her a better life than this.'

We're interrupted by a colleague of Rowda's, who stands behind her and sorts through documents until he finds what he wants, leaves with a kiss on her suddenly reddened, upturned cheek. She turns to me, unable to disguise the smile in her voice.

'I'm not debating whether or not you have the funds. I'm sure you can get all you need from your Israeli boyfriend. What I object to is a white woman, such as you, presuming to know what's best for a Palestinian orphan.'

'But you're white.'

'I am not. I'm an Arab. These are my roots.'

'Look.' I lean forward over the desk and try to catch her eye. 'I'm not going to play these games. All I need from you is a simple reference after you've seen the apartment. Come on, you're a counsellor. You've known them both a long time. This is your job.'

'Don't tell me what my job is or isn't! Whether you like it or not, Anoush, you're a white woman, with a white woman's education, privileges and prejudices. How do you think you can bring up a child like that? I'm only saying this for your own good. And most of all Inam's.'

'It's Chaim you object to, isn't it? You haven't even met him, how do you know what he's like? You're a grown woman. And I hope with all my heart that Inam will see lots of him and that he'll be supportive of my decision. He'll be the best thing that's ever happened to her. So she won't grow up as narrow-minded as you.'

'Say what you like. I don't care.'

I sigh.

'Just write me the reference, Rowda. I can go to somebody else for one if you don't, you know.'

'Not if I have anything to do with it. Not here.'

I let out another long, broken sigh that seems to spur Rowda on to new fits of anger.

'You're a Westerner. You pretend you're just like these poor, oppressed people but you have no idea.'

'What about you? You were brought up in Australia! At least I lived the first sixteen years of my life here.'

'The difference is I don't presume to be the great white hope for them. Do you see me adopting any Palestinian orphans? I just help in small, modest ways – in any way I can. You're only interested in the grand gesture.'

I stand up.

'Well, I tried. There's nothing more I can say to convince you.'

'No, there isn't.'

'How sad, Rowda, to be so young and yet so rigid.'

'What did you say?'

'Whatever. You live with it.'

Rowda gets up from behind the desk and sees me to the door.

'Your lawyer will get a copy of my report in the mail tomorrow. Advising against you. I'll send another to the Camp Authority.'

✻ I walk out of the Red Crescent office without looking where I'm going. Rowda's voice and face and her strident view of the world overwhelm the narrow street, the listing buildings, the people hurrying from kerb to kerb. Dust blows onto my face, hair, all over the crisp white trousers I put on this morning, thinking to intimidate Rowda with my linen freshness. Rowda is not to be intimidated by anything. Fearlessness seems to be one of the few virtues of doing away with personal doubt and replacing it with an iron-clad certainty.

I find a cafe, sit at one of the outdoor tables. The pollution is unbearable. I move inside. The cigarette smoke drives me out again.

'Staying?' The waiter chuckles.

I nod.

'You seem pretty uncomfortable,' he says in English.

'I'm sorry. I just need a bottle of mineral water, thank you.'

The Italian water arrives on a napkin. I wipe my face with the minuscule square, sit and look at the smears of dirt from my cheeks for a long time. A car backfiring jolts me out of my reverie. I take out the sheaf of adoption papers, booklets and official forms from my bag. It looks so easy. So easy for a Western woman to do. And what if I was poor, uneducated and Muslim?

I leave all the dotted lines blank but fill in details of marital status, age, rental income in US dollars, my dwindling savings in the bank, my assets, liabilities, references, place of residence. My pen hovers over the page at this last question, undecided. I don't know where I should live anymore. I need somebody's help with this. Inam needs some kind of father. I can't do it on my own. Or can I? It's really not about Sayed, or Chaim, I suppose. It's about helping Inam to rise above her prejudices – about trying to live what I teach her.

I haven't told Chaim about the adoption yet. Sometimes I think I'm only doing this to sabotage my relationship still further. It all seems so crazy. I'm in love with an Israeli and adopting a Palestinian. The butt of one of those mixed-race jokes. Any man would be confused by my decision, if not plain angry. Am I pushing him away by doing this? And if so, why? Is it because of Sayed? Or my father? In no way is Chaim anything like his distorted memory. Issa Ali? I've resolved that pain by now. Or at least enough to keep moving. Inam is not Issa, just as I am not Selim.

I pay for the water, stuff the papers into my bag, and punch Chaim's work number into the cafe payphone. Engaged. Breathing out, I shock myself by being glad for the reprieve.

✳ A week later I stand before Chaim in my new apartment. It feels surreal: as though it is not me but someone else signing rental agreements, cleaning out cupboards, buying linen and crockery that may be discarded before this time next year. Inam is spending the day with Amal, and I've had the chance to ponder what I've done – and scare myself.

'Please,' Chaim says. 'Come and sit down. I even brought my own kitchen chairs for you.'

He tries to laugh, but the sound dies on his lips. He looks at my face and his eyes harden. I know how hurt he is that I'm not living with him anymore. But I can't smooth it over – there's nothing to absolve me. I place a pot of tea on a low table of hammered copper, clichéd scenes of oases and camels, the only piece of furniture I've bought so far. I bring out green olives from the bar fridge that came with the apartment, some bread, a pat of smooth white cheese.

'I'm not that hungry,' he says. 'But I'll pick. You eat. I never see you eat anymore.'

I come behind him where he sits, and put my hands on his shoulders. He closes his eyes, surrendering.

'Come on, won't you eat something with me?' he asks.

'You know I can't. My stomach.'

With his eyes still closed he takes an olive from the bowl on the table, reaches up and shoves it into my mouth. I spit it out, heaving, leaning over the sink.

'You're a middle-aged man! Don't be so immature.'

'And you waste no opportunity to remind me of it. What is this upset stomach? Surely by now you should be used to the food here. It's anxiety, isn't it? You're afraid. Admit it.'

'Afraid of what?'

'Me. Committing. Being open. Everything.'

'Maybe. But I have every reason to be afraid. Of you, for a start.'

'Come on, what's wrong with me? I thought you were in love, but now, in the past few weeks – this is pure indifference.'

'How can you say that?' I spit back. 'How do you know what goes on inside me? Of course I still love you.'

He shrugs. 'You don't even know yourself. Please sit down, stop hovering.' I move closer, sit opposite. He passes the teapot, a glass. 'Like I said, you do need to eat sometimes as well. You've got so thin since I first met you. Brittle.'

'Chaim, listen to me. I've made arrangements to adopt her.'

'What? You're joking.'

He puts his tea glass down, looks away as if he can't trust himself to speak.

'Do you really think that's a good idea? I thought you would know better than that. And why didn't you tell me first?'

'She has nobody to care for her now. She loves me. I love her.'

'Yes, but why didn't you tell me first?'

'I'm sorry. I knew you would disapprove.'

'I do. And it's not that easy. You say you love her? What are you talking about? You hardly know the kid.'

'I know her. I know she feels as abandoned as I was.'

'So what? How about when she's a teenager? In only a couple of years? When she tells you she hates you? When she despises you for not being Palestinian, or Muslim? And why adopt her when you can have your own? You're so young. And I—I've not given up hope of a child of my own.'

'That's not what I want right now. A baby. With you. Or anyone.'

'Oh, so that's how it is, is it?'

'At the moment I want to adopt Inam. Or foster her at least. It's my only chance to change things. To really help someone who needs me. To right those wrongs.'

'*Right those wrongs*. Listen to yourself. Could you be any more self-satisfied? And what about me, in this ideal world of yours? Are you saying you and I won't be together?'

'No. Of course not. Well, I don't know.' I stop, tracing the shape of the kitchen tile with the toe of my slipper. 'I'm not sure.'

I watch his face, the soft lines of cheek and chin, the patrician mouth.

'Chaim, I'm sorry. Chaim! Please look at me.'

'Yes?'

His eyes are shining with unshed tears.

'I care for you, Chaim. I love you.'

'And you know I love you more than you love me. And I can't figure out why you're doing this to me now.'

'I'm being insufferable. But—Inam needs me more than you do. And she loves me. I know it. And I love her, like a sister and a mother.'

'How can you talk about love for a child you hardly know? So what now, are you going to take her back to the States? She's a refugee, Anoush. Remember? She can't even get a passport.'

'I can help her, Chaim. And you can too, if you let yourself.'

'For God's sake! Who do you think you are? Really?'

I wait, breathing hard.

'Right then,' he says. 'You want me to help. To right those fucking wrongs. And dammit, you know I'll do it, for your sake. Then hate myself for being such a pushover.'

'I'm not asking you to, okay? I can do it without you.'

'Look, Anoush. I don't want to force myself on you. Maybe— maybe you do need someone of your own age.'

'That's not the issue—'

'No – listen to me. For once, you need to be clear. I'm going away to Nabatiye for two weeks. Giving you space, time, all that crap. No pressure. Think about me … and that other guy. I'll help you a little with Inam when I come back, I'll give you that; but as for everything else, it's up to you.'

I stand up, put my hand out to him. He waves me away and gets up to go. Before he leaves, he turns at the door and takes my shoulders in both hands. His grip is tight, almost hurting me, but I don't say anything. I circle his waist with my arms and for the first time ever, he seems diminished instead of me.

BEIRUT, 1984

Issa's dead body was everywhere. When Sanaya went downstairs to hang washing on the line it was there, dangling among satin slips and nappies and underpants. He seemed to be beckoning her to him with the muteness of his expression. To where, she was not so eager to find out anymore. Much as she missed and longed for him, the pull of the present in her baby girl was too strong. She was moored to life now – a bloated, unsteady boat with its importunate cargo, unable to contemplate any change.

Yet when she woke in the morning Issa's corpse lay between her and their child, a dead, sweaty weight, and she had to shove it over to get out of bed. Most of all it was there at night, confronting her at three in the morning while she stood at the kitchen counter, baby in arms, making sage tea to keep herself awake as she breastfed, peering at her from the dark mirror of the window, in the new television screen behind smiling faces of presidents and military leaders, in the murky depths of the toilet before she sat down.

She was too immersed in her grief to take note of what she really wanted. Even sleep eluded her, as if that too was a surrendering of the body into death. The first tinge of dawn, with the sun split slowly open like a winter pomegranate, awoke in her a feeling of dread. Time passed; her desolation increased with it. How, like this, would she be able to suffer the rest of her life? Better to end it now. But her baby. Inam relied on her for everything. Yet how could she get through the next day and the next, and the night to follow? She looked in the bathroom mirror by the pale rays of the morning sun, and always expected to see a face grown old and desiccated by pain and fatigue. Yet she was shocked each time to see a woman looking younger than even a year ago, a little tired about the eyes perhaps, but untouched by Issa or Selim.

Rouba and Bilqis had moved into her apartment since heating had become so expensive this winter. The Druze family downstairs had managed to escape to Cyprus by boat and donated their TV and sofa bed, their tapestry quilts. Everyone crooned over the baby, covering her thin blue legs with more blankets and putting a finger in her constantly sucking mouth.

'A house of four women,' Rouba said. 'And little Inam rules us all.'

Islamic Jihad sent Bilqis food: hessian sacks of beans and lentils and two-litre tins of the finest Italian tomatoes. At first Sanaya had protested at accepting this blood bribery but, as the city's situation became more desperate and her milk ceased flowing for the baby, she relented and began using the powdered farina, olive oil, rice. The organisation even sent Bilqis a parcel of Issa's personal effects: three changes of underwear, dirty socks, those tight jeans that were still so stiff and new. Sanaya gasped when she saw a silver bracelet wrapped in a square of newspaper. It was so much like Selim's. She felt it in her hands, examining the large ropy links, the finely wrought crosses, wondering whether this meant he too was dead. There was an inscription on its side in strange characters she knew were Armenian. She didn't tell the other women what she suspected, merely released the bracelet to watch Bilqis fasten it on her own wrist. 'To remind me of my boy,' she sobbed, and Sanaya could only stand aside and nod in sympathy.

The multinational force was finally gone, leaving the Lebanese to govern themselves. There were still more abductions of Westerners, pointless deaths under torture. The Israelis refused to leave the south then suddenly turned about and withdrew from Sidon, while fighting for every other square inch of land in its vicinity. Suicide bombers attacked Israeli positions in the southern villages. There was still no running water in the apartment block and electricity was intermittent at best. Even candles had gone up in price.

Inam celebrated her first birthday with an iced cake Rouba managed to make with no eggs or butter. The icing smelled suspiciously of glue. The fat white candle stuck into it was too large and made a gaping hole on the smooth pink surface when it was removed.

'Don't look at me,' Rouba said. 'Not my fault it looks so bad.'

'Funeral candle,' Bilqis replied. 'Christian candle. Bad omen.'

Rouba leered at her, hurt. She cut a large slice and bit into it.

'Stop! Nobody move.'

Her mouth hung half-open with its morsel of cake, before she spluttered and spat it out onto the plate. Amid the laughter of Bilqis and Sanaya she yelled out from her position at the sink.

'Don't eat it, it might kill you.'

The other women nibbled at the corners of their pieces of cake, tossing the rest to the stray dogs in the courtyard.

Inam grew and took her first faltering steps in her grandmother's hands. Issa's dead body lay draped on the divan, where he would often sit, reading the Koran. *God brought you out of your mother's wombs devoid of all knowledge, and gave you ears and eyes and hearts, so that you may give thanks.* His body lolled uncomfortably and Sanaya leaned forward and tried to straighten the bloated marionette legs.

'I think I'm going mad,' she whispered.

The other women looked at her, clucked in sympathy.

'Go to sleep,' Bilqis said. 'You're worn out, that's what's wrong with you. We'll look after our darling girl till she asks for you.'

'Can't any of you see? He's right there, watching us. I see him everywhere.'

She pointed to the empty divan. Rouba patted her on the shoulder.

'You really need a night out, honey.'

'Is it safe to go out these days?' Bilqis asked.

Sanaya gave Inam some wooden spoons and a saucepan to play with, watched her throw them to the ground and clap her hands, then reach to do it all over again. She cupped the small, tapered head in one hand.

'I've been walking out there alone for the whole of this damned war,' she said. 'Nothing can touch me.'

✳ She tried not to be angry with Issa but it was no use. When she lay in bed and Inam was finally asleep, she conducted frenzied, private debates with his dead body. *Why did you leave me? Wasn't I enough for you?* She thought of those last few months before he vanished and then kidnapped Selim. Was there anything she didn't notice? Was he any different?

He read the Koran no more than usual. Had the same nightmares, the same bouts of stifled breathing and talking in his sleep. He spent a night away at HQ – that was normal. He came home the next morning at dawn after morning prayers at the mosque. He was singing, playful, ready for fun, but she was tired and sleepy and told him to shut up and come to bed. He was immediately angry. His happiness was always jittery, brittle, a thin veneer masking an abyss.

She wanted to find him alive again just so she could shake him. No, that was not entirely true. She wanted to shake him hard, yes, but she also wanted to touch him, kiss his mouth, grasp his head in her hands and ask him why he really did it. Why he thought he was so right. *Why did you kill, Issa? Why did you kill so many people? Why did you kill Selim? Why did you kill yourself?*

Now she hit out at his imaginary corpse with her elbow. She whispered to him. *You're taking up too much of the bed. Selfish, that's what you are. Well, you've got what you want now. Raised up to Paradise amid clouds of spiritual glory. Good luck to you. And what about us?*

S
K
Y

BEIRUT, 1995

Chaim lies in bed. It's the only day off he's had for a fortnight. He's been in Nabatiye as promised, and is planning to confront Anoush tonight. Has she finally decided? He pretends to be asleep as she opens the door with her old key. She creeps into his bedroom, leans over his warm body, the sheet pulled tight to his neck.

'I know what you're going to say, but I need a big favour. Please, please go and see Inam today. There's a morning tea for the prospective parents and I said I would be there.'

Chaim turns over, rolls the blanket all the way to the other side of the bed.

'Why can't you go?'

'I got a call at dawn from one of the nurses at the hospice. She said Bilqis is asking for me, panicking. They assume she thinks she's back in the camp. During the massacres.'

'I don't see how I can go. The girl hates me, Anoush. Remember, it was intimated to me very clearly that it's only you wanting to adopt her, not *us*.'

'Well, I can't be there. So you're the only one left.'

He mumbles something into the sheet, turns over and away from the filaments of light escaping from the curtains. She leans further and peers into his face. He puts a hand out from the folds to touch her mouth. Before she can plead one more time he sits up and stretches.

'Okay. I'll do my best.'

'Thank you,' Anoush says, and he hears the door shut carefully behind her. 'I'll see you tonight.'

Chaim gathers gardenias from the pots on his balcony into a bouquet. A peace offering. A measure of his respect. *Inam may appreciate it*, he thinks, *or else she may throw it to the floor*. She's that sort of girl.

Some of the petals are already creased and splitting, but he ties them all together into a hard-packed wheel. He begins by feeling self-conscious carrying them on the bus, but in the next breath feels proud when Muslim women around him smile, open-faced and unsuspicious. Usually he only gets scowls for looking so evidently foreign.

✳ I walk with trembling knees to Bilqis's ward. The contrast with the heat outside never fails to astonish me: cathode blue of fluorescent lights, iciness of walls and floors and the nurses' immovable features. I shiver as I hurry down the corridors, pressing my hands to my arms for warmth.

'Didn't you bring a jacket?'

The Irish nurse who rang me stands at the side of a patient's bed, taking a vial of blood. She jabs at the old man's arm, trying to find a vein. He mews quietly, like a kitten. I stand and watch the slow drip-drip of blood thickly collecting, clotting to the sides of the glass. The nurse finishes and wriggles her own cardigan off in one gesture.

'Here. I'm hot anyway. Give it back to me when you leave.'

I take the cardigan thankfully and put it on, inhaling the nurse's scent of disinfectant and cheap soap and tobacco smoke. She jerks her head in the direction of Bilqis's bed.

'She's still in the same place. Been screaming and raving all night. We didn't know what to do with her.'

As I slide down the smooth linoleum to Bilqis's bed, I hear the nurse call after me.

'We gave her another shot about an hour ago, so she may still be a bit drowsy.'

Bilqis stares rigidly at me. Her face is a mask of pain, drawn-out mouth dribbling and eyes that dart about, trying to find some respite. I put both my hands on her cheeks.

'Oh, Bilqis, what have they done to you?'

✳ Chaim sits in the row of chairs provided for the would-be adoptive parents and foster families. The chairs are small and wooden and his legs buckle under him so grotesquely that he'd be better off kneeling upright on the floor. Some of the other men are having the same trouble, balancing cups of milky coffee and slices of cake on their distorted laps. Chaim clutches the bouquet so hard his knuckles turn white.

The French headmistress claps her hands gracefully, as with everything she does. The children, in various states of shyness and reluctance, file into the room hand in hand. They are all girls, all aged between four and twelve and all dressed identically in white starched pinafores and shirts with pale-blue cuffs. Chaim can hardly recognise Inam. She catches his eye, embarrassed and subdued by her scrubbed pink face and plaited hair, and grimaces. She mouths exaggeratedly at him. 'Where's Anoush?'

He shakes his head and shrugs his shoulders as if to say, *I'm all you've got today, sorry.* He lifts up the bouquet and gives a self-deprecating grin. The headmistress claps her hands once more.

'*Mes enfants, attention!*'

The children stand still in perfect formation. Another teacher bends over a piano and begins to play, badly, out of tune. *Il etait une bergeré et ron, ron, ron, petit patapon.* The children sing along in muted tones and with expressionless faces. Except for Inam. Although she suffers the same severe stance as the rest of them, feet splayed out in her ugly shoes and hands behind her back, she's singing completely different words. Her mouth is moving silently and she is singing in Arabic. She faces Chaim and smiles wide as she sings.

✳ I feed Bilqis a mush of hashed meat with flecks of something orange through it, using the moulded plastic spoon the nurse has suggested so it's easier on Bilqis's tender, exposed mouth. I put some of the food on the spoon – 'Just enough and not too much,' the nurse cautions – wait for Bilqis to wearily open up again, and stick the spoon almost as far down as her gullet. It's the only way she can eat. She's lost any ability to chew.

Most attempts fail. The spoon isn't down far enough; its contents spill over onto her tongue and down the chafed sides of her mouth, mixed with saliva and the half-digested remnants of yesterday's dinner. I despair, feel tears forming in my eyes. Bilqis gazes at me, steadfast as a lover. *It's okay,* she seems to be saying. *I have patience.* I try again. I gulp down a sob, load up one more spoonful.

'One more,' I whisper to Bilqis. 'Only one more to go.'

Just as I do, the Irish nurse enters the enclosed little world I've created by pulling plastic curtains around the bed.

'You're taking too long, honey. Her food's gone cold. Kitchen staff want to wash up as well.'

She draws aside the curtains with a decisive slash and settles herself down near me. She takes the spoon and basin and proceeds to dose Bilqis with the last spoonful, forcefully and without compunction. I sit aside and watch in shame, as if I've betrayed Bilqis to her Phalangist torturers.

✳ Inam sits on a chair next to Chaim, twirling her paper plate faultlessly on one hand. She hasn't touched her slice of cake. She's professing to be bored with anything he says. When Chaim told her Anoush couldn't make it because Bilqis had been asking for her, Inam changed the subject without the flicker of an eyelash. She accepted the flowers with something bordering on cautious delight, making a huge to-do of finding a vase for them. They repose now in a chipped mug on the laden trestle table, among filled baguettes and tinned sardines and jugs of bright-yellow custard from a packet.

Chaim eyes her revolving slice of cake.

'Can I have it, if you're not eating?'

She passes it to him without a word. Chaim swallows in silence for a few seconds.

'Anoush will bring you to my place one weekend and you can get acquainted with my dog again.'

Inam raises her eyebrow. 'He's such a big dog. I'm scared of him.'

'Well … yes, he is big. But he would never hurt you. He likes little girls.'

Inam sighs, worldly. 'I'm not a little girl anymore. And I don't like dogs.'

'Come on, you like Julius. Even more than you like me. Do you like me, even a little bit?

'Hmmm …' Inam pauses.

'So why don't you like me, Inam?'

'Because.'

'Tell me, I won't be offended.'

'Grandma told me all Israelis are bad.'

'You know that's not true. Not every person from one place can be bad.'

'The ones at the prison were. They had big, nasty dogs too. And they swore at Anoush.'

'Did they? She didn't tell me that.'

Inam nods, self-consciously serious.

'My father would go out and kill them every day. I heard Grandma saying to Aunty Amal. Before he died.'

'And do you want to kill me?'

Inam ignores the question, fixing her blue eyes on his.

'I heard them talking. Grandma and Anoush. My father killed her father. Then he killed himself too.'

✳   I sit by Bilqis's bed. My buttocks are stuck to the cushioned plastic seat.

'Bilqis? If you're tired out, I might go home now.'

Bilqis doesn't open her eyes but her mouth works with the effort to speak. With her head flung right back on the pillow, her skin so white, she could be a corpse waiting to be laid out. I stand up and lean close to her face. The swollen eyelids blue and heavy.

'What is it? What can I do for you?'

Bilqis tries to raise her left arm, the better one, but it flops onto the blanket after a brief struggle. I stroke her hand, breakable but heavy, the texture of crepe. Bilqis manages a sound, a bellowing cry. A word forms from it.

'Can't—'

Another word.

'—breathe.'

'She can't breathe! Come quickly!'

I run out into the middle of the ward. Nurses rush past, attending to other patients, and I grab one by the arm.

'She needs oxygen! She can't breathe!'

The girl runs after me to the bed. Bilqis is choking, great globules of food and spit being expelled as she gasps for air, skewed arms clutching at nothing.

✳ 'What do you mean, your father killed hers?' Chaim narrows his eyes and glares at Inam. *Is she lying? Making things up?*

Inam leans forward, confidingly.

'I told you. It was in the war.'

She pronounces the word *war* as if uncertain of its precise meaning. Chaim rubs his eyes, tries to take her nail-bitten hand. She pulls it out of his reach with a grand gesture.

'Are you sure, Inam? Are you sure you're telling me the truth?'

'Of course I am. But Anoush still loves me, doesn't she?'

Chaim speaks automatically.

'Yes, she loves you. Was her father a militiaman, then?'

'I don't know.'

He grasps her by the shoulder, bringing her closer. She lets him.

'Did you hear them say he was a soldier, you know, with a gun?'

Inam opens her mouth, hesitates.

'I—I think so.'

'Remember!'

'Yeah. Yeah, a what-do-you-call-em, Pha-lang-ist, they said.'

Chaim leans back, expels the air he's been keeping tight inside his chest. Inam studies him and a ripple of doubt passes over her face.

'It doesn't matter, does it, Chaim? It doesn't matter what happened then.'

Chaim repeats it after her – *doesn't matter what happened then* – believing something else entirely.

✳ I slump in the matron's office, am handed a cup of cold tea, another cardigan draped across my shoulders. I'm shaking so much I can't hold the cup and a nurse takes it from me with painful solicitude. The matron speaks, breaking through the only sound in the tiny room, that of my teeth chattering.

'I'm sorry, Ms Pakradounian. There was nothing we could do.'

I nod, look down at the linoleum floor, at the strip running from the door to the desk that is somehow lighter than the rest.

'Is there anyone we can call, Ms Pakradounian?'

I try to think. I'm numb. After a while I open my mouth.

'Her sister Amal. Her nephew, Sayed Ali.'

✳ Chaim rushes home from the orphanage. He kicks at loose rubbish, rolled-up newspapers, a garbage bag's contents spilled across the street. He stands for a minute, controlling his breath, looking out at the blackness of sea beyond the Corniche. A beggar comes toward him and Chaim gives him such a look of contempt he doesn't even attempt to ask for any money, backing away and shaking his head. Chaim fumes, left alone.

He sits on the sea wall, attempts to gather his thoughts. After taunting him about his own father and brother, making him feel like the enemy, like she was sacrificing so many of her principles to be with him. He too is a child of survivors, of genocide. Victims and perpetrators. How different are they? Her subtle rejection, renting her own apartment, wanting to have a separate life. And now this.

'Anoush,' Chaim screws his mouth up to silently form the sound. 'I don't care if your father was a Phalangist or a terrorist or a dictator. It's your attitude I'm so pissed about. You didn't trust me enough to tell me the truth. Now I can't trust you. So what the hell does that say about any future for us?'

He knocks on her front door feverishly, waits. Nothing. He tries the knob, bursts into her bare living room. There are no lights turned on. She has Julius with her. He barks once, a sharp, exhausted cry. In the beam from the promenade below he can discern her huddled form on the floorboards. *What right does she have to be upset over an old Arab woman? The murderer's mother.* Her self-indulgence enrages him all the more.

'Why did you hide it from me?'

She silences him with an upraised hand.

'She's dead.'

✳ On the way to Bilqis's memorial in a hired limousine, Chaim is coldly silent. It's been seven days since Bilqis's death and burial. I stood aside while Amal and the other women of the camp ritually washed the pallid body, folding her limbs – grown so thin in death – and wrapping them in a white shroud, clinging in all the wrong places like a little girl's sundress. Rowda stood aside as well, her lips as tight as the arms across her chest. She didn't speak to me.

Bilqis was buried the next day before sundown, with her head turned to face Mecca. Chaim didn't come.

'It's not right,' I can remember him saying. 'You'll end up resenting the kid for what her father did. Now it's all new and happy, but just wait a few years.'

I glance toward the front seat; Inam is happily ensconced with the driver. He's letting her choose which radio station she wants to listen to. Until now I've been looking out my window at the glaring streets, still heat-dazed in early winter: nougat sellers thrusting their wares into the car, the sudden smell of nuts and scorched sugar, vendors of feather dusters preening their borrowed plumage before presenting them to me through the open window like bouquets.

The car stops in traffic and an old woman looks up from selling herbs – feathery rocket, basil, fronds of coriander – from a hessian sack as she squats on the kerb. She holds up a bunch and smiles at me, gap-toothed, overly familiar, knowing I won't buy. An ironic greeting, a fitting farewell for Bilqis.

I whisper with violence into Chaim's ear. He jumps.

'If I don't help Inam now I'll dry up and become self-obsessed and shallow. I don't want to die like my father.'

He seems surprised. 'How do you know what state of mind he was in when he died?'

'I can guess.'

'And what good will it do to take her away from everything she's known? Don't you want to go back to the States?'

'I told you, I won't go, not now. You know I've decided to stay here in Beirut. A year, at least. For Inam's sake and for my grandmother. At least until she dies too.'

'And for me?'

I look at him, a different expression on my face. The tears of the last week still fresh in my eyes.

'Well, not with your attitude of the last few days.'

'Do you still want me?'

We stare at each other, not sure what to say next. The air around us grows heavy, the sounds of babbling humanity from outside increasing. I remember the excitement I felt when he first told me he loved me, the comfort of lying in bed beside him late at night, my head resting in the hollow made by his collarbones. I feel the thrill again of imagining a future together. A future with Chaim and Inam. I brush my hand against his freshly shaven face. Smoothness of a pebble.

'I'm sorry, Chaim. I still don't know yet. You need to give me some more time. It's not just about you and me anymore. It's about Inam too.'

The driver stops at the mosque. I draw my white veil around my head and shoulders mechanically, get out of the car in a daze. The imam I requested is waiting outside; he sees me and rushes forward. Chaim sits. He can't seem to move his legs. After a while, he rouses himself, opens the door for Inam.

Rowda is outside as well, with a group of Red Crescent workers. Her veil is wrapped so completely around her head I can only recognise her by the slash of red that's her mouth. I begin to follow the imam inside without another glance at her.

'Wait,' Rowda hisses, putting out her arm. 'Do you mind if I'm here?'

'What do I care? It's a memorial, Rowda. This mosque doesn't belong to me. This is Bilqis's memorial.'

As I say Bilqis's name, the tears I've been trying to hold back all morning – for Inam's sake, for Chaim's, for my own – come all in a rush. At the mention of her name, Rowda murmurs *Rahimaha Allah*, the traditional prayer: *Allah be merciful upon the deceased.* I turn away and wipe my cheeks with my veil, embarrassed for Rowda to see me like this.

'It doesn't matter whether or not I mind.'

But my words are crushed against her shoulder as she draws me close. The group huddles around us, screening my tears from passers-by.

'I'm sorry,' Rowda says. 'I'm so sorry.'

Somewhere in my half-hysterical state, I'm trying to figure out why Rowda is saying this. *Sorry for what? For Bilqis's death; for your prejudices; for everyone here?* All I'm aware of are the two strong hands holding my head down, the musty hashish sweetness of Rowda's clothes, the swishing, smacking sounds from people's bare feet as they discard their sandals and step over the entrance to the mosque. I pull away.

'Thank you. I'm sorry too. I—I need to go inside now.'

I sit at the back of the mosque, near the open doors. My veil damp and clammy, a dead weight around my neck. As I kneel and bend my head I can see Chaim walking through the entrance with Inam running behind. I beckon to them but they don't see. Inam's tugging on his jacket as they make their way closer, and he stops and looks back at her, exasperated.

Then I see him bend down and twine his fingers with hers, leading her to me.

❋ The adoption process was surprisingly easy, even with Rowda's negative report. I managed to find another Muslim social worker, who came to my new apartment and stayed for three days, writing a glowing account of my living arrangements. Julius and his good-natured antics obviously helped. My job and apartment in America helped. I referred to Chaim as an 'honorary uncle' to the social worker, saying that Inam could rely on him for friendship and support as she grew older. He didn't object to this, but in his heart I can see he mourns what could have been. Or maybe could still be – he hasn't given up hope. Nor have I. I'm a mystery to myself these days, but I know I still feel so much love for him. It increases every day, changes. If he and Inam can learn to love each other too, then I can see a future for us. The healing of my father's wound has left a bigger hole: a hole that's surprisingly light, and spacious, and free. I'm letting it be. For now.

The court saw fit to milk the situation as a political coup, a best-case scenario of Israeli–Arab relations. As did the fact that I was staying in Beirut. I wasn't going to take the orphan away to a foreign country of infidels. After all, it wasn't as if rich Westerners were clamouring to take away Palestinian children. Unless they were newborn babies, of course. The babies didn't even make it to the orphanage. They were especially sought after, being adequately unformed, pale-skinned, pliable. Easy to pretend with.

I sat in the office of the orphanage and the French headmistress handed me paper after paper to sign. I could see Amal's and Sayed's signatures on the line above mine: Sayed's a flourish, Amal's a thin, shaky cross. I kept on scribbling my initials at the bottom of each page, anxious to get it all over with, to take Inam home.

✽   I show Inam her bedroom – tiny, almost a cupboard, but perfumed with triangles of incense I've burnt to chase away the past. I switch on a lamp, pale-blue and beaded, with silk fringing Inam caresses as she stands looking at the oval side table, the tiny writing desk against the high, pointed window, a flat ultramarine square of sky.

'Do you like it?'

Inam wanders to the centre of the room, sits down on the bed, gazing around and up at the ceiling.

'It's beautiful.'

I'm relieved at her reaction.

'This is your room now. There are fresh sheets on the bed, more blankets in the linen cupboard if you get cold.'

Inam nods. She's overwhelmed by the immensity of the situation. She grasps my hand.

'Is it really true? I'm living here with you – forever?'

I laugh.

'Don't know if we'll be living here forever, sweetheart. But we'll definitely be together, you and me, for a very long time.'

Inam thinks for a moment.

'And Julius?'

'Well, Julius is Chaim's dog, and I don't really know what Chaim will do next. But he'll always be our dear friend, I hope. Do you like Chaim better now?'

'I like him so much more now I've met Julius. He's such a good dog – better than the ones at the prison.'

Chaim hears this from the open door, where he's come with a tray of baked eggplant for dinner.

'We always liked each other a little bit, didn't we, Inam?'

Inam shouts back, 'Whatever you want. Nothing matters anymore now I'm here.'

✽   Inam and I walk arm in arm along the beach. Julius has raced on before us, sniffing at seaweed and sea urchins rotting on the shore. I'm tired. We've scaled the split white rocks in bare feet and made it down to the water's edge. Far away now, obdurate buildings and noiseless cars make no impact. Here we can splash in the foamy waves, watching out all the while for drowned garbage and discarded syringes, feel the hot wind from Africa sting our faces and a hotter sun burn the tops of our heads. We can talk in whispers. Talk about Bilqis.

Since the funeral six months ago, all we talk about when we're alone together is Bilqis. Whether she's happy wherever she is, whether she can see us and know how much we miss her now she's gone. Amal visits once or twice a week but her great-aunt's presence seems to make Inam's grief worse. She looks like Bilqis but isn't – and Inam can't bear the trick. Yet her grief is always more manageable in the daytime: when she's at school or after-school activities, when I traipse around the city interviewing people and filing stories for *The Star*. But in the evening, when dinner is over, when she's had her shower and is allowed to read for an hour in bed, the tears and disbelief well up and Bilqis is too far away.

Inam wails for me then and I bring her into the big bed. Some nights Chaim is staying over, and I can't help but feel ashamed. So I ask him to go back to his own apartment and Inam snuggles into the warmth he's left behind. It's the only way she can fall asleep for a few hours and be half-awake for school the next day. I worry that Chaim will soon become fed up with the nightly situation and go away to Nabatiye, never to return. Then I reason that it wouldn't be so bad after all, that at least the situation will be resolved that way.

Some nights I wait until I think Inam is sound asleep, legs and arms kicked out to the far edges of the bed, frail mouth quivering in her dreams. Then I tiptoe silently out to the hall and phone Chaim to come back. I slip down beside him in Inam's single bed. On some nights he refuses to come back. On others he kisses the back of my neck, breathing comfort into me. When dawn steals through the curtains, I always make sure I'm back in bed with Inam, and Chaim is back in his apartment.

'Put your sandals back on,' I say now. 'I'm scared you'll step on a syringe and catch something.'

'I won't. I'm being careful.'

Inam looks up at my face, pleading. I sigh, feel the responsibility weigh heavy on my chest, hesitate, nod my head. Inam will never know what it costs me to do this.

'Okay. Just this once.'

Inam sighs, happily. She threads her arm still tighter through mine and hops a little from foot to foot.

'She might be looking down on us now and smiling.'

'Won't she have better things to do, don't you think?'

'No. Nothing better than watching over us. She must miss home.'

Inam skips over the pebbles, splashing herself a little around the hem of her dress. Julius joins in the fun with more enthusiasm than is necessary, almost knocking her over into the waves. She pushes him away and hums, crouching low near the water. I look at her, drink her in: the peach-dark skin, the long-limbed grace, the kiss-curls at the nape of her neck. I can't get used to this miracle. Inam is not family yet I love her with a ferocity only blood and pain can impart. There's plenty of that between us, even without the mess of birth.

She plucks pebbles from the shore like flowers, fat stones fall as she wades in further. Up to her hands, her brown wrists. Fingers submerged, silver-finned, and she shakes them free, singing. An unintelligible song, obscured beat by beat as she advances into the blueness, so blue; her voice covered by the lapping of waves then finally increasing in volume, unfolding into the air.

I can't hear her anymore. Panic makes my voice sharp.

'Hey! Get back here now.'

She wrinkles her nose and returns, protesting with the slowness of her movements.

'I wasn't going far. And you know I'm old enough to be careful.'

She flits up and down, humming the song under her breath, clapping her hands to the quiet rhythm of the music.

'What's that song?'

'I made it up.'

She continues singing, but softer now.

'I know that tune from somewhere. But I've never heard you sing it before.'

'I used to hear the old men sing it in the camp.'

'Did you know it's Armenian originally? There's also a Turkish version. It's not in Arabic.'

'No. I never thought about it.'

'I'm sure your grandma would have told you. She knew some

Turkish, from her days in Palestine. So tell me, isn't paradise preferable to the camp? She must feel as if she's gone home to Jaffa.'

'Not if we're not there to enjoy it with her.'

'But she's with her son, my darling. And with your mother too.'

Inam stops and stares up at me.

'But Anoush, my father's not in paradise. He killed too many people. So he must be in hell. Like your father. They're both in hell.'

'Who's been telling you such lies?'

'Nobody. I worked it out myself.'

I bend down, fix her with a stern eye.

'Are you sure about that? Nobody said this – not the French teachers at the orphanage, other kids at school?'

Inam shakes her head from side to side, as if mesmerised. I draw her closer, rest the burnished head against my chest.

'Nobody knows where your father is, Inam. Not me, not you, not Chaim, not the teacher. Only Allah knows. Okay?'

Inam nods and clutches tighter. She seems relieved. I stand up with her arm still about me. We walk slowly. Inam breaks away and paddles in the foam, teasing Julius, and all the while I'm thinking, *I said 'Allah'. I said something I don't know if I believe. I relinquished control to something higher.*

I stop at the water's edge and Inam runs closer, splashing me as she goes.

✳   'I got all your messages. They wouldn't let me out – even for half an hour – to go to the memorial.'

Sayed directs his remark solely to me. He seems to look right through Chaim, who gets up to go.

'I think I'll wait outside.'

I put out a restraining arm without looking at him.

'No. Please stay. Sayed, this is Chaim, my—my … my boyfriend.'

Chaim smiles. Sayed glares but he puts out his hand to Chaim, then jerks it back again when the guard moves forward.

'I'm sorry,' Chaim says. 'Sorry about your aunt.'

Sayed looks down, fiddles with nothing on the tabletop. I try to lighten his mood.

'I wrote another article about you. Look.' I fish it out of my bag, unfold the headline. 'Look, Sayed. *Wrongly accused in Israeli jail.* It's in *The Star,* as you know, and in *The Globe.* But I also managed to get it into *The Florida Times.* I have a friend who works there.'

Sayed smiles wryly. 'Not much sympathy for me over there, I expect?'

'No, I suppose not.'

All three of us laugh, sourly. When it subsides there's silence. Sayed clears his throat and looks at Chaim.

'Listen, thanks for being a friend to Anoush – and to Inam. I don't know how I would have felt if she was in an orphanage. And by the time I get out—'

Chaim interrupts. 'They might still be able to do something. Anoush has been talking to your lawyer.'

'We can't even appeal. Or so they say.'

'You can. He's working on taking your case to the civilian Supreme Court here in Jerusalem.'

'On what grounds? They all think I had a big part in it. Being Palestinian is enough.'

'On the grounds that the facts were unfairly represented by the prosecution.'

Sayed seems unimpressed. He sighs. 'I'm so tired of it all.'

'Your presence in court isn't even necessary,' I say. 'The case will be argued on a purely academic level.'

Sayed sighs again, looks around at the guards' impassive expressions, takes a soft packet of cigarettes and lighter out of his breast pocket. 'Anyone?'

We shake our heads. Sayed proceeds to drag at the cigarette with energy, waving the smoke away from my face. I lean over the table.

'How are you going, anyway? In here, I mean.'

Sayed stubs the cigarette out on the tabletop with a disgusted expression.

'I get three meals a day. Exercise. Not much torture, only the psychological kind.'

He glances up sharply to see if any of the guards have heard. Their faces remain cool. I put my hands out flat on the table.

Nobody speaks, and the silence becomes uncomfortable. When I remove them, the formica top is marked by my two handprints made of sweat.

'Be serious,' I say finally.

'I am.'

'Are you depressed? How are your sessions with the counsellor?'

'I can deal with it.'

'What do you want me to do?'

'There's nothing you can do. Keep talking to this lawyer of yours. Come and see me sometimes. Bring me smokes, books, my laptop if they let you. Bring Inam next month if you can.'

✳ I lean over Chaim's shoulder. Today is a rare, festive weekend day: he's in my apartment and frying a breakfast dish involving a vast amount of maple syrup and eggs. He plays the chef, tea towel over one shoulder and warmed plates waiting in the oven.

'What are you making, Chaim? French toast! Are we turning into real Americans, then?'

'I like American food,' Inam says. 'Hot dogs with ketchup and hamburgers too.'

She waits at the kitchen table, knife and fork clutched upright in each hand. At her feet, Julius begs with one paw on each of her knees, and she leans down and whispers in his alert ear, 'Don't worry, my darling, you'll get some too.'

'And where have you eaten junk like that?' I ask. 'There could be pork in it.'

'After school. The other kids buy them and then give me some.'

I telegraph a look to Chaim, *I knew I shouldn't have chosen that international school*, smooth a cloth napkin onto Inam's lap and prod Chaim in the kidneys.

'Mademoiselle is waiting to be served.'

I'm remembering Rowda, her fierce comfort at the memorial, her tense apology. Could we be friends, she and I? Or do I just want her approval for what I've done?

'Inam, what do you think? Should we invite Rowda to come here for tea one day?'

Chaim butts in over the sound of butter sizzling in the pan. He slaps more bread on.

'Who's this Rowda?'

Inam answers, 'That lady at Grandma's funeral. The pretty one. Don't you remember? She came and kissed me and ignored you.'

'Don't remember,' Chaim mumbles.

He's busy attending to his cooking, arranging thick slices of French toast onto a plate and sprinkling them with cinnamon. A deluge of syrup and three fanned strawberries, thrown on for the hell of it.

'Did she really ignore Chaim, Inam?'

'Mmm.'

Inam begins attacking the huge portion Chaim has placed in front of her. She speaks through a full mouth.

'Rowda hates Jews.'

Chaim wheels around from the stove and stares at her. 'What did you say?'

Inam repeats the phrase in a small voice. 'She says she hates Jews.'

Behind Chaim, the bread in the frying pan sputters. He brings his hand down to the edge of the stove with force, making the pan and empty plates rattle. Julius growls and flees to the balcony. A stink of burning fills the room. I open the kitchen window. Chaim comes closer to Inam and rests his hand on her shoulder.

'Inam, I don't want you to ever say things like that again.'

I inch around him and turn off the gas on the stove.

'Chaim, the child is only repeating what she hears. Inam, look at me. Chaim, please sit down. Let's talk about this. '

He turns away from us with an exasperated movement, takes the handle of the frying pan to empty the mess into the bin.

'Fuck! I burnt myself.'

Inam giggles into her plate then looks up at him, afraid, waiting for a reaction. He sits, breathing heavily.

'Inam, grab some ice from the fridge, will you?' I ask her.

I take his hand and look at where he's burnt himself, run the cold-water tap. As I speak, I tend to it, immersing his hand in a bowl of cold water, pressing ice to his palm. The way he lets himself be cared for is touching, almost voluptuous, as if he's surrendered to me completely. I look up at Inam.

'Sweetheart, is Chaim a Jew?'

She nods.

'Is there anything about him to hate?'

She shakes her head. 'I like you, Chaim. I really like you now. You're kind. Anoush lets me stay up late when you're here.'

'So why do you think Rowda hates Jews?' I ask.

'Because she's never met one like Chaim?'

Chaim looks at me, gives a half-smile. I grin back.

'Inam, what do you think we should say to someone who uses that word – hate – all the time?'

'I don't know. I'm sick of all this talk.'

Chaim leans forward, gently taking Inam's hand in his good one, as he did at the funeral.

'I think we need to show them there's another way. A way where we can all be friends.'

She shifts her hand in his. 'We're still friends, aren't we? Even if I said that just now?'

'Indeed we are. I hope we'll still be friends when I'm an old man and you're all grown up.'

'We will,' she says. 'I promise.'

At that, she unlooses her hand from his and continues to sit at the table, serenely eating her French toast with sticky fingers. The knife and fork lie on either side of her plate, untouched and clean. I look from one to the other, child and lover, collapse in my chair and begin to laugh.

Soon all three of us are laughing, even Chaim, who resumes his cooking, breaking eggs into a bowl and shaking his head. Inam doesn't know why we're all laughing but she sees no reason anymore to be sad, and laughs the longest between mouthfuls of syrup-soaked toast.

✳ Rowda perches on the edge of Chaim's broken couch. Just his luck she's decided to come early today, making lame excuses of a last-minute meeting at the Red Crescent office tonight and no way she can get out of it. She tells him she knocked at Anoush's door, didn't have any paper to leave a note. And here she is, asking him for some. Anoush and Inam aren't home yet, belly dance lessons or martial arts, too many after-school activities to keep track of. He'd wanted to sit around and watch bad cable this afternoon, order kebabs from downstairs. His only day off this fortnight. He's gone back to his bachelor ways now that Anoush has moved into her own apartment. Today he feels deflated, as if no amount of trying will get him anywhere. He hasn't seen Anoush for a few days, she's been so busy with Inam. And now look.

Rowda accepts tea from him graciously, says no to a biscuit or sugar, and he tries not to bare his teeth and snarl. He wishes Julius would but the damned dog just lies there in the corner and sleeps. *Tolerance*, Chaim thinks. *Compassion. Charity.*

'I hear Anoush's been helping Sayed Ali,' she says.

'Her lawyer's working on an appeal. He says there's a good chance Sayed will be out of prison in seven years, maybe less.'

'And Inam? Will he take custody of her?'

'She'll be a grown woman by then. Almost nineteen and able to decide for herself.'

'Is she settling in well with Anoush?'

'Is this a counsellor asking or a friend?'

'Both, I hope.'

'She's happy, I think. She and Anoush are fast friends. She even spares a kind word for me at times. They may be going on a little trip early next year, maybe in the spring – a holiday. I may go as well, if work permits.'

'Not back to the Zionist entity, I hope.'

He decides not to let it pass.

'Sorry? Are you serious? Can't you understand basic facts? Israel is a true democracy, unlike here. Or the Territories. All sorts of people live in Israel, and not all of them are Zionists.'

She gulps down her tea. 'No, I'm not sorry, actually. You think you're not a Zionist. You are. As far as I'm concerned, anyone who lives or has lived in Israel is a Zionist.'

He lets out a whistle.

'Shit, you're loopier than I thought. Here's your piece of paper. You can go now. There's no use arguing with you. By the way, Anoush will be taking Inam to Turkey. Armenia, really. Anoush's ancestral home.'

'Is Inam happy about that?'

'Of course she is. She's never been outside Beirut her whole life. She can get a passport now. She's also looking forward to my mother coming to stay for a few weeks. Another grandma, she says. A real Jewish grandma.'

Rowda surveys him with her head turned to one side.

'I already know you're a Jew. You don't have to make such a point of it.'

Chaim wills himself to be cold and steady.

'Why do you feel the need to make me excuse myself for it?'

Rowda puts down her tea glass. Some of it sloshes onto the saucer.

'It's your own insecurity that makes you feel that. Self-hating Jew.'

Chaim can feel his eyes bulge. *The bitch.* When he speaks, his voice is slow, correct.

'I don't hate, Rowda. I don't hate myself, or you. I don't hate Palestinians or Lebanese or Arabs. I don't even hate the terrorists and governments who kill innocent people every single day. What I do despair of is this ignorance, this pig-headedness that can't see people for who they really are. What I fear is the possibility of another Holocaust. And deep down, I know it's not even about hatred. It's about fear. I hope we'll all stop being afraid of each other all the time. I want better than that, for you and me, and Inam – for everyone.'

She simpers, runs her hand over the worn linen of his couch. He feels affronted by this as well.

'Enough of the fine words, Chaim. I'll say I'm sorry, if you like. I didn't intend to insult you.'

She looks at him for a moment, her eyes travelling over his set shoulders, his frozen eyes. He can feel she's having trouble discerning his expression. He could go either way. She tosses her hair over her shoulder.

'Could you please tell Anoush and Inam that I came? I'm sorry I missed them.'

She gets up. Before she can make for the door Chaim stands up too, blocking her way.

'Don't you think I need more of an apology than that?'

Rowda crumples her mouth, ironically obsequious. 'I see I've hit a nerve.'

Chaim becomes more solid, weighty. 'Apologise.'

Rowda stands her ground. Julius wakes up and barks, his tail flapping wildly, as if he can't work out whether to be cruel or kind. The door opens. Inam stands there, takes in the scene. Chaim turns to her, afraid she may fly at him. Condemn him. He opens his mouth to plead his case; his face wrinkles with the effort.

'Where's Anoush?'

Inam ignores him. Instead, she plants her feet on the welcome mat and points a finger at Rowda.

'I was listening in the corridor. You were rude to Chaim.'

Rowda opens her mouth to say something, turns away and walks quickly down the stairs.

✳ There's still tension, but it's manageable. There are disagreements, fights, tears, but they're usually over by nightfall. Inam spends inordinate amounts of time in the downstairs courtyard whispering to Julius when she feels she's been wronged. The dog rests his head in her lap and snuffles, humouring her complaints, his tail beating an upbeat tattoo on the tiles. There are long periods of sullen silence and stubbornness, but I'm becoming good at taking her for a walk down to the sea and coaxing the bad mood out of her.

Our city is waking as if from a long sleep. The Corniche hosts a carnival atmosphere every night, with food stalls and tea-sellers and buskers from all over the world. Chaim complains about music keeping him awake past midnight. But I like it, feel like going down there and making some noise myself. Downtown cafes are open all hours, dancing spills onto rubbled streets; the bookstalls and antique shops lining Rue Hamra are doing a roaring trade. I take Inam to the American University campus and we sit on the grass with an afternoon picnic, watching students loll about and kiss in secret, notebooks aflutter in the sea breeze. We check out the noticeboard, discussing the different subjects on offer. Inam wants to go to university one day, she says, to study history.

At her age, Inam shouldn't fully understand what history is. Not yet. But when I sit on the side of her bed at night, watching her sleep, I study her young yet troubled face. I watch the lidded pebble eyes, the knowing brow, the map of time smoothed out across her features.

Other times, other people's histories. Inam was born with them, has first-hand knowledge of homelands, territories, injustices and desires. Intimations of her father and mother, in the flick of a hand, the crazy shapes of her elegant toes, the sharpness of her language. In the sly way she licks her forefinger to smooth down her eyebrows with the glue of her own saliva. The sticky mass of history. Inam surely knows more than enough about that.

She's celebrating her twelfth birthday. She's enjoying her new school – American, non-denominational, co-ed – has many friends her age, moderate Muslims and Christians of all stripes, Lebanese, Palestinian, Armenian, Greek. At our apartment, they crowd around her and the magnificent, lighted cake, a gooey thing of Belgian chocolate and Grand Marnier.

'Are you sure you should put that much alcohol in it?' Chaim asked me the day before. Anxious, licking at a smear of icing with his finger. I flicked a lump at him, laughed.

'I'm not Muslim, you know.' As soon as I heard myself say the words, I felt in the wrong. Am I dishonouring Inam's past, in this way and countless others? These doubts are unanswerable, an unease I know will follow me until Inam is grown up, maybe beyond, until I can feel my choices have been justified.

Chaim sat at the kitchen table and half-watched me ice the cake. He was absently building a little tower out of the beach pebbles Inam had gathered and left strewn there. Like the memorials of the Holocaust: each cairn a generation, each pebble a soul.

Inam stands at the head of the table and poses for photographs, ready to cut the cake. Chaim stands on a chair with the camera. 'Look up!'

The girlish singing – the boys refuse to join in – is deafening, raucous.

'*Happy birthday to you! Happy birthday!*'

Inam closes her eyes, just for a moment, and I close mine too. The song wobbles and changes, our grandmothers' voices cracking, calling: *My darling, my love, your sufferings and joys will be many.* We remember; do we really remember or would we merely like to? The strength of our desire to know overcomes reality. Another room, another time, a beautiful mother dimly known from photographs and Bilqis and a fat white candle, funereal tones, a corpse-like father grinning from the corner.

Hot wax drips onto the icing. Inam cuts the cake and makes a silent wish; I gather up the spent candles and take them to the kitchen, to save them for next year. Standing at the counter, I break off a piece, the wax warm and yielding in my palm. Alive. I roll it between my fingers, making a tiny, perfect ball. I can try to tell Inam about hatred, about mistakes and lies. What I can't tell her is how to avoid them. I see Lilit led away by Turkish men, flushed face in her palms. Split pomegranates and the solid ball, like this wax, that water gruel makes when it cools, Minas stuffing it into his mouth in the death camp. I think of Chaim, and last night: the trail of his semen on my thighs so thin, so translucent I took it between my fingers for only a moment before it vanished. All of us, here for a single moment, then gone.

✳ Late that night, when the girls and boys have all gone home clutching paper plates of leftovers and moist parcels of cake, I sit on the edge of Inam's bed and tuck the sheets down over the still-flat chest.

'Before you go to sleep, there's something I need to give you.'

'Another present?'

'No – not really another present. Haven't you had enough?'

I laugh. Inam laughs too, holding up her wrist with its Armenian bracelet, so that the heavy silver links and crosses sparkle in the lamp's dim light.

'This one's my favourite.'

'It was my father's for a while. An antique from the forties. One day I'll tell you the story of your father and this bracelet too.'

'Not now? I hate it when people tell me I'm not old enough to know things. I understand *everything*.'

'I'm sure you do. But maybe not this – not yet. Isn't it gorgeous? My grandfather made it himself. Apparently my mother wore this bracelet originally, even when she was a little girl.'

'The mumma you never knew?'

I try to speak softly. 'That's right, Inam.'

'Just like me.'

'Just like you. And now we have each other.'

Inam sighs, but it's a sigh of contentment and tiredness. I squeeze the thin, braceleted wrist.

'Time for some sleep now. But first, our secret. Actually, it's a little like a present.'

Inam sits up in bed and looks at the envelope. On it is a message in Arabic, scrawled in black pencil: *For my darling Inam. Don't open until you turn twelve.*

'Your grandmother gave it to me before they took her to the hospice. It's from your mother.'

I bend down and kiss her on the forehead. 'Do you need me to be here while you read it?'

Inam shakes her head, slowly. I get up to leave, come back on an irresistible impulse and kiss her again, holding her so tight she can't breathe.

'Call me if you need to talk about anything in the letter.'

I close the door.

✻   Inam sits very still for a while, until she's certain Anoush has gone down the hall and into her own bedroom. She then opens the envelope with small, careful tears where it's been glued down, and takes out a smooth, flat pebble. Not stopping to examine it further, she lays it on the bedspread as she unfolds the letter. Her eyes scan the closely written page in Arabic, searching for the last line. *With great and everlasting love, Your mother, Sanaya.* She winces when she sees the handwriting, can't recall if she's ever seen anything written by her mother at all.

14 November 1983

My darling Inam,

Now that you're twelve, no longer a child, not yet a woman, I'm writing this to you. Writing, not speaking, in case in these uncertain times, you find yourself alone without me to guide you and tell you a little of your history.

We're a historic people, all of us, and we allow this to shape our actions and emotions and the very stuff we suppose we are made of. When we allow history to shape us in this way we sometimes lose our humanity, our compassion, our logic, and we can commit any crime in the name of ignorance. All those little, messy truths and that one big lie – the lie of who is right and who is wrong. Nobody is right, my darling Inam. We're all right and we are all, too often, and tragically, wrong.

Your father loved you although he never knew you. I'm sure of that. I'm sure he looks over you from wherever he is and smiles. He hated injustice and this hatred consumed him, but he also felt a deep love for the smallest objects: the soft line of a woman's veil, a piece of fruit, the bird outside his window.

He loved more often than he hated, but hatred became so much easier to fall into. Please don't judge him.

With great and everlasting love,

Your mother,

Sanaya

Inam isn't sure what to feel after reading this. Part of her would like to understand; the other part shuns this raw, new knowledge. She puts the letter back inside the envelope, licks it shut again and wedges it under her mattress. The pebble she looks at carefully now: greyish-blue, shiny as a mirror, perfect as a peach. She holds it tight in her hand as she falls asleep.

BEIRUT, 1984

Rouba leaned into a seated Sanaya, applying electric-blue mascara to her widened eyes.

'Now look up. That's better. I don't want my friends thinking you're half asleep.'

She stood back, surveyed Sanaya's make-up with her head to one side, came closer to apply another coat of mascara. She murmured under her breath, lips an inch away from Sanaya's cheek.

'You haven't been looking your best lately, poor thing.'

Their physical proximity was oddly comforting, but tonight Sanaya was not in the mood. She suffered Rouba's attentions, swivelled in her seat. This morning, as she woke before dawn to breastfeed Inam, she found the canary on the floor of its cage, claws curled in the spasm of death.

'It's not a good sign, Rouba,' she murmured, as the other woman turned away toward the mirror to pat at her own face with powder.

'What's not?'

'The dead bird. It was healthy for so long.'

'What, you're still going on about that? Canaries are not known for their longevity, darling.'

She dabbed glitter cream on Sanaya's bottom lip, feathered some rouge on her cheeks.

'That'll make you look more alive.'

Sanaya kissed Inam, hugged her with an intensity that surprised her. She and Rouba made for the door. She stopped and shouted down the hall.

'Please Bilqis, don't let her stay up too late! You know how unsettled she gets when we overstimulate her. I need her in bed by eight.'

Bilqis looked up from her game with Inam and chuckled.

The two women walked to the party all the way, enjoying the spring gusts caressing their necks, ruffling their shiny satin blouses. Rouba sewed them herself from the gaudy pink-and-gold quilts abandoned by the Druze family downstairs. She flapped her headscarf about, making little puffs of air beneath the fabric. Then she decided to take it off. In one movement, she crumpled it up and dropped it into her handbag. Sanaya gasped and then cheered.

'I don't need it anymore,' Rouba said.

Sanaya felt more vital now they were outside. She suppressed a deep flash of separation-pain from her baby, close to guilt, then reasoned with herself that Inam was with her grandmother, who loved her, that she wouldn't even notice her mother was gone. She and Rouba both laughed loudly, drawing attention to themselves, clutching their mesh handbags to their hips. Rouba made a passing commentary on every man who walked by.

Sanaya told her to shut up between giggles. 'I'd forgotten what it was like to feel so alive.'

They walked through a Shia neighbourhood, careful not to offend the black-veiled women, the milling white-suited men, tiny children cloaked in floor-length chadors. Here they walked faster, not speaking, holding hands in order not to be separated in the crowd.

As they passed a parked BMW Rouba paused to check her hair in the tinted windows, teasing out the gelled strands that had fallen limp. She sprayed some perfume on Sanaya's inner elbow and Sanaya sprang back, rubbing at the sudden stinging coolness.

As she did so, the car exploded. Both women were flung forward then back among the debris.

LAKE VAN, TURKEY, 1996

I lead the way into town by following the pale thread of lake. Inam wants to drive into the centre – says she's tired of walking, all this holiday has been is walking – but I feel that approaching Van on foot will reveal more, so we leave the car behind.

On the distant island of Akdamar all that can be seen is a triangle-topped dome. The rest of the tenth-century church is obscured by vapour rising from the surface of the water. I have no desire to go there, to ache again for the loss of so many looted treasures, vandalised icons, mosaics gone dull with age. I remember Lilit telling me about the carvings – delicate reliefs of Adam and Eve, Samson, Jonah and his whale, with the head of a perplexed dog. Does Inam want to go and see them? But she's strangely afraid of the cone-shaped, rickety boats moored at the shore, making her displeasure known until the sailors shrink away, muttering.

The lake is a mirror. I look into it, Inam by my side, and feel ashamed. Guilty I've managed to survive, that I can stand here with unmarked skin, healthy limbs wrapped in micro-fibres from the sweatshops of the Third World. What trick of fate has left a few Armenians to survive, to have children, grandchildren, to keep the pain and anger and disbelief alive? In another time, I would have been the bound woman marched through blood and sand, torn from home, trembling in fear of the final blow. Yet from the destruction of my race, tribe, family – I've survived. Survived to bear this guilt, this sense of unworthiness. Such a statement sounds so trite on this bare earth, among this bitter history. Psychobabble. As does the political, the economic, the aesthetic universe I float in like a fish underwater.

This is the Armenia of my childhood then. It became Turkey eighty years ago. This lake and its town, uneven rows of skinny houses with carved timber balconies, window frames, studded doors, the slow piling of brick upon hand-hewn brick by Armenians not so long ago. Dirt roads that join remote villages with their Armenian names, old Armenian inscriptions. Defaced words, names since changed, slightly wrong. The memory of oil lamps tended and candles lit in mountain chapels: burnt now, desecrated, their frescoes hacked away. How did we let this happen?

The lake is silent. Inam and I wear sandals too flimsy for this stony bank: a land that seems determined to devour, to reduce me to itself. All I can remember now is Lilit's mouth: an old scar that cut her bottom lip in half and became white then whiter whenever she cried.

'So, Inam,' I finally say. 'Will you be glad to go home tomorrow?'

'I miss Beirut,' she replies. 'I miss school and I'm sure they're all ahead of me by now.'

'After only a week? Surely you're too clever for that.'

She smiles at the compliment. 'And you? What do you miss?'

I pause. *I miss my grandmother*, I want to say. *I miss the father I never knew. But most of all, I miss knowing who's right and who is wrong.* I miss the heaviness of womanhood too, the pull of biology. No time for that yet. I have Inam to look after, work, my responsibility to the past. I have Siran. I feel a pinch of anxiety when I think of going back to Beirut, as if the flamboyant city with all its conflict and chaos has become too much for me. I don't know what I'm doing with Chaim, whether I'm big enough to wait for Sayed to come out of prison. Whether I love them both in different ways. Or if I can just be alone.

My womb is empty for now – and if full at all, would be papery, rectangular, stretched tight by words, stories, swollen with competing versions of the past. No unborn child with its secrets. I have my own living, breathing child now. No infant who knows the world before all worlds. I carry my own worlds now. Worlds of difference, foreign languages, warring tribes.

'You know, Inam, I think I might miss Beirut too.'

Across the lake, the island starts to rise from the mist as if by some blind force of will. This lake with all its colours of bone and ash and sky. Blue as Lilit's eyes when she was fifteen, still unclouded by horror. Bone. Ash. Sky. Someone keeps saying it. Repeating it, over and over. Bone and ashes. Sky – that's all there is. And the lapping of water, like a lullaby that puts me in mind of Lilit – again – singing the high-pitched songs of childhood. I can hear those songs: distant monks from the island's church chanting in accents plaintive and half-familiar. But there are no more monks on Akdamar, only an abandoned ruin and a story I'd rather forget.

Genocide. A race wiped out. I try on various emotions and the faces that go with them: terror, outrage, acceptance, grief. None of them fit the sense, beneath it all, that I'm repeating empty gestures, the movements of somebody else, on the edge of this same lake, sometime in the past. Could it be possible so much killing took place here? Mass graves shouldn't be this beautiful. On this serene, cloud-curdled day the atrocities seem a fabrication, tales told to frighten children. Now Inam is uncharacteristically silent. As we walk hand in hand we bend down and comb through the sand, finding smooth treasures, pebbles fragile as bird-bone. I want this ancestral earth to be rich, evocative; soil I can only hope will give birth to something new. We find a sweet wrapper, crudely pink; a Turkish cola can squashed so flat it could be tribal jewellery, millennial old. A clod of earth, a grave of rubbish. A thin human wrist-joint severed from the arm. I fall to my knees now, digging, with unexpected tears blurring my vision. Inam stops, frightened. I'm digging deeper. Fast, faster. She kneels down to help. Brown shards, soft as clay, our fingers crumbling them into unrecognisable splinters. The broken ends of bone are creamy, bleached white. I sift through, more careful now. Teeth, jaw, eye-sockets. These were once skin, fat, hair, a face.

My disbelief at the scale of my discovery attacks me somewhere under the breastbone.

'It's okay, Inam. It's okay. Let's just place them in the earth again, say a prayer.'

She studies my face, concerned. 'Why are you crying? There's nothing to cry about.'

The lake now so still. We get up, hold hands. Not even a bird, not a leaf stirring.

S
K
Y

477

In the long evenings … there was time enough to consider where the core of the tragedy lay. In the age of the Assyrians, the Empire of Rome, in the 1860s perhaps? In the French mandate? In Auschwitz? In Palestine? In those rusting front door keys now buried deep in the rubble of Chatila? In the 1978 Israeli invasion? The 1982 invasion? Was there a point where one could have said: Stop, beyond this point there is no future?

Robert Fisk, *Pity the Nation*

ACKNOWLEDGEMENTS

Three men have believed in my work over many years.

My husband, Nick Georges, who allowed me to drag him to deserts and war zones for the sake of love and research, who printed out countless copies of my manuscript and brings home tulips and poppies on days when my writing has gone stale.

My literary agent, Tim Curnow, whose humorous, experienced and authentic encouragement has for twelve years pushed me toward deeper truths, and who has now become more than an agent to me – family friend, mentor and wise counsel.

Peter Bishop, formerly of Varuna, The Writers' House, Australia's patron saint of writers, who went beyond the course of duty to read this book in its very early stages.

Thanks to Dr Izzeldin Abuelaish, who took the time to read the entire manuscript and provide such heartfelt praise. Also the *Independent*'s foreign correspondent Robert Fisk – who not only read the sample my agent sent him, but went to the trouble of phoning me personally right away – for being so generous with his time, his knowledge of the Middle East and his contacts, and for making suggestions for the chapters he read.

The whole team at Hardie Grant Australia and the UK – from CEO to sales, marketing, publicity and proofreading – have my eternal gratitude: firstly, for being brave and far-sighted enough to take on this difficult and controversial book during such tough times in publishing, and for nurturing me with such enthusiasm and kindness.

Special gratitude to the wonderful Rose Michael, my editor and publisher. Without her bold commitment to the book in the beginning, and the intense energy she brought to championing it, editing it, promoting it and believing in it throughout the whole process, none of this would have occurred. Thanks also to my fellow writer Libby-Jane Charleston, for, without a chance conversation between Rose and her, this partnership would never have come to fruition.

Huge thanks to Nicola Redhouse, for her insightful and exhaustive thematic and line-editing. Sometimes I felt she cared as much – if not more – for the book as I did.

Kenneth Hachikian, chairman of the Armenian National Committee of America (ANCA) has gone far beyond the call of duty to be a passionate advocate of my novel in the US and overseas. Varant Mergueditchian, executive director of the Armenian National Committee of Australia (ANC) was also supportive and enthusiastic about this work in his former role. Vache Kahramanian, his successor, has also been a tireless advocate for me and the book. Khatchig Mouradian, editor of the US-based *Armenian Weekly*, has also been a great supporter and help – and a fount of knowledge about the genocide. Thank you all for your incredible generosity and belief in my retelling of your story, and for welcoming a non-Armenian into the fold.

I would like to thank the Australia Council for a generous year-long grant and a residency at the Tyrone Guthrie Centre in County Monaghan, Ireland, in 2003, where I began this novel. I would also like to express my appreciation for a three-year Australian Postgraduate Award (APA) scholarship that allowed me to complete my doctorate at the University of Technology, Sydney, and to pave the way for this book. My mentors and colleagues at UTS, particularly Dr John Dale, were an invaluable source of inspiration throughout this process, as were my early workshop partners, Heather Banyard, Libby-Jane Charleston and Dr Carol Major.

Fellow writer Christopher Cyril fully inhabited the 'dream' of the novel, as he so beautifully termed it, and gave me fresh insights when I was at a low ebb.

Huge, humbling thanks to Sophie Haythornthwaite, who read the manuscript countless times (with much brainstorming for titles) between the demands of children and her own need to paint. Also to Anyo Geddes, who gave me valuable feedback when I asked her to read many chapters at the last minute.

Thanks to Dr Martes Alison for reading an early draft.

Also to Hugh Barrett in London, who always reads with a fresh eye and an inexhaustible knowledge of culture and geo-politics.

Big thanks to Armen Gakavian, who read the novel in its final stages and made sure my Armenian content and language was correct.

Shukran to Omran Matar, who read with an eye to correcting my Arabic and any strange ideas I had about Lebanese culture, religion(s) and customs.

Also to Michael Lever, who did the same for the Israeli/Jewish sections.

I would also like to thank Dr Charles Herdy, who helped me immensely with matters military.

All mistakes and misconceptions are mine.

A special, heartfelt thank you to Jane Turner, who graciously allowed me to leave our business partnership at Gertrude and Alice Café Bookstore to pursue my writing ambitions.

To my dear friend Larissa Reid: it was in your home that I finished one of the many drafts of this book. Thank you for your gentleness and generosity of spirit.

The people of Lebanon, Syria, Turkey, Morocco, the Gulf and Armenia speeded the progress of this book with their recollections, hopes, honesty and hospitality. I thank every one of them for sharing their stories and lives with me in 1995, 1998, 2002, 2004 and 2010.

Aghapi to my mother Anastasia Bakas and my father Graham Cosgrove, whose unobtrusive support smoothed the writer's path.

To my sister Annette Livas, who died in October 2010, my deepest thanks for the many times I needed to hear your voice over the phone: for your strength, serenity and sheer will. Thank you for the beautiful example that was your life.

Finally, I am blessed with my daughter Damascin, who, with her devastating mixture of innocence and intensity, has taught me a new – and more time-efficient! – way to write.

483

For further reading, sources and articles go to
www.katerinacosgrove.com

Praise for *The Glass Heart*

'*The Glass Heart* shimmers with Cosgrove's evocative powers …
Visceral images of eating, drinking, love-making, giving birth
and dying are treated with an unerring eye. Cosgrove's writing has
beautiful, poetic flourishes so it's not surprising her name has been
coupled with the likes of Allende and Garcia Marquez.'
The Age

'Cancel that trip to the Greek islands and read this book instead … this
is as real as it gets. It would be difficult to surpass Katerina Cosgrove's
intense evocation … This book will erase your sense of the here and
now … Cosgrove does not flinch from offsetting the good with the
bad, powerfully rendering the difficulty and rawness … intimately,
jaggedly female in its bias, scored with eroticism, pain and loss … this
is a captivating read.'
The Australian

'When you read a book that's fantastic it takes – perhaps unfairly
– from those around it. And so *The Glass Heart* draws an invisible
line around itself that says, this book is special, take it slowly, enjoy
it, remember it … The measured prose links past and present with
parallels in plot, subtle shifts in imagery and the constant counter-
balance of two different lives …'
The Canberra Times

'This is a provocative, sensual telling of relationships and bonds that
defy generations … Cosgrove's telling is tantalisingly ripe with the tastes
and smells of Greece … Her characters are drawn with honesty and
rawness as she digs a finger into the dark and brittle places of the heart.'
The Sunday Mail

'Cosgrove is … a young writer who truly does fulfil that most
hackneyed phrase "an exciting new talent".'
The Gold Coast Bulletin

Praise for *Intimate Distance*

'a tale of infidelity and parenthood ... Cosgrove's loving depiction of the Greek setting and her sophisticated craftsmanship help ground the controversial, motherhood–parenthood theme.'
The Sydney Morning Herald

'Cosgrove's unchronological narrative is vastly effective in charting the protagonist's confused state of jumbled emotions, displacement and disarray. With its overarching themes of forbidden love, abandonment, filial duty versus individual needs, and unresolved passion, *Intimate Distance* effectively delves into the dichotomy between the individualistic societies of the West and the more family-oriented, collective societies of Greece.'
ArtsHub

'*Intimate Distance* by Katerina Cosgrove is ... a page turner ... packed with dynamite charges. [Moving] back and forth through three time zones and three countries ... [a] complex web of family loyalties and conflicts emerge. This is a story that lingers in the mind long after it is read.'
M/C Reviews

Katerina has been a Sydney bookseller (Sappho Books and Gertrude & Alice cafe bookstore), university tutor and has completed a doctorate in Creative Arts. Her first novel, *The Glass Heart* (2000), was published by HarperCollins in Australia and Govostis in Greece to critical acclaim and in 2012 Katerina was one of the winners of the Griffith Review/CAL Novella Prize, for *Intimate Distance*. She began *Bone Ash Sky* with the aid of an Australia Council grant and a residency at the Tyrone Guthrie Centre in Ireland and travelled to Armenia, Turkey, Lebanon and Syria for research. In 2010 she published a controversial article in *The Australian*, 'Turkey must lift veil on first Holocaust'. An earlier of *Bone Ash Sky* version was shortlisted for the Writing Australia unpublished manuscript prize. For more about Katerina, go to www.katerinacosgrove.com or like her on www.facebook.com/AuthorCosgrove.